DON QUIXOTE
DE LA
MANCHA

THE FIRST PART OF
THE LIFE AND ACHIEVEMENTS
OF THE RENOWNED
DON QUIXOTE
DE LA MANCHA

—

MIGUEL DE CERVANTES SAAVEDRA

TRANSLATED BY PETER MOTTEUX

ILLUSTRATED WITH WOOD ENGRAVINGS BY
HANS ALEXANDER MUELLER

1941

RANDOM HOUSE · NEW YORK

FOREWORD

In the year 1605, in the Spanish city of Valladolid, an unsuccessful writer and former soldier by the name of Miguel de Cervantes Saavedra published a book that was to place his name forever in the pantheon of the immortals.

The book was an immediate and extraordinary success, although —such were the times—the author profited little thereby. Six editions were printed during the first year and translations into foreign languages quickly followed. (Thomas Shelton began work on his famous translation into English, which quite possibly Shakespeare may have read, two years after the original was published in Spain.) The story was pirated on all sides. Indeed, there was even a very popular "sequel" published before the author had finished writing the second part of his own book.

Cervantes' novel—for such we call it, although there is no book quite like it in all literature—told of the adventures of an eccentric hidalgo who adopted the name of Don Quixote de la Mancha, when his brain had become so addled from reading too many romances on knighthood that his "wit was wholly extinguished" and he "fell into one of the strangest conceits that ever madman stumbled on in this world."

What that conceit was, what was the nature of Don Quixote's madness, is by now a matter of general contention, if not of general knowledge. Cervantes himself was more explicit than most of his commentators. "To wit," he wrote, "it seemed unto him (Don Quixote) very requisite and behooveful, as well for the augmentation of his honor as also for the benefit of the commonwealth, that he himself should become a knight-errant, and go throughout the world with his horse and armour, to seek adventures, and practise in person all that he had read was used by knights of yore; revenging of all kinds of injuries, and offering himself to occasions and dangers, which, being once happily achieved, might gain him eternal renown."

This, then, was the specific madness as the author conceived it, only to have his hero grow enormously out of hand—as is the way of the greatest characters in fiction—until today Don Quixote has come to mean all things to all men, and his absurd adventures tragic or comic, the butt of ridicule or the symbol of adoration, in proportion to the way the vision of life burgeons in the soul of each of us.

In the three hundred years that have elapsed since the Knight of the Rueful Countenance first rode upon the scene on his woebegone Rosinante, numberless volumes have been written about him, until he has become the best-known character in all literature, as unquestionably he is the most living and the most endearing.

What manner of man was this Miguel de Cervantes who at the age of fifty-seven, in desperate financial straits and with an almost continuous record of failure and misfortune behind him, could bring into the world a book that has helped men to laugh at their own troubles ever since?

"Every production must resemble its author," he wrote in a wry preface to the reader, "and my barren and unpolished understanding can produce nothing but what is very dull, very impertinent and extravagant beyond imagination. You may suppose it the child of disturbance, engendered in some dismal prison." And quite possibly *Don Quixote* actually was begun in jail, for its author was given ample opportunity by his masters to know what the inside of a prison looks like.

6

A contemporary of Shakespeare—in fact, the two greatest writers of their respective countries died in the same year—Cervantes lived a continual struggle against poverty, debt and sheer bad luck. Born in the year 1547, the son of a poor surgeon, he had not the means to attend the local university. Instead he became a soldier and in 1571, at the naval battle of Lepanto, was so severely wounded that he lost the use of his left hand. Returning from the wars at the age of twenty-eight, he was taken prisoner by Berber pirates and held for ransom for five years, narrowly missing being sold into slavery in the public mart of Constantinople.

Cervantes had risked his life for his king, but that did not prevent his being thrust into prison for bad debts, when at last he returned home. Perhaps he could redeem himself with his pen. In six years he wrote thirty plays and all were failures. He even "ghosted" for more fortunate authors and wrote advertisements for their books and dramas. In 1588 he was a commissary in Seville and four years later was in prison for having bungled a sale of wheat. If only he could get away to try his luck elsewhere, perhaps in the New World! But though he endeavored to get a post in Guatemala, he had not the necessary influence.

In 1594 he served as a tax-collector in Granada. Once more he was in disgrace; once more in prison. Released on his word that he would make good the deficit to the treasury of the King, he nevertheless ended up in jail again, when the bank in which he had deposited government funds had to close its doors. Small wonder if *Don Quixote* was begun behind lock and key.

For more than twenty years Cervantes' daily bread had been the bitter fare of shame and defeat. We can imagine in what mood he must have set himself the task of writing his book. Yet even the tremendous victory he wrested from adversity brought him scant relief. Despite the fact that during the last years of his life his fame resounded not only through Spain but throughout all Europe,

Cervantes was acquainted with humiliation and starvation until the end.

His memory, however, is hardly in need of our pity. This old soldier, plagued with more than his share of the world's burdens and suffering from dropsy, remained to the end a human being of dignity and spirit. At sixty-six, to use his own words, he was "a man of aquiline visage, with chestnut hair, smooth and unruffled brow, with sparkling eyes, and a nose arched, although well proportioned, a silver beard, although not twenty years ago it was golden, large moustache, small mouth, teeth not important, for there are but six of them and those in ill condition and worse placed because they do not correspond the one with the other, the body between two extremes, neither large nor small, the complexion bright, rather white than brown, somewhat heavy shouldered, and not very nimble on the feet."

Cervantes, we may assume, started work on *Don Quixote* with no higher purpose than to write a satirical burlesque. Even the extraordinary character of Sancho Panza, second only in significance to Don Quixote, did not occur to him until he was well along with his story and suddenly realized that a knight was always accompanied by a squire in the romances of chivalry.

But somewhere in the writing, Cervantes' book underwent a sea-change. Something rich and strange happened, and what was begun as a burlesque grew into "an analogue of all mankind's adventures on this earth." Cervantes' satire on the books that had addled the brains of his hero became only the jumping-off place for what is, after all, the core of the novel—the humorous and enchanting contrast between the nature of the haggard and lantern-jawed Knight and that of his faithful Sancho.

But even when we have said this, when we have said with Henry Edward Watts that it is "the human element which is the perennial

8

charm of *Don Quixote*," we have hardly begun to tell why it should have a more universal appeal than any other book. Surely the fact that it is peerless entertainment is not enough.

Don Quixote is the inspiration of an old man, an old soldier of the world who has known most of the misfortunes that can befall a man and has yet remained of good humor and stout heart. Cervantes had known what it was to be buffeted and kicked around for all his pains, to sally forth again and again with fond hopes and high purpose, only to come limping home with standard muddied and bedraggled, amidst the world's indifference or ribald laughter If, then, as the English critic Sir Walter Raleigh has said, Cervantes' masterpiece is "the wisest and most splendid book in the world," perhaps it is because the way of the Knight parallels so closely the tragically absurd progress of all of us pilgrims on this earth.

But in the last analysis, it is impossible wholly to encompass the greatness of a book like *Don Quixote*. As impossible as it is to encompass the wholeness of life. For just as the sum of life is greater than any combination of all its parts, so, too, the work of Cervantes, like the work of Shakespeare, is greater than any combination of characters, or incidents, or beautiful or striking passages contained therein.

With a book of so wide an appeal it is hardly necessary to offer an explanation for the appearance of another edition. It seems particularly fitting, in fact, that such an edition should appear just now.

If, as is at least arguable, the greatest novels of our time— Marcel Proust's *Remembrance of Things Past*, for instance, or James Joyce's *Ulysses*, or Thomas Mann's magnificent *Joseph* series—are terminal works in a literary genre that has enjoyed some three centuries of uninterrupted growth, how right and proper that the first great example of this genre should be commended anew to our attention.

In an age of social upheaval like our own, when the individual tends to be submerged in the mass, when the mass is fostered at the expense of the individual and when, indeed, the individual may suffer punishment for merely being himself, it is heartening to read again a book which so preëminently celebrates the unique and solitary human being.

A few further words should be said, in closing, about the present edition of Part One. Although the second part of *Don Quixote* has its own particular glories, it is in the nature of a sequel to Part One, which is complete in itself. *Don Quixote* has been translated into every known language, but no nation has printed more volumes and brought out more editions than the English. Indeed, the foremost authorities on Cervantes are not Spanish, but English. Approximately one hundred years after the publication of Thomas Shelton's pioneer translation, Peter Motteux began work on his version which to this day remains the one most commonly read, as it is "by far the most spirited," and was therefore used for this edition.

It is impossible to end these notes without mention of Hans Alexander Mueller's beautiful engravings. Not since the drawings of Gustave Doré, it seems to me, have there been any illustrations for *Don Quixote* that can match these, while perhaps only Daumier, in the few sketches he made for Cervantes, has equalled the purity and tenderness of Mr. Mueller's conceptions.

EDWIN SEAVER

CONTENTS

BOOK THREE

BOOK FOUR

DON QUIXOTE
DE LA
MANCHA

THE AUTHOR'S PREFACE
TO THE READER

YOU MAY DEPEND *upon my bare word, reader, without any further security, that I could wish this offspring of my brain were as ingenious, sprightly, and accomplished as yourself could desire; but the mischief of it is, nature will have its course: every production must resemble its author, and my barren and unpolished understanding can produce nothing but what is very dull, very impertinent, and extravagant beyond imagination. You may suppose it the child of disturbance, engendered in some dismal prison,[1] where wretchedness keeps its residence, and every dismal sound its habitation. Rest and ease, a convenient place, pleasant fields and groves, murmuring springs, and a sweet repose of mind, are helps that raise the fancy, and impregnate even the*

[1] The author is said to have written this satirical romance in a prison.

17

most barren muses with conceptions that fill the world with admiration and delight. Some parents are so blinded by a fatherly fondness, that they mistake the very imperfections of their children for so many beauties; and the folly and impertinence of the brave boy, must pass upon their friends and acquaintance for wit and sense. But I, who am only a step-father, disavow the authority of this modern and prevalent custom; nor will I earnestly beseech you, with tears in my eyes, which is many a poor author's case, dear reader, to pardon or dissemble my child's faults; for what favor can I expect from you, who are neither his friend nor relation? You have a soul of your own, and the privilege of free-will, whoever you be, as well as the proudest he that struts in a gaudy outside: you are a king by your own fireside, as much as any monarch in his throne: you have liberty and property, which set you above favor or affection, and may therefore freely like or dislike this history, according to your humor.

I had a great mind to have exposed it as naked as it was born, without the addition of a preface, or the numberless trumpery of commendatory sonnets, epigrams, and other poems that usually usher in the conceptions of authors. For I dare boldly say, that though I bestowed some time in writing the book, yet it cost me not half so much labor as this very preface. I very often took up my pen, and as often laid it down, and could not for my life think of anything to the purpose. Sitting once in a very studious posture, with my paper before me, my pen in my ear, my elbow on the table, and my cheek on my hand, considering how I should begin, a certain friend of mine, an ingenious gentleman, and of a merry disposition, came and surprised me. He asked me what I was so very intent and thoughtful upon. I was so free with him as not to mince the matter, but told him plainly I had been puzzling my brain for a preface to Don Quixote, and had made myself so uneasy about it, that I was now resolved to trouble my head no further either with preface or book, and even to let the achievements of that noble Knight remain unpublished: "For," continued I, "why should I expose myself to the lash of the old legislator, the vulgar? They will say, I have spent my youthful days very finely, to have nothing to *recommend my gray hairs to the world, but a dry, insipid legend, not worth a rush, wanting good language as well as invention, barren of conceits or pointed wit, and without either quotations on the margin, or annotations at the end, which other books, though never so fabulous and profane, have to set them off. Other authors can pass upon the public, by stuffing their books from Aristotle, Plato, and the whole company of ancient philosophers; thus amusing their readers into a great opinion of their prodigious reading. Plutarch and Cicero are slurred on the public for as orthodox doctors as St. Thomas, or any of the Fathers. And then the method of these moderns is so wonderfully agreeable and full of variety, that they cannot fail to please. In one line, they will describe you a whining amorous coxcomb, and the next shall be some dry scrap of a homily, with such ingenious turns as cannot choose but ravish the reader. Now I want all these embellishments and graces: I have neither marginal notes nor critical remarks; I do not so much as know what authors I follow, and consequently, can have no formal index, as it is the fashion now, methodically strung on the letters of the alphabet, beginning with Aristotle, and ending with Xenophon, or Zoilus, or Zeuxis; which last two are commonly crammed into the same piece, though one of them was a famous painter, and the other a saucy critic. I shall want also the pompous preliminaries of commendatory verses sent to me by the right honorable my Lord such a one, by the honorable the Lady such a one, or the most ingenious Master such a one; though I know I might have them at an easy rate from two or three brothers of the quill of my acquaintance, and better, I am sure, than the best quality in Spain can compose.*

"In short, my friend," said I, "the great Don Quixote may lie buried in the musty records of La Mancha, till Providence has ordered some better hand to fit him out as he ought to be; for I must own myself altogether incapable of the task; besides, I am naturally lazy, and love my ease too well to take the pains of turning over authors for those things which I can express as well without it. And these are the considerations that made me so thoughtful when you came in." The gentleman, after a long and loud fit of laughing, rubbing his forehead:

19

"O my conscience, friend," said he, "your discourse has freed me from a mistake that has a great while imposed upon me: I always took you for a man of sense, but now I am sufficiently convinced to the contrary. What! puzzled at so inconsiderable a trifle! a business of so little difficulty confound a man of such deep sense and searching thought as once you seemed to be!

"I am sorry, sir, that your lazy humor and poor understanding should need the advice I am about to give you, which will presently solve all your objections and fears concerning the publishing of the renowned Don Quixote, the luminary and mirror of all knight-errantry." *"Pray, sir,"* said I, *"be pleased to instruct me in whatever you think may remove my fears, or solve my doubts."* *"The first thing you object,"* replied he, *"is your want of commendatory copies from persons of figure and quality: there is nothing sooner helped. It is but taking a little pains in writing them yourself, and clapping whose name you please to them; you may father them on Prester John of the Indies, or on the emperor of Trebizond, whom I know to be most celebrated poets: but suppose they were not, and that some presuming pedantic critics might snarl, and deny this notorious truth, value it not two farthings; and though they should convict you of forgery, you are in no danger of losing the hand with which you wrote* [2] *them.*

"As to marginal notes and quotations from authors for your history, it is but dropping here and there some scattered Latin sentences that you have already by rote, or may have with little or no pains. For example, treating of liberty and slavery, clap me in, non bene pro toto libertas venditur auro; *and, at the same time, make Horace, or some other author vouch it in the margin. If you treat of the power of death, come round with this close,* pallida mors æquo pulsat pede pauperum tabernas, regumque turres. *If of loving our enemies, as Heaven enjoins, you may, if you have the least curiosity, presently turn to the divine precept, and say,* ego autem dico vobis, diligite inimicos vestros; *or, if you discourse of bad thoughts, bring in this passage,* de corde exeunt cogitationes malæ. *If the uncertainty of friendship be your theme,*

2 He lost his left hand (*izquierda*) in the sea-fight at Lepanto against the Turks.

20

Cato offers you his old couplet with all his heart, donec eris felix multos numerabis amicos: Tempora si fuerint nubila, solus eris: *and so proceed. These scraps of Latin will at least gain you the credit of a great grammarian, which, I will assure you, is no small accomplishment in this age. As to annotations or remarks at the end of your book, you may safely take this course. If you have occasion for a giant in your piece, be sure you bring in Goliah, and on this very Goliah (who will not cost you one farthing) you may spin out a swinging annotation. You may say, 'The giant Goliah, or Goliat, was a Philistine, whom David the shepherd slew with the thundering stroke of a pebble in the valley of Terebinthus:* Vide "Kings," *in such a chapter, and such a verse, where you may find it written.' If, not satisfied with this, you would appear a great humanist, and would show your knowledge in geography, take some occasion to draw the river Tagus into your discourse, out of which you may fish a most notable remark: 'The river Tagus,' say you, 'was so called from a certain king of Spain. It takes its rise from such a place, and buries its waters in the ocean, kissing first the walls of the famous city of Lisbon; and some are of opinion that the sands of this river are gold,' etc. If you have occasion to talk of robbers, I can presently give you the history of Cacus, for I have it by heart. If you would descant upon whores, or women of the town, there is the bishop of Mondonedo, who can furnish you with Lamia, Laïs, and Flora, courtesans, whose acquaintance will add very much to your reputation. Ovid's Medea can afford you a good example of cruelty. Calypso from Homer, and Circe out of Virgil, are famous instances of witchcraft or enchantment. Would you treat of valiant commanders? Julius Caesar has writ his Commentaries on purpose; and Plutarch can furnish you with a thousand Alexanders. If you would mention love, and have but three grains of Italian, you may find Leon the Jew ready to serve you most abundantly. But if you keep nearer home, it is but examining Fonseca of Divine Love, which you have here in your study; and you need go no further, for all that can be said on that copious subject. In short, it is but quoting these authors in your book, and let me alone to make large annotations; I will engage to*

21

*crowd your margin sufficiently, and scribble you four or five sheets
besides at the end of your book. And for the citation of so many
authors, it is the easiest thing in nature. Find out one of those books
with an alphabetical index, and without any further ceremony, remove
it verbatim into your own: and though the world will not believe you
have occasion for such lumber, yet there are fools enough to be thus
drawn into an opinion of the work; at least, such a flourishing train of
attendants will give your book a fashionable air, and recommend it to
sale; for few chapmen will stand to examine it, and compare the authorities upon the compter, since they can expect nothing but their labor
for their pains. But, after all, sir, if I know anything of the matter,
you have no occasion for any of those things; for your subject, being a
satire on knight-errantry, is so absolutely new, that neither Aristotle,
St. Basil, nor Cicero ever dreamed or heard of it. Those fabulous extravagancies have nothing to do with the impartial punctuality of true
history; nor do I find any business you can have either with astrology,
geometry, or logic; and I hope you are too good a man to mix sacred
things with profane. Nothing but pure nature is your business; her
you must consult, and the closer you can imitate, your picture is the
better. And since this writing of yours aims at no more than to destroy
the authority and acceptance the books of chivalry have had in the
world, and among the vulgar, you have no need to go begging sentences
of philosophers, passages out of holy writ, poetical fables, rhetorical
orations, or miracles of saints. Do but take care to express yourself in
a plain, easy manner, in well-chosen, significant, and decent terms, and
to give an harmonious and pleasing turn to your periods: study to
explain your thoughts, and set them in the truest light, laboring, as
much as possible, not to leave them dark nor intricate, but clear and
intelligible: let your diverting stories be expressed in diverting terms,
to kindle mirth in the melancholic, and heighten it in the gay: let mirth
and humor be your superficial design, though laid on a solid foundation,
to challenge attention from the ignorant, and admiration from the
judicious; to secure your work from the contempt of the graver sort,
and deserve the praises of men of sense; keeping your eye still fixed on*

22

the principal end of your project, the fall and destruction of that monstrous heap of ill-contrived romances, which, though abhorred by many, have so strangely infatuated the greater part of mankind. Mind this, and your business is done."

I listened very attentively to my friend's discourse, and found it so reasonable and convincing, that without any reply, I took his advice, and have told you the story by way of preface; wherein you may see, gentlemen, how happy I am in so ingenious a friend, to whose seasonable counsel you are all obliged for the omission of all this pedantic garniture in the history of the renowned Don Quixote de la Mancha, whose character among all the neighbors about Montiel, is, that he was the most chaste lover, and the most valiant knight, that has been known in those parts these many years. I will not urge the service I have done you by introducing you into so considerable and noble a knight's acquaintance, but only beg the favor of some small acknowledgment for recommending you to the familiarity of the famous Sancho Panza his squire; in whom, in my opinion, you will find united and described all the squire-like graces which are scattered up and down in the whole bead-roll of books of chivalry. And now I take my leave, entreating you not to forget your humble servant.

BOOK ONE

I

THE QUALITY AND MANNER OF LIFE OF THE RENOWNED DON QUIXOTE DE LA MANCHA

A T A CERTAIN VILLAGE in La Mancha,[1] which I shall not name, there lived not long ago one of those old-fashioned gentlemen who are never without a lance upon a rack, an old target, a lean horse, and a greyhound. His diet consisted more of beef than mutton; and with minced meat on most nights, lentils on Fridays, eggs and bacon on Saturdays, and a pigeon extraordinary on Sundays, he consumed three quarters of his revenue; the rest was laid out in a plush coat, velvet breeches, with slippers of the same, for holidays; and a suit of the very best homespun cloth, which he bestowed on himself for working days. His whole family was a

[1] *A small territory, partly in the kingdom of Arragon, and partly in Castile.*

housekeeper something turned of forty, a niece not twenty, and a man that served him in the house and in the field, and could saddle a horse, and handle the pruning-hook. The master himself was nigh fifty years of age, of a hale and strong complexion, lean-bodied, and thin-faced, an early riser, and a lover of hunting. Some say his surname was Quixada, or Quesada (for authors differ in this particular) : however, we may reasonably conjecture he was called Quixana (*i.e.* lanthorn-jaws) though this concerns us but little, provided we keep strictly to the truth in every point of this history.

You must know then, that when our gentleman had nothing to do (which was almost all the year round), he passed his time in reading books of knight-errantry; which he did with that application and delight, that at last he in a manner wholly left off his country sports, and even the care of his estate; nay, he grew so strangely besotted with those amusements, that he sold many acres of arable land to purchase books of that kind; by which means he collected as many of them as were to be had: but among them all, none pleased him like the works of the famous Feliciano de Silva; for the clearness of his prose, and those intricate expressions with which it is interlaced, seemed to him so many pearls of eloquence, especially when he came to read the challenges; and the amorous addresses, many of them in this extraordinary style, "The reason of your unreasonable usage of my reason, does so enfeeble my reason, that I have reason to expostulate with your beauty:" and this, "The sublime heavens, which with your divinity divinely fortify you with the stars, and fix you the deserver of the desert that is deserved by your grandeur." These and such-like expressions, strangely puzzled the poor gentleman's understanding, while he was breaking his brain to unravel their meaning, which Aristotle himself could never have found, though he should have been raised from the dead for that very purpose.

He did not so well like those dreadful wounds which Don Belianis gave and received; for he considered that all the art of surgery could never secure his face and body from being strangely disfigured with scars. However, he highly commended the author for concluding his book with a promise to finish that unfinishable adventure; and many times he had a desire to put pen to paper, and faithfully and literally finish it himself: which he had certainly done, and doubtless with good success, had not his thoughts been wholly engrossed in much more important designs.

He would often dispute with the curate of the parish, a man of learning, that had taken his degrees at Ciguenza, who was the better knight, Palmerin of England, or Amadis de Gaul, but master Nicholas, the barber[2] of the same town, would say, that none of them could compare with the Knight of the Sun; and that if any-one came near him, it was certainly Don Galaor, the brother of Amadis de Gaul; for he was a man of a most commodious temper, neither was he so cynical, nor such a puling whining lover as his brother; and as for courage, he was not a jot behind him.

In fine, he gave himself up so wholly to the reading of romances, that a-nights he would pore on until it was day, and a-days he would read on until it was night; and thus, by sleeping little and reading much, the moisture of his brain was exhausted to that degree, that at last he lost the use of his reason. A world of disorderly notions, picked out of his books, crowded into his imagination; and now his head was full of nothing but enchantments, quarrels, battles, challenges, wounds, complaints, amours, torments, and abundance of stuff and impossibilities; insomuch, that all the fables and fantastical tales which he read seemed to him now as true as the most authentic histories. He would say, that the Cid Ruy Diaz was a very brave knight, but not worthy to stand in competition with the Knight of the Burning Sword, who with a single back-stroke had cut in sunder two fierce and mighty giants. He

2 *The barber in country towns in Spain is also the surgeon.*

liked yet better Bernardo del Carpio, who at Roncesvalles deprived of life the enchanted Orlando, having lifted him from the ground, and choked him in the air, as Hercules did Anteus the son of the earth.

As for the giant Morgante, he always spoke very civil things of him; for, though he was one of that monstrous brood who ever were intolerably proud and brutish, he still behaved himself like a civil and well-bred person.

But of all men in the world he admired Rinaldo of Montalban, and particularly his sallying out of his castle to rob all he met; and then again, when abroad, he carried away the idol Mahomet, which was all massy gold, as the history says: but he so hated that traitor Galalon,[3] that for the pleasure of kicking him handsomely, he would have given up his housekeeper, nay, and his niece into the bargain.

Having thus lost his understanding, he unluckily stumbled upon the oddest fancy that ever entered into a madman's brain; for now he thought it convenient and necessary, as well for the increase of his own honor, as the service of the public, to turn knight-errant, and roam through the whole world, armed *cap-à-pie* and mounted on his steed, in quest of adventures; that thus imitating those knights-errant of whom he had read, and following their course of life, redressing all manner of grievances, and exposing himself to danger on all occasions, at last, after a happy conclusion of his enterprises, he might purchase everlasting honor and renown. Transported with these agreeable delusions, the poor gentleman already grasped in imagination the imperial scepter of Trebizond; and, hurried away by his mighty expectations, he prepares with all expedition to take the field.

The first thing he did was to scour a suit of armor that had be-

[3] *Galalon, the Spaniards say, betrayed the French army at Roncesvalles.*

28

longed to his great-grandfather, and had lain time out of mind carelessly rusting in a corner; but, when he had cleaned and repaired it as well as he could, he perceived there was a material piece wanting; for instead of a complete helmet, there was only a single head-piece: however, his industry supplied that defect; for, with some pasteboard, he made a kind of half-beaver, or vizor, which being fitted to the head-piece, made it look like an entire helmet. Then, to know whether it was cutlass-proof, he drew his sword, and tried its edge upon the pasteboard vizor; but, with the first stroke, he unluckily undid in a moment what he had been a whole week a-doing. He did not like its being broke with so much ease, and therefore to secure it from the like accident, he made it anew, and fenced it with thin plates of iron, which he fixed in the inside of it so artificially, that at last he had reason to be satisfied with the solidity of the work; and so, without any experiment, he resolved it should pass to all intents and purposes for a full and sufficient helmet.

The next moment he went to view his horse, whose bones stuck out like the corners of a Spanish real, being a worse jade than Gonela's, *qui tantum pellis et ossa fuit;* however, his master thought that neither Alexander's Bucephalus, nor the Cid's Babieca could be compared with him. He was four days considering what name to give him; for, as he argued with himself, there was no reason that a horse bestrid by so famous a knight, and withal so excellent in himself, should not be distinguished by a particular name; and therefore he studied to give him such a one as should demonstrate as well what kind of horse he had been before his master was a knight-errant, as what he was now; thinking it but just, since the owner had changed his profession, that the horse should also change his title, and be dignified with another; a sonorous word, such a one as should fill the mouth, and seem consonant with the quality and profession of his master. And thus after many

29

names which he devised, rejected, changed, liked, disliked, and pitched upon again, he concluded to call him Rozinante;[4] a name, in his opinion, lofty sounding, and significant of what he had been before, and also of what he was now; in a word, a horse before or above all the vulgar breed of horses in the world.

When he had thus given his horse a name so much to his satisfaction, he thought of choosing one for himself; and having seriously pondered on the matter eight whole days more, at last he determined to call himself Don Quixote. Whence the author of this most authentic history draws this inference, that his name was Quixada, and not Quesada, as others obstinately pretend. And observing that the valiant Amadis, not satisfied with the bare appellation of Amadis, added to it the name of his country, that it might grow more famous by his exploits, and styled himself Amadis de Gaul; so he, like a true lover of his native soil, resolved to call himself Don Quixote de la Mancha; which addition, to his thinking, denoted very plainly his parentage and country, and consequently would fix a lasting honor on that part of the world.

And now, his armor being scoured, his head-piece improved to a helmet, his horse and himself new-named, he perceived he wanted nothing but a lady, on whom he might bestow the empire of his heart; for he was sensible that a knight-errant without a mistress was a tree without either fruit or leaves, and a body without a soul. "Should I," said he to himself, "by good or ill fortune chance to encounter some giant, as it is common in knight-errantry, and happen to lay him prostrate on the ground, transfixed with my lance, or cleft in two, or, in short, overcome and have him at my mercy, would it not be proper to have some lady to whom I may send him as a trophy of my valor? That, when he comes into her presence,

4 Rozin *commonly means an "ordinary horse"*; Ante *signifies "before" and "formerly." Thus the word Rozinante may imply, that he was formerly an ordinary horse, and also, that he is now an horse that claims the precedence from all other ordinary horses.*

throwing himself at her feet, he may thus make his humble submission: 'Lady, I am the giant Caraculiambro, lord of the island of Malindrania, vanquished in single combat by that never-deservedly-enough-extolled knight-errant Don Quixote de la Mancha, who has commanded me to cast myself most humbly at your feet, that it may please your honor to dispose of me according to your will.'" Oh! how elevated was the Knight with the conceit of this imaginary submission of the giant; especially having bethought himself of a person on whom he might confer the title of mistress which, it is believed, happened thus. Near the place where he lived dwelt a good likely country lass, for whom he had formerly had a sort of an inclination, though it is believed she never heard of it, nor regarded it in the least. Her name was Aldonza Lorenzo, and this was she whom he thought he might entitle to the sovereignty of his heart: upon which he studied to find her out a new name, that might have some affinity with her old one, and yet at the same time sound somewhat like that of a princess, or lady of quality: so at last he resolved to call her Dulcinea, with the addition of del Toboso, from the place where she was born; a name, in his opinion, sweet, harmonious, extraordinary, and no less significant than the others which he had devised.

II: OF DON QUIXOTE'S FIRST SALLY

These preparations being made, he found his designs ripe for action, and thought it now a crime to deny himself any longer to the injured world, that wanted such a deliverer; the more when he considered what grievances he was to redress, what wrongs and injuries to remove, what abuses to correct, and what duties to discharge. So one morning before day, in the greatest heat of July, without acquainting any one with his design, with all the secrecy

imaginable, he armed himself *cap-à-pie*, laced on his ill-contrived helmet, braced on his target, grasped at his lance, mounted Rozinante, and at the private door of his back yard sallied out into the fields, wonderfully pleased to note with how much ease he had succeeded in the very beginning of his enterprise. But he had not gone far ere a terrible thought alarmed him, a thought that had like to have made him renounce his great undertaking; for now it came into his mind that the honor of knighthood had not yet been conferred upon him, and therefore, according to the laws of chivalry, he neither could nor ought to appear in arms against any professed knight: nay, he also considered, that though he were already knighted, it would become him to wear white armor, and not to adorn his shield with any device, till he had deserved one by some extraordinary demonstration of his valor.

These thoughts staggered his resolution; but his folly prevailing more than any reason, he resolved to be dubbed a knight by the first he should meet, after the example of several others, who, as his distracting romances informed him, had formerly done the like. As for the other difficulty about wearing white armor, he proposed to overcome it by scouring his own at leisure till it should look whiter than ermine. And having thus dismissed these busy scruples, he very calmly rode on, leaving it to his horse's discretion to go which way he pleased; firmly believing that in this consisted the very being of adventures. And as he thus went on, "I cannot but believe," said he to himself, "that when the history of my famous achievements shall be given to the world, the learned author will begin it in this very manner, when he comes to give an account of this my early setting out: 'Scarce had the ruddy-colored Phoebus begun to spread the golden tresses of his lovely hair over the vast surface of the earthly globe, and scarce had those feathered poets of the grove, the pretty painted birds, tuned their little pipes, to sing their early welcomes in soft melodious strains to the beautiful Aurora, who having left her jealous husband's bed, displayed her rosy graces to mortal eyes from the gates and balconies of the Manchegan Horizon, when the renowned knight Don Quixote de la Mancha, disdaining soft repose, forsook the voluptuous down, and mounting his famous steed Rozinante, entered the ancient and celebrated plains of Montiel.' " [1] This was indeed the very road he took; and then proceeding, "O happy age! O fortunate times!" cried he, "decreed to usher into the world my famous achievements; achievements worthy to be engraven on brass, carved on marble, and delineated in some masterpiece of painting, as monuments of my glory, and examples for posterity! And thou, venerable sage, wise enchanter, whatever be thy name; thou whom fate has ordained to be the compiler of this rare history, forget not, I beseech thee, my trusty Rozinante, the eternal companion of all my adventures." After this, as if he had been really in love: "O princess Dulcinea," cried he, "lady of this captive heart, much sorrow and woe you have doomed me to in banishing me thus, and imposing on me your rigorous commands, never to appear before your beauteous face! Remember, lady, that loyal heart your slave, who for your love submits to so many miseries." To these extravagant conceits he added a world of others, all in imitation, and in the very

[1] *Montiel, a proper field to inspire courage, being the ground upon which Henry the Bastard slew his legitimate brother Don Pedro, whom our brave black prince Edward had set upon the throne of Spain.*

33

style of those which the reading of romances had furnished him with; and all this while he rode so softly, and the sun's heat increased so fast, and was so violent, that it would have been sufficient to have melted his brains, had he had any left.

He traveled almost all that day without meeting any adventure worth the trouble of relating; which put him into a kind of despair; for he desired nothing more than to encounter immediately some person, on whom he might try the vigor of his arm.

Some authors say, that his first adventure was that of the pass called Puerto Lapice; others, that of the windmills; but all that I could discover of certainty in this matter, and that I meet with in the annals of La Mancha, is, that he traveled all that day; and, towards the evening, he and his horse being heartily tired, and almost famished, Don Quixote, looking about him in hopes to discover some castle, or at least some shepherd's cottage, there to repose and refresh himself; at last, near the road which he kept, he espied an inn, as welcome a sight to his longing eyes, as if he had discovered a star directing him to the gate, nay, to the palace of his redemption. Thereupon hastening towards the inn with all the speed he could, he got thither just at the close of the evening. There stood by chance at the inn-door, two young female adventurers, alias common wenches, who were going to Seville with some carriers, that happened to take up their lodgings there that very evening; and, as whatever our knight-errant saw, thought, or imagined, was all of a romantic cast, and appeared to him altogether after the manner of the books that had perverted his imagination, he no sooner saw the inn, but he fancied it to be a castle fenced with four towers and lofty pinnacles, glittering with silver, together with a deep moat, drawbridge, and all those other appurtenances peculiar to such kind of places.

Therefore when he came near it, he stopped a while at a distance from the gate, expecting that some dwarf would appear on the battlements, and sound his trumpet to give notice of the arrival of a knight; but finding that nobody came, and that Rozinante was for making the best of his way to the stable, he advanced to the inn-door, where, spying the two young doxies, they seemed to him two beautiful damsels, or graceful ladies, taking the benefit of the fresh air at the gate of the castle. It happened also at the very moment, that a swine-herd, getting together his hogs (for, without begging pardon, so they are called) [2] from the stubble-field, winded his horn; and Don Quixote presently imagined this was the wished-for signal, which some dwarf gave to notify his approach; therefore, with the greatest joy in the world he rode up to the inn. The wenches, affrighted at the approach of a man cased in iron, and armed with a lance and target, were for running into their lodging; but Don Quixote, perceiving their fear by their flight, lifted up the pasteboard beaver of his helmet, and discovering his withered, dusty face, with comely grace and grave delivery accosted them in this manner. "I beseech ye, ladies, do not fly, nor fear the least offense: the order of knighthood, which I profess, does not permit me to countenance or offer injuries to anyone in the universe, and least of all to virgins of such high rank as your presence denotes." The wenches looked earnestly upon him, endeavoring to get a glimpse of his face, which his ill-contrived beaver partly hid; but when they heard themselves styled virgins, a thing so out of the way of their profession, they could not forbear laughing outright; which Don Quixote resented as a great affront. "Give me leave to tell ye, ladies," cried he, "that modesty and civility are very becoming in the fair sex; whereas laughter without ground is the highest piece of indiscretion: however," added he, "I do not presume to say this to offend you, or incur your displeasure; no, ladies, I assure you I have no other design but to do you service."

2 *Our author here ridicules the affected delicacy of the Spaniards and Italians, who look upon it as ill manners to name the word hog or swine, as too gross an image.*

This uncommon way of expression, joined to the Knight's scurvy figure, increased their mirth; which incensed him to that degree, that this might have carried things to an extremity, had not the innkeeper luckily appeared at that juncture. He was a man whose burden of fat inclined him to peace and quietness, yet when he had observed such a strange disguise of human shape, in his old armor and equipage, he could hardly forbear keeping the wenches company in their laughter; but, having the fear of such a warlike appearance before his eyes, he resolved to give him good words, and therefore accosted him civilly: "Sir Knight," said he, "if your worship be disposed to alight, you will fail of nothing here but of a bed; as for all other accommodations, you may be supplied to your mind." Don Quixote observing the humility of the governor of the castle (for such the innkeeper and inn seemed to him), "Signor Castellano," said he, "the least thing in the world suffices me; for arms are the only things I value, and combat is my bed of repose." The innkeeper thought he had called him Castellano,[3] as taking him to be one of the true Castilians, whereas he was indeed of Andalusia, nay, of the neighborhood of St. Lucar, no less thievish than Cacus, or less mischievous than a truant scholar or court page; and therefore he made him this reply: "At this rate, Sir Knight, your bed might be a pavement, and your rest to be still awake; you may then safely alight, and I dare assure you, you can hardly miss being kept awake all the year long in this house, much less one single night." With that he went and held Don Quixote's stirrup, who having not broke his fast that day, dismounted with no small trouble or difficulty. He immediately desired the governor (that is, the innkeeper) to take especial care of his steed, assuring him that there was not a better in the universe; upon which the innkeeper viewed him narrowly, but could not think him to be half so

[3] *Castellano signifies both a constable or governor of a castle, and an inhabitant of the kingdom of Castile in Spain.*

good as Don Quixote said: however, having set him up in the stable, he came back to the Knight to see what he wanted, and found him pulling off his armor by the help of the good-natured wenches, who had already reconciled themselves to him; but, though they had eased him of his corslet and back-plate, they could by no means undo his gorget, nor take off his ill-contrived beaver, which he had tied so fast with green ribbons, that it was impossible to get it off without cutting them; now he would by no means permit that, and so was forced to keep on his helmet all night, which was one of the most pleasant sights in the world; and while his armor was being taken off by the two kind lasses, imagining them to be persons of quality, and ladies of that castle, he very gratefully made them the following compliment (in imitation of an old romance):

> *"There never was on earth a knight*
> *So waited on by ladies fair,*
> *As once was he, Don Quixote hight,*
> *When first he left his village dear:*
> *Damsels to serve him ran with speed,*
> *And princesses to dress his steed.*

"O Rozinante! for that is my horse's name, ladies, and mine Don Quixote de la Mancha; I never thought to have discovered it, till some feats of arms, achieved by me in your service, had made me better known to your ladyships; but necessity forcing me to apply to present purpose that passage of the ancient romance of Sir Lancelot, which I now repeat, has extorted the secret from me before its time; yet a day will come, when you shall command, and I obey, and then the valor of my arm shall evince the reality of my zeal to serve your ladyships."

The two females, who were not used to such rhetorical speeches, could make no answer to this; they only asked him whether he would eat anything. "That I will with all my heart," cried Don Quixote, "whatever it be, for I am of opinion, nothing can come to

37

me more seasonably." Now, as ill-luck would have it, it happened to be Friday, and there was nothing to be had at the inn but some pieces of fish, which is called Abadexo in Castile, Bacalloa in Andalusia, Curadillo in some places, and in others Truchuela or Little Trout, though, after all, it is but Poor Jack: so they asked him whether he could eat any of that Truchuela, because they had no other fish to give him. Don Quixote, imagining they meant a small trout, told them, that, provided there were more than one, it was the same thing to him, they would serve him as well as a great one; "for," continued he, "it is all one to me whether I am paid a piece of eight in one single piece, or in eight small reals, which are worth as much: besides, it is probable these small trouts may be like veal, which is finer meat than beef; or like the kid, which is better than the goat. In short, let it be what it will, so it comes quickly, for the weight of armor and the fatigue of travel are not to be supported without recruiting food." Thereupon they laid the cloth at the inn-door, for the benefit of the fresh air, and the landlord brought him a piece of that salt fish, but ill-watered and as ill-dressed; and, as for the bread, it was as moldy and brown as the Knight's armor: but it would have made one laugh to have seen him eat; for, having his helmet on, with his beaver lifted up, it was impossible for him to feed himself without help, so that one of those ladies had that office; but there was no giving him drink that way, and he must have gone without it, had not the innkeeper bored a cane, and setting one end of it to his mouth, poured the wine in at the other; all which the Knight suffered patiently, because he would not cut the ribbons that fastened his helmet.

While he was at supper, a sow-gelder happened to sound his cane-trumpet, or whistle of reeds, four or five times as he came near the inn; which made Don Quixote the more positive of his being in a famous castle, where he was entertained with music at supper, that the Poor Jack was young trout, the bread of the finest flour, the wenches great ladies, and the innkeeper the governor of the castle; which made him applaud himself for his resolution, and his setting out on such an account. The only thing that vexed him was, that he was not dubbed a knight; for he fancied he could not lawfully undertake any adventure till he had received the order of knighthood.

III: AN ACCOUNT OF THE PLEASANT METHOD TAKEN BY DON QUIXOTE TO BE DUBBED A KNIGHT

Don Quixote's mind being disturbed with that thought, he abridged even his short supper; and as soon as he had done, he called his host, then shut him and himself up in the stable, and falling at his feet, "I will never rise from this place," cried he, "most valorous knight, till you have graciously vouchsafed to grant me a boon, which I will now beg of you, and which will redound to your honor and the good of mankind." The landlord, strangely at a loss to find his guest at his feet, and talking at this rate, endeavored to make him rise, but all in vain till he had promised to grant him what he asked. "I expected no less from your great magnificence, noble sir," replied Don Quixote, "and therefore I make bold to tell you, that the boon which I beg, and you generously condescend to grant me, is, that tomorrow you will be pleased to bestow the honor of knighthood upon me. This night I will watch my armor in the chapel of your castle, and then in the morning you shall gratify me, as I passionately desire that I may be duly qualified to seek out adventures in every corner of the universe, to relieve the distressed, according to the laws of chivalry, and the inclinations of knights-errant like myself." The innkeeper, who, as I said, was a sharp fellow, and had already a shrewd suspicion of the disorder in his guest's understanding, was fully convinced of it when he heard him talk after this manner; and, to make sport that night, resolved to humor him in his desires, telling him he was highly to be commended for his choice of such an employment, which was altogether worthy a knight of the first order, such as his gallant deportment discovered him to be: that he himself had in his youth followed that honorable profession, ranging through many parts of the world in search of adventures, without so much as forgetting to visit the Percheles [1] of Malaga, the isles of Riaran, the compass of Seville, the quicksilver house of Segovia, the olive-field of Valencia, the circle of Granada, the coast of St. Lucar, the potro of Cordova, [2] the hedge-taverns of Toledo, and divers other places, where he had exercised the nimbleness of his feet, and the subtilty of his hands, doing wrongs in abundance, soliciting many widows, undoing some damsels, bubbling young heirs, and, in a word, making himself famous in most of the courts of judicature in Spain, till at length he retired to this castle, where he lived on his own estate and those of others, entertaining all knights-errant of what quality or condition soever, merely for the great affection he bore them, and to partake of what they got in recompense of his good-will. He added, that his castle at present had no chapel, where the Knight might keep his vigil of arms, it being pulled down in order to be new-built; but that he knew they might lawfully be watched in any other place in a case of necessity, and therefore he might do it that night in the court-yard of the castle; and in the morning (God willing) all the necessary ceremonies should be performed, so that he might assure himself he should be dubbed a knight, nay, as much a knight as anyone in the world could be. He then asked Don Quixote, whether he had any money. "Not a cross," replied the Knight, "for I never read in any history of chivalry that any knight-errant

1 *These are all places noted for rogueries.*
2 *A square in the city of Cordova, where a fountain gushes out from the mouth of a horse, near which is also a whipping-post.*

40

ever carried money about him." "You are mistaken," cried the innkeeper; "for admit the histories are silent in this matter, the authors thinking it needless to mention things so evidently necessary as money and clean shirts, yet there is no reason to believe the knights went without either; and you may rest assured that all the knights-errant, of whom so many histories are full, had their purses well lined to supply themselves with necessaries, and carried also with them some shirts, and a small box of salves to heal their wounds; for they had not the conveniency of surgeons to cure them every time they fought in fields and deserts, unless they were so happy as to have some sage or magician for their friend, to give them present assistance, sending them some damsel or dwarf through the air in a cloud, with a small bottle of water of so great a virtue, that they no sooner tasted a drop of it, but their wounds were as perfectly cured as if they had never received any. But when they wanted such a friend in former ages, the knights thought themselves obliged to take care that their squires should be provided with money and other necessaries, as lint and salves to dress their wounds; and, if those knights ever happened to have no squires, which was but very seldom, then they carried those things behind them in a little bag,[3] as if it had been something of greater value, and so neatly fitted to their saddle that it was hardly seen; for, had it not been upon such an account, the carrying of wallets was not much allowed among knights-errant. I must therefore advise you," continued he, "nay, I might even charge and command you, as you are shortly to be my son in chivalry, never from this time forwards to ride without money, nor without the other necessaries of which I spoke to you, which you will find very beneficial when you least expect it." Don Quixote promised to perform very punctually all his injunctions; and so they disposed everything in order to his watching his arms in a great yard that adjoined to the

[3] *Of striped stuff, which Spaniards carry when they travel.*

inn. To which purpose the Knight, having got them all together, laid them in a cistern close by a well in that yard; then, bracing his target and grasping his lance, just as it grew dark, he began to walk about by the horse-trough with a graceful deportment. In the meanwhile the innkeeper acquainted all those that were in the house with the extravagancies of his guest, his watching his arms,

and his hopes of being made a knight. They all admired very much at so strange a kind of folly, and went on to observe him at a distance; where they saw him sometimes walk about with a great deal of gravity, and sometimes lean on his lance, with his eyes all the while fixed upon his arms. It was now undoubted night, but yet the moon did shine with such a brightness as might almost have vied with that of the luminary which lent it her; so that the Knight was wholly exposed to the spectators' view. While he was thus employed, one of the carriers who lodged in the inn came out to water his mules, which he could not do without removing the arms out of the trough. With that Don Quixote, who saw him make towards him, cried out to him aloud, "O thou, whoever thou art, rash knight, that prepares to lay thy hands on the arms of the most valorous knight-errant that ever wore a sword, take heed; do not audaciously attempt to profane them with a touch, lest instant death be the too-sure reward of thy temerity." But the carrier never regarded these dreadful threats; and, laying hold on the armor by the straps, without any more ado threw it a good way from him; though it had been better for him to have let it alone: for Don Quixote no sooner saw this, but lifting up his eyes to heaven, and addressing his thoughts, as it seemed, to his lady Dulcinea, "Assist me, lady," cried he, "in the first opportunity that offers itself to your faithful slave; nor let your favor and protection be denied me in this first trial of my valor!" Repeating such like ejaculations, he let slip his target, and lifting up his lance with both his hands, he gave the carrier such a terrible knock on his inconsiderate pate with his lance, that he laid him at his feet in a woeful condition; and, had he backed that blow with another, the fellow would certainly have had no need of a surgeon. This done, Don Quixote took up his armor, laid it again in the horse-trough, and then walked on, backwards and forwards, with as great unconcern as he did at first.

Soon after another carrier, not knowing what had happened, came also to water his mules, while the first yet lay on the ground in a trance; but, as he offered to clear the trough of the armor, Don Quixote, without speaking a word or imploring anyone's assistance, once more dropped his target, lifted up his lance, and then let it fall so heavily on the fellow's pate, that, without damaging his lance, he broke the carrier's head in three or four places. His outcry soon alarmed and brought thither all the people in the inn, and the landlord among the rest; which Don Quixote perceiving, "Thou queen of beauty," cried he, bracing on his shield, and drawing his sword, "thou courage and vigor of my weakened heart, now is the time when thou must enliven thy adventurous slave with the beams of thy greatness, while this moment he is engaging in so terrible an adventure!" With this, in his opinion, he found himself supplied with such an addition of courage, that, had all the carriers in the world at once attacked him, he would undoubtedly have faced them all. On the other side, the carriers, enraged to see their comrades thus used, though they were afraid to come near, gave the Knight such a volley of stones, that he was forced to shelter himself as well as he could under the covert of his target, without daring to go far from the horse-trough, lest he should seem to abandon his arms. The innkeeper called to the carriers as loud as he could to let him alone; that he had told them already that he was mad, and consequently the law would acquit him, though he should kill them. Don Quixote also made yet more noise, calling them false and treacherous villains, and the lord of the castle a base, inhospitable, and discourteous knight, for suffering a knight-errant to be so abused. "I would make thee know," cried he, "what a perfidious wretch thou art, had I but received the order of knighthood; but for you, base, ignominious rabble! fling on, do your worst; come on, draw nearer if you dare, and receive the reward of your indiscretion and insolence." This he spoke with so much spirit and undauntedness, that he struck a terror into all his assailants; so that, partly through fear and partly through the innkeeper's persuasions, they gave over flinging stones at him; and he, on his side, permitted the enemy to carry off their wounded, and then returned to the guard of his arms as calm and composed as before.

The innkeeper, who began somewhat to disrelish these mad tricks of his guest, resolved to dispatch him forthwith, and bestow on him that unlucky knighthood, to prevent further mischief: so, coming to him, he excused himself for the insolence of those base scoundrels, as being done without his privity or consent; but their audaciousness, he said, was sufficiently punished. He added, that he had already told him there was no chapel in his castle; and that indeed there was no need of one to finish the rest of the ceremony of knighthood, which consisted only in the application of the sword to the neck and shoulders, as he had read in the register of the ceremonies of the order; and that this might be performed as well in a field as anywhere else. That he had already fulfilled the obligation of watching his arms, which required no more than two hours' watch, whereas he had been four hours upon the guard. Don Quixote, who easily believed him, told him he was ready to obey him, and desired him to make an end of the business as soon as possible; for, if he were but knighted, and should see himself attacked, he believed he should not leave a man alive in the castle, except those whom he should desire him to spare for his sake.

Upon this the innkeeper, lest the Knight should proceed to such extremities, fetched the book in which he used to set down the carriers' accounts for straw and barley; and having brought with him the two kind females, already mentioned, and a boy that held a piece of lighted candle in his hand, he ordered Don Quixote to kneel: then reading in his manual, as if he had been repeating some pious oration, in the midst of his devotion, he lifted up his hand, and gave him a good blow on the neck, and then a gentle slap on the back with the flat of his sword, still mumbling some words between his teeth in the tone of a prayer. After this he ordered one of the wenches to gird the sword about the Knight's waist; which she did with much solemnity, and, I may add, discretion, considering how hard a thing it was to forbear laughing at every circumstance of the ceremony. It is true, the thoughts of the Knight's late prowess did not a little contribute to the suppression of their mirth. As she girded on his sword, "Heaven," cried the kind lady, "make your worship a lucky knight, and prosper you wherever you go." Don Quixote desired to know her name, that he might understand to whom he was indebted for the favor she had bestowed upon him, and also make her partaker of the honor he was to acquire by the strength of his arm. To which the lady answered with all humility, that her name was Tolosa, a cobbler's daughter, that kept a stall among the little shops of Sanchobinaya at Toledo; and that, whenever he pleased to command her, she would be his

45

humble servant. Don Quixote begged of her to do him the favor to add hereafter the title of Lady to her name, and for his sake to be called from that time the Lady Tolosa; which she promised to do. Her companion, having buckled on his spurs, occasioned a like conference between them; and, when he had asked her name, she told him she went by the name of Miller, being the daughter of an honest miller of Antequera. Our new Knight entreated her also to style herself the Lady Miller, making her new offers of service. These extraordinary ceremonies (the like never seen before) being thus hurried over in a kind of post-haste, Don Quixote could not rest till he had taken the field in quest of adventures; therefore, having immediately saddled his Rozinante, and being mounted, he embraced the innkeeper, and returned him so many thanks at so extravagant a rate, for the obligation he had laid upon him in dubbing him a knight, that it is impossible to give a true relation of them all: to which the innkeeper, in haste to get rid of him, returned as rhetorical, though shorter answers; and, without stopping his horse for the reckoning, was glad with all his heart to see him go.

IV: WHAT BEFELL THE KNIGHT AFTER HE HAD LEFT THE INN

Aurora began to usher in the morn, when Don Quixote sallied out of the inn, so well pleased, so gay, and so overjoyed to find himself knighted, that he infused the same satisfaction into his horse, who seemed ready to burst his girths for joy. But calling to mind the admonitions which the innkeeper had given him, concerning the provision of necessary accommodations in his travels, particularly money and clean shirts, he resolved to return home to furnish himself with them, and likewise get him a squire, designing to entertain,

46

as such, a laboring man, his neighbor, who was poor and had a charge of children, but yet very fit for the office. With this resolution he took the road which led to his own village; and Rozinante, that seemed to know his will by instinct, began to carry him a round trot so briskly, that his heels seemed scarcely to touch the ground. The Knight had not traveled far, when he fancied he heard an effeminate voice complaining in a thicket on his right hand. "I thank heaven," said he, when he heard the cries, "for favoring me so soon with an opportunity to perform the duty of my profession, and reap the fruit of my desires! For these complaints are certainly the moans of some distressed creature who wants my present help." Then turning to that side with all the speed which Rozinante could make, he no sooner came into the wood but he saw a mare tied to an oak, and to another a young lad, about fifteen years of age, naked from the waist upwards. This was he who made such a lamentable outcry; and not without cause, for a lusty country-fellow was strapping him soundly with a girdle, at every stripe putting him in mind of a proverb, "Keep your mouth shut, and your eyes open, sirrah." "Good master," cried the boy, "I'll do so no more; as I hope to be saved, I'll never do so again! Indeed, master, hereafter I'll take more care of your goods." Don Quixote seeing this, cried, in an angry tone, "Discourteous Knight, it is an unworthy act to strike a person who is not able to defend himself: come, bestride thy steed, and take thy lance" (for the farmer had something that looked like one leaning to the same tree to which his mare was tied), "then I'll make thee know thou hast acted the part of a coward." The country-fellow, who gave himself for lost at the sight of an apparition in armor brandishing his lance at his face, answered him in mild and submissive words: "Sir Knight," cried he, "this boy, whom I am chastising, is my servant, employed by me to look after a flock of sheep, which I have not far off; but he is so heedless, that I lose some of them every day. Now, because I correct

47

him for carelessness or his knavery, he says I do it out of covetousness, to defraud him of his wages; but, upon my life and soul, he belies me." "What! the lie in my presence, you saucy clown," cried Don Quixote; "by the sun that shines I have a good mind to run thee through the body with my lance. Pay the boy this instant, without more words, or, by the Power that rules us all, I will immediately dispatch and annihilate thee: come, unbind him this moment." The countryman hung down his head, and, without any further reply, unbound the boy; who, being asked by Don Quixote what his master owed him, told him it was nine months' wages, at seven reals a month. The Knight, having cast it up, found it came to sixty-three reals in all; which he ordered the farmer to pay the fellow immediately, unless he intended to lose his life that very moment. The poor countryman, trembling for fear, told him, that, as he was on the brink of death, by the oath he had sworn (by the bye, he had not sworn at all) he did not owe the lad so much: for there was to be deducted for three pair of shoes which he had bought him, and a real for his being let blood twice when he was sick. "That may be," replied Don Quixote; "but, set the price of the shoes and the bleeding against the stripes which you have given him without cause: for, if he has used the leather which you paid for, you have in return misused and impaired his skin sufficiently; and, if the surgeon let him blood when he was sick, you have drawn blood from him now he is in health; so that he owes you nothing on that account." "The worst is, Sir Knight," cried the farmer, "that I have no money about me; but let Andrew go home with me, and I'll pay him every piece out of hand." "What! I go home with him!" cried the youngster, "the devil a bit, sir! not I truly, I know better things; for he would no sooner have me by myself but he would flea me alive, like another St. Bartholomew." "He will never dare to do it," replied Don Quixote; "I command him, and that is sufficient to restrain him: therefore, provided he will swear by the

48

order of knighthood which has been conferred upon him, that he will duly observe this regulation, I will freely let him go, and then thou art secure of thy money." "Good sir, take heed what you say," cried the boy; "for my master is no knight, nor ever was of any order in his life: he is John Haldudo, the rich farmer of Quintinar." "This signifies little," answered Don Quixote, "for there may be knights among the Haldudos; besides, the brave man carves out his fortune, and every man is the son of his own works." "That's true, sir," quoth Andrew; "but of what works can this master of mine be the son, who denies me my wages, which I have earned with the sweat of my brow?" "I do not deny to pay thee thy wages, honest Andrew," cried the master; "be but so kind as to go along with me, and by all the orders of knighthood in the world, I swear, I will pay thee every piece, as I said, nay, and perfumed to boot."[1] "You may spare your perfume," said Don Quixote; "do but pay him in reals, and I am satisfied; but be sure you perform your oath, for if you fail, I myself swear by the same oath to return and find you out, and punish you, though you should hide yourself as close as a lizard. And if you will be informed who it is that lays these injunctions on you, that you may understand how highly it concerns you to observe them; know, I am the valorous Don Quixote de la Mancha, the righter of wrongs, the revenger and redresser of grievances; and so farewell: but remember what you have promised and sworn, as you will answer the contrary at your peril." This said, he clapped spurs to Rozinante, and quickly left the master and the man a good way behind him.

The countryman, who followed him with both his eyes, no sooner perceived that he was passed the woods and quite out of sight, but he went back to his boy Andrew. "Come, child," said he, "I will

[1] *To pay or return a thing perfumed is a Spanish expression signifying it shall be done to content or with advantage to the receiver. It is also said to be intended as a satire on the effeminate custom of wearing everything perfumed, insomuch that the very money in their pockets was scented.*

pay thee what I owe thee, as that righter of wrongs and redresser of grievances has ordered me." "Ay," quoth Andrew, "on my word, you will do well to fulfill the commands of that good Knight, whom Heaven grant long to live; for he is so brave a man, and so just a judge, that, adad, if you do not pay me he will come back and make his words good." "I dare swear as much," answered the master; "and to show thee how much I love thee, I am willing to increase the debt, that I may enlarge the payment." With that, he caught the youngster by the arm, and tied him again to the tree; where he handled him so unmercifully, that scarce any signs of life were left in him. "Now call your Righter of Wrongs, Mr. Andrew," cried the farmer, "and you shall see he will never be able to undo what I have done; though I think it is but a part of what I ought to do, for I have a good mind to flea you alive, as you said I would, you rascal." However, he untied him at last, and gave him leave to go and seek out his judge, in order to have his decree put in execution. Andrew went his ways, not very well pleased you may be sure, yet fully resolved to find out the valorous Don Quixote de la Mancha, and give him an exact account of the whole transaction, that he might pay the abuse with sevenfold usury; in short, he crept off sobbing and weeping, while his master stayed behind laughing. And in this manner was this wrong redressed by the valorous Don Quixote de la Mancha.

In the meantime, being highly pleased with himself and what had happened, imagining he had given a most fortunate and noble beginning to his feats of arms, as he went on towards his village, "O most beautiful of beauties," said he with a low voice, "Dulcinea del Toboso! well mayest thou deem thyself most happy, since it was thy good fortune to captivate and hold a willing slave to thy pleasure, so valorous and renowned a knight as is, and ever shall be, Don Quixote de la Mancha; who, as all the world knows, had the honor of knighthood bestowed on him but yesterday, and this

day redressed the greatest wrong and grievance that ever injustice could design, or cruelty commit; this day has he wrested the scourge out of the hands of that tormentor, who so unmercifully treated a tender infant, without the least occasion given." Just as he had said this, he found himself at a place where four roads met; and this made him presently bethink of those crossways which often used to put knights-errant to a stand, to consult with themselves which way they should take; and that he might follow their example, he stopped a while, and after he had seriously reflected on the matter, gave Rozinante the reins, subjecting his own will to that of his horse, who pursuing his first intent, took the way that led to his own stable.

Don Quixote had not gone above two miles, but he discovered a company of people riding towards him, who proved to be merchants of Toledo, that were going to buy silks in Murcia. They were six in all, every one screened with an umbrella, besides four servants on horseback, and three muleteers [2] on foot. The Knight no sooner perceived them, but he imagined this to be some new adventure; and, because he was resolved to imitate as much as possible the passages he had read in his books, he was pleased to represent this to himself as such a particular adventure as he had a singular desire to meet with; and so, with a dreadful grace and assurance, fixing himself in his stirrups, couching his lance, and covering his breast with his target, he posted himself in the middle of the road, expecting the coming up of the supposed knights-errant. As soon as they came within hearing, with a loud voice and haughty tone, "Hold," cried he, "let all mankind stand, nor hope to pass on further, unless all mankind acknowledge and confess, that there is not in the universe a more beautiful damsel than the Empress of La Mancha, the peerless Dulcinea del Toboso." At those words they made a halt to view the unaccountable figure of their opponent; and easily conjecturing, both by his expression and disguise, that the poor gentleman had lost his senses, they were willing to understand the meaning of that strange confession which he would force from them; and therefore one of the company, who loved and understood raillery, having discretion to manage it, undertook to talk to him. "Signor cavalier," cried he, "we do not know this worthy lady you talk of; but be pleased to let us see her, and then if we find her possessed of those matchless charms, of which you assert her to be the mistress, we will freely, and without the least compulsion, own the truth which you would extort from us." "Had I once showed you that beauty," replied Don Quixote, "what wonder would it be to acknowledge so notorious a truth? The impor-

2 *Mule-boys conducted travelers through Spain, brought back the mules, and took care of them all the way.*

52

tance of the thing lies in obliging you to believe it, confess it, affirm it, swear it, and maintain it, without seeing her; and therefore make this acknowledgment this very moment, or know, that it is with me you must join in battle, ye proud and unreasonable mortals. Come one by one, as the laws of chivalry require, or all at once, according to the dishonorable practice of men of your stamp; here I expect you all my single self, and will stand the encounter, confiding in the justness of my cause." "Sir Knight," replied the merchant, "I beseech you, in the name of all the princes here present, that for the discharge of our consciences, which will not permit us to affirm a thing we never heard or saw, and which, besides, tends so much to the dishonor of the Empresses and Queens of Alcaria and Estremadura, your worship will vouchsafe to let us see some portraiture of that lady, though it were no bigger than a grain of wheat; for by a small sample we may judge of the whole piece, and by that means rest secure and satisfied, and you contented and appeased. Nay, I verily believe, that we all find ourselves already so inclined to comply with you, that though her picture should represent her to be blind of one eye, and distilling vermilion and brimstone at the other, yet to oblige you, we should be ready to say in her favor whatever your worship desires." "Distill, ye infamous scoundrels!" replied Don Quixote, in a burning rage, "distill, say you? know that nothing distills from her but amber and civit; neither is she defective in her make or shape, but more straight than a Guadaramin spindle. But you shall all severely pay for the horrid blasphemy which thou hast uttered against the transcendent beauty of my incomparable lady." Saying this, with his lance couched, he ran so furiously at the merchant who thus provoked him, that, had not good fortune so ordered it that Rozinante should stumble and fall in the midst of his career, the audacious trifler had paid dear for his raillery; but as Rozinante fell, he threw down his master, who rolled and tumbled a good way on the ground, without being able to get upon his legs, though he used all his skill and strength to effect it, so encumbered he was with his lance, target, spurs, helmet, and the weight of his rusty armor. However, in this helpless condition he played the hero with his tongue: "Stay," cried he, "cowards, rascals, do not fly! It is not through my fault that I lie here, but through that of my horse, ye poltroons!"

One of the grooms, who was none of the best-natured creatures, hearing the overthrown Knight thus insolently treat his master, could not bear it without returning him an answer on his ribs; and therefore, coming up to him as he lay wallowing, snatched his lance, and, having broken it to pieces, he so belabored Don Quixote's sides with one of them, that, in spite of his arms, he thrashed him like a wheat-sheaf. His master indeed called to him not to lay on him so vigorously, and to let him alone; but the fellow, whose hand was in, would not give over rib-roasting the Knight, till he had tired out his passion and himself; and therefore, running to the other pieces of the broken lance, he fell to it again without ceasing, until he had splintered them all on the Knight's iron enclosure. He, on his side, notwithstanding all this storm of bastinadoes, lay all the while bellowing, threatening heaven and earth, and those villainous ruffians, as he took them to be. At last the mule-driver was tired, and the merchants pursued their journey, sufficiently furnished with matter of discourse at the poor Knight's expense. When he found himself alone, he tried once more to get on his feet; but when he could not do it when he had the use of his limbs, how should he do it now, bruised and battered as he was? But yet, for all this, he esteemed himself a happy man, being still persuaded that his misfortune was one of those accidents common in knight-errantry, and such a one as he could wholly attribute to the falling of his horse; nor could he possibly get up, so sore and mortified was his body all over.

V: A FURTHER ACCOUNT OF OUR KNIGHT'S MISFORTUNES

Don Quixote, perceiving that he was not able to stir, resolved to have recourse to his usual remedy, which was to bethink himself what passage in his books might afford him some comfort: and presently his folly brought to his remembrance the story of Baldwin and the Marquis of Mantua, when Charlotte left the former wounded on the mountain; a story learned and known by little children, not unknown to young men and women, celebrated, and even believed by the old, and yet not a jot more authentic than the miracles of Mahomet. This seemed to him as if made on purpose for his present circumstances, and therefore he fell a-rolling and tumbling up and down, expressing the greatest pain and resentment, and breathing out, with a languishing voice, the same complaints which the wounded knight of the wood is said to have made.

> *"Alas! where are you, lady dear,*
> *That for my woe you do not moan?*
> *You little know what ails me here,*
> *Or are to me disloyal grown!"*

Thus he went on with the lamentations in that romance, till he came to these verses:

> *"O thou, my uncle and my prince,*
> *Marquis of Mantua, noble lord!"*—

when kind fortune so ordered it, that a plowman, who lived in the same village, and near his house, happened to pass by, as he came from the mill with a sack of wheat. The fellow seeing a man lie at his full length on the ground, asked him who he was, and why he made such a sad complaint. Don Quixote, whose distempered brain presently represented to him the countryman for the Marquis of Mantua, his imaginary uncle, made him no answer, but went on with the romance, giving him an account of his misfortunes, and of the loves of his wife, and the emperor's son, just as the book relates them. The fellow stared, much amazed to hear a man talk such unaccountable stuff; and, taking off the vizor of his helmet, broken all to pieces with blows bestowed upon it by the mule-driver, he wiped off the dust that covered his face, and presently knew the gentleman. "Master Quixada!" cried he (for so he was properly called when he had the right use of his senses, and had not yet from a sober gentleman transformed himself into a wandering knight), "how came you in this condition?" But the other continued his romance, and made no answers to all the questions the countryman put to him, but what followed in course in the book; which the good man perceiving, he took off the battered adventurer's armor, as well as he could, and fell a-searching for his wounds; but finding no sign of blood, or any other hurt, he endeavored to set him upon his legs; and at last, with a great deal of trouble, he heaved him upon his own ass, as being the more easy and gentle carriage. He also got all the Knight's arms together, not leaving behind so much as the splinters of his lance; and having tied them up, and laid them on Rozinante, which he took by the bridle, and his ass by the halter, he led them all towards the village, and trudged afoot himself very pensive, while he reflected on the extravagancies which he heard Don Quixote utter. Nor was Don Quixote himself less melancholy, for he felt himself so bruised and battered, that he could hardly sit on the ass; and now and then he breathed such grievous sighs, as seemed to pierce the very skies, which moved his compassionate neighbor once more to entreat him to declare to him the cause of his grief: but one would have imagined the devil prompted him with stories, that had some resemblance of his circumstances; for in that instant, wholly forgetting Baldwin, he bethought himself of the Moor Abindaraez, whom Rodrigo de Narvaez, Alcaide of Antequera, took and carried prisoner to his castle; so that, when the husbandman asked him how he did, and what ailed him, he answered word for word as the prisoner Abindaraez replied to Rodrigo de Narvaez, in the "Diana" of George de Montemayor, where that adventure is related; applying it so properly to his purpose, that the countryman wished himself at the devil rather than within the hearing of such strange nonsense; and, being now fully convinced that his neighbor's brains were turned, he made all the haste he could to the village, to be rid of his troublesome impertinencies. Don Quixote in the meantime thus went on: "You must know, Don Rodrigo de Narvaez, that this beautiful Xerifa, of whom I gave you an account, is at present the most lovely Dulcinea del Toboso, for whose sake I have done, still do, and will achieve the most famous deeds of chivalry that ever were, are, or ever shall be seen in the universe." "Good sir," replied the husbandman, "as I am a sinner, I am not Don Rodrigo de Narvaez, nor the Marquis of Mantua, but Pedro Alonzo by name, your worship's neighbor; nor are you Baldwin, nor Abindaraez, but only that worthy gentleman Signor Quixada." "I know very well who I am," answered Don Quixote, "and what is more, I know, that I may not only be the persons I have named, but also the twelve peers of France, nay, and the nine worthies all in one; since my achievements will out-rival not only the famous exploits which made any of them singly illustrious, but all their mighty deeds accumulated together."

Thus discoursing, they at last got near their village about sunset, but the countryman stayed at some distance till it was dark, that the distressed gentleman might not be seen so scurvily mounted, and then he led him home to his own house, which he found in great confusion. The curate and the barber of the village, both of them Don Quixote's intimate acquaintances, happened to be there at that juncture, as also the housekeeper, who was arguing with them.

57

"What do you think, pray good doctor Perez," said she (for this was the curate's name), "what do you think of my master's mischance? neither he nor his horse, nor his target, lance, nor armor, have been seen these six days. What shall I do, wretch that I am! I dare lay my life, and it is as sure as I am a living creature, that those cursed books of errantry, which he used to be always poring

upon, have set him besides his senses; for, now I remember, I have heard him often mutter to himself, that he had a mind to turn knight-errant, and jaunt up and down the world to find out adventures. May Satan and Barabbas even take all such books that have thus cracked the best head-piece in all La Mancha!" His niece said as much, addressing herself to the barber: "You must know, Mr. Nicholas," quoth she (for that was his name), "that many times my uncle would read those unconscionable books of disventures for eight and forty hours together, then away he would throw his book, and, drawing his sword, he would fall a-fencing against the walls, and when he had tired himself with cutting and slashing, he would cry he had killed four giants as big as any steeples; and the sweat which he put himself into, he would say, was the blood of the wounds he had received in the fight; then would he swallow a huge jug of cold water, and presently he would be as quiet and as well as ever he was in his life; and he said that this same water was a sort of precious drink brought him by the sage Esquife,[1] a great magician, and his special friend. Now it is I who am the cause of all this mischief, for not giving you timely notice of my uncle's raving, that you might have put a stop to it ere it was too late, and have burnt all these excommunicated books; for there are I do not know how many of them that deserve as much to be burned, as those of the rankest heretics." "I am of your mind," said the curate, "and verily tomorrow shall not pass over before I have fairly brought them to a trial, and condemned them to the flames, that they may not minister occasion to such as would read them, to be perverted after the example of my good friend." The countryman, who with Don Quixote stood without listening to all this discourse, now perfectly understood by this the cause of his neighbor's disorder, and therefore, without any more ado, he called out aloud, "Here! house! open the gates there, for the Lord Baldwin, and the Lord Marquis of Mantua, who is coming sadly wounded; and for the Moorish Lord Abindaraez, whom the valorous Don Rodrigo de Narvaez, Alcaide of Antequera, brings prisoner." At which words they all got out of doors; and the one finding it to be her uncle, and the other to be her master, and the rest their friend, who had not yet alighted from the ass, because indeed he was not able, they all ran to embrace him; to whom Don Quixote, "Forbear," said he, "for I am sorely hurt, by reason that my horse failed me; carry me to bed, and if it be possible, let the enchantress Urganda be sent for to cure my wounds." "Now, in the name of mischief," quoth the housekeeper, "see whether I did not guess right, on which foot my

[1] *She means Alquife, a famous enchanter in "Amadis de Gaul" and "Don Belianis of Greece," husband to the no less famous Urganda the sorceress.*

master halted! Come, get you to bed, I beseech you, and, my life for yours, we will take care to cure you without sending for that same Urganda. A hearty curse, and the curse of curses, I say it again and again a hundred times, light upon those books of chivalry that have put you in this pickle." Thereupon they carried him up to his bed, and searched for his wounds, but could find none; and then he told them he was only bruised, having had a dreadful fall from his horse Rozinante, while he was fighting ten giants, the most outrageous and audacious that ever could be found upon the face of the earth. "How!" cried the curate, "have we giants too in the dance?[2] Nay then, by the holy sign of the Cross, I will burn them all by tomorrow night." Then did they ask the Don a thousand questions, but to every one he made no other answer, but that they should give him something to eat, and then leave him to his repose, a thing which was to him of the greatest importance. They complied with his desires; and then the curate informed himself at large in what condition the countryman had found him; and having had a full account of every particular, as also of the Knight's extravagant talk, both when the fellow found him and as he brought him home, this increased the curate's desire of effecting what he had resolved to do the next morning; at which time he called upon his friend Mr. Nicholas, the barber, and went with him to Don Quixote's house.

[2] *Alluding to a passage in "Amadis," where several giants are mixed with ladies and knights, at Constantinople, in a dance.*

VI: OF THE PLEASANT AND CURIOUS SCRUTINY WHICH THE CURATE AND THE BARBER MADE OF THE LIBRARY OF OUR INGENIOUS GENTLEMAN

The Knight was yet asleep, when the curate came attended by the barber, and desired his niece to let him have the key of the room where her uncle kept his books, the author of his woes: she readily consented; and so in they went, and the housekeeper with them. There they found above a hundred large volumes neatly bound, and a good number of small ones: as soon as the housekeeper had spied them out, she ran out of the study, and returned immediately with a holy water-pot and a sprinkler. "Here, doctor," cried she, "pray sprinkle every crack and corner in the room, lest there should lurk in it some one of the many sorcerers these books swarm with, who might chance to bewitch us, for the ill-will we bear them, in going about to send them out of the world." The curate could not forbear smiling at the good woman's simplicity, and desired the barber to reach him the books one by one, that he might peruse the title-pages, for perhaps he might find some among them, that might not deserve to be committed to the flames. "Oh, by no means," cried the niece, "spare none of them, they all help somehow or other to crack my uncle's brain. I fancy we had best throw them all out at the window in the yard, and lay them together in a heap, and then set them on fire, or else carry them into the back yard, and there make a pile of them, and burn them, and so the smoke will offend nobody": the housekeeper joined with her, so eagerly bent they were both upon the destruction of those poor innocents; but the curate would not condescend to those irregular proceedings, and resolved first to read at least the title-page of every book.

The first that Mr. Nicholas put into his hands was "Amadis de Gaul," in four volumes. "There seems to be some mystery in this book's being the first taken down," cried the curate as soon as he had looked upon it, "for I have heard it is the first book of knight-

errantry that ever was printed in Spain, and the model of all the rest; and therefore I am of opinion, that, as the first teacher and author of so pernicious a sect, it ought to be condemned to the fire without mercy." "I beg a reprieve for him," cried the barber, "for I have been told it is the best book that has been written in that kind; and therefore, as the only good thing of that sort, it may deserve a pardon." "Well then," replied the curate, "for this time let him have it. Let us see that other, which lies next to him." "These," said the barber, "are the exploits of Esplandian, the lawful begotten son of Amadis de Gaul." "Verily," said the curate, "the father's goodness shall not excuse the want of it in the son; here, good mistress housekeeper, open that window, and throw it into the yard, and let it serve as a foundation to that pile we are to set a-blazing presently." She was not slack in her obedience; and thus "Don Esplandian" was sent headlong into the yard, there patiently to wait the time of his fiery trial. "To the next," cried the curate. "This," said the barber, "is 'Amadis of Greece'; and I am of opinion, that all those that stand on this side are of the same family." "Then let them all be sent packing into the yard," replied the curate, "for rather than
lose the satisfaction of
burning queen Pinti-

62

quiniestra, [1] and the shepherd Darinel with his eclogues, and the confounded unintelligible discourses of the author, I think I should burn my own father along with them, if I met him in the disguise of a knight-errant." "I am of your mind," cried the barber; "and I too," said the niece. "Nay then," quoth the old female, "let them come, and down with them all into the yard." They were delivered to her accordingly, and many they were; so that, to save herself the labor of carrying them down-stairs, she fairly sent them flying out at the window.

"What tun of an author have we here?" cried the curate: "'Olivante de Laura,'" returned the barber. "The same author wrote 'The Garden of Flowers'; and, to deal ingenuously with you, I cannot well tell which of the two books has most truth in it, or, to speak more properly, less lies; but this I know for certain, that he shall march into the back yard like a nonsensical arrogant blockhead as he is."

"The next," cried the barber, "is 'Florismarte of Hyrcania.'" "How! my lord Florismarte, is he here?" replied the curate, "nay, then truly he shall even follow the rest to the yard, in spite of his wonderful birth and incredible adventures; for his rough, dull, and insipid style deserves no better usage. Come, toss him into the yard, and this other too, good mistress." "With all my heart," quoth the governess; and straight she was as good as her word.

"Here is the noble 'Don Platir,'" cried the barber. "It is an old book," replied the curate, "and I can think of nothing in him that deserves a grain of pity; away with him, without any more word"; and down he went accordingly.

Another book was opened, and it proved to be "The Knight of the Cross." "The holy title," cried the curate, "might in some meas-

[1] *A terrible fighting giantess in "Amadis de Gaul," and one of the most ridiculous characters imaginable.*

ure atone for the badness of the book; but then, as the saying is, 'The devil lurks behind the Cross!' To the flames with him."

Then the barber taking down another book, cried, "Here is 'The Mirror of Knighthood.'" "Oh! I have the honor to know him," replied the curate; "there you will find the lord Rinaldo of Montalban, with his friends and companions, all of them greater thieves than Cacus, together with the twelve peers of France, and that faithful historian Turpin. Truly, I must needs say, I am only for condemning them to perpetual banishment, at least, because their story contains something of the famous Boyardo's invention, out of which the Christian poet Ariosto also spun his web; yet, if I happened to meet with him in this bad company, and speaking in any other language than his own, I will show him no manner of favor; but, if he talks in his own native tongue, I will then treat him with all the respect imaginable." "I have him at home in Italian," said the barber, "but I cannot understand him." "Neither is it any great matter whether you do or not," replied the curate; "and I could willingly have excused the good captain who translated it that trouble of attempting to make him speak Spanish, for he has deprived him of a great deal of his primitive graces; a misfortune incident to all those who presume to translate verses, since their utmost wit and industry can never enable them to preserve the native beauties and genius that shine in the original. For this reason, I am for having not only this book, but likewise all those which we shall find here treating of French affairs, laid up and deposited to some dry vault, till we have maturely determined what ought to be done with them; yet give me leave to except 'Bernardo del Carpio' and 'Roncesvalles,' who must be somewhere here among the rest; for whenever I meet with them, I will certainly deliver them up into the hands of the housekeeper, who shall toss them into the fire." The barber gave his approbation to every particular, well knowing that the curate was so good a Christian, and so great a lover of truth, that he would not have uttered a falsity for all the world. Then, opening another volume, he found it to be "Palmerin de Oliva," and the next to that "Palmerin of England." "Ha! have I found you!" cried the curate. "Here take that 'Oliva,' let him be torn to pieces, then burnt, and his ashes scattered in the air; but let 'Palmerin of England' be preserved as a singular relic of antiquity; and let such a costly box be made for him, as Alexander found among the spoils of Darius, which he devoted to inclose Homer's works; for, I must tell you, neighbor, that book deserves particular respect for two things; first, for its own excellencies; and, secondly, for the sake of its author, who is said to have been a learned king of Portugal; then all the adventures of the Castle of Miraguarda are well and artfully managed, the dialogue very courtly and clear, and the decorum strictly observed in equal character, with equal propriety and judgment. Therefore, Mr. Nicholas," continued he, "with submission to your better advice, this and 'Amadis de Gaul' shall be exempted from the fire; and let all the rest be condemned without any further inquiry or examination." "By no means, I beseech you," returned the barber, "for this which I have in my hands is the famous 'Don Belianis.'" "Truly," cried the curate, "he with his second, third, and fourth parts, had need of a dose of rhubarb to purge his excessive choler; besides, his Castle of Fame should be demolished, and a heap of other rubbish removed, in order to which I give my vote to grant them the benefit of a reprieve; and, as they show signs of amendment, so shall mercy or justice be used towards them. In the meantime, neighbor, take them into custody, and keep them safe at home; but let none be permitted to converse with them." "Content," cried the barber; and to save himself the labor of looking on any more books of that kind, he bid the housekeeper take all the great volumes and throw them into the yard. This was not spoken to one stupid or deaf, but to one who had a greater mind to be burning them than weaving the finest and largest web; so that, laying hold of no less than eight volumes at once, she presently made them leap towards the place of execution; but as she went too eagerly to work, taking more books than she could conveniently carry, she happened to drop one at the barber's feet, which he took up out of curiosity to see what it was, and found it to be the "History of the Famous Knight Tirante the White." "Good-lack-a-day," cried the curate, "is 'Tirante the White' here? Oh! pray good neighbor, give it me by all means, for I promise myself to find in it a treasure of delight and a mine of recreation. There we have the valorous knight Don Kyrie-Eleison [2] of Montalban, with his brother Thomas of Montalban, and the knight Fonseca; the combat between the valorous Detriente and Alano; the dainty and witty conceits of the damsel Plazerdemivida, with the loves and guiles of the widow Reposada; together with the lady Empress, that was in love with Hippolito her gentleman-usher. I vow and protest to you, neighbor," continued he, "that in its way there is not a better book in the world; why, here the knights eat and drink, sleep and die natural deaths in their beds, nay, and make their last wills and testaments; with a world of other things, of which all the rest of these sorts of books do not say one syllable. Yet, after all, I must tell you, that for willfully taking the pains to write so many foolish things, the worthy author fairly deserves to be sent to the galleys for all the days of his life. Take it home with you and read it, and then tell me whether I have told you the truth or no." "I believe you," replied the barber, "but what shall we do with all these smaller books that are left?" "Certainly," replied the curate, "these cannot be books of knight-errantry, they are too small; you will find they are only poets": and so opening one, it happened to be the "Diana" of Mon-

[2] *Most of these names are significant, and are qualities personified; as* Kyrie-Eleison, *Greek for "Lord have mercy upon us";* Alano *is a mastiff-dog;* Plazerdemivida, *"pleasure of my life";* Reposada, *sedate or quiet.*

temayor; which made him say (believing all the rest to be of that stamp), "These do not deserve to be punished like the others, for they neither have done, nor can do that mischief which those stories of chivalry have done, being generally ingenious books, that can do nobody any prejudice." "Oh! good sir," cried the niece, "burn them with the rest, I beseech you; for should my uncle get cured of his knight-errant frenzy, and betake himself to the reading of these books, we should have him turn shepherd, and so wander through the woods and fields; nay, and what would be worse yet, turn poet, which they say is a catching and an incurable disease." "The gentlewoman is in the right," said the curate, "and it will not be amiss to remove that stumbling-block out of our friend's way; and, since we began with the 'Diana' of Montemayor, I am of opinion we ought not to burn it, but only take out that part of it which treats of the Magician Felicia, and the enchanted water, as also all the longer poems; and let the work escape with its prose, and the honor of being the first of that kind." "Here is another 'Diana,'" quoth the barber, "the second of that name, by Salmantino (of Salamanca); nay, and a third too by Gil Polo." "Pray," said the curate, "let Salmantino increase the number of the criminals in the yard; but, as for that Gil Polo, preserve it as charily as if Apollo himself had written it; and go on as fast as you can, I beseech you, good neighbor, for it grows late." "Here," quoth the barber, "I have a book called the 'Ten Books of the Fortunes of Love,' by Anthony de Lofraso, a Sardinian poet." "Now, by my holy orders," cried the curate, "I do not think since Apollo was Apollo, the muses muses, and the poets poets, there ever was a more comical, more whimsical book. Of all the works of the kind commend me to this, for, in its way, it is certainly the best and most singular that ever was published, and he that never read it, may safely think he never in his life read anything that was pleasant. Give it me, neighbor," continued he, "for I am more glad to have found it, than if any one had given me a cassock of the best Florence serge." With that he laid it aside with extraordinary satisfaction, and the barber went on. "These that follow," cried he, "are 'The Shepherd of Iberia,' 'The Nymphs of Enares,' and the 'Cures of Jealousy.'" "Take them, jailer," quoth the curate, "and never ask me why, for then we shall never have done." "The next," said the barber, "is 'The Shepherd of Filida.'" "He is no shepherd," returned the curate, "but a very discreet courtier; keep him as a precious jewel." "Here is a bigger," cried the barber, "called the 'Treasure of Divers Poems.'" "Had there been fewer of them," said the curate, "they would have been more esteemed. It is fit the book should be pruned and cleared of several trifles that disgrace the rest: keep it, however, because the author is my friend, and for the sake of his other more heroic and lofty productions." "Here is a book of songs by Lopez Maldonado," cried the barber. "He is also my particular friend," said the curate: "his verses are well liked when he reads them himself, and his voice is so excellent, that they charm whenever he sings them. He seems indeed to be somewhat too long in his eclogues; but can we ever have too much of a good thing? Let him be preserved among the best. What is the next book?" "The 'Galatea' of Miguel de Cervantes," replied the barber. "That Cervantes has been my intimate acquaintance these many years," cried the curate, "and I know he has been more conversant with misfortunes than with poetry. His book, indeed, has I do not know what that looks like a good design; he aims at something, but concludes nothing: therefore we must stay for the second part, which he has promised us; perhaps he may make us amends, and obtain a full pardon, which is denied him for the present; till that time, keep him close prisoner at your house." "I will," quoth the barber: "but see, I have here three more for you, the 'Araucana' of Don Alonso de Ercilla, the 'Austriada' of Juan Rufo, a magistrate of Cordova, and the 'Monserrato' of Christoval de Virves, a Valentian poet." "These," cried the curate, "are the best heroic poems we have in Spanish, and may vie with the most celebrated of Italy; reserve them as the most valuable performance which Spain has to boast of in poetry."

At last the curate grew so tired with prying into so many volumes, that he ordered all the rest to be burnt at a venture. But the barber showed him one which he had opened by chance ere the dreadful sentence was past. "Truly," said the curate, who saw by the title it was "The Tears of Angelica," "I should have wept myself, had I caused such a book to share the condemnation of the rest; for the author was not only one of the best poets in Spain, but in the whole world, and translated some of Ovid's fables with extraordinary success."

VII: DON QUIXOTE'S SECOND SALLY IN QUEST OF ADVENTURES

While they were thus employed, Don Quixote, in a raving fit, began to talk aloud to himself: "Here, here, valorous knights," cried he, "now is the time that you must exert the strength of your mighty arms; for lo, the courtiers bear away the honor of the tournament." This amazing outcry called away the inquisitors from any further examination of the library; and therefore, the housekeeper and the niece being left to their own discretion, it is thought the "Carolea" and "Leon of Spain," with the deeds of the Emperor, written by Don Luis de Avila, which to be sure were part of the collection, were committed to the flames unseen and unheard, without any legal trial; a fate which perhaps they might have escaped, had the curate been there to have weighed what might have been urged in their defense.

When they came into Don Quixote's chamber, they found him

risen out of his bed as mad as ever he was, tearing his throat, and making a heavy bustle, laying about him with his sword, back-stroke and fore-stroke, as broad awake as if he had never slept. They ran in upon him, caught him in their arms, and carried him to bed again by main force; where, after he was somewhat quiet and settled, turning himself to the curate, "Certainly," cried he, "my Lord Archbishop Turpin, it is a great dishonor to us who are called the twelve peers, to suffer the knights of the court to bear away the honor of the tournament without any further opposition, after we the knight-adventurers had carried it for three days before." "Be pacified, my good friend," replied the curate; "fortune may have yet a better success in reserve for you, and they who lose today may win tomorrow. At present think on your health, for doubtless you must needs be now extremely tired, if not very much wounded." "Wounded!" replied Don Quixote, "no; but as for being bruised, I will not deny it, for that base-born knight, Don Orlando, has battered all my limbs with the trunk of an oak, out of mere envy, because he sees that I only dare rival his exploits: but, may I be no more called Rinaldo of Montalban, if, in spite of his enchantments, I do not make him severely pay for this as soon as I can leave my bed; and therefore let my dinner be brought in, for it is what I want most at this juncture, and then let me alone to revenge this abuse." Accordingly they brought him some victuals, which, when he had eaten, he fell asleep again; and they left him, all of them strangely amazed at his uncommon madness. That night the housekeeper burnt all the books, not only those in the yard, but all those that were in the house; and several suffered in the general calamity, that deserved to have been treasured up in everlasting archives, had not their fate and the remissness of the inquisitors ordered it other-wise. And thus they verified the proverb, "That the good often fare the worse for the bad."

One of the expedients which the curate and the barber bethought themselves of, in order to aid their friend's recovery, was to stop up the door of the room where his books lay, that he might not find it, nor miss them when he rose; for they hoped the effect would cease when they had taken away the cause; and they ordered, that if he inquired about it, they should tell him that a certain enchanter had carried away study, books and all. Two days after, Don Quixote having gotten up, the first thing he did was to go visit his darling books; and, as he could not find the study in the place where he had left it, he went up and down, and looked for it in every room. Sometimes he came to the place where the door used to stand, and then stood feeling and groping about a good while, then cast his eyes, and stared on every side, without speaking a word. At last, after a long deliberation, he thought fit to ask his housekeeper which was the way to his study. "What study," answered the woman, according to her instructions, "or rather, what nothing is it you look for? Alas! there is neither study nor books in the house now, for the devil has run away with them all." "No, it was not the devil," said the niece, "but a conjuror, or an enchanter, as they call them, who, since you went, came hither one night mounted on a dragon on the top of a cloud, and then, alighting, went into your study, where what he did, he and the devil best can tell; for a while after, he flew out at the roof of the house, leaving it full of smoke; and, when we went to see what he had done, we could neither find the books, nor so much as the very study; only the housekeeper and I very well remember, that when the old thief went away, he cried out aloud that out of a private grudge which he bore in his mind to the owner of those books, he had done the house a mischief, as we should soon perceive, and then, I think, he called himself the Sage Muniaton." "Not Muniaton, but Freston,[1] you should have said," cried Don Quixote. "Truly," quoth the niece, "I cannot tell whether it was Freston or Friston, but sure I am that his name ended with

[1] An enchanter in "Don Belianis of Greece."

71

a ton." "It is so," returned Don Quixote, "for he is a famous necromancer, and my mortal enemy, and bears me a great deal of malice; for, seeing by his art, that, in spite of all his spells, in process of time I shall fight and vanquish in single combat a knight whose interest he espouses, therefore he endeavors to do me all manner of mischief; but, I dare assure him, he strives against the stream, nor can his power reverse the first decrees of fate." "Who doubts of that?" cried the niece. "But, dear uncle, what makes you run yourself into these quarrels? Had you not better stay at home, and live in peace and quietness, than go rambling up and down like a vagabond, and seeking for better bread than is made of wheat, without once so much as considering that many go to seek wool and come home shorn themselves?" "Oh, good niece," replied Don Quixote, "how ill thou understandeth these matters! Know, that before I will suffer myself to be shorn, I will tear and pluck off the beards of all those audacious mortals that shall attempt to profane the tip of one single hair within the verge of these mustaches." To this neither the niece nor the governess thought fit to make any reply, for they perceived the Knight to grow angry. Full fifteen days did our Knight remain quietly at home, without betraying the least sign of his desire to renew his rambling; during which time there passed a great deal of pleasant discourse between him and his two friends, the curate and the barber; while he maintained, that there was nothing the world stood so much in need of as knights-errant; wherefore he was resolved to revive the order. In which disputes Mr. Curate sometimes contradicted him, and sometimes submitted; for had he not now and then given way to his fancies, there would have been no conversing with him.

In the meantime, Don Quixote earnestly solicited one of his neighbors, a country laborer, and a good honest fellow, if we may call a poor man honest, for he was poor indeed, poor in purse, and

poor in brains;
and, in short, the
Knight talked so long to him,
plied him with so many arguments, and made him so many fair
promises, that at last the poor silly clown consented to go along
with him, and become his squire. Among other inducements to en-
tice him to do it willingly, Don Quixote forgot not to tell him, that
it was likely such an adventure would present itself, as might secure
him the conquest of some island, in the time he might be picking up
a straw or two, and then the squire might promise himself to be
made governor of the place. Allured with these large promises, and

many others, Sancho Panza (for that was the name of the fellow) forsook his wife and children to be his neighbor's squire.

This done, Don Quixote made it his business to furnish himself with money; for which purpose, selling one house, mortgaging another, and losing by all, he at last got a pretty good sum together. He also borrowed a target of a friend, and having patched up his head-piece and beaver as well as he could, he gave his squire notice of the day and hour when he intended to set out, that he might also furnish himself with what he thought necessary; but, above all, he charged him to provide himself with a wallet; which Sancho promised him to do, telling him he would also take his ass along with him, which, being a very good one, might be a great ease to him, for he was not used to travel much a-foot. The mentioning of the ass made the noble Knight pause a while; he mused, and pondered whether he had ever read of any knight-errant whose squire used to ride upon an ass; but he could not remember any precedent for it: however, he gave him leave at last to bring his ass, hoping to mount him more honorably with the first opportunity, by unhorsing the next discourteous knight he should meet. He also furnished himself with shirts, and as many other necessaries as he could conveniently carry, according to the innkeeper's injunctions. Which being done, Sancho Panza, without bidding either his wife or children good-by, and Don Quixote, without taking any more notice of his housekeeper or of his niece, stole out of the village one night, not so much as suspected by anybody, and made such haste, that by break of day they thought themselves out of reach, should they happen to be pursued. As for Sancho Panza, he rode like a patriarch, with his canvas knapsack, or wallet, and his leathern bottle, having a huge desire to see himself governor of the island, which his master had promised him.

Don Quixote happened to strike into the same road which he took the time before, that is, the plains of Montiel, over which he traveled with less inconveniency than when he went alone, by reason it was yet early in the morning; at which time the sunbeams, being almost parallel to the surface of the earth, and not directly darted down, as in the middle of the day, did not prove so offensive. As they jogged on, "I beseech your worship, Sir Knight-errant," quoth Sancho to his master, "be sure you do not forget what you promised me about the island; for, I dare say, I shall make shift to govern it, let it be never so big." "You must know, friend Sancho," replied Don Quixote, "that it has been the constant practice of knights-errant, in former ages, to make their squires governors of the islands or kingdoms they conquered: now, I am not only resolved to keep up that laudable custom, but even to improve it, and outdo my predecessors in generosity: for whereas sometimes, or rather most commonly, other knights delayed rewarding their squires till they were grown old, and worn out with service, bad days, worse nights, and all manner of hard duty, and then put them off with some title, either of Count, or at least Marquis of some valley or province of great or small extent; now, if thou and I do but live, it may happen, that before we have passed six days together, I may conquer some kingdom, having many other kingdoms annexed to its imperial crown; and this would fall out most luckily for thee; and then would I presently crown thee king of one of them. Nor do thou imagine this to be a mighty matter; for so strange accidents and revolutions, so sudden and so unforeseen, attend the profession of chivalry, that I might easily give thee a great deal more than I have promised." "Why, should this come to pass," quoth Sancho Panza, "and I be made a king by some such miracle as your worship says, then happy-be-lucky, my Whither-d'ye-go Mary Gutierrez would be at least a queen, and my children infantas and princes, if it like your worship." "Who doubts of that?" cried Don Quixote. "I doubt of it," replied Sancho, "for I cannot help believing, that though it should rain kingdoms down upon the

75

face of the earth, not one of them would fit well upon Mary Gutierrez's head; for, I must needs tell you, she is not worth two brass jacks to make a queen of: no, Countess would be better for her, if it please you; and that too, God help her, will be as much as she can handsomely manage." "Recommend the matter to providence," returned Don Quixote, "it will be sure to give what is most expedient for thee; but yet disdain to entertain inferior thoughts, and be not tempted to accept less than the dignity of a viceroy." "No more I will, sir," quoth Sancho, "especially since I have so rare a master as your worship, who will take care to give me whatever may be fit for me, and what I may be able to deal with."

VIII: OF THE GOOD SUCCESS WHICH THE VALOROUS DON QUIXOTE HAD IN THE MOST TERRIFYING AND NEVER-TO-BE-IMAGINED ADVENTURE OF THE WINDMILLS, WITH OTHER TRANSACTIONS WORTHY TO BE TRANSMITTED TO POSTERITY

As they were thus discoursing, they discovered some thirty or forty windmills that are in that plain; and, as soon as the Knight had spied them, "Fortune," cried he, "directs our affairs better than we ourselves could have wished: look yonder, friend Sancho, there are at least thirty outrageous giants, whom I intend to encounter; and, having deprived them of life, we will begin to enrich ourselves with their spoils: for they are lawful prize; and the extirpation of that cursed brood will be an acceptable service to Heaven." "What giants?" quoth Sancho Panza. "Those whom thou seest yonder," answered Don Quixote, "with their long-extended arms; some of that detested race have arms of so immense a size, that sometimes they reach two leagues in length." "Pray, look better, sir," quoth Sancho; "those things yonder are no giants, but windmills, and the arms you fancy, are their sails, which, being whirled about by the wind, make the mill go." "It is a sign," cried Don Quixote, "thou art but little acquainted with adventures. I tell thee they are giants; and therefore, if thou art afraid, go aside and say thy prayers, for I am resolved to engage in a dreadful, unequal combat against them all." This said, he clapped spurs to his horse

Rozinante, without giving ear to his squire Sancho, who bawled out to him, and assured him that they were windmills, and no giants. But he was so fully possessed with a strong conceit of the contrary, that he did not so much as hear his squire's outcry, nor was he sensible of what they were, although he was already very near them; far from that. "Stand, cowards," cried he as loud as he could; "stand your ground, ignoble creatures, and fly not basely from a single knight, who dares encounter you all." At the same time the wind rising, the mill-sails began to move, which, when Don Quixote spied, "Base miscreants," cried he, "though you move more arms than the giant Briareus, you shall pay for your arrogance." He most devoutly recommended himself to his lady Dulcinea, imploring her assistance in this perilous adventure; and so, covering himself with his shield, and couching his lance, he rushed with Rozinante's utmost speed upon the first windmill he could come at, and, running his lance into the sail, the wind whirled about with such swiftness, that the rapidity of the motion presently broke the lance into shivers, and hurled away both knight and horse along with it, till down he fell, rolling a good way off in the field. Sancho Panza ran as fast as his ass could drive to help his master, whom he found lying, and not able to stir, such a blow he and Rozinante had received. "Mercy on me!" cried Sancho, "did I not give your worship fair warning? did not I tell you they were windmills, and that nobody could think otherwise, unless he had also windmills in his head?" "Peace, friend Sancho," replied Don Quixote: "there is nothing so subject to the inconstancy of fortune as war. I am verily persuaded, that cursed necromancer Freston, who carried away my study and books, has transformed these giants into windmills, to deprive me of the honor of the victory; such is his inveterate malice against me; but, in the end, all his pernicious wiles and stratagems shall prove ineffectual against the prevailing edge of my sword." "Amen, say I," replied Sancho; and so heaving him up again upon his legs, once more the Knight mounted poor Rozinante, that was half shoulder-slipped with his fall.

This adventure was the subject of their discourse, as they made the best of their way towards the pass of Lapice; for Don Quixote took that road, believing he could not miss of adventures in one so mightily frequented. However, the loss of his lance was no small affliction to him; and, as he was making his complaint about it to his squire, "I have read," said he, "friend Sancho, that a certain Spanish knight, whose name was Diego Perez de Vargas, having broken his sword in the heat of an engagement, pulled up by the roots a huge oak-tree, or at least tore down a massy branch, and did such wonderful execution, crushing and grinding so many Moors with it that day, that he won himself and his posterity the surname of The Pounder or Bruiser. I tell thee this, because I intend to tear up the next oak, or crab-tree we meet; with the trunk whereof I hope to perform such wondrous deeds, that thou wilt esteem thyself particularly happy in having had the honor to behold them, and been the ocular witness of achievements which posterity will scarce be able to believe." "Heaven grant you may," cried Sancho. "I believe it all, because your worship says it. But, if it please you, sit a little more upright in your saddle; you ride sidelong, methinks; but that, I suppose, proceeds from your being bruised by the fall." "It does so," replied Don Quixote; "and, if I do not complain, it is because a knight-errant must never complain of his wounds, though his bowels were dropping out through them." "Then I have no more to say," quoth Sancho; "and yet, heaven knows my heart, I should be glad to hear your worship hone a little now and then, when something ails you. For my part, I shall not fail to bemoan myself when I suffer the smallest pain, unless indeed it can be proved, that the rule of not complaining extends to the squires as well as knights." Don Quixote could not forbear smiling at the simplicity of his squire; and told him he gave him leave to complain not only when he pleased, but as much as he pleased, whether he had any cause or no; for he had never yet read anything to the contrary in any books of chivalry. Sancho desired him, however, to consider that it was high time to go to dinner; but his master answered him, that he might eat whenever he pleased; as for himself, he was not yet disposed to do it. Sancho, having thus obtained leave, fixed himself as orderly as he could upon his ass, and, taking some victuals out of his wallet, fell to munching lustily as he rode behind his master; and ever and anon he lifted his bottle to his nose, and fetched such hearty pulls, that it would have made the best-

pampered vintner in Malaga a-dry to have seen him. While he thus
went on stuffing and swilling, he did not think in the least of all his
master's great promises; and was so far from esteeming it a trouble
to travel in quest of adventures, that he fancied it to be the greatest
pleasure in the world, though they were never so dreadful.

In fine, they passed that night under some trees; from one of
which Don Quixote tore a withered branch, which in some sort was
able to serve him for a lance, and to this he fixed the head or spear
of his broken lance. But he did not sleep all that night, keeping his
thoughts intent on his dear Dulcinea, in imitation of what he had
read in books of chivalry, where the knights pass that time, without
sleep, in forests and deserts, wholly taken up with the entertaining
thoughts of their absent mistresses. As for Sancho, he did not spend
the night at that idle rate; for, having his paunch well stuffed with
something more substantial than dandelion-water, he made but
one nap of it; and, had not his master waked him, neither the
sprightly beams which the sun darted on his face, nor the melody
of the birds, that cheerfully on every branch welcomed the smiling
morn, would have been able to have made him stir. As he got up to
clear his eye-sight, he took two or three long-winded swigs at his
friendly bottle, for a morning's draught; but he found it somewhat lighter than it was the night before; which misfortune went
to his very heart, for he shrewdly mistrusted that he was not in a
way to cure it of that distemper as soon as he could have wished. On
the other side, Don Quixote would not break fast, having been
feasting all night on the more delicate and savory thoughts of his
mistress; and therefore they went on directly towards the pass of
Lapice, which they discovered about three o'clock. When they came
near it, "Here it is, brother Sancho," said Don Quixote, "that we
may wanton, and as it were, thrust our arms up to the very elbows,
in that which we call adventures. But let me give thee one necessary
caution; know that though thou shouldest see me in the greatest

extremity of danger, thou must not offer to draw thy sword in my defense, unless thou findest me assaulted by base plebeians and vile scoundrels; for, in such a case, thou mayest assist thy master: but if those with whom I am fighting are knights, thou must not do it; for the laws of chivalry do not allow thee to encounter a knight, till thou art one thyself." "Never fear," quoth Sancho; "I will be sure to obey your worship in that, I warrant you; for I have ever loved peace and quietness, and never cared to thrust myself into frays and quarrels; and yet I do not care to take blows at anyone's hands neither; and should any knight offer to set upon me first, I fancy I should hardly mind your laws; for all laws, whether of God or man, allow one to stand in his own defense, if any offer to do him a mischief." "I agree to that," replied Don Quixote; "but, as for helping me against any knights, thou must set bounds to thy natural impulses." "I will be sure to do it," quoth Sancho; "never trust me if I do not keep your commandment as well as I do the Sabbath."

As they were talking, they spied coming towards them two monks of the order of St. Benedict, mounted on two dromedaries, for the mules on which they rode were so high and stately, that they seemed little less. They wore riding-masks, with glasses at the eyes, against the dust, and umbrellas to shelter them from the sun. After them came a coach, with four or five men on horseback, and two muleteers on foot. There proved to be in the coach a Biscayan lady, who was going to Seville to meet her husband, who was there in order to embark for the Indies, to take possession of a considerable post. Scarce had Don Quixote perceived the monks, who were not of the same company, though they went the same way, but he cried to his squire, "Either I am deceived, or this will prove the most famous adventure that ever was known; for, without question, those two black things that move towards us must be some necromancers, that are carrying away by force some princess in that coach; and it is my duty to prevent so great an injury." "I fear me this will prove

81

a worse job than the windmills," quoth Sancho. " 'Slife, sir, do not you see these are Benedictine friars, and it is likely the coach belongs to some travelers that are in it; therefore once more take warning, and do not you be led away by the devil." "I have already told thee, Sancho," replied Don Quixote, "thou art miserably ignorant in matters of adventures; what I say is true, and thou shalt find it so presently." This said, he spurred on his horse, and posted himself just in the middle of the road where the monks were to pass: and when they came within hearing, "Cursed implements of hell," cried he in a loud and haughty tone, "immediately release those high-born princesses, whom you are violently conveying away in the coach, or else prepare to meet with instant death, as the just punishment of your pernicious deeds." The monks stopped their mules, no less astonished at the figure, than at the expressions of the speaker. "Sir Knight," cried they, "we are no such persons as you are pleased to term us, but religious men of the order of St. Benedict, that travel about our affairs, and are wholly ignorant whether or no there are any princesses carried away by force in that coach." "I am not to be deceived with fair words," replied Don Quixote; "I know you well enough, perfidious caitiffs"; and immediately, without expecting their reply, he set spurs to Rozinante and ran so furiously, with his lance couched, against the first monk, that, if he had not prudently flung himself off to the ground, the Knight would certainly have laid him either dead or grievously wounded. The other, observing the discourteous usage of his companion, clapped his heels to his over-grown mule's flanks, and scoured over the plain as if he had been running a race with the wind. Sancho Panza no sooner saw the monk fall, but he nimbly skipped off his ass, and running to him, began to strip him immediately, but then the two muleteers, who waited on the monks, came up to him, and asked why he offered to strip him. Sancho told them that this belonged to him as lawful plunder, being the spoils won

82

in battle by his lord and master Don Quixote. The fellows, with whom there was no jesting, not knowing what he meant by his spoils and battle, and seeing Don Quixote at a good distance in deep discourse by the side of the coach, both fell upon poor Sancho, threw him down, tore his beard from his chin, trampled on his stomach, thumped and mauled him in every part of his carcass, and there left him sprawling without breath or motion. In the meanwhile the monk, scared out of his wits, and as pale as a ghost, got upon his mule again as fast as he could, and spurred after his friend, who stayed for him at a distance, expecting the issue of this strange adventure: but, being unwilling to stay to see the end of it, they made the best of their way, making more signs of the Cross than if the devil had been posting after them.

Don Quixote, as I said, was all that while engaged with the lady in the coach. "Lady," cried he, "your discretion is now at liberty to dispose of your beautiful self as you please; for the presumptuous arrogance of those who attempted to enslave your person lies prostrate in the dust, overthrown by this my strenuous arm; and that you may not be at a loss for the name of your deliverer, know I am called Don Quixote de la Mancha, by profession a knight-errant and adventurer, captive to that peerless beauty Donna Dulcinea del Toboso: nor do I desire any other recompense for the service I have done you, but that you return to Toboso to present yourselves to that lady, and let her know what I have done to purchase your deliverance." To this strange talk, a certain Biscainer, the lady's squire, gentleman-usher, or what you will please to call him, who rode along with the coach, listened with great attention; and perceiving that Don Quixote not only stopped the coach, but would have it presently go back to Toboso, he bore briskly up to him, and laying hold on his lance, "Get gone," cried he to him in bad Spanish and worse Biscayan; "get gone, thou knight, and devil go with thou; or, by He who me create, if thou do not leave

83

the coach, me kill thee now so sure as me be a Biscayan." Don
Quixote, who made shift to understand him well enough, very calmly made him this answer. "Wert thou a gentleman, as thou art not,
ere this I would have chastised thy insolence and temerity, thou
inconsiderable mortal." "What! me no gentleman?" replied the
Biscainer; "I swear thou be liar, as me be Christian. If thou throw
away lance, and draw sword, me will make no more of thee than cat
does of mouse, me will show thee me be Biscayan, and gentleman by
land, gentleman by sea, gentleman in spite of devil; and thou lie
if thou say contrary." "I will try titles with you, as the man said,"
replied Don Quixote: and, with that, throwing away his lance, he
drew his sword, grasped his target, and attacked the Biscainer,
fully bent on his destruction. The Biscainer seeing him come on so
furiously, would gladly have alighted, not trusting to his mule,
which was one of those scurvy jades that are let out to hire; but all
he had time to do was only to draw his sword, and snatch a cushion
out of the coach, to serve him instead of a shield; and immediately
they assaulted one another with all the fury of mortal enemies. The
bystanders did all they could to prevent their fighting; but it was
in vain, for the Biscainer swore in his gibberish, he would kill his
very lady, and all those who presumed to hinder him, if they would
not let him fight. The lady in the coach being extremely affrighted
at these passages, made her coachman drive out of harm's way, and
at a distance was an eye-witness of the furious combat. At the same
time the Biscainer let fall such a mighty blow on Don Quixote's
shoulder, over his target, that had not his armor been sword-proof,
he would have cleft him down to the very waist. The Knight, feeling
the weight of that unmeasurable blow, cried out aloud, "Oh! lady
of my soul, Dulcinea! flower of all beauty, vouchsafe to succor
your champion in this dangerous combat, undertaken to set forth
your worth." The breathing out of this short prayer, the gripping
fast of his sword, the covering of himself with his shield, and the

charging of his enemy, was but the work of a moment; for Don Quixote was resolved to venture the fortune of the combat all upon one blow. The Biscainer, who read his design in his dreadful countenance, resolved to face him with equal bravery and stand the terrible shock with uplifted sword, covered with the cushion, not being able to manage his jaded mule, who defying the spur, and not being cut out for such pranks, would move neither to the right nor to the left. While Don Quixote, with his sword aloft, was rushing upon the wary Biscainer, with a full resolution to cleave him asunder, all the spectators stood trembling with terror and amazement, expecting the dreadful event of those prodigious blows which threatened the two desperate combatants: the lady in the coach, with the women, were making a thousand vows and offerings to all the images and places of devotion in Spain, that Providence might deliver them and the squire out of the great danger that threatened them.

But here we must deplore the abrupt end of this history, which the author leaves off just at the very point when the fortune of the battle is going to be decided, pretending he could find nothing more recorded of Don Quixote's wondrous achievements than what he had already related. However, the second undertaker of this work could not believe that so curious a history could lie for ever inevitably buried in oblivion; or that the learned of La Mancha were so regardless of their country's glory, as not to preserve in their archives, or at least in their closets, some memoirs, as monuments of this famous knight; and therefore he would not give over inquiring after the continuation of this pleasant history, till at last he happily found it, as the next book will inform the reader.

BOOK TWO

I

THE EVENT OF THE MOST STUPENDOUS COMBAT BETWEEN THE BRAVE BISCAINER AND THE VALOROUS DON QUIXOTE

IN THE FIRST BOOK of this history, we left the valiant Biscainer and the renowned Don Quixote with their swords lifted up, and ready to discharge on each other two furious and most terrible blows, which, had they fallen directly, and met with no opposition, would have cut and divided the two combatants from head to heel, and have split them like a pomegranate; but, as I said before, the story remained imperfect; neither did the author inform us where we might find the remaining part of the relation. This vexed me extremely, and turned the pleasure which the perusal of the beginning had afforded me into disgust, when I had reason to despair of ever seeing the rest. Yet, after all, it seemed to me no less impossible than unjust, that so valiant a knight should have been destitute of some learned person to record his incomparable exploits; a misfortune which never attended any of his predecessors, I mean the knights-adventurers, each of whom was always provided with one or two learned men, who were always at hand to write not only their wondrous deeds, but also to set down their thoughts and childish petty actions, were they never so hidden. Therefore, as I could not imagine that so worthy a knight should be so unfortunate, as to want that which had been so profusely lavished even on such a one as Platyr,[1] and others of that stamp, I could not induce myself to believe that so admirable a history was ever left unfinished, and rather chose to think that time, the devourer of all things, had hidden or consumed it. On the other side, when I considered that several modern books were found in his study, as "The Cures of Jealousy," and "The Nymphs and Shepherds of Henares," [2] I had reason to think that the history of our Knight could be of no very ancient date; and that, had it never been continued, yet his neighbors and friends could not have forgotten the most remarkable passages of his life. Full of this thought I resolved to make it my business to make a particular and exact inquiry into the life and miracles of our renowned Spaniard Don Quixote, that refulgent glory and mirror of the knighthood of La Mancha, and the first who in these depraved and miserable times devoted himself to the neglected profession of knight-errantry, to redress wrongs and injuries, to relieve widows, and defend the honor of damsels; such of them, I mean, who in former ages rode up and down over hills and dales, with whip in hand, mounted on their palfreys, with all their virginity about them, secure from all manner of danger; and who,

[1] *A second-rate knight in "Palmerin of England."*
[2] *Henares runs by the University of Alcala in Old Castile.*

unless they happened to be ravished by some boisterous villain or huge giant, were sure, at fourscore years of age (all which time they never slept one night under a roof) to be decently laid in their graves, as pure virgins as the mothers that bore them. For this reason and many others, I say, our gallant Don Quixote is worthy of everlasting and universal praise: nor ought I to be denied my due commendation for my indefatigable care and diligence, in seeking and finding out the continuation of this delightful history; though, after all, I must confess that, had not Providence, chance, or fortune, as I will now inform you, assisted me in the discovery, the world had been deprived of two hours' diversion and pleasure, which it is likely to afford to those who will read it with attention. One day, being in the Alcala at Toledo, I saw a young lad offer to sell a parcel of old written papers to a shopkeeper. Now I, being apt to take up the least piece of written or printed paper that lies in my way, though it were in the middle of the street, could not forbear laying my hands on one of the manuscripts, to see what it was; and I found it to be written in Arabic, which I could not read. This caused me to look about, to see whether I could ever find a Morisco that understood Spanish, to read it for me and give me some account of it; nor was it very difficult to meet with an interpreter there; for, had I wanted one for a better and more ancient tongue, that place would have infallibly supplied me. It was my good fortune to find one immediately; and, having informed him of my desire, he no sooner read some lines than he began to laugh. I asked him what he laughed at. "At a certain remark here in the margin of the book," said he. I prayed him to explain it, whereupon, still laughing, he did it in these words: "This Dulcinea del Toboso, so often mentioned in this history, is said to have had the best hand at salting of pork of any woman in La Mancha." I was surprised when I heard him name Dulcinea del Toboso, and presently imagined that those old papers contained the history of Don Quixote. This

89

made me press him to read the title of the book, which he did, turning it thus extempore out of Arabic: "The History of Don Quixote de la Mancha, written by Cid Hamet Benengeli, an Arabian historian." I was so overjoyed when I heard the title, that I had much ado to conceal it; and presently, taking the bargain out of the shopkeeper's hand, I agreed with the young man for the whole, and bought that for half a real, which he might have sold me for twenty times as much had he but guessed at the eagerness of his chapman. I immediately withdrew with my purchase to the cloister of the great church, taking the Moor with me, and desired him to translate to me those papers that treated of Don Quixote, without adding or omitting the least word, offering him any reasonable satisfaction. He asked me but two Arrobes [3] of raisins, and two bushels of wheat, and promised to do it faithfully with all expedition. In short, for the quicker dispatch and the greater security, being unwilling to let such a lucky prize go out of my hands, I took the Moor to my own house, where, in less than six weeks he finished the whole translation.

Don Quixote's fight with the Biscainer was exactly drawn on one of the leaves of the first quire, in the same posture as we left them, with their swords lifted up over their heads, the one guarding himself with his shield, the other with his cushion. The Biscainer's mule was so pictured to the life, that with half an eye you might have known it to be a hired mule. Under the Biscainer was written, "Don Sancho de Azpetia," and under Rozinante, "Don Quixote." Rozinante was so admirably delineated, so slim, so stiff, so lean, so jaded, with so sharp a ridge-bone, and altogether so like one wasted with an incurable consumption, that any one must have owned, at first sight, that no horse ever better deserved that name. Not far off stood Sancho Panza,[4] holding his ass by the halter, at whose feet there was a scroll, in which was written "Sancho Canças" [5]; and, if

[3] *An Arrobe is about 32 lb. weight.*   [4] *"Paunch."*
[5] *"Haunches," or rather "thigh-bones."*

90

we may judge of him by his picture, he was thick and short, paunch-bellied, and long-haunched; so that, in all likelihood, for this reason he is sometimes called Panza and sometimes Cança in the History. There were some other niceties to be seen in that piece, but hardly worth observation, as not giving any light into this true history, otherwise they had not passed unmentioned; for none can be amiss, so they are authentic. I must only acquaint the reader, that if any objection is to be made as to the veracity of this, it is only that the author is an Arabian, and those of that country are not a little addicted to lying: but yet, if we consider that they are our enemies, we should sooner imagine that the author has rather suppressed the truth than added to the real worth of our Knight; and I am the more inclined to think so, because it is plain that where he ought to have enlarged on his praises, he maliciously chooses to be silent; a proceeding unworthy of an historian, who ought to be exact, sincere, and impartial; free from passion, and not to be biased either by interest, fear, resentment, or affection, to deviate from truth, which is the mother of history, the preserver and eternizer of great actions, the professed enemy of oblivion, the witness of things passed, and the director of future times. As for the History, I know it will afford you as great variety as you could wish, in the most entertaining manner; and if in any point it falls short of your expectation, I am of opinion it is more the fault of the Infidel, its author, than the subject; and so let us go to the second book, which, according to our translation, began in this manner:

Such were the bold and formidable looks of the two enraged combatants that, with uplifted arms and with destructive steel, they seemed to threaten heaven, earth, and the infernal mansions; while the spectators seemed wholly lost in fear and astonishment. The choleric Biscainer discharged the first blow, and that with such a force and so desperate a fury that, had not his sword turned in his hand, that single stroke had put an end to the dreadful combat and

91

all our Knight's adventures. But fate, that reserved him for greater things, so ordered it, that his enemy's sword turned in such a manner, that though it struck him on the left shoulder, it did him no other hurt than to disarm that side of his head, carrying away with it a great part of his helmet, and one half of his ear, which, like a dreadful ruin, fell together to the ground. Assist me, ye powers!—but it is in vain! The fury which then engrossed the breast of our hero of La Mancha is not to be expressed; words would but wrong it: for what color of speech can be lively enough to give but a slight sketch or faint image of his unutterable rage? Exerting all his valor, he raised himself upon his stirrups, and seemed even greater than himself; and, at the same instant, gripping his sword fast with both hands, he discharged such a tremendous blow full on the Biscainer's cushion and his head, that in spite of so good a defense, as if a whole mountain had fallen upon him, the blood gushed out at his mouth, nose, and ears all at once; and he tottered so in his saddle, that he had fallen to the ground immediately, had he not caught hold of the neck of his mule: but the dull beast itself, being roused out of its stupidity with that terrible blow, began to run about the fields; and the Biscainer, having lost his stirrups and his hold, with two or three winces the mule shook him off, and threw him on the ground. Don Quixote beheld the disaster of his foe with the greatest tranquillity and unconcern imaginable; and, seeing him down, slipped nimbly from his saddle, and running to him, set the point of his sword to his throat, and bid him yield, or he would cut off his head. The Biscainer was so stunned that he could make him no reply; and Don Quixote had certainly made good his threats, so provoked was he, had not the ladies in the coach, who, with great uneasiness and fear, beheld the sad transaction, hastened to beseech Don Quixote very earnestly to spare his life. "Truly, beautiful ladies," said the victorious Knight, with a deal of loftiness and gravity, "I am willing to grant your request; but upon condition that this same knight shall pass his word of honor to go to Toboso, and there present himself, in my name, before the peerless lady Donna Dulcinea, that she may dispose of him as she shall see convenient." The lady, who was frightened almost out of her senses, without considering what Don Quixote enjoined, or inquiring who the lady Dulcinea was, promised in her squire's behalf a punctual obedience to the Knight's commands. "Let him live then," replied Don Quixote, "upon your word, and owe to your intercession that pardon which I might justly deny his arrogance."

II: OF THE PLEASANT DISCOURSES WHICH PASSED BETWEEN DON QUIXOTE AND SANCHO PANZA, HIS SQUIRE

Sancho Panza had gotten up again before this, not much the better for the kicks and thumps bestowed on his carcass by the monk's grooms; and, seeing his master engaged in fight, he went devoutly to prayers, beseeching Heaven to grant him victory, that he might now win some island, in order that he might be made governor of it according to his promise. At last, perceiving the danger was over, the combat at an end, and his master ready to mount again, he ran in all haste to help him; but, ere the Knight put his foot in the stirrup, Sancho fell on his knees before him, and kissing his hand, "If it please your worship," cried he, "my good Lord Don Quixote, I beseech you make me governor of the island you have won in this dreadful and bloody fight; for, though it were never so great, I find myself able to govern it as well as the best he that ever went

93

about to govern an island in the world." "Brother Sancho," replied Don Quixote, "these are no adventures of islands; these are only re-encounters on the road, where little is to be got besides a broken head, or the loss of an ear: therefore have patience, and some adventure will offer itself, which will not only enable me to prefer thee to a government, but even to something more considerable."

Sancho gave him a world of thanks; and, having once more kissed his hand, and the skirts of his coat of armor, he helped him to get upon Rozinante; and then, leaping on his ass, he followed the hero, who, without taking leave of those in the coach, put on a good round pace, and rode into a wood, that was not far off. Sancho made after him as fast as his ass would trot; but, finding that Rozinante was like to leave him behind, he was forced to call to his master to stay for him. Don Quixote accordingly checked his horse, and soon gave Sancho leisure to overtake him. "Methinks, sir," said the fearful squire, as soon as he come up with him, "it will not be amiss for us to betake ourselves to some church, to get out of harm's way; for, if that same man whom you have fought with should do otherwise than well, I dare lay my life they will get a warrant from the Holy Brotherhood,[1] and have us taken up; which if they do, on my word, it will go hard with us ere we can get out of their clutches." "Hold thy tongue," cried Don Quixote: "where didst thou ever read, or find that a knight-errant was ever brought before any judge for the homicides which he committed?" "I cannot tell what you mean by your homilies," replied Sancho; "I do not know that ever I saw one in my born days, not I: but well I wot, that the law lays hold on those that go to murder one another in the fields; and, for your what-do-you-call-'ems, I have nothing to say to them." "Then be not afraid, good Sancho," cried Don Quixote; "for I would deliver thee out of the hands of the Chaldeans, and with much more ease out of those of the Holy Brotherhood. But come, tell me truly, dost thou believe that the whole world can boast of another knight that may pretend to rival me in valor? Didst thou ever read in history, that any other ever showed more resolution to undertake, more vigor to attack, more breath to hold out, more dexterity and activity to strike, and more art and force to overthrow his enemies?" "Not I, by my troth," replied Sancho. "I never did meet anything like you in history, for I neither can read nor write; but that which I dare wager is, that I never in my life served a bolder master than your worship: pray Heaven this same boldness may not bring us to what I bid you beware of. All I have to put you in mind of now, is, that you get your ear dressed, for you lose a deal of blood; and by good luck I have here some lint and a little white salve in my wallet." "How needless would all this have been," cried Don Quixote, "had I but bethought myself of making a small bottleful of the balsam of Fierabras, a single drop of which would have spared us a great deal of time and medicaments." "What is that same balsam, if it please you?" cried Sancho. "A balsam," answered Don Quixote, "of which I have the receipt in my head; he that hath some of it may defy death itself, and dally

---

[1] *An institution spread through all Spain, to suppress robbers, and make the roads safe to travelers.*

with all manner of wounds: therefore, when I have made some of it, and given it thee, if at any time thou happenest to see my body cut in two, by some unlucky back-stroke, as it is common among us knights-errant, thou hast no more to do but to take up nicely that half of me which is fallen to the ground, and clap it exactly to the other half on the saddle, before the blood is congealed, always taking care to lay it just in its proper place: then thou shalt give me two drops of that balsam, and thou shalt immediately see me become whole and sound as an apple." "If this be true," quoth Sancho, "I will quit you of your promise about the island this minute of an hour, and will have nothing of your worship for what service I have done, and am to do you, but the receipt of that same balsam; for, I dare say, let me go wherever I will, it will be sure to yield me three good reals an ounce; and thus I shall make shift to pick a pretty good livelihood out of it. But stay though," continued he, "does the making stand your worship in much, sir?" "Three quarts of it," replied Don Quixote, "may be made for three reals." "Body of me," cried Sancho, "why do not you make some out of hand, and teach me how to make it?" "Say no more, friend Sancho," returned Don Quixote; "I intend to teach thee much greater secrets, and design thee nobler rewards; but, in the meantime, dress my ear, for it pains me more than I could wish." Sancho then took his lint and ointment out of his wallet; but, when Don Quixote perceived the visor of his helmet was broken, he had like to have run stark-staring mad; straight, laying hold on his sword, and lifting up his eyes to heaven, "By the great Creator of the universe," cried he, "by every syllable contained in the four holy evangelists, I swear to lead a life like the great Marquis of Mantua, when he made a vow to revenge the death of his cousin Baldwin, which was never to eat bread on a tablecloth, never to lie with the dear partner of his bed, and other things, which, though they are now at present slipped out of my memory, I comprise in my vow no less than if I had now mentioned them; and this I bind myself to, till I have fully revenged myself on him that has done me this injury."

"Good your worship," cried Sancho (amazed to hear him take such a horrid oath), "think on what you are doing; for if that same knight has done as you bid him, and has gone and cast himself before my Lady Dulcinea del Toboso, I do not see but you and he are quit; and the man deserves no further punishment, unless he does you some new mischief." "It is well observed," replied Don Quixote; "and therefore, as to the point of revenge, I revoke my oath; but I renew and confirm the rest, protesting solemnly to lead the life I mentioned, till I have by force of arms despoiled some knight of as good a helmet as mine was. Neither do thou fancy, Sancho, that I make this protestation lightly, or make a smoke of straw: no, I have a laudable precedent for it, the authority of which will sufficiently justify my imitation; for the very same thing happened about Mambrino's helmet, which cost Sacripante so dear." [2] "Good sir," quoth Sancho, "let all such cursing and swearing go to the devil; there is nothing can be worse for your soul's health, nay, for your bodily health either. Besides, suppose we should not this good while meet anyone with a helmet on, what a sad case should we then be in? Will your worship then keep your oath in spite of so many hardships, such as to lie rough for a month together, far from any inhabited place, and a thousand other idle penances which that mad old Marquis of Mantua punished himself with by his vow? Do but consider, that we may ride I do not know how long upon this road without meeting any armed knight to pick a quarrel with; for here are none but carriers and wagoners, who are so far from wearing any helmets, that it is ten to one whether they ever heard of such a thing in their lives." "Thou art mistaken, friend Sancho," replied Don Quixote; "for we shall not be two hours this way without meeting more men in arms than there were at the siege of

[2] *The story is in Ariosto's "Orlando Furioso."*

97

Albraca, to carry off the fair Angelica." [3] "Well then, let it be so," quoth Sancho; "and may we have the luck to come off well, and quickly win that island which costs me so dear, and then I do not matter what befalls me." "I have already bid thee not trouble thyself about this business, Sancho," said Don Quixote; "for should we miss an island, there is either the kingdom of Denmark, or that of Sobradisa,[4] as fit for thy purpose as a ring to thy finger; and, what ought to be no small comfort to thee, they are both upon *terra firma*.[5] But we will talk of this in its proper season: at this time I would have thee see whether thou hast anything to eat in thy wallet, that we may afterwards seek for some castle, where we may lodge this night, and make the balsam I told thee; for I protest my ear smarts extremely." "I have here an onion," replied the squire, "a piece of cheese, and a few stale crusts of bread; but sure such coarse fare is not for such a brave knight as your worship." "Thou art grossly mistaken, friend Sancho," answered Don Quixote: "know, that it is the glory of knights-errant to be whole months without eating: and when they do, they fall upon the first thing they meet with, though it be never so homely. Hadst thou but read as many books as I have done, thou hadst been better informed as to that point; for though I think I have read as many histories of chivalry in my time as any other man, I never could find that the knights-errant ever ate, unless it were by mere accident, or when they were invited to great feasts and royal banquets; at other times they indulged themselves with little other food besides their thoughts. Though it is not to be imagined they could live without supplying the exigencies of human nature, as being after all no more than mortal

3 *Meaning king Marsilio, and the thirty-two kings, his tributaries, with all their forces.—Ariosto.*

4 *A fictitious kingdom in "Amadis de Gaul."*

5 *In allusion to the famous Firm Island in "Amadis de Gaul," the land of promise to the faithful squires of knights-errant.*

men; yet it is likewise to be supposed, that, as they spent the greatest part of their lives in forests and deserts, and always destitute of a cook, consequently their usual food was but such coarse country fare as thou now offerest me. Never then make thyself uneasy about what pleases me, friend Sancho, nor pretend to make a new world, or unhinge the very constitution and ancient customs of knight-errantry." "I beg your worship's pardon," cried Sancho; "for, as I was never bred a scholar, I may chance to have missed in some main point of your laws of knighthood; but, from this time forward, I will be sure to stock my wallet with all sorts of dry fruits for you, because your worship is a knight; as for myself, who am none, I will provide good poultry and other substantial victuals." "I do not say, Sancho," replied Don Quixote, "that a knight-errant is obliged to feed altogether upon fruit; I only mean, that this was their common food, together with some roots and herbs, which they found up and down the fields, of all which they had a perfect knowledge, as I myself have." "It is a good thing to know those herbs," cried Sancho; "for I am much mistaken, or that kind of knowledge will stand us in good stead ere long. In the meantime," continued he, "here is what good Heaven has sent us." With that he pulled out the provision he had, of which they ate heartily together. But their impatience to find out a place where they might be harbored that night, made them shorten their sorry meal and mount again, for fear of being benighted; so away they put on in search of a lodging. But the sun and their hopes failed them at once, as they came to a place where some goatherds had set up some small huts; and therefore they concluded to take up their lodging there that night. This was as great a mortification to Sancho, who was altogether for a good town, as it was a pleasure to his master, who was for sleeping in the open field, as believing, that as often as he did it, he confirmed his title to knighthood by a new act of possession.

The Knight was very courteously received by the goatherds, and as for Sancho, after he had set up Rozinante and his ass, as well as he could, he presently repaired to the attractive smell of some pieces of kid's flesh, which stood boiling in a kettle over the fire. The hungry squire would immediately have tried whether they were fit to be removed out of the kettle into the stomach, but was not put to that trouble; for the goatherds took them off the fire, and, spreading some sheep-skins on the ground, soon got their rural feast ready, and cheerfully invited his master and him to partake of what they had. Next, with some coarse compliment, after the country way, they desired Don Quixote to sit down on a trough with the bottom upwards; and then six of them, who were all that belonged to that fold, squatted them down round the skins, while Sancho stood to wait upon his master, and give him drink in a horn cup, which the goatherds used. But he, seeing his man stand behind, said to him, "That thou mayest understand, Sancho, the benefits of knight-errantry, and how the meanest retainers to it have a fair prospect of being speedily esteemed and honored by the world, it is my pleasure that thou sit thee down by me in the company of those good people; and that there be no difference now observed between thee and me, thy natural lord and master, that thou eat in the same dish, and drink in the same cup; for it may be said of knight-errantry as of love, that it makes all things equal." "I thank your worship," cried Sancho; "but yet I must needs own, had I but a good deal of meat before me, I would eat it as well, or rather better, standing, and by myself, than if I sat by an emperor; and, to deal plainly and truly with you, I had rather munch a crust of brown bread and an onion in a corner, without any more ado and ceremony, than feed upon turkey at another man's table, where one is fain to sit mincing and chewing his meat an hour together, drink little, be always wiping his fingers and his chops, and never dare to cough nor sneeze, though he has never so much a mind to do it, nor do many things which a body may do freely by one's self; therefore, good sir, change those tokens of your kindness, which I have a right to by being your worship's squire, into something that may do me more good. As for these same honors, I heartily thank you as much as if I had accepted them, but yet I give up my right to them from this time to the world's end." "Talk no more," replied Don Quixote, "but sit thee down, for the humble shall be exalted"; and so, pulling him by the arm, he forced him to sit by him.

All this while the goatherds, who did not understand this jargon of knights-errant, chivalry, and squires, fed heartily and said nothing, but stared upon their guests, who very fairly swallowed whole luncheons, as big as their fists, with a mighty appetite. The first course being over, they brought in the second, consisting of dried acorns, and half a cheese as hard as a brick. Nor was the horn idle all the while, but went merrily round up and down so many times, sometimes full and sometimes empty, like the two buckets of a well, that they made shift at last to drink off one of the two skins of wine which they had there. And now, Don Quixote having satisfied his appetite, he took a handful of acorns, and looking earnestly upon them: "O happy age," cried he, "which our first parents called the age of gold! Not because gold, so much adored in this iron age, was then easily purchased, but because those two fatal words *mine* and *thine*, were distinctions unknown to the people of those fortunate times; for all things were in common in that holy age: men, for their sustenance, needed only to lift their hands and take it from the sturdy oak, whose spreading arms liberally invited them to gather the wholesome savory fruit; while the clear springs, and silver rivulets, with luxuriant plenty, offered them their pure refreshing water. In hollow trees, and in the clefts of rocks, the laboring and

101

industrious bees erected their little commonwealths, that men might reap with pleasure and with ease the sweet and fertile harvest of their toils. The tough and strenuous cork-trees did of themselves, and without other art than their native liberality, dismiss and impart their broad light bark, which served to cover these lowly huts, propped up with rough-hewn stakes, that were first built as a

shelter against the inclemencies of the air. All then was union, all peace, all love and friendship in the world; as yet no rude plow-share presumed with violence to pry into the pious bowels of our mother earth, for she, without compulsion, kindly yielded from every part of her fruitful and spacious bosom, whatever might at once satisfy, sustain, and indulge her frugal children. Then was the time when innocent, beautiful young shepherdesses went tripping over the hills and vales; their lovely hair sometimes plaited, sometimes loose and flowing, clad in no other vestment but what was necessary to cover decently what modesty would always have concealed. The Tyrian dye and the rich glossy hue of silk, martyred and dissembled into every color, which are now esteemed so fine and magnificent, were unknown to the innocent plainness of that age; yet bedecked with more becoming leaves and flowers, they may be said to outshine the proudest of the vain-dressing ladies of our age, arrayed in the most magnificent garbs, and all the most sumptuous adornings which idleness and luxury have taught succeeding pride: lovers then expressed the passion of their souls in the unaffected language of the heart, with the native plainness and sincerity in which they were conceived, and divested of all that artificial contexture, which enervates what it labors to enforce: imposture, deceit and malice had not yet crept in and imposed themselves unbribed upon mankind in the disguise of truth and simplicity: justice, unbiased either by favor or interest, which now so fatally pervert it, was equally and impartially dispensed; nor was the judge's fancy law, for then there were neither judges nor causes to be judged: the modest maid might walk wherever she pleased alone, free from the attacks of lewd, lascivious importuners. But, in this degenerate age, fraud and a legion of ills infecting the world, no virtue can be safe, no honor be secure; while wanton desires, diffused into the hearts of men, corrupt the strictest watches, and the closest retreats; which, though as intricate and unknown as the labyrinth of Crete, are no security for chastity. Thus that primitive innocence being vanished, the oppression daily prevailing, there was a necessity to oppose the torrent of violence: for which reason the order of knighthood-errant was instituted to defend the honor of virgins, protect widows, relieve orphans, and assist all the distressed in general. Now I myself am one of this order, honest friends; and though all people are obliged by the law of nature to be kind to persons of my order, yet, since you, without knowing anything of this obligation, have so generously entertained me, I ought to pay you my utmost acknowledgment; and, accordingly, return you my most hearty thanks for the same."

All this long oration, which might very well have been spared, was owing to the acorns, that recalled the golden age to our Knight's remembrance, and made him thus hold forth to the goatherds, who devoutly listened, but edified little, the discourse not being suited to their capacities. Sancho, as well as they, was silent all the while, eating acorns, and frequently visiting the second skin of wine, which, for coolness' sake, was hung upon a neighboring cork-tree. As for Don Quixote, he was longer, and more intent, upon his speech than upon his supper. When he had done, one of the goatherds, addressing himself to him, "Sir Knight," said he, "that you may be sure you are heartily welcome, we will get one of our fellows to give us a song; he is just a-coming: a good notable young lad he is, I will say that for him, and up to the ears in love. He is a scholar, and can read and write, and plays so rarely upon the rebec, that it is a charm but to hear him." No sooner were the words out of the goatherd's mouth, but they heard the sound of the instrument he spoke of, and presently appeared a good comely young man of about two-and-twenty years of age. The goatherds asked him if he had supped, and he having told them he had, "Then, dear Antonio," says the first speaker, "prithee sing us a song, to let this gentleman, our guest, see that we have those among us who know somewhat of music, for all we live amidst woods and mountains. We have told him of thee already; therefore prithee make our words good, and sing us the ditty thy uncle, the prebendary, made of thy love, that was so liked in our town." "With all my heart," replied Antonio; and so, without any further entreaty, sitting down on the stump of an oak, he tuned his fiddle, and very handsomely sung the following song:

ANTONIO'S AMOROUS COMPLAINT

Tho' love ne'er prattles at your eyes,
(The eyes those silent tongues of love)
Yet sure, Olalia, you're my prize:
For truth with zeal ev'n Heav'n can move.

104

I think, my love, you only try,
    Ev'n while I fear you've seal'd my doom;
So, tho' involv'd in doubts I lie,
    Hope sometimes glimmers thro' the gloom.
A flame so fierce, so bright, so pure,
    No scorn can quench, or art improve;
Thus like a martyr I endure,
    For there's a heaven to crown my love.
In dress and dancing I have strove
    My proudest rivals to outvie;
In serenades I've breath'd my love,
    When all things slept but love and I.
I need not add, I speak your praise
    Till every nymph's disdain I move;
Tho' thus a thousand foes I raise,
    'Tis sweet to praise the fair I love.
Teresa once your charms debas'd,
    But I her rudeness soon reprov'd;
In vain her friend my anger fac'd,
    For then I fought for her I lov'd.
Dear cruel fair, why then so coy?
    How can you so much love withstand?
Alas! I crave no lawless joy,
    But with my heart would give my hand.
Soft, easy, strong is Hymen's tie;
    Oh! then no more the bliss refuse;
Oh! wed me, or I swear to die,
    Or linger wretched and recluse.

Here Antonio ended his song. Don Quixote entreated him to sing another, but Sancho Panza, who had more mind to sleep than to hear the finest singing in the world, told his master there was enough. "Good sir," quoth he, "your worship had better go and lie down where you are to take your rest this night; besides, these good people are tired with their day's labor, and rather want to go to sleep, than to sit up all night to hear ballads." "I understand thee, Sancho," cried Don Quixote; "and indeed, I thought thy frequent visiting the bottle would make thee fonder of sleep than of music." "Make us thankful," cried Sancho, "we all liked the wine well enough." "I do not deny it," replied Don Quixote; "but go thou and lay thee down where thou pleasest; as for me, it better becomes a man of my profession to wake than to sleep: yet stay and dress my ear before thou goest, for it pains me extremely." Thereupon one of the goatherds, beholding the wound as Sancho offered to dress it, desired the Knight not to trouble himself, for he had a remedy that would quickly cure him; and then fetching a few rosemary leaves, which grew in great plenty thereabout, he bruised them, and mixed a little salt among them, and having applied the medicine to the ear, he bound it up, assuring him he needed no other remedy; which, in a little time, proved very true.

IV: THE STORY WHICH A YOUNG GOATHERD TOLD TO THOSE THAT WERE WITH DON QUIXOTE

A young fellow, who used to bring them provisions from the next village, happened to come while this was doing, and addressing himself to the goatherds, "Hark ye, friends," said he, "do you hear the news?" "What news?" cried one of the company. "That fine shepherd and scholar Chrysostom died this morning," answered the other; "and they say it was for love of that devilish untoward lass Marcella, rich William's daughter, that goes up and down the country in the habit of a shepherdess." "For Marcella!" cried one of the goatherds. "I say for her," replied the fellow, "and what is more, it is reported, he has ordered, by his will, they should bury him in the fields like any Heathen Moor, just at the foot of the rock, hard by the cork-tree fountain, where they say he had the first sight of her. Nay, he has likewise ordered many other strange things to be done, which the heads of the parish will not allow of, for they seem to be after the way of the Pagans. But Ambrose, the other scholar, who likewise appareled himself like a shepherd, is resolved to have his friend Chrysostom's will fulfilled in everything, just as he has ordered it. All the village is in an uproar. But after all, it is thought Ambrose and his friends will carry the day; and, tomorrow morning, he is to be buried in great state where I told you: I fancy it will be worth seeing; howsoever, be it what it will, I will ev'n go and see it, even though I should not get back again tomorrow." "We will all go," cried the goatherds, "and cast lots who shall tarry to look after the goats." "Well said, Peter," cried one of the goatherds; "but, as for casting of lots, I will save you that labor, for I will stay myself, not so much out of kindness to you neither, or want of curiosity, as because of the thorn in my toe, that will not let me go." "Thank you, however," quoth Peter. Don Quixote, who heard all this, entreated Peter to tell him who the deceased was, and also to give him a short account of the shepherdess.

Peter made answer, that all he knew of the matter was, that the deceased was a wealthy gentleman, who lived not far off, that he had been several years at the university of Salamanca, and then came home mightily improved in his learning. "But above all," quoth he, "it was said of him, that he had great knowledge in the stars, and whatsoever the sun and moon do in the skies; for he would tell us to a title the clip of the sun and moon." "We call it an eclipse," cried Don Quixote, "and not a clip, when either of these great luminaries are darkened." "He would also," continued Peter, who did not stand upon such nice distinctions, "foretell when the year would be plentiful or 'estil.'" "You would say 'sterile,'" cried Don Quixote. "'Sterile' or 'estil,'" replied the fellow, "that is all one to me; but this I say, that his parents and friends, being ruled by him, grew extremely rich in a short time; for he would tell them, 'This year

107

sow barley, and no wheat; in this you may sow peas and no barley; next year will be a good year for oil; the three after that, you shall not gather a drop': and whatsoever he said would certainly come to pass." "That science," said Don Quixote, "is called astrology." "I do not know what you call it," answered Peter, "but I know he knew all this, and a deal more. But, in short, within some few months after he had left the Versity, on a certain morning we saw him come dressed, for all the world like a shepherd, and driving his flock, having laid down the long gown which he used to wear as a scholar. At the same time one Ambrose, a great friend of his, who had been his fellow-scholar, also took upon him to go like a shepherd, and bear him company; which we all did not a little marvel at. I had almost forgot to tell you, how he that is dead was a mighty man for making of verses, insomuch that he commonly made the carols, which we sung on Christmas-eve; and the plays which the young lads in our neighborhood enacted on Corpus-Christi-day, and everyone would say, that nobody could mend them. Somewhat before that time Chrysostom's father died, and left him a deal of wealth, both in land, money, cattle, and other goods, whereof the young man remained absolute master; and in truth he deserved it all, for he was as good-natured a soul as ever trod on shoe-leather; mighty good to the poor, a main friend to all honest people, and had a face like a blessing. At last it came to be known, that the reason of his altering his garb in that fashion, was only that he might go up and down after that shepherdess Marcella, whom our comrade told you of before, for he was fallen mightily in love with her. And now I will tell you such a thing you never heard the like in your born days, and may not chance to hear of such another while you breathe, though you were to live as long as Sarna." "Say Sarah," cried Don Quixote, who hated to hear him blunder thus. "The Sarna, or the itch (for that is all one with us)," quoth Peter, "lives long enough too; but if you go on thus, and make me break off my tale at every

108

word, we are not like to have done this twelvemonth." "Pardon me, friend," replied Don Quixote; "I only spoke to make thee understand that there is a difference between Sarna and Sarah: however, thou sayest well; for the Sarna (that is, the itch) lives longer than Sarah; therefore pray make an end of thy story, for I will not interrupt thee any more." "Well then," quoth Peter, "you must know, good master of mine, that there lived near us one William, a yeoman, who was richer yet than Chrysostom's father; now he had no child in the 'versal world but a daughter; her mother died in childbed of her (rest her soul) and was as good a woman as ever went upon two legs; methinks I see her yet standing before me, with that blessed face of hers, the sun on one side, and the moon on the other. She was a main housewife, and did a deal of good among the poor; for which I dare say she is at this minute in Paradise. Alas! her death broke poor William's heart; he soon went after her, poor man, and left all to his little daughter, that Marcella by name, giving charge of her to her uncle, the parson of our parish. Well, the girl grew such a fine child, and so like her mother, that it used to put us in mind of her every foot: however, it was thought she would make a finer woman yet; and so it happened indeed; for, by that time she was fourteen or fifteen years of age, no man set his eyes on her, that did not bless Heaven for having made her so handsome; so that most men fell in love with her, and were ready to run mad for her. All this while her uncle kept her up very close; yet the report of her great beauty and wealth spread far and near, insomuch, that she had I do not know how many sweethearts, almost all the young men in our town asked her of her uncle; nay, from I do not know how many leagues about us, there flocked whole droves of suitors, and the very best in the country too, who all begged, and sued, and teased her uncle to let them have her. But though he would have been glad to have got fairly rid of her, as soon as she was fit for a husband, yet would not he advise, or marry her against her will;

109

for he is a good man, I will say that for him, and a true Christian every inch of him, and scorns to keep her from marrying, to make a benefit of her estate; and, to his praise be it spoken, he has been mainly commended for it more than once, when the people of our parish meet together. For, I must tell you, Sir Errant, that here in the country, and in our little towns, there is not the least thing can be said or done, but people will talk and find fault: but let busy-bodies prate as they please, the parson must have been a good body indeed, who could bring his whole parish to give him a good word, especially in the country." "Thou art in the right," cried Don Quixote, "and therefore go on, honest Peter, for the story is pleasant, and thou tellest it with a grace." "May I never want God's grace," quoth Peter, "for that is most to the purpose; but, for our parson, as I told you before, he was not for keeping his niece from marrying, and therefore he took care to let her know of all those that would have taken her to wife, both what they were, and what they had, and he was at her, to have her pitch upon one of them for a husband; yet would she never answer otherwise, but that she had no mind to wed as yet, as finding herself too young for the burden of wedlock. With these and such-like come-offs, she got her uncle to let her alone, and wait till she thought fit to choose for herself: for he was wont to say, that parents are not to bestow their children where they bear no liking; and, in that, he spoke like an honest man. And thus it happened, that when we least dreamed of it, that coy lass, finding herself at liberty, would needs turn shepherdess, and neither her uncle, nor all those of the village who advised her against it, could work anything upon her, but away she went to the fields, to keep her own sheep, with the other young lasses of the town. But then it was ten times worse; for no sooner was she seen abroad, when I cannot tell how many spruce gallants, both gentlemen and rich farmers, changed their garb for love of her, and followed her up and down in shepherd's guise. One of them, as I have

110

told you, was this same Chrysostom who now lies dead, of whom it is said, he not only loved but worshiped her. However, I would not have you think or surmise, because Marcella took that course of life, and was, as it were, under no manner of keeping, that she gave the least token of naughtiness or light behavior; for she ever was, and is still so coy, and so watchful to keep her honor pure and free from evil tongues, that among so many wooers who suitor her, there is not one can make his brags of having the least hope of ever speeding with her. For though she does not shun the company of shepherds, but uses them courteously, so far as they behave themselves handsomely; yet whensoever any one of them does but offer to break his mind to her, be it never so well meant, and only in order to marry, she casts him away from her, as with a fling, and will never have any more to say to him.

"And thus this fair maiden does more harm in this country, than the plague would do; for her courteousness and fair looks draw on everybody to love her; but then her dogged stubborn coyness breaks their hearts, and makes them ready to hang themselves; and all they can do, poor wretches, is to make a heavy complaint, and call her cruel, unkind, ungrateful, and a world of such names; whereby they plainly show what a sad condition they are in. Were you but to stay

here some time, you would hear these hills and valleys ring again with the doleful moans of those she has denied, who yet cannot for the blood of them give over sneaking after her. We have a place not far off, where there are some two dozen of beech-trees, and on them all you may find I do not know how many Marcellas cut in the smooth bark. On some of them there is a crown carved over the name; as much as to say that Marcella bears away the crown, and deserves the garland of beauty. Here sighs one shepherd, there another whines; here is one singing doleful ditties, there another is wringing his hands and making woeful complaints. You shall have one lay him down at night at the foot of a rock, or some oak, and there lie weeping and wailing without a wink of sleep, and talking to himself till the sun finds him the next morning; you shall have another lie stretched upon the hot sandy ground, breathing his sad lamentations to heaven, without heeding the sultry heat of the summer sun. And, all this while, the hard-hearted Marcella never minds any one of them, and does not seem to be the least concerned for them. We are all mightily at a loss to know what will be the end of all this pride and coyness, who shall be the happy man that shall at last tame her and bring her to his lure. Now, because there is nothing more certain than all this, I am the more apt to give credit to what our comrade has told us as to the occasion of Chrysostom's death; and, therefore, I would needs have you go and see him laid in his grave tomorrow; which I believe will be worth your while, for he had many friends, and it is not half a league to the place where it was his will to be buried." "I intend to be there," answered Don Quixote, "and, in the meantime, I return thee many thanks for the extraordinary satisfaction this story has afforded me." "Alas! Sir Knight," replied the goatherd, "I have not told you half the mischiefs this proud creature hath done here, but tomorrow mayhap we shall meet some shepherd by the way that will be able to tell you more. Meanwhile it will not be amiss for you to take your

112

rest in one of the huts; for the open air is not good for your wound, though what I have put to it is so special a medicine that there is not much need to fear but it will do well enough." Sancho, who was quite out of patience with the goatherd's long story, and wished him at the devil for his pains, at last prevailed with him to lie down in Peter's hut, where Don Quixote, in imitation of Marcella's lovers, devoted the remainder of the night to amorous expostulations with his dear Dulcinea. As for Sancho, he laid himself down between Rozinante and his ass, and slept it out, not like a disconsolate lover, but like a man that had been soundly kicked and bruised in the morning.

V: A CONTINUATION OF THE STORY OF MARCELLA

Scarce had day begun to appear from the balconies of the east, when five of the goatherds got up, and having waked Don Quixote, asked him if he held his resolution of going to the funeral, whither they were ready to bear him company. Thereupon the Knight, who desired nothing more, presently arose, and ordered Sancho to get Rozinante and the ass ready immediately; which he did with all expedition, and then they set forwards. They had not yet gone a quarter of a league, before they saw advancing towards them, out of a cross path, six shepherds clad in black skins, their heads crowned with garlands of cypress and bitter rose-bay-tree, with long holly staves in their hands. Two gentlemen on horseback, attended by three young lads on foot, came immediately after them: as they drew near, they saluted one another civilly, and after the usual question, "Which way do ye travel?" they found they were all going the same way to see the funeral, and so they all joined company. "I fancy, Signor Vivaldo," said one of the gentlemen, addressing himself to the other, "we shall not think our time misspent in going

113

to see this famous funeral; for it must of necessity be very extraordinary, according to the account which these men have given us of the dead shepherd and his murdering mistress." "I am so far of your opinion," answered Vivaldo, "that I would not only stay one day, but a whole week rather than miss the sight." This gave Don Quixote occasion to ask them what they had heard concerning Chrysostom and Marcella. One of the gentlemen made answer, that, having met that morning with those shepherds, they could not forbear inquiring of them, why they wore such a mournful dress. Whereupon one of them acquainted them with the sad occasion, by relating the story of a certain shepherdess, named Marcella, no less lovely than cruel, whose coyness and disdain has made a world of unfortunate lovers, and caused the death of that Chrysostom, to whose funeral they were going. In short, he repeated to Don Quixote all that Peter had told him the night before. After this, Vivaldo asked the Knight why he traveled so completely armed in so peaceable a country. "My profession," answered the champion, "does not permit me to ride otherwise. Luxurious feasts, sumptuous dresses, and downy ease, were invented for effeminate courtiers; but labor, vigilance, and arms are the portion of those whom the world calls knights-errant, of which number I have the honor to be one, though the most unworthy, and the meanest of the fraternity." He needed to say no more to satisfy them his brains were out of order; however, that they might the better understand the nature of his folly, Vivaldo asked him what he meant by a knight-errant. "Have you not read then," cried the famous Don Quixote, "the annals and history of Britain, where are recorded the famous deeds of King Arthur, who, according to an ancient tradition in that kingdom, never died, but was turned into a crow by enchantment, and shall one day resume his former shape, and recover his kingdom again? For which reason since that time, the people of Great Britain dare not offer to kill a crow. In this good king's time, the most noble order of the Knights

114

of the Round Table was first instituted, and then also the amours between Sir Lancelot of the Lake and Queen Guinever were really transacted, as that history relates; they being managed and carried on by the mediation of that honorable matron the Lady Quintaniona; which produced that excellent history in verse, so sung and celebrated here in Spain:

> " 'There never was on earth a knight
> So waited on by ladies fair,
> As once was he Sir Lancelot hight,
> When first he left his country dear.'

"And the rest, which gives so delightful an account, both of his loves and feats of arms. From that time the order of knight-errantry began by degrees to dilate and extend itself into most parts of the world. Then did the great Amadis de Gaul signalize himself by heroic exploits, and so did his offspring to the fifth generation. The valorous Felixmarte of Hyrcania then got immortal fame, and that undaunted knight Tirante the White, who never can be applauded to his worth. Nay, had we but lived a little sooner, we might have been blessed with the conversation of that invincible knight of our modern times, the valorous Don Belianis of Greece. And this, gentlemen, is that order of chivalry, which, as much a sinner as I am, I profess, with a due observance of the laws which those brave knights observed before me; and, for that reason I choose to wander through these solitary deserts, seeking adventures, fully resolved to expose my person to the most formidable dangers which fortune can obtrude on me, that by the strength of my arm I may relieve the weak and the distressed."

After all this stuff, you may be sure the travelers were sufficiently convinced of Don Quixote's frenzy. Nor were they less surprised than were all those who had hitherto discovered so unaccountable a distraction in one who seemed a rational creature. However Vivaldo, who was of a gay disposition, had no sooner made the discovery, but he resolved to make the best advantage of it, that the shortness of the way would allow him.

Therefore, to give him further occasion to divert them with his whimsies, "Methinks, Sir Knight-errant," said he to him, "you have taken up one of the strictest and most mortifying professions in the world. I do not think but that a Carthusian friar has a better time of it than you have." "Perhaps," answered Don Quixote, "the profession of a Carthusian may be as austere, but I am within two fingers' breadth of doubting whether it may be as beneficial to the world as ours. For, if we must speak the truth, the soldier, who puts his captain's command in execution, may be said to do as much at least as the captain who commanded him. The application is easy; for, while those religious men have nothing to do, but with all quietness and security to say their prayers for the prosperity of the world, we knights, like soldiers, execute what they do but pray for, and procure those benefits to mankind, by the strength of our arms, and at the hazard of our lives, for which they only intercede. Nor do we do this sheltered from the injuries of the air, but under no other roof than that of the wide heavens, exposed to summer's scorching heat and winter's pinching cold. So that we may justly style ourselves the ministers of Heaven, and the instruments of its justice upon earth; and as the business of war is not to be compassed without vast toil and labor, so the religious soldier must undoubtedly be preferred before the religious monk, who living still quiet and at ease, has nothing to do but to pray for the afflicted and distressed. However, gentlemen, do not imagine I would insinuate that the profession of a knight-errant was a state of perfection equal to that of a holy recluse: I would only infer from what I have said, and what I myself endure, that ours, without question, is more laborious, more subject to the discipline of heavy blows, to maceration, to the penance of hunger and thirst, and, in a word, to rags, to want, and misery. For if you find that some knights-errant have

116

at last, by their valor, been raised to thrones and empires, you may be sure it has been still at the expense of much sweat and blood. And had even those happier knights been deprived of those assisting sages and enchanters, who helped them in all emergencies, they would have been strangely disappointed of their mighty expectations." "I am of the same opinion," replied Vivaldo, "but one thing, among many others, which I can by no means approve in your profession, is, that when you are just going to engage in some very hazardous adventure, where your lives are evidently to be much endangered, you never once remember to commend yourselves to God, as every good Christian ought to do on such occasions, but only recommend yourselves to your mistresses, and that with as great zeal and devotion as if you worshiped no other deity; a thing which, in my opinion, strongly relishes of Paganism." "Sir," replied Don Quixote, "there is no altering that method; for, should a knight-errant do otherwise, he would too much deviate from the ancient and established customs of knight-errantry, which inviolably oblige him, just in the moment when he is rushing on, and giving birth to some dubious achievement, to have his mistress still before his eyes, still present to his mind, by a strong and lively imagination, and with soft, amorous, and energetic looks, imploring her favor and protection in that perilous circumstance. Nay, if nobody can overhear him, he is obliged to whisper, or speak between his teeth, some short ejaculations, to recommend himself with all the fervency imaginable to the lady of his wishes, and of this we have innumerable examples in history. Nor are you for all this to imagine that knights-errant omit recommending themselves to Heaven, for they have leisure enough to do it even in the midst of the combat."

"Sir," replied Vivaldo, "you must give me leave to tell you, I am not yet thoroughly satisfied in this point; for I have often observed in my reading, that two knights-errant, having first talked a little together, have fallen out presently, and been so highly provoked, that having turned their horses' heads, to gain room for the career, they have wheeled about, and then with all speed run full tilt at one another, hastily recommending themselves to their mistresses, in the midst of their career; and the next thing has commonly been, that one of them has been thrown to the ground, over the crupper of his horse, fairly run through and through with his enemy's lance; and the other forced to catch hold of his horse's mane to keep himself from falling. Now, I cannot apprehend how the knight that was slain had any time to recommend himself to Heaven, when his business was done so suddenly. Methinks, those hasty invocations, which in his career were directed to his mistress, should have been directed to Heaven, as every good Christian would have done. Besides, I fancy every knight-errant has not a mistress to invoke, nor is every one of them in love." "Your conjecture is wrong," replied Don Quixote; "a knight-errant cannot be without a mistress; it is not more essential for the skies to have stars, than it is to us to be in love. Insomuch, that, I dare affirm, no history ever made mention of any knight-errant that was not a lover; for were any knight free from the impulses of that generous passion, he would not be allowed to be a lawful knight; but a misborn intruder, and one who was not admitted within the pale of knighthood at the door, but leaped the fence, and stole in like a robber and a thief." "Yet, sir," replied the other, "I am much mistaken, or I have read, that Don Galaor, the brother of Amadis, never had any certain mistress to recommend himself to, and yet for all that he was not the less esteemed." "One swallow never makes a summer," answered Don Quixote, "besides, I know that knight was privately very much in love; and, as for his making his addresses wherever he met with beauty, this was an effect of his natural inclination, which he could not easily restrain. But, after all, it is an undeniable truth, that he had a favorite lady, whom he had crowned empress of his will; and to her he frequently recommended himself in private, for he did not a little value himself upon his discretion and secrecy in love." "Then, sir," said Vivaldo, "since it is so much the being of knight-errantry to be in love, I presume, you, who are of that profession, cannot be without a mistress. And therefore, if you do not set up for secrecy as much as Don Galaor did, give me leave to beg of you, in the name of all the company, that you will be pleased so far to oblige us, as to let us know the name and quality of your mistress, the place of her birth, and the charms of her person. For, without doubt, the lady cannot but esteem herself happy in being known to all the world, to be the object of the wishes of a knight so accomplished as yourself." With that Don Quixote, breathing out a deep sigh, "I cannot tell," said he, "whether this lovely enemy of my repose, is the least affected with the world's being informed of her power over my heart; all I dare say, in compliance with your request is, that her name is Dulcinea, her country La Mancha, and Toboso the happy place which she honors with her residence. As for her quality, it cannot be less than princess, seeing she is my mistress and my queen. Her beauty transcends all the united charms of her whole sex; even those chimerical perfections, which the hyperbolical imaginations of poets in love have assigned to their mistresses, cease to be incredible descriptions when applied to her, in whom all those miraculous endowments are most divinely centered. The curling locks of her bright flowing hair are purest gold; her smooth forehead the Elysian Plain; her brows are two celestial bows; her eyes two glorious suns; her cheeks two beds of roses; her lips are coral; her teeth are pearl; her neck is alabaster; her breasts marble; her hands ivory; and snow would lose its whiteness near her bosom. Then, for the parts which modesty has veiled, my imagination, not to wrong them, chooses to lose itself in silent admiration; for nature boasts nothing that may give an idea of their incomparable worth." "Pray, sir," cried Vivaldo, "oblige us with an account of her parentage, and the place of her birth, to

119

complete the description." "Sir," replied Don Quixote, "she is not descended from the ancient Curtii, Caii, nor Scipios of Rome, nor from the more modern Colonnas, nor Ursinis; nor from the Moncadas, and Requesenes of Catalonia; nor from the Rebellas and Villanovas of Valencia; nor from the Palafoxes, Nuças, Rocabertis, Corellas, Lunas, Alagones, Urreas, Foçes, or Gurreas of Arragon; nor from the Cerdas, Manriques, Mendoças, and Gusmans of Castile; nor from the Alencastros, Pallas, and Menezes of Portugal; but she derives her great original from the family of Toboso in La Mancha, a race, which, though it be modern, is sufficient to give a noble beginning to the most illustrious progenies of succeeding ages. And let no man presume to contradict me in this, unless it be upon these conditions, which Zerbin fixed at the foot of Orlando's armor:

" 'Let none but he these arms displace,
Who dares Orlando's fury face.' "

"I draw my pedigree from the Cachopines of Laredo," replied Vivaldo, "yet I dare not make any comparisons with the Tobosos of La Mancha; though, to deal sincerely with you, it is a family I never heard of till this moment." "It is strange," said Don Quixote, "you should never have heard of it before."

All the rest of the company gave great attention to this discourse; and even the very goatherds and shepherds were now fully convinced that Don Quixote's brains were turned topsy-turvy. But Sancho Panza believed every word that dropped from his master's mouth to be truth, as having known him from his cradle to be a man of sincerity. Yet that which somewhat staggered his faith, was this story of Dulcinea of Toboso; for he was sure he had never heard before of any such princess, nor even of the name, though he lived hard by Toboso.

As they went on thus discoursing, they saw upon the hollow road,

between the neighbor-
ing mountains, about
twenty shepherds more,
all accoutered in black
skins with garlands on
their heads, which, as
they shortly afterwards
perceived, were all of
yew or cyprus: six of
them carried a bier cov-
ered with several sorts
of branches and blos-
soms; which one of the
goatherds observing it,
"Those are they that
are carrying our poor
Chrysostom to an early
grave," cried he, "and
it was in yonder bottom that he gave charge they should bury his
corpse." This made them all double their pace, that they might get
thither in time; and so they arrived just as the bearers had set
down the bier upon the ground, and four of them had begun to
open the ground with their spades, just at the foot of a rock. They
all saluted each other courteously, and condoled their mutual loss;
and then Don Quixote, with those who came with him, went to view
the bier, where they saw the dead body of a young man in shepherd's weeds all strewn over with flowers. The deceased seemed to
be about thirty years old; and, dead though he was, it was easily
perceived that both his face and shape were extraordinarily handsome. Within the bier were some few books and several papers,
some open, and the rest folded up. This doleful object so strangely
filled all the company with sadness, that not only the beholders,

121

but also the grave-makers, and all the mourning shepherds remained a long time silent; till at last one of the bearers, addressing himself to one of the rest: "Look, Ambrose," cried he, "whether this be the place which Chrysostom meant, since you must needs have his will so punctually performed?" "This is the very place," answered the other: "there it was that my unhappy friend many times told me the sad story of his cruel fortune; and there it was that he first saw that mortal enemy of mankind; there it was that he made the first discovery of his passion, no less innocent than violent; there it was that the relentless Marcella last denied, shunned him, and drove him to that extremity of sorrow and despair that hastened the sad catastrophe of his tragical and miserable life; and there it was, that, in token of so many misfortunes, he desired to be committed to the bowels of eternal oblivion."

Then, addressing himself to Don Quixote and the rest of the travelers, "This body, gentlemen," said he, "which here you now behold, was once enlivened by a soul which Heaven had enriched with the greatest part of its most valuable graces. This is the body of that Chrysostom, who was unrivaled in wit, matchless in courteousness, incomparable in gracefulness, a phœnix in friendship, generous and magnificent without ostentation, prudent and grave without pride, modest without affectation, pleasant and complaisant without meanness: in a word, the first in every esteemable qualification, and second to none in misfortune: he loved well, and was hated; he adored, and was disdained; he begged pity of cruelty itself; he strove to move obdurate marble; pursued the wind; made his moans to solitary deserts; was constant to ingratitude; and for the recompense of his fidelity, became a prey to death in the flower of his age, through the barbarity of a shepherdess, whom he strove to immortalize by his verse; as these papers which are here deposited might testify, had he not commanded me to sacrifice them to the flames, at the same time that his body was committed to the earth."

"Should you do so," cried Vivaldo, "you would appear more cruel to them than their exasperated unhappy parent. Consider, sir, it is not consistent with discretion, not even with justice, so nicely to perform the request of the dead, when it is repugnant to reason. Augustus Cæsar himself would have forfeited his title to wisdom, had he permitted that to have been effected which the divine Virgil had ordered by his will. Therefore, sir, now that you resign your friend's body to the grave, do not hurry thus the noble and only remains of that dear unhappy man to a worse fate, the death of oblivion. What though he has doomed them to perish in the height of his resentment, you ought not indiscreetly to be their executioner; but rather reprieve and redeem them from eternal silence, that they may live, and, flying through the world, transmit to all ages the dismal story of your friend's virtue, and Marcella's ingratitude, as a warning to others, that they may avoid such tempting snares and enchanting destructions; for not only to me, but to all here present, is well known the history of your enamored and desperate friend: we are no strangers to the friendship that was between you, as also to Marcella's cruelty, which occasioned his death. Last night, being informed that he was to be buried here today, moved not so much by curiosity as pity, we are come to behold with our eyes that which gave us so much trouble to hear. Therefore, in the name of all the company, like me deeply affected with a sense of Chrysostom's extraordinary merit and his unhappy fate, and desirous to prevent such deplorable disasters for the future, I beg that you will permit me to save some of these papers, whatever you resolve to do with the rest." And so, without expecting an answer, he stretched out his arm, and took out those papers which lay next to his hand. "Well, sir," said Ambrose, "you have found a way to make me submit, and you may keep those papers; but, for the rest, nothing shall make me alter my resolution of burning them." Vivaldo said no more; but, being impatient to see what those papers were which he had rescued

123

from the flames, he opened one of them immediately, and read the title of it, which was, "The Despairing Lover." "That," said Ambrose, "was the last piece my dear friend ever wrote; and therefore, that you may all hear to what a sad condition his unhappy passion had reduced him, read it aloud, I beseech you, sir, while the grave is making." "With all my heart," replied Vivaldo: and so the company, having the same desire, presently gathered round, and he read as follows:

VI: THE UNFORTUNATE SHEPHERD'S VERSES, AND OTHER UNEXPECTED MATTERS

THE DESPAIRING LOVER

Relentless tyrant of my heart,
Attend, and hear thy slave impart
   The matchless story of his pain.
In vain I labor to conceal
What my extorted groans reveal;
   Who can be rack'd, and not complain?
But oh! who fully can express
Thy cruelty, and my distress?
   No human art, no human tongue.
Then fiends assist, and rage infuse!
A raving fury be my muse,
   And hell inspire the dismal song!
Owls, ravens, terrors of the night,
Wolves, monsters, fiends, with dire affright,
   Join your dread accents to my moans!
Join, howling winds, your sullen noise;
Thou, grumbling thunder, join thy voice;
   Mad seas, your roar, and hell, thy groans.
Tho' still I moan in dreary caves,
To desert rocks, and silent graves,
   My loud complaints shall wander far;

124

Borne, by the winds, they shall survive,
By pitying echoes kept alive,
    And fill the world with my despair.
Love's deadly cure is fierce disdain,
Distracting fear a dreadful pain,
    And jealousy a matchless woe;
Absence is death, yet while it kills,
I live with all these mortal ills,
    Scorn'd, jealous, loath'd, and absent too.
No dawn of hope e'er cheer'd my heart,
No pitying ray e'er sooth'd my smart,
    All, all the sweets of life are gone;
Then come despair, and frantic rage,
With instant fate my pain assuage,
    And end a thousand deaths by one.
But even in death let love be crown'd,
My fair destruction guiltless found,
    And I be thought with justice scorn'd:
Thus let me fall unlov'd, unbless'd,
With all my load of woes oppress'd,
    And even too wretched to be mourn'd.
O! thou, by whose destructive hate,
I'm hurry'd to this doleful fate,
    When I'm no more, thy pity spare!
I dread thy tears; oh spare 'em then—
But oh! I rave, I was too vain,
    My death can never cost a tear.
Tormented souls, on you I call,
Hear one more wretched than you all;
    Come howl as in redoubled flames.
Attend me to th' eternal night,
No other dirge, no fun'ral rite,
    A poor despairing lover claims.
And thou, my song, sad child of woe,
When life is gone, and I'm below,
    For thy lost parent cease to grieve:

125

With life and thee my woes increase,
And should they not by dying cease,
Hell has no pain like these I leave.

These verses were well approved by all the company; only Vivaldo observed, that the jealousies and fears, of which the shepherd complained, did not very well agree with what he had heard of Marcella's unspotted modesty and reservedness. But Ambrose, who had been always privy to the most secret thoughts of his friend, informed him, that the unhappy Chrysostom wrote those verses when he had torn himself from his adored mistress, to try whether absence, the common cure of love, would relieve him, and mitigate his pain. And as everything disturbs an absent lover, and nothing is more usual than for him to torment himself with a thousand chimeras of his own brain, so did Chrysostom perplex himself with jealousies and suspicions, which had no ground but in his distracted imagination; and therefore whatever he said in those uneasy circumstances could never affect, or in the least prejudice, Marcella's virtuous character, upon whom, setting aside her cruelty and her disdainful haughtiness, envy itself could never fix the least reproach. Vivaldo being thus convinced, they were going to read another paper, when they were unexpectedly prevented by a kind of apparition that offered itself to their view. It was Marcella herself, who appeared at the top of the rock, at the foot of which they were digging the grave; but so beautiful, that fame seemed rather to have lessened than to have magnified her charms: those who had never seen her before, gazed on her with silent wonder and delight: nay, those who used to see her every day seemed no less lost in admiration than the rest. But scarce had Ambrose spied her, when, with anger and indignation in his heart, he cried out, "What makest thou there, thou fierce, thou cruel basilisk of these mountains! comest thou to see whether the wounds of this murdered wretch will bleed afresh at thy presence? or comest thou, thus

126

mounted aloft, to glory in the fatal effects of thy native inhumanity, like another Nero at the sight of flaming Rome? or is it to trample on this unfortunate corpse, as Tarquin's ungrateful daughter did her father's? Tell us quickly why thou comest, and what thou yet desirest? For, since I know that Chrysostom's whole study was to serve and please thee while he lived, I am willing to dispose all his friends to pay thee the like obedience now he is dead." "I come not here to any of these ungrateful ends, Ambrose," replied Marcella, "but only to clear my innocence, and show the injustice of all those who lay their misfortunes and Chrysostom's death to my charge: therefore, I entreat you all, who are here at this time, to hear me a little, for I shall not need to use many words to convince people of sense of an evident truth. Heaven, you are pleased to say, has made me beautiful, and that to such a degree that you are forced, nay, as it were, compelled to love me, in spite of your endeavors to the contrary; and, for the sake of that love, you say I ought to love you again. Now, though I am sensible that whatever is beautiful is lovely, I cannot conceive, that what is loved for being handsome should be bound to love that by which it is loved, merely because it is loved. He that loves a beautiful object may happen to be ugly: and as what is ugly deserves not to be loved, it would be ridiculous to say, 'I love you because you are handsome, and therefore you must love me again, though I am ugly.' But suppose two persons of different sexes are equally handsome, it does not follow that their desires should be alike and reciprocal; for all beauties do not kindle love; some only recreate the sight, and never reach nor captivate the heart. Alas! should whatever is beautiful beget love, and enslave the mind, mankind's desires would ever run confused and wandering, without being able to fix their determinate choice: for, as there is an infinite number of beautiful objects, the desires would consequently be also infinite; whereas, on the contrary, I have heard that true love is still confined to one, and voluntary and unforced. This being granted, why would you have me force my inclinations for no other reason but that you say you love me? Tell me, I beseech you, had Heaven formed me as ugly as it has made me beautiful, could I justly complain of you for not loving me? Pray consider also, that I do not possess those charms by choice; such as they are, they were freely bestowed on me by Heaven: and as the viper is not to be blamed for the poison with which she kills, seeing it was assigned her by nature, so I ought not to be censured for that beauty which I derive from the same cause: for beauty in a virtuous woman is but like a distant flame, or a sharp-edged sword, and only burns and wounds those who approach too near it. Honor and virtue are the ornaments of the soul, and that body that is destitute of them cannot be esteemed beautiful, though it be naturally so. If, then, honor be one of those endowments which most adorn the body, why should she that is beloved for her beauty expose herself to the loss of it, merely to gratify the loose desires of one who, for his own selfish ends, uses all the means imaginable to make her lose it? I was born free, and that I might continue so I retired to these solitary hills and plains, where trees are my companions, and clear fountains my looking-glasses. With the trees and with the waters I communicate my thoughts and my beauty. I am a distant flame, and a sword far off: those whom I have attracted with my sight, I have undeceived with my words; and if hope be the food of desire, as I never gave any encouragement to Chrysostom, nor to any other, it may well be said it was rather his own obstinacy than my cruelty that shortened his life. If you tell me that his intentions were honest, and therefore ought to have been complied with, I answer, that when, at the very place where his grave is making, he discovered his passion, I told him I was resolved to live and die single, and that the earth alone should reap the fruit of my reservedness, and enjoy the spoils of my beauty; and if, after all the admonitions I gave him, he would persist in his obstinate pursuit, and sail against

128

the wind, what wonder is it he should perish in the waves of his indiscretion? Had I ever encouraged him, or amused him with ambiguous words, then I had been false; and had I gratified his wishes, I had acted contrary to my better resolves. He persisted, though I had given him a due caution, and he despaired without being hated. Now I leave you to judge, whether I ought to be blamed for his sufferings? If I have deceived anyone, let him complain; if I have broke my promise to anyone, let him despair; if I encourage anyone, let him presume; if I entertain anyone, let him boast: but let no man call me cruel nor murderer, until I either deceive, break my promise, encourage, or entertain him. Heaven has not been pleased to show whether it is its will I should love by destiny, and it is vain to think I will ever do it by choice: so let this general caution serve everyone of those who make their addresses to me for their own ends. And, if anyone hereafter dies on my account, let not their jealousy, nor my scorn or hate, be thought the cause of their death; for she who never pretended to love, cannot make anyone jealous, and a free and generous declaration of our fixed resolution ought not to be counted hate or disdain. In short, let him that calls me a tigress, and a basilisk, avoid me as a dangerous thing; and let him that calls me ungrateful, give over serving me; I assure them I will never seek nor pursue them. Therefore, let none hereafter make it their business to disturb my ease, nor strive to make me hazard among men the peace I now enjoy, which I am persuaded is not to be found with them. I have wealth enough: I neither love nor hate anyone. The innocent conversation of the neighboring shepherdesses, with the care of my flocks, help me to pass away my time, without either coquetting with this man, or practicing arts to ensnare that other. My thoughts are limited by these mountains; and if they wander further, it is only to admire the beauty of Heaven, and thus, by steps, to raise my soul towards her original dwelling."

129

As soon as she had said this, without expecting any answer, she left the place, and ran into the thickest of the adjoining wood, leaving all that heard her charmed with her discretion as well as with her beauty.

However, so prevalent were the charms of the latter, that some of the company, who were desperately struck, could not forbear offering to follow her, without being the least deterred by the solemn protestations which they had heard her make that very moment. But Don Quixote, perceiving their design, and believing he had now a fit opportunity to exert his knight-errantry: "Let no man," cried he, "of what quality or condition soever, presume to follow the fair Marcella, under the penalty of incurring my furious displeasure. She has made it appear, by undeniable reasons, that she was not guilty of Chrysostom's death; and has positively declared her firm resolution never to condescend to the desires of any of her admirers: for which reason, instead of being importuned and persecuted, she ought to be esteemed and honored by all good men, as being perhaps the only woman in the world that ever lived with such virtuous reservedness." Now, whether it were that Don Quixote's threats terrified the amorous shepherds, or that Ambrose's persuasion prevailed with them to stay and see their friend interred, none of the shepherds left the place, till, the grave being made and the papers burnt, the body was deposited into the bosom of the earth, not without many tears from all the assistants. They covered the grave with a great stone till a monument was made, which Ambrose said he designed to have set up there, with the following epitaph upon it:

CHRYSOSTOM'S EPITAPH

Here of a wretched swain
The frozen body's laid,
Kill'd by the cold disdain
Of an ungrateful maid.

130

Here first love's pow'r he try'd,
  Here first his pains express'd;
Here first he was deny'd,
  Here first he chose to rest.
You who the shepherd mourn,
  From coy Marcella fly;
Who Chrysostom could scorn,
  May all mankind destroy.

The shepherds strewed the grave with many flowers and boughs; and everyone, having condoled awhile with his friend Ambrose, they took their leave of him, and departed. Vivaldo and his companion did the like; as did also Don Quixote, who was not a person to forget himself on such occasions: he likewise bid adieu to the kind goatherds, that had entertained him, and to the two travelers who desired him to go with them to Seville, assuring him there was no place in the world more fertile in adventures, every street and every corner there producing some. Don Quixote returned them thanks for their kind information; but told them he neither would, nor ought to go to Seville, till he had cleared all those mountains of the thieves and robbers, which he heard very much infested all those parts. Thereupon the travelers, being unwilling to divert him from so good a design, took their leaves of him once more, and pursued their journeys, sufficiently supplied with matter to discourse on from the story of Marcella and Chrysostom, and Don Quixote's follies. As for him, he resolved to find out the shepherdess Marcella, if possible, to offer her his service to protect her to the utmost of his power: but he happened to be crossed in his designs, as you shall hear in the sequel of this true history: for here ends the second book.

BOOK THREE

I

GIVING AN ACCOUNT OF DON QUIXOTE'S UNFORTUNATE RENCOUNTER WITH CERTAIN BLOODY-MINDED AND WICKED YANGUESIAN[1] CARRIERS

THE SAGE CID HAMET BENENGELI relates, that when Don Quixote had taken leave of all those that were at Chrysostom's funeral, he and his squire went after Marcella into the wood; and, having ranged it above two hours without being able to find her, they came at last to a meadow, whose springing green, watered with a delightful and refreshing rivulet, invited, or rather pleasantly forced them to alight and give way to the heat of the day, which began to be very violent: so, leaving the ass and Rozinante

[1] *Carriers of the kingdom of Galicia.*

133

to graze at large, they ransacked the wallet; and without ceremony, the master and the man fell to, and fed lovingly on what they found. Now Sancho had not taken care to tie up Rozinante, knowing him to be a horse of that sobriety and chastity, that all the mares in the pastures of Cordova could not have raised him to attempt an indecent thing. But either fortune, or the devil, who seldom sleeps, so ordered it, that a good number of Galician mares, belonging to some Yanguesian carriers, were then feeding in the same valley, it being the custom of those men, about the hottest time of the day, to stop wherever they met with grass and water to refresh their cattle: nor could they have found a fitter place than that where Don Quixote was. Rozinante, as I said before, was chaste and modest; however, he was flesh and blood; so that, as soon as he had smelt the mares, forsaking his natural gravity and reservedness, without asking his master's leave, away he trots it briskly to make them sensible of his little necessities: but they, who it seems had more mind to feed than to be merry, received their gallant so rudely with their heels and teeth, that in a trice they broke his girths, threw down his saddle, and left him disrobed of all his equipage. And, for an addition to his misery, the carriers perceiving the violence that was offered to their mares, flew to their relief with poles and pack-staves, and so belabored poor Rozinante, that he soon sank to the ground under the weight of their unmerciful blows.

Don Quixote and Sancho, perceiving at a distance the ill-usage of Rozinante, ran with all speed to his rescue; and as they came near the place, panting, and almost out of breath, "Friend Sancho," cried Don Quixote, "I perceive these are no knights, but only a pack of scoundrels and fellows of the lowest rank; I say it, because thus thou mayest lawfully help me to revenge the injury they have done Rozinante before our faces." "What a devil do ye talk of revenge?" quoth Sancho, "we are like to revenge ourselves finely! You see they are above twenty, and we are but two; nay, perhaps but one and

134

a half." "I alone am worth a hundred," replied Don Quixote; then without any more words, he drew his sword, and flew upon the Yanguesians. Sancho, encouraged by his master's example, did the like; and with the first blow which Don Quixote gave one of them, he cut through his leathern doublet, and gave him a deep slash in the shoulder. The Yanguesians, seeing themselves thus rudely handled, betook themselves to their levers and pack-staves, and then all at once, surrounding the valiant Knight and his trusty squire, they charged them and laid on with great fury. At the second round, down they settled poor Sancho, and then Don Quixote himself, who, as chance would have it, fell at the feet of Rozinante, that had not yet recovered his legs; neither could the Knight's courage nor his skill avail against the fury of a number of rustical fellows armed with pack-staves. The Yanguesians, fearing the ill consequences of the mischief they had done, made all the haste they could to be gone, leaving our two adventurers in a woeful condition. The first that came to himself was Sancho Panza; who, finding himself near his master, called to him thus, with a weak and doleful voice: "Ah, master! master! Sir, Sir Knight!" "What is the matter, friend Sancho?" asked the Knight in the same feeble and lamentable tone. "I could wish," replied Sancho, "that your worship would help me to two good draughts of the liquor you talk on, if you have any by you; perhaps it is as good to cure broken bones, as it is to heal outward wounds." "Oh! that I had some of it here now!" cried Don Quixote; "we could not then be said to want anything: but I swear to thee, honest Sancho, by the faith of a knight-errant, within these two days (if no other disaster prevent me) I will have some at my disposal, or it shall hardly escape my hands." "Two days, sir!" replied Sancho: "why, pray, how many days do you think it will be before we are able to stir our feet?" "As for myself," answered the bruised Don Quixote, "I must own I cannot set a certain term to the days of our recovery; but it is I who am the fatal cause of all this mischief; for I ought not to have drawn my sword against a company of fellows, upon whom the honor of knighthood was never conferred; and I do not doubt but that the Lord of Hosts suffered this punishment to befall me, for transgressing thus the laws of chivalry. Therefore, friend Sancho, observe what I am going to tell thee, for it is a thing that highly concerns the welfare of us both: it is, that for the future, whenever thou perceivest us to be anyways abused by such inferior fellows, thou art not to expect I should offer to draw my sword against them; for I will not do it in the least: no, do thou then draw, and chastise them as thou thinkest fit: but if any knights come to take their parts, then will I be sure to step between thee and danger, and assault them with the utmost vigor and intrepidity. Thou hast already had a thousand proofs of the greatness of my valor, and the prevailing strength of my most dreadful arm" (so arrogant the Knight was grown since his victory over the bold Biscainer); but Sancho was not so well pleased with his master's admonitions, but that he thought fit to answer him. "Sir," says he, "I am a peaceful man, a harmless quiet fellow, do you see; I can make shift to pass by an injury as well as any man, as having a wife to maintain, and children to bring up; and therefore pray take this from me, by the way of advice (for I will not offer to command my master), that I will not in any wise draw my sword neither against knight nor clown, not I. I freely forgive all mankind, high and low, rich and poor, lords and beggars, whatever wrongs they ever did or may do me, without the least exception." "Sancho," said his master, hearing this, "I heartily wish I had breath enough to answer thee effectually, or that the pain which I feel in one of my short ribs would leave me but for so long as might serve to convince thee of thy error. Come, suppose, thou silly wretch, that the gale of fortune, which has hitherto been so contrary to us, should at last turn favorable, swelling the sails of our desires, so that we might with as much security as ease arrive at some of those

136

islands which I have promised thee; what would become of thee, if after I had conquered one of them, I were to make thee lord of it? Thou wouldest certainly be found not duly qualified for that dignity, as having abjured all knighthood, all thoughts of honor, and all intention to revenge injuries, and defend thy own dominions. For thou must understand, that in kingdoms and provinces newly conquered, the hearts and minds of the inhabitants are never so thoroughly subdued, or wedded to the interests of their new sovereign, but that there is reason to fear they will endeavor to raise some commotions to change the face of affairs, and, as men say, once more try their fortune. Therefore it is necessary that the new possessor have not only understanding to govern, but also valor to attack his enemies, and defend himself on all occasions." "I would I had had that understanding and valor you talk of," quoth Sancho; "but now, sir, I must be free to tell you, I have more need of a surgeon than of a preacher. Pray, try whether you can rise, and we will help Rozinante, though he does not deserve it; for he is the chief cause of all this beating. For my part, I could never have believed the like of him before, for I always took him for as chaste and sober a person as myself. In short, it is a true saying, that 'a man must eat a peck of salt with his friend, before he knows him'; and I find 'there is nothing sure in this world': for who would have thought, after the dreadful slashes you gave to that knight-errant, such a terrible shower of bastinadoes would so soon have fallen upon our shoulders?" "As for thine," replied Don Quixote, "I doubt they are used to endure such sort of showers; but mine, that were nursed in soft linen, will most certainly be longer sensible of this misfortune; and were it not that I imagine (but why do I say imagine?), were it not that I am positively sure, that all these inconveniences are inseparable from the profession of chivalry, I would abandon myself to grief, and die of mere despair on this very spot." "I beseech you, sir," quoth Sancho, "since these rubs are

137

the vails of your trade of knighthood, tell me whether they seem to come often, or whether we may look for them at set times: for, I fancy, if we meet but with two such harvests more, we shall never be able to reap the third, unless God of His infinite mercy assist us." "Know, friend Sancho," returned Don Quixote, "that the lives of knights-errant are subject to a thousand hazards and misfortunes: but, on the other side, they may at any time suddenly become kings and emperors, as experience has demonstrated in many knights, of whose histories I have a perfect knowledge. And I could tell thee now (would my pain suffer me) of some of them, who have raised themselves to those high dignities only by the valor of their arm; and those very knights, both before and after their advancement, were involved in many calamities: for, the valorous Amadis de Gaul saw himself in the power of his mortal enemy Archelaus the enchanter, of whom it is credibly reported, that when he held him prisoner, he gave him above two hundred stripes with his horse bridle, after he had tied him to a pillar in the court-yard of his house. There is also a secret author of no little credit who relates, that the Knight of the Sun, being taken in a trap in a certain castle, was hurried to a deep dungeon, where, after they had bound him hand and foot, they forcibly gave him a clyster of snow-water and sand, which would probably have cost him his life, had he not been assisted in that distress by a wise magician, his particular friend. Thus I may well bear my misfortune patiently, since those which so many greater persons have endured may be said to outdo it: for, I would have thee to know, that those wounds that are given with the instruments and tools which a man happens to have in his hand, do not really disgrace the person struck. We read it expressly in the laws of duels, 'That if a shoe-maker strikes another man with his last which he held in his hand, though it be of wood, as a cudgel is, yet the party who was struck with it shall not be said to have been cudgeled.' I tell thee this, that thou may not think we are in the

138

least dishonored, though we have been horribly beaten in this rencounter: for the weapons which those men used were but instruments of their profession, and not one of them, as I very well remember, had either tuck, or sword, or dagger." "They gave me no leisure," quoth Sancho, "to examine things so narrowly; for I had no sooner laid my hand on my cutlass,[2] but they crossed my shoulders with such a wooden blessing, as settled me on the ground without sense or motion, where you see me lie, and where I do not trouble my head whether it be a disgrace to be mauled with cudgels or with pack-staves: let them be what they will, I am only vexed to feel them so heavy on my shoulders, where I am afraid they are imprinted as deep as they are on my mind." "For all this," replied Don Quixote, "I must inform thee, friend Sancho, that there is no remembrance which time will not deface, nor no pain to which death will not put a period." "Thank you for nothing!" quoth Sancho, "what worse can befall us, than to have only death to trust to? Were our affliction to be cured with a plaster or two, a man might have some patience; but, for aught I see, all the salves in a hospital will not set us on our best legs again." "Come, no more of this," cried Don Quixote; "take courage, and make a virtue of necessity; for it is what I am resolved to do. Let us see how it fares with Rozinante; for, if I am not mistaken, the poor creature has not been the least sufferer in this adventure." "No wonder at that," quoth Sancho; "seeing he is a knight-errant too; I rather wonder how my ass has escaped so well, while we have fared so ill." "In our disasters," returned Don Quixote, "fortune leaves always some door open to come at a remedy. I say it, Sancho, because that little beast may now supply the want of Rozinante, to carry me to some castle, where I may get cured of my wounds. Nor do I esteem this kind of riding dishonorable; for I remember, that the good old Silenus, tutor and

[2] *"Tizona": the romantic name of the sword which the Spanish general, Roderick Diaz de Bivar, used against the Moors.*

governor to the jovial God of Wine, rode very fairly on a goodly ass, when he made his entry into the city with a hundred gates." "Ay," quoth Sancho, "it will do well enough, could you ride as fairly on your ass as he did on his; but there is a deal of difference between riding and being laid across the pannel like a pack of rubbish." "The wounds which are received in combat," said Don Quixote, "rather add to our honor than deprive us of it; therefore, good Sancho, trouble me with no more replies, but, as I said, endeavor to get up, and lay me as thou pleasest upon thy ass, that we may leave this place ere night steal upon us." "But, sir," cried Sancho, "I have heard you say, that it is a common thing among you knights-errant to sleep in the fields and deserts the best part of the year, and that you look upon it to be a very happy kind of life." "That is to say," replied Don Quixote, "when we can do no better, or when we are in love; and this is so true, that there have been knights who have dwelt on rocks, exposed to the sun, and other inclemencies of the sky, for the space of two years, without their lady's knowledge: one of those was Amadis, when, assuming the name of 'The Lovely Obscure,' he inhabited the bare rock, either eight years or eight months, I cannot now punctually tell which of the two; for I do not thoroughly remember that passage. Let it suffice that there he dwelt, doing penance, for I do not know what unkindness his Lady Oriana had showed him. But, setting these discourses aside, pray thee dispatch, lest some mischief befall the ass, as it has done Rozinante." "That would be the devil indeed," replied Sancho, and, so breathing out some thirty lamentations, threescore sighs, and a hundred and twenty plagues and poxes on those that had decoyed him thither, he at last got upon his legs, yet not so but that he went stooping, with his body bent like a Turk's bow, not being able to stand upright. Yet, in this crooked posture, he made a shift to harness his ass, who had not forgot to take his share of licentiousness that day. After this, he helped up Rozinante,

140

who, could his tongue have expressed his sorrows, would certainly not have been behind-hand with Sancho and his master. After many bitter Ohs, and screwed faces, Sancho laid Don Quixote on the ass, tied Rozinante to its tail, and then, leading the ass by the halter, he took the nearest way that he could guess to the high road; to which he luckily came before he had traveled a short league, and then he discovered an inn; which, in spite of all he could say, Don Quixote was pleased to mistake for a castle. Sancho swore bloodily it was an inn, and his master was as positive of the contrary. In short, their dispute lasted so long, that before they could decide it they reached the inn-door, where Sancho straight went in, with all his train, without troubling himself any further about the matter.

II: WHAT HAPPENED TO DON QUIXOTE IN THE INN WHICH HE TOOK FOR A CASTLE

The innkeeper, seeing Don Quixote lying quite athwart the ass, asked Sancho what ailed him. Sancho answered, it was nothing, only his master had got a fall from the top of a rock to the bottom, and had bruised his sides a little. The innkeeper had a wife very different from the common sort of hostesses, for she was of a charitable nature, and very compassionate of her neighbor's affliction: which made her immediately take care of Don Quixote, and call her daughter (a good handsome girl) to set her helping hand to his cure. One of the servants in the inn was an Asturian wench, a broad-faced, flat-headed, saddle-nosed dowdy, blind of one eye, and the other almost out. However, the activity of her body supplied all other defects. She was not above three feet high from her heels to her head; and her shoulders, which somewhat loaded her, as having too much flesh upon them, made her look downwards oftener than she could have wished. This charming original likewise assisted the

141

mistress and the daughter; and, with the latter, helped to make the Knight's bed, and a sorry one it was; the room where it stood was an old gambling cock-loft, which by manifold signs seemed to have been, in the days of yore, a repository for chopped straw. Somewhat further, in a corner of that garret, a carrier had his lodging; and, though his bed was nothing but the pannels and coverings of his mules, it was much better than that of Don Quixote, which only consisted of four rough-hewn boards laid upon two uneven tressels, a flock-bed, that, for thinness, might well have passed for a quilt, and was full of knobs and bunches, which, had they not peeped out through many a hole, and shown themselves to be of wool, might well have been taken for stones. The rest of that extraordinary bed's furniture was a pair of sheets, which rather seemed to be of leather than of linen-cloth, and a coverlet whose every individual thread you might have told, and never have missed one in the tale.

In this ungracious bed was the Knight laid to rest his belabored carcass, and presently the hostess and her daughter anointed and plastered him all over, while Maritornes (for that was the name of the Asturian wench) held the candle. The hostess, while she greased him, wondering to see him so bruised all over: "I fancy," said she, "those bumps look much more like a dry beating than a fall." "It was no dry beating, mistress, I promise you," quoth Sancho, "but the rock had I know not how many cragged ends and knobs, whereof every one gave my master a token of his kindness. And by the way, forsooth," continued he, "I beseech you save a little of that same tow and ointment for me too; for I do not know what is the matter with my back, but I fancy I stand mainly in want of a little greasing too." "What! I suppose you fell too?" quoth the landlady. "Not I," quoth Sancho, "but the very fright that I took to see my master tumble down the rock has so wrought upon my body, that I am as sore as if I had been sadly mauled." "It may well be as you say," cried the innkeeper's daughter, "for I have dreamed sev-

142

eral times that I have been falling from the top of a high tower without ever coming to the ground; and, when I waked, I have found myself as out of order, and as bruised, as if I had fallen in good earnest." "That is even my case, mistress," quoth Sancho; "only ill luck would have it so, that I should find myself even almost as battered and bruised as my lord Don Quixote, and yet all the while be as broad awake as I am now." "How do you call this same gentleman?" quoth Maritornes. "He is Don Quixote de la Mancha," replied Sancho; "and he is a knight-errant, and one of the primest and stoutest that ever the sun shined on." "A knight-errant," cried the wench, "pray, what is that?" "Heyday!" cried Sancho, "does the wench know no more of the world than that comes to? Why, a knight-errant is a thing which in two words you see well cudgeled, and then an emperor. Today there is not a more wretched thing upon the earth, and yet tomorrow he will have you two or three kingdoms to give away to his squire." "How comes it to pass, then," quoth the landlady, "that thou, who are this great person's squire, hast not yet got thee at least an earldom?" "Fair and softly goes far," replied Sancho; "why, we have not been a month in our gears, so that we have not yet encountered any adventure worth the naming; besides, many a time we look for one thing, and light on another. But if my lord Don Quixote happens to get well again, and I escape remaining a cripple, I will not take the best title in the land for what I am sure will fall to my share."

Here Don Quixote, who had listened with great attention to all these discourses, raised himself up in his bed with much ado, and taking the hostess in a most obliging manner by the hand, "Believe me," said he, "beautiful lady, you may well esteem it a happiness that you have now the opportunity to entertain my person in your castle. Self praise is unworthy a man of honor, and therefore I shall say no more of myself, but my squire will inform you who I am; only thus much let me add, that I will eternally preserve your kindness in the treasury of my remembrance, and study all occasions to testify my gratitude: and I wish," continued he, "the Powers above had so disposed my fate, that I were not already love's devoted slave, and captivated by the charms of the disdainful beauty who engrosses all my softer thoughts; for then would I be proud to sacrifice my liberty to this beautiful damsel." The hostess, her daughter, and the kind-hearted Maritornes stared on one another, quite at a loss for the meaning of this high-flown language, which they understood full as well as if it had been Greek. Yet, conceiving these were words of compliment and courtship, they looked upon him, and admired him as a man of another world: and so, having made him such returns as innkeeper's breeding could afford, they left him to his rest; only Maritornes stayed to rub down Sancho, who wanted her help no less than his master.

Now you must know, that the carrier and she had agreed to pass the night together; and she had given him her word that, as soon as all the people in the inn were in bed, she would be sure to come to him, and be at his service. And it is said of this good-natured thing, that whenever she had passed her word in such cases, she was sure to make it good, though she had made the promise in the midst of a wood, and without any witness at all: for she stood much upon her gentility, though she undervalued herself so far as to serve in an inn; often saying, that nothing but crosses and necessity could have made her stoop to it.

Don Quixote's hard, scanty, beggarly, miserable bed was the first of the four in that wretched apartment; next to that was Sancho's kennel, which consisted of nothing but a bed-mat and a coverlet, that rather seemed shorn canvas than a rug. Beyond these two beds was that of the carrier, made, as we have said, of the pannels and furniture of two of the best of twelve mules which he kept, every one of them goodly beasts, and in special good case; for he was one of the richest muleteers of Arevalo, as the Moorish author

144

of this history relates, who makes particular mention of him, as having been acquainted with him; nay, some do not stick to say, he was somewhat of kin to him. However it be, it appears that Cid Hamet Benengeli was a very exact historian, since he takes care to give us an account of things that seem so inconsiderable and trivial. A laudable example which these historians should follow, who usually relate matters so concisely, that we have scarcely a smack of them, leaving the most essential part of the story drowned in the bottom of the ink-horn, either through neglect, malice, or ignorance. A thousand blessings then be given to the curious author of Tablante of Ricamonte, and to that other indefatigable sage who recorded the achievements of Count Tomillas; for they have described even the most minute and trifling circumstances with a singular preciseness. But, to return to our story, you must know, that, after the carrier had visited his mules, and given them their second course,[1] he laid himself down upon his pannels, in expectation of the most punctual Maritornes's kind visit. By this time Sancho, duly greased and anointed, had crept into his sty, where he did all he could to sleep, but his aching ribs did all they could to prevent him. As for the Knight, whose sides were in as bad circumstances as his squire's, he lay with both his eyes open like a hare. And now was every soul in the inn gone to bed, nor any light to be seen, except that of a lamp which hung in the middle of the gate-way. This general tranquillity setting Don Quixote's thoughts at work, offered to his imagination one of the most absurd follies that ever crept into a distempered brain from the perusal of romantic whimsies. Now he fancied himself to be in a famous castle (for, as we have already said, all the inns he lodged in seemed no less than castles to him) and that the innkeeper's daughter (consequently daughter to the lord of the castle), strangely captivated with his graceful presence and gal-

[1] *In Spain they get up in the night to dress their cattle, and give them barley and straw, in place of oats and hay.*

lantry, had promised him the pleasure of her embraces, as soon as her father and mother were gone to rest. This chimera disturbed him, as if it had been a real truth; so that he began to be mightily perplexed, reflecting on the danger to which his honor was exposed. But at last his virtue overcame the powerful temptation, and he firmly resolved not to be guilty of the least infidelity to his lady Dulcinea del Toboso, though Queen Guinever herself, with her trusty Matron Quintaniona, should join to decoy him into the alluring snare.

While these wild imaginations worked in his brain, the gentle Maritornes was mindful of her assignation, and with soft and wary steps, bare-foot, and in her smock, with her hair gathered up in a fustian coif, stole into the room, and felt about for her beloved carrier's bed: but scarce had she got to the door, when Don Quixote, whose ears were on the scout, was sensible that something was coming in: and therefore, having raised himself in his bed, sore and wrapped up in plasters as he was, he stretched out his arms to receive his fancied damsel, and caught hold of Maritornes by the wrist, as she was, with her arms stretched, groping her way to her paramour; he pulled her to him, and made her sit down by his bed's side, she not daring to speak a word all the while. Now, as he imagined her to be the lord of the castle's daughter, her smock, which was of the coarsest canvas, seemed to him of the finest holland; and the glass beads about her wrist, precious oriental pearls; her hair, that was almost as rough as a horse's mane, he took to be soft flowing threads of bright curling gold; and her breath, that had a stronger hogo than stale venison, was to him a grateful compound of the most fragrant perfumes of Arabia. In short, flattering imagination transformed her into the likeness of those romantic beauties, one of whom, as he remembered to have read, came to pay a private visit to a wounded knight, with whom she was desperately in love; and the poor gentleman's obstinate folly had so infatuated

146

his outward sense, that his feeling and his smell could not in the least undeceive him, and he thought he had no less than a balmy Venus in his arms, while he hugged a fulsome bundle of deformities, that would have turned any man's stomach but a sharp-set carrier's. Therefore clasping her still closer, with a soft and amorous whisper: "Oh! thou most lovely temptation," cried he; "oh! that I

now might but pay a warm acknowedgment for the mighty blessing which your extravagant goodness would lavish on me; yes, most beautiful charmer, I would give an empire to purchase your more desirable embraces: but fortune, madam, fortune, that tyrant of my life, that unrelenting enemy to the truly deserving, has maliciously hurried and riveted me to this bed, where I lie so bruised and macerated, that, though I were eager to gratify your desires, I should at this dear unhappy minute be doomed to impotence; nay, to that unlucky bar fate has added a yet more invincible obstacle; I mean my plighted faith to the unrivaled Dulcinea del Toboso,

147

the sole mistress of my wishes, and absolute sovereign of my heart. Oh! did not this oppose my present happiness, I could never be so dull and insensible a knight, as to lose the benefit of this extraordinary favor which you have now condescended to offer me."

Poor Maritornes all this while sweated for fear and anxiety, to find herself thus locked in the Knight's arms; and without either understanding, or being willing to understand his florid excuses, she did what she could to get from him, and sheer off without speaking a word. On the other side, the carrier, whose lewd thoughts kept him awake, having heard his trusty lady when she first came in, and listened ever since to the Knight's discourse, began to be afraid that she had made some other assignation; and so, without any more ado he crept softly to Don Quixote's bed, where he listened a while to hear what would be the end of all this talk, which he could not understand. But perceiving at last, by the struggling of his faithful Maritornes, that it was none of her fault, and that the Knight strove to detain her against her will, he could by no means bear his familiarity; and therefore, taking it in mighty dudgeon, he up with his fist, and hit the enamored Knight such a swinging blow on the jaws, that his face was all over blood in a moment. And, not satisfied with this, he got on the top of the Knight, and with his splayfeet betrampled him as if he had been trampling a hay-mow. With that the bed, whose foundations were none of the best, sunk under the additional load of the carrier, and fell with such a noise, that it waked the innkeeper, who presently suspects it to be one of Maritornes's nightly skirmishes; and therefore, having called her aloud, and finding that she did not answer, he lighted a lamp, and made to the place where he heard the bustle. The wench, who heard him coming, knowing him to be of a passionate nature, was scared out of her wits, and fled for shelter to Sancho's sty, where he lay snoring to some tune: there she pigged in, and slunk under the coverlet, where she lay snug, and trussed up as round as an egg. Presently

148

her master came in, in a mighty heat: "Where is this damned whore?" cried he. "I dare say, this is one of her pranks." By this, Sancho awoke; and feeling that unusual lump, which almost overlaid him, he took it to be the nightmare, and began to lay about him with his fists, and thumped the wench so unmercifully, that at last flesh and blood were no longer able to bear it; and, forgetting the danger she was in, and her dear reputation, she paid him back his thumps as fast as her fists could lay them on, and soon roused the drowsy squire out of his sluggishness, whether he would or no: who, finding himself thus pommeled by he did not know who, bustled up in his nest, and catching hold of Maritornes, they began the most pleasant skirmish in the world. When the carrier perceiving, by the light of the innkeeper's lamp, the dismal condition that his dear mistress was in, presently took her part; and leaving the Knight, whom he had more than sufficiently mauled, flew at the squire, and paid him confoundedly. On the other hand, the innkeeper, who took the wench to be the cause of all this hurly-burly, cuffed and kicked, and kicked and cuffed her over and over again: and so there was a strange multiplication of fisticuffs and drubbings. The carrier pommeled Sancho, Sancho mauled the wench, the wench belabored the squire, and the innkeeper thrashed her again: and all of them laid on with such expedition, that you would have thought they had been afraid of losing time. But the jest was, that in the heat of the fray the lamp went out, so that being now in the dark, they plied one another at a venture: they struck and tore, all went to rack, while nails and fists flew about without mercy.

There happened to lodge that night in the inn one of the officers belonging to that society which they call the old Holy Brotherhood of Toledo, whose chief office is to look after thieves and robbers. Being waked with the heavy bustle, he presently jumped out of his bed, and, with his short staff in one hand, and a tin-box with his commission in it in the other, he groped out his way; and, having

149

entered the room in the dark, cried out, "I charge ye all to keep the peace: I am an officer of the Holy Brotherhood." The first he popped his hand upon happened to be the poor battered Knight, who lay upon his back at his full length, without any feeling, upon the ruins of his bed. The officer, having caught him by the beard, presently cried out, "I charge you to aid and assist me": but finding he could not stir, though he gripped him hard, he presently imagined him to be dead, and murdered by the rest in the room. With that he bawled out to have the gates of the inn shut. "Here is a man murdered," cried he; "look that nobody makes his escape." These words struck all the combatants with such a terror, that as soon as they reached their ears, they gave over, and left the argument undecided. Away stole the innkeeper to his own room, the carrier to his pannels, and the wench to her kennel; only the unfortunate Knight, and his as unfortunate squire, remained where they lay, not being able to stir; while the officer, having let go Don Quixote's beard, went out for a light, in order to apprehend the supposed murderers: but the innkeeper having wisely put out the lamp in the gate-way, as he sneaked out of the room, the officer was obliged to repair to the kitchen-chimney, where, with much ado, puffing and blowing a long while amidst the embers, he at last made shift to get a light.

III: A FURTHER ACCOUNT OF THE INNUMERABLE
HARDSHIPS WHICH THE BRAVE DON QUIXOTE,
AND HIS WORTHY SQUIRE SANCHO, UNDER-
WENT IN THE INN, WHICH THE KNIGHT
UNLUCKILY TOOK FOR A CASTLE

Don Quixote, who by this time was come to himself, began to call Sancho with the same lamentable tone as the day before, when he had been beaten by the carriers in the meadow. "Sancho," cried he,

150

"friend Sancho! art thou asleep? art thou asleep, friend Sancho?" "Sleep!" replied Sancho, mightily out of humor, "may Old Nick rock my cradle then: why, how the devil should I sleep, when all the imps of hell have been tormenting me tonight?" "Nay, thou art in the right," answered Don Quixote, "for either I have no skill in these matters, or this castle is enchanted. Hear what I say to thee, but first swear thou wilt never reveal it till after my death." "I swear it," quoth Sancho. "I am thus cautious," said Don Quixote, "because I hate to take away the reputation of any person." "Why," quoth Sancho, "I tell you again, I swear never to speak a word of the matter while you live; and I wish I may be at liberty to talk on it tomorrow." "Why!" cried Don Quixote, "have I done thee so much wrong, Sancho, that you would have me die so soon?" "Nay, it is not for that neither," quoth Sancho; "but because I cannot abide to keep things long, for fear they should grow moldy." "Well, let it be as thou pleasest," said Don Quixote: "for I dare trust greater concerns to thy courtesy and affection. In short, know, that this very night there happened to me one of the strangest adventures that can be imagined; for the daughter of the lord of this castle came to me, who is one of the most engaging and most beautiful damsels that ever nature has been proud to boast of: what could I not tell thee of the charms of her shape and face, and the perfections of her mind! what could I not add of other hidden beauties, which I condemn to silence and oblivion, lest I endanger my allegiance and fidelity to my lady Dulcinea del Toboso! I will only tell thee, that the Heavens, envying the inestimable happiness which fortune had thrown into my hand; or rather, because this castle is enchanted, it happened, that in the midst of the most tender and passionate discourses that passed between us, the profane hand of some mighty giant, which I could not see, nor imagine whence it came, hit me such a dreadful blow on the jaws, that they are still embrued with blood; after which the discourteous wretch, presum-

151

ing on my present weakness, did so barbarously bruise me, that I feel myself in a worse condition now than I did yesterday, after the carriers had so roughly handled me for Rozinante's incontinency: from which I conjecture, that the treasure of this damsel's beauty is guarded by some enchanted Moor, and not reserved for me."

"Nor for me neither," quoth Sancho; "for I have been rib-roasted by above four hundred Moors, who have hammered my bones in such guise, that I may safely say, the assault and battery made on my body by the carriers' poles and pack-staves, were but ticklings and strokings with a feather to this. But, sir, pray tell me, do you call this such a pleasant adventure, when we are so lamentably pounded after it? And yet your hap may well be accounted better than mine, seeing you have hugged that fair maiden in your arms. But I, what have I had, I pray you, but the heaviest blows that ever fell on a poor man's shoulders? Woe is me and the mother that bore me, for I neither am, nor ever mean to be a knight-errant; and yet, of all the misadventures, the greater part falls still to my lot." "What, hast thou been beaten as well as I?" said Don Quixote. "What a plague," cried Sancho, "have not I been telling you so all this while!" "Come, never let it trouble thee, friend Sancho," replied Don Quixote; "for I will immediately make the precious balsam, that will cure thee in the twinkling of an eye."

By this time the officer, having lighted his lamp, came into the room, to see who it was that was murdered. Sancho seeing him enter in his shirt, a napkin wrapped about his head like a turban, and the lamp in his hand, he being also an ugly ill-looked fellow: "Sir," quoth the squire to his master, "pray see whether this be not the enchanted Moor, that is come again to have the other bout with me, and try whether he has not left some place unbruised for him now to maul as much as the rest." "It cannot be the Moor," replied Don Quixote; "for persons enchanted are to be seen by nobody." "If they do not suffer themselves to be seen," quoth Sancho, "at least they suffer themselves to be felt: if not, let my carcass bear witness." "So might mine," cried Don Quixote: "yet this is no sufficient reason to prove, that what we see is the enchanted Moor."

While they were thus arguing, the officer advanced, and wondered to hear two men talk so calmly to one another there: yet finding the unfortunate Knight lying in the same deplorable posture as he left him, stretched out like a corpse, bloody, bruised and beplastered, and not able to stir himself, "How is it, honest fellow," quoth he to the champion, "how do you find yourself?" "Were I your fellow," replied Don Quixote, "I would have a little more manners than you have, you blockhead, you; is that your way of approaching knights-errant in this country?" The officer could not bear such a reprimand from one who made so scurvy a figure, and lifting up the lamp, oil and all, hit Don Quixote such a blow on the head with it, that he had reason to fear he had made work for the surgeon, and therefore stole presently out of the room, under the protection of the night. "Well, sir," quoth Sancho, "do you think now it was the enchanted Moor, or no? For my part, I think he keeps the treasure you talk of for others, and reserves only kicks, cuffs, thumps and knocks for your worship and myself." "I am now convinced," answered Don Quixote; "therefore let us waive that resentment of these injuries, which we might otherwise justly show; for considering these enchanters can make themselves invisible when they please, it is needless to think of revenge. But I pray thee rise, if thou canst, Sancho, and desire the governor of the castle to send me some oil, salt, wine and rosemary, that I may make my healing balsam; for truly I want it extremely, so fast the blood flows out of the wound which the phantasm gave me just now."

Sancho then got up as fast as his aching bones would let him, and with much ado made shift to crawl out of the room to look for the

153

innkeeper, and stumbling by the way on the officer, who stood hearkening to know what mischief he had done. "Sir," quoth he to him,
"for heaven's sake, do so much as help us to a little oil, salt, wine
and rosemary, to make a medicine for one of the best knights-errant
that ever trod one shoe of leather, who lies yonder grievously
wounded by the enchanted Moor of this inn." The officer hearing
him talk at that rate, took him to be one out of his wits; and it beginning to be daylight, he opened the inn-door, and told the innkeeper what Sancho wanted. The host presently provided the desired ingredients, and Sancho crept back with them to his master,
whom he found holding his head and sadly complaining of the
pain which he felt there; though, after all, the lamp had done him
no more harm than only raising of two huge bumps; for that which
he fancied to be blood was only sweat, and the oil of the lamp, that
had liquored his hair and face.

The Knight took all the ingredients, and having mixed them together, he had them set over the fire, and there kept them boiling
till he thought they were enough. That done, he asked for a vial to
put this precious liquor in: but there being none to be got, the innkeeper presented him with an old earthen jug, and Don Quixote
was forced to be contented with that. Then he mumbled over the
pot above fourscore *paternosters*, and as many *ave-marias*, *salve
reginas*, and *credos*, making the sign of the Cross at every word, by
way of benediction. At which ceremony Sancho, the innkeeper, and
the officer were present; for, as for the carrier, he was gone to look
after his mules, and took no manner of notice of what passed. This
blessed medicine being made, Don Quixote resolved to make an
immediate experiment of it on himself; and to that purpose he took
off a good draught of the overplus, which the pot would not hold:
but he had scarce gulped it down, when it set him a-vomiting so
violently, that you would have thought he would have cast up his

heart, liver, and guts; and his reaching and straining put him into such a sweat that he desired to be covered up warm, and left to his repose. With that they left him, and he slept three whole hours; and then waking, found himself so wonderfully eased, that he made no question but he had now the right balsam of Fierabras; and therefore he thought he might safely undertake all the most dangerous adventures in the world, without the least hazard of his person.

Sancho, encouraged by the wonderful effect of the balsam on his master, begged that he would be pleased to give him leave to sip up what was left in the pot, which was no small quantity; and the Don having consented, honest Sancho lifted it up with both his hands, and, with a strong faith and better will, poured every drop down his throat. Now the man's stomach not being so nice as his master's, the drench did not set him a-vomiting after that manner, but caused such a wambling in his stomach, such a bitter loathing, kecking, and reaching, and such grinding pangs, with cold sweats and swoonings, that he verily believed his last hour was come, and in the midst of his agony gave both the balsam and him that made it to the devil. "Friend," said Don Quixote, seeing him in that condition, "I begin to think all this pain befalls thee, only because thou hast not received the order of knighthood; for, it is my opinion, this balsam ought to be used by no man that is not a professed knight." "What a plague did you mean then by letting me drink it?" quoth Sancho. "A murrain on me and all my generation, why did not you tell me this before?" At length the dose began to work to some purpose, and forced its way at both ends so copiously, that both his bed-mat and coverlet were soon made unfit for any further use; and all the while he strained so hard, that not only himself but the standers-by thought he would have died. This dreadful hurricane lasted about two hours; and then, too, instead of finding himself as free from

155

pain as his master, he felt himself as feeble, and so far spent, that he was not able to stand.

But Don Quixote, as we have said, found himself in an excellent temper; and his active soul loathing an inglorious repose, he presently was impatient to depart to perform the duties of his adventurous profession: for he thought those moments that were trifled away in amusements or other concerns, only a blank in life; and all delays a depriving distressed persons, and the world in general, of his needed assistance. The confidence which he reposed in his balsam, heightened, if possible, his resolution; and thus, carried away by his eager thoughts, he saddled Rozinante himself, and then put the pannel upon the ass, and his squire upon the pannel, after he had helped him to huddle on his clothes: that done, he mounted his steed; and, having spied a javelin that stood in a corner, he seized and appropriated it to himself, to supply the want of his lance. Above twenty people that were in the inn stood spectators of all these transactions; and among the rest the innkeeper's daughter, from whom Don Quixote had not power to withdraw his eyes, breathing out at every glance a deep sigh from the very bottom of his heart; which those who had seen him so mortified the night before, took to proceed from the pain of his bruises.

And now, being ready to set forwards, he called for the master of the house, and with a grave delivery: "My Lord Governor," cried he, "the favors I have received in your castle are so great and extraordinary, that they bind my grateful soul to an eternal acknowledgment: therefore that I may be so happy as to discharge part of the obligation, think if there be ever a proud mortal breathing on whom you desire to be revenged for some affront or other injury, and acquaint me with it now, and by my order of knighthood which binds me to protect the weak, relieve the oppressed, and punish the bad, I promise you I will take effectual care, that you shall have ample satisfaction to the utmost of your wishes." "Sir Knight,"

156

answered the innkeeper, with an austere gravity, "I shall not need your assistance to revenge any wrong that may have been offered to my person; for I would have you to understand, that I am able to do myself justice, whenever any man presumes to do me wrong: therefore all the satisfaction I desire is, that you will pay your reckoning for horse meat and man's meat, and all your expenses in my inn." "How!" cried Don Quixote, "is this an inn?" "Yes," answered the host, "and one of the most noted, and of the best repute upon the road." "How strangely have I been mistaken then!" cried Don Quixote; "upon my honor I took it for a castle, and a considerable one too: but, if it be an inn, and not a castle, all I have to say is, that you must excuse me from paying anything; for I would by no means break the laws which we knights-errant are bound to observe: nor was it ever known, that they ever paid in any inn whatsoever; for this is the least recompense that can be allowed them for the intolerable labors they endure day and night, winter and summer, on foot and on horseback, pinched with hunger, choked with thirst, and exposed to all the injuries of the air, and all the inconveniences in the world." "I have nothing to do with all this," cried the innkeeper: "pay your reckoning, and do not trouble me with your foolish stories of a cock and a bull: I cannot afford to keep house at that rate." "Thou art both a fool and a knave of an innkeeper," replied Don Quixote: and with that, clapping spurs to Rozinante, and brandishing his javelin at his host, he rode out of the inn without any opposition, and got a good way from it, without so much as once looking behind him to see whether his squire came after him.

The Knight having marched off, there remained only the squire, who was stopped for the reckoning. However, he swore bloodily he would not pay a cross; for the self-same law that acquitted the Knight acquitted the squire. This put the innkeeper into a great passion, and made him threaten Sancho very hard, telling him, if

157

he would not pay him by fair means, he would have him laid by the heels that moment. Sancho swore by his master's knighthood, he would sooner part with his life than his money on such an account: nor should the squires in after ages ever have occasion to upbraid him with giving so ill a precedent, or breaking their rights. But, as ill luck would have it, there happened to be in the inn four Segovia clothiers, three Cordova point-makers, and two Seville hucksters, all brisk, gamesome, arch fellows; who, agreeing all in the same design, encompassed Sancho, and pulled him off his ass, while one of them went and got a blanket. Then they put the unfortunate squire into it, and observing the roof of the place they were in to be somewhat too low for their purpose, they carried him into the back yard, which had no limits but the sky, and there they tossed him for several times together in the blanket, as they do dogs on Shrove Tuesday. Poor Sancho made so grievous an outcry all the while, that his master heard him, and imagined those lamentations were of some person in distress, and consequently the occasion of some

adventure: but, having at last distinguished the voice, he made to the inn with a broken gallop; and, finding the gates shut, he rode about to see whether he might not find some other way to get in. But he no sooner came to the back-yard wall, which was none of the highest, when he was an eye-witness of the scurvy trick that was put upon his squire. There he saw him ascend and descend, and frolic and caper in the air with so much nimbleness and agility, that it is thought the Knight himself could not have forborne laughing, had he been anything less angry. He did his best to get over the wall, but alas! he was so bruised, that he could not so much as alight from his horse. This made him fume and chaff, and vent his passion in a thousand threats and curses, so strange and various, that it is impossible to repeat them. But the more he stormed, the more they tossed and laughed, Sancho, on his side, begging, and howling, and threatening, and damning to as little purpose as his master, for it was weariness alone could make the tossers give over. Then they charitably put an end to his high dancing, and set him upon his ass again, carefully wrapped in his mantle. But Maritornes's tender soul made her pity a male creature in such tribulation; and thinking he had danced and tumbled enough to be a-dry, she was so generous as to help him to a draught of water, which she purposely drew from the well that moment, that it might be the cooler. Sancho clapped the pot to his mouth, but his master made him desist: "Hold, hold," cried he, "son Sancho, drink no water, child, it will kill thee: behold, I have here the most holy balsam, two drops of which will cure thee effectually." "Ha!" replied Sancho, shaking his head, and looking sourly on the Knight with a side-face, "have you again forgot that I am no knight? or would you have me cast up the few guts I have left since yesternight's job? Keep your brewings for yourself, in the devil's name, and let me alone." With that he lifted up the jug to his nose, but finding it to be mere element, he squirted out again the little he had tasted, and desired the wench to

159

help him to some better liquor: so she went and fetched him wine to make him amends, and paid for it too out of her own pocket: for, to give the devil his due, it was said of her, that though she was somewhat too free of her favors, yet she had something of Christianity in her. As soon as Sancho had tipped off his wine, he visited his ass's ribs twice or thrice with his heels; and, free egress being granted him, he trooped off mightily tickled with the thoughts of having had his ends, and got off shot-free; though at the expense of his shoulders, his usual sureties. It is true, the innkeeper kept his wallet for the reckoning; but the poor squire was so dismayed, and in such haste to be gone, that he never missed it. The host was for shutting the inn-doors after him, for fear of the worst; but the tossers would not let him, being a sort of fellows that would not have worried a straw about Don Quixote, though he had really been one of the knights of the round-table.

IV: OF THE DISCOURSE BETWEEN THE KNIGHT AND THE SQUIRE, WITH OTHER MATTERS WORTH RELATING

Sancho overtook his master, but so pale, so dead-hearted, and so mortified, that he was hardly able to sit on his ass. "My dear Sancho," said Don Quixote, seeing him in that condition, "I am now fully convinced that this castle, or inn, is enchanted; for what could they be that made themselves such barbarous sport with thee, but spirits and people of the other world? And I the rather believe this, seeing, that when I looked over the wall, I saw thee thus abused, I strove to get over it, but could not stir, nor by any means alight from Rozinante. For, by my honor, could I either have got over the wall or dismounted, I would have revenged thee so effectually on those discourteous wretches, that they should never have forgot the severity of their punishment, though for once I had infringed the laws of chivalry; which, as I have often informed thee, do not permit any knight to lay hands on one that is not knighted, unless it be in his own defense, and in case of great necessity." "Nay," quoth Sancho, "I would have paid them home myself, whether knight or no knight, but it was not in my power; and yet I dare say, those that made themselves so merry with my carcass were neither spirits nor enchanted folks, as you will have it, but mere flesh and blood as we be. I am sure they called one another by their Christian names and surnames, while they made me vault and frisk in the air: one was called Pedro Martinez, the other Tenorio Hernandez; and, as for our dog of a host, I heard them call him Juan Palomeque the Left-handed. Then pray do not you fancy, that your not being able to get over the wall, nor to alight, was some enchanter's trick. It is a folly to make many words; it is as plain as the nose in a man's face, that these same adventures which we hunt for up and down, are like to bring us at last into a peck of troubles, and such a plaguy deal of mischief, that we shall not be able to set one foot afore the other. The short and the long is, I take it to be the wisest course to jog home and look after our harvest, and not to run rambling from Ceca to Mecca,[1] lest 'we leap out of the frying-pan into the fire,' or 'out of God's blessing into the warm sun.'" "Poor Sancho," cried Don Quixote, "how ignorant thou art in matters of chivalry! Come say no more, and have patience. A day will come when thou shalt be convinced how honorable a thing it is to follow this employment. For, tell me, what satisfaction in this world, what pleasure can equal that of vanquishing and triumphing over one's enemy? None without doubt." "It may be so for aught I know," quoth Sancho, "though I know nothing of the matter. However, this I may venture to say, that ever since we have turned knights-errant (your

[1] *Ceca was a place of devotion among the Moors, in the city of Cordova, to which they were accustomed to go on pilgrimage from many other places, as Mecca is among the Turks: whence the proverb comes to signify, "Sauntering about to no purpose."*

worship I mean, for it is not for such scrubs as myself to be named the same day with such folk) the devil of any fight you have had the better in, unless it be that with the Biscayan; and in that too you came off with the loss of one ear and the vizor of your helmet. And what have you got ever since, pray, but blows, and more blows; bruises, and more bruises? Besides this tossing in a blanket, which fell all to my share, and for which I cannot be revenged, because they were hobgoblins that served me so, though I hugely long to be even with them, that I may know the pleasure you say there is in vanquishing one's enemy." "I find, Sancho," cried Don Quixote, "thou and I are both sick of the same disease; but I will endeavor with all speed to get me a sword made with so much art, that no sort of enchantment shall be able to hurt whosoever shall wear it: and perhaps fortune may put into my hand that which Amadis de Gaul wore when he styled himself, 'The Knight of the Burning Sword,' which was one of the best blades that ever was drawn by knight: for besides the virtue I now mentioned, it had an edge like a razor, and would enter the strongest armor that ever was tempered or enchanted." "I will lay anything," quoth Sancho, "when you have found this sword, it will prove just such another help to me as your balsam; that is to say, it will stand nobody in any stead but your dubbed knights, let the poor devil of a squire shift how he can." "Fear no such thing," replied Don Quixote; "heaven will be more propitious to thee than thou imaginest."

Thus they went on discoursing, when Don Quixote, perceiving a thick cloud of dust arise right before them in the road: "The day is come," said he, turning to his squire, "the day is come, Sancho, that shall usher in the happiness which fortune has reserved for me: this day shall the strength of my arm be signalized by such exploits as shall be transmitted even to the latest posterity. Seest thou that cloud of dust, Sancho? It is raised by a prodigious army marching this way, and composed of an infinite number of nations." "Why then, at this rate," quoth Sancho, "there should be two armies; for yonder is as great a dust on the other side." With that Don Quixote looked, and was transported with joy at the sight, firmly believing that two vast armies were ready to engage each other in that plain. For his imagination was so crowded with those battles, enchantments, surprising adventures, amorous thoughts, and other whimsies which he had read of in romances, that his strong fancy changed everything he saw into what he desired to see; and thus he could not conceive that the dust was only raised by two large flocks of sheep that were going the same road from different parts, and could not be discerned till they were very near. He was so positive that they were two armies that Sancho firmly believed him at last. "Well, sir," quoth the squire, "what are we to do, I beseech you?" "What shall we do," replied Don Quixote, "but assist the weaker and the injured side? For know, Sancho, that the army which now moves toward us is commanded by the great Alifanfaron, emperor of the vast island of Taprobana: the other that advances behind us is his enemy, the king of the Garamantians, Pentapolin with the naked arm; so called, because he always enters into battle with his right arm bare." [2] "Pray, sir," quoth Sancho, "why are these two great men going together by the ears?" "The occasion of their quarrel is this," answered Don Quixote, "Alifanfaron, a strong Pagan, is in love with Pentapolin's daughter, a very beautiful lady and a Christian: now her father refuses to give her in marriage to the heathen prince, unless he abjure his false belief, and embrace the Christian religion." "Burn my beard," said Sancho, "if Pentapolin be not in the right on it; I will stand by him, and help him all I may." "I commend thy resolution," replied Don Quixote, "it is not only lawful, but requisite; for there is no need of being a knight to fight in such battles." "I guessed as much," quoth Sancho: "but where shall we leave my ass in the meantime, that I may be sure to

2 *Alluding to the story of Scanderbeg, king of Epirus.*

find him again after the battle; for I fancy you never heard of any man that ever charged upon such a beast." "It is true," answered Don Quixote, "and therefore I would have you turn him loose, though thou wert sure never to find him again; for we shall have so many horses after we have got the day, that even Rozinante himself will be in danger of being changed for another." Then, mounting to the top of a hillock, whence they might have seen both the flocks, had not the dust obstructed their sight, "Look yonder, Sancho," cried Don Quixote, "that knight whom thou seest in the gilded arms, bearing in his shield a crowned lion couchant at the feet of a lady, is the valiant Laurealco, lord of the Silver Bridge.

"He in the armor powdered with flowers of gold, bearing three crows argent in a field azure, is the formidable Micocolembo, great duke of Quiracia. That other of a gigantic size that marches on his right, is the undaunted Brandabarbaran of Boliche, sovereign of the three Arabias; he is arrayed in a serpent's skin, and carries instead of a shield a huge gate, which they say belonged to the temple which Samson pulled down at his death, when he revenged himself upon his enemies. But cast thy eyes on this side, Sancho, and, at the head of the other army, see the ever-victorious Timonel of Carcajona, prince of New Biscay, whose armor is quartered azure, vert, or, and argent, and who bears in his shield a cat, or, in a field gules, with these four letters, 'MIAU,' for a motto, being the beginning of his mistress's name, the beautiful Miaulina, daughter to Alpheniquen, duke of Algarva. That other monstrous load upon the back of yonder wild horse, with arms as white as snow and a shield without any device, is a Frenchman, new created knight, called Pierre Papin, baron of Utrique. He whom you see pricking that pied courser's flanks with his armed heels, is the mighty duke of Nerbia, Espartafilardo of the Wood, bearing in his shield a field of pure azure, powdered with asparagus (*Esparago* [3]) with this

[3] *The jingle between the duke's name Espartafilardo and Esparago (his arms) is a*

164

motto in Castilian, *Rastrea mi suerte:* 'Thus trails or drags my fortune.' " And thus he went on, naming a great number of others in both armies, to every one of whom his fertile imagination assigned arms, colors, impresses, and mottoes, as readily as if they had really been that moment extant before his eyes.

And then, proceeding without the least hesitation: "That vast body," said he, "now just opposite to us, is composed of several nations. There you see those who drink the pleasant stream of the famous Xanthus; there the mountaineers that till the Massilian [4] fields; those that sift the pure gold of Arabia Fælix; those that inhabit the renowned and delightful banks of Thermodon. Yonder, those who so many ways sluice and drain the golden Pactolus for its precious sand; the Numidians, unsteady and careless of their promises; the Persians, excellent archers; the Medes and Parthians, who fight flying; the Arabs, who have no fixed habitations; the Scythians, cruel and savage, though fair complexioned; the sooty Æthiopians, that bore their lips; and a thousand other nations whose countenances I know, though I have forgotten their names. On the other side, come those whose country is watered with the crystal streams of Betis, shaded with olive-trees; those who bathe their limbs in the rich flood of the golden Tagus; those whose mansions are laved by the profitable stream of the divine Genil; those who range the verdant Tartesian meadows; those who indulge their luxurious temper in the delicious pastures of Xereza; the wealthy inhabitants of the Mancha, crowned with golden ears of corn; the ancient offspring of the Goths, cased in iron; those who wanton in the lazy current of Pisuerga; those who feed their numerous flocks

ridicule upon the foolish quibbles so frequent in heraldry; and probably this whole catalogue is a satire upon several great names and sounding titles in Spain, whose owners were beggars. The trailing of his fortune may allude to the word Esparto, a sort of rush they make ropes with. Or perhaps he was without a mistress, to which the asparagus may allude: for in Spain they have a proverb, Solo comes el Esparago: "As solitary as asparagus," *because every one of them springs up by itself.*
[4] *An imitation of Homer's catalogue of ships.*

in the ample plains where the Guadiana, so celebrated for its hidden course, pursues its wandering race; those who shiver with extremity of cold, on the woody Pyrenean hills, or on the hoary tops of the snowy Apennine. In a word, all that Europe includes within its spacious bounds, half a world in an army."

It is scarce to be imagined how many countries he ran over, how many nations he enumerated, distinguishing every one by what is peculiar to them, with an incredible vivacity of mind, and that still in the puffy style of his fabulous books. Sancho listened to all this romantic muster-roll as mute as a fish, with amazement; all that he could do was now and then to turn his head on this side and the other side, to see if he could discern the knights and giants whom his master named. But at length, not being able to discover any: "Why," cried he, "you had as good tell me it snows; the devil of any knight, giant, or man can I see, of all those you talk of now; who knows but all this may be witchcraft and spirits, like yesternight?" "How," replied Don Quixote, "dost thou not hear their horses neigh, their trumpets sound, and their drums beat?" "Not I," quoth Sancho, "I prick up my ears like a sow in the beans, and yet I can hear nothing but the bleating of sheep." Sancho might justly say so indeed, for by this time the two flocks were got very near them. "Thy fear disturbs thy senses," said Don Quixote, "and hinders thee from hearing and seeing right: but it is no matter; withdraw to some place of safety, since thou art so terrified; for I alone am sufficient to give the victory to that side which I shall favor with my assistance." With that he couched his lance, clapped spurs to Rozinante, and rushed like a thunder-bolt from the hillock into the plain. Sancho bawled after him as loud as he could: "Hold, sir," cried Sancho, "for Heaven's sake come back. What do you mean? As sure as I am a sinner, those you are going to maul are nothing but poor harmless sheep. Come back, I say. Woe be to him that begot me! Are you mad, sir? There are no giants, no knights, no cats, no asparagus gardens, no golden quarters, nor what-do-you-call-thems. Does the devil possess you? You are leaping over the hedge before you come at the stile. You are taking the wrong sow by the ear. Oh, that I was ever born to see this day!" But Don Quixote, still riding on, deaf and lost to good advice, outroared his expostulating squire. "Courage, brave knights," cried he: "march up, fall on, all you who fight under the standard of the valiant Pentapolin with the naked arm: follow me, and you shall see how easily I will revenge him on that infidel Alifanfaron of Taprobana"; and, so saying, he charged the squadron of sheep with that gallantry and resolution, that he pierced, broke, and put it to flight in an instant, charging through and through, not without a great slaughter of his mortal enemies, whom he laid at his feet, biting the ground and wallowing in their blood. The shepherds seeing their sheep go to rack, called out to him; till, finding fair means ineffectual, they unloosed their slings, and began to ply him with stones as big as their fists. But the champion, disdaining such a distant war, in spite of their showers of stones, rushed among the routed sheep, trampling both the living and the slain in a most terrible manner, impatient to meet the general of the enemy, and end the war at once. "Where, where art thou," cried he, "proud Alifanfaron? Appear! see here a single knight who seeks thee everywhere, to try now, hand to hand, the boasted force of thy strenuous arm, and deprive thee of life, as a due punishment for the unjust war which thou hast audaciously waged with the valiant Pentapolin." Just as he had said this, while the stones flew about his ears, one unluckily fell upon his small ribs, and had like to have buried two of the shortest deep in the middle of his body. The Knight thought himself slain, or at least desperately wounded; and, therefore, calling to mind his precious balsam, and pulling out his earthen jug, he clapped it to his mouth: but, before he had swallowed a sufficient dose, souse comes another of those bitter almonds

167

that spoiled his draught, and hit him so pat upon the jug, hand, and teeth, that it broke the first, maimed the second, and struck out three or four of the last. These two blows were so violent, that the boisterous Knight, falling from his horse, lay upon the ground as quiet as the slain; so that the shepherds, fearing he was killed, got their flock together with all speed, and carrying away their dead, which were no less than seven sheep, they made what haste they could out of harm's way, without looking any further into the matter.

All this while Sancho stood upon the hill, mortified upon the sight of this mad adventure. There he stamped, swore, and banned his master to the bottomless pit; he tore his beard for madness, and cursed the moment he first knew him: but seeing him at last knocked down, and settled, the shepherds being scampered, he thought he might venture to come down; and found him in a very ill plight, though not altogether senseless. "Ah! master," quoth he, "this comes of not taking my counsel. Did I not tell you it was a flock of sheep, and no army?" "Friend Sancho," replied Don Quixote, "know it is an easy matter for necromancers to change the shapes of things as they please: thus that malicious enchanter, who is my inveterate enemy, to deprive me of the glory which he saw me ready to acquire, while I was reaping a full harvest of laurels, transformed in a moment the routed squadrons into sheep. If thou wilt not believe me, Sancho, yet do one thing for my sake: do but take thy ass, and follow those supposed sheep at a distance, and I dare engage thou shalt soon see them resume their former shapes, and appear such as I described them. But stay, do not go yet, for I want thy assistance: draw near, and see how many cheek-teeth and others I want; for, by the dreadful pain in my jaws and gums, I fear there is a total dilapidation in my mouth." With that the Knight opened his mouth as wide as he could, while the squire gaped to tell his grinders, with his snout almost in his chops: but just in

168

that fatal moment the balsam that lay wambling and fretting in Don Quixote's stomach, came up with an unlucky hickup; and, with the same violence that the powder flies out of a gun, all that he had in his stomach discharged itself upon the beard, face, eyes, and mouth of the officious squire. "Santa Maria," cried poor Sancho, "what will become of me! my master is a dead man! he is vomiting his very heart's blood!" but he had hardly said this, when the color, smell, and taste soon undeceived him; and finding it to be his master's loathsome drench, it caused such a sudden rumbling in his maw, that before he could turn his head he unladed the whole cargo of his stomach full in his master's face, and put him in as delicate a pickle as he was himself. Sancho having thus paid him in his own coin, half-blinded as he was, ran to his ass, to take out something to clean himself and his master: but when he came to look for his wallet, and found it missing, not remembering till then that he had unhappily left it in the inn, he was ready to run quite

169

out of his wits. He stormed and stamped, and cursed him worse than before, and resolved with himself to let his master go to the devil, and even trudge home by himself, though he was sure to lose his wages, and his hopes of being governor of the promised island.

Thereupon Don Quixote got up with much ado, and clapping his left hand before his mouth, that the rest of his loose teeth might not drop out, he laid his right hand on Rozinante's bridle (for such was the good nature of the creature, that he had not budged a foot from his master); then he crept along to squire Sancho, that stood lolling on his ass's pannel, with his face in the hollow of both his hands, in a doleful, moody, melancholy fit. "Friend Sancho," said he, seeing him thus abandoned to sorrow, "learn of me, that one man is no more than another, if he do no more than what another does. All these storms and hurricanes are but arguments of the approaching calm: better success will soon follow our past calamities; good and bad fortune have their vicissitudes; and it is a maxim, that nothing violent can last long; and therefore we may well promise ourselves a speedy change in our fortune, since our afflictions have extended their reign beyond the usual stint; besides, thou oughtest not to afflict thyself so much for my misfortunes, of which thou hast no share, but what friendship and humanity bid thee take." "How," quoth Sancho, "have I no other share in them? Was not he that was tossed in the blanket this morning, the son of my father? And did not the wallet, and all that was in it, which I have lost, belong to the son of my mother?" "How," asked Don Quixote, "hast thou lost thy wallet?" "I do not know," said Sancho, "whether it is lost or no, but I am sure I cannot tell what is become of it." "Nay, then," replied Don Quixote, "I find we must fast to-day." "Ay, marry must we," quoth Sancho, "unless you take care to gather in these fields some of those roots and herbs which I have heard you say you know, and which use to help such unlucky knights-errant as yourself at a dead lift." "For all that," cried

170

Don Quixote, "I would rather have at this time a good luncheon of bread, or a cake and two pilchards' heads, than all the roots and simples in Dioscorides's herbal, and Doctor Laguna's supplement and commentary: I pray thee, therefore, get upon thy ass, good Sancho, and follow me once more; for God's providence, that relieves every creature, will not fail us, especially since we are about a work so much to His service; thou seest He even provides for the little flying insects in the air, the wormlings in the earth, and the spawnlings in the water; and, in His infinite mercy, He makes His sun shine on the righteous and on the unjust, and rains upon the good and the bad." "Many words will not fill a bushel," quoth Sancho, interrupting him; "you would make a better preacher than a knight-errant, or I am plaguedly out." "Knights-errant," replied Don Quixote, "ought to know all things; there have been such in former ages, that have delivered as ingenious and learned a sermon or oration at the head of an army, as if they had taken their degrees at the University of Paris: from which we may infer, that the lance never dulled the pen, nor the pen the lance." "Well then," quoth Sancho, "for once let it be as you would have it; let us even leave this unlucky place, and seek out a lodging; where, I pray God, there may be neither blankets, nor blanket-heavers, nor hobgoblins, nor enchanted Moors; for, before I will be hampered as I have been, may I be cursed with bell, book and candle, if I do not give the trade to the devil." "Leave all things to Providence," replied Don Quixote, "and for once lead which way thou pleasest, for I leave it wholly to thy discretion to provide us a lodging. But first, I pray thee, feel a little how many teeth I want in my upper jaw on the right side, for there I feel most pain." With that Sancho, feeling with his finger in the Knight's mouth: "Pray, sir," quoth he, "how many grinders did your worship use to have on that side?" "Four," answered Don Quixote, "besides the eye-tooth, all of them whole and sound." "Think well on what you say," cried Sancho. "I say four,"

171

replied Don Quixote, "if there were not five; for I never in all my life have had a tooth drawn or dropped out, or rotted by the worm, or loosened by rheum." "Bless me!" quoth Sancho, "why, you have in this nether-jaw on this side but two grinders and a stump; and in that part of your upper jaw, never a stump, and never a grinder: alas! all is leveled there as smooth as the palm of one's hand." "Oh, unfortunate Don Quixote!" cried the Knight, "I had rather have lost an arm, so it were not my sword-arm, for a mouth without cheek-teeth is like a mill without a mill-stone, Sancho; and every tooth in a man's head is more valuable than a diamond. But we that profess this strict order of knight-errantry, are all subject to these calamities; and therefore, since the loss is irretrievable, mount, my trusty Sancho, and go thy own pace; I will follow thee." Sancho obeyed, and led the way, still keeping the road they were in, which being very much beaten, promised to bring him soonest to a lodging. Thus pacing along very softly, for Don Quixote's gums and ribs would not suffer him to go faster, Sancho, to divert his uneasy thoughts, resolved to talk to him all the while of one thing or other, as the next chapter will inform you.

V: OF THE WISE DISCOURSE BETWEEN SANCHO AND HIS MASTER; AS ALSO OF THE ADVENTURE OF THE DEAD CORPSE, AND OTHER FAMOUS OCCURRENCES

"Now, sir," quoth Sancho, "I cannot help thinking but that all the mishaps that have befallen us of late, are a just judgment for the grievous sin you have committed against the order of knighthood, in not keeping the oath you swore, not to eat bread at board, nor to have a merry bout with the queen, and the Lord knows what more, until you had won what-do-you-call-him, the Moor's helmet,[1] I

1 *Mambrino.*

think you named him." "Truly," answered Don Quixote, "thou art much in the right, Sancho, and, to deal ingenuously with thee, I wholly forgot that: and now thou mayest certainly assure thyself, thou wert tossed in a blanket for not remembering to put me in mind of it. However, I will take care to make due atonement; for knight-errantry has ways to conciliate all sorts of matters." "Why," quoth Sancho, "did I ever swear to mind you of your vow?" "It is nothing to the purpose," replied Don Quixote, "whether thou sworest or no: let it suffice that I think thou art not very clear from being accessory to the breach of my vow; and therefore to prevent the worst, there will be no harm in providing for a remedy." "Hark you then," cried Sancho, "be sure you do not forget your atonement, as you did your oath, lest those confounded hobgoblins come and maul me, and mayhap you too, for being a stubborn sinner."

Insensibly night overtook them before they could discover any lodging; and which was worse, they were almost hunger-starved, all their provision being in the wallet which Sancho had unluckily left behind; and, to complete their distress, there happened to them an adventure, or something that really looked like one.

While our benighted travelers went on dolefully in the dark, the Knight very hungry, and the squire very sharp set, what should they see moving towards them but a great number of lights, that appeared like so many wandering stars. At this strange apparition, down sunk Sancho's heart at once, and even Don Quixote himself was not without some symptoms of surprise. Presently the one pulled to him his ass's halter, the other his horse's bridle, and both made a stop. They soon perceived that the lights made directly towards them, and the nearer they came the bigger they appeared. At the terrible wonder Sancho shook and shivered every joint, like one in a palsy, and Don Quixote's hair stood up on end; however, heroically shaking off the amazement which that sight stamped upon his soul, "Sancho," said he, "this must doubtless be a great and most perilous adventure, where I shall have occasion to exert the whole stock of my courage and strength." "Woe's me," quoth Sancho, "should this happen to be another adventure of ghosts, as I fear it is, where shall I find ribs to endure it?" "Come all the fiends in hell," cried Don Quixote, "I will not suffer them to touch a hair of thy head. If they insulted thee lately, know there was then between thee and me a wall, over which I could not climb; but now we are in the open field, where I shall have liberty to make use of my sword." "Ay," quoth Sancho, "you may talk; but, should they bewitch you as they did before, what the devil would it avail us to be in the open field?" "Come, Sancho," replied Don Quixote, "be of good cheer; the event will soon convince thee of the greatness of my valor." "Pray Heaven it may," quoth Sancho; "I will do my best." With that they rode a little out of the way, and gazing earnestly at the lights, they soon discovered a great number of persons all in white. At the dreadful sight, all poor Sancho's shuffling courage basely deserted him. His teeth began to chatter as if he had been in an ague fit, and as the objects drew nearer his chattering increased. And now they could plainly distinguish about twenty men on horseback, all in white, with torches in their hands, followed by a hearse covered over with black, and six men in deep mourning, whose mules were also in black down to their very heels. Those in white moved slowly, murmuring from their lips something in a low and lamentable tone. This dismal spectacle, at such a time of night, in the midst of such a vast solitude, was enough to have shipwrecked the courage of a stouter squire than Sancho, and even of his master, had he been any other than Don Quixote: but as his imagination straight suggested to him, that this was one of those adventures of which he had so often read in his books of chivalry, the hearse appeared to him to be a litter, where lay the body of some knight either slain or dangerously wounded, the revenge of whose misfortunes was reserved for his prevailing arm; and so, without

174

any more ado, couching his lance, and seating himself firm in his saddle, he posted himself in the middle of the road, where the company were to pass. As soon as they came near, "Stand," cried he to them in a haughty tone, "whoever you be, and tell me who you are, whence you come, whither you go, and what you carry in that litter? for there is all the reason in the world to believe, that you have either done or received a great deal of harm; and it is requisite I should be informed of the matter, in order either to punish you for the ill you have committed, or else to revenge you of the wrong you have suffered." "Sir," answered one of the men in white, "we are in haste; the inn is a great way off, and we cannot stay to answer so many questions"; and with that, spurring his mule, he moved forwards. But Don Quixote, highly dissatisfied with the reply, laid hold on the mule's bridle and stopped him. "Stay," cried he, "proud, discourteous knight, mend your behavior, and give me instantly an account of what I asked of ye, or here I defy you all to mortal combat." Now the mule, that was shy and skittish, being thus rudely seized by the bridle, was presently scared, and rising up on her hinder legs, threw her rider to the ground. Upon this, one of the footmen that belonged to the company gave Don Quixote ill language; which so incensed him, that being resolved to be revenged upon them all, in a mighty rage he flew at the next he met, who happened to be one of the mourners. Him he threw to the ground very much hurt; and then turning to the rest, with a wonderful agility, he fell upon them with such fury, that he presently put them all to flight. You would have thought Rozinante had wings at that time, so active and so fierce he then approved himself.

It was not indeed for men unarmed, and naturally fearful, to maintain the field against such an enemy; no wonder then if the gentlemen in white were immediately dispersed: some ran one way, some another, crossing the plain with their lighted torches: you would now have taken them for a parcel of frolicsome masqueraders, gamboling and scouring on a carnival night. As for the mourners, they, poor men, were so muffled up in their long, cumbersome cloaks, that not being able to make their party good, nor defend themselves, they were presently routed, and ran away like the rest, the rather, for that they thought it was no mortal creature, but the devil himself, that was come to fetch away the dead body which they were ac-

companying to the grave. All the while Sancho was lost in admiration and astonishment, charmed with the sight of his master's valor; and now concluded him to be the formidable champion he boasted himself.

After this the Knight, by the light of a torch that lay burning upon the ground, perceiving the man who was thrown by his mule lying near it, he rode up to him, and setting his lance to his throat, "Yield," cried he, "and beg thy life, or thou diest." "Alas, sir," cried the other, "what need you ask me to yield? I am not able to stir, for one of my legs is broken; and I beseech you, if you are a

Christian, do not kill me. I am a master of arts, and in holy orders; it would be a heinous sacrilege to take away my life." "What a devil brought you hither then, if you are a clergyman?" cried Don Quixote. "What else but my ill fortune," replied the supplicant. "A worse hovers over thy head," cried Don Quixote, "and threatens thee, if thou dost not answer this moment to every particular question I ask." "I will, I will, sir," replied the other; "and first I must beg your pardon for saying I was a master of arts, for I have yet but taken my bachelor's degree. My name is Alonzo Lopez: I am of Alcovendas, and came now from the town of Baeça, with eleven other clergymen, the same that now ran away with the torches. We were going to Segovia to bury the corpse of a gentleman of that town, who died at Baeça, and lies now in yonder hearse." "And who killed him?" asked Don Quixote. "Heaven, with a pestilential fever," answered the other. "If it be so," said Don Quixote, "I am discharged of revenging his death. Since Heaven did it, there is no more to be said; had it been its pleasure to have taken me off so, I too must have submitted. I would have you informed, reverend sir, that I am a knight of La Mancha, my name Don Quixote; my employment is to visit all parts of the world in quest of adventures, to right and relieve injured innocence, and punish oppression." "Truly, sir," replied the clergyman, "I do not understand how you can call that to right and relieve men, when you break their legs: you have made that crooked which was right and straight before; and Heaven knows whether it can ever be set right as long as I live. Instead of relieving the injured, I fear you have injured me past relief; and while you seek adventures, you have made me meet with a very great misadventure."[2] "All things," replied Don Quixote, "are not blessed alike with a prosperous

<hr>

[2] *The author's making the bachelor quibble so much, under such improper circumstances, was properly designed as a ridicule upon the younger students of the universities, who are so apt to run into an affectation that way, and to mistake it for wit; as also upon the dramatic writers, who frequently make their heroes, in their greatest distresses, guilty of the like absurdity.*

event, good Mr. Bachelor. You should have taken care not to have thus gone a-processioning in these desolate plains, at this suspicious time of night, with your white surplices, burning torches, and sable weeds, like ghosts and goblins, that went about to scare people out of their wits; for I could not omit doing the duty of my profession, nor would I have forborne attacking you, though you had really been all Lucifer's infernal crew; for such I took you to be, and till this moment could have no better opinion of you." "Well, sir," said the Bachelor, "since my bad fortune has so ordered it, I must desire you, as you are a knight-errant, who have made mine so ill an errand, to help me to get from under my mule, for it lies so heavy upon me that I cannot get my foot out of the stirrup." "Why did not you acquaint me sooner with your grievances?" cried Don Quixote. "I might have talked on till tomorrow morning and never have thought on it." With that he called Sancho, who made no great haste, for he was much better employed in rifling a load of choice provisions, which the holy men carried along with them on a sumpter-mule. He had spread his coat on the ground, and having laid on it as much food as it would hold, he wrapped it up like a bag, and laid the booty on his ass; and then away he ran to his master, and helped him to set the Bachelor upon his mule: after which he gave him his torch, and Don Quixote bade him follow his company, and excuse him for his mistake, though, all things considered, he could not avoid doing what he had done. "And, sir," quoth Sancho, "if the gentlemen would know who it was that so well threshed their jackets, you may tell them it was the famous Don Quixote de la Mancha, otherwise called the Knight of the Woeful Figure."

When the Bachelor was gone, Don Quixote asked Sancho why he called him the Knight of the Woeful Figure. "I will tell you why," quoth Sancho; "I have been staring upon you this pretty

178

while by the light of that unlucky priest's torch, and may I never stir if ever I set eyes on a more dismal figure in my born-days; and I cannot tell what should be the cause of it, unless your being tired after this fray, or the want of your worship's teeth." "That is not the reason," cried Don Quixote; "no, Sancho, I rather conjecture, that the sage who is commissioned by fate to register my achievements, thought it convenient I should assume a new appellation, as all the knights of yore: for one was called the Knight of the Burning Sword, another of the Unicorn, a third of the Phœnix, a fourth the Knight of the Damsels, another of the Griffin, and another the Knight of Death; by which by-names and distinctions they were known all over the globe. Therefore, doubtless, that learned sage, my historian, has inspired thee with the thought of giving me that additional appellation of the Knight of the Woeful Figure: and accordingly I assume the name, and intend henceforwards to be distinguished by that denomination. And, that it may seem the more proper, I will with the first opportunity have a most woeful face painted on my shield." "On my word," quoth Sancho, "you may even save the money, and instead of having a woeful face painted, you need no more but only show your own. I am but in jest, as a body may say, but what with the want of your teeth, and what with hunger, you look so queerly and so woefully, that no painter can draw you a figure so fit for your purpose as your worship's." This merry conceit of Sancho extorted a smile from his master's austere countenance: however, he persisted in his resolution about the name and the picture; and after a pause, a sudden thought disturbing his conscience, "Sancho," cried he, "I am afraid of being excommunicated for having laid violent hands upon a man in holy orders, *Juxta illud; siquis suadente diabolo*, etc.[3] But yet, now I think better of it, I never

[3] *Canon. 72. Distinct. 134.*

179

touched him with my hands, but only with my lance; besides, I did not in the least suspect I had to do with priests, whom I honor and revere as every good Catholic and faithful Christian ought to do, but rather took them to be evil spirits. Well, let the worst come to the worst, I remember what befell the Cid Ruy Diaz, when he broke to pieces the chair of a king's ambassador in the Pope's presence, for which he was excommunicated; which did not hinder the worthy Roderigo de Vivar from behaving himself that day like a valorous knight, and a man of honor."

This said, Don Quixote was for visiting the hearse, to see if what was in it were only dead bones: but Sancho would not let him: "Sir," quoth he, "you are come off now with a whole skin, and much better than you have done hitherto. Who knows but these same fellows that are now scampered off, may chance to bethink themselves what a shame it is for them to have suffered themselves to be thus routed by a single man, and so come back, and fall upon us all at once; then we shall have work enough upon our hands. The ass is in good case; there is a hill not far off, and our bellies cry 'Cupboard.' Come, let us even keep out of harm's way, 'and not let the plow stand to catch a mouse,' as the saying is; 'to the grave with the dead, and the living to the bread.'" With that he put on a dog-trot with his ass, and his master, bethinking himself that he was in the right, put on after him without replying.

After they had ridden a little way, they came to a valley that lay skulking between two hills; there they alighted, and Sancho having opened his coat and spread it on the grass, with the provision which he had bundled up in it, our two adventurers fell to; and their stomachs being sharpened with the sauce of hunger, they ate their breakfast, dinner, afternoon's luncheon, and supper, all at the same time, feasting themselves with variety of cold meats, which you may be sure were the best that could be got, the priests, who had brought it for their own eating, being like the rest of their coat, none of the worst stewards for their bellies, and knowing how to make much of themselves.

But now they began to grow sensible of a very great misfortune, and such a misfortune as was bemoaned by poor Sancho, as one of the saddest that ever could befall him; for they found they had not one drop of wine or water to wash down their meat and quench their thirst, which now scorched and choked them worse than hunger had pinched them before. However, Sancho considering they were in a place where the grass was fresh and green, said to his master what you shall find in the following chapter.

VI: OF A WONDERFUL ADVENTURE ACHIEVED BY THE VALOROUS DON QUIXOTE DE LA MANCHA; THE LIKE NEVER COMPASSED WITH LESS DANGER BY ANY OF THE MOST FAMOUS KNIGHTS IN THE WORLD

"The grass is so fresh," quoth Sancho, half choked with thirst, "that I dare lay my life we shall light on some spring or stream hereabouts; therefore, sir, let us look, I beseech you, that we may quench this confounded thirst that plagues our throats ten times worse than hunger did our guts." Thereupon Don Quixote, leading Rozinante by the bridle, and Sancho his ass by the halter, after he had laid up the reversion of their meal, they went feeling about, only guided by their guess; for it was so dark they scarce could see their hands. They had not gone above two hundred paces before they heard a noise of a great waterfall; which was to them the most welcome sound in the world: but then, listening with great attention to know on which side the grateful murmur came, they on a sudden heard another kind of noise that strangely allayed the pleasure of the first, especially in Sancho, who was naturally fearful and pusillanimous. They heard a terrible din of obstreperous

181

blows, struck regularly, and a more dreadful rattling of chains and irons, which, together with the roaring of the waters, might have filled any other heart but Don Quixote's with terror and amazement. Add to this the horrors of a dark night and solitude, in an unknown place, the loud rustling of the leaves of some lofty trees under which fortune brought them at the same unlucky moment, the whistling of the wind, which concurred with the other dismaying sounds; the fall of the waters, the thundering thumps and the clinking of chains aforesaid. The worst too was, that the blows were redoubled without ceasing, the wind blew on, and daylight was far distant. But then it was, Don Quixote, secured by his intrepidity (his inseparable companion), mounted his Rozinante, braced his shield, brandished his lance, and showed a soul unknowing fear, and superior to danger and fortune. "Know, Sancho," cried he, "I was born in this iron age, to restore the age of gold, or the golden age, as some choose to call it. I am the man for whom fate has reserved the most dangerous and formidable attempts, the most stupendous and glorious adventures, and the most valorous feats of arms. I am the man who must revive the order of the round-table, the twelve peers of France, and the nine worthies, and efface the memory of your Platirs, your Tablantes, your Olivantes, and your Tirantes. Now must your Knights of the Sun, your Belianises, and all the numerous throng of famous heroes, and knights-errant of former ages, see the glory of all their most dazzling actions eclipsed and darkened by more illustrious exploits. Do but observe, O thou my faithful squire, what a multifarious assemblage of terrors surrounds us! A horrid darkness, a doleful solitude, a confused rustling of leaves, a dismal rattling of chains, a howling of the winds, an astonishing noise of cataracts, that seem to fall with a boisterous rapidity from the steep mountains of the moon, a terrible sound of redoubled blows, still wounding our ears like furious thunder-claps, and a dead and universal

182

silence of those things that might buoy up the sinking courage of frail mortality. In this extremity of danger, Mars himself might tremble with the affright: yet I, in the midst of all these unutterable alarms, still remain undaunted and unshaken. These are but incentives to my valor, and but animate my heart the more; it grows too big and mighty for my breast, and leaps at the approach of this threatening adventure, as formidable as it is like to prove. Come, gird Rozinante straighter, and then Providence protect thee: thou mayest stay for me here; but if I do not return in three days, go back to our village; and from thence, for my sake, to Toboso, where thou shalt say to my incomparable lady Dulcinea, that her faithful Knight fell a sacrifice to love and honor, while he attempted things that might have made him worthy to be called her adorer."

When Sancho heard his master talk thus, he fell a-weeping in the most pitiful manner in the world. "Pray, sir," cried he, "why will you thus run yourself into mischief? Why need you go about this rueful misadventure? It is main dark, and there is never a living soul sees us; we have nothing to do but to sheer off, and get out of harm's way, though we were not to drink a drop these three days. Who is there to take notice of our flinching? I have heard our parson, whom you very well know, say in his pulpit, that he who seeks danger perishes therein: and therefore we should not tempt Heaven by going about a thing that we cannot compass but by a miracle. Is it not enough, think you, that it has preserved you from being tossed in a blanket, as I was, and made you come off safe and sound from among so many goblins that went with the dead man? If all this will not work upon that hard heart of yours, do but think of me, and rest yourself assured that when once you have left your poor Sancho, he will be ready to give up the ghost for very fear, to the next that will come for it: I left my house and home, my wife, children, and all to follow you, hoping to be the better for it, and not the worse; but as covetousness breaks the sack, so has it broke me and my hopes; for while I thought myself cocksure of that unlucky and accursed island, which you so often promised me, in lieu thereof you drop me here in a strange place. Dear master, do not be so hard-hearted; and if you won't be persuaded not to meddle with this ungracious adventure, do but put it off till daybreak, to which, according to the little skill I learned when a shepherd, it cannot be above three hours; for the muzzle of the lesser bear is just over our heads, and makes midnight in the line of the left arm." "How can you see the muzzle of the bear?" asked Don Quixote; "there is not a star to be seen in the sky." "That is true," quoth Sancho, "but fear is sharpsighted, and can see things underground, and much more in the skies." "Let day come, or not come, it is all one to me," cried the champion; "it shall never be recorded of Don Quixote, that either tears or entreaties could make him neglect the duty of a knight. Then, Sancho, say no more; for Heaven, that has inspired me with a resolution of attempting this dreadful adventure, will certainly take care of me and thee: come quickly, gird my steed, and stay here for me; for you will shortly hear of me again, either alive or dead."

Sancho, finding his master obstinate, and neither to be moved with tears nor good advice, resolved to try a trick of policy to keep him there till daylight. And accordingly, when he pretended to fasten the girths, he slily tied Rozinante's hinder legs with his ass's halter, without being so much as suspected, so that when Don Quixote thought to have moved forwards, he found his horse would not go a step without leaping, though he spurred him on smartly. Sancho, perceiving his plot took, "Look you, sir," quoth he, "Heaven is on my side, and won't let Rozinante budge a foot forwards; and now, if you will still be spurring him, I dare pawn my life it will be but striving against the stream; or, as the saying is, but kicking against the pricks." Don Quixote fretted and chafed, and raved, and was in a desperate fury, to find his horse so stubborn; but at last, observing that the more he spurred and galled his sides, the more resty he proved, and he, though unwillingly, resolved to have patience till it was light. "Well," said he, "since Rozinante will not leave this place, I must tarry in it till the dawn, though its slowness will cost me some sighs." "You shall not need to sigh nor be melancholy," quoth Sancho, "for I will undertake to tell you stories, till it be day, unless your worship had rather get off your horse, and take a nap upon the green grass, as knights-errant are wont, that you may be the fresher, and the better able in the morning to go through that monstrous adventure that waits for you." "What dost thou mean by this alighting and sleeping?" replied Don Quixote. "Thinkest thou I am one of those carpet-knights that abandon themselves to sleep and lazy ease, when danger is at hand? No, sleep thou, thou art born to sleep; or do what thou wilt. As for myself, I know what I have to do." "Good sir!" quoth Sancho, "do not put yourself into a passion, I meant no such thing, not I"; saying this, he clapped one of his hands upon the pummel of Rozinante's saddle, and the other upon the crupper, and thus he stood embracing his master's left thigh, not daring to budge an inch, for fear of the blows that dinned continually in his ears. Don Quixote then thought fit to claim his promise, and desired him to tell some of his stories to help to pass away the time. "Sir," quoth Sancho, "I am woefully frightened, and have no heart to tell stories; however, I will do my best; and now I think on it, there is one come into my head, which, if I can but hit on it right, and nothing happen to put me out, is the best story you ever heard in your life; therefore listen, for I am going to begin. 'In the days of yore, when it was as it was, good betide us all, and evil to him that evil seeks.' And here, sir, you are to take notice that they of old did not begin their tales in an ordinary way; for it was

185

a saying of a wise man whom they called Cato, the Roman Tonsor,[1] that said, 'Evil to him that evil seeks,' which is as pat for your purpose as a ring for the finger, that you may neither meddle nor make, nor seek evil and mischief for the worse, but rather get out of harm's way; for nobody forces us to run into the mouth of all the devils in hell that wait for us yonder." "Go on with thy story, Sancho," cried Don Quixote, "and leave the rest to my discretion." "I say then," quoth Sancho, "that in a country town in Estremadura, there lived a certain shepherd, goatherd I should have said; which goatherd, as the story has it, was called Lope Ruiz; and this Lope Ruiz was in love with a shepherdess, whose name was Toralva, the which shepherdess, whose name was Toralva, was the daughter of a wealthy grazier, and this wealthy grazier—" "If thou goest on at this rate," cried Don Quixote, "and makest so many needless repetitions, thou wilt not have told thy story these two days. Pray thee tell it concisely, and like a man of sense, or let it alone." "I tell it you," quoth Sancho, "as all stories are told in our country, and I cannot for the blood of me tell it any other way, nor is it fit I should alter the custom." "Why then, tell it how thou wilt," replied Don Quixote, "since my ill fortune forces me to stay and hear thee." "Well then, dear sir," quoth Sancho, "as I was saying, this same shepherd, goatherd I should have said, was extremely in love with that same shepherdess, Toralva, who was a well-trussed, round, crummy strapping wench, coy and froppish, and somewhat like a man, for she had a kind of beard on her upper lip; methinks I see her now standing before me." "Then I suppose thou knewest her," said Don Quixote. "Not I," answered Sancho, "I never set eyes on her in my life; but he that told me the story said this was so true, that I might vouch it for a real truth, and even swear I had seen it all myself. Well—but, as you know, days go and come, and time and straw make medlars ripe; so it happened,

[1] *A mistake for Cato, the Roman Censor.*

186

that after several days coming and going, the devil, who seldom lies dead in a ditch, but will have a finger in every pie, so brought it about, that the shepherd fell out with his sweetheart, insomuch that the love he bore her turned into dudgeon and ill-will; and the cause was, by report of some mischievous tale-carriers that bore no good-will to either party, for that the shepherd thought her no better than she should be, a little loose in the hilts, and free of her hips.[2] Thereupon, being grievous in the dumps about it, and now bitterly hating her, he even resolved to leave that country to get out of her sight: for now, as every dog has his day, the wench perceiving he came no longer a-suitoring her, but rather tossed his nose at her, and shunned her, she began to love him, and doat upon him like anything." "That is the nature of women," cried Don Quixote, "not to love when we love them, and to love when we love them not. But go on." "The shepherd then gave her the slip," continued Sancho, "and driving his goats before him, went trudging through Estremadura, on his way to Portugal. But Toralva, having a long nose, soon smelt his design; and then what does she do, think ye, but comes after him bare-foot and bare-legged, with a pilgrim's staff in her hand, and a wallet at her back, wherein they say she carried a piece of looking-glass, half a comb, a broken pot with paint, and I do not know what other trinkumstrankums, to prink herself up. But let her carry what she would, it is no bread and butter of mine; the short and the long is, that they say the shepherd with his goats got at last to the river Guadiana, which happened to be overflowed at that time, and, what is worse than ill luck, there was neither boat nor bark to ferry him over; which vexed him the more, because he perceived Toralva at his heels, and he feared to be teased and plagued with her weeping and

2 *In the original it runs, "She gave him a certain quantity of little jealousies, above measure, and within the prohibited degrees," alluding to certain measures not to be exceeded (in Spain) on pain of forfeiture and corporal punishment, as swords above such a standard, etc.*

187

wailing. At last he spied a fisherman in a little boat, but so little it was, that it would carry but one man and one goat at a time. Well, for all that he called to the fisherman, and agreed with him to carry him and his three hundred goats, over the water. The bargain being struck, the fisherman came with his boat, and carried over one goat; then he rowed back and fetched another goat, and after that another goat. Pray, sir," quoth Sancho, "be sure you keep a good account how many goats the fisherman ferries over; for if you happen to miss one, my tale is at an end, and the devil a word have I more to say. Well then, whereabout was I?—Ho! I have it.— Now the landing-place on the other side was very muddy and slippery, which made the fisherman be a long while in going and coming; yet for all that he took heart of grace, and made shift to carry over one goat, then another, and then another." "Come," said Don Quixote, "we will suppose he has landed them all on the other side of the river; for, as thou goest on one by one, we shall not have done these twelve months." "Pray let me go on in my own way," quoth Sancho. "How many goats are got over already?" "Nay, how the devil can I tell!" replied Don Quixote. "There it is!" quoth Sancho: "did I not bid you keep count? On my word the tale is at an end, and now you may go whistle for the rest." "Ridiculous!" cried Don Quixote: "pray thee is there no going on with the story unless I know exactly how many goats are wafted over?" "No, Mary is there not!" quoth Sancho, "for as soon as you answered, that you could not tell, the rest of the story quite and clean slipped out of my head; and in truth, it is a thousand pities, for it was a special one." "So then," cried Don Quixote, "the story is ended." "Ah, marry is it!" quoth Sancho, "it is no more to be fetched to life than my dead mother." "Upon my honor," cried Don Quixote, "a most extraordinary story, and told and concluded in as extraordinary a manner! It is a nonesuch, I assure ye; though truly I expected no less from a man of such

188

uncommon parts. Alas! poor Sancho, I am afraid this dreadful noise has turned thy brain." "That may well be," quoth Sancho, "but, as for my story, I am sure there is nothing more to be said, for where you lose the account of the goats, there it ends." "Let

it be so," replied Don Quixote, "but now let us try whether Rozinante be in humor to march." With that he gave Rozinante two spurs, and the high-mettled jade answered with one bound, and then stood stock-still, not having the command of his hind legs.

Much about this time, whether it was the coolness of the night, or that Sancho had eaten some loosening food at supper, or, which seems more probable, that nature, by a regular impulse, gave him notice of her desire to perform a certain function that follows the

189

third concoction, it seems, honest Sancho found himself urged to do that which nobody could do for him; but such were his fears that he durst not for his life stir the breadth of a straw from his master; yet, to think of bearing the intolerable load that pressed him so, was to him as great an impossibility. In this perplexing exigency (with leave be it spoken) he could find no other expedient but to take his right hand from the crupper of the saddle, and softly untying his breeches, let them drop down to his heels; having done this, he as silently took up his shirt, and exposed his posteriors, which were none of the least, to the open air: but the main point was how to ease himself of this terrible burden without making a noise; to which purpose he clutched his teeth close, screwed up his face, shrunk up his shoulders, and held in his breath as much as possible: yet see what misfortunes attend the best projected undertakings! When he had almost compassed his design, he could not hinder an obstreperous sound, very different from those that caused his fear, from unluckily bursting out. "Hark!" cried Don Quixote, who heard it, "what noise is that, Sancho?" "Some new adventures, I will warrant you," quoth Sancho, "for ill-luck, you know, seldom comes alone." Having passed off the thing thus, he even ventured the other strain, and did it so cleverly, that without the least rumor or noise, his business was done effectually, to the unspeakable ease of his body and mind.

But Don Quixote having the sense of smelling as perfect as that of hearing, and Sancho standing so very near, or rather tacked to him, certain fumes, that ascended perpendicularly, began to regale his nostrils with a smell not so grateful as amber. No sooner the unwelcome steams disturbed him, but, having recourse to the common remedy, he stopped his nose, and then, with a snuffling voice, "Sancho," said he, "thou art certainly in great bodily fear." "So I am," quoth Sancho; "but what makes your worship perceive it now more than you did before?" "Because," replied Don Quixote,

190

"thou smellest now more unsavorily than thou didst before." "Ho! that may be," quoth Sancho; "but whose fault is that? you may even thank yourself for it. Why do you lead me a wild-goose chase, and bring me at such unseasonable hours to such dangerous places? you know I am not used to it." "Pray thee," said Don Quixote, still holding his nose, "get thee three or four steps from me; and for the future take more care, and know your distance; for I find, my familiarity with thee has bred contempt." "I warrant," quoth Sancho, "you think I have been doing something I should not have done." "Come, say no more," cried Don Quixote, "the more you stir, the worse it will be."

This discourse, such as it was, served them to pass away the night; and now Sancho, feeling the morning arise, thought it time to untie Rozinante's feet, and do up his breeches; and he did both with so much caution that his master suspected nothing. As for Rozinante, he no sooner felt himself at liberty, but he seemed to express his joy by pawing the ground, for, with his leave be it spoken, he was a stranger to curveting and prancing. Don Quixote also took it as a good omen, that his steed was now ready to move, and believed it was a signal given him by kind fortune, to animate him to give birth to the approaching adventure.

Now had Aurora displayed her rosy mantle over the blushing skies, and dark night withdrawn her sable veil; all objects stood confessed to human eyes, and Don Quixote could now perceive he was under some tall chestnut-trees, whose thick spreading boughs diffused an awful gloom around the place, but he could not yet discover whence proceeded the dismal sound of those incessant strokes. Therefore, being resolved to find it out, once more he took his leave of Sancho, with the same injunctions as before; adding withal, that he should not trouble himself about the recompense of his services, for he had taken care of that in his will, which he had providently made before he left home; but, if he came off victorious from this adventure, he might most certainly expect to be gratified with the promised island. Sancho could not forbear blubbering again, to hear these tender expressions of his master, and resolved not to leave him till he had finished this enterprise. And from that deep concern, and this nobler resolution to attend him, the author of this history infers, that the squire was something of a gentleman by descent, or at least the offspring of the old Christians. Nor did his good nature fail to move his master more than he was willing to show, at a time when it behoved him to shake off all softer thoughts; for now he rode towards the place whence the noise of the blows and the water seemed to come, while Sancho trudged after him, leading by the halter the inseparable companion of his good and bad fortune.

After they had gone a pretty way under a pleasant covert of chestnut-trees, they came into a meadow adjoining to certain rocks, from whose top there was a great fall of waters. At the foot of those rocks they discovered certain old ill-contrived buildings, that rather looked like ruins than inhabited houses; and they perceived that the terrifying noise of the blows, which yet continued, issued out of that place. When they came nearer, even patient Rozinante himself started at the dreadful sound; but, being heartened and pacified by his master, he was at last prevailed with to draw nearer and nearer with wary steps; the Knight recommending himself all the way most devoutly to his Dulcinea, and now and then also to Heaven in short ejaculations. As for Sancho, he stuck close to his master, peeping all the while through Rozinante's legs, to see if he could perceive what he dreaded to find out. When a little further, at the doubling of the point of a rock, they plainly discovered (kind reader, do not take it amiss) six huge fulling-mill hammers, which, interchangeably thumping several pieces of cloth, made the terrible noise that caused all Don Quixote's anxieties and Sancho's tribulation that night.

Don Quixote was struck dumb at this unexpected sight, and was ready to drop from his horse with shame and confusion. Sancho stared upon him, and saw him hang down his head, with a desponding, dejected countenance, like a man quite dispirited with this cursed disappointment. At the same time he looked upon Sancho, and seeing by his eyes, and his cheeks swelled with laughter, that he was ready to burst, he could not forbear laughing himself in spite of all his vexation; so that Sancho, seeing his master begin, immediately gave a loose to his mirth, and broke out into such a fit of laughing, that he was forced to hold his sides with both his knuckles, for fear of bursting his aching paunch. Four times he ceased, and four times renewed his obstreperous laughing; which sauciness Don Quixote began to resent with great indignation; and the more when Sancho, in a jeering tone, presumed to ridicule him with his own words, repeating part of the vain speech he made when first they heard the noise: "Know, Sancho, I was born in this iron age to restore the age of gold. I am the man for whom Heaven has reserved the most dangerous and glorious adventures," etc. Thus he went on, till his master, dreadfully enraged at his insolence, hit him two such blows on the shoulders with his lance, that, had they fallen upon his head, they had saved Don Quixote the trouble of paying him his wages, whatever he must have done to his heirs. Thereupon Sancho, finding his jest turn to earnest, begged pardon with all submission. "Mercy, good your worship," cried he, "spare my bones, I beseech you! I meant no harm, I did but joke a little." "And because you joke, I do not," cried Don Quixote. "Come hither, good Mr. Jester, you who pretend to rally, tell me, had this been a dangerous adventure, as well as it proves only a false alarm, have I not shown resolution enough to undertake and finish it! Am I, who am a knight, bound to know the meaning of every mechanic noise, and distinguish between sound and sound? Besides, it might happen, as really it is, that I had never seen a

193

fulling-mill before, though thou, like a base scoundrel as thou art, wert born and brought up among such mean implements of drudgery. But let the six fulling-hammers be transformed into so many giants, and then set them at me one by one, or all together; and if I do not lay them all at my feet with their heels upwards, then I will give thee leave to exercise thy ill-bred raillery as much as thou pleasest."

"Good your worship," quoth Sancho, "talk no more of it, I beseech you; I confess I carried the jest too far. But now all is hushed and well; pray tell me in sober sadness, as you hope to speed in all adventures, and come off safe and sound as from this, do not you think but that the fright we were in, I mean that I was in, would be a good subject for people to make sport with?" "I grant it," answered Don Quixote, "but I would not have it told; for all people are not so discreet as to place things, or look upon them in the position in which they should be considered." "I will say that for you," quoth Sancho, "you have shown you understand how to place things in their right position, when aiming at my head, you hit my shoulders; had not I ducked a little on one side, I had been in a fine condition! But let that pass, it will wash out in the bucking. I have heard my grannum say, 'That man loves thee well, who makes thee to weep.' Good masters may be hasty sometimes with a servant, but presently after a hard word or two they commonly give him a pair of cast breeches: what they give after a basting, Heaven knows; all I can tell is, that knights-errant, after bastinadoes, give you some cast island, or some old-fashioned kingdom upon the mainland."

"Fortune," said Don Quixote, "will perhaps order everything thou hast said to come to pass; therefore, Sancho, I pray thee think no more of my severity; thou knowest a man cannot always command the first impulse of his passions. On the other side, let me

194

advise thee not to be so saucy for the future, and not assume that strange familiarity with me which is so unbecoming in a servant. I protest, in such a vast number of books of knight-errantry as I have read, I never found that any squire was ever allowed so great a freedom of speech with his master as thou takest with me; and truly I look upon it to be a great fault in us both; in thee for disrespecting me, and in me for not making myself be more respected. Gandalin, Amadis de Gaul's squire, though he was earl of the Firm Island, yet never spoke to his master but with cap in hand, his head bowed, and his body half bent, after the Turkish manner. But what shall we say of Gasabal, Don Galaor's squire, who was such a strict observer of silence, that, to the honor of his marvelous taciturnity, he gave the author occasion to mention his name but once in that voluminous authentic history? From all this, Sancho, I would have thee make this observation, that there ought to be a distance kept between the master and the man, the knight and the squire. Therefore, once more I tell thee, let us live together for the future more according to the due decorum of our respective degrees, without giving one another any further vexation on this account; for, after all, it will always be the worse for you, on whatsoever occasion we happen to disagree. As for the rewards I promised you, they will come in due time; and should you be disappointed that way, you have your salary to trust to, as I have told you."

"You say very well," quoth Sancho; "but now, sir, suppose no rewards should come, and I should be forced to stick to my wages, I would fain know how much a squire-errant used to earn in the days of yore? Did they go by the month, or by the day, like our laborers?" "I do not think," replied Don Quixote, "they ever went by the hire, but rather that they trusted to their master's generosity. And if I have assigned thee wages in my will, which I left sealed up at home, it was only to prevent the worst, because I do not know yet what success I may have in chivalry in these depraved times; and I would not have my soul suffer in the other world for such a trifling matter; for there is no state of life so subject to dangers as that of a knight-errant." "Like enough," quoth Sancho, "when merely the noise of the hammers of a fulling-mill is able to trouble and disturb the heart of such a valiant knight as your worship! But you may be sure, I will not hereafter so much as offer to open my lips to gibe or joke at your doings, but always stand in awe of you, and honor you as my Lord and Master." "By doing so," replied Don Quixote, "thy days shall be long on the face of the earth; for next to our parents we ought to respect our masters, as if they were our fathers."

VII: OF THE HIGH ADVENTURE AND CONQUEST OF MAMBRINO'S HELMET, WITH OTHER EVENTS RELATING TO OUR INVINCIBLE KNIGHT

At the same time it began to rain, and Sancho would fain have taken shelter in the fulling-mills: but Don Quixote had conceived such an antipathy against them for the shame they had put upon him, that he would by no means be prevailed with to go in; and turning to the right hand, he struck into a highway, where they had not gone far before he discovered a horseman, who wore upon his head something that glittered like gold. The Knight had no sooner spied him, but turning to his squire, "Sancho," cried he, "I believe there is no proverb but what is true; they are all so many sentences and maxims drawn from experience, the universal mother of sciences: for instance, that saying, 'That where one door shuts, another opens.' Thus fortune, that last night deceived us with the false prospect of an adventure, this morning offers us a real one to

196

make us amends; and such an adventure, Sancho, that if I do not gloriously succeed in it, I shall have now no pretense to an excuse, no darkness, no unknown sounds to impute my disappointment to: in short, in all probability yonder comes the man who wears on his head Mambrino's helmet,[1] and thou knowest the vow I have made." "Good sir," quoth Sancho, "mind what you say, and take heed what you do; for I would willingly keep my carcass and the case of my understanding from being pounded, mashed, and crushed with fulling-hammers." "Hell take the block-head!" cried Don Quixote: "is there no difference between a helmet and a fulling-mill?" "I do not know," says Sancho, "but I am sure, were I suffered to speak my mind now as I was wont, mayhaps I would give you such main reasons, that yourself should see you are wide of the matter." "How can I be mistaken, thou eternal misbeliever?" cried Don Quixote. "Dost thou not see that knight that comes riding up directly towards us upon a dapple-gray steed, with a helmet of gold on his head?" "I see what I see," replied Sancho, "and the devil of anything I can spy but a fellow on such another gray ass as mine is, with something that glistens on the top of his head." "I tell thee, that is Mambrino's helmet," replied Don Quixote: "do thou stand at a distance, and leave me to deal with him; thou shalt see, that without trifling away so much as a moment in needless talk, I will finish this adventure, and possess myself of the desired helmet." "I shall stand at a distance, you may be sure," quoth Sancho; "but I wish this may not prove another blue bout, and a worse job than the fulling-mills." "I have warned you already, fellow," said Don Quixote, "not so much as to name the fulling-mills; dare but once more to do it, nay, but to think on it, and I vow to— I say no more; but I will full and pound your dogship into jelly!" These threats were more than sufficient to padlock Sancho's lips, for he had no

[1] *Mambrino, a Saracen of great valor, who had a golden helmet, which Rinaldo took from him. See "Orlando Furioso," Canto I.*

mind to have his master's vow fulfilled at the expense of his bones.

Now the truth of the story was this: There were in that part of the country two villages; one of which was so little, that it had not so much as a shop in it, nor any barber; so that the barber of the greater village served also the smaller. And thus a person happening to have occasion to be let blood, and another to be shaved, the barber was going thither with his brass basin, which he had clapped upon his head to keep his hat, that chanced to be a new one, from being spoiled by the rain; and as the basin was newly scoured, it made a glittering show a great way off. As Sancho had well observed, he rode upon a gray ass, which Don Quixote as easily took for a dapple-gray steed, as he took the barber for a knight, and his brass basin for a golden helmet; his distracted brain easily applying every object to his romantic ideas. Therefore, when he saw the poor imaginary knight draw near, he fixed his lance, or javelin, to his thigh, and without staying to hold a

parley with his thoughtless adversary, flew at him as fiercely as Rozinante would gallop, resolved to pierce him through and through; crying out in the midst of his career, "Caitiff! wretch! defend thyself, or yield to me immediately that which is so justly my due!" The barber, who as he peaceably went along saw that terrible apparition come thundering upon him at unawares, had no other

198

way to avoid being run through with the lance, but to throw himself off from his ass to the ground; and then as hastily getting up, he took to his heels, and ran over the fields swifter than the wind, leaving his ass and his basin behind him. Don Quixote finding himself thus master of the field, and of the basin: "The miscreant!" cried he, "who has left this helmet, has shown himself as prudent as the beaver, who finding himself hotly pursued by the hunters, to save his life, tears and cuts off with his teeth that for which his natural instinct tells him he was followed." Then he ordered Sancho to take up the helmet. "On my word," quoth Sancho, having taken it up, "it is a special basin, and as well worth a piece of eight as a thief is worth a halter." With that he gave it to his master, who presently clapped it on his head, turning it every way to find out the beaver or vizor; and at last, seeing it had none, "Doubtless," said he, "the Pagan for whom this famous helmet was first made, had a head of a prodigious size; but the worst is, that there is at least one half of it wanting." Sancho could not forbear smiling to hear his master call the barber's basin a helmet, and had not his fear dashed his mirth, he had certainly laughed outright. "What does the fool grin at now?" cried Don Quixote. "I laugh," said he, "to think what a hugeous jolt-head he must needs have had who was the owner of this same helmet, that looks for all the world like a barber's basin." "I fancy," said Don Quixote, "this enchanted helmet has fallen by some strange accident into the hands of some person, who, not knowing the value of it, for the lucre of a little money, finding it to be of pure gold, melted one half, and of the other made this head-piece, which, as thou sayest, has some resemblance of a barber's basin. But to me, who know the worth of it, the metamorphosis signifies little; for as soon as ever I come to some town where there is an armorer, I will have it altered so much for the better, that then even the helmet which the God of Smiths made for

199

the God of War shall not deserve to be compared with it. In the meantime I will wear it as it is; it is better than nothing, and will serve at least to save part of my head from the violent encounter of a stone." "Ay, that it will," quoth Sancho, "so it is not hurled out of a sling, as were those at the battle between the two armies, when they hit you that confounded dowse on the chops, that saluted your worship's cheek-teeth, and broke the pot about your ears in which you kept that blessed drench that made me bring up my inside." "True," cried Don Quixote, "there I lost my precious balsam indeed; but I do not much repine at it, for thou knowest I have the receipt in my memory." "So have I too," quoth Sancho, "and shall have while I have breath to draw; but if ever I make any of that stuff, or taste it again, may I give up the ghost with it. Besides, I do not intend ever to do anything that may give occasion for the use of it. For my fixed resolution is, with all my five senses, to preserve myself from hurting and from being hurt by anybody. As to being tossed in a blanket again, I have nothing to say to that, for there is no remedy for accidents but patience, it seems: so if it ever be my lot to be served so again, I will even shrink up my shoulders, hold my breath, and shut my eyes, and then happy be lucky, let the blanket and fortune even toss on to the end of the chapter."

"Truly," said Don Quixote, "I am afraid thou art no good Christian, Sancho; thou never forgettest injuries. Let me tell thee, it is the part of noble and generous spirits to pass by trifles. Where art thou lame? which of thy ribs is broken? or what part of thy skull is bruised? that you can never think on that jest without malice. For, after all, it was nothing but a jest, a harmless piece of pastime: had I looked upon it otherwise, I had returned to that place before this time, and had made more noble mischief in revenge of the abuse than ever the incensed Grecians did at Troy, for the detention of their Helen, that famed beauty of the ancient world,

200

who, however, had she lived in our age, or had my Dulcinea adorned hers, would have found her charms outrivaled by my mistress's perfections": and saying this, he heaved up a deep sigh. "Well, then," quoth Sancho, "I will not rip up old sores; let it go for a jest, since there is no revenging it in earnest. But what shall we do with this dapple-gray steed that is so like a gray ass? You see, that same poor devil-errant has left it to shift for itself, poor thing, and by his haste to run off, I do not think he means to come back for it, and, by my beard, the gray beast is a special one." "It is not my custom," replied Don Quixote, "to plunder those whom I overcome; nor is it usual among us knights, for the victor to take the horse of his vanquished enemy and let him go on foot, unless his own steed be killed or disabled in the combat: therefore, Sancho, leave the horse, or the ass, whatever thou pleasest to call it, the owner will be sure to come for it as soon as he sees us gone." "I have a huge mind to take him along with us," quoth Sancho, "or at least to exchange him for my own, which is not so good. What, are the laws of knight-errantry so strict, that a man must not exchange one ass for another? At least I hope they will give me leave to swop one harness for another." "Truly, Sancho," replied Don Quixote, "I am not so very certain as to this last particular, and, therefore, till I am better informed, I give thee leave to exchange the furniture, if thou hast absolutely occasion for it." "I have so much occasion for it," quoth Sancho, "that though it were for my own very self I could not need it more." So, without any more ado, being authorized by his master's leave, he made *mutatio caparum* (a change of caparisons), and made his own beast three parts in four better[2] for his new furniture. This done, they breakfasted upon what they left at supper, and quenched their thirst at the stream that turned the fulling-mills, towards which they took care

2 *Literally leaving him better by a* tierce *and a* quint. *Alluding to the game of* piquet, *in which a* tierce *or a* quint *may be gained by putting out bad cards, and taking in better.*

not to cast an eye, for they abominated the very thoughts of them. Thus their spleen being eased, their choleric and melancholic humors assuaged, up they got again, and never minding their way, were all guided by Rozinante's discretion, the depository of his master's will, and also of the ass's, that kindly and sociably always followed his steps wherever he went. Their guide soon brought them again into the high road, where they kept on a slow pace, not caring which way they went.

As they jogged on thus, quoth Sancho to his master, "Pray, sir, will you give me leave to talk to you a little; for since you have laid that bitter command upon me, to hold my tongue, I have had four or five quaint conceits that have rotted in my gizzard, and now I have another at my tongue's end that I would not for anything should miscarry." "Say it," cried Don Quixote, "but be short, for no discourse can please when too long."

"Well, then," quoth Sancho, "I have been thinking to myself of late how little is to be got by hunting up and down those barren woods and strange places, where, though you compass the hardest and most dangerous jobs of knight-errantry, yet no living soul sees or hears of it, and so it is every bit as good as lost; and therefore methinks it were better (with submission to your worship's better judgment be it spoken) that we even went to serve some emperor, or other great prince that is at war; for there you might show how stout, and how wondrous strong and wise you be; which, being perceived by the lord we shall serve, he must needs reward each of us according to his deserts; and there you will not want a learned scholar to set down all your high deeds, that they may never be forgotten: as for mine I say nothing, since they are not to be named the same day with your worship's; and yet I dare a-vouch, that if any notice be taken in knight-errantry of the feats of squires, mine will be sure to come in for a share." "Truly, Sancho," replied Don Quixote, "there is some reason in what thou sayest; but first of all it is requisite that a knight-errant should spend some time in various parts of the world, as a probationer, in quest of adventures, that, by achieving some extraordinary exploits, his renown may diffuse itself through neighboring climes and distant nations: so, when he goes to the court of some great monarch, his fame flying before him as his harbinger, secures him such a reception, that the knight has scarce reached the gates of the metropolis of the kingdom, when he finds himself attended and surrounded by admiring crowds, pointing and crying out, 'There, there rides the Knight of the Sun (or of the Serpent, or whatever other title the knight takes upon him): that is he,' they will cry, 'who vanquished in single combat the huge giant Brocabruno, surnamed of the Invincible Strength; that is he that freed the great Mamaluco of Persia from the enchantment that had kept him confined for almost nine hundred years together.' Thus, as they relate his achievements with loud acclamations, the spreading rumor at last reaches the king's palace, and the monarch of that country being desirous to be informed with his own eyes, will not fail to look out of his window. As soon as he sees the knight, knowing him by his arms, or by the device on his shield, he will be obliged to say to his attendants, 'My lords and gentlemen, haste all of you, as many as are knights, go and receive the flower of chivalry that is coming to our court.' At the king's command, away they all run to introduce him; the king himself meets him halfway on the stairs, where he embraces his valorous guest, and kisses his cheek: then, taking him by the hand, he leads him directly to the queen's apartment; where the knight finds her attended by the princess her daughter, who must be one of the most beautiful and most accomplished damsels in the whole compass of the universe. At the same time fate will so dispose of everything, that the princess shall gaze on the knight, and the knight on the princess, and each shall admire one another as persons rather angelical than human;

and then, by an accountable charm, they shall both find themselves caught and entangled in the inextricable net of love, and wondrously perplexed for want of an opportunity to discover their amorous anguish to one another. After this, doubtless, the knight is conducted by the king to one of the richest apartments in the palace; where, having taken off his armor, they will bring him a rich scarlet vestment lined with ermine; and if he looked so graceful cased in steel, how lovely will he appear in all the heightening ornaments of courtiers! Night being come, he shall sup with the king, the queen, and the princess; and shall all the while be feasting his eyes with the sight of the charmer, yet so as nobody shall perceive it; and she will repay him his glances with as much discretion; for, as I have said, she is a most accomplished person. After supper a surprising scene is unexpectedly to appear: enter first an ill-favored dwarf, and after him a fair damsel between two giants, with the offer of a certain adventure, so contrived by an ancient necromancer, and so difficult to be performed, that he who shall undertake and end it with success, shall be esteemed the best knight in the world. Presently it is the king's pleasure that all his courtiers should attempt it; which they do, but all of them unsuccessfully; for the honor is reserved for the valorous stranger, who effects that with ease which the rest essayed in vain; and then the princess shall be overjoyed, and esteem herself the most happy creature in the world, for having bestowed her affections on so deserving an object.

"Now by the happy appointment of fate, this king, or this emperor, is at war with one of his neighbors as powerful as himself; and the knight being informed of this, after he has been some few days at court, offers the king his service, which is accepted with joy, and the knight courteously kisses the king's hand in acknowledgment of so great a favor. That night the lover takes his leave of the princess at the iron grate before her chamber window, looking into the garden, where he and she have already had several interviews, by means of the princess's confidante, a damsel who carries on the intrigue between them. The knight sighs, the princess swoons, the damsel runs for cold water to bring her to life again, very uneasy also because the morning light approaches, and she would not have them discovered, lest it should reflect on her lady's honor. At last the princess revives, and gives the knight her lovely hand to kiss through the iron grate, which he does a thousand and a thousand times, bathing it all the while with his tears. Then they agree how to transmit their thoughts with secrecy to each other, with a mutual intercourse of letters, during this fatal absence. The princess prays him to return with all the speed of a lover; the knight promises it with repeated vows, and a thousand kind protestations. At last the fatal moment being come that must tear him from all he loves, and from his very self, he seals once more his love on her soft snowy hand, almost breathing out his soul, which mounts to his lips, and even would leave its body to dwell there; and then he is hurried away by the fearful confidante. After this cruel separation he retires to his chamber, throws himself on his bed; but grief will not suffer sleep to close his eyes. Then, rising with the sun, he goes to take his leave of the king and the queen: he desires to pay his compliment of leave to the princess, but he is told she is indisposed; and as he has reason to believe that his departing is the cause of her disorder, he is so grieved at the news, that he is ready to betray the secret of his heart; which the princess's confidante observing, she goes and acquaints her with it, and finds the lovely mourner bathed in tears, who tells her, that the greatest affliction of her soul is her not knowing whether her charming knight be of royal blood; but the damsel pacifies her, assuring her that so much gallantry, and such noble qualifications, were unquestionably derived from an illustrious and royal original. This comforts the afflicted fair, who does all she can to compose her looks, lest the king or the queen should suspect the cause of their alteration; and so some days after she appears in public as before. And now the knight, having been absent for some time, meets, fights, and overcomes the king's enemies, takes I do not know how many cities, wins I do not know how many battles, returns to court, and appears before his mistress laden with honor. He visits her privately as before, and they agree that he shall demand her of the king her father in marriage, as the reward of all his services; but the king will not grant his suit, as being unacquainted with his birth; however, whether it be that the princess suffers herself to be privately carried away, or that some other means are used, the knight marries her, and in a little time the king is very well pleased with the match; for now the knight appears to be the son of a mighty king, of I cannot tell you what country, for I think it is not in the map. Sometime after, the father dies, the princess is heiress, and thus in a trice our knight comes to be king. Having thus completed his happiness, his next thoughts are to gratify his squire, and of all those who have been instrumental in his advancement to the throne: thus he marries his squire to one of the princess's damsels, and most probably to her favorite, who had been privy to the amours, and who is daughter to one of the most considerable dukes in the kingdom."

"That is what I have been looking for all this while," quoth Sancho, "give me but that, and let the world rub, there I will stick; for every title of this will come to pass, and be your worship's case, as sure as a gun, if you will take upon you that same nick-name of the Knight of the Woeful Figure." "Most certainly, Sancho," replied Don Quixote; "for by the same steps, and in that very manner, knights-errant have always proceeded to ascend to the throne: therefore our chief business is to find out some great potentate, either among the Christians or the Pagans, that is at war with his neighbors, and has a fair daughter. But we shall have time enough

206

to inquire after that; for, as I have told thee, we must purchase fame in other places, before we presume to go to court. Another thing makes me more uneasy. Suppose we have found out a king and a princess, and I have filled the world with the fame of my unparalleled achievements, yet cannot I tell how to find out that I am of royal blood, though it were but second cousin to an emperor: for it is not to be expected that the king will ever consent that I should wed his daughter till I have made this out by authentic proofs, though my service deserve it never so much; and thus, for want of a punctilio, I am in danger of losing what my valor so justly merits. It is true, I am a gentleman, and of a noted ancient family, and possessed of an estate of a hundred and twenty crowns a year; nay, perhaps, the learned historiographer, who is to write the history of my life, will so improve and beautify my genealogy, that he will find me to be the fifth, or sixth, at least, in descent from a king: for, Sancho, there are two sorts of originals in the world; some who sprung from mighty kings and princes, by little and little have been so lessened and obscured, that the estate and titles of the following generations have dwindled to nothing, and ended in a point like a pyramid; others, who from mean and low beginnings, still rise and rise, till at last they are raised to the very top of human greatness: so vast the difference is, that those who were something are now nothing, and those that were nothing are now something. And therefore who knows but that I may be one of those whose original is so illustrious; which being handsomely made out, after due examination, ought undoubtedly to satisfy the king, my father-in-law. But even supposing he were still refractory, the princess is to be so desperately in love with me, that she will marry me without his consent, though I were a son of the meanest water-carrier; and if her tender honor scruples to bless me against her father's will, then it may not be amiss to put a pleasant constraint upon her, by conveying her by force out of the reach of her father, to whose persecutions either time or death will be sure to put a period."

"Ay," quoth Sancho, "your rake-helly fellows have a saying that is pat to your purpose, 'Never cringe nor creep for what you by force may reap'; though I think it were better said, 'A leap from a hedge is better than the prayer of a good man.'[3] No more to be said, if the king, your father-in-law, will not let you have his daughter by fair means, never stand shall I, but fairly and square-ly run away with her. All the mischief that I fear is, only, that while you are making your peace with him, and waiting after a dead man's shoes, as the saying is, the poor dog of a squire is like to go long bare-foot, and may go hang himself for any good you will be able to do him, unless the damsel go-between, who is to be his wife, run away too with the princess, and he solace himself with her till a better time comes: for I do not see but that the knight may clap up the match between us without any more ado." "That is most certain," answered Don Quixote. "Why then," quoth Sancho, "let us even take our chance, and let the world rub." "May fortune crown our wishes," cried Don Quixote, "and let him be a wretch who thinks himself one." "Amen, say I," quoth Sancho, "for I am one of your old Christians, and that is enough to qualify me to be an earl." "And more than enough," said Don Quixote, "for though thou wert not so well descended, being a king, I could bestow nobility on thee, without putting thee to the trouble of buying it, or doing me the least service; and making thee an earl, men must call thee My Lord, though it grieves them never so much." "And do you think," quoth Sancho, "I would not become my equality main well?" "Thou shouldest say quality," said Don Quixote, "and not equality." "Even as you will," returned Sancho: "but, as I was saying, I should become an earldom rarely; for I was once beadle to a brotherhood, and the beadle's gown did so

[3] *Better to rob than to ask charity.*

208

become me, that everybody said I had the presence of a warden. Then how do you think I shall look with a duke's robes on my back, all bedaubed with gold and pearl like any foreign count? I believe we shall have folks come an hundred leagues to see me." "Thou wilt look well enough," said Don Quixote, "but then thou must shave that rough bushy beard of thine at least every other day, or people will read thy beginning in thy face as soon as they see thee." "Why then," quoth Sancho, "it is but keeping a barber in my house; and, if needs be, he shall trot after me wherever I go, like a grandee's master of the horse." "How camest thou to know," said Don Quixote, "that grandees have their masters of the horse to ride after them?" "I will tell you," quoth Sancho: "some years ago I happened to be about a month among your court-folks, and there I saw a little dandiprat riding about, who, they said, was a hugeous great lord: there was a man on horseback that followed him close wherever he went, turning and stopping as he did; you would have thought he had been tied to his horse's tail. With that I asked why that hind man did not ride by the other, but still came after him thus, and they told me he was master of his horses, and that the grandees have always such kind of men at their tail; and I marked this so well, that I have not forgotten it since." "Thou art in the right," said Don Quixote, "and thou mayest as reasonably have thy barber to attend thee in this manner. Customs did not come up all at once, but rather started up and were improved by degrees; so thou mayest be the first earl that rode in state with his barber behind him; and this may be said to justify thy conduct, that it is an office of more trust to shave a man's beard than to saddle a horse." "Well," quoth Sancho, "leave the business of the cut-beard to me, and do but take care you be a king and I an earl." "Never doubt," replied Don Quixote; and with that, looking about, he discovered—what the next chapter will tell you.

Cid Hamet Benengeli, an Arabian and Manchegan author, relates in this most grave, high-sounding, minute, soft, and humorous history, that after this discourse between the renowned Don Quixote and his squire, Sancho Panza, which we laid down at the end of the seventh chapter, the Knight lifting up his eyes, saw about twelve men a-foot, trudging in the road, all in a row, one behind another, like beads upon a string, being linked together by the neck to a huge iron chain, and manacled besides. They were guarded by two horsemen, armed with carbines, and two men a-foot, with swords and javelins. As soon as Sancho spied them, "Look ye, sir," cried he, "here is a gang of wretches hurried away by main force to serve the king in the galleys." "How!" replied Don Quixote, "is it possible the king will force anybody?" "I do not say so," answered Sancho; "I mean these are rogues whom the law has sentenced for their misdeeds, to row in the king's galleys." "However," replied Don Quixote, "they are forced, because they do not go of their own free will." "Sure enough," quoth Sancho. "If it be so," said Don Quixote, "they come within the verge of my office, which is to hinder violence and oppression, and succor all people in misery." "Ay, sir," quoth Sancho, "but neither the king nor law offer any violence to such wicked wretches, they have but their deserts." By this the chain of slaves came up, when Don Quixote, in very civil terms, desired the guards to inform him why these poor people were led along in that manner. "Sir," answered one of the horsemen, "they are criminals condemned to serve the king in his galleys. That is all that I have to say to you, and you need inquire no further." "Nevertheless, sir," replied Don Quixote, "I have a great desire to know in few words the cause of their misfortune, and I will esteem it an extraordinary favor, if you will let me have that satisfaction." "We have here the copies and certificates of their several sentences," said the other horseman, "but we cannot stand to pull them out and read them now; you may draw near and examine the men yourself: I suppose they themselves will tell you why they are condemned; for they are such honest people, they are not ashamed to boast of their rogueries." With this permission, which Don Quixote would have taken of himself had they denied it him, he rode up to the chain, and asked the first, for what crimes he was in these miserable circumstances. The galley-slave answered him, that it was for being in love. "What, only for being in love!" cried Don Quixote; "were all those that are in love to be thus used, I myself might have been long since in the galleys." "Ay, but," replied the slave, "my love was not of that sort which you conjecture: I was so desperately in love with a basket of linen, and embraced it so close, that had not the judge taken it from me by force, I would not have parted with it willingly. In short, I was taken in the fact, and so there was no need to put me to the rack, it was proved so plain upon me. So I was committed, tried, condemned, had the gentle lash; and besides that, was sent, for three years, to be an element-dasher, and there is an end of the business." "An element-dasher!" cried Don Quixote, "what do you mean by that?" "A galley-slave," answered the criminal, who was a young fellow, about four-and-twenty years old, and said he was born at Piedra-Hita.

Then Don Quixote examined the second, but he was so sad and desponding, that he would make no answer; however, the first rogue informed the Knight of his affairs. "Sir," said he, "this canary-bird keeps us company for having sung too much." "Is it

211

possible!" cried Don Quixote; "are men sent to the galleys for singing?" "Ay, Mary are they," quoth the arch rogue; "for there is nothing worse than to sing in anguish." "How!" cried Don Quixote, "that contradicts the saying, 'Sing away sorrow, cast away care.'" "Ay, but with us the case is different," replied the slave, "'he that sings in disaster, weeps all his life after.'" "This is a riddle which I cannot unfold," cried Don Quixote. "Sir," said one of the guards, "singing in anguish, among these jail-birds, means to confess upon the rack: this fellow was put to the torture, and confessed his crime, which was stealing of cattle; and because

he squeaked, or sung, as they call it, he was condemned to the galleys for six years, besides an hundred jerks with a cat-o'-nine-tails that have whisked and powdered his shoulders already. Now the reason why he goes thus mopish and out of sorts, is only because his comrogues jeer and laugh at him continually for not having had the courage to deny: as if it had not been as easy for him to say No as Yes; or, as if a fellow, taken up on suspicion, were not a lucky rogue, when there is no positive evidence can come in against him but his own tongue; and in my opinion they are somewhat in the right." "I think so too," said Don Quixote.

Thence addressing himself to the third, "And you," said he,

"what have you done?" "Sir," answered the fellow, readily and pleasantly enough, "I must mow the great meadow for five years together, for want of twice five ducats." "I will give twenty with all my heart," said Don Quixote, "to deliver thee from that misery." "Thank you for nothing," quoth the slave; "it is just like the proverb, 'After meat comes mustard'; or, like money to a starving man at sea, when there are no victuals to be bought with it. Had I had the twenty ducats you offer me before I was tried, to have greased the clerk's, or recorder's, fist, and have whetted my lawyer's wit, I might have been now at Toledo in the market-place of Zocodover, and not have been thus led along like a dog in a string. But Heaven is powerful, Basta; I say no more."

Then passing to the fourth, who was a venerable old Don, with a gray beard that reached to his bosom, he put the same question to him; whereupon the poor creature fell a-weeping, and was not able to give him an answer. So the next behind him lent him a tongue. "Sir," said he, "this honest person goes to the galleys for four years, having taken his progress through the town in state, and rested at the usual stations." "That is," quoth Sancho, "as I take it, after he had been exposed to public shame."[1] "Right," replied the slave; "and all this he is condemned to for being a broker of human flesh: for, to tell you the truth, the gentleman is a pimp, and, besides that, he has a smack of conjuring." "If it were not for that addition of conjuring," cried Don Quixote, "he ought not to have been sent to the galleys, purely for being a pimp, unless it were to be general of the galleys: for, the profession of a bawd, pimp, or messenger of love, is not like other common employments, but an office that requires a great deal of prudence and sagacity; an office of trust and weight, and most highly necessary in a well-

[1] *Instead of the pillory, in Spain, they carry that sort of malefactors on an ass, and in a particular habit, along the streets, the crier going before and proclaiming their crime.*

213

regulated commonwealth; nor should it be executed but by civil well-descended persons of good natural parts, and of a liberal education. Nay, it were requisite there should be a comptroller and surveyor of the profession, as there are of others; and a certain and settled number of them, as there are of exchange-brokers. This would be a means to prevent an infinite number of mischiefs that happen every day, because the trade or profession is followed by poor ignorant pretenders, silly waiting women, young giddy-brained pages, shallow footmen, and such raw inexperienced sort of people, who in unexpected turns and emergencies stand with their fingers in their mouths, know not their right hand from their left, but suffer themselves to be surprised, and spoil all for want of quickness of invention either to conceal, carry on, or bring off a thing artificially. Had I but time I would point out what sort of persons are best qualified to be chosen professors of this most necessary employment in the commonwealth; however, at some fitter season I will inform those of it who may remedy this disorder. All I have to say now, is, that the grief I had to see those venerable gray hairs in such distress, for having followed that no less useful than ingenious vocation of pimping, is now lost in my abhorrence of his additional character of a conjurer; though I very well know that no sorcery in the world can affect or force the will, as some ignorant credulous persons fondly imagine: for our will is a free faculty, and no herb nor charms can constrain it. As for philters and such-like compositions which some silly women and designing pretenders make, they are nothing but certain mixtures and poisonous preparations, that make those who take them run mad; though the deceivers labor to persuade us they can make one person love another; which, as I have said, is an impossible thing, our will being a free, uncontrollable power." "You say very well, sir," cried the old coupler; "and, upon my honor, I protest I am wholly innocent as to the imputation of witchcraft. As for the business of pimping, I cannot deny it, but I never took it to be a criminal function; for my intention was, that all the world should taste the sweets of love, and enjoy each other's society, living together in friendship and in peace, free from those griefs and jars that unpeople the earth. But my harmless design has not been so happy as to prevent my being sent now to a place whence I never expect to return, stooping as I do under the heavy burden of old age, and being grievously afflicted with the strangury, which scarce affords me a moment's respite from pain." This said, the reverend procurer burst out afresh into tears and lamentations, which melted Sancho's heart so much, that he pulled a piece of money out of his bosom and gave it to him as an alms.

Then Don Quixote turned to the fifth, who seemed to be nothing at all concerned. "I go to serve his majesty," said he, "for having been somewhat too familiar with two of my cousin-germans, and two other kind-hearted virgins that were sisters; by which means I have multiplied my kind, and begot so odd and intricate a medley of kindred, that it would puzzle a convocation of casuists to resolve their degrees of consanguinity. All this was proved upon me. I had no friends, and what was worse, no money, and so was like to have hung for it: however, I was only condemned to the galleys for six years, and patiently submitted to it. I feel myself yet young, to my comfort; so if my life but does hold out, all will be well in time. If you will be pleased to bestow something upon poor sinners, Heaven will reward you; and when we pray, we will be sure to remember you, that your life may be as long and prosperous, as your presence is goodly and noble." This brisk spark appeared to be a student by his habit, and some of the guards said he was a fine speaker, and a good Latinist.

After him came a man about thirty years old, a clever, well-set, handsome fellow, only he squinted horribly with one eye: he was strangely loaded with irons; a heavy chain clogged his leg, and

215

was so long, that he twisted it about his waist like a girdle: he had
a couple of collars about his neck, the one to link him to the rest
of the slaves, and the other, one of those iron-ruffs which they call
a keep-friend, or a friend's foot; from whence two irons went down
to his middle, and to their two bars were riveted a pair of manacles
that gripped him by the fists, and were secured with a large padlock; so that he could neither lift his hands to his mouth, nor bend
down his head towards his hands. Don Quixote inquiring why he
was worse hampered with irons than the rest, "Because he alone
has done more rogueries than all the rest," answered one of the
guards. "This is such a reprobate, such a devil of a fellow, that no
jail nor fetters will hold him; we are not sure he is fast enough,
for all he is chained so." "What sort of crimes then has he been
guilty of," asked Don Quixote, "that he is only sent to the galleys?" "Why," answered the keeper, "he is condemned to ten years'
slavery, which is no better than a civil death: but I need not stand
to tell you any more of him, but that he is that notorious rogue
Gines de Passamonte, alias Ginesillo de Parapilla." "Hark you,
sir," cried the slave, fair and softly; "what a pox makes you give a
gentleman more names than he has? Gines is my Christian name,
and Passamonte my surname, and not Ginesillo, nor Parapilla, as
you say. Blood! let every man mind what he says, or it may prove
the worse for him." "Do not you be so saucy, Mr. Crack-rope,"
cried the officer to him, "or I may chance to make you keep a better
tongue in your head." "It is a sign," cried the slave, "that a man is
fast, and under the lash; but one day or other somebody shall know
whether I am called Parapilla or no." "Why, Mr. Slip-string,"
replied the officer, "do not people call you by that name?" "They
do," answered Gines, "but I will make them call me otherwise, or I
will fleece and bite them worse than I care to tell you now. But you,
sir, who are so inquisitive," added he, turning to Don Quixote, "if
you have a mind to give us anything, pray do it quickly, and go

216

your ways; for I do not like to stand here answering questions; broil me! I am Gines de Passamonte, I am not ashamed of my name. As for my life and conversation, there is an account of them in black and white, written with this numerical hand of mine." "There he tells you true," said the officer, "for he has written his own history himself, without omitting a tittle of his roguish pranks; and he has left the manuscript in pawn in the prison for two hundred reals." "Ay," said Gines, "and will redeem it, burn me! though it lay there for as many ducats." "Then it must be an extraordinary piece," cried Don Quixote. "So extraordinary," replied Gines, "that it far outdoes not only Lazarillo de Tormes, but whatever has been, and shall be written in that kind: for mine is true every word, and no invented stories can compare with it for variety of tricks and accidents." "What is the title of the book?" asked Don Quixote. " 'The Life of Gines de Passamonte,' " answered the other. "Is it quite finished?" asked the Knight. "How the devil can it be finished and I yet living?" replied the slave. "There is in it every material point from my cradle, to this my last going to the galleys." "Then it seems you have been there before," said Don Quixote. "To serve God and the king, I was some four years there once before," replied Gines: "I already know how the biscuit and the bull's-pizzle agree with my carcass: it does not grieve me much to go there again, for there I shall have leisure to give a finishing stroke to my book. I have the devil knows what to add; and in our Spanish galleys there is always leisure and idle time enough in conscience: neither shall I want so much for what I have to insert, for I know it all by heart."

"Thou seemest to be a witty fellow," said Don Quixote. "You should have said unfortunate too," replied the slave; "for the bitch fortune is still unkind to men of wit." "You mean to such wicked wretches as yourself," cried the officer. "Look you, Mr. Commissary," said Gines, "I have already desired you to use good language; the law did not give us to your keeping for you to abuse us, but only to conduct us where the king has occasion for us. Let every man mind his own business, and give good words, or hold his tongue: for by the blood—I will say no more, murder will out; there will be a time when some people's rogueries may come to light, as well as those of other folks." With that the officer, provoked by the slave's threats, held up his staff to strike him; but Don Quixote stepped between them, and desired him not to do it, and to consider, that the slave was the more to be excused for being too free of his tongue, since he had never another member at liberty. Then addressing himself to all the slaves, "My dearest brethren," cried he, "I find, by what I gather from your own words, that though you deserve punishment for the several crimes of which you stand convicted, yet you suffer execution of the sentence by constraint, and merely because you cannot help it. Besides, it is not unlikely but that this man's want of resolution upon the rack, the other's want of money, the third's want of friends and favor, and, in short, the judges' perverting and wresting the law to your great prejudice, may have been the cause of your misery. Now, as Heaven has sent me into the world to relieve the distressed, and free suffering weakness from the tyranny of oppression, according to the duty of my profession of knight-errantry, these considerations induce me to take you under my protection—but, because it is the part of a prudent man not to use violence where fair means may be effectual, I desire you, gentlemen of the guard, to release these poor men, there being people enough to serve his majesty in their places; for it is a hard case to make slaves of men whom God and nature made free; and you have the less reason to use these wretches with severity, seeing they never did you any wrong. Let them answer for their sins in the other world: Heaven is just, you know, and will be sure to punish the wicked, as it will certainly reward the good. Consider besides, gentlemen, that it is neither a

218

Christian-like, nor an honorable action, for men to be the butchers and tormentors of one another; particularly, when no advantage can arise from it. I choose to desire this of you, with so much mildness, and in so peaceable a manner, gentlemen, that I may have occasion to pay you a thankful acknowledgment, if you will be pleased to grant so reasonable a request: but, if you provoke me by refusal, I must be obliged to tell ye, that this lance, and this sword, guided by this invincible arm, shall force you to yield that to my valor which you deny to my civil entreaties."

"A very good jest indeed," cried the officer, "what a devil makes you dote at such a rate? Would you have us set at liberty the king's prisoners, as if we had authority to do it, or you to command it? Go, go about your business, good Sir Errant, and set your basin right upon your empty pate; and pray do not meddle any further in what does not concern you, for those who will play with cats must expect to be scratched."

"Thou art a cat, and rat, and a coward also," cried Don Quixote; and with that he attacked the officer with such a sudden and surprising fury, that before he had any time to put himself into a posture of defense, he struck him down dangerously wounded with his lance, and as fortune had ordered it, this happened to be the horseman who was armed with a carbine. His companions stood astonished at such a bold action, but at last fell upon the champion with their swords and darts, which might have proved fatal to him, had not the slaves laid hold of this opportunity to break the chain, in order to regain their liberty: for, the guards perceiving their endeavors to get loose, thought it more material to prevent them, than to be fighting a madman. But as he pressed them vigorously on one side, and the slaves were opposing them and freeing themselves on the other, the hurly-burly was so great, and the guards so perplexed, that they did nothing to the purpose. In the meantime Sancho was helping Gines de Passamonte to get off his chain, which he did sooner than can be imagined; and then that active desperado having seized the wounded officer's sword and carbine, he joined with Don Quixote, and sometimes aiming at one, and sometimes at the other, as if he had been ready to shoot them, yet still without letting off the piece, the other slaves at the same time pouring volleys of stone-shot at the guards, they betook themselves to their heels, leaving Don Quixote and the criminals masters of the field. Sancho, who was always for taking care of the main chance, was not at all pleased with this victory; for he guessed that the guards who were fled would raise a hue and cry, and soon be at their heels with the whole posse of the Holy Brotherhood, and lay them up for a rescue and rebellion. This made him advise his master to get out of the way as fast as he could, and hide himself in the neighboring mountains. "I hear you," answered Don Quixote to this motion of his squire, "and I know what I have to do." Then calling to him all the slaves, who by this time had uncased the keeper to his skin, they gathered about him to know his pleasure, and he spoke to them in this manner: "It is the part of generous spirits to have a grateful sense of the benefits they receive, no crime being more odious than ingratitude. You see, gentlemen, what I have done for your sakes, and you cannot but be sensible how highly you are obliged to me. Now all the recompense I require is only, that everyone of you, loaded with that chain from which I have freed your necks, do instantly repair to the city of Toboso; and there, presenting yourselves before the Lady Dulcinea del Toboso, tell her, that her faithful votary, the Knight of the Woeful Countenance, commanded you to wait on her, and assure her of his profound veneration. Then you shall give her an exact account of every particular relating to this famous achievement, by which you once more taste the sweets of liberty; which done, I give you leave to seek your fortunes where you please."

To this the ringleader and master-thief, Gines de Passamonte, made answer for all the rest. "What you would have us do," said he, "our noble deliverer, is absolutely impracticable and impossible; for we dare not be seen all together for the world. We must rather part, and skulk some one way, some another, and lie snug in creeks and corners underground, for fear of those damned manhounds that will be after us with a hue and cry; therefore all we can, and ought to do in this case, is to change this compliment and homage which you would have us pay to the Lady Dulcinea del Toboso, into a certain number of Ave Marias and Creeds, which we will say for your worship's benefit; and this may be done by night or by day, walking or standing, and in war as well as in peace: but to imagine we will return to our flesh-pots of Egypt, that is to say, take up our chains again, and lug them the devil knows where, is as unreasonable as to think it is night now at ten o'clock in the morning. 'Sdeath, to expect this from us, is to expect pears from an elm-tree." "Now, by my sword," replied Don Quixote, "Sir son of a whore, Sir Ginesillo de Parapilla, or whatever be your name, you yourself, alone, shall go to Toboso, like a dog that has scalded his tail, with the whole chain about your shoulders." Gines, who was naturally very choleric, judging, by Don Quixote's extravagance in freeing them, that he was not very wise, winked on his companions, who, like men that understood signs, presently fell back to the right and left, and pelted Don Quixote with such a shower of stones, that all his dexterity to cover himself with his shield was now ineffectual, and poor Rozinante no more obeyed the spur, than if he had been only the statue of a horse. As for Sancho, he got behind his ass, and there sheltered himself from the volleys of flints that threatened his bones, while his master was so battered, that in a little time he was thrown out of his saddle to the ground. He was no sooner down, but the student leaped on him, took off his

221

basin from his head, gave him three or four thumps on the shoulders with it, and then gave it so many knocks against the stones, that he almost broke it to pieces. After this, they stripped him of his upper coat, and had robbed him of his hose too, but that his greaves hindered them. They also eased Sancho of his upper coat, and left him in his doublet: then, having divided the spoils, they shifted everyone for himself, thinking more how to avoid being taken up, and linked again in the chain, than of trudging with it to my Lady Dulcinea del Toboso. Thus the ass, Rozinante, Sancho, and Don Quixote remained indeed masters of the field, but in an ill condition: the ass hanging his head, and pensive, shaking his ears now and then, as if the volleys of stones had still whizzed about them; Rozinante lying in a desponding manner, for he had been knocked down as well as his unhappy rider; Sancho uncased to his doublet, and trembling for fear of the Holy Brotherhood; and Don Quixote filled with sullen regret, to find himself so barbarously used by those whom he had so highly obliged.

IX: WHAT BEFELL THE RENOWNED DON QUIXOTE IN THE SIERRA MORENA (BLACK MOUNTAIN), BEING ONE OF THE RAREST ADVENTURES IN THIS AUTHENTIC HISTORY

Don Quixote finding himself so ill-treated, said to his squire: "Sancho, I have always heard it said, that to do a kindness to clowns is like throwing water into the sea. Had I given ear to thy advice, I had prevented this misfortune: but, since the thing is done, it is needless to repine; this shall be a warning to me for the future." "That is," quoth Sancho, "when the devil is blind: but, since you say you had escaped this mischief had you believed me, good sir, believe me now, and you will escape a greater; for I must tell you that those of the Holy Brotherhood do not stand in awe of your chivalry, nor do they care a straw for all the knights-errant in the world. Methinks I already hear their arrows whizzing about my ears."[1] "Thou art naturally a coward, Sancho," cried Don Quixote; "nevertheless, that thou mayest not say that I am obstinate, and never follow thy advice, I will take thy counsel, and for once convey myself out of the reach of this dreadful brotherhood that so strangely alarms thee; but upon this condition, that thou never tell any mortal creature, neither while I live nor after my death, that I withdraw myself from this danger through fear, but merely to comply with thy entreaties: for if thou ever presume to say otherwise, thou wilt belie me; and from this time to that time, and from that time to the world's end, I give thee the lie, and thou liest, and shalt lie in thy throat, as often as thou sayest or but thinkest to the contrary. Therefore do not offer to reply; for shouldst thou but surmise, that I would avoid any danger, and especially this, which seems to give some occasion or color for fear, I would certainly stay here, though unattended and alone, and expect and face not only the Holy Brotherhood, which thou dreadest so much, but also the fraternity, or twelve heads of the tribes of Israel, the seven Maccabees, Castor and Pollux, and all the brothers and brotherhoods in the universe." "If it please your worship," quoth Sancho, "to withdraw is not to run away, and to stay is no wise action when there is more reason to fear than to hope. It is the part of a wise man to keep himself today for tomorrow, and not venture all his eggs in one basket. And though I am

[1] *The troopers of the Holy Brotherhood ride with bows and arrows.*

but a clown, or a bumpkin, as you may say, yet I would have you
to know I know what is what, and have always taken care of the
main chance; therefore do not be ashamed of being ruled by me,
but even get on horseback if you are able: come, I will help you,
and then follow me; for my mind plaguely misgives me that now
one pair of heels will stand us in more stead than two pair of hands."

Don Quixote, without any reply, made shift to mount Rozinante,
and Sancho on his ass led the way to the neighboring mountainous
desert, called Sierra Morena,[2] which the crafty squire had a design
to cross over, and get out at the furthest end, either at Viso or Almodovar del Campo, and in the meantime to lurk in the craggy and
almost inaccessible retreats of that vast mountain, for fear of falling into the hands of the Holy Brotherhood. He was the more eager
to steer this course, finding that the provision which he had laid on

2 *Sierra, though Spanish for a mountain, properly means (not a chain, but) a saw,
from Latin* Serra, *because of its ridges rising and falling like the teeth of a saw. This
mountain (called Morena, from its Moorish or swarthy color) parts the kingdom of
Castile from the province of Andalusia.*

his ass had escaped plundering, which was a kind of miracle, considering how narrowly the galley-slaves had searched everywhere for booty. It was night before our two travelers got to the middle and most desert part of the mountain; where Sancho advised his master to stay some days, at least as long as their provisions lasted; and accordingly that night they took up their lodging between two rocks, among a great number of cork-trees: but Fortune, which, according to the opinion of those that have not the light of true faith, guides, appoints, and contrives all things as she pleases, directed Gines de Passamonte (that master rogue, who, thanks be to Don Quixote's force and folly, had been put in a condition to do him a mischief) to this very part of the mountain, in order to hide himself till the heat of the pursuit, which he had just cause to fear, was over. He discovered our adventurers much about the time that they fell asleep; and, as wicked men are always ungrateful, and urgent necessity prompts many to do things, at the very thoughts of which they perhaps would start at other times, Gines, who was a stranger both to gratitude and humanity, resolved to ride away with Sancho's ass; for, as for Rozinante, he looked upon him as a thing that would neither sell nor pawn: so while poor Sancho lay snoring, he spirited away his darling beast, and made such haste that before day he thought himself and his prize secure from the unhappy owner's pursuit.

Now Aurora with her smiling face returned to enliven and cheer the earth; but, alas! to grieve and affright Sancho with a dismal discovery: for he had no sooner opened his eyes, but he missed his ass, and finding himself deprived of that dear partner of his fortunes, and best comfort in his peregrinations, he broke out into the most pitiful and sad lamentations in the world; insomuch that he waked Don Quixote with his moans. "O dear child of my bowels," cried he, "born and bred under my roof, my children's playfellow, the comfort of my wife, the envy of my neighbors, the ease of my burdens, the staff of my life, and, in a word, half my maintenance! for, with six-and-twenty maravedis, which were daily earned by thee, I made shift to keep half my family." Don Quixote, who easily guessed the cause of these complaints, strove to comfort him with kind, condoling words, and learned discourses upon the uncertainty of human happiness: but nothing proved so effectual to assuage his sorrow, as the promise which his master made him of drawing a bill of exchange on his niece for three asses out of five which he had at home, payable to Sancho Panza, or his order; which prevailing argument soon dried up his tears, hushed his sighs and moans, and turned his complaints into thanks to his generous master for so unexpected a favor.

And now, as they wandered further in these mountains, Don Quixote was transported with joy to find himself where he might flatter his ambition with the hopes of fresh adventures to signalize his valor; for these vast deserts made him call to mind the wonderful exploits of other knights-errant performed in such solitudes. Filled with those airy notions, he thought on nothing else: but Sancho was for more substantial food; and now thinking himself quite out of the reach of the Holy Brotherhood, his only care was to fill his belly with the relics of the clerical booty; and thus, sitting sideling, as women do, upon his beast,[3] he slily took out now one piece of meat, then another, and kept his grinders going faster than his feet. Thus plodding on, he would not have given a rush to have met with any other adventure.

While he was thus employed, he observed that his master en-

[3] *It is scarce twenty lines since Sancho lost his ass and here he is upon his back again. This is a blunder, intentional or otherwise on the part of Cervantes.*

226

deavored to take up something that lay on the ground with the end of his lance: this made him run to help him to lift up the bundle, which proved to be a portmanteau and the seat of a saddle, that were half, or rather quite rotten with lying exposed to the weather. The portmanteau was somewhat heavy; and Don Quixote having ordered Sancho to see what it contained, though it was shut with a chain and a padlock, he easily saw what was in it through the cracks, and pulled out four fine holland shirts, and other clean and fashionable linen, besides a considerable quantity of gold tied up in a handkerchief. "Bless my eyesight!" quoth Sancho; "and now, Heaven, I thank thee for sending us such a lucky adventure once in our lives": with that, groping further in the portmanteau, he found a table-book richly bound. "Give me that," said Don Quixote, "and do thou keep the gold." "Heaven reward your worship," quoth Sancho, kissing his master's hand, and at the same time clapping up the linen and the other things into the bag where he kept the victuals. "I fancy," said Don Quixote, "that some person, having lost his way in these mountains, has been met by robbers who have murdered him, and buried his body somewhere hereabouts." "Sure your worship's mistaken," answered Sancho; "for had they been highwaymen, they would never have left such a booty behind them." "Thou art in the right," replied Don Quixote; "and therefore I cannot imagine what it must be. But stay, I will examine the table-book, perhaps we shall find something written in that which will help us to discover what I would know." With that he opened it, and the first thing he found was the following rough draft of a sonnet, fairly enough written to be read with ease: so he read it aloud, that Sancho might know what was in it as well as himself.

A SONNET

"Love is a god ne'er knows our pain,
Or cruelty's his darling attribute;
Else he'd ne'er force me to complain,
And to his spite my raging pain impute.
But sure, if Love's a god, he must
Have knowledge equal to his pow'r;
And 'tis a crime to think a god unjust:
Whence then the pains that now my heart devour?
From Phyllis? No: why do I pause?
Such cruel ills ne'er boast so sweet a cause;
Nor from the gods such torments we do bear,
Let death then quickly be my cure.
When thus we ills unknown endure,
'Tis shortest to despair."

"The devil of anything can be picked out of this," quoth Sancho, "unless you can tell who that same Phyll is." "I did not read 'Phyll,' but 'Phyllis,'" said Don Quixote. "Oh, then, mayhap, the man has lost his filly-foal." "Phyllis," said Don Quixote, "is the name of a lady that is beloved by the author of this sonnet, who truly seems to be a tolerable poet,[4] or I have but little judgment." "Why then," quoth Sancho, "belike your worship understands how to make verses, too?" "That I do," answered Don Quixote, "and better than thou imaginest, as thou shalt see, when I shall give thee a letter written all in verse to carry to my Lady Dulcinea del Toboso; for I must tell thee, friend Sancho, all the knights-errant, or at least, the greatest part of them, in former times, were great poets, and as great musicians: those qualifications, or, to speak better, those two gifts or accomplishments, being almost insepar-able from amorous adventures: though, I must confess, the

4 *Cervantes himself.*

verses of the knights in former ages are not altogether so polite, nor so adorned with words, as with thoughts and inventions."

"Good sir," quoth Sancho, "look again into the pocket-book, mayhap you will find somewhat that will inform you of what you would know." With that Don Quixote, turning over the leaf, "Here is some prose," cried he, "and I think it is the sketch of a love-letter." "O! good your worship," quoth Sancho, "read it out by all means; for I mightily delight in hearing of love-stories."

Don Quixote read it aloud, and found what follows:

"The falsehood of your promises, and my despair, hurry me from you forever; and you shall sooner hear the news of my death, than the cause of my complaints. You have forsaken me, ungrateful fair, for one more wealthy indeed, but not more deserving than your abandoned slave. Were virtue esteemed a treasure equal to its worth by your unthinking sex, I must presume to say, I should have no reason to envy the wealth of others, and no misfortune to bewail. What your beauty has raised, your actions have destroyed; the first made me mistake you for an angel, but the last convince me you are a very woman. However, O! too lovely disturber of my peace, may uninterrupted rest and downy ease engross your happy hours; and may forgiving Heaven still keep your husband's perfidiousness concealed, lest it should cost your repenting heart a sigh for the injustice you have done to so faithful a lover, and so I should be prompted to a revenge which I do not desire to take. Farewell."

"This letter," quoth Don Quixote, "does not give us any further insight into the things we would know; all I can infer from it is, that the person who wrote it was a betrayed lover"; and so, turning over the remaining leaves, he found several other letters and verses, some of which were legible, and some so scribbled, that he could

229

make nothing of them. As for those he read, he could meet with nothing in them but accusations, complaints, and expostulations, distrusts and jealousies, pleasures and discontents, favors and disdain, the one highly valued, the other as mournfully resented. And while the Knight was poring on the table-book, Sancho was rummaging the portmanteau and the seat of the saddle, with that exactness, that he did not leave a corner unsearched, nor a seam unripped, nor a single lock of wool unpicked; for the gold he had found, which was above a hundred ducats, had but whetted his greedy appetite, and made him wild for more. Yet though this was all he could find, he thought himself well paid for the more than Herculean labors he had undergone; nor could he now repine at his being tossed in a blanket, the straining and gripping operation of the balsam, the benedictions of pack-staves and levers, the fisticuffs of the lewd carrier, the loss of his cloak, his dear wallet, and of his dearer ass, and all the hunger, thirst, and fatigue which he had suffered in his kind master's service. On the other side, the Knight of the Woeful Figure strangely desired to know who was the owner of the portmanteau, guessing by the verses, the letter, the linen, and the gold, that he was a person of worth, whom the disdain and unkindness of his mistress had driven to despair. At length, however, he gave over the thoughts of it, discovering nobody through that vast desert; and so he rode on, wholly guided by Rozinante's discretion, which always made the grave sagacious creature choose the plainest and smoothest way; the master still firmly believing, that in those woody, uncultivated forests he should infallibly start some wonderful adventure.

And indeed, while these hopes possessed him, he spied upon the top of a stony crag just before him, a man that skipped from rock to rock, over briers and bushes, with wonderful agility. He seemed to him naked from the waist upwards, with a thick black beard, his hair long, and strangely tangled, his head, legs, and feet bare; on his hips a pair of breeches, that appeared to be of sad-colored velvet, but so tattered and torn, that they discovered his skin in many places. These particulars were observed by Don Quixote while he passed by: and he followed him, endeavoring to overtake him; for he presently guessed this was the owner of the portmanteau. But Rozinante, who was naturally slow and phlegmatic, was in too weak a case besides to run races with so swift an apparition: yet the Knight of the Woeful Figure resolved to find out that unhappy creature, though he were to bestow a whole year in the search; and, to that intent, he ordered Sancho to beat one side of the mountain, while he hunted the other. "In good sooth," quoth Sancho, "your worship must excuse me as to that; for if I but offer to stir an inch from you, I am almost frighted out of my seven senses: and let this serve you hereafter for a warning, that you may not send me a nail's breadth from your presence." "Well," said the Knight, "I will take thy case into consideration; and it does not displease me, Sancho, to see thee thus rely upon my valor, which I dare assure thee shall never fail thee, though thy very soul should be scared out of thy body. Follow me, therefore, step by step, with as much haste as is consistent with good speed; and let thy eyes pry everywhere while we search every part of this rock, where, it is probable, we may meet with that wretched mortal, who, doubtless, is the owner of the portmanteau."

"Odsnigs, sir," quoth Sancho, "I had rather get out of his way; for should we chance to meet him, and he lay claim to the portmanteau, it is a plain case I shall be forced to part with the money: and therefore I think it much better, without making so much ado, to let me keep it *bona fide*, till we can light on the right owner some more easy way, and without dancing after him; which may not happen till we spend all the money; and in that case I am free from the law, and he may go whistle for it." "Thou art mistaken, Sancho," cried Don Quixote; "for, seeing we have some reason to think that

231

we know who is the owner, we are bound in conscience to endeavor to find him out, and restore it to him; the rather, because should we not now strive to meet him, yet the strong presumption we have that the goods belong to him, would make us possessors of them *mala fide,* and render us as guilty as if the party whom we suspect to have lost the things were really the right owner; therefore, friend Sancho, do not think much of searching for him, since if we find him out, it will extremely ease my mind." With that he spurred Rozinante; and Sancho, not very well pleased, followed him, comforting himself, however, with the hopes of the three asses which his master had promised him. So when they had ridden over the greatest part of the mountain, they came to a brook, where they found a mule lying dead, with her saddle and bridle about her, and herself half devoured by beasts and birds of prey; which discovery further confirmed them in their suspicion, that the man who fled so nimbly from them was the owner of the mule and portmanteau. Now, as they paused and pondered upon this, they heard a whistling like that of some shepherd keeping his flocks; and presently after, upon their left hand, they spied a great number of goats, with an old herdsman after them, on the top of the mountain. Don Quixote called out to him, and desired him to come down; but the goatherd, instead of answering him, asked them in as loud a tone, how they came thither in those deserts, where scarce any living creatures resorted except goats, wolves, and other wild beasts? Sancho told him they would satisfy him as to that point, if he would come where they were. With that the goatherd came down to them; and seeing them look upon the dead mule, "That dead mule," said the old fellow, "has lain in that very place these six months; but pray tell me, good people, have you not met the master of it by the way?" "We have met nobody," answered Don Quixote; "but we found a portmanteau and a saddle-cushion not far from this place." "I have seen it too," quoth the goatherd, "but I never durst meddle with it, nor so much as come near it, for fear of some misdemeanor, lest I should be charged with having stolen somewhat out of it: for who knows what might happen? The devil is subtle, and sometimes lays baits in our way to tempt, or blocks to make us stumble." "It is just so with me, gaffer," quoth Sancho; "for I saw the portmanteau too, do ye see, but the devil a bit would I come within a stone's throw of it; no, there I found it, and there I left it; in faith, it shall even lie there still for me. He that steals a bellwether shall be discovered by the bell." "Tell me, honest friend," asked Don Quixote, "dost thou know who is the owner of those things?" "All I know of the matter," answered the goatherd, "is, that it is now six months, little more or less, since to a certain sheep-fold, some three leagues off, there came a young, well-featured, proper gentleman in good clothes, and under him the same mule that now lies dead here, with the cushion and cloak-bag, which you say you met, but touched not. He asked us which was the most desert and least frequented part of these mountains; and we told him this where we are now; and in that we spoke the plain truth, for should you venture to go but half a league further, you would hardly be able to get back again in haste; and I marvel how you could get even thus far; for there is neither highway nor footpath that may direct a man this way. Now as soon as the young gentleman had heard our answer, he turned about his mule, and made to the place we showed him, leaving us all with a hugeous liking for his comeliness, and strangely marveling at his demand, and the haste he made towards the middle of the mountain. After that we heard no more of him for a great while, till one day by chance one of the shepherds coming by, he fell upon him, without saying why, or wherefore, and beat him without mercy: after that he went to the ass that carried our victuals, and taking away all the bread and cheese that was there, he tripped back again to the mountain with wondrous speed. Hearing this, a good number of us together

233

resolved to find him out; and when we had spent the best part of two days in the thickest of the forest, we found him at last lurking in the hollow of a huge cork-tree, from whence he came forth to meet us as mild as could be. But then he was so altered, his face was so disfigured, wan, and sunburnt, that had it not been for his attire, which we made shift to know again, though it was all in rags and tatters, we could not have thought it had been the same man. He saluted us courteously, and told us, in few words, mighty handsomely put together, that we were not to marvel to see him in that manner, for that it behoved him so to be, that he might fulfill a certain penance enjoined him for the great sins he had committed. We prayed him to tell us who he was, but he would by no means do it: we likewise desired him to let us know where we might find him, that whensoever he wanted victuals we might bring him some, which we told him we would be sure to do; for otherwise he would be starved in that barren place; requesting him, that if he did not like that motion neither, he would, at least, come and ask us for what he wanted, and not take it by force as he had done. He thanked us heartily for our offer, and begged pardon for that injury, and promised to ask it henceforwards as an alms, without setting upon anyone. As for his place of abode, he told us, he had none certain, but wherever night caught him, there he lay: and he ended his discourse with such bitter moans, that we must have had hearts of flint had we not had a feeling of them, and kept him company therein; chiefly, considering him so strangely altered from what we had seen him before: for, as I said, he was a very fine comely young man, and by his speech and behavior we could guess him to be wellborn, and a court-like sort of a body: for though we were but clowns, yet such was his genteel behavior, that we could not help being taken with it. Now as he was talking to us, he stopped of a sudden, as if he had been struck dumb, fixing his eyes steadfastly on the ground; whereat we all stood in amaze. After he had thus

234

stared a good while he shut his eyes, then opened them again, bit his lips, knit his brows, clutched his fists; and then rising from the ground, whereon he had thrown himself a little before, he flew at the man that stood next to him with such fury that if we had not pulled him off by main force, he would have bit and thumped him to death; and all the while he cried out, 'Ah! traitor Ferdinand, here, here thou shalt pay for the wrong thou hast done me: I must rip up that false heart of thine!' And a deal more he added, all in dispraise of that same Ferdinand. After that he flung from us without saying a word, leaping over the bushes and brambles at such a strange rate, that it was impossible for us to come at him; from which we gathered that his madness comes on him by fits, and that same one called Ferdinand had done him an ill-turn that hath brought the poor young man to this pass. And this hath been confirmed since that many and many times; for when he is in his right senses he will come and beg for victuals, and thank us for it with tears. But when he is in his mad fit, he will beat us, though we proffer him meat civilly: and to tell you the truth, sirs," added the goatherd, "I and four others, of whom two are my men, and the other two my friends, yesterday agreed to look for him till we should find him out, either by fair means or by force to carry him to Almodovar town, that is but eight leagues off; and there we will have him cured, if possible, or at least we shall learn what he is when he comes to his wits, and whether he has any friends to whom he may be sent back. This is all I know of the matter; and I dare assure you that the owner of those things which you saw in the way, is the self-same body that went so nimbly by you"; for Don Quixote had by this time acquainted the goatherd of his having seen that man skipping among the rocks.

The Knight was wonderfully concerned when he had heard the goatherd's story, and renewed his resolution of finding out that distracted wretch, whatever time and pains it might cost him. But

235

fortune was more propitious to his desires than he could reasonably have expected: for, just as they were speaking, they spied him right against the place where they stood, coming towards them out of the cleft of a rock, muttering somewhat to himself, which they could not well have understood had they stood close by him, much less could they guess his meaning at that distance. His apparel was such as has already been said, only Don Quixote observed, when he drew nearer, that he had on a shamoy waistcoat torn in many places, which yet the Knight found to be perfumed with amber; and by this, as also by the rest of his clothes, and other conjectures, he judged him to be a man of some quality. As soon as the unhappy creature came near them, he saluted them very civilly, but with a hoarse voice. Don Quixote returned his civilities, and, alighting from Rozinante, accosted him in a very graceful manner, and hugged him close in his arms, as if he had been one of his intimate acquaintance. The other, whom we may venture to call the Knight of the Ragged Figure, as well as Don Quixote the Knight of the Woeful Figure, having got loose from that embrace, could not forbear stepping back a little, and laying his hands on the champion's shoulders, he stood staring in his face, as if he had been striving to call to mind whether he had known him before, probably wondering as much to behold Don Quixote's countenance, armor, and strange figure, as Don Quixote did to see his tattered condition: but the first that opened his mouth after this pause was the ragged knight, as you shall find by the sequel of the story.

X: THE ADVENTURE IN THE SIERRA MORENA CONTINUED

The history relates, that Don Quixote listened with great attention to the disastrous knight of the mountain, who made him the following compliment, "Truly, sir, whoever you be (for I have not the honor to know you) I am much obliged to you for your expressions of civility and friendship; and I could wish I were in a condition to convince you otherwise than by words of the deep sense I have of them! But my bad fortune leaves me nothing to return for so many favors, but unprofitable wishes." "Sir," answered Don Quixote, "I have so hearty a desire to serve you, that I was fully resolved not to depart from these mountains till I had found you out, that I might know from you whether the discontents that have urged you to make choice of this unusual course of life, might not admit of a remedy; for, if they do, assure yourself I will leave no means untried, till I have purchased you that ease which I heartily wish you: or if your disasters are of that fatal kind that exclude you for ever from the hopes of comfort or relief, then will I mingle sorrows with you, and by sharing your load of grief, help you to bear the oppressing weight of affliction: for it is the only comfort of the miserable to have partners in their woes. If then good intentions may plead merit, or a grateful requital, let me entreat you, sir, by that generous nature that shoots through the gloom with which adversity has clouded your graceful outside; nay, let me conjure you by the darling object of your wishes, to let me know who you are, and what strange misfortunes have urged you to withdraw from the converse of your fellow-creatures, to bury yourself alive in this horrid solitude, where you linger out a wretched being, a stranger to ease, to all mankind, and even to your very self. And I solemnly swear," added Don Quixote, "by the order of knighthood, of which I am an unworthy professor, that if you so far gratify my desires, I will assist you to the utmost of my capacity, either by remedying your disaster, if it is not past redress; or at least, I will become your partner in sorrow, and strive to ease it by a society in sadness."

The Knight of the Wood, hearing the Knight of the Woeful

Figure talk at that rate, looked upon him steadfastly for a long time, and viewed and reviewed him from head to foot; and when he had gazed a great while upon him, "Sir," cried he, "if you have anything to eat, for Heaven's sake give it me, and when my hunger is abated, I shall be better able to comply with your desires, which your great civilities and undeserved offers oblige me to satisfy." Sancho and the goatherd hearing this, presently took out some victuals, the one out of his bag, the other out of his scrip, and gave it to the ragged knight to allay his hunger, who immediately fell on with that greedy haste, that he seemed rather to devour than to feed; for he used no intermission between bite and bite, so greedily he chopped them up: and all the time he was eating, neither he, nor the by-standers, spoke the least word. When he had assuaged his voracious appetite, he beckoned to Don Quixote and the rest to follow him; and after he had brought them to a neighboring meadow, he laid himself at his ease on the grass, where the rest of the company sitting down by him, neither he nor they having yet spoken a word since he fell to eating, he began in this manner:

"Gentlemen," said he, "if you intend to be informed of my misfortunes, you must promise me before-hand not to cut off the thread of my doleful narration with any questions, or any other interruption; for in the very instant that any of you do it, I shall leave off abruptly; and will not afterwards go on with the story." This preamble put Don Quixote in mind of Sancho's ridiculous tale, which by his neglect in not telling the goats, was brought to an untimely conclusion. "I only use this precaution," added the ragged knight, "because I would be quick in my relation; for the very remembrance of my former misfortune proves a new one to me, and yet I promise you I will endeavor to omit nothing that is material, that you may have as full an account of my disasters as I am sensible you desire." Thereupon Don Quixote, for himself and the rest, having promised him uninterrupted attention, he proceeded in this manner: "My name is Cardenio, the place of my birth one of the best cities in Andalusia; my descent noble,[1] my parents wealthy; but my misfortunes are so great, that they have doubtless filled my relations with the deepest of sorrows; nor are they to be remedied with wealth, for goods of fortune avail but little against the anger of Heaven. In the same town dwelt the charming Lucinda, the most beautiful creature that ever nature framed, equal in descent and fortune to myself, but more happy and less constant. I loved, nay adored her almost from her infancy; and from her tender years she blessed me with as kind a return as is suitable with the innocent freedom of that age. Our parents were conscious of that early friendship; nor did they oppose the growth of this inoffensive passion, which they perceived could have no other consequences than a happy union of our families by marriage; a thing which the equality of our births and fortunes did indeed of itself almost invite us to. Afterwards our loves so grew up with our years, that Lucinda's father, either judging our usual familiarity prejudicial to his daughter's honor, or for some other reasons, sent to desire me to discontinue my frequent visits to his house: but this restraint proved but like that which was used by the parents of that loving Thisbe, so celebrated by the poets, and but added flames to flames, and impatience to desires. As our tongues were now debarred their former privilege, we had recourse to our pens, which assumed the greater freedom to disclose the most hidden secrets of our hearts; for the presence of the beloved object often heightens a certain awe and bashfulness, that disorders, confounds and strikes dumb even the most passionate lover. How many letters have I writ to that lovely charmer! how many soft moving verses have I addressed to her! what kind, yet honorable returns have I received from her! The mutual pledges of our secret loves, and the innocent consolations of a violent passion. At length, lan-

[1] *In Spain all the gentry are called noble.*

239

guishing and wasting with desire, deprived of that reviving comfort of my soul, I resolved to remove those bars with which her father's care and decent caution obstructed my only happiness, by demanding her of him in marriage. He very civilly told me, that he thanked me for the honor I did him, but that I had a father alive, whose consent was to be obtained as well as his, and who was the most proper person to make such a proposal. I thanked him for his civil answer, and thought it carried some show of reason, not doubting but my father would readily consent to the proposal. I therefore immediately went to wait on him, with a design to beg his approbation and assistance. I found him in his chamber, with a letter opened before him, which, as soon as he saw me, he put into my hand, before I could have time to acquaint him with my business. 'Cardenio,' said he, 'you will see by this letter the extraordinary kindness that Duke Ricardo has for you.' I suppose I need not tell you, gentlemen, that this Duke Ricardo is a grandee of Spain, most of whose estate lies in the best part of Andalusia. I read the letter, and found it contained so kind and advantageous an offer, that my father could not but accept of it with thankfulness: for the Duke entreated him to send me to him with all speed, that I might be the companion of his eldest son, promising withal to advance me to a post answerable to the good opinion he had of me. This unexpected news struck me dumb; but my surprise and disappointment were much greater, when I heard my father say to me, 'Cardenio, you must get ready to be gone in two days: in the meantime, give Heaven thanks for opening you a way to that preferment which I am so sensible you deserve.' After this he gave me several wise admonitions, both as a father and a man of business, and then he left me. The day fixed for my journey quickly came; however, the night that preceded it, I spoke to Lucinda at her window, and told her what had happened. I also gave her father a visit, and informed him of it too, beseeching him to preserve his good opinion of me, and defer the bestowing of his daughter till I had been with Duke Ricardo, which he kindly promised me: and then Lucinda and I, after an exchange of vows and protestations of eternal fidelity, took our leaves of each other with all the grief which two tender and passionate lovers can feel at a separation.

"I left the town, and went to wait upon the Duke, who received and entertained me with that extraordinary kindness and civility that soon raised the envy of his greatest favorites. But he that most endearingly caressed me, was Don Ferdinand, the Duke's second son, a young, airy, handsome, generous gentleman, and of a very amorous disposition: he seemed to be overjoyed at my coming, and in a most obliging manner told me, he would have me one of his most intimate friends. In short, he so really convinced me of his affection, that though his elder brother gave me many testimonies of love and esteem, yet could I easily distinguish between their favors. Now, as it is common for bosom friends to keep nothing secret from each other, Don Ferdinand relying as much on my fidelity, as I had reason to depend on his, revealed to me his most private thoughts; and among the rest, his being in love with the daughter of a very rich farmer, who was his father's vassal. The beauty of that lovely country maid, her virtue, her discretion, and the other graces of her mind, gained her the admiration of all those who approached her; and those uncommon endowments had so charmed the soul of Don Ferdinand, that, finding it absolutely impossible to corrupt her chastity, since she would not yield to his embraces as a mistress, he resolved to marry her. I thought myself obliged by all the ties of gratitude and friendship to dissuade him from so unsuitable a match; and therefore I made use of such arguments as might have diverted anyone but so confirmed a lover from such an unequal choice. At last, finding them all ineffectual, I resolved to inform the Duke, his father, with his inten-

241

tions: but Don Ferdinand was too clear-sighted not to read my design in my great dislike of his resolutions; and dreading such a discovery, which he knew my duty to his father might well warrant, in spite of our intimacy, since I looked upon such a marriage as highly prejudicial to them both, he made it his business to hinder me from betraying his passion to his father, assuring me there would be no need to reveal it to him. To blind me the more effectually, he told me he was willing to try the power of absence, that common cure of love, thereby to wear out and lose his unhappy passion; and that in order to do this, he would take a journey with me to my father's house, pretending to buy horses in our town, where the best in the world are bred. No sooner had I heard this plausible proposal but I approved it, swayed by the interest of my own love, that made me fond of an opportunity to see my absent Lucinda. I have heard since, that Don Ferdinand had already been blessed by his mistress with all the liberty of boundless love, upon a promise of marriage, and that he only waited an opportunity to discover it with safety, being afraid of incurring his father's indignation. But as what we call love in young men, is too often only an irregular passion, and boiling desire, that has no other object than sensual pleasure, and vanishes with enjoyment, while real love, fixing itself on the perfections of the mind, is still improving and permanent; as soon as Don Ferdinand had accomplished his lawless desires, his strong affection slackened, and his hot love grew cold: so that if at first his proposing to try the power of absence was only a pretense, to get rid of his passion, there was nothing now which he more heartily coveted, than that he might thereby avoid fulfilling his promise. And therefore, having obtained the Duke's leave, away we posted to my father's house, where Don Ferdinand was entertained according to his quality; and I went to visit my Lucinda, who, by a thousand innocent endearments, made me sensible, that her love, like mine, was rather heightened than weakened by absence, if anything could heighten a love so great and so perfect. I then thought myself obliged by the laws of friendship, not to conceal the secrets of my heart from so kind and intimate a friend, who had so generously entrusted me with his; and therefore, to my eternal ruin, I unhappily discovered to him my passion. I praised Lucinda's beauty, her wit, her virtue, and praised them so like a lover, so often, and so highly, that I raised in him a great desire to see so accomplished a lady; and, to gratify his curiosity, I showed her to him by the help of a light one evening, at a low window, where we used to have our amorous interviews. She proved but too charming, and too strong a temptation to Don Ferdinand; and her prevailing image made so deep an impression on his soul, that it was sufficient to blot out of his mind all those beauties that had till then employed his wanton thoughts: he was struck dumb with wonder and delight, at the sight of the ravishing apparition; and, in short, to see her and to love her proved with him the same thing: and, when I say to love her, I need not add to desperation, for there is no loving her but to an extreme. If her face made him so soon take fire, her wit quickly set him all in a flame. He often importuned me to communicate to him some of her

243

letters, which I indeed would never expose to any eyes but my own; but unhappily one day he found one, wherein she desired me to demand her of her father, and to hasten the marriage. It was penned with that tenderness and discretion, that when he had read it, he presently cried out, that the amorous charms which were scattered and divided among other beauties, were all divinely centered in Lucinda, and in Lucinda alone. Shall I confess a shameful truth? Lucinda's praises, though never so deserved, did not sound pleasantly to my ears out of Don Ferdinand's mouth. I began to entertain I know not what distrusts and jealous fears, the rather, because he would be still improving the least opportunity of talking of her, and insensibly turning the discourse he held of other matters, to make her the subject, though never so far fetched, of our constant talk. Not that I was apprehensive of the least infidelity from Lucinda: far from it; she gave me daily fresh assurances of her inviolable affection; but I feared everything from my malignant stars, and lovers are commonly industrious to make themselves uneasy.

"It happened one day, that Lucinda, who took great delight in reading books of knight-errantry, desired me to lend her the 'Romance of Amadis de Gaul'——"

Scarce had Cardenio mentioned knight-errantry, when Don Quixote interrupted him: "Sir," said he, "had you but told me, when you first mentioned the lady Lucinda, that she was an admirer of books of knight-errantry, there had been no need of using any amplification to convince me of her being a person of uncommon sense: yet, sir, had she not used those mighty helps, those infallible guides to sense, though indulgent nature had strove to bless her with the richest gifts she can bestow, I might justly enough have doubted whether her perfections could have gained her the love of a person of your merit: but now you need not employ your eloquence to set forth the greatness of her beauty, the excellence of her worth, or the depth of her sense: for, from this account which I have of her taking great delight in reading books of chivalry, I dare pronounce her to be the most beautiful, nay, the most accomplished lady in the universe: and I heartily could have wished that with 'Amadis de Gaul' you had sent her the worthy 'Don Rugel of Greece'; for I am certain the lady Lucinda would have been extremely delighted with Daryda and Garaya, as also with the discreet Darinel, and those admirable verses of his Bucolics, which he sung and repeated with so good a grace: but a time may yet be found to give her the satisfaction of reading those master-pieces, if you will do me the honor to come to my house; for there I may supply you with above three hundred volumes, which are my soul's greatest delight, and the darling comfort of my life; though now I remember myself, I have just reason to fear there is not one of them left in my study, thanks to the malicious envy of wicked enchanters. I beg your pardon for giving you this interruption, contrary to my promise; but when I hear the least mention made of knight-errantry, it is no more in my power to forbear speaking, than it is in the sunbeams not to warm, or in those of the moon not to impart her natural humidity; and therefore, sir, I beseech you to go on."

While Don Quixote was running on with this impertinent digression, Cardenio hung down his head on his breast with all the signs of a man lost in sorrow; nor could Don Quixote with repeated entreaties persuade him to look up, or answer a word. At last, after he had stood thus a considerable while, he raised his head, and suddenly breaking silence, "I am positively convinced," cried he, "nor shall any man in the world ever persuade me to the contrary; and he is a blockhead who says, that great villain Mr. Elisabat[2] never lay with Queen Madasima."

2 *Elisabat is a skillful physician in "Amadis de Gaul," who performs wonderful cures; and Queen Madasima is wife to Gantasis, and makes a great figure in the aforesaid romance. They travel and lie together in woods and deserts, without any imputation on her honor.*

"It is false!" cried Don Quixote, in a mighty heat: "by all the powers above, it is all scandal and base detraction to say this of Queen Madasima. She was a most noble and virtuous lady; nor is it to be presumed that so great a princess would ever debase herself so far as to fall in love with a quack. Whoever dares to say she did, lies like an arrant villain; and I will make him acknowledge it either on foot or horseback, armed or unarmed, by night or by day, or how he pleases." Cardenio very earnestly fixed his eyes on Don Quixote, while he was thus defying him and taking Queen Madasima's part, as if she had been his true and lawful princess; and being provoked by these abuses into one of his mad fits, he took up a great stone that lay by him, and hit Don Quixote such a blow on his breast with it, that it beat him down backwards. Sancho, seeing his lord and master so roughly handled, fell upon the mad knight with his clenched fists; but he beat him off at the first onset, and laid him at his feet with a single blow, and then fell a-trampling on his guts, like a baker in a dough-trough. Nay, the goatherd who was offering to take Sancho's part, had like to have been served in the same manner. So the ragged knight, having tumbled them one over another and beaten them handsomely, left them, and ran into the wood without the least opposition.

Sancho got up when he saw him gone, and being very much out of humor to find himself so roughly handled without any manner of reason, began to pick a quarrel with the goatherd, railing at him for not forewarning them of the ragged knight's mad fits, that they might have stood upon their guard. The goatherd answered, he had given them warning at first, and, if he could not hear, it was no fault of his. To this Sancho replied, and the goatherd made a rejoinder, till from *pro* and *con* they fell to a warmer way of disputing, and went to fisticuffs together, catching one another by the beards, and tugging, hauling, and belaboring one another so unmercifully, that had not Don Quixote parted them, they would

have pulled one another's chins off. Sancho in great wrath, still
keeping his hold, cried to his master, "Let me alone, Sir Knight
of the Woeful Figure. This is no dubbed knight, but an ordinary
fellow like myself; that I may be revenged on him for the wrong
he has done me, let me box it out, and fight him fairly hand to fist
like a man." "Thou mayest fight him as he is thy equal," answered

Don Quixote, "but thou oughtest not to do it, since he has done us
no wrong." After this he pacified them; and then, addressing himself to the goatherd, he asked him whether it were possible to find
out Cardenio again, that he might hear the end of his story? The
goatherd answered that, as he already told him, he knew of no
settled place he used, but that if they made any stay thereabouts,
he might be sure to meet with him, mad or sober, sometime or other.

XI: OF THE STRANGE THINGS THAT HAPPENED TO THE VALIANT KNIGHT OF LA MANCHA IN THE BLACK MOUNTAIN: AND OF THE PENANCE HE DID THERE, IN IMITATION OF BELTENEBROS, OR THE LOVELY OBSCURE

Don Quixote took leave of the goatherd, and having mounted Rozinante, commanded Sancho to follow him, which he did, but with no very good will, his master leading him into the roughest and most craggy part of the mountain. Thus they traveled for a while without speaking a word to each other. Sancho, almost dead, and ready to burst for want of a little chat, waited with great impatience till his master should begin, not daring to speak first, since his strict injunction of silence. But at last, not being able to keep his word any longer, "Good your worship," quoth he, "give me your blessing and leave to begone, I beseech you, that I may go home to my wife and children, where I may talk till I am weary, and nobody can hinder me; for I must needs tell you, that for you to think to lead me a jaunt through hedge and ditch, over hills and dales, by night and by day, without daring to open my lips, is to bury me alive. Could beasts speak, as they did in Æsop's time, it would not have been half so bad with me; for then might I have communed with my ass as I pleased, and have forgot my ill-fortune: but to trot on in this fashion all the days of my life, after adventures, and to light on nothing but thumps, kicks, cuffs, and be tossed in a blanket; and after all, forsooth, to have a man's mouth sewed up, without daring to speak one's mind, I say it again, no living soul can endure it." "I understand thee, Sancho," answered Don Quixote, "thou lingerest with impatience to exercise thy talking faculty. Well, I am willing to free thy tongue from this restraint that so cruelly pains thee, upon condition, that the time of this license shall not extend beyond that of our continuance in these mountains." "A match," quoth Sancho; "let us make hay while the sun shines, I will talk whilst I may; what I may do hereafter Heaven knows best." And so beginning to take the benefit of his privilege, "Pray, sir," quoth he, "what occasion had you to take so hotly the part of Queen Magimasa, or what do ye call her? What a devil was it to you, whether that same master Abbot [1] was her friend in a corner or no? Had you taken no notice of what was said, as you might well have done, seeing it was no business of yours, the madman would have gone on with his story, you had missed a good thump on the breast, and I had escaped some five or six good dowses on the chaps, besides the trampling of my puddings." "Upon my honor, friend Sancho," replied Don Quixote, "didst thou but know, as well as I do, what a virtuous and eminent lady Queen Madasima was, thou wouldst say I had a great deal of patience, seeing I did not strike that profane wretch on the mouth, out of which such blasphemies proceeded: for, in short, it was the highest piece of detraction, to say that a queen was scandalously familiar with a barber-surgeon: for the truth of the story is, that this Mr. Elisabat, of whom the madman spoke, was a person of extraordinary prudence and sagacity, and physician to that queen, who also made use of his advice in matters of importance; but to say she gave him up her honor, and prostituted herself to the embraces of a man of such an inferior degree, was an impudent, groundless, and slanderous accusation, worthy the severest punishment. Neither can I believe that Cardenio knew what he said, when he charged the queen with that debasing guilt: for, it is plain that his raving fit had disordered the seat of his understand-

[1] *Sancho, remembering only the latter part of Mr. Elisabat's name, pleasantly calls him "Abad," which is Spanish for an Abbot. Abad sounds like the end of Elisabat.*

ing." "Why, there it is," quoth Sancho; "who but a madman would have minded what a madman said? What if the flint that hit you on the breast had dashed out your brains? we had been in a dainty pickle for taking the part of that same lady, with a pease-cod in her: nay, and Cardenio would have come off too, had he knocked you on the head; for the law has nothing to do with madmen." "Sancho," replied Don Quixote, "we knights-errant are obliged to vindicate the honor of women of what quality soever, as well against madmen as against men in their senses; much more queens of that magnitude and extraordinary worth, as Queen Madasima, for whose rare endowments I have a peculiar veneration; for she was a most beautiful lady, discreet and prudent to admiration, and behaved herself with an exemplary patience in all her misfortunes. It was then that the company and wholesome counsels of Mr. Elisabat proved very useful to alleviate the burden of her afflictions: from which the ignorant and ill-meaning vulgar took occasion to suspect and rumor, that she was guilty of an unlawful commerce with him. But I say once more, they lie, and lie a thousand times, whoever they be, that shall presumptuously report, or hint, or so much as think or surmise so base a calumny."

"Why," quoth Sancho, "I neither say nor think one way nor the other, not I: let them that say it, eat the lie, and swallow it with their bread. If they lay together, they have answered for it before now. I never thrust my nose into other men's porridge. It is no bread and butter of mine. Every man for himself, and God for us all, say I; for he that buys and lies, finds it in his purse. Let him that owns the cow take her by the tail. Naked came I into the world, and naked must I go out. Many think to find flitches of bacon, where there is not so much as the racks to lay them on: but who can hedge in a cuckoo? Little said is soon mended. It is a sin to belie the devil, but misunderstanding brings lies to the town, and there is no padlocking of people's mouths: for a close mouth catches no flies."

"Bless me," cried Don Quixote, "what a catalogue of musty proverbs hast thou run through! What a heap of frippery-ware hast thou threaded together, and how wide from the purpose! I pray thee have done, and for the future let thy whole study be to spur thy ass, nor do thou concern thyself with things that are out of thy sphere: and with all thy five senses remember this, that whatsoever I do, have done, and shall do, is no more than what is the result of mature consideration, and strictly conformable to the laws of chivalry, which I understand better than all the knights that ever professed knight-errantry." "Ay, ay, sir," quoth Sancho; "but, pray, is it a good law of chivalry that says we shall wander up and down, over bushes and briars, in this rocky wilderness, where there is neither footpath nor horse-way, running after a madman; who, if we light on him again, may chance to make an end of what he has begun, not of his tale of a roasted horse I mean, but of belaboring you and me thoroughly, and squeezing out my guts at both ends?" "Once more, I pray thee, have done," said Don Quixote. "I have business of greater moment than the finding this frantic man. It is not so much that business that detains me in this barren and desolate wild, as a desire I have to perform a certain and heroic deed that shall immortalize my fame, and make it fly to the remotest regions of the habitable globe; nay, it shall seal and confirm the most complete and absolute knight-errant in the world." "But is not this same adventure very dangerous?" asked Sancho. "Not at all," replied Don Quixote; "though, as fortune may order it, our expectations may be baffled by disappointing accidents, but the main thing consists in thy diligence." "My diligence?" quoth Sancho. "I mean," said Don Quixote, "that if thou returnest with all the speed imaginable from the place whither I design to send thee, my pain will soon be at an end, and

251

my glory begin. And because I do not doubt thy zeal for advancing thy master's interest, I will no longer conceal my design from thee. Know then, my faithful squire, that Amadis de Gaul was one of the most accomplished knights-errant; nay, I should not have said he was one of them, but the most perfect, the chief, and prince of them all. And let not the Belianises, nor any others, pretend to stand in competition with him for the honor of priority; for, to my knowledge, should they attempt it, they would be egregiously in the wrong. I must also inform thee that when a painter studies to excel and grow famous in his art, he takes care to imitate the best originals; which rule ought likewise to be observed in all other arts and sciences that serve for the ornament of well-regulated commonwealths. Thus he that is ambitious of gaining the reputation of a prudent and patient man, ought to propose to himself to imitate Ulysses, in whose person and troubles Homer has admirably delineated a perfect pattern and prototype of wisdom and heroic patience. So Virgil, in his Æneas, has given the world a rare example of filial piety, and of the sagacity of a valiant and experienced general, both the Greek and Roman poets representing their heroes not such as they really were, but such as they should be, to remain examples of virtue to ensuing ages. In the same manner, Amadis, having been the Polar star, and sun, of valorous and amorous knights, it is him we ought to set before our eyes as our great example, all of us that fight under the banner of love and chivalry; for it is certain that the adventurer who shall emulate him best, shall consequently arrive nearest the perfection of knight-errantry. Now, Sancho, I find that among the things which most displayed that champion's prudence and fortitude, his constancy and love, and his other heroic virtues, none was more remarkable than his retiring from his disdainful Oriana, to do penance on the Poor Rock, changing his name into that of Beltenebros, or The Lovely Obscure, a title certainly most significant, and adapted to the life which he then intended to lead. So I am resolved to imitate him in this, the rather because I think it a more easy task than it would be to copy after his other achievements, such as cleaving the bodies of giants, cutting off the heads of dragons, killing dreadful monsters, routing armies, dispersing navies, and breaking the force of magic spells. And, since these mountainous wilds offer me so fair an opportunity, I see no reason why I should neglect it; and therefore I will lay hold on it now." "Very well," quoth Sancho; "but pray, sir, what is that you mean to do in this fag-end of the world?" "Have I not already told thee," answered Don Quixote, "that I intend to copy Amadis in his madness, despair, and fury? Nay, at the same time I will imitate the valiant Orlando Furioso's extravagance, when he ran mad, after he had found the unhappy tokens of the fair Angelica's dishonorable commerce with Medoro at the fountain; at which time, in his frantic despair, he tore up trees by the roots, troubled the waters of the clear fountains, slew the shepherds, destroyed their flocks, fired their huts, demolished houses, drove their horses before him, and committed a hundred thousand other extravagancies worthy to be recorded in the eternal register of fame. Not that I intend, however, in all things to imitate Roldan, or Orlando, or Rotoland (for he had all those names), but only to make choice of such frantic effects of his amorous despair, as I shall think most essential and worthy imitation. Nay, perhaps, I shall wholly follow Amadis, who, without launching out into such destructive and fatal ravings, and only expressing his anguish in complaints and lamentations, gained nevertheless, a renown equal, if not superior, to that of the greatest heroes."

"Sir," quoth Sancho, "I dare say the knights who did these penances had some reason to be mad; but what need have you to be mad too? What lady has sent you a-packing, or so much as slighted you? When did you ever find that my Lady Dulcinea del

253

Toboso did otherwise than she should do, with either Moor[2] or Christian?" "Why, there is the point!" cried Don Quixote. "In this consists the singular perfection of my undertaking: for, mark me, Sancho, for a knight-errant to run mad upon any just occasion, is neither strange nor meritorious; no, the rarity is to run mad without a cause, without the least constraint or necessity. There is a refined and exquisite passion for you, Sancho! For thus my mistress must needs have a vast idea of my love, since she may guess what I should perform in the wet, if I do so much in the dry.[3] But, besides, I have but too just a motive to give a loose to my raving grief, considering the long date of my absence from my ever-supreme Lady Dulcinea del Toboso; for, as the shepherd in 'Matthias Ambrosio' has it:

> " 'Poor lovers, absent from the darling fair,
>   All ills not only dread, but bear.'

Then do not lavish any more time in striving to divert me from so rare, so happy, and so singular an imitation. I am mad, and will be mad, until thy return with an answer to the letter which thou must carry from me to the Lady Dulcinea; and, if it be as favorable as my unshaken constancy deserves, then my madness and my penance shall end; but if I find she repays my vows and services with ungrateful disdain, then will I be emphatically mad, and screw up my thoughts to such an excess of distraction, that I shall be insensible of the rigor of my relentless fair. Thus what return soever she makes to my passion, I shall be eased one way or other of the anxious thoughts that now divide my soul; either entertaining the welcome news of her reviving pity with demonstrations of sense,

2 *Sancho says Moor for Medoro, in his blundering way.*
3 *A profane allusion to a text in Scripture, Luke xxiii, 31—"For if they do these things in a green tree, what shall be done in the dry?" So here Don Quixote's meaning is—"My mistress may guess what I would do where occasion should be given me, since I can do so much without any."*

254

or else showing my insensibility of her cruelty by the height of my distraction. But, in the meantime, Sancho, tell me, hast thou carefully preserved Mambrino's helmet? I saw thee take it up the other day, after that monster of ingratitude had spent his rage in vain endeavors to break it; which, by the way, argues the most excellent temper of the metal." "Body of me," quoth Sancho, "Sir Knight of the Woeful Figure, I can no longer bear to hear you run on at this rate! Why, this were enough to make any man believe that all your bragging and bouncing of your knight-errantry, your winning of kingdoms, and bestowing of islands, and Heaven knows what upon your squire, are mere flim-flam stories, and nothing but shams and lies: for who the devil can hear a man call a barber's basin a helmet, nay, and stand to it, and vouch it four days together, and not think him that says it to be stark mad or without brains? I have the basin safe enough here in my pouch, and I will get it mended for my own use, if ever I have the luck to get home to my wife and children." "Now, as I love bright arms," cried Don Quixote, "I swear thou art the shallowest, silliest, and most stupid fellow of a squire that ever I heard or read of in my life. How is it possible for thee to be so dull of apprehension as not to have learnt, in all this time that thou hast been in my service, that all the actions and adventures of us knights-errant seem to be mere chimeras, follies, and impertinencies? Not that they are so, indeed, but either through the officious care, or else through the malice and envy of those enchanters that always haunt and persecute us unseen, and by their fascinations change the appearance of our actions into what they please, according to their love or hate. This is the very reason why that which I plainly perceive to be Mambrino's helmet, seems to thee to be only a barber's basin, and perhaps another man may take it to be something else. And in this I can never too much admire the prudence of the sage who espouses my interests in making that inestimable helmet seem a basin: for, did it appear in its proper shape, its tempting value would raise me as many enemies as there are men in the universe, all eager to snatch from me so desirable a prize: but so long as it shall seem to be nothing else but a barber's basin, men will not value it, as is manifest from the fellow's leaving it behind him on the ground. For, had he known what it really was, he would sooner have parted with his life. Keep it safe then, Sancho, for I have no need of it at present; far from it, I think to put off my armor, and strip myself as naked as I came out of my mother's womb, in case I determine to imitate Orlando's fury, rather than the penance of Amadis."

This discourse brought them to the foot of a high rock, that stood by itself, as if it had been hewn out, and divided from the rest; by the skirt of it glided a purling stream, that softly took its winding course through an adjacent meadow. The verdant freshness of the grass, the number of wild trees, plants, and flowers, that feasted the eyes in that pleasant solitude, invited the Knight of the Woeful Figure to make choice of it to perform his amorous penance; and therefore, as soon as his ravished sight had roved a while over the scattered beauties of the place, he took possession of it with the following speech, as if he had utterly lost the small share of reason he had left. "Behold, O Heavens!" cried he, "the place which an unhappy lover has chosen to bemoan the deplorable state to which you have reduced him: here shall my flowing tears swell the liquid veins of this crystal rill, and my deep sighs perpetually move the leaves of these shady trees, in testimony of the anguish and pain that harrows up my soul! Ye rural deities, whoever you be, that make these unfrequented deserts your abode, hear the complaints of an unfortunate lover, whom a tedious absence, and some slight impressions of a jealous mistrust, have driven to these regions of despair, to bewail his rigorous destiny, and deplore the distracting cruelty of that ungrateful fair, who is the perfection of all human beauty. Ye pitying Napæan nymphs and dryads, silent inhabitants of the woods and groves, assist me to lament my fate, or at least attend the mournful story of my woes: so may no designing beastly satyrs, those just objects of your hate, ever have power to interrupt your rest.—Oh, Dulcinea del Toboso! thou sun that turnest my gloomy night to day! glory of my pain! north star of my travels, and reigning planet that controllest my heart! Pity, I conjure thee, the unparalleled distress to which thy absence has reduced the faithfulest of lovers, and grant to my fidelity that kind return which it so justly claims! So may indulgent fate shower on thee all the blessings thou ever canst desire, or Heaven grant!—Ye lonesome trees, under whose spreading branches I come to linger out the gloomy shadow of a tedious being; let the soft language of your rustling leaves, and the kind nodding of your springing boughs, satisfy me that I am welcome to your shady harbors! O thou, my trusty squire, the inseparable companion of my adventures, diligently observe what thou shalt see me do in this lonely retreat, that thou mayest inform the dear cause of my ruin with every particular." As he said this, he alighted, and presently taking off his horse's bridle and saddle, "Go, Rozinante," said he, giving the horse a clap on the posteriors, "he that has lost his freedom gives thee thine; thou steed, as renowned for thy extraordinary actions, as for thy misfortunes, go, rear thy awful front wherever thou pleasest, secure that neither the Hippogryphon of Astolpho, nor the renowned Frontino, which Bradamante purchased at so high a price, could ever be thought thy equals."

"Well fare him," cried Sancho, "that saved me the trouble of sending my ass to grass too: poor thing, had I him here, he should not want two or three claps on the buttocks, nor a fine speech in his praise neither, while I took off his pannel. But stay, were he here, what need would there be to strip him of his harness: alas, he never had anything to do with these mad pranks of love, no more than myself, who was his master when fortune pleased. But do ye hear me, now I think on it, Sir Knight of the Woeful Figure, if your worship is resolved to be mad, and send me away in good earnest, we must even clap the saddle again on Rozinante's back; for to tell you the truth, I am but a sorry footman, and if I do not ride home, I do not know when I shall be able to come back again." "Do as thou thinkest fit for that, Sancho," answered Don Quixote, "for I design thou shalt set forward about three days hence. In the meanwhile thou shalt be a witness of what I will do for my lady's sake, that thou mayest give her an account of it." "Bless my eyesight," quoth Sancho, "what can I see more than I have seen already?" "Thou hast seen nothing yet," answered Don Quixote; "thou must see me throw away my armor, tear my clothes, knock my head against the rocks, and do a thousand other things of that kind, that will fill thee with astonishment." "For goodness' sake, sir," quoth Sancho, "take heed how you quarrel with those ungracious rocks; you may chance to get such a crack on the crown at the very first rap, as may spoil your penance at one dash. No, I do not like that way by no means; if you must needs be knocking your noddle, to go through-stitch with this ugly job, seeing it is all but a mockery, or as it were between jest and earnest, why cannot you as well play your tricks on something that is softer than these unconscionable stones: you may run your head against water, or rather against cotton, or the stuffing of Rozinante's saddle; and then let me alone with the rest: I will be sure to tell my lady Dulcinea, that you bumped your pole against the point of a rock that is harder than a diamond."

"I thank thee for thy good-will, dear Sancho," replied Don Quixote: "but I assure thee, that all these seeming extravagancies that I must run through, art no jests: far from it, they must all be performed seriously and solemnly; for otherwise we should transgress the laws of chivalry, that forbid us to tell lies upon pain of degradation. Now to pretend to do one thing, and effect another, is an evasion, which I esteem to be as bad as lying. Therefore the blows which I must give myself on the head, ought to be real, substantial, sound ones, without any trick, or mental reservation; for which reason I would have thee leave me some lint and salve, since fortune has deprived us of the sovereign balsam which we lost." "It was a worse loss to lose the ass," quoth Sancho, "for with him we have lost bag and baggage, lint and all: but no more of your damned drench, if you love me; the very thoughts of it are enough not only to turn my stomach, but my soul, such a rumbling I feel in my guts at the name of it. Then, as for the three days you would have me loiter here to mind your mad tricks, you had as good make account they are already over; for I hold them for done, unsight unseen, and will tell wonders to my lady: wherefore write you your letter, and send me away with all haste; for let me be hanged if I do not long already to be back, to take you out of this purgatory wherein I leave you."

"Dost thou only call it purgatory, Sancho!" cried Don Quixote; "call it hell rather, or something worse, if there be in nature a term expressive of a more wretched state." "Nay, not so neither," quoth Sancho, "I would not call it hell; because, as I heard our parson say, 'There is no retention [4] out of hell.'" "Retention!" cried Don Quixote, "what dost thou mean by that word?" "Why," quoth Sancho, "retention is retention: it is, that whosoever is in hell never comes, nor can come out of it; which shall not be your case this bout, if I can stir my heels, and have but spurs to tickle Rozinante's flanks, till I come to my lady Dulcinea: for I will tell her such strange things of your maggoty tricks, your folly, and your madness, for indeed they are no better, that I will lay my head to a hazel nut, I will make her as supple as a glove, though I found her at first as tough-hearted as a cork; and when I have wheedled an

4 *No redemption, he means.*

259

answer out of her, all full of sweet honey words, away will I whisk it back to you, cutting the air as swift as a witch upon a broomstick, and free you out of your purgatory; for a purgatory I will have it to be in spite of hell, nor shall you gainsay me in that fancy; for, as I have told you before, there is some hope of your retention out of this place."

"Well, be it so," said the Knight of the Woeful Figure: "but how shall I do to write this letter?" "And the order for the three asses," added Sancho. "I will not forget it," answered Don Quixote; "but, since we have here no paper, I must be obliged to write on the leaves or bark of trees, or on wax, as they did in ancient times; yet, now I consider of it, we are here as ill-provided with wax as with paper: but stay, now I remember, I have Cardenio's pocket-book, which will supply that want in this exigence, and then thou shalt get the letter fairly transcribed at the first village, where thou canst meet with a schoolmaster; or, for want of a schoolmaster, thou mayest get the clerk of the parish to do it: but by no means give it to any notary or scrivener to be written out; for they commonly write such confounded hands, that the devil himself would scarce be able to read it." "Well," quoth Sancho, "but what shall I do for want of your name to it?" "Why," answered Don Quixote, "Amadis never used to subscribe his letters." "Ay," replied Sancho, "but the bill of exchange for the three asses must be signed; for should I get it copied out afterwards, they would say it is not your hand, and so I shall go without the asses." "I will write and sign the order for them in the table-book," answered Don Quixote, "and as soon as my niece sees the hand she will never scruple the delivery of the asses: and, as for the love-letter, when thou gettest it transcribed, thou must get it thus underwritten, 'Yours till death, the Knight of the Woeful Figure.' It is no matter whether the letter and subscription be written by the same hand or no; for, as I remember, Dulcinea can neither read nor write, nor

260

did she ever see any of my letters, nay, not so much as any of my writing in her life: for my love and hers have always been purely Platonic, never extending beyond the lawful bounds of a modest look; and that, too, so very seldom, that I dare safely swear that, though for these twelve years she has been dearer to my soul than light to my eyes, yet I never saw her four times in my life; and perhaps of those few times that I have seen her, she has scarcely perceived once that I beheld her: so strictly Lorenzo Corchuelo, her father, and Aldonza Nagales, her mother, have kept and educated her." "Heigh-day!" quoth Sancho, "did you ever hear the like! and is my lady Dulcinea del Toboso, at last, the daughter of Lorenzo Corchuelo, she that is otherwise called Aldonza Lorenzo?" "The same," answered Don Quixote; "and it is she that merits to be the sovereign mistress of the universe." "Udsdaggers," quoth Sancho, "I know her full well; she is a strapping wench, in faith, and pitches the bar with e'er a lusty young fellow in our parish. By the Mass, she is a notable, strong-built, sizable, sturdy, manly lass, and one that will keep her chin out of the mire, I warrant her; nay, and hold the best knight-errant to it that wears a head, if ever he venture upon her. Body o' me, what a pair of lungs and a voice she has, when she sets up her throat! I saw her one day perched up on the top of our steeple, to call to some plowmen that were at work in a fallow-field: and though they were half a league off, they heard her as plain as if they had been in the churchyard under her. The best of her is, that she is neither coy nor frumpish, she is a tractable lass, and fit for a courtier, for she will play with you like a kitten, and gibes and jokes with everybody. And now, in good truth, Sir Knight of the Woeful Figure, you may even play at your gambols as you please; you may run mad, you may hang yourself for her sake; there is nobody will say but you even took the wisest course, though the devil himself should carry you away a-pick-a-pack. Now am I even wild to be gone, though it were for nothing else but to see her, for I have not seen her this many a day: I fancy I shall hardly know her again, for a woman's face strangely alters by her being always in the sun, and drudging and moiling in the open fields. Well, I must needs own I have been mightily mistaken all along: for I durst have sworn this lady Dulcinea had been some great princess with whom you were in love, and such a one as deserved those rare gifts you bestowed on her, as the Biscainer, the galley-slaves, and many others, that, for aught I know, you may have sent her before I was your squire. I cannot choose but laugh to think how my lady Aldonza Lorenzo (my lady Dulcinea del Toboso, I should have said) would behave herself, should any of those men which you have sent, or may send to her, chance to go and fall down on their marrow-bones before her: for it is ten to one they may happen to find her a-carding of flax, or threshing in the barn, and then how finely baulked they will be! As sure as I am alive, they must needs think the devil owed them a shame; and she herself will but flout them, and mayhap be somewhat nettled at it."

"I have often told thee, Sancho," said Don Quixote, "and I tell thee again, that thou oughtest to bridle or immure thy saucy prating tongue: for though thou art but a dull-headed dunce, yet now and then thy ill-mannered jests bite too sharp. But that I may at once make thee sensible of thy folly and my discretion, I will tell thee a short story. A handsome, brisk, young, rich widow, and withal no prude, happened to fall in love with a well-set, lusty lay-brother.[5] His superior hearing of it, took occasion to go to her, and said to her, by way of charitable admonition, 'I mightily wonder, madam, how a lady of your merit, so admired for beauty and for sense, and withal so rich, could make so ill a choice, and dote on a mean, silly, despicable fellow, as I hear you do, while we have in

[5] Motillon, *a lay-brother, or servant in the convent or college, so called from* Motilo, *a cropped head; his hair being cropped short, he has no crown like those in orders.*

262

our house so many masters of art, bachelors, and doctors of divinity, among whom your ladyship may pick and choose, as you would among pears, and say, "This I like, that I do not like."' But she soon answered the officious, grave gentleman: 'Sir,' said she, with a smile, 'you are much mistaken, and think altogether after the old out-of-fashion way, if you imagine I have made so ill a choice; for though you fancy the man is a fool, yet, as to what I take him for, he knows as much, or rather more philosophy than Aristotle himself.' So, Sancho, as to the use which I make of lady Dulcinea, she is equal to the greatest princess in the world. Pray thee, tell me, dost thou think the poets, who every one of them celebrate the praises of one lady or other, had all real mistresses? Or that the Amaryllises, the Phyllises, the Sylvias, the Dianas, the Galateas, the Alidas, and the like, which you shall find in so many poems, romances, songs, and ballads, upon every stage, and even in every barber's shop, were creatures of flesh and blood, and mistresses to those that did and do celebrate them? No, no, never think it; for I dare assure thee, the greatest part of them were nothing but the mere imaginations of the poets, for a groundwork to exercise their wits upon, and give to the world occasion to look on the authors as men of an amorous and gallant disposition: and so it is sufficient for me to imagine, that Aldonza Lorenzo is beautiful and chaste; as for her birth and parentage, they concern me but little: for there is no need to make an inquiry about a woman's pedigree, as there is of us men, when some badge of honor is bestowed on us; and so she is to me the greatest princess in the world: for thou oughtest to know, Sancho, if thou knowest it not already, that there are but two things that chiefly excite us to love a woman, an attractive beauty, an unspotted fame. Now these two endowments are happily reconciled in Dulcinea; for, as for the one, she has not her equal, and few can vie with her in the other: but, to cut off all objections at once, I imagine, that all I say of her is really so, without the least addition or diminution: I fancy her to be just such as I would have her for beauty and quality. Helen cannot stand in competition with her; Lucretia cannot rival her; and all the heroines which antiquity has to boast, whether Greeks, Romans or Barbarians, are at once out-done by her incomparable perfections. Therefore let the world say what it will; should the ignorant vulgar foolishly censure me, I please myself with the assurances I have of the approbation of men of the strictest morals, and the nicest judgment." "Sir," quoth Sancho, "I knock under: you have reason on your side in all you say, and I own myself an ass. Nay, I am an ass to talk of an ass; for it is ill talking of halters in the house of a man that was hanged. But where is the letter-will all this while, that I may be jogging?" With that Don Quixote pulled out the table-book, and retiring a little aside, he very seriously began to write the letter; which he had no sooner finished, but he called Sancho, and ordered him to listen while he read it over to him, that he might carry it as well in his memory as in his pocket-book, in case he should have the ill-luck to lose it by the way: for so cross was fortune to him, that he feared every accident. "But, sir," said Sancho, "write it over twice or thrice there in the book, and give it me, and then I will be sure to deliver the message safe enough, I warrant ye: for it is folly to think I can get it by heart; alas, my memory is so bad, that many times I forget my own name! But yet, for all that, read it out to me, I beseech you, for I have a hugeous mind to hear it. I dare say, it is as fine as though it were in print." "Well then, listen," said Don Quixote.

"DON QUIXOTE DE LA MANCHA
to
DULCINEA DEL TOBOSO

"*High and Sovereign Lady,*
"*He that is stabbed to the quick with the poniard of absence, and wounded to the heart with love's most piercing darts, sends you*

that health which he wants himself, sweetest Dulcinea del Toboso. If your beauty reject me, if your virtue refuse to raise my fainting hopes, if your disdain exclude me from relief, I must at last sink under the pressure of my woes, though much inured to sufferings: for my pains are not only too violent, but too lasting. My trusty squire Sancho will give an exact account of the condition to which love and you have reduced me, too beautiful ingrate! If you relent at last, and pity my distress, then I may say I live, and you preserve, what is yours. But, if you abandon me to despair, I must patiently submit, and by ceasing to breathe, satisfy your cruelty and my passion.

> *"Yours till death,*
> *"The Knight of the Woeful Figure"*

"By the life of my father," quoth Sancho, "if I ever saw a finer thing in my born days! How neatly and roundly you tell your mind, and how cleverly you bring in at last, 'The Knight of the Woeful Figure!' Well, I say it again in good earnest, you are a devil at everything, and there is no kind of thing in the 'versal world but what you can turn your hand to." "A man ought to have some knowledge of everything," answered Don Quixote, "if he would be duly qualified for the employment I profess." "Well then," quoth Sancho, "do so much as write the warrant for the three asses on the other side of that leaf; and pray write it mighty plain, that they may know it is your hand at first sight." "I will," said Don Quixote, and with that he wrote it accordingly, and then read it in this form:

"My dear Niece,
"Upon sight of this my first bill of asses, be pleased to deliver three of the five which I left at home in your custody, to Sancho Panza

265

my squire, for the like number received of him here in tale; and this, together with his receipt, shall be your discharge. Given in the very bowels of Sierra Morena, the 22nd of August, in the present year."

"It is as it should be," quoth Sancho; "there only wants your name at the bottom." "There is no need to set my name," answered Don Quixote, "I will only set the two first letters of it, and it will be as valid as if written at length, though it were not only for three asses, but for three hundred." "I dare take your Worship's word," quoth Sancho, "and now I am going to saddle Rozinante, and then you shall give me your blessing; for I intend to set out presently, without seeing any of your mad tricks; and I will relate, that I saw you perform so many, that she can desire no more." "Nay," said Don Quixote, "I will have thee stay a while, Sancho, and see me stark-naked; it is also absolutely necessary thou shouldest see me practice some twenty or thirty mad gambols; I shall have dispatched them in less than half an hour: and when thou hast been an eye witness of that essay, thou mayest with a safe conscience swear thou hast seen me play a thousand more; for I dare assure thee, for thy encouragement, thou never canst exceed the number of those I shall perform." "Good sir," quoth Sancho, "as you love me, do not let me stay to see you naked; it will grieve me so to the heart, that I shall cry my eyes out; and I have blubbered and howled but too much since yesternight for the loss of my ass. My head is so sore with it, I am not able to cry any longer: but, if you will needs have me see some of your antics, pray do them in your clothes out of hand, and let them be such as are most to the purpose; for the sooner I go, the sooner I shall come back; and the way to be gone, is not to stay here. I long to bring you an answer to your heart's content: and I will be sure to do it,

266

or let the Lady Dulcinea look to it; for if she does not answer as she should do, I protest solemnly I will force an answer out of her guts by dint of good kicks and fisticuffs: for it is not to be endured, that such a notable knight-errant as your worship is, should thus run out of his wits without knowing why or wherefore, for such a—odsbobs! I know what I know; she had not best provoke me to speak it out; for, by the Lord, I shall let fly, and out with it by wholesale, though it spoil the market."

"I protest, Sancho," said Don Quixote, "I think thou art as mad as myself." "Nay, not so mad neither," replied Sancho, "but somewhat more choleric. But talk no more of that: let us see, how will you do for victuals when I am gone? Do you mean to do like the other madman yonder, rob upon the highway, and snatch the goatherds' victuals from them by main force?" "Never let that trouble thy head," replied Don Quixote; "for though I had all the dainties that can feast a luxurious palate, I would feed upon nothing but the herbs and fruits which this wilderness will afford me: for the singularity of my present task consists in fasting, and half-starving myself, and in the performance of other austerities." "But there is another thing come into my head," quoth Sancho; "how shall I do to find the way hither again, it is such a by-place?" "Take good notice of it beforehand," said Don Quixote, "and I will endeavor to keep hereabouts till thy return: besides, about the time when I may reasonably expect thee back, I will be sure to watch on the top of yonder high rock for thy coming. But now I bethink myself of a better expedient; thou shalt cut down a good number of boughs, and strew them in the way as thou ridest along, till thou gettest to the plains, and this will serve thee to find me again at thy return, like Perseus's clue to the labyrinth in Crete."

"I will go about it out of hand," quoth Sancho. With that he went and cut down a bundle of boughs, then came and asked his master's blessing, and after a shower of tears shed on both sides, mounted Rozinante, which Don Quixote very seriously recommended to his care, charging him to be as tender of that excellent steed as of his own person. After that he set forward toward the plains, strewing several boughs as he rode, according to order. His master importuned him to stay and see him do two or three of his antic postures before he went, but he could not prevail with him: however, before he was got out of sight, he considered of it, and rode back: "Sir," quoth he, "I have thought better of it, and believe I had best take your advice, that I may swear with a safe conscience I have seen you play your mad tricks; therefore I would see you do one of them, though I think I have seen you do a very great one already, I mean your staying by yourself in this desert."

"I had advised thee right," said Don Quixote; "and therefore stay but while a man may repeat the Creed, and I will show thee what thou wouldst see." With that, slipping off his breeches and stripping himself naked to the waist, he gave two or three frisks in the air, and then pitching on his hands he fetched his heels over his head twice together; and as he tumbled with his legs aloft, discovered such rarities, that Sancho even made haste to turn his horse's head, that he might no longer see them, and rode away full satisfied, that he might swear his master was mad. And so we will leave him to make the best of his way till his return, which will be more speedy than might be imagined.

XII: A CONTINUATION OF THE REFINED EXTRAVAGANCIES BY WHICH THE GALLANT KNIGHT OF LA MANCHA CHOSE TO EXPRESS HIS LOVE IN THE SIERRA MORENA

The history relates, that as soon as the Knight of the Woeful Figure saw himself alone, after he had taken his frisks and leaps naked as he was, the prelude to his amorous penance, he ascended the top of a high rock, and there began seriously to consider with himself what resolution to take in that nice dilemma, which had already so perplexed his mind; that is, whether he should imitate Orlando in his wild ungovernable fury, or Amadis in his melancholy mood. To which purpose, reasoning with himself, "I do not much wonder," said he, "at Orlando's being so very valiant, considering he was enchanted in such a manner, that he could not be slain but by the thrust of a long pin through the bottom of his foot, which he sufficiently secured, always wearing seven iron soles to his shoes; and yet this availed him nothing against Bernardo del Carpio, who, knowing what he depended upon, squeezed him to death between his arms at Roncesvalles. But, setting aside his valor, let us examine his madness; for that he was mad, is an unquestionable truth; nor is it less certain, that his frenzy was occasioned by the assurances he had that the fair Angelica had resigned herself up to the unlawful embraces of Medoro, that young Moor with curled locks, who was page to Agramante. Now, after all, seeing he was too well convinced of his lady's infidelity, it is not to be admired he should run mad: but how can I imitate him in his furies, if I cannot imitate him in their occasion? For I dare swear my Dulcinea del Toboso never saw a downright Moor in his own garb since she first beheld light, and that she is at this present speaking as right as the mother that bore her: so that I should do her a great injury, should I entertain any dishonorable thoughts of her behavior, and

fall into such a kind of madness as that of Orlando Furioso. On the other side, I find that Amadis de Gaul, without punishing himself with such distraction or expressing his resentments in so boisterous and raving a manner, got as great a reputation for being a lover as anyone whatsoever; for what I find in history as to his abandoning himself to sorrow, is only this: 'he found himself disdained, his lady Oriana having charged him to get out of her sight, and not to presume to appear in her presence till she gave him leave; and this was the true reason why he retired to the Poor Rock with the hermit, where he gave up himself wholly to grief, and wept a deluge of tears, till pitying Heaven at last, commiserating his affliction, sent him relief in the height of his anguish.' Now then, since this is true, as I know it is, what need have I to tear off my clothes, to rend and root up these harmless trees, or trouble the water of these brooks, that must give me drink when I am thirsty? No, long live the memory of Amadis de Gaul, and let him be the great example which Don Quixote de la Mancha chooses to imitate in all things that will admit of a parallel. So may it be said of the living copy, as was said of the dead original, that if he did not perform great things, yet no man was more ambitious of undertaking them than he; and though I am not disdained nor discarded by Dulcinea, yet it is sufficient that I am absent from her. Then it is resolved! And now the famous actions of the great Amadis occur to my remembrance, and be my trusty guides to follow his example." This said, he called to mind, that the chief exercise of that hero in his retreat was prayer: to which purpose, our modern Amadis presently made himself a rosary of galls instead of beads; but he was extremely troubled for want of an hermit to hear his confession, and comfort him in his affliction. However, he entertained himself with his amorous contemplations, walking up and down the meadow, and writing some poetical conceptions in the smooth sand, and upon the barks of trees, all of them expressive of his sorrows, and the praises of Dulcinea; but unhappily none were found entire and legible, but these stanzas that follow:

> Ye lofty trees with spreading arms,
>   The pride and shelter of the plain;
> Ye humbler shrubs, and flow'ry charms
>   Which here in springing glory reign!

271

If my complaints may pity move,
Hear the sad story of my love,
 While with me here you pass your hours.
Should you grow faded with my cares,
 I'll bribe you with refreshing show'rs;
You shall be water'd with my tears.
  Distant, tho' present in idea,
  I mourn my absent Dulcinea
     Del Toboso.

Love's truest slave despairing chose
 This lonely wild, this desert plain,
The silent witness of the woes
 Which he, tho' guiltless, must sustain.
Unknowing why those pains he bears,
He groans, he raves, and he despairs:
 With ling'ring fires love racks my soul,
In vain I grieve, in vain lament;
 Like tortur'd fiends I weep, I howl,
And burn, yet never can repent.
  Distant, tho' present in idea,
  I mourn my absent Dulcinea
     Del Toboso.

While I thro' honor's thorny ways,
 In search of distant glory rove,
Malignant fate my toil repays
 With endless woes, and hopeless love.
Thus I on barren rocks despair,
And curse my stars, yet bless my fair.
 Love arm'd with snakes has left his dart,
And now does like a fury rave,
 And scourge and sting in every part,
And into madness lash his slave.
  Distant, tho' present in idea,
  I mourn my absent Dulcinea
     Del Toboso.

This addition of Del Toboso to the name of Dulcinea, made those who found these verses laugh heartily; and they imagined, that when Don Quixote made them, he was afraid those who should happen to read them would not understand on whom they were made, should he omit the place of his mistress's birth and residence: and this was indeed the true reason, as he himself afterwards confessed. With this employment did our disconsolate Knight beguile the tedious hours; sometimes also he expressed his sorrows in prose, sighed to the winds, and called upon the sylvan gods, the fauns, the naïades, the nymphs of the adjoining groves, and the mournful echo, imploring their attention and condolement with repeated supplications: at other times he employed himself in gathering herbs for the support of languishing nature, which decayed so fast, with his slender diet and his studied anxiety and intenseness of thinking, that had Sancho stayed but three weeks from him, whereas by good fortune he stayed but three days, the Knight of the Woeful Figure would have been so disfigured, that his mother would never have known the child of her own womb.

But now it is necessary we should leave him a while to his sighs, his sobs, and his amorous expostulations, and see how Sancho Panza behaved himself in his embassy. He made all the haste he could to get out of the mountain; and then, taking the direct road to Toboso, the next day he arrived near the inn where he had been tossed in a blanket. Scarce had he descried the fatal walls, but a sudden shivering seized his bones, and he fancied himself to be again dancing in the air; so that he had a good mind to ride still farther before he baited, though it was dinner-time, and his mouth watered strangely at the thoughts of a hot bit of meat, the rather, because he had lived altogether upon cold victuals for a long while. This greedy longing drew him near the inn, in spite of his aversion to the place; but yet when he came to the gate he had not the courage to go in, but stopped there, not knowing whether he had best enter or no. While he sat musing, two men happened to come out, and, believing they knew him, "Look, master doctor," cried one to the other, "is not that Sancho Panza, whom the housekeeper told us her master had inveigled to go along with him?" "The same," answered the other; "and more than that, he rides on Don Quixote's horse." Now these two happened to be the curate and the barber, who had brought his books to a trial and passed sentence on them: therefore they had no sooner said this, but they called to Sancho, and asked him where he had left his master? The trusty squire presently knew them, and having no mind to discover the place and condition he left his master in, told them he was taken up with certain business of great consequence at a certain place which he durst not discover for his life. "How! Sancho," cried the barber, "you must not think to put us off with a flim-flam story; if you will not tell us where he is, we shall believe you have murdered him, and robbed him of his horse; therefore, either satisfy us where you did leave him, or we will have you laid by the heels."

"Look you, neighbor," quoth Sancho, "I am not afraid of words, do ye see: I am neither a thief nor a manslayer; I kill nobody, so nobody kills me: I leave every man to fall by his own fortune, or by the hand of Him that made him. As for my master, I left him frisking and doing penance in the midst of yonder mountain, to his heart's content." After this, without any further entreaty, he gave them a full account of that business, and of all their adventures; how he was then going from his master to carry a letter to my lady Dulcinea del Toboso, Lorenzo Corchuelo's daughter, with whom Don Quixote was up to the ears in love. The curate and barber stood amazed, hearing all these particulars: and, though they already knew his madness but too well, they wondered more and more at the increase of it, and at so strange a cast and variety of extravagance. Then they desired Sancho to show them the letter. He told them it was written in a pocket-book, and that his

274

master had ordered him to get it fairly transcribed upon paper at the next village he should come at. Whereupon the curate promising to write it out very fairly himself, Sancho put his hand into his bosom to give him the table-book; but, though he fumbled a great while for it, he could find none of it. He searched and searched again, but it had been in vain though he had searched till Doomsday, for he came away from Don Quixote without it. This put him into a cold sweat, and made him turn as pale as death; he searched his clothes, turned his pockets inside outwards, and fumbled in his bosom again; but, being at last convinced he had it not about him, he fell a-raving and stamping, and cursing himself like a madman: he rent his beard from his chin with both hands, befisted his own forgetful skull and his blubber cheeks, and gave himself a bloody nose in a moment. The curate and the barber asked him what was the matter with him, and why he punished himself at that strange rate? "I deserve it all," quoth Sancho, "like a blockhead as I am, for losing at one cast no less than three asses, of which the least was worth a castle." "How so?" quoth the barber. "Why," cried Sancho, "I have lost that same table-book, wherein was written Dulcinea's letter and a bill of exchange drawn by my master upon his niece, for three of the five asses which he has at home"; and with that he told them how he had lost his own ass. But the curate cheered him up, and promised him to get another bill of exchange from his master written upon paper, whereas that in the table-book, not being in due form, would not have been accepted. With that Sancho took courage, and told them, if it were so, he cared not a straw for Dulcinea's letter, for he knew it almost all by rote. "Then prithee let us hear it," said the barber, "and we will see and write it." In order to this, Sancho paused, and began to study for the words. Presently he fell a-scratching his head, stood first upon one leg, and then upon another, gaped sometimes upon the skies and sometimes upon the ground: at length, after he had gnawed

away the top of his thumb, and quite tired out the curate and barber's patience, "Before George," cried he, "Mr. Doctor, I believe
the devil is in it; for may I be choked if I remember a word of this
confounded letter, but only, that there was at the beginning, 'High
and subterrene lady.'" "'Sovereign, or superhuman lady,' you
would say," quoth the barber. "Ay, ay," quoth Sancho, "you are in
the right—but stay, now I think I can remember some of that which
followed. Ho! I have it, I have it now—'He that is wounded, and
wants sleep, sends you the dagger—which he wants himself—that
stabbed him to the heart—and the hurt man does kiss your ladyship's hand'; and at last, after a hundred hums and haws, 'sweetest
Dulcinea del Toboso.' And thus he went on rambing a good while
with I do not know what more of fainting, and relief, and sinking,
till at last he ended with 'Yours till death, the Knight of the Woeful Figure.'" The curate and the barber were mightily pleased
with Sancho's excellent memory; insomuch that they desired him
to repeat the letter twice or thrice more, that they might also get it
by heart, and write it down; which Sancho did very freely, but
every time he made many odd alterations and additions, as pleasant as the first. Then he told them many other things of his master,
but spoke not a word of his own being tossed in a blanket at that
very inn. He also told them, that, if he brought a kind answer from
the lady Dulcinea, his master would forthwith set out to see and
make himself an emperor, or at least a king; for so they two had
agreed between themselves, he said; and that, after all, it was a
mighty easy matter for his master to become one, such was his
prowess and the strength of his arm: which being done, his master
would marry him to one of the empress's damsels; and that fine
lady was to be heiress to a large country on the mainland, but not
to any island, or islands, for he was out of conceit with them. Poor
Sancho spoke all this so seriously and so feelingly, ever and anon

wiping his nose, and stroking his beard, that now the curate and the barber were more surprised than they were before, considering the prevalent influences of Don Quixote's folly upon that silly credulous fellow. However, they did not think it worth their while to undeceive him yet, seeing this was only a harmless delusion, that might divert them a while; and therefore they exhorted him to pray for his master's health and long life, seeing it was no impossible thing, but that he might in time become an emperor, as he said, or at least an archbishop, or somewhat else equivalent to it.

"But pray, good Mr. Doctor," asked Sancho, "should my master have no mind to be an emperor, and take a fancy to be an archbishop, I would fain know what your archbishops-errant are wont to give their squires?" "Why," answered the curate, "they used to give them some parsonage, or sinecure, or some other benefice, or church-living, which, with the profits of the altar, and other fees, brings them in a handsome revenue." "Ay, but," says Sancho, "to put in for that, the squire must be a single man, and know how to answer and assist at mass at least; and how shall I do then, seeing I have the ill-luck to be married? Nay, and besides, I do not so much as know the first letter of my Christcross-row. What will become of me, should it come into my master's head to make himself an archbishop, and not an emperor, as it is the custom of knights-errant?" "Do not let that trouble thee, friend Sancho," said the barber, "we will talk to him about it, and advise him, nay, urge him to it as a point of conscience to be an emperor and not an archbishop, which will be better for him, by reason he has more courage than learning."

"Truth, I am of your mind," quoth Sancho, "though he is such a head-piece that I dare say he can turn himself to anything; nevertheless, I mean to make it the burden of my prayers, that Heaven may direct him to that which is best for him, and what may enable

277

him to reward me most." "You speak like a wise man, and a good Christian," said the curate, "but all we have to do at present is to see how we shall get your master to give over that severe unprofitable penance which he has undertaken; and therefore let us go on to consider about it, and also to eat our dinner, for I fancy it is ready by this time." "Do you two go in, if you please," quoth Sancho, "but as for me, I had rather stay without; and anon I will tell you why I do not care to go within doors; however, pray send me a piece of hot victuals to eat here, and some provender for Rozinante." With that they went in, and a while after the barber brought him out some meat; and returning to the curate, they consulted how to compass their design. At last the latter luckily bethought himself of an expedient that seemed most likely to take, as exactly fitting Don Quixote's humor; which was that he should disguise himself in the habit of a damsel-errant, and the barber should alter his dress as well as he could, so as to pass for a squire, or gentleman-usher. "In that equipage," added he, "we will go to Don Quixote, and feigning myself to be a distressed damsel, I will beg a boon of him, which he, as a valorous knight-errant, will not fail to promise me. By this means I will engage him to go with me to redress a very great injury done me by a false and discourteous knight, beseeching him not to desire to see my face, nor ask anything about my circumstances, till he has revenged me of that wicked knight. This bait will take, I dare engage, and by this stratagem we will decoy him back to his own house, where we will try to cure him of his romantic frenzy."

The curate's project was so well liked by the barber, that they
instantly put it into practice. First they borrowed a complete
woman's apparel of the hostess, leaving her in pawn a new cassock of the curate's; and the barber made himself a long beard with
a grizzled ox's tail, in which the innkeeper used to hang his combs.

The hostess being desirous to know what they intended to do with
those things, the curate gave her a short account of Don Quixote's
distraction, and their design. Whereupon the innkeeper and his
wife presently guessed this was their romantic knight, that made
the precious balsam; and accordingly they told them the whole
story of Don Quixote's lodging there, and of Sancho's being tossed
in a blanket. Which done, the hostess readily fitted out the curate
at such a rate, that it would have pleased anyone to have seen him;
for she dressed him up in a cloth gown, trimmed with borders of
black velvet, the breadth of a span, all pinked and jagged; and a

pair of green velvet bodice, with sleeves of the same, and faced with white satin; which accouterments probably had been in fashion in old King Bamba's [1] days. The curate would not let her encumber his head with a woman's headgear, but only clapped upon his crown a white quilted cap which he used to wear a-nights, and bound his forehead with one of his garters, that was of black taffeta, making himself a kind of muffler and vizard mask with the other: then he half-buried his head under his hat, pulling it down to squeeze in his ears; and as the broad brim flapped down over his eyes, it seemed a kind of umbrella. This done, he wrapped his cloak about him, and seated himself on his mule sideways like a woman; then the barber clapped on his ox-tail beard, half red and half grizzled, which hung from his chin down to his waist; and, having mounted his mule, they took leave of their host and hostess, as also of the good-conditioned Maritornes, who vowed, though she was a sinner, to tumble her beads, and say a rosary to the good success of so arduous and truly Christian an undertaking.

But scarce were they got out of the inn, when the curate began to be troubled with a scruple of conscience about his putting on women's apparel, being apprehensive of the indecency of the disguise in a priest, though the goodness of his intention might well warrant a dispensation from the strictness of decorum: therefore he desired the barber to change dresses, for that in his habit of a squire he should less profane his own dignity and character, to which he ought to have a greater regard than to Don Quixote; withal assuring the barber, that unless he consented to this exchange, he was absolutely resolved to go no further, though it were to save Don Quixote's soul from hell. Sancho came up with them just upon their demur, and was ready to split his sides with laughing at the sight of these strange masqueraders. In short, the

[1] *An ancient Gothic king of Spain, concerning whom several fables are written; wherefore the Spaniards, to express anything exceeding old, say it was in being in his time.*

barber consented to be the damsel, and to let the curate be the squire. Now, while they were thus changing sexes, the curate offered to tutor him how to behave himself in that female attire, so as to be able to wheedle Don Quixote out of his penance; but the barber desired him not to trouble himself about that matter, assuring him, that he was well enough versed in female affairs, to be able to act a damsel without any directions; however, he said he would not now stand fiddling and managing his pins to prink himself up, seeing it would be time enough to do that when they came near Don Quixote's hermitage; and therefore, having folded up his clothes, and the curate his beard, they spurred on, while their guide Sancho entertained them with a relation of the mad, tattered gentleman whom they had met in the mountain; however, without mentioning a word of the portmanteau or the gold, for, as much a fool as he was, he loved money, and knew how to keep it when he had it, and was wise enough to keep his own counsel.

They got the next day to the place where Sancho had strewed the boughs to direct him to Don Quixote; and therefore he advised them to put on their disguises, if it were, as they told him, that their design was only to make his master leave that wretched kind of life, in order to become an emperor. Thereupon they charged him on his life not to take the least notice who they were. As for Dulcinea's letter, if Don Quixote asked him about it, they ordered him to say he had delivered it; but by reason she could neither write nor read, she had sent him her answer by word of mouth; which was, that on pain of her indignation, he should immediately put an end to his severe penance, and repair to her presence. This, they told Sancho, together with what they themselves designed to say, was the only way to oblige his master to leave the desert, that he might prosecute his design of making himself an emperor; assuring him they would take care he should not entertain the least thought of an archbishopric.

281

Sancho listened with great attention to all these instructions, and treasured them up in his mind, giving the curate and the barber a world of thanks for their good intention of advising his master to become an emperor, and not an archbishop; for, as he said, he imagined in his simple judgment, that an emperor-errant was ten times better than an archbishop-errant, and could reward his squire a great deal better.

He likewise added, that he thought it would be proper for him to go to his master somewhat before them, and give him an account of his lady's kind answer; for, perhaps, that alone would be sufficient to fetch him out of that place, without putting them to any further trouble. They liked this proposal very well, and therefore agreed to let him go, and wait there till he came back to give them an account of his success. With that Sancho rode away, and struck into the clefts of the rock, in order to find out his master, leaving the curate and the barber by the side of a brook, where the neighboring hills and some trees that grew along its banks, combined to make a cool and pleasant shade. There they sheltered themselves from the scorching beams of the sun, that commonly shines intolerably hot in those parts at that time, being about the middle of August, and hardly three o'clock in the afternoon. While they quietly refreshed themselves in that delightful place, where they agreed to stay till Sancho's return, they heard a voice, which, though unattended with any instrument, ravished their ears with its melodious sound: and, what increased their surprise and their admiration, was to hear such artful notes, and such delicate music in so unfrequented and wild a place, where scarce any rustics ever straggled, much less such skillful songsters, as the person whom they heard unquestionably was; for, though the poets are pleased to fill the fields and woods with swains and shepherdesses, that sing with all the sweetness and delicacy imaginable, yet it is well enough known that those gentlemen deal more in fiction than in truth, and

282

love to embellish the descriptions they make with things that have
no existence but in their own brain. Nor could our two listening
travelers think it the voice of a peasant, when they began to distinguish the words of the song, for they seemed to relish more of a
courtly style than a rural composition. These were the verses:

A SONG

I

What makes me languish and complain?
                                Oh, 'tis disdain!
What yet more fiercely tortures me?
                                'Tis jealousy.
How have I patience lost?
                                By absence crost.
  Then hopes farewell, there's no relief;
  I sink beneath oppressing grief;
  Nor can a wretch, without despair,
  Scorn, jealousy, and absence bear.

II

What in my breast this anguish drove?
                                Intruding love.
Who could such mighty ills create?
                                Blind fortune's hate.
What cruel pow'rs my fate approve?
                                The powers above.
  Then let me bear, and cease to moan;
  'Tis glorious thus to be undone:
  When these invade, who dares oppose?
  Heaven, love and fortune are my foes.

III

Where shall I find a speedy cure?
                                Death is sure.
No milder means to set me free?
                                Inconstancy.

283

Can nothing else my pains assuage?
                              Distracting rage.
  What die or change? Lucinda lose;
  Oh let me rather madness choose!
  But judge ye gods, what we endure,
  When death or madness are a cure!

The time, the hour, the solitariness of the place, the voice and agreeable manner with which the unseen musician sung, so filled the hearers' minds with wonder and delight, that they were all attention; and when the voice was silent, they continued so too a pretty while, watching with listening ears to catch the expected sounds, expressing their satisfaction best by that dumb applause. At last, concluding the person would sing no more, they resolved to find out the charming songster; but, as they were going so to do, they heard the wished-for voice begin another air, which fixed them where they stood till it had sung the following sonnet:

A SONNET

  O sacred friendship, Heaven's delight,
    Which, tir'd with man's unequal mind,
  Took to thy native skies thy flight,
    While scarce thy shadow's left behind!
  From thee, diffusive good below,
    Peace and her train of joys we trace.
  But falsehood, with dissembl'd show
    Too oft usurps thy sacred face.
  Bless'd genius, then resume thy seat!
  Destroy imposture and deceit,
    Which in thy dress confound the ball!
  Harmonious peace and truth renew,
  Show the false friendship from the true,
    Or nature must to chaos fall.

This sonnet concluded with a deep sigh, and such doleful throbs, that the curate and the barber now, out of pity as well as curiosity, resolved instantly to find out who this mournful songster was. They had not gone far, when by the side of a rock they discovered a man, whose shape and aspect answered exactly to the description Sancho had given them of Cardenio. They observed he stopped short as soon as he spied them, yet without any signs of fear; only he hung down his head, like one abandoned to sorrow, never so much as lifting up his eyes to mind what they did. The curate, who was a good and a well-spoken man, presently guessing him to be the same of whom Sancho had given them an account, went towards him, and addressing himself to him with great civility and discretion, earnestly entreated him to forsake this desert, and a course of life so wretched and forlorn, which endangered his title to a better, and from a willful misery might make him fall into greater and ever-lasting woes. Cardenio was then free from the distraction that so often disturbed his senses; yet seeing two persons in a garb wholly different from that of those few rustics who frequented those deserts, and hearing them talk as if they were no strangers to his concerns, he was somewhat surprised at first; however, having looked upon them earnestly for some time, "Gentlemen," said he, "whoever ye be, I find Heaven, pitying my misfortunes, has brought ye to these solitary regions, to retrieve me from this fright-ful retirement, and recover me to the society of men; but because you do not know how unhappy a fate attends me, and that I never am free from one affliction but to fall into a greater, you perhaps take me for a man naturally endowed with a very small stock of sense, and what is worse, for one of those wretches who are alto-gether deprived of reason. And indeed I cannot blame anyone that entertains such thoughts of me; for even I myself am convinced, that the bare remembrance of my disasters often distracts me to that degree, that losing all sense of reason and knowledge, I unman myself for the time, and launch into those extravagancies which nothing but height of frenzy and madness would commit: and I am the more sensible of my being troubled with this distemper, when people tell me what I have done during the violence of that terrible accident, and give me too certain proofs of it. And after all, I can allege no other excuse but the cause of my misfortune, which occasioned that frantic rage, and therefore tell the story of my hard fate to as many as have the patience to hear it; for men of sense, perceiving the cause, will not wonder at the effects; and though they can give me no relief, yet at least they will cease to condemn me; for a bare relation of my wrongs must needs make them lose their resentments of the effects of my disorder into a compassion of my miserable fate. Therefore, gentlemen, if you came here with that design, I beg that before you give yourselves the trouble of reproving or advising me, you will be pleased to attend to the relation of my calamities; for perhaps, when you have heard it, you will think them past redress, and so will save yourselves the labor you would take." The curate and the barber, who desired nothing more than to hear the story from his own mouth, were extremely glad of his proffer; and, having assured him they had no design to aggravate his miseries with pretending to remedy them, nor would they cross his inclinations in the least, they entreated him to begin his relation.

The unfortunate Cardenio then began his story, and went on with the first part of it, almost in the same words, as far as when he related it to Don Quixote and the goathered, when the Knight, out of superstitious niceness to observe the decorum of chivalry, gave an interruption to the relation, by quarreling about master Elizabat, as we have already said. Then he went on with that passage concerning the letter sent him by Lucinda, which Don Ferdinand had unluckily found, happening to be by, to open the book of "Amadis de Gaul" first, when Lucinda sent it back to Cardenio with that letter in it between the leaves; which Cardenio told them was as follows:

"'*LUCINDA TO CARDENIO.*

"'*I discover in you every day so much merit, that I am obliged, or rather forced, to esteem you more and more. If you think this acknowledgment to your advantage, make that use of it which is most consistent with your honor and mine. I have a father that knows you, and is too kind a parent ever to obstruct my designs, when he shall be satisfied with their being just and honorable: so that it is now your part to show you love me, as you pretend, and I believe.*'

"This letter," continued Cardenio, "made me resolve once more to demand Lucinda of her father in marriage, and was the same that increased Don Ferdinand's esteem for her, by that discovery of her sense and discretion, which so inflamed his soul, that from that moment he secretly resolved to destroy my hopes before I could be so happy as to crown them with success. I told that perfidious friend what Lucinda's father had advised me to do, when I had rashly asked her for my wife before, and that I durst not now impart this to my father, lest he should not readily consent I should marry yet. Not but that he knew, that her quality, beauty, and virtue were sufficient to make her an ornament to the noblest house in Spain, but because I was apprehensive he would not let me marry till he saw what the Duke would do for me. Don Ferdinand, with a pretended officiousness, proffered me to speak to my father, and persuade him to treat with Lucinda's. Ungrateful man! deceitful friend! ambitious Marius! cruel Cataline! wicked Sylla! perfidious Galalon! faithless Vellido! malicious Julian! [2] treacherous, covetous Judas! thou, all those fatal hated men in one, false Ferdinand!

[2] *Count Julian brought the Moors into Spain, because King Roderigo had ravished his daughter. Galalon and Vellido are explained elsewhere. Marius, Cataline, etc., are well known.*

287

what wrongs had that fond confiding wretch done thee, who thus to thee unbosomed all his cares, all the delights and secrets of his soul? What injury did I ever utter, or advice did I ever give, which were not all directed to advance thy honor and profit? But oh! I rave, unhappy wretch! I should rather accuse the cruelty of my stars, whose fatal influence pours mischiefs on me, which no earthly force can resist, or human art prevent. Who would have thought that Don Ferdinand, whose quality and merit entitled him to the lawful possession of beauties of the highest rank, and whom I had engaged by a thousand endearing marks of friendship and services, should forfeit thus his honor and his truth, and lay such a treacherous design to deprive me of all the happiness of my life? But I must leave expostulating, to end my story. The traitor Ferdinand, thinking his project impracticable while I stayed near Lucinda, bargained for six fine horses the same day he promised to speak to my father, and presently desired me to ride away to his brother for money to pay for them. Alas! I was so far from suspecting his treachery, that I was glad of doing him a piece of service. Accordingly I went that very evening to take my leave of Lucinda, and to tell her what Don Ferdinand had promised to do. She bid me return with all the haste of an expecting lover, not doubting but our lawful wishes might be crowned as soon as my father had spoken for me to be hers. When she had said this, I marked her trickling tears, and a sudden grief so obstructed her speech, that though she seemed to strive to tell me something more, she could not give it utterance. This unusual scene of sorrow strangely amazed and moved me; yet because I would not murder hope, I chose to attribute this to the tenderness of her affection, and unwillingness to part with me. In short, away I went, buried in deep melancholy, and full of fears and imaginations, for which I could give no manner of reason. I delivered Don Ferdinand's letter to his brother, who received me with all the kindness imaginable, but did not dispatch me as I expected. For, to my sorrow, he enjoined me to tarry a whole week, and to take care the Duke might not see me, his brother having sent for money unknown to his father: but this was only a device of false Ferdinand's; for his brother did not want money, and might have dispatched me immediately, had he not been privately desired to delay my return.

"This was so displeasing an injunction, that I was ready to come away without the money, not being able to live so long absent from my Lucinda, principally considering in what condition I had left her. Yet at last I forced myself to stay, and my respect for my friend prevailed over my impatience: but, before four tedious days were expired, a messenger brought me a letter, which I presently knew to be Lucinda's hand. I opened it with trembling hands, and an aching heart, justly imagining it was no ordinary concern that could urge her to send thither to me: and before I read it, I asked the messenger who had given it him? He answered me, 'that, going by accidentally in the street about noon, in our town, a very handsome lady, all in tears, had called him to her window, and with great precipitation, "Friend," said she, "if you be a Christian, as you seem to be, for Heaven's sake take this letter, and deliver it with all speed into the person's own hand to whom it is directed: I assure you in this, you will do a very good action; and that you may not want means to do it, take what is wrapped up in this;" and so saying, she threw me a handkerchief, wherein I found a hundred reals, this gold ring which you see, and the letter which I now brought you: which done, I having made her signs to let her know I would do as she desired, without so much as staying for an answer, she went from the grate. This reward, but much more the beautiful lady's tears, and earnest prayers, made me post away to you that very minute, and so in sixteen hours I have traveled eighteen long leagues.' While the messenger spoke, I was seized with sad apprehensions of some fatal news; and such a

289

trembling shook my limbs, that I could scarce support my fainting body. However, taking courage, at last I read the letter, the contents of which were these:

"'Don Ferdinand, according to his promise, has desired your father to speak to mine; but he has done that for himself which you had engaged him to do for you: for he has demanded me for his wife; and my father, allured by the advantages which he expects from such an alliance, has so far consented, that two days hence the marriage is to be performed, and with such privacy, that only Heaven and some of the family are to be witnesses. Judge of the affliction of my soul by that concern which I guess fills your own; and therefore haste to me, my dear Cardenio. The issue of this business will show how much I love you: and grant, propitious Heaven, this may reach your hand before mine is in danger of being joined with his who keeps his promises so ill.'

"I had no sooner read the letter," added Cardenio, "but away I flew, without waiting for my dispatch: for then I too plainly discovered Don Ferdinand's treachery, and that he only sent me to his brother, to take the advantage of my absence. Revenge, love, and impatience gave me wings, so that I got home privately the next day, just when it grew duskish, in good time to speak with Lucinda; and, leaving my mule at the honest man's house who brought me the letter, I went to wait upon my mistress, whom I luckily found at the window,[3] the only witness of our loves. She presently knew me, and I her, but she did not welcome me as I expected, nor did I find her in such a dress as I thought suitable to our circumstances. But what man has assurance enough not to pretend to know thoroughly the riddle of a woman's mind, and who could ever hope to

[3] A la rexa, "at the iron grate." In Spain, the lovers make their courtship at a low window that has a grate before it, having seldom admission into the house till the parents on both sides have agreed.

fix her mutable nature? 'Cardenio,' said Lucinda to me, 'my wedding clothes are on, and the perfidious Ferdinand, with my covetous father and the rest, stay for me in the hall, to perform the marriage-rites; but they shall sooner be witnesses of my death than of my nuptials. Be not troubled, my dear Cardenio; but rather strive to be present at that sacrifice. I promise thee, if entreaties and words cannot prevent it, I have a dagger that shall do me justice; and my death, at least, shall give thee undeniable assurances of my love and fidelity.' 'Do, madam,' cried I to her with precipitation, and so disordered that I did not know what I said, 'let your actions verify your words: let us leave nothing unattempted which may serve our common interests; and I assure you, if my sword does not defend them well, I will turn it upon my own breast, rather than outlive my disappointment.' I cannot tell whether Lucinda heard me, for she was called away in great haste, the bridegroom impatiently expecting her. My spirit forsook me when she left me, and my sorrows and confusion cannot be expressed. Methought I saw the sun set forever; and my eyes and my senses partaking of my distraction, I could not so much as spy the door to go into the house, and seemed rooted to the place where I stood. But at last, the consideration of my love having roused me out of this stupefying astonishment, I got into the house without being discovered, everything there being in a hurry; and going into the hall, I hid myself behind the hangings, where two pieces of tapestry met, and gave me liberty to see, without being seen. Who can describe the various thoughts, the doubts, the fears, the anguish that perplexed and tossed my soul, while I stood waiting there! Don Ferdinand entered the hall, not like a bridegroom, but in his usual habit, with only a cousin-german of Lucinda's, the rest were the people of the house: some time after came Lucinda herself, with her mother, and two waiting-women. I perceived she was as richly dressed, as was consistent with her quality, and the solemnity of the ceremony; but the distraction that possessed me, lent me no time to note particularly the apparel she had on: I only marked the colors, which were carnation and white, and the splendor of the jewels that enriched her dress in many places; but nothing equaled the luster of her beauty, that adorned her person much more than all those ornaments. Oh, memory! thou fatal enemy of my ease, why dost thou now so faithfully represent to the eyes of my mind Lucinda's incomparable charms? Why dost thou not rather show me what she did then; that, moved by so provoking a wrong, I may endeavor to revenge it, or at least to die. Forgive me these tedious digressions, gentlemen. Alas! my woes are not such as can or ought to be related with brevity; for to me every circumstance seems worthy to be enlarged upon."

The curate assured Cardenio that they attended every word with a mournful pleasure, that made them greedy of hearing the least passage. With that Cardenio went on. "All parties being met," said he, "the priest entered, and taking the young couple by the hands, he asked Lucinda whether she were willing to take Don Ferdinand for her wedded husband? With that I thrust out my head from between the two pieces of tapestry, listening with anxious heart to hear her answer, upon which depended my life and happiness. Dull-heartless wretch that I was! why did I not then show myself? why did I not call to her aloud? 'Consider what thou dost, Lucinda; thou art mine, and cannot be another man's: nor canst thou speak now the fatal Yes, without injurying Heaven, thyself, and me, and murdering thy Cardenio! And thou perfidious Ferdinand, who darest to violate all rights, both human and divine, to robe me of my treasure; canst thou hope to deprive me of the comfort of my life with impunity? Or thinkest thou that any consideration can stifle my resentments, when my honor and my love lie at stake?' Fool that I am! now that is too late, and danger is far distant; I say what I should have done, and not what I did then: after I have suffered the treasure of my soul to be stolen, I exclaim against the thief, whom I might have punished for the base attempt, had I had but so much resolution to revenge as I have now to complain. Then let me rather accuse my faint heart that durst not do me right, and let me die here like a wretch, void both of sense and honor, the outcast of society and nature. The priest stood waiting for Lucinda's answer a good while before she gave it: and all that time I expected she would have pulled out her dagger, or unloosed her tongue to plead her former engagement to me. But, alas! to my eternal disappointment, I heard her at last, with a feeble voice, pronounce the fatal Yes; and then Don Ferdinand, saying the same and giving her the ring, the sacred knot was tied which death alone can dissolve. Then did the faithless bridegroom advance to embrace his bride; but she, laying her hand upon her heart, in that very moment swooned away in her mother's arms. Oh what confusion seized me, what pangs, what torments racked me, seeing the falsehood of Lucinda's promises, all my hopes shipwrecked, and the only thing that made me wish to live, forever ravished from me! Confounded and despairing, I looked upon myself as abandoned by Heaven to the cruelty of my destiny; and the violence of my griefs stifling my sighs, and denying a passage to my tears, I felt myself transfixed with killing anguish, and burning with jealous rage and vengeance! In the meantime, the whole company was troubled at Lucinda's swooning; and, as her mother unclasped her gown before, to give her air, a folded paper was found in her bosom, which Don Ferdinand immediately snatched; then, stepping a little aside, he opened it and read it by the light of one of the tapers: and as soon as he had done, he, as it were, let himself fall upon a chair, and there he sat with his hand upon the side of his face, with all the signs of melancholy and discontent, as unmindful of his bride as if he had been insensible of her accident. For my own part, seeing all the house thus in an uproar, I resolved to leave the hated place, without caring whether I was seen or not, and in case I were seen, I resolved to act such a desperate part in punishing the traitor Ferdinand, that the world should at once be informed of his perfidiousness, and the severity of my just resentment; but my destiny, that preserved me for greater woes (if greater can be) allowed me then the use of that small remainder of my senses, which afterwards quite forsook me: so that I left the house, without revenging myself on my enemies, whom I could easily have sacrificed to my rage in this unexpected disorder; and I chose to inflict upon myself, for my credulity, the punishment which their infidelity deserved. I went to the messenger's house where I had left my mule, and without so much as bidding him adieu, I mounted, and left the town like another Lot, without turning to give it a parting look; and as I rode along the fields, darkness and silence round me, I vented my passions in execrations against the treacherous Ferdinand, and in as loud complaints of Lucinda's breach of vows and ingratitude. I called her cruel, ungrateful, false, but above all, covetous and sordid, since the wealth of my enemy was what had induced her to forget her vows to me; but then again, said I to myself, it is no strange thing for a young lady, that was so strictly educated, to yield herself up to the guidance of her father and mother, who had provided her a husband of that quality and fortune. But yet with truth and justice she might have pleaded, that she was mine before. In fine, I concluded that ambition had got the better of her love, and made her forget her promises to Cardenio. Thus abandoning myself to these tempestuous thoughts, I rode on all that night, and about break of day I struck into one of the passes that lead into these mountains; where I wandered for three days together, without keeping any road, till at last, coming to a certain valley that lies somewhere hereabouts, I met some shepherds, of whom I inquired the way to the most craggy and inaccessible part of these rocks. They

directed me, and I made all the haste I could to get thither, resolved to linger out my hated life far from the converse of false
ungrateful mankind. When I came among these deserts, my mule,
through weariness and hunger, or rather to get rid of so useless a
load as I was, fell down dead, and I myself was so weak, so tired
and dejected, being almost famished, and withal destitute and
careless of relief, that I soon laid myself down, or rather fainted on
the ground, where I lay a considerable while, I do not know how
long, extended like a corpse. When I came to myself again, I got
up, and could not perceive I had any appetite to eat: I found some
goatherds by me, who, I suppose, had given me some sustenance,
though I was not sensible of their relief: for they told me in what
a wretched condition they found me, staring, and talking so
strangely, that they judged I had quite lost my senses. I have
indeed since that had but too much cause to think, that my reason
sometimes leaves me, and that I commit those extravagancies which
are only the effects of senseless rage and frenzy; tearing my
clothes, howling through these deserts, filling the air with curses
and lamentations, and idly repeating a thousand times Lucinda's
name; all my wishes at that time being to breathe out my soul with
the dear word upon my lips; and when I come to myself, I am commonly so weak, and so weary, that I am scarce able to stir. As for
my place of abode, it is usually some hollow cork-tree, into which I
creep at night; and there some few goatherds, whose cattle browse
on the neighboring mountains, out of pity and Christian charity,
sometimes leave some victuals for the support of my miserable life:
for, even when my reason is absent, nature performs its animal
functions, and instinct guides me to satisfy it. Sometimes these
good people meet me in my lucid intervals, and chide me for taking
that from them by force and surprise, which they are always so
ready to give me willingly; for which violence I can make no other
excuse, but the extremity of my distraction. Thus must I drag a

295

miserable being, until Heaven, pitying my afflictions, will either put a period to my life, or blot out of my memory perjured Lucinda's beauty and ingratitude, and Ferdinand's perfidiousness. Could I but be so happy ere I die, I might then hope to be able, in time, to compose my frantic thoughts: but if I must despair of such a favor, I have no other way but to recommend my soul to Heaven's mercy; for I am not able to extricate my body or my mind out of that misery in which I have unhappily plunged myself.

"Thus, gentlemen, I have given you a faithful account of my misfortunes. Judge now whether it was possible I should relate them with less concern. And, pray do not lose time to prescribe remedies to a patient who will make use of none: I will, and can have no health without Lucinda; since she forsakes me, I must die: she has convinced me, by her infidelity, that she desires my ruin; and by my unparalleled sufferings to the last, I will strive to convince her I deserved a better fate. Let me then suffer on, and may I be the only unhappy creature whom despair could not relieve, while the impossibility of receiving comfort brings cure to so many other wretches!"

Here Cardenio made an end of his mournful story; and just as the curate was preparing to give him some proper consolation, he was prevented by the doleful accents of another complaint that engaged them to new attention. But the account of that adventure is reserved for the fourth book of this history; for our wise and judicious historian, Cid Hamet Benengeli, puts here a period to the third.

BOOK FOUR

I

THE PLEASANT NEW ADVENTURE THE CURATE AND BARBER MET WITH IN SIERRA MORENA, OR BLACK MOUNTAIN

MOST FORTUNATE and happy was the age that ushered into the world that most daring Knight, Don Quixote de la Mancha! for from his generous resolution to revive and restore the ancient order of knight-errantry, that was not only wholly neglected, but almost lost and abolished, our age, barren in itself of pleasant recreations, derives the pleasure it reaps from his true history, and the various tales and episodes thereof, in some respects, no less pleasing, artful, and authentic than the history itself. We told you that as the curate was preparing to give Cardenio some seasonable consolation, he was prevented by a voice, whose doleful complaints reached his ears. "O heavens!" cried the unseen mourner, "is it possible I have at last found out a place that will afford a private grave to this miserable body, whose load I so repine to bear? Yes, if the silence and solitude of these deserts do not deceive me, here I may die concealed from human eyes. Ah me! ah wretched creature! to what extremity has affliction driven me, reduced to think these hideous woods and rocks a kind retreat! 'Tis true indeed, I may here freely complain to Heaven, and beg for that relief which I might ask in vain of false mankind: for it is vain, I find, to seek below either counsel, ease, or remedy." The curate and his company, who heard all this distinctly, justly conjectured they were very near the person who thus expressed his grief, and therefore rose to find him out. They had not gone above twenty paces, before they spied a youth in a country habit, sitting at the foot of a rock, behind an ash-tree; but they could not well see his face, being bowed almost upon his knees, as he sat washing his feet in a rivulet that glided by. They approached him so softly that he did not perceive them: and, as he was gently paddling in the clear water, they had time to discern that his legs were as white as alabaster, and so taper, so curiously proportioned, and so fine, that nothing of the kind could appear more beautiful. Our observers were amazed at this discovery, rightly imagining that such tender feet were not used to trudge in rugged ways, or measure the steps of oxen at the plow, the common employments of people in such apparel; and therefore the curate, who went before the rest, whose curiosity was heightened by this sight, beckoned to them to step aside, and hide themselves behind some of the little rocks that were by; which they did, and from thence making a stricter observation, they found he had on a gray double-skirted jerkin, girt tight about his body with a linen towel. He wore also a pair of breeches, and gamashes of gray cloth, and a gray huntsman's cap on his head. His gamashes were now pulled up to the middle of his leg, which

298

really seemed to be of snowy alabaster. Having made an end of washing his beauteous feet, he immediately wiped them with a handkerchief, which he pulled out from under his cap; and with that, looking up, he discovered so charming a face, so accomplished a beauty, that Cardenio could not forbear saying to the curate, that since this was not Lucinda, it was certainly no human form, but an angel. And then the youth taking off his cap, and shaking his head, an incredible quantity of lovely hair flowed down upon his shoulders, and not only covered them, but almost all his body; by which they were now convinced, that what they at first took to be a country lad, was a young woman, and one of the most beautiful creatures in the world. Cardenio was not less surprised than the other two, and once more declared that no face could vie with hers but Lucinda's. To part her disheveled tresses, she only used her slender fingers, and at the same time discovered so fine a pair of arms and hands, so white and lovely, that our three admiring gazers grew more impatient to know who she was, and moved forwards to accost her. At the noise they made, the pretty creature started; and, peeping through her hair, which she hastily removed from before her eyes with both her hands, she no sooner saw three men coming towards her, but in a mighty fright she snatched up a little bundle that lay by her, and fled as fast as she could, without so much as staying to put on her shoes, or do up her hair. But alas! scarce had she gone six steps, when her tender feet not being able to endure the rough encounter of the stones, the poor affrighted fair fell on the hard ground; so that those from whom she fled hastening to help her: "Stay, madam," cried the curate, "whoever you be, you have no reason to fly; we have no other design but to do you service." With that, approaching her, he took her by the hand, and perceiving she was so disordered with fear and confusion, that she could not answer a word, he strove to compose her mind with kind expressions. "Be not afraid, madam," continued

299

he, "though your hair has betrayed what your disguise concealed from us, we are but the more disposed to assist you, and do you all manner of service. Then, pray, tell us how we may best do it. I imagine it was no slight occasion that made you obscure your singular beauty under so unworthy a disguise, and venture into this desert, where it was the greatest chance in the world that ever you met with us. However, we hope it is not impossible to find a remedy for your misfortunes, since there are none which reason and time will not at last surmount: and therefore, madam, if you have not absolutely renounced all human comfort, I beseech you tell us the cause of your affliction, and assure yourself we do not ask this out of mere curiosity, but a real desire to serve you, and either to condole or assuage your grief."

While the curate endeavored thus to remove the trembling fair one's apprehension, she stood amazed, staring, without speaking a word, sometimes upon one, sometimes upon another, like one scarce well awake, or like an ignorant clown who happens to see some strange sight. But at last, the curate having given her time to recollect herself, and persisting in his earnest and civil entreaties, she fetched a deep sigh, and then, unclosing her lips, broke silence in this manner: "Since this desert has not been able to conceal me, and my hair has betrayed me, it would be needless now for me to dissemble with you; and, since you desire to hear the story of my misfortunes, I cannot in civility deny you, after all the obliging offers you have been pleased to make me: but yet, gentlemen, I am much afraid, what I have to say will but make you sad, and afford you little satisfaction; for you will find my disasters are not to be remedied. There is one thing that troubles me yet more; it shocks my nature to think I must be forced to reveal to you some secrets, which I had a design to have buried in my grave; but yet, considering the garb and the place you have found me in, I fancy it will be better for me to tell you all, than to give occasion to doubt

300

of my past conduct and my present designs, by an affected reservedness." The disguised lady having made this answer, with a modest blush and extraordinary discretion, the curate and his company, who now admired her the more for her sense, renewed their kind offers and pressing solicitations; and then they modestly let her retire a moment to some distance, to put herself in decent order. Which done, she returned, and being all seated on the grass, after she had used no small violence to smother her tears, she thus began her story:

"I was born in a certain town of Andalusia, from which a duke takes his title, that makes him a grandee of Spain. This duke has two sons, the eldest heir to his estate, and as it may be presumed, of his virtues; the youngest heir to nothing I know of, but the treachery of Vellido,[1] and the deceitfulness of Galalon.[2] My father, who is one of his vassals, is but of low degree; but so very rich, that had fortune equaled his birth to his estate, he could have wanted nothing more, and I perhaps, had never been so miserable; for I verily believe, my not being of noble blood is the chief occasion of my ruin. True it is, my parents are not so meanly born as to have any cause to be ashamed of their originals, nor so high as to alter the opinion I have, that my misfortune proceeds from their lowness. It is true, they have been farmers from father to son, yet without any mixture or stain of infamous or scandalous blood. They are old rusty [3] Christians (as we call our true primitive Spaniards), and the antiquity of their family, together with their large possessions and the port they live in, raises them much above their profession, and has by little and little almost universally gained them the name of Gentlemen, setting them, in a manner, equal to

1 *Who murdered Sancho, King of Castile, as he was easing himself, at the siege of Camora.*
. 2 *Who betrayed the French army at Roncesvalles.*
3 Ranciofos *in the original; a metaphor taken from rusty bacon, yellow and moldy, as it were with age. It is a farmer's daughter speaks this.*

many such in the world's esteem. As I am their only child, they ever loved me with all the tenderness of indulgent parents; and their great affection made them esteem themselves happier in their daughter, than in the peaceable enjoyment of their large estate. Now as it was my good fortune to be possessed of their love, they were pleased to trust me with their substance. The whole house and estate was left to my management, and I took such care not to abuse the trust reposed in me, that I never forfeited their good opinion of my discretion. The time I had to spare from the care of the family, I commonly employed in the usual exercises of young women, sometimes making bone-lace, or at my needle, and now and then reading some good book, or playing on the harp; having experienced that music was very proper to recreate the wearied mind: and this was the innocent life I led. I have not descended to these particulars out of vain ostentation, but merely that, when I come to relate my misfortunes, you may observe I do not owe them to my ill-conduct. While I thus lived the life of a nun, unseen, as I thought, by anybody but our own family, and never leaving the house but to go to church, which was commonly betimes in the morning, and always with my mother, and so close hid in a veil that I could scarce find my way; notwithstanding all the care that was taken to keep me from being seen, it was unhappily rumored abroad that I was handsome, and to my eternal disquiet, love intruded into my peaceful retirement. Don Ferdinand, second son to the Duke I have mentioned, had a sight of me—" Scarce had Cardenio heard Don Ferdinand named, but he changed color, and betrayed such a disorder of body and mind, that the curate and the barber were afraid he would have fallen into one of those frantic fits that often used to take him; but by good fortune it did not come to that, and he only set himself to look steadfastly on the country-maid, presently guessing who she was; while she continued her story, without taking any notice of the alterations of his countenance.

302

"No sooner had he seen me," said she, "but, as he since told me, he felt in his breast that violent passion of which he afterwards gave me so many proofs. But, not to tire you with a needless relation of every particular, I will pass over all the means he used to inform me of his love: he purchased the good-will of all our servants with private gifts; he made my father a thousand kind offers of service; every day seemed a day of rejoicing in our neighborhood, every evening ushered in some serenade, and the continual music was even a disturbance in the night. He got an infinite number of love-letters transmitted to me, I do not know by what means, every one full of the tenderest expressions, promises, vows, and protestations. But all this assiduous courtship was so far from inclining my heart to a kind return, that it rather moved my indignation; insomuch that I looked upon Don Ferdinand as my greatest enemy, and one wholly bent on my ruin: not but that I was well enough pleased with his gallantry, and took a secret delight in seeing myself thus courted by a person of his quality. Such demonstrations of love are never altogether displeasing to women, and the most disdainful, in spite of all their coyness, reserve a little complaisance in their hearts for their admirers. But the disproportion between our qualities was too great to suffer me to entertain any reasonable hopes, and his gallantry too singular not to offend me. Besides, my father, who soon made a right construction of Don Ferdinand's pretensions, with his prudent admonitions concurred with the sense I ever had of my honor, and banished from my mind all favorable thoughts of his addresses. However, like a kind parent, perceiving I was somewhat uneasy, and imagining the flattering prospect of so advantageous a match might still amuse me, he told me one day he reposed the utmost trust in my virtue, esteeming it the strongest obstacle he could oppose to Don Ferdinand's dishonorable designs; yet, if I would marry, to rid me at once of his unjust pursuit, and prevent the ruin of my reputation,

I should have liberty to make my own choice of a suitable match, either in our own town or the neighborhood; and that he would do for me whatever could be expected from a loving father. I humbly thanked him for his kindness, and told him, that as I had never yet had any thoughts of marriage, I would try to rid myself of Don Ferdinand some other way. Accordingly I resolved to shun him with so much precaution, that he should never have the opportunity to speak to me: but all my reservedness, far from tiring out his passion, strengthened it the more. In short, Don Ferdinand, either hearing or suspecting I was to be married, thought of a contrivance to cross a design that was likely to cut off all his hopes. One night, therefore, when I was in my chamber, nobody with me but my maid, and the door double locked and bolted that I might be secured against the attempts of Don Ferdinand, whom I took to be a man who would stick at nothing to compass his designs, unexpectedly I saw him just before me; which amazing sight so surprised me, that I was struck dumb, and fainted away with fear. So I had not power to call for help, nor do I believe he would have given me time to have done it, had I attempted it; for he presently ran to me, and taking me in his arms, while I was sinking with the fright, he spoke to me in such endearing terms, and with so much address and pretended tenderness and sincerity, that I did not dare to cry out when I came to myself. His sighs, and yet more his tears, seemed to me undeniable proofs of his vowed integrity; and I being but young, bred up in perpetual retirement from all society but my virtuous parents, and unexperienced in those affairs, in which even the most knowing are apt to be mistaken, my reluctancy abated by degrees, and I began to have some sense of compassion, yet none but what was consistent with my honor. However, when I was pretty well recovered from my first fright, my former resolution returned; and then, with more courage than I thought I should have had, 'My lord,' said I, 'if, at the same time that you offer

304

me your love, and give me such strange demonstrations of it, you would also offer me poison, and leave to take my choice, I would soon resolve which to accept, and convince you, by my death, that my honor is dearer to me than my life. To be plain, I can have no good opinion of a presumption that endangers my reputation; and, unless you leave me this moment, I will so effectually make you know how much you are mistaken in me, that if you have but the least sense of honor left, you will repent the driving me to that extremity as long as you live. I was born your vassal, but not your slave; nor does the greatness of your birth privilege you to injure your inferiors, or exact from me more than the duties which all vassals pay; that excepted, I do not esteem myself less in my low degree, than you have reason to value yourself in your high rank. Do not then think to awe or dazzle me with your grandeur, or fright or force me into a base compliance; I am not to be tempted with titles, pomp and equipage; nor weak enough to be moved with vain sighs and false tears. In short, my will is wholly at my father's disposal, and I will not entertain any man as a lover, but by his appointment. Therefore, my lord, if you would have me believe you so sincerely love me, give over your vain and injurious pursuit; suffer me peaceably to enjoy the benefits of life in the free possession of my honor, the loss of which forever embitters all life's sweets; and since you cannot be my husband, do not expect from me that affection which I cannot pay to any other.' 'What do you mean, charming Dorothea?' cried the perfidious lord, 'cannot I be yours by the sacred title of husband? Who can hinder me, if you will but consent to bless me on those terms? Too happy if I have no other obstacle to surmount, I am yours this moment, beautiful Dorothea. See, I give you here my hand to be yours, and yours alone forever; and let all-seeing Heaven, and this holy image here on your oratory, witness the solemn truth.'"

Cardenio, hearing her call herself Dorothea, was now fully satisfied she was the person whom he took her to be: however, he would not interrupt her story, being impatient to hear the end of it; only addressing himself to her, "Is then your name Dorothea, madam?" cried he; "I have heard of a lady of that name, whose misfortunes have a great resemblance with yours. But proceed, I beseech you, and when you have done, I may perhaps surprise you with an account of things that have some affinity with those you relate." With that Dorothea made a stop, to study Cardenio's face, and his wretched attire; and then earnestly desired him, if he knew anything that concerned her, to let her know it presently; telling him, that all the happiness she had left, was only the courage to bear with resignation all the disasters that might befall her, well assured that no new one could make her more unfortunate than she was already. "Truly, madam," replied Cardenio, "I would tell you all I know, were I sure my conjectures were true; but, so far as I may judge by what I have heard hitherto, I do not think it material to tell it you yet, and I shall find a more proper time to do it." Then Dorothea, resuming her discourse, "Don Ferdinand," said she, "repeated his vows of marriage in the most serious manner; and giving me his hand, plighted me his faith in the most binding words, and sacred oaths. But before I would let him engage himself thus, I advised him to have a care how he suffered an unruly passion to get the ascendant over his reason, to the endangering of his future happiness. 'My lord,' said I, 'let not a few transitory and imaginary charms, which could never excuse such an excess of love, hurry you to your ruin: spare your noble father the shame and displeasure of seeing you married to a person so much below you by birth; and do not rashly do a thing of which you may repent, and that may make my life uncomfortable.' I added several other reasons to dissuade him from that hasty match, but they were all unregarded. Don Ferdinand, deaf to everything but to his desires, engaged and bound himself like an inconsiderate

306

lover, who sacrifices all things to his passion, or rather like a cheat, who does not value a breach of vows. When I saw him so obstinate, I began to consider what I had to do. I am not the first, thought I to myself, whom marriage has raised to unhoped-for greatness, and whose beauty alone has supplied her want of birth and merit; thousands besides Don Ferdinand have married merely for love, without any regard to the inequality of wealth or birth. The opportunity was fair and tempting; and as fortune is not always favorable, I thought it an imprudent thing to let it slip. Thought I to myself, while she kindly offers me a husband who assures me of an inviolable affection, why should I by an unreasonable denial make myself an enemy of such a friend? And then there was one thing more: I apprehended it would be dangerous to drive him to despair by an ill-timed refusal; nor could I think myself safe alone in his hands, lest he should resolve to satisfy his passion by force; which done, he might think himself free from performing a promise which I would not accept, and then I should be left without either honor or an excuse; for it would be no easy matter to persuade my father, and the censorious world, that this nobleman was admitted into my chamber without my consent. All these reasons, which in a moment offered themselves in my mind, shook my former resolves; and Don Ferdinand's sighs, his tears, his vows, and the sacred witnesses by which he swore, together with his graceful mien, his extraordinary accomplishments, and the love which I fancied I read in all his actions, helped to bring on my ruin, as I believe they would have prevailed with anyone's heart as free and as well guarded as was mine. Then I called my maid to be witness to Don Ferdinand's vows and sacred engagements, which he reiterated to me, and confirmed with new oaths and solemn promises: he called again on Heaven, and on many particular saints, to witness his sincerity, wishing a thousand curses might fall on him, in case he ever violated his word. Again he sighed, again he wept, and moved me

307

more and more with fresh marks of affection; and the treacherous maid having left the room, the perfidious lord, presuming on my weakness, completed his pernicious design. The day which succeeded that unhappy night had not yet begun to dawn, when Don Ferdinand, impatient to be gone, made all the haste he could to leave me. For after the gratifications of brutish appetite are past, the greatest pleasure then is to get rid of that which entertained it. He told me, though not with so great a show of affection, nor so warmly as before, that I might rely on his honor, and on the sincerity of his vows and promises; and, as a further pledge, he pulled off a ring of great value from his finger, and put it upon mine. In short, he went away; and my maid, who, as she confessed it to me, let him in privately, took care to let him out into the street by break of day, while I remained so strangely concerned at the thoughts of all these passages, that I cannot well tell whether I was sorry or pleased. I was in a manner quite distracted, and either forgot, or had not the heart to chide my maid for her treachery, not knowing yet whether she had done me good or harm. I had told Don Ferdinand before he went, that, seeing I was now his own, he might make use of the same means to come again to see me, till he found it convenient to do me the honor of owning me publicly for his wife: but he came to me only the next night, and from that time I never could see him more, neither at church nor in the street, though, for a whole month together, I tired myself endeavoring to find him out: being credibly informed he was still near us, and went a-hunting almost every day, I leave you to think with what uneasiness I passed those tedious hours, when I perceived his neglect, and had reason to suspect his breach of faith. So unexpected a flight, which I looked upon as the most sensible affliction that could befall me, had like to have quite overwhelmed me. Then it was that I found my maid had betrayed me; I broke out into severe complaints of her presumption, which I had smothered till that time. I exclaimed against Don Ferdinand, and exhausted my sighs and tears without assuaging my sorrow. What was worse, I found myself obliged to set a guard upon my very looks, for fear my father and mother should inquire into the cause of my discontent, and so occasion my being guilty of shameful lies and evasions to conceal my more shameful disaster. But at last I perceived it was in vain to dissemble, and I gave a loose to my resentments; for I could no longer hold, when I heard that Don Ferdinand was married in a neighboring town to a young lady of rich and noble parentage, and extremely handsome, whose name is Lucinda." Cardenio, hearing Lucinda named, felt his former disorder; but, by good fortune, it was not so violent as it used to be, and he only shrugged up his shoulders, bit his lips, knit his brows, and a little while after let fall a shower of tears, which did not hinder Dorothea from going on. "This news," continued she, "instead of freezing up my blood with grief and astonishment, filled me with burning rage. Despair took possession of my soul, and in the transports of my fury I was ready to run raving through the streets, and publish Don Ferdinand's disloyalty, though at the expense of my reputation. I do not know whether a remainder of reason stopped these violent motions, but I found myself mightily eased, as soon as I had pitched upon a design that presently came into my head. I discovered the cause of my grief to a young country-fellow that served my father, and desired him to lend me a suit of man's apparel, and to go along with me to the town where I heard Don Ferdinand was. The fellow used the best arguments he had to hinder me from so strange an undertaking; but, finding I was inflexible in my resolution, he assured me he was ready to serve me. Thereupon I put on this habit, which you see, and taking with me some of my own clothes, together with some gold and jewels, not knowing but I might have some occasion for them, I set out that very night, attended with that servant and many

309

anxious thoughts, without so much as acquainting my maid with my design. To tell you the truth, I did not well know myself what I went about; for, as there could be no remedy, Don Ferdinand being actually married to another, what could I hope to get by seeing him, unless it were the wretched satisfaction of upbraiding him with his infidelity? In two days and a half we got to the town, where the first thing I did was to inquire where Lucinda's father lived. That single question produced a great deal more than I desired to hear: for the first man I addressed myself to showed me the house, and informed me of all that happened at Lucinda's marriage; which, it seems, was grown so public, that it was the talk of the whole town. He told me how Lucinda had swooned away as soon as she answered the priest that she was contented to be Don Ferdinand's wife; and how, after he had approached to open her stays to give her more room to breathe, he found a letter in her own hand, wherein she declared she could not be Don Ferdinand's wife, because she was already contracted to a considerable gentleman of the same town, whose name was Cardenio; and that she had only consented to that marriage in obedience to her father. He also told me, that it appeared by the letter, and a dagger which was found about her, that she designed to have killed herself after the ceremony was over; and that Don Ferdinand, enraged to see himself thus deluded, would have killed her himself with that very dagger, had he not been prevented by those that were present. He added, it was reported, that upon this Don Ferdinand immediately left the town; and that Lucinda did not come to herself till the next day; and then she told her parents that she was really Cardenio's wife, and that he and she were contracted before she had seen Don Ferdinand. I heard also that this Cardenio was present at the wedding; and that as soon as he saw her married, which was a thing he never could have believed, he left the town in despair, leaving a letter behind him full of complaints of Lucinda's breach of faith, and to inform his friends of his resolution to go to some place where they should never hear of him more. This was all the discourse of the town when I came thither; and, soon after, we heard that Lucinda also was missing, and that her father and mother were grieving almost to distraction, not being able to learn what was become of her. For my part, this news revived my hopes, having reason to be pleased to find Don Ferdinand unmarried. I flattered myself that Heaven had perhaps prevented this second marriage to make him sensible of his violating the first, and to touch his conscience, in order to his acquitting himself of his duty like a Christian and a man of honor. So I strove to beguile my cares with an imaginary prospect of a far distant change of fortune, amusing myself with vain hopes that I might not sink under the load of affliction, but prolong life; though this was only a lengthening of my sorrows, since I have now but the more reason to wish to be eased of the trouble of living. But while I stayed in that town, not knowing what I had best to do, seeing I could not find Don Ferdinand, I heard a crier publicly describe my person, my clothes, and my age, in the open street, promising a considerable reward to any that could bring tidings of Dorothea. I also heard that it was rumored I was run away from my father's house with the servant who attended me; and that report touched my soul as much as Don Ferdinand's perfidiousness; for thus I saw my reputation wholly lost, and that too for a subject so base and so unworthy of my nobler thoughts. Thereupon I made all the haste I could to get out of the town with my servant, who, even then, to my thinking, began by some tokens to betray a faltering in the fidelity he had promised me. Dreading to be discovered, we reached the most desert part of this mountain that night: but, as it is a common saying, that misfortunes seldom come alone, and the end of one disaster is often the beginning of a greater, I was no sooner got to that place, where I thought myself safe, but the fellow, whom

311

I had hitherto found to be modest and respectful, now rather incited by his own villainy, than my beauty, and the opportunity which that place offered than by anything else, had the impudence to talk to me of love; and, seeing I answered him with anger and contempt, he would no longer lose time in clownish courtship, but resolved to use violence to compass his wicked design. But just Heaven, which seldom or never fails to succor just designs, so assisted mine, and his brutish passion so blinded him, that, not perceiving he was on the brink of a steep rock, I easily pushed him down; and then, without looking to see what was become of him, and with more nimbleness than could be expected from my surprise and weariness, I ran into the thickest part of the desert to secure myself. The next day I met a countryman, who took me to his house amidst these mountains, and employed me ever since in quality of his shepherd. There I have continued some months, making it my business to be as much as possible in the fields, the better to conceal my sex: but, notwithstanding all my care and industry, he at last discovered I was a woman; which made him presume to importune me with beastly offers. So that, fortune not favoring me with the former opportunity of freeing myself, I left his house, and chose to seek a sanctuary among these woods and rocks, there with sighs and tears to beseech Heaven to pity me, and to direct and relieve me in this forlorn condition: or at least to put an end to my miserable life, and bury in this desert the very memory of an unhappy creature, who, more through ill fortune than ill intent, has given the idle world occasion to be too busy with her fame."

"This, gentlemen," continued Dorothea, "is a true history of my tragical adventure; and now be you judges, whether I had reason to make the complaint you overheard, and whether so unfortunate and hopeless a creature be in a condition to admit of comfort. I have only one favor to beg of you: be pleased to direct me to some place where I may pass the rest of my life, secure from the search and inquiry of my parents; not but their former affection is a sufficient warrant for my kind reception, could the sense I have of the thoughts they must have of my past conduct permit me to return to them; but, when I think they must believe me guilty, and can now have nothing but my bare word to assure them of my innocence, I can never resolve to stand their sight." Here Dorothea stopped, and the blushes that overspread her cheeks were certain signs of the discomposure of her thoughts, and the unfeigned modesty of her soul. Those who had heard her story were deeply moved with compassion for her hard fate, and the curate would not delay any longer to give her some charitable comfort and advice. But scarce had he begun to speak, when Cardenio, addressing himself to her, interrupted him: "How, madam," said he, taking her by the hand, "are you then the beautiful Dorothea, the only daughter of the rich Cleonardo?" Dorothea was strangely surprised to hear her father named, and by one in so tattered a garb. "And pray who are you, friend," said she to him, "that know so well my father's name? for I think I did not mention it once throughout the whole relation of my afflictions?" "I am Cardenio," replied the other, "that unfortunate person, whom Lucinda, as you told us, declared to be her husband: I am that miserable Cardenio, whom the perfidiousness of the man who has reduced you to this deplorable condition, has also brought to this wretched state, to rags, to nakedness, to despair, nay to madness itself, and all hardships and want of human comforts; only enjoying the privilege of reason by short intervals, to feel and bemoan my miseries the more. I am the man, fair Dorothea, who was the unhappy eyewitness of Don Ferdinand's unjust nuptials, and who heard my Lucinda give her consent to be his wife; that heartless wretch, who, unable to bear so strange a disappointment, lost in amazement and trouble, flung out of the house, without staying to know what would follow her trance, and what the paper that was taken out of her bosom would produce. I abandoned myself to despair, and, having left a letter with a person whom I charged to deliver it into Lucinda's own hands, I hastened to hide myself from the world in this desert, resolved to end there a life, which from that moment I had abhorred as my greatest enemy. But fortune has preserved me, I see, that I may venture it upon a better cause: for, from what you have told us now, which I have no reason to doubt, I am emboldened to hope that Providence may yet reserve us both to a better fate than we durst have expected; Heaven will restore to you Don Ferdinand, who cannot be Lucinda's, and to me Lucinda, who cannot be Don Ferdinand's. For my part, though my interests were not linked with yours, as they are, I have so deep a sense of your misfortunes, that I would expose myself to any dangers to see you righted by Don Ferdinand: and here, on the word of a gentleman and a Christian, I vow and promise not to forsake you till he has done you justice, and to oblige him to do it at the hazard of my life, should reason and generosity prove ineffectual to force him to be blessed with you." Dorothea, ravished with joy, and not knowing how to express a due sense of Cardenio's obliging offers, would have thrown herself at his feet, had he not civilly hindered it. At the same time the curate, discreetly speaking for them both, highly applauded Cardenio for his generous resolution, and comforted

Dorothea. He also very heartily invited them to his house, where they might furnish themselves with necessaries, and consult together how to find out Don Ferdinand, and bring Dorothea home to her father; which kind offer they thankfully accepted. Then the barber, who had been silent all this while, put in for a share, and handsomely assured them, he would be very ready to do them all the service that might lie in his power. After these civilities, he acquainted them with the design that had brought the curate and him to that place; and gave them an account of Don Quixote's strange kind of madness, and of their staying there for his squire. Cardenio, hearing him mentioned, remembered something of the scuffle he had with them both, but only as if it had been a dream; so that, though he told the company of it, he could not let them know the occasion. By this time they heard somebody call, and, by the voice, knew that it was Sancho Panza, who, not finding them where he had left them, tore his very lungs with hallooing. With that they all went to meet him; which done, they asked him what was become of Don Quixote? "Alas," answered Sancho, "I left him yonder, in an ill plight: I found him in his shirt, lean, pale, and almost starved, sighing and whining for his lady Dulcinea. I told him, how that she would have him come to her presently to Toboso, where she looked for him out of hand; yet for all this he would not budge a foot, but even told me he was resolved he would never set eyes on her sweet face again, till he had done some feats that might make him worthy of her goodness. So that," added Sancho, "if he leads this life any longer, I fear me my poor master is never like to be an emperor, as he is bound in honor to be, nay not so much as an archbishop, which is the least thing he can come off with; therefore, good sir, see and get him away by all means, I beseech you." The curate bid him be of good cheer, for they would take care to make him leave that place whether he would or

315

not; and then, turning to Cardenio and Dorothea, he informed them of the design which he and the barber had laid in order to effect his cure, or at least to get him home to his house. Dorothea, whose mind was much eased with the prospect of better fortune, kindly undertook to act the distressed lady herself, which she said she thought would become her better than the barber, having a dress very proper for that purpose; besides, she had read many books of chivalry, and knew how the distressed ladies used to express themselves when they came to beg some knight-errant's assistance. "This is obliging, madam," said the curate, "and we want nothing more: so let us to work as fast as we can; we may now hope to succeed, since you thus happily facilitate the design." Presently Dorothea took out of her bundle a petticoat of very rich stuff, and a gown of very fine green silk; also a necklace, and several other jewels out of a box; and with these in an instant she so adorned herself, and appeared so beautiful and glorious, that they all stood in admiration that Don Ferdinand should be so injudicious, to slight so accomplished a beauty. But he that admired her most was Sancho Panza; for he thought he had never set eyes on so fine a creature, and perhaps he thought right: which made him earnestly ask the curate who that fine dame was, and what wind had blown her thither among woods and rocks? "Who, that fine lady, Sancho?" answered the curate; "she is the only heiress in a direct line to the vast kingdom of Micomicon: moved by the fame of your master's great exploits, that spreads itself over all Guinea, she comes to seek him out, and beg a boon of him; that is, to redress a wrong which a wicked giant has done her." "Why, that is well," quoth Sancho: "a happy seeking and a happy finding. Now if my master be but so lucky as to right that wrong, by killing that son of a whore of a giant you tell me of, I am a made man: yes, he will kill him, that he will, if he can but come at him, and he be not a hobgoblin; for my master can do no good with

316

hobgoblins. But, Mr. Curate, if it please you, I have a favor to ask of you: I beseech you put my master out of conceit with all archbishoprics, for that is what I dread; and therefore to rid me of my fears, put it into his head to clap up a match with this same princess: for by that means it will be past his power to make himself archbishop, and he will come to be emperor, and I a great man as sure as a gun. I have thought well of the matter, and I find it is not at all fitting he should be an archbishop for my good; for what should I get by it? I am not fit for Church preferment, I am a married man; and now for me to go trouble my head with getting a license to hold Church-livings, it would be an endless piece of business; therefore, it will be better for him to marry out of hand this same princess, whose name I cannot tell, for I never heard it." "They call her the Princess Micomicona," said the curate; "for her kingdom being called Micomicon, it is a clear case she must be called so." "Like enough," quoth Sancho; "for I have known several men in my time go by the names of the places where they were born, as Pedro de Alcala, Juan de Ubeda, Diego de Valladolid; and mayhap the like is done in Guinea, and the queens go by the name of their kingdoms." "It is well observed," replied the curate: "as for the match, I will promote it to the utmost of my power." Sancho was heartily pleased with this promise; and, on the other side, the curate was amazed to find the poor fellow so strangely infected with his master's mad notions, as to rely on his becoming an emperor. By this time Dorothea being mounted on the curate's mule, and the barber having clapped on his ox-tail beard, nothing remained but to order Sancho to show them the way, and to renew their admonitions to him, lest he should seem to know them, and to spoil the plot, which if he did, they told him it would be the ruin of all his hopes and his master's empire. As for Cardenio, he did not think fit to go with them, having no business there; besides, he could not tell but that Don Quixote might remember their late

317

fray. The curate, likewise not thinking his presence necessary, resolved to stay to keep Cardenio company; so, after he had once more given Dorothea her cue, she and the barber went before with Sancho, while the two others followed on foot at a distance.

Thus they went on for about three-quarters of a league, and then, among the rocks, they spied Don Quixote, who had by this time put on his clothes, though not his armor. Immediately Dorothea, understanding he was the person, whipped her palfrey, and when she drew near Don Quixote, her squire alighted, and took her from her saddle. When she was upon her feet, she gracefully advanced towards the Knight, and, with her squire, falling on her knees before him, in spite of his endeavors to hinder her: "Thrice valorous and invincible knight," said she, "never will I rise from this place, till your generosity has granted me a boon, which shall redound to your honor, and the relief of the most disconsolate and most injured damsel that the sun ever saw: and indeed if your valor and the strength of your formidable arm be answerable to the extent of your immortal renown, you are bound by the laws of honor, and the knighthood which you profess, to succor a distressed princess, who, led by the resounding fame of your marvelous and redoubted feats of arms, comes from the remotest regions, to implore your protection." "I cannot," said Don Quixote, "make you any answer, most beautiful lady, nor will I hear a word more, unless you vouchsafe to rise." "Pardon me, noble knight," replied the petitioning damsel; "my knees shall first be rooted here, unless you will courteously condescend to grant me the boon which I humbly request." "I grant it then, lady," said Don Quixote, "provided it be nothing to the disservice of my king, my country, and that beauty who keeps the key of my heart and liberty." "It shall not tend to the prejudice or detriment of any of these," cried the lady. With that Sancho, closing up to his master, and whispering him in the ear, "Grant it, sir," quoth he, "grant it,

I tell ye; it is but a trifle next
to nothing, only to kill a great
looby of a giant; and she that asks this, is the high and mighty
Princess Micomicona, queen of the huge kingdom of Micomicon in
Æthiopia." "Let her be what she will," replied Don Quixote, "I will
discharge my duty, and obey the dictates of my conscience, according to the rules of my profession." With that, turning to the damsel, "Rise, lady, I beseech you," cried he: "I grant you the boon
which your singular beauty demands." "Sir," said the lady, "the
boon I have to beg of your magnanimous valor is, that you will be
pleased to go with me instantly whither I shall conduct you, and
promise me not to engage in any other adventure, till you have
revenged me on a traitor who usurps my kingdom, contrary to all
laws both human and divine." "I grant you all this, lady," quoth

Don Quixote; "and therefore from this moment shake off all desponding thoughts that sit heavy upon your mind, and study to revive your drooping hopes; for, by the assistance of Heaven, and my strenuous arm, you shall see yourself restored to your kingdom, and seated on the throne of your ancestors, in spite of all the traitors that dare oppose your right. Let us then hasten our performance; delay always breeds danger; and to protract a great design is often to ruin it." The thankful princess, to speak her grateful sense of his generosity, strove to kiss the Knight's hand; however he, who was in everything the most gallant and courteous of all knights, would, by no means, admit of such a submission; but having gently raised her up, he embraced her with an aweful grace and civility, and then called to Sancho for his arms. Sancho went immediately, and having fetched them from a tree, where they hung like trophies, armed his master in a moment. And now the champion being completely accoutered, "Come on," said he, "let us go and vindicate the rights of this dispossessed princess." The barber was all this while upon his knees, and had enough to do to keep himself from laughing, and his beard from falling, which, if it had dropped off, as it threatened, would have betrayed his face and their whole plot at once. But, being relieved by Don Quixote's haste to put on his armor, he rose up, and taking the princess by the hand, they both together set her upon her mule. Then the Knight mounted his Rozinante, and the barber got on his beast. Only poor Sancho was forced to foot it, which made him fetch many a heavy sigh for the loss of his dear Dapple: however, he bore his crosses patiently, seeing his master in so fair a way of being next door to an emperor; for he did not question but he would marry that princess, and so be, at least, king of Micomicon. But yet it grieved him, to think his master's dominions were to be in the land of the negroes, and that, consequently, the people, over whom he was to be governor, were all to be black. But he presently bethought himself of a good remedy for that: "What care I," quoth he, "though they be blacks? best of all; it is but loading a ship with them, and having them into Spain, where I shall find chapmen enough to take them off my hands and pay me ready money for them; and so I will raise a good round sum, and buy me a title or an office to live upon frank and easy all the days of my life. Hang him that has no shifts, say I; it is a sorry goose that will not baste herself. Why, what if I am not so book-learned as other folks, sure I have a head-piece good enough to know how to sell thirty or ten thousand slaves in the turn of a hand. Let them even go higgledy-piggledy, little and great. What though they be as black as the devil in hell, let me alone to turn them into white and yellow boys: I think I know how to lick my own fingers." Big with these imaginations, Sancho trudged along so pleased and light-hearted, that he forgot his pain of traveling a-foot. Cardenio and the curate had beheld the pleasant scene through the bushes, and were at a loss what they should do to join companies. But the curate, who had a contriving head, at last bethought himself of an expedient; and pulling out a pair of scissors, which he used to carry in his pocket, he snipped off Cardenio's beard in a trice: and having pulled off his black cloak, and a sad-colored riding-coat, which he had on, he equipped Cardenio with them, while he himself remained in his doublet and breeches. In which new garb Cardenio was so strangely altered, that he would not have known himself in a looking-glass. This done, they made to the highway, and there stayed till Don Quixote and his company were got clear of the rocks and bad ways, which did not permit horsemen to go so fast as those on foot. When they came near, the curate looked very earnestly upon Don Quixote, as one that was in a study whether he might not know him; and then, like one that had made a discovery, he ran towards the Knight

321

with open arms, crying out, "Mirror of chivalry, my noble country-man Don Quixote de la Mancha! the cream and flower of gentility! the shelter and relief of the afflicted, and quintessence of knight-errantry! how overjoyed am I to have found you!" At the same time he embraced his left leg. Don Quixote, admiring what adorer of his heroic worth this should be, looked on him earnestly; and at last calling him to mind, would have alighted to have paid him his respects, not a little amazed to meet him there. But the curate hindering him, "Reverend sir," cried the Knight, "I beseech you let me not be so rude as to sit on horseback, while a person of your worth and character is on foot." "Sir," replied the curate, "you shall by no means alight: let your excellency be pleased to keep your saddle, since thus mounted you every day achieve the most stupendous feats of arms and adventures that were ever seen in our age. It will be honor enough for an unworthy priest, like me, to get up behind some of your company, if they will permit me; and I will esteem it as great a happiness as to be mounted upon Pegasus, or the Zebra, or the fleet mare of the famous Moor Musaraque, who to this hour lies enchanted in the dreary cavern of Zulema, not far distant from the great Compluto."[1] "Truly, good sir, I did not think of this," answered Don Quixote; "but, I suppose, my lady the princess will be so kind as to command her squire to lend you his saddle, and to ride behind himself, if his mule be used to carry double." "I believe it will," cried the princess; "and my squire, I suppose, will not stay for my commands to offer his saddle, for he is too courteous and well-bred to suffer an ecclesiastical person to go a-foot, when we may help him to a mule." "Most certainly," cried the barber; and with that, dismounting, he offered the curate his saddle, which was accepted without much entreaty. By ill fortune the mule was a hired beast, and consequently unlucky; so, as

[1] *An university of Spain, now called Alcala de Henares.*

322

the barber was getting up behind the curate, the resty jade gave two or three jerks with her hinder legs, that, had they met with master Nicholas's skull or ribs, he would have bequeathed his rambling after Don Quixote to the devil. However, he flung himself nimbly off, and was more afraid than hurt: but yet, as he fell, his beard dropped off, and being presently sensible of that accident, he could not think of any better shift than to clap both his hands before his cheeks, and cry out he had broken his jaw-bone. Don Quixote was amazed to see such an overgrown bush of beard lie on the ground without jaws and bloodless. "Bless me," cried he, "what an amazing miracle is this! Here is a beard as cleverly taken off by accident, as if a barber had mowed it." The curate perceiving the danger they were in of being discovered, hastily caught up the beard, and, running to the barber, who lay all the while roaring and complaining, he pulled his head close to his own breast, and then muttering certain words, which he said were a charm appropriated to fastening on of fallen beards, he fixed it on again so handsomely, that the squire was presently then as bearded and as well as ever he was before; which raised Don Quixote's admiration, and made him engage the curate to teach him the charm at his leisure, not doubting but its virtue extended further than to the fastening on of beards, since it was impossible that such a one could be torn off without fetching away flesh and all; and, consequently, such a sudden cure might be beneficial to him upon occasion. And now, everything being set to rights, they agreed that the curate should ride first by himself, and then the other two, by turns relieving one another, sometimes riding, sometimes walking, till they came to their inn, which was about two leagues off. So Don Quixote, the princess, and the curate, being mounted, and Cardenio, the barber, and Sancho ready to move forwards on foot, the Knight addressing himself to the distressed damsel: "Now, lady," said he, "let me entreat your greatness to tell me which way we must go, to do you service." The curate, before she could answer, thought fit to ask her a question, that might the better enable her to make a proper reply. "Pray, madam," said he, "towards what country is it your pleasure to take your progress? is it not towards the kingdom of Micomicon? I am very much mistaken if that be not the part of the world whither you desire to go." The lady, having got her cue, presently understood the curate, and answered that he was in the right. "Then," said the curate, "your way lies directly through the village where I live, from whence we have a straight road to Carthagena, where you may conveniently take shipping; and if you have a fair wind and good weather, you may, in something less than nine years, reach the vast lake Meona, I mean the Palus Meotis, which lies somewhat more than a hundred days' journey from your kingdom." "Surely, sir," replied the lady, "you are under a mistake; for it is not quite two years since I left the place; and besides, we have had very little fair weather all the while, and yet I am already got hither, and have so far succeeded in my designs, as to have obtained the sight of the renowned Don Quixote de la Mancha, the fame of whose achievements reached my ears as soon as I landed in Spain, and moved me to find him out, to throw myself under his protection, and commit the justice of my cause to his invincible valor." "No more, madam, I beseech you," cried Don Quixote; "spare me the trouble of hearing myself praised, for I mortally hate whatever may look like adulation; and though your compliments may deserve a better name, my ears are too modest to be pleased with any such discourse; it is my study to deserve and to avoid applause. All I will venture to say is, that whether I have any valor or no, I am wholly at your service, even at the expense of the last drop of my blood; and therefore, waving all these matters till a fit opportunity, I would gladly know of this reverend clergyman what brought him hither, unattended by any of his servants, alone, and so slenderly clothed; for I must confess, I am not a little surprised to meet him in this condition." "To tell you the reason in a few words," answered the curate, "you must know, that Mr. Nicholas, our friend and barber, went with me to Seville, to receive some money which a relation of mine sent me from the Indies, where he has been settled these many years; neither was it a small sum, for it was no less than seventy thousand pieces of eight, and all of due weight, which is no common thing, you may well judge: but upon the road hereabouts we met four highwaymen that robbed us of all we had, even to our very beards, so that the poor barber was forced to get him a chin-periwig. And, for that young gentleman whom you see there," continued he, pointing to Cardenio, "after they had stripped him to his shirt, they transfigured him as you see.[2] Now everybody hereabouts says, that those who robbed us were certainly a pack of rogues condemned to the galleys, who, as they were going to punishment, were rescued by a single man, not far from this place, and that with so much courage, that, in spite of the king's officer and his guards, he alone set them all at liberty. Certainly that man was either mad, or as great a rogue as any of them; for would anyone that had a grain of sense or honesty, have let loose a company of wolves among sheep, foxes among innocent poultry, and wasps among the honey-pots? He has hindered public justice from taking its course, broke his allegiance to his lawful sovereign, disabled the strength of his galleys, rebelled against him, opposed his officers in contempt of the law, and alarmed the Holy Brotherhood, that had lain quiet so long; nay, what is yet worse, he has endangered his life upon earth, and his salvation hereafter." Sancho had given the curate an account of the adventure of the galley-slaves, and this made him lay it on thick in the relation, to try how Don Quixote would bear it. The Knight changed color at every word,

2 *The priest had clipped off Cardenio's beard in haste.*

not daring to confess he was the pious knight-errant who had delivered those worthy gentlemen out of bondage. "These," said the curate, by way of conclusion, "were the men that reduced us to this condition; and may Heaven in mercy forgive him that freed them from the punishment they so well deserved."

III: THE PLEASANT STRATAGEMS USED TO FREE THE ENAMOURED KNIGHT FROM THE RIGOROUS PENANCE WHICH HE HAD UNDERTAKEN

Scarce had the curate made an end, when Sancho, addressing himself to him, "Faith and truth," quoth he, "Master Curate, he that did that rare job was my master his own self, and that not for want of fair warning; for I bid him have a care what he did, and told him over and over, it would be a grievous sin to put such a gang of wicked wretches out of durance, and that they all went to the galleys for their roguery." "You buffle-headed clown," cried Don Quixote, "is it for a knight-errant when he meets with people laden with chains, and under oppression, to examine whether they are in those circumstances for their crimes, or only through misfortune? We are only to relieve the afflicted, to look on their distress, and not on their crimes. I met a company of poor wretches, who went along sorrowful, dejected and linked together like the beads of a rosary; thereupon I did what my conscience and my profession obliged me to do. And what has any man to say to this? If anyone dares say otherwise, saving this reverend clergyman's presence and the holy character he bears, I say, he knows little of knight-errantry, and lies like a son of a whore, and a base-born villain; and this I will make him know more effectually with the convincing edge of my sword!" This said, with a grim look, he fixed himself in his stirrups, and pulled his helmet over his brows, for the basin, which he took to be Mambrino's helmet, hung at his saddle-bow, in order to have the damage repaired which it had received from the galley-slaves. Thereupon Dorothea, by this time well acquainted with his temper, seeing him in such a passion, and that everybody except Sancho Panza, made a jest of him, resolved, with her native sprightliness and address, to carry on the humor. "I beseech you, sir," cried she, "remember the promise you have made me, and that you cannot engage in any adventure whatsoever, till you have performed that we are going about. Therefore pray assuage your anger; for had master curate known the galley-slaves were rescued by your invincible arm, I am sure he would rather have stitched up his lips, or bit off his tongue, than have spoken a word that should make him incur your displeasure." "Nay, I assure you," cried the curate, "I would sooner have twitched off one of my mustachios into the bargain." "I am satisfied, madam," cried Don Quixote, "and for your sake the flame of my just indignation is quenched; nor will I be induced to engage in any quarrel, till I have fulfilled my promise to your highness. Only in recompense of my good intentions, I beg you will give us the story of your misfortunes, if this will not be too great a trouble to you; and let me know who and what, and how many are the persons of whom I must have due and full satisfaction on your behalf." "I am very willing to do it," replied Dorothea; "but yet I fear a story like mine, consisting only of afflictions and disasters, will prove but a tedious entertainment." "Never fear that, madam," cried Don Quixote. "Since then it must be so," said Dorothea, "be pleased to lend me your attention." With that Cardenio and the barber gathered up to her, to hear what kind of story she had provided so soon; Sancho also hung his ears upon her side-saddle, being no less deceived in her than his master: and the lady having seated herself well on her mule, after coughing once or twice, and other preparations, very gracefully began her story.

"First, gentlemen," said she, "you must know my name is——"
Here she stopped short, and could not call to mind the name the
curate had given her; whereupon, finding her at a non-plus, he
made haste to help her out. "It is not at all strange," said he,
"madam, that you should be so discomposed by your disasters, as
to stumble at the very beginning of the account you are going to
give of them; extreme affliction often distracts the mind to that
degree, and so deprives us of memory, that sometimes we for a while
can scarce think on our very names: no wonder then, that the
Princess Micomicona, lawful heiress to the vast kingdom of Micomicon, disordered with so many misfortunes, and perplexed with
so many various thoughts for the recovery of her crown, should
have her imagination and memory so encumbered; but I hope you
will now recollect yourself, and be able to proceed." "I hope so
too," said the lady, "and I will try to go through with my story
without any further hesitation. Know then, gentlemen, that the
king, my father, who was called Tinacrio the Sage, having great
skill in the magic art, understood by his profound knowledge in
that science, that Queen Xaramilla, my mother, should die before
him, that he himself should not survive her long, and I should be
left an orphan. But he often said, that this did not so much trouble
him as the foresight he had by his speculations, of my being threatened with great misfortunes, which would be occasioned by a certain giant, lord of a great island near the confines of my kingdom,
his name Pandafilando, surnamed of the Gloomy Aspect; because,
though his eyeballs are seated in their due place, yet he affects to
squint and look askew, on purpose to fright those on whom he
stares. My father, I say, knew that this giant, hearing of his death,
would one day invade my kingdom with a powerful army, and drive
me out of my territories, without leaving me so much as the least
village for a retreat; though he knew withal that I might avoid
that extremity, if I would but consent to marry him; but as he

found out by his art, he had reason to think I never would incline to such a match. And indeed I never had any thoughts of marrying this giant, nor really any other giant in the world, how unmeasurably great and mighty soever he were. My father therefore charged me to bear my misfortunes patiently, and abandon my kingdom to Pandafilando for a time, without offering to keep him out by force of arms, since this would be the best means to prevent my own death and the ruin of my subjects, considering the impossibility of withstanding the devilish force of the giant. But withal, he ordered me to direct my course towards Spain, where I should be sure to meet with a powerful champion, in the person of a knight-errant, whose fame should at that time be spread over all the kingdom; and his name, my father said, should be, if I forget not, Don Azote,[1] or Don Gigote." "And if it please you, forsooth," quoth Sancho, "you would say Don Quixote, otherwise called the Knight of the Woeful Figure." "You are right," answered Dorothea, "and my father also described him, and said he should be a tall thin-faced man, and that on his right side, under the left shoulder, or somewhere thereabouts, he should have a tawny mole overgrown with a tuft of hair, not much unlike that of a horse's mane." With that Don Quixote, calling for his squire to come to him: "Here," said he, "Sancho, help me off with my clothes, for I am resolved to see whether I be the knight of whom the necromantic king has prophesied." "Pray, sir, why would you pull off your clothes?" cried Dorothea. "To see whether I have such a mole about me as your father mentioned," replied the Knight. "Your worship need not strip to know that," quoth Sancho; "for, to my knowledge, you have just such a mark as my lady says, on the small of your back, which betokens you to be a strong-bodied man." "That is enough," said Dorothea; "friends may believe one another without such a

[1] *Don Azote, is Don Horse-whip; and Don Gigote, Don Hash or Minced Meat: willful mistakes upon likeness of the words.*

strict examination; and, whether it be on the shoulder or on the back-bone, it is not very material. In short, I find my father aimed right in all his predictions, and so do I in recommending myself to Don Quixote, whose stature and appearance so well agree with my father's description, and whose renown is so far spread, not only in Spain, but over all La Mancha, that I had no sooner landed at Ossuna, but the fame of his prowess reached my ears; so that I was satisfied in myself he was the person in quest of whom I came." "But pray, madam," cried Don Quixote, "how came you to land at Ossuna, since it is no seaport town?" "Doubtless, sir," said the curate, before Dorothea could answer for herself, "the princess would say, that after she landed at Malaga, the first place where she heard of your feat of arms, was Ossuna." "That is what I would have said," replied Dorothea. "It is easily understood," said the curate; "then pray let your majesty be pleased to go on with your story." "I have nothing more to add," answered Dorothea, "but that fortune has at last so far favored me, as to make me find the noble Don Quixote, by whose valor I look upon myself as already restored to the throne of my ancestors; since he has so courteously and magnanimously vouchsafed to grant me the boon I begged, to go with me whithersoever I should guide him. For all I have to do is to show him this Pandafilando of the Gloomy Aspect, that he may slay him, and restore that to me of which he has so unjustly deprived me. For all this will certainly be done with the greatest ease in the world, since it was foretold by Tinacrio the Sage, my good and royal father, who has also left a prediction written either in Chaldean or Greek characters (for I cannot read them) which denotes, that after the knight of the prophecy has cut off the giant's head, and restored me to the possession of my kingdom, if he should ask me to marry him, I should by no means refuse him, but instantly put him in possession of my person and kingdom." "Well, friend Sancho," said Don Quixote, hearing this and turning to the squire, "what thinkest thou now? Dost thou not hear how matters go? Did not I tell thee as much before! See now, whether we have not a kingdom which we may command, and a queen whom we may espouse." "Ah, marry have you!" replied Sancho, "and a pox take the son of a whore, I say, that will not wed and bed her majesty's grace as soon as master Pandafilando's windpipes are slit. Look what a dainty bit she is! Ha! would I never had a worse flea in my bed!" With that, to show his joy, he cut a couple of capers in the air; and, turning to Dorothea, laid hold on her mule by the bridle, and flinging himself down on his knees, begged she would be graciously pleased to let him kiss her hand, in token of his owning her for his sovereign lady. There was none of the beholders but was ready to burst for laughter, having a sight of the master's madness and the servant's simplicity. In short, Dorothea was obliged to comply with his entreaties, and promised to make him a grandee, when fortune should favor her with the recovery of her lost kingdom. Whereupon Sancho gave her his thanks, in such a manner as obliged the company to a fresh laughter. Then going on with her relation, "Gentlemen," said she, "this is my history; and among all my misfortunes, this only has escaped a recital: that not one of the numerous attendants I brought from my kingdom has survived the ruins of my fortune, but this good squire with the long beard: the rest ended their days in a great storm, which dashed our ship to pieces in the very sight of the harbor; and he and I had been sharers in the destiny, had we not laid hold of two planks, by which assistance we were driven to land, in a manner altogether miraculous, and agreeable to the whole series of my life, which seems, indeed, but one continued miracle. And if in any part of my relation I have been tedious, and not so exact as I should have been, you must impute it to what master curate observed to you, in the beginning of my story, that continual troubles oppress the senses, and weaken the memory."

"Those pains and afflictions, be they ever so intense and difficult," said Don Quixote, "shall never deter me (most virtuous and high-born lady) from adventuring for your service, and enduring whatever I shall suffer in it: and therefore I again ratify the assurances I have given you, and swear that I will bear you company, though to the end of the world, in search of this implacable enemy of yours, till I shall find him; whose insulting head, by the help of Heaven, and my own invincible arm, I am resolved to cut off, with the edge of this (I will not say good) sword: a curse on Gines de Passa-monte, who took away my own!" This he spoke murmuring to himself, and then prosecuted his discourse in this manner: "And after I have divided it from the body, and left you quietly possessed of your throne, it shall be left at your own choice to dispose of your person, as you shall think convenient: for, as long as I shall have my memory full of her image, my will captivated, and my understanding wholly subjected to her, whom I now forbear to name, it is impossible I should in the least deviate from the affection I bear to her, or be induced to think of marrying, though it were a phœnix."

The close of Don Quixote's speech, which related to his not marrying, touched Sancho so to the quick, that he could not forbear bawling out his resentments: "Body of me, Sir Don Quixote," cried he, "you are certainly out of your wits, or how is it possible you should stick at striking a bargain with so great a lady as this is? Do you think, sir, fortune will put such dainty bits in your way at every corner? Is my lady Dulcinea handsomer, do you think? No, marry is she not half so handsome: I could almost say she is not worthy to tie this lady's shoe-latchets. I am likely indeed to get the earldom I have fed myself with hopes of, if you spend your time in fishing for mushrooms in the bottom of the sea. Marry, marry out of hand, or Old Nick take you for me: lay hold of the kingdom, which is ready to leap into your hands; and, as soon as you are a king, even make me a marquis, or a peer of the land; and afterwards let things go at sixes and sevens, it will be all one case to Sancho." Don Quixote, quite divested of all patience, at the blasphemies which were spoken against his lady Dulcinea, could bear with him no longer; and therefore, without so much as a word to give him notice of his displeasure, gave him two such blows with his lance, that poor Sancho measured his length on the ground, and had certainly there breathed his last, had not the Knight desisted, through the persuasions of Dorothea. "Thinkest thou," said he, after a considerable pause, "most infamous peasant, that I shall always have leisure and disposition to put up thy affronts; and that thy whole business shall be to study new offenses, and mine to give thee new pardons? Dost thou not know, excommunicated traitor (for certainly excommunication is the least punishment can fall upon thee, after such profanations of the peerless Dulcinea's name), and art thou not assured, vile slave and ignominious vagabond, that I should not have strength sufficient to kill a flea, did not she give strength to my nerves, and infuse vigor into my sinews? Speak, thou villain with the viper's tongue; who doth thou imagine has restored the queen to her kingdom, cut off the head of a giant, and made thee a marquis (for I count all this is done already), but the power of Dulcinea, who makes use of my arm, as the instrument of her act in me? She fights and overcomes in me, and I live and breathe in her, holding life and being from her. Thou base-born wretch! art thou not possessed of the utmost ingratitude, thou who seest thyself exalted from the very dregs of the earth to nobility and honor, and yet dost repay so great a benefit with obloquies against the person of thy benefactress."

Sancho was not so mightily hurt, but he could hear what his master said well enough; wherefore, getting upon his legs in all haste, he ran for shelter behind Dorothea's palfrey; and being got thither, "Hark you, sir," cried he to him, "if you have no thought of marrying this same lady, it is a clear case that the kingdom will never be yours; and, if it be not, what good can you be able to do me? Then let anyone judge whether I have not cause to complain. Therefore, good your worship, marry her once for all, now we have her rained down, as it were, from heaven to us, and you may after keep company with my lady Dulcinea: for, I guess, you will not be the only king in the world that has kept a miss or two in a corner. As for beauty, do you see, I will not meddle nor make, for (if I must say the truth) I like both the gentlewomen well enough in conscience; though, now I think on it, I have never seen the lady Dulcinea." "How, not seen her, blasphemous traitor," replied Don Quixote, "when just now you brought me a message from her!" "I say," answered Sancho, "I have not seen her so leisurely as to take notice of her features and good parts one by one; but yet, as I saw them at a blush, and all at once, methought I had no reason to find fault with them." "Well, I pardon thee now," quoth Don Quixote, "and you must excuse me for what I have done to you; for the first motions are not in our power." "I perceive that well enough," said Sancho, "and that is the reason my first motions are always in my tongue; and I cannot for my life help speaking what comes uppermost." "However, friend Sancho," said Don Quixote, "you had better think before you speak; for the pitcher goes so often to the well—I need say no more." "Well, what must be must be," answered Sancho, "there is Somebody above who sees all, and will one day judge which hath most to answer for, whether I for speaking amiss, or you for doing so." "No more of this, Sancho," said Dorothea, "but run and kiss your lord's hands, and beg his pardon; and for the time to come, be more advised and cautious how you run into the praise or dispraise of any person; but especially take care you do not speak ill of that lady of Toboso, whom I do not know, though I am ready to do her any service; and, for your own part, trust in Heaven; for you shall infallibly have a lordship, which shall enable you to live like a prince." Sancho shrugged up his shoulders, and, in a sneaking posture, went and asked his master for his hand, which he held out to him with a grave countenance; and, after the squire had kissed the back of it, the Knight gave him his blessing, and told him he had a word or two with him, bidding him come nearer, that he might have the better convenience of speaking to him. Sancho did as his master commanded, and, going a little from the company with him: "Since thy return," said Don Quixote, applying himself to him, "I have neither had time nor opportunity to inquire into the particulars of thy embassy, and the answer thou hast brought; and therefore, since fortune has now befriended us with convenience and leisure, deny me not the satisfaction you may give me by the rehearsal of thy news." "Ask what you will," cried Sancho, "and you shall not want for an answer: but, good your worship, for the time to come, I beseech you do not be too hasty." "What occasion hast thou, Sancho, to make this request?" replied Don Quixote. "Reason good enough, truly," said Sancho; "for the blows you gave me even now, were rather given me on account of the quarrel which the devil stirred up between your worship and me the other night, than for your dislike of anything which was spoken against my lady Dulcinea." "I pray thee, Sancho," cried Don Quixote, "be careful of falling again into such irreverent ex-pressions; for they provoke me to anger, and are highly offensive. I pardoned thee then for being a delinquent, but thou art sensible that a new offense must be attended with a new punishment." As they were going on in such discourse as this, they saw at a distance a person riding up to them on an ass, who, as he came near enough to be distinguished, seemed to be a gipsy by his habit. But Sancho Panza, who, whenever he got sight of any asses, followed them with his eyes and his heart, as one whose thoughts were ever fixed on his own, had scarce given him half an eye, but he knew him to be Gines de Passamonte, and by the looks of the gipsy found out the visage

of his ass; as really it was the
very same which Gines had got under him; who, to conceal himself
from the knowledge of the public, and have the better opportunity
of making a good market of his beast, had clothed himself like a
gipsy; the cant of that sort of people, as well as the languages of
other countries, being as natural and familiar to them as their own.
Sancho saw him, and knew him; and, scarce had he seen and taken
notice of him, when he cried out as loud as his tongue would permit: "Ah! thou thief Ginesillo, leave my goods and chattels behind
thee; get off from the back of my own dear life: thou hast nothing
to do with my poor beast, without whom I cannot enjoy a moment's ease: away from my Dapple, away from my comfort; take
to thy heels, thou villain; hence thou hedge-bird, leave what is
none of thine!" He had no occasion to use so many words; for
Gines dismounted as soon as he heard him speak, and taking to
his heels, got from them, and was out of sight in an instant.
Sancho ran immediately to his ass, and embraced him: "How hast
thou done?" cried he, "since I saw thee, my darling and treasure,
my dear Dapple, the delight of my eyes, and my dearest companion!" And then he stroked and slabbered him with kisses, as

336

if the beast had been a rational creature. The ass, for his part, was as silent as could be, and gave Sancho the liberty of as many kisses as he pleased, without the return of so much as one word to the many questions he had put to him. At sight of this the rest of the company came up with him, and paid their compliments of congratulation to Sancho, for the recovery of his ass, especially Don Quixote, who told him, that though he had found his ass again, yet would not he revoke the warrant he had given him for the three asses; for which favor Sancho returned him a multitude of thanks.

While they were traveling together, and discoursing after this manner, the curate addressed himself to Dorothea, and gave her to understand, that she had excellently discharged herself of what she had undertaken, as well in the management of the history itself, as in her brevity, and adapting her style to the particular terms made use of in books of knight-errantry. She returned for answer, that she had frequently conversed with such romances, but that she was ignorant of the situation of the provinces and the sea-ports, which occasioned the blunder she had made, by saying that she landed at Ossuna. "I perceived it," replied the curate, "and therefore I put in what you heard, which brought matters to rights again. But is it not an amazing thing, to see how ready this unfortunate gentleman is to give credit to these fictitious reports, only because they have the air of the extravagant stories in books of knight-errantry?" Cardenio said that he thought this so strange a madness, that he did not believe the wit of man, with all the liberty of invention and fiction, capable of hitting so extraordinary a character. "The gentleman," replied the curate, "has some qualities in him, even as surprising in a madman, as his unparalleled frenzy: for, take him but off from his romantic humor, discourse with him of any other subject, you will find him to handle it with a great deal of reason, and show himself, by his conversation, to have very clear and entertaining conceptions: insomuch, that if knight-errantry bears no relation to his discourse, there is no man but will esteem him for his vivacity of wit, and strength of judgment." While they were thus discoursing, Don Quixote prosecuted his converse with his squire: "Sancho," said he, "let us lay aside all manner of animosity, let us forget and forgive injuries; [2] and answer me as speedily as you can, without any remains of thy last displeasure, how, when, and where didst thou find my lady Dulcinea? What was she doing when you first paid thy respects to her? How didst thou express thyself to her? What answer was she pleased to make thee? What countenance did she put on at the perusal of my letter? Who transcribed it fairly for thee? And everything else which has any relation to this affair, without addition, lies, or flattery. On the other side, take care thou lose not a tittle of the whole matter, by abbreviating it, lest thou rob me of part of that delight, which I propose to myself from it." "Sir," answered Sancho, "if I must speak the truth, and nothing but the truth, nobody copied out the letter for me; for I carried none at all." "That is right," cried Don Quixote, "for I found the pocket-book, in which it was written, two days after thy departure, which occasioned exceeding grief in me, because I knew not what thou couldest do, when you found yourself without the letter; and I could not but be induced to believe that you would have returned, in order to take it with thee." "I had certainly done so," replied Sancho, "were it not for this head of mine, which kept it in remembrance ever since your worship read it to me, and helped me to say it over to a parish-clerk, who writ it out for me word for word, so purely, that he swore, though he had written out many a letter of excommunication in his time, he never in all the days of his life had read or seen anything so well spoken as it was." "And do you still retain the memory of it, my dear Sancho?" cried Don Quixote.

2 *In the original Spanish it is* Echemos pelillos a la mar: *i.e. literally, let us throw small hairs into the sea; but figuratively, let us renew our friendship and forget past differences.*

"Not I," quoth Sancho, "for as soon as I had given it her, and your turn was served, I was very willing to forget it. But, if I remember anything, what was on the top was thus, 'High and Subterrene,' I mean 'sovereign lady': and at the bottom, 'Yours till death, the Knight of the Woeful Figure'; and I put between these two things, three hundred souls, and lives, and dear eyes."

IV: THE PLEASANT DIALOGUE BETWEEN DON QUIXOTE AND HIS SQUIRE CONTINUED, WITH OTHER ADVENTURES

"All this is mighty well," said Don Quixote, "proceed, therefore: you arrived, and how was that queen of beauty then employed? On my conscience thou found her stringing of orient pearls, or embroidering some curious device in gold for me, her captive knight: was it not so, my Sancho?" "No, faith," answered the squire, "I found her winnowing a parcel of wheat very seriously in the back yard." "Then," said the Don, "you may rest assured, that every corn of that wheat was a grain of pearl, since she did it the honor of touching it with her divine hand. Did you observe the quality of the wheat; was it not of the finest sort?" "Very indifferent, I thought," said the squire. "Well, this at least, you must allow; it must make the finest, whitest bread, if sifted by her white hands. But go on; when you delivered my letter, did she kiss it? Did she treasure it in her bosom, or what ceremony did she use worthy such a letter? How did she behave herself?" "Why truly, sir," answered Sancho, "when I offered her the letter she was very busy handling her sieve; and, 'Prithee, honest friend,' said she, 'do so much as lay that letter down upon the sack there; I cannot read it till I have winnowed out what is in my hands.'" "O unparalleled discretion!" cried Don Quixote, "she knew that a perusal required leisure, and therefore deferred it for her more pleasing and private hours. But oh! my squire, while she was thus employed, what conferences passed? What did she ask about her knight, and what did you reply? Say all, say all, my dearest Sancho; let not the smallest circumstance escape thy tongue; speak all that thought can frame, or pen describe." "Her questions were easily answered, sir," said Sancho, "for she asked me none at all: I told her, indeed, in what a sad pickle I had left you for her sake, naked to the waist; that you ate and slept like the brute beasts; that you would let a razor as soon touch your throat as your beard; that you were still blubbering and crying, or swearing, and cursing your fortune." "There you mistook," replied Don Quixote. "I rather bless my fortune, and always shall, while life affords me a breath, since I am thought

to merit the esteem of so great a lady as my Dulcinea del Toboso." "There you hit it," said Sancho; "she is a high lady indeed, sir, for she is taller than I am by a handsbreadth." "Why, how now, Sancho," said the Knight, "hast thou measured up with her?" "Ah, marry did I, sir," said the squire: "for you should know that she desired me to lend her a hand in lifting a sack of wheat on an ass; so we buckled about it, and I came so close to her, that I found she was taller than I by a full span at least." "Right," answered Don Quixote; "but thou art also conscious that the uncommon stature of her person is adorned with innumerable graces and endowments of soul! But, Sancho, when you approached the charming she, did not an aromatic smell strike thy sense, a scent so odoriferous, pleasing, and sweet, that I want a name for it; sweet as ———— you understand me, as the richest fragrancy diffused around a perfumer's magazine of odors? This, at least, you must grant me." "I did, indeed, feel a sort of scent a little unsavory," said Sancho, "somewhat vigorous or so; for I suppose she had wrought hard, and sweat somewhat plentifully." "It is false," answered the Knight, "thy smelling has been debauched by thy own scent, or some canker in thy nose; if thou couldest tell the scent of opening roses, fragrant lilies, or the choicest amber, then you might guess at hers." "Cry ye mercy, sir," said Sancho, "it may be so indeed, for I remember that I myself have smelt very oft just as Madam Dulcinea did then, and that she should smell like me, is no such wondrous thing neither, since there is never a barrel the better herring [1] of us." "But now," said the Knight, "supposing the corn winnowed and dispatched to the mill; what did she, after she had read my letter?" "Your letter, sir," answered Sancho, "your letter was not read at all, sir; as for her part, she said she could neither read nor write, and she would trust nobody else, lest they should tell tales, and so she cunningly tore your letter. She said, that what I told her by word of mouth of your love and penance was enough: to make short now, she gave her service to you, and said she had rather see you than hear from you; and she prayed you, if ever you loved her, upon sight of me, forthwith to leave your madness among the bushes here, and come straight to Toboso (if you be at leisure), for she has something to say to you, and has a huge mind to see you. She had like to burst with laughing, when I called you the Knight of the Woeful Figure. She told me the Biscainer whom you mauled so was there, and that he was a very

[1] *An obsolete proverb meaning "never one better than another"—"nothing to choose between them."*

341

honest fellow; but that she heard no news at all of the galley-slaves."

"Thus far all goes well," said Don Quixote; "but tell me, pray, what jewel did she present you at your departure, as a reward for the news you brought? for it is a custom of ancient standing among knights- and ladies-errant to bestow on squires, dwarfs, or damsels, who bring them good news of their ladies or servants, some precious jewel as a grateful reward of their welcome tidings." "Ah, sir," said Sancho, "that was the fashion in the days of yore, and a very good fashion I take it: but all the jewels Sancho got was a luncheon of bread and a piece of cheese, which she handed to me over the wall when I was taking my leave, by the same token (I hope there is no ill-luck in it), the cheese was made of sheep's milk." "It is strange," said Don Quixote, "for she is liberal, even to profuseness; and if she presented thee not a jewel, she certainly had none about her at that time; but what is deferred is not lost, sleeves are good after Easter.[2] I shall see her, and matters shall be accommodated. Knowest thou, Sancho, what raises my astonishment? It is thy sudden return; for, proportioning thy short absence to the length of thy journey, Toboso being at least thirty leagues distant, thou must have ridden on the wind; certainly the sagacious enchanter, who is my guardian and friend (for doubtless such a one there is and ought to be, or I should not be a true knight-errant) ; certainly, I say, that wise magician has furthered thee on thy journey unawares: for there are sages of such incredible power, as to take up a knight-errant sleeping in his bed, and waken him next morning a thousand leagues from the place where he fell asleep. By this power knights-errant succor one another in their most dangerous exigents, when and where they please. For instance, suppose me fighting in the mountains of Armenia, with some hellish monster, some dreadful sprite, or fierce gigantic

2 *A proverbial expression, signifying that a good thing is always seasonable.*

342

knight, where perhaps I am like to be worsted (such a thing may happen), when just in the very crisis of my fate, when I least expect it, behold on the top of a flying cloud, or riding in a flaming chariot, another knight, my friend, who but a minute before was in England perhaps; he sustains me, delivers me from death, and returns that night to his own lodging, where he sups with a very good appetite after his journey, having ridden two or three thousand leagues that day; and all this performed by the industry and wisdom of these knowing magicians, whose only business and charge is glorious knight-errantry. Some such expeditious power, I believe, Sancho, though hidden from you, has promoted so great a dispatch in your late journey." "I believe, indeed," answered Sancho, "that there was witchcraft in the case, for Rozinante went without spur all the way, and was as mettlesome as though he had been a gipsy's ass with quicksilver in his ears." "Quicksilver! you coxcomb," said the Knight, "ay, and a troop of devils besides; and they are the best horse-coursers in nature, you must know, for they must needs go whom the devil drives; but no more of that. What is thy advice as to my lady's commands to visit her? I know her power should regulate my will; but then my honor, Sancho, my solemn promise has engaged me to the princess's service that comes with us, and the law of arms confines me to my word; love draws me one and glory the other way; on this side Dulcinea's strict commands, on the other my promised faith; but—it is resolved. I will travel night and day, cut off this giant's head, and having settled the princess in her dominions, will presently return to see that sun which enlightens my senses: she will easily condescend to excuse my absence, when I convince her it was for her fame and glory; since the past, present, and future success of my victorious arms depends wholly on the gracious influences of her favor, and the honor of being her knight." "Oh sad, oh sad!" said Sancho, "I doubt your worship's head is much the worse for wearing: are you mad, sir, to take so long a voyage for nothing? why do not you catch at this preferment that now offers, where a fine kingdom is the portion, twenty thousand leagues round, they say; nay, bigger than Portugal and Castile both together—good your worship! hold your tongue, I wonder you are not ashamed— take a fool's counsel for once, marry her by the first priest you meet; here is our own curate can do the job most curiously: come, master, I have hair enough in my beard to make a counselor, and my advice is as fit for you as your shoe is for your foot; a bird in hand is worth two in the bush, and

> " 'He that will not when he may,
>   When he would, he shall have nay.' "

"Thou advisest me thus," answered Don Quixote, "that I may be able to promote thee according to my promise: but that I can do without marrying this lady; for I shall make this the condition of entering into battle; that after my victory, without marrying the princess, she shall leave part of her kingdom at my disposal, to gratify whom I please; and who can claim any such gratuity but thyself?" "That is plain," answered Sancho, "but pray, sir, take care that you reserve some part near the seaside for me; that, if the air does not agree with me, I may transport my black slaves, make my profit of them, and go live somewhere else; so that I would have you resolve upon it presently; leave the lady Dulcinea for the present, and go kill this same giant, and make an end of that business first; for I dare swear it will yield you a good market." "I am fixed in thy opinion," said Don Quixote; "but I admonish thee not to whisper to any person the least hint of our conference; for, since Dulcinea is so cautious and secret, it is proper that I and mine should follow her example." "Why the devil, then," said Sancho, "should you send everybody you overcome packing to Madam Dulcinea, to fall down before her, and tell her they came from you to pay their obedience, when this tells all the world that she is your mistress as much as if they had it under your hand?" "How dull of apprehension and stupid thou art," said the Knight; "hast thou not sense to find that all this redounds to her greater glory? Know that, in proceedings in chivalry, a lady's honor is calculated from the number of her servants, whose services must not tend to any reward, but the favor of her acceptance, and the pure honor of performing them for her sake, and being called her servants." "I have heard our curate," answered Sancho, "preach up this doctrine of loving for love's sake, and that we ought to love our Maker so for His own sake, without either hope of good, or fear of pain: though, for my part, I would love and serve Him for what I could get." "Thou art an unaccountable fellow," cried Don Quixote: "thou talkest sometimes with so much sense, that one would imagine thee to be something of a scholar." "A scholar, sir," answered Sancho, "lack-a-day, I do not know, as I am an honest man, a letter in the book." Master Nicholas, seeing them so deep in discourse, called to them to stop and drink at a little fountain by the road: Don Quixote halted, and Sancho was very glad of the interruption, his stock of lies being almost spent, and he stood in danger besides of being trapped in his words, for he had never seen Dulcinea, though he knew she lived at Toboso. Cardenio by this time had changed his clothes for those Dorothea wore, when they found her in the mountains; and, though they made but an ordinary figure, they looked much better than those he had put off.[3] They all stopped at the fountain, and fell aboard the curate's provision, which was but a snap among so many, for they were all very hungry. While they sat refreshing themselves, a young lad, traveling that way, observed them, and, looking earnestly on the whole company, ran

3 *These must be the ragged apparel Cardenio wore before he was dressed in the priest's short cassock and cloak.*

suddenly and fell down before Don Quixote, addressing him in a very doleful manner. "Alas, good sir," said he, "do not you know me? do not you remember poor Andrew, whom you caused to be untied from the tree?" With that the Knight knew him; and, raising him up, turned to the company, "That you may all know," said he, "of how great importance, to the redressing of injuries, punishing vice, and the universal benefit of mankind, the business of knight-errantry may be, you must understand, that riding through a desert some days ago, I heard certain lamentable shrieks and outcries: prompted by the misery of the afflicted, and borne away by the zeal of my profession, I followed the voice, and found this boy, whom you all see, bound to a great oak: I am glad he is present, because he can attest the truth of my relation. I found him, as I told you, bound to an oak, naked from the waist upwards, and a bloody-minded peasant scourging his back unmercifully with the reins of a bridle. I presently demanded the cause of his severe chastisement. The rude fellow answered, that he had liberty to punish his own servant, whom he thus used for some faults that argued him more knave than fool. 'Good sir,' said the boy, 'he can lay nothing to my charge, but demanding my wages.' His master made some reply, which I would not allow as a just excuse, and ordered him immediately to unbind the youth, and took his oath that he would take him home and pay him all his wages upon the nail, in good and lawful coin. Is not this literally true, Andrew? Did you not mark, besides, with what face of authority I commanded, and with how much humility he promised to obey all I imposed, commanded, and desired? Answer me, boy, and tell boldly all that passed to this worthy company, that it may appear how necessary the vocation of knights-errant is up and down the high roads."

"All you have said is true enough," answered Andrew, "but the business did not end after that manner you and I hoped it would."

"How?" said the Knight, "has not the peasant paid you?" "Ay, he has paid me with a vengeance," said the boy; "for, no sooner was your back turned, but he tied me again to the same tree, and lashed me so cursedly, that I looked like St. Bartholomew flayed alive; and at every blow he had some joke or another to laugh at you; and, had he not laid on me as he did, I fancy I could not have helped laughing myself. At last he left me in so pitiful a case, that I was forced to crawl to an hospital, where I have lain ever since to get cured, so woefully the tyrant had lashed me. And now I may thank you for this, for had you ridden on your journey, and neither meddled nor made, seeing nobody sent for you, and it was none of your business, my master, perhaps, had been satisfied with giving me ten or twenty lashes, and after that would have paid me what he owed me; but you was so huffy, and called him so many names, that it made him mad, and so he vented all his spite against you upon my poor back, as soon as yours was turned, insomuch that I fear I shall never be my own man again." "The miscarriage," answered the Knight, "is only chargeable on my departure before I saw my orders executed; for I might, by experience, have remembered, that the word of a peasant is regulated not by honor but by profit. But you remember, Andrew, how I swore if he disobeyed, that I would return and seek him through the universe, and find him, though hid in a whale's belly." "Ah, sir," answered Andrew, "but that is no cure for my sore shoulders." "You shall be redressed," answered the Knight, starting fiercely up, and commanding Sancho immediately to bridle Rozinante, who was baiting as fast as the rest of the company. Dorothea asked what he intended to do? He answered, that he intended to find out the villain and punish him severely for his crimes, then force him to pay Andrew his wages to the last maravedi,[4] in spite of all the peasants in the universe. She then desired him to remember his engagements to

4 *Near the value of a farthing.*

her, which withheld him from any new achievement till that was finished; that he must therefore suspend his resentments till his return from her kingdom. "It is but just and reasonable," said the Knight, "and therefore Andrew must wait with patience my return; but, when I do return, I do hereby ratify my former oath and promise, never to rest till he be fully satisfied and paid." "I dare not trust to that," answered Andrew; "but, if you will bestow on me as much money as will bear my charges to Seville, I shall thank your worship more than for all the revenge you tell me of. Give me a snap to eat, and a bit in my pocket, and so Heaven be with you and all other knights-errant, and may they prove as errant fools in their own business as they have been in mine."

Sancho took a crust of bread and a slice of cheese, and reaching it to Andrew, "There, friend," said he, "there is something for thee; on my word, we have all of us a share of thy mischance." "What share?" said Andrew. "Why the curst mischance of parting with this bread and cheese to thee; for, my head to a halfpenny, I may live to want it; for thou must know, friend of mine, that we, the squires of knights-errant, often pick our teeth without a dinner, and are subject to many other things, which are better felt than told." Andrew snatched at the provender, and seeing no likelihood of any more, he made his leg and marched off. But, looking over his shoulder at Don Quixote, "Hark ye, you sir knight-errant," cried he, "if ever you meet me again in your travels, which I hope you never shall, though I were torn in pieces, do not trouble me with your plaguy help, but mind your own business; and so fare you well, with a curse upon you and all the knights-errant that ever were born." The Knight thought to chastise him, but the lad was too nimble for any there, and his heels carried him off; leaving Don Quixote highly incensed at his story, which moved the company to hold their laughter, lest they should raise his anger to a dangerous height.

When they had eaten plentifully, they left that place, and traveled
all that day and the next, without meeting anything worth notice,
till they came to the inn, which was so frightful a sight to poor
Sancho, that he would willingly not have gone in, but could by
no means avoid it. The innkeeper, the hostess, her daughter, and
Maritornes, met Don Quixote and his squire with a very hearty
welcome: the Knight received them with a face of gravity and
approbation, bidding them prepare him a better bed than their
last entertainment afforded him. "Sir," said the hostess, "pay us
better than you did then, and you shall have a bed for a prince";
and, upon the Knight's promise that he would, she promised him a
tolerable bed, in the large room where he lay before: he presently
undressed, and being heartily crazed in body, as well as in mind,
he went to bed. He was scarcely got to his chamber, when the
hostess flew suddenly at the barber, and catching him by the beard,
"On my life," said she, "you shall use my tail no longer for a beard:
pray, sir, give me my tail, my husband wants it to stick his thing
into, his comb I mean, and my tail I will have, sir!" The barber held
tug with her till the curate advised him to return it, telling him
that he might now undisguise himself, and tell Don Quixote, that
after the galley-slaves had pillaged him, he fled to that inn; and if
he should ask for the princess's squire, he should pretend that he
was dispatched to her kingdom before her, to give her subjects an
account of her arrival, and of the power she brought to free them
all from slavery. The barber, thus schooled, gave the hostess her
tail, with the other trinkets which he had borrowed to decoy
Don Quixote out of the desert. Dorothea's beauty, and Cardenio's
handsome shape surprised everybody. The curate bespoke supper,
and the host, being pretty secure of his reckoning, soon got them

a tolerable entertainment. They would not disturb the Knight, who slept very soundly, for his distemper wanted rest more than meat; but they diverted themselves with the hostess's account of his encounter with the carriers, and of Sancho's being tossed in a blanket. Don Quixote's unaccountable madness was the principal subject of their discourse, upon which the curate insisting, and arguing it to proceed from his reading romances, the innkeeper took him up. "Sir," said he, "you cannot make me of your opinion; for, in my mind, it is the pleasantest reading that ever was. I have now in the house, two or three books of that kind, and some other pieces, that really have kept me, and many others, alive. In harvest time, a great many of the reapers come to drink here in the heat of the day, and he that can read best among us takes up one of these books; and all the rest of us, sometimes thirty or more, sit round about him, and listen with such pleasure, that we think neither of sorrow nor care; as for my own part, when I hear the mighty blows and dreadful battles of those knights-errant, I have half a mind to be one myself, and am raised to such a life and briskness, that I frighten away old age. I could sit and hear them from morning till night." "I wish you would, husband," said the hostess, "for then we should have some rest; for at all other times you are so out of humor, and so snappish, that we lead a hellish life with you." "That is true enough," said Maritornes; "and for my part, I think there are mighty pretty stories in those books, especially that one about the young lady who is hugged so sweetly by her knight under the orange-tree, when the damsel watches lest somebody comes, and stands with her mouth watering all the while; and a thousand such stories, which I would often forego my dinner and my supper to hear." "And what think you of this matter, young miss?" said the curate to the innkeeper's daughter. "Alack-a-day, sir!" said she, "I do not understand those things, and yet I love to hear them: but I do not like that frightful ugly fighting that

350

so pleases my father. Indeed, the sad lamentations of the poor knights for the loss of their mistresses, sometimes makes me cry like anything." "I suppose then, young gentlewoman," said Dorothea, "you will be tender-hearted, and will never let a lover die for you?" "I do not know what may happen as to that," said the girl; "but this I know, that I will never give anybody reason to call me tigress and lioness, and I do not know how many other ugly names, as those ladies are often called; and I think they deserve yet worse, so they do; for they can never have soul nor conscience to let such fine gentlemen die or run mad for a sight of them. What signifies all their fiddling and coyness? If they are civil women, why do not they marry them, for that is all their knights would be at?" "Hold your prating, mistress," said the hostess. "How came you to know all this? It is not for such as you to talk of these matters." "The gentleman only asked me a question," said she, "and it would be uncivil not to answer him." "Well," said the curate, "do me the favor, good landlord, to bring out these books that I may have a sight of them."

"With all my heart," said the innkeeper; and, with that, stepping to his chamber, he opened a little portmanteau that shut with a chain, and took out three large volumes, with a parcel of manuscripts in a fair legible letter: the title of the first was "Don Cirongilio of Thrace"; the second "Felixmarte of Hyrcania"; and the third was the "History of the great Captain Gonzalo Fernandez de Cordova," and the "Life of Diego Garcia de Paredes," bound together.[1] The curate, reading the titles, turned to the barber, and told him they wanted now Don Quixote's housekeeper and his niece. "I shall do as well with the books," said the barber,

1 *These were such famous leaders, as the great captain who conquered Naples for King Ferdinand of Spain and Diego Garcia before him; but authors have added such monstrous fables to their true actions, that there is no more believing any of them, than the fables of Guy of Warwick, or the like romantic heroes, as may appear by what the curate speaks in their praise.*

"for I can find the way to the back yard or the chimney; there is a good fire that will do their business." "Business!" said the inn-keeper, "I hope you would not burn my books." "Only two of them," said the curate, "this same Don Cirongilio and his friend Felixmarte." "I hope, sir," said the host, "they are neither heretics nor flegmatics." "Schismatics you mean," said the barber. "I mean so," said the innkeeper; "and, if you must burn any, let it be this of Gonzalo Fernandez and Diego Garcia, for you should sooner burn one of my children than the others." "These books, honest friend," said the curate, "that you appear so concerned for, are senseless rhapsodies of falsehoods and folly; and this which you so despise is a true history, and contains a true account of two cele-brated men; the first by his bravery and courage purchased immortal fame, and the name of the Great General, by the universal consent of mankind. The other, Diego Garcia de Paredes, was of noble extraction, and born in Truxillo, a town of Estremadura, and was a man of singular courage, and such mighty strength, that with one of his hands he could stop a mill-wheel in its most rapid motion; and with his single force defended the passage of a bridge against a great army. Several other great actions are related in the memoirs of his life, but all with so much modesty and unbiased truth, that they easily pronounce him his own historiographer; and, had they been written by anyone else, with freedom and impartiality, they might have eclipsed your Hectors, Achilleses and Orlandos, with all their heroic exploits." "That is a fine jest, faith," said the innkeeper, "my father could have told you another tale, sir. Holding a mill-wheel? Why, is that such a mighty matter! Odds fish, do but turn over a leaf of Felixmarte there; you will find how, with one single back-stroke, he cut five swinging giants off by the middle, as if they had been so many bean-cods, of which the children make little puppet-friars;[2] and read how, at another time, he charged a most mighty and powerful army of above a million and six hundred thousand fighting men, all armed *cap-à-pie*, and routed them all like so many sheep. And what can you say of the worthy Cirongilio of Thrace who, as you may read there, going by water one day, was assaulted by a fiery serpent in the middle of the river; he presently leaped nimbly upon her back, and hanging by her scaly neck, grasped her throat fast with both his arms, so that the serpent, finding herself almost strangled, was forced to dive into the water to save herself and carried the knight, who would not quit his hold, to the very bottom, where he found a stately palace, and such pleasant gardens, that it was a wonder;

2 *Children, in Spain, we are told, make puppets resembling friars, out of bean-cods, by breaking as much of the upper end as to discover part of the first bean, which is to represent the bald head, and letting the broken cod hang back like a cowl.*

and straight the serpent turned into a very old man, and told him such things as were never heard nor spoken.—Now a fig for your Great Captain, and your Diego Garcia." Dorothea, hearing this, said softly to Cardenio, that the host was capable of making a second part to Don Quixote. "I think so too," cried Cardenio, "for it is plain he believes every tittle contained in those books, nor can all the Carthusian friars in the world persuade him otherwise." "I tell thee, friend," said the curate, "there were never any such persons, as your books of chivalry mention, upon the face of the earth: your Felixmarte of Hyrcania, and your Cirongilio of Thrace, are all but chimeras and fictions of idle and luxuriant wits, who wrote them for the same reason that you read them, because they had nothing else to do." "Sir," said the innkeeper, "you must angle with another bait, or you will catch no fish. I know what is what, as well as another: I can tell where my own shoe pinches me; and you must not think, sir, to catch old birds with chaff; a pleasant jest, faith, that you should pretend to persuade me now that these notable books are lies and stories; why, sir, are they not in print? are they not published according to order? licensed by authority from the privy-council? And do you think that they would permit so many untruths to be printed, and such a number of battles and enchantments, to set us all a-madding?" "I have told you already, friend," replied the curate, "that this is licensed for our amusement in our idle hours, for the same reason that tennis, billiards, chess, and other recreations are tolerated, that men may find a pastime for those hours they cannot find employment for. Neither could the government foresee this inconvenience from such books that you urge, because they could not reasonably suppose any rational person would believe their absurdities. And, were this a proper time, I could say a great deal in favor of such writings, and how, with some regulations, they might be made both instruct-

354

ive and diverting; but I design, upon the first opportunity, to communicate my thoughts on this head to some that may redress it: in the meantime, honest landlord, you may put up your books, and believe them true if you please, and much good may they do you. And I wish you may never halt of the same foot as your guest Don Quixote." "There is no fear of that," said the innkeeper, "for I never design to turn knight-errant, because I find the customs that supported that noble order are quite out of doors."

About the middle of their discourse entered Sancho, who was very uneasy at hearing that knights-errant were out of fashion, and books of chivalry full of nothing but folly and fiction; he resolved, however (in spite of all their contempt of chivalry), still to stick by his master; and if his intended expedition failed of success, then to return to his family and plow. As the innkeeper was carrying away the books, the curate desired his leave to look over those manuscripts which appeared in so fair a character; he reached them to him, to the number of eight sheets, on one of which there was written in a large hand, "The Novel of the Curious Impertinent." "The title," said the curate, "promises something, perhaps it may be worth reading through." "Your reverence," said the innkeeper, "may be worse employed; for that novel has received the approbation of several ingenious guests of mine who have read it, and who would have begged it of me; but I would by no means part with it, till I deliver it to the owner of this portmanteau, who left it here with these books and papers: I may perhaps see him again, and restore them honestly; for I am as much a Christian as my neighbors, though I am an innkeeper." "But I hope," said the curate, "if it pleases me you will not deny me a copy of it." "Nay, as to that matter," said the host, "we shall not fall out." Cardenio, having by this perused it a little, recommended it to the curate, and entreated him to read it for the entertainment of the

355

company. The curate would have excused himself, by urging the unseasonable time of night, and that sleep was then more proper, especially for the lady. "A pleasant story," said Dorothea, "will prove the best repose for some hours to me; for my spirits are not composed enough to allow me to rest, though I want it." Mr. Nicholas and Sancho joined in the request. "To please ye then, and satisfy my own curiosity," said the curate, "I will begin, if you will but give your attention."

VI: THE NOVEL OF THE CURIOUS IMPERTINENT

Anselmo and Lothario, considerable gentlemen of Florence, the capital city of Tuscany in Italy, were so eminent for their friendship, that they were called nothing but the Two Friends. They

were both young and unmarried, of the same age and humor, which did not a little concur to the continuance of their mutual affection, though, of the two, Anselmo was the most amorously inclined, and Lothario the greater lover of hunting; yet they loved one another above all other considerations, and mutually quitted their own pleasure for their friend's; and their very wills, like the different motions of a well-regulated watch, were always subservient to their unity, and still kept time with one another. Anselmo, at last, fell desperately in love with a beautiful lady of the same city; so eminent for her fortune and family, that he resolved by the consent of his friend (for he did nothing without his advice), to demand her in marriage. Lothario was the person employed in this affair, which he managed with that address, that in few days he put his friend into possession of Camilla, for that was the lady's name; and this so much to their satisfaction, that he received a thousand acknowledgments from both, for the equal happiness they derived from his endeavors. Lothario, as long as the nuptials lasted, was every day at Anselmo's, and did all he could to add to the sports and diversions of the occasion. But as soon as the new-married pair had received the congratulation of their friends, and the nuptial ceremonies were over, Lothario retired, with the rest of their acquaintance, and forbore his visits, because he prudently imagined that it was not at all proper to be so frequent at his friend's house after marriage as before: for, though true friendship entirely banishes all suspicion and jealousy, yet the honor of a married man is of so nice and tender a nature, that it has been sometimes sullied by the conversation of the nearest relations, and therefore more liable to suffer from that of a friend. Anselmo observed this remissness of Lothario; and, fond as he was of his wife, showed by his tender complaints how much it affected him. He told him that, if he could have believed he must also have left so dear a correspondence by marriage, as much as he loved, he would never have paid so great a price for the satisfaction of his passion; and that he would never, for the idle reputation of a cautious husband, suffer so tender and agreeable a name to be lost, as that of the Two Friends, which, before his marriage, they had so happily obtained; and therefore, he begged him, if that were a term lawful to be used betwixt them two, to return to his former familiarity and freedom of conversation; assuring him, that his wife's will and pleasure were entirely

357

formed by his; and that, being acquainted with their ancient and strict friendship, she was equally surprised at so unexpected a change. Lothario replied to these endearing persuasions of his friend with such prudence and discretion, that he convinced him of the sincerity of his intentions in what he had done; and so, in conclusion, they agreed that Lothario should dine twice a week at his house, besides holy days. Yet Lothario's compliance with this resolution being only not to disoblige his friend, he designed to observe it no further than he should find it consistent with Anselmo's honor, whose reputation was as dear to him as his own; and he used to tell him, that the husband of a beautiful wife ought to be as cautious of the friends whom he carried home to her himself, as other female acquaintance and visitants. For a friend's or relation's house often renders the contrivance of those things easy, and not suspected, which could not be compassed either in the church, the markets, or at public entertainments and places of resort, which no man can entirely keep a woman from frequenting. To this Lothario said also, that every married man ought to have some friend to put him in mind of the defects of his conduct; for a husband's fondness many times makes him either not see, or at least, for fear of displeasing his wife, not command or forbid her what may be advantageous or prejudicial to his reputation. In all which, a friend's warning and advice might supply him with a proper remedy. But where shall we find a friend so qualified with wisdom and truth as Anselmo demands? I must confess I cannot tell, unless it were Lothario, whose care of his friend's honor made him so cautious as not to comply with his promised visiting days, lest the malicious observers should give a scandalous censure of the frequent admission of so well-qualified a gentleman, both for his wit, fortune, youth, and address, to the house of a lady of so celebrated a beauty as Camilla: for, though his virtue was sufficiently known to check the growth of any malignant report, yet he would not

358

suffer his friend's honor nor his own, to run the hazard of being called in question; which made him spend the greatest part of those days he had by promise devoted to his friend's conversation, in other places and employments; yet excusing his absence so agreeably, that Anselmo could not deny the reasonableness of what he alleged. And thus the time passed away in pathetic accusations of want of love and friendship on one side, and plausible excuses on the other.

"I know very well," said Anselmo, walking one day in the fields with his friend, "that of all the favors and benefits for which Heaven commands my gratitude, as the advantage of my birth, fortune and nature, the greatest and most obliging is the gift of such a wife and such a friend; being both of you pledges of so great value, that though it is impossible for me to raise my esteem and love equal to your deserts, yet is no man capable of having a greater. And yet, while I am in possession of all that can or usually does make a man happy, I live the most discontented life in the world. I am not able to tell you when my misery began, which now inwardly torments me with so strange, extravagant and singular a desire, that I never reflect on it, but I wonder at myself, and condemn and curb my folly, and would fain hide my desires even from myself: and yet I have received no more advantage from this private confusion than if I had published my extravagance to all the world. Since therefore it is evident that it will at last break out, dear Lothario, I would have it go no further than thy known fidelity and secrecy; for that and thy own industry (which, as my friend, thou wilt turn to my assistance) will quickly, I hope, free me from the anguish it now gives me, and restore that tranquillity of which my own folly has deprived me."

Lothario stood in great suspense, unable to guess at the consequence of so strange and prolix an introduction. In vain he racked his imagination for the causes of his friend's affliction; the truth was the last thing he could think of: but, no longer to remain in doubt, he told Anselmo, that he did his friendship a particular injury in not coming directly to the point in the discovery of his thoughts to him, since his counsels might enable him to support, and, perhaps, to lose or compass such importunate desires.

"It is very true," replied Anselmo, "and with that assurance I must inform you, that the desire that gives me so much pain, is to know whether Camilla be really as virtuous as I think her. Nor can this be made evident but by such a trial, that, like gold by the fire, the standard and degree of her worth be discovered. For in my opinion, no woman has more virtue than she retains, after the force of the most earnest solicitations. *Casta est, quam nemo rogavit;* and she only may be said to be chaste, who has withstood the force of tears, vows, promises, gifts, and all the importunities of a lover that is not easily denied: for where is the praise of a woman's virtue, whom nobody has ever endeavored to corrupt? Where is the wonder if a wife be reserved, when she has no temptation nor opportunity of being otherwise, especially if she have a jealous husband, with whom the least suspicion goes for a reality, and who therefore punishes the least appearance with death? Now I can never so much esteem her, who owes her virtue merely to fear or want of opportunity of being false, as I would one who victoriously surmounts all the assaults of a vigorous and watchful lover, and yet retains her virtue entire and unshaken. These, and many other reasons which I could urge to strengthen my opinion, make me desire that my Camilla's virtue may pass through the fiery trial of vigorous solicitations and addresses, and these offered by a gallant who may have merit enough to deserve her good opinion; and if, as I am confident she will, she be able to resist so agreeable a temptation, I shall think myself the most happy man in the world, and attain to the height and utmost aim of my desires, and shall

360

say, that a virtuous woman is fallen to my lot, of whom the Wise Man says, 'Who can find her?' If she yields, I shall, at least, have the satisfaction of finding my opinion of women justified, and not be imposed on by a foolish confidence that abuses most men; which consideration will be sufficient to make me support the grief I shall derive from so expensive an experiment. And, assuring myself that nothing which you can say can dissuade me from my resolution, I desire that you yourself, my dear friend, would be the person to put my design in execution. I will furnish you with opportunities enough of making your addresses, in which I would have you omit nothing you may suppose likely to prevail with and work upon a woman of quality, who is modest, virtuous, reserved, and discreet by nature. The most prevailing reason that makes me choose you for this affair, above all others, is, because if she should prove so frail as to be overcome by addresses and importunities, the victory will not cost me so dear, since I am secured from your taking that advantage, of which another might make no scruple. And so my honor will remain untouched, and the intended injury a secret, in the virtue of thy silence; for I know my friend so well, that death and the grave will as soon divulge my affairs. Wherefore, if you would give me life indeed, and deliver me from the most perplexing torment of doubt, you will immediately begin this amorous assault, with all that warmth, assiduity, and courage I expect from that confidence I put in your friendship."

Lothario gave so great an attention to Anselmo's reasons, that he gave him no other interruption than what we mentioned. But now, finding his discourse was at an end, full of amazement at the extravagance of the proposal, he thus replied: "Could I, my dear Anselmo, persuade myself that what you have said were any more than a piece of raillery, I should not have been so long silent; no, I should have interrupted you at the beginning of your speech. Sure you know neither yourself nor me, Anselmo, or you would never have employed me on such an affair, if you had not thought me as much altered from what I was, as you seem to be; for, as the poet has it, *usque ad aras;* a true friend ought to desire nothing of his friend that is offensive to Heaven. But should a man so far exert his friendship, as to deviate a little from the severity of religion in compliance to his friend, no trifling motives can excuse the transgression, but such only as concern at least his friend's life and honor. Which therefore of these, Anselmo, is in danger, to warrant my undertaking so detestable a thing as you desire? Neither, I dare engage: on the contrary, you would make me the assaulter of both, in which my own is included; for, to rob you of your reputation, is to take away your life, since an infamous life is worse than death; and by making me the guilty instrument of this, as you would have me, you make me worse than a dead man, by the murder of my reputation. Therefore I desire you will hear with patience what I have to urge against your extravagant desire, and I shall afterwards hear your reply without interruption." Anselmo having promised his attention, Lothario proceeded in this manner: "In my opinion, you are not unlike the Moors, who are incapable of being convinced of the error of their religion, by Scripture, speculative reasons, or those drawn immediately from the articles of our faith; and will yield to nothing but demonstrations as evident as those of the mathematics, and which can as little be denied, as when we say, if from two equal parts we take away two equal parts, the parts that remain are also equal. And when they do not understand this proposition, which they seldom do, we are obliged, by operation, to make it yet more plain and obvious to their senses: and yet, all this labor will at last prove ineffectual to convince them of the verities of our religion. The same must be my method with you, since your strange desire is so very foreign to all manner of reason, that I very much fear I shall spend my time and labor in vain, in endeavoring to convince you of your own folly, for I can afford it no other name. Nay, did I not love you as I do, I should leave you to the prosecution of your own odd humor, which certainly tends to your ruin. But, to lay your folly a little more open, you bid me, Anselmo, attempt a woman of honor, cautious of her reputation, and one who is not much inclined to love; for all these good qualifications you allowed her. If therefore you already know your wife is possessed of all these advantages of prudence, discretion, honor, and reservedness, what have you more to inquire after? And if you believe, as I myself do, that she will be impregnable to all my assaults, what greater and better names will you give her than she already deserves? Either you pretend to think better of her than really you do, or else you desire you know not what yourself. But then, if you do not believe her as virtuous as you pretend, why would you put it to the trial? why do you not rather use her as you think she deserves? On the other hand, if she be as good as you profess you believe her, why would you go to tempt truth and goodness itself, without any reasonable prospect of advantage? For, when the trial is over, she will be but the same virtuous woman she was before. Wherefore, it is allowed, that it is the effect of temerity, and want of reason, to attempt what is likely to produce nothing but danger and detriment to the undertaker, especially when there is no necessity for it, and when we may easily foresee the folly of the undertaking. There are but these motives to incite us to difficult attempts, religion, interest, or both together. The first makes the saints endeavor to lead angelic lives in these frail bodies: the second makes us expose ourselves to the hazards of long voyages and travels, in pursuit of riches: the third motive is compounded of both, and prompts us to act as well for the honor of God, as for our own particular glory and interests; as, for example, the daring adventures of the valiant soldier, who, urged by his duty to God, his

363

prince, and his country, fiercely runs into the midst of a dreadful breach, unterrified with any considerations of the danger that threatens him. These are things done every day, and let them be never so dangerous, they bring honor, glory, and profit, to those that attempt them. But, by the project you design to reduce to an experiment, you will never obtain either the glory of Heaven, profit, or reputation: for, should the experiment answer your expectation, it will make no addition, either to your content, honor, or riches; but, if it disappoints your hopes, it makes you the most miserable man alive. And the imaginary advantage of no man's knowing your disgrace will soon vanish, when you consider, that, to know it yourself, will be enough to supply you perpetually with all the tormenting thoughts in the world. A proof of this is what the famous poet Ludovico Tansilo, at the end of his first part of 'St. Peter's Tears,' says, in these words:

> " 'Shame, grief, remorse in Peter's breast increase,
>   Soon as the blushing morn his crime betrays:
> When most unseen, then most himself he sees,
>   And with due horror all his soul surveys.

> ' For a great spirit needs no cens'ring eyes
>   To wound his soul, when conscious of a fault;
> But self-condemn'd, and e'en self-punish'd lies,
>   And dreads no witness like upbraiding thought.'

So that your boasted secrecy, far from alleviating your grief, will only serve to increase it; and, if your eyes do not express it by outward tears, they will flow from your very heart in blood. So wept that simple doctor, who, as our poet tells us, made that experiment on the brittle vessel, which the more prudent Reinaldo excused himself from doing. This, indeed, is but a poetical fiction, but yet the moral which it enforces is worthy to be observed and imitated.

And accordingly, I hope, you will discover the strange mistake into which you would run precipitantly, when you have heard what I have further to say to you.

"Suppose, Anselmo, you had a diamond, as valuable, in the judgment of the best jewelers, as such a stone could be; would you not be satisfied with their opinion, without trying its hardness on the anvil? You must own that, should it be proof against your blows, it would not be one jot the more valuable than really it was before your foolish trial; but should it happen to break, as well it might, the jewel was then entirely lost, as well as the sense and reputation of the owner. This precious diamond, my friend, is your Camilla, for so she ought to be esteemed in all men's opinion as well as your own; why then would you imprudently put her in danger of falling, since your trial will add no greater value to her than she has already? But, if she should prove frail, reflect with yourself on the unhappiness of your condition, and how justly you might complain of your being the cause of her ruin and your own. Consider that, as a modest and honest woman is the most valuable jewel in the world, so all women's virtue and honor consist in the opinion and reputation they maintain with other people; and, since that of your wife is perfect both in your own and all other men's opinion, why will you go, to no purpose, to call the reality of it in question? You must remember, my friend, that the nature of woman is, at best, but weak and imperfect; and, for that reason, we should be so far from casting rubs in its way, that we ought, with all imaginable care, to remove every appearance that might hinder its course to that perfection it wants, which is virtue.

"If you believe the naturalists, the ermine is a very white little creature; when the hunters have found its haunts, they surround it almost with dirt and mire, toward which the ermine being forced to fly, rather than sully its native white with dirt, it suffers itself

365

to be taken, preferring its color to its liberty and life. The virtuous woman is our ermine, whose chastity is whiter than snow; but, to preserve its color unsullied, you must observe just a contrary method: the addresses and services of an importunate lover, are the mire into which you should never drive a woman; for it is ten to one she will not be able to free herself and avoid it, being but too apt to stumble into it; and therefore that should be always removed, and only the candor and beauty of virtue, and the charms of a good fame and reputation placed before her. A good woman is also not unlike a mirror of crystal, which will infallibly be dimmed and stained by breathing too much upon it: she must rather be used like the relics of saints, adored, but not touched; or, like a garden of curious tender flowers, that may at a distance gratify the eye, but are not permitted by the master to be trampled on, or touched by every beholder. I shall add but a few verses out of a late new play, very fit for our present purpose, where a prudent old man advises his neighbor, that had a daughter, to lock her up close; and gives these reasons for it, besides several others:

> " 'Since nothing is frailer than woman and glass,
> He that wou'd expose 'em to fall is an ass:
> And sure the rash mortal is yet more unwise,
> Who on bodies so ticklish experiments tries.
>
> 'With ease both are damag'd; then keep that with care,
> Which no art can restore, nor no solder repair.
> Fond man, take my counsel, watch what is so frail;
> For where Danaës lie, golden show'rs will prevail.'

All I have hitherto urged relates only to you. I may now at last be allowed to consider what regards myself; and, if I am tedious, I hope you will pardon me; for, to draw you out of the labyrinth into which you have run yourself, I am forced on that prolixity. You call me friend, yet, which is absolutely inconsistent with friendship,

366

you would rob me of my honor; nay, you stop not here, but would oblige me to destroy yours. First, that you would rob me of mine is evident; for what will Camilla think, when I make a declaration of love to her, but that I am a perfidious villain, that makes no scruple of violating the most sacred laws of friendship, and who sacrifices the honor and reputation of my friend to a criminal passion: secondly, that I destroy yours is as evident; for, when she sees me take such a liberty with her, she will imagine that I have discovered some weakness in her, that has given me assurance to make her so guilty a discovery, by which she esteems herself injured in her honor; you, being the principal part of her, must of necessity be affected with the affronts she receives. For this is the reason why the husband, though never so deserving, cautious and careful, suffers the infamy of a scandalous name, if his wife goes astray; whereas, in reason, he ought rather to be an object of compassion than contempt, seeing the misfortune proceeds from the vice and folly of the wife, not his own defects. But, since the reason and justice of the man's suffering for the wife's transgression may be serviceable to you, I will give you the best account of it I can; and pray do not think me tedious, since this is meant for your good. When woman was given to man, and marriage first ordained in Paradise, man and wife were made and pronounced one flesh; the husband therefore being of a piece with the wife, whatever affects her affects him, as a part of her; though, as I have said, he has been no occasion of it: for, as the whole body is affected by the pain of any part, as the head will share the pain of the foot, though it never caused that pain, so is the husband touched with his wife's infamy, because she is part of him. And, since all worldly honors and dishonors are derived from flesh and blood, and the scandalous baseness of an unfaithful wife proceeds from the same principle, it necessarily follows, that the husband, though no party in the offense, and entirely ignorant and innocent of it, must have his

367

share of the infamy. Let what I have said, my dear Anselmo, make you sensible of the danger into which you would run, by endeavoring thus to disturb the happy tranquillity and repose that your wife at present enjoys; and for how vain a curiosity, and extravagant a caprice, you would rouse and awake those peccant humors which are now lulled asleep by the power of an unattempted chastity. Reflect further, how small a return you can expect from so hazardous a voyage, and such valuable commodities as you venture; for the treasure you will lose is so great, and ought to be so dear, that all words are too inexpressive to show how much you ought to esteem it. But, if all I have said be too weak to destroy your foolish resolve, employ some other instrument of your disgrace and ruin: for, though I should lose your friendship, a loss which I must esteem the greatest in the world, I will have no hand in an affair so prejudicial to your honor."

Lothario said no more, and Anselmo, discovering a desponding melancholy in his face, remained a great while silent and confounded. "At least I have," said he, "my friend, listened to your discourse, as you might observe, with all the attention in nature, and every part of what you have said convinces me of the greatness of your wisdom and friendship; and I must own, that if I suffer my desires to prevail over your reasons, I shun the good and pursue the evil. But yet, my friend, you ought, on the other side, to reflect, that my distemper is not much unlike that of those women, who sometimes long for coals, lime, nay, some things that are loathsome to the very sight; and therefore some little arts should be used to endeavor my cure, which might easily be effected, if you would but consent to solicit Camilla, though it were but weakly and remissly; for, I am sure, she will not be so frail to surrender at the first assault, which yet will be sufficient to give me the satisfaction I desire; and in this you will fulfill the duty of our friendship, in restoring me to life, and securing my honor, by your powerful and persuasive reasons. And you are indeed bound, as my friend, to do thus much to secure me from betraying my defects and follies to a stranger, which would hazard that reputation which you have taken so much pains to preserve; since I am so bent on this experiment, that, if you refuse me, I shall certainly apply myself elsewhere: and though, awhile, your reputation may suffer in Camilla's opinion, yet, when she has once proved triumphant, you may cure that wound, and recover her good opinion by a sincere discovery of your design. Wherefore I conjure you to comply with my importunity, in spite of all the obstacles that may present themselves to you, since what I desire is so little, and the pleasure I shall derive from it so great; for, as I have promised, your very first attempt shall satisfy me as much as if you had gone through the whole experiment."

Lothario plainly saw that Anselmo's resolution was too much fixed for anything he could say to alter it; and, finding that he threatened to betray his folly to a stranger, if he persisted in a refusal, to avoid greater inconveniences, he resolved to seem to comply with his desires, privately designing to satisfy Anselmo's caprice, without giving Camilla any trouble; and therefore he desired him to break the matter to nobody else, since he would himself undertake it, and begin as soon as he pleased. Anselmo embraced him with all the love and tenderness imaginable, and was as prodigal of his thanks, as if the very promise had been the greatest obligation that could be laid on him. They immediately agreed on the next day for the trial, at which time Anselmo should give him the opportunity of being alone with her, and gold and jewels to present her with. He advised him to omit no point of gallantry, as serenades, songs, and verses in her praise; offering to make them himself, if Lothario would not be at the trouble. But Lothario promised him to do all himself, though his design was far different from Anselmo's.

Matters being thus adjusted, they returned to Anselmo's house, where they found the beautiful Camilla sad with concern for the absence of her husband beyond his usual hour. Lothario left him there, and retired home, as pensive how to come off handsomely in this ridiculous affair, as he had left Anselmo pleased and contented with his undertaking it. But, that night, he contrived a way of imposing on Anselmo to his satisfaction, without offending Camilla. So next day he went to Anselmo's, and was received by Camilla with a civility and respect answerable to the uncommon friendship she knew was between him and her husband. Dinner being over, Anselmo desired his friend to keep his lady company, till his return from an extraordinary affair that would require his absence about an hour and a half. Camilla desired him not to go: Lothario offered to go with him; but he, pleading peculiar business, entreated his friend to stay, and enjoined his wife not to leave him alone till his return. In short, he knew so well how to counterfeit a necessity for his absence, though that necessity proceeded only from his own folly, that no one could perceive it was feigned. And so he left them together, without anyone to observe their actions, all the servants being retired to dinner.

Thus Lothario found himself entered the lists, his adversary before him terribly armed with a thousand piercing beauties, sufficient to overcome all the men she should encounter, which gave him cause enough to fear his own fate. The first thing he did, in this first onset, was to lean his head carelessly on his hand, and beg her leave to take a nap in his chair till his friend came back: Camilla told him she thought he might rest with more ease on the couch [1] in the next room: he declared himself satisfied with the place where he was, and so slept till his friend came back. Anselmo, finding his wife in her chamber, and Lothario asleep at his return, con-

[1] Estrado: *a space of the visiting-rooms of ladies, raised a foot above the floor of the rest of the room, covered with carpets or mats, on which the ladies sit on cushions laid along by the wall, or low stools.*

cluded that he had given them time enough both for discourse and repose; and therefore waited with a great deal of impatience for his friend's awaking, that they might retire, and he might acquaint him with his success. Lothario at last awaked, and going out with his friend, he answered his inquiry to this purpose: That he did not think it convenient to proceed further, at that time, than in some general praise of her wit and beauty, which would best prepare his way for what he might do hereafter, and dispose her to give a more easy and willing ear to what he should say to her: as the devil, by laying a pleasing and apparent good at first before us, insinuates himself into our inclinations, so he generally gains his point before we discover the cloven foot, if his disguise pass on us in the beginning. Anselmo was extremely satisfied with what Lothario said, and promised him every day as good an opportunity; and, though he could not go every day abroad, yet he would manage his conduct so well, that Camilla should have no cause of suspicion. He took care to do as he said. But Lothario willfully lost the frequent opportunities he gave him; however, he soothed him still with assurances, that his lady was inflexible, her virtue not to be surmounted, and that she had threatened to discover his attempts to her husband, if ever he presumed to be so insolent again; so far was she from giving the least hope or encouragement. "Thus far it is well," said Anselmo, "but yet Camilla has resisted nothing but words; we must now see what proof she has against more substantial temptations. Tomorrow I will furnish you with two thousand crowns in gold, to present her with; and, as a further bait, you shall have as much more for jewels. For women, especially if they are handsome, naturally love to go gaily and richly dressed, be they never so chaste and virtuous; and, if she has power to overcome this temptation, I will give you no further trouble." "Since I have begun this adventure," replied Lothario, "I will make an end of it, though I am sure her repulses

371

will tire out my patience, and her virtue overcome any temptation, and baffle my endeavors."

The next day Anselmo delivered him the four thousand crowns, and with them as many perplexing thoughts, not knowing how to supply his invention with some new story to amuse his friend. However, at last, he resolved to return the money, with assurance that Camilla was as unmoved with presents as with praise, and as untouched with promises as with vows and sighs of love; and therefore all further attempts would be but a fruitless labor. This was his intention; but fortune that meddled too much in these affairs disappointed his designs. For Anselmo, having left him alone with his wife one day, as he used to do, privately conveyed himself into the closet, and through the chinks of the door set himself to observe what they did; he found, that, for one half hour, Lothario said not one word to Camilla; from whence he concluded that all the addresses, importunities, and repulses, with which he had amused him, were pure fictions. But, that he might be fully satisfied in the truth of his surmise, coming from his covert he took his friend aside, and inquired of him what Camilla had then said to him, and how he now found her inclined? Lothario replied, that he would make no further trial of her, since her answer had now been so severe and awful, that he durst not for the future venture upon a discourse so evidently her aversion.

"Ah! Lothario, Lothario!" cried Anselmo, "is it thus that you keep your promises? Is this what I should expect from your friendship? I observed you through that door, and found that you said not a word to Camilla; and, from thence, I am very well satisfied, that you have only imposed on me all the answers and relations you have made. Why did you hinder me from employing some other, if you never intended to satisfy my desire?" Anselmo said no more, but this was enough to confound Lothario, and cover him with shame for being found in a lie. Therefore, to appease his friend, he swore to him, from that time forward to set in good earnest about the matter, and that so effectually, that he himself, if he would again give himself the trouble of observing him, should find proof enough of his sincerity. Anselmo believed him; and, to give him the better opportunity, he engaged a friend of his to send for him, with a great deal of importunity, to come to his house at a village near the city, where he meant to spend eight days, to take away all apprehension and fear from both his friend and his wife.

Was ever man so unhappy as Anselmo, who industriously contrived the plot of his own ruin and dishonor? He had a very good wife, and possessed her in quiet, without any other man's mingling in his pleasures; her thoughts were bounded with her own house, and her husband, the only earthly good she hoped or thought on, and her only pleasure and desire; his will the rule of hers, and measure of her conduct. When he possessed love, honor, beauty and discretion, without pain or toil, what should provoke him to seek, with so much danger and hazard of what he had already, that which was not to be found in nature! He that aims at things impossible, ought justly to lose those advantages which are within the bounds of possibility. As the poet sings:

I

"In death I seek for life,
In a disease for health,
For quietness in strife,
In poverty for wealth,
And constant truth in an inconstant wife.

II

But sure the fates disdain
My mad desires to please,
Nor shall I e'er obtain
What others get with ease,
Since I demand what no man e'er cou'd gain."

373

The next day Anselmo went out of town; having first informed Camilla, that his friend Lothario would look after his affairs, and keep her company in his absence, and desired her to make as much of him as of himself. His lady, like a discreet woman, begged him to consider how improper a thing it was for any other to take his place in his absence; and told him, that if he doubted her ability in managing her house, he should try her but this time, and she questioned not but he would find she had capacity to acquit herself to his satisfaction in greater matters. Anselmo replied that it was her duty not to dispute, but obey his command: to which she returned that she would comply, though much against her will. In short, her husband left the town. Lothario, the next day, was received at her house with all the respect that could be paid a friend so dear to her husband; but yet with so much caution, that she never permitted herself to be left alone with him, but kept perpetually some of her maids in the room, and chiefly Leonela, for whom she had a particular love, as having been bred in her father's house with her from her infancy.

Lothario said nothing to her the first three days, notwithstanding he might have found an opportunity when the servants were gone to dinner; for, though the prudent Camilla had ordered Leonela to dine before her, that she might have no occasion to go out of the room; yet she, who had other affairs to employ her thoughts, more agreeable to her inclinations (to gratify which that was usually the only convenient time she could find), was not so very punctually obedient to her lady's commands, but that she sometimes left them together. Lothario did not yet make use of these advantages, as I have said, being awed by the virtue and modesty of Camilla. But this silence, which she thus imposed on Lothario, had at last a quite contrary effect. For, though he said nothing, his thoughts were active, his eyes were employed to see and survey the outward charms of a form so perfect, that it was enough to fire the most cold, and soften the most obdurate heart. In these intervals of silence, he considered how much she deserved to be beloved; and these considerations, by little and little, undermined and assaulted the faith which he owed to his friend. A thousand times he resolved to leave the city, and retire where Anselmo should never see him, and where he should never more behold the dangerous face of Camilla; but the extreme pleasure he found in seeing her, soon destroyed so feeble a resolve. When he was alone he would accuse his want of friendship and religion, and run into frequent comparisons betwixt himself and Anselmo, which generally concluded that Anselmo's folly and madness was greater than his breach of faith; and that, would Heaven as easily excuse his intentions as man, he had no cause to fear any punishment for the crime he was going to commit. In fine, Camilla's beauty, and the opportunity given him by the husband himself, wholly vanquished his faith and friendship. And now, having an eye only to the means of obtaining that pleasure, to which he was prompted with so much violence, after he had spent the first three days of Anselmo's absence in a conflict betwixt love and virtue, he attempted, by all means possible, to prevail with Camilla, and discovered so much passion in his words and actions, that Camilla, surprised with the unexpected assault, flung from him out of the room, and retired with haste to her chamber. Hope is always born with love, nor did this repulse in the least discourage Lothario from further attempts on Camilla, who by this appeared more charming, and more worthy his pursuit. She, on the other hand, knew not what to do upon the discovery of that in Lothario, which she never could have imagined. The result of her reflections was this, that since she could not give him any opportunity of speaking to her again, without the hazard of her reputation and honor, she would send a letter to her husband to solicit his return to his house. The letter she sent by a messenger that very night; and it was to the following purpose:

"As it is very improper to leave an army without a general, and a garrison without its governor, so, to me, it seems much more imprudent to leave a young married woman without her husband; especially when there are no affairs of consequence to plead for his absence. I find myself so ill in yours, and so impatient, and unable to endure it any longer, that if you come not home very quickly, I shall be obliged to return to my father's, though I leave your house without anyone to look after it: for the person to whom you have entrusted the care of your family, has, I believe, more regard to his own pleasure than your concerns. You are wise and prudent, and therefore I shall say no more, nor is it convenient I should."

Anselmo was not a little satisfied at the receipt of this letter, which assured him that Lothario had begun the attempt, which she had repelled according to his hopes; and therefore he sent her word not to leave his house, assuring her it should not be long before he returned. Camilla was surprised with his answer, and more perplexed than before, being equally afraid of going to her father, and of staying at home; in the first she disobeyed her husband, in the latter ran the risk of her honor. The worst resolution prevailed, which was to stay at her own house, and not avoid Lothario's company, lest it should give some cause of suspicion to her servants. And now she repented her writing to Anselmo, lest he should suspect that Lothario had observed some indiscretion in her, that made him lose the respect due to her, and gave him assurance to offer at the corrupting her virtue: but, confiding in Heaven and her own innocence, which she thought proof against all Lothario's attempts, she resolved to make no answer to whatever he should say to her, and never more to trouble her husband with complaints, for fear of engaging him in disputes and quarrels with his friend. For that reason she considered how she might best excuse him to Anselmo, when he should examine the cause of her writing to him in that manner. With a resolution so innocent and dangerous, the next day she gave ear to all that Lothario said: and he gave the assault with such force and vigor, that Camilla's constancy could not stand the shock unmoved, and her virtue could do no more than guard her eyes from betraying that tender compassion, of which his vows, and entreaties, and all his sighs and tears had made her heart sensible. Lothario discovered this with an infinite satisfaction, and no less addition to his flame; and found that he ought to make use of this opportunity, of Anselmo's absence, with all his force and importunity, to win so valuable a fortress. He began with the powerful battery of the praise of her beauty, which being directly pointed on the weakest part of woman, her vanity, with the greatest ease and facility in the world makes a breach as great as a lover would desire. Lothario was not unskillful or remiss in the attack, but followed his fire so close, that let Camilla's integrity be built on never so obdurate a rock, it must at last have fallen. He wept, prayed, flattered, promised, swore, vowed, and showed so much passion and truth in what he said, that, beating down the care of her honor, he, at last, triumphed over what he scarce durst hope, though what he most of all desired; for she, at last, surrendered, even Camilla surrendered. Nor ought we to wonder if she yielded, since even Lothario's friendship and virtue were not able to withstand the terrible assault: an evident proof that love is a power too strong to be overcome by anything but flying, and that no mortal creature ought to be so presumptuous as to stand the encounter, since there is need of something more than human, and indeed a heavenly force, to confront and vanquish that human passion. Leonela was the only confidante of this amour, which these new lovers and faithless friends could not by any means conceal from her knowledge. Lothario would not discover to Camilla, that her husband, for her trial, had designedly given him this opportunity, to which he owed so extreme a happiness; she should not think he lacked love to solicit her himself with importunity, or that she was gained on too easy terms.

Anselmo came home in a few days, but discovered not what he had lost, though it was what he most valued and esteemed: from thence he went to Lothario, and, embracing him, begged of him to let him know his fate. "All I can tell you, my friend," answered Lothario, "is that you may boast yourself of the best wife in the world, the ornament of her sex, and the pattern which all virtuous women ought to follow. Words, offers, presents, all is ineffectual, the tears I pretended to shed moved only her laughter. Camilla is not only mistress of the greatest beauty, but of modesty, discretion, sweetness of temper, and every other virtue and perfection that add to the charms of a woman of honor. Therefore, my friend, here take back your money, I have had no occasion to lay it out, for Camilla's integrity cannot be corrupted by such base and mercenary things as gifts and promises. And now, Anselmo, be at last content with the trial you have already made; and having so luckily got over the dangerous quicksands of doubts and suspicions that are to be met with in the ocean of matrimony, do not venture out again, with another pilot, that vessel whose strength you have sufficiently experienced; but believe yourself, as you are, securely anchored in a safe harbor, at pleasure and ease, till death, from whose force no title, power, nor dignity can secure us, does come and cut the cable." Anselmo was extremely satisfied with Lothario's discourse and believed it as firmly as if it had been an oracle; yet desired him to continue his pursuit, if it were but to pass away the time: he did not require he should press Camilla with those importunities he had before used, but only make some verses in her praise, under the name of Cloris; and he would make Camilla believe he

378

celebrated a lady he loved under that name, to secure her honor and reputation from the censure which a more open declaration would expose her to: he added, that if Lothario would not be at the expense of so much trouble and time as to compose them himself, he would do it for him with a great deal of pleasure. Lothario told him there was no need of that, since he himself was sometimes poetically given: "Do you but tell Camilla of my pretended love, as you say you will, and I will make the verses as well as I can, though not so well as the excellency of the subject requires." The Curious Impertinent and his treacherous friend having thus agreed the matter, Anselmo went home, and then asked Camilla on what occasion she sent him the letter? Camilla, who wondered that this question had not been asked her before, replied, that the motive that prevailed with her to write in that manner to him, was a jealousy she had entertained that Lothario, in his absence, looked on her with more criminal and desiring eyes than he used to do when he was at home; but that, since, she had reason to believe that suspicion but weakly grounded, seeing he discovered rather an aversion than love, as avoiding all occasions of being alone with her. Anselmo told her she had nothing to apprehend from Lothario on that account, since he knew his affections engaged on one of the noblest young ladies of the city, whose praise he wrote under the name of Cloris; but, were he not thus engaged, there was no reason to suspect Lothario's virtue and friendship. Camilla, at this discourse, without doubt, would have been very jealous of Lothario, had he not told her his design of abusing her husband with the pretense of another love, that he might, with the greater liberty and security, express her praise and his passion. The next day, at dinner, Anselmo desired him to read some of the verses he had made on his beloved Cloris; telling him, he might say anything of her before Camilla, since she did not know who the lady was. "Did Camilla know her," replied Lothario, "that should not make me

379

pass over in silence any part of that praise which was her due; for if a lover complains of his mistress's cruelty while he is praising her perfections, she can never suffer in her reputation. Therefore, without any fear, I shall repeat a sonnet which I made yesterday on the ingratitude of Cloris:

A SONNET

"At dead of night, when ev'ry troubl'd breast
By balmy sleep is eas'd of anxious pain,
*   When slaves themselves in pleasing dreams are blest,*
Of Heaven and Cloris, restless, I complain.
*   The rosy morn dispels the shades of night,*
The sun, the pleasures, and the day return;
*   All nature's cheer'd with the reviving light,*
I, only I, can never cease to mourn.

At noon, in vain I bid my sorrow cease,
The heat increases, and my pains increase,
*   And still my soul in the mild evening grieves:*
The night returns, and my complaints renew,
No moment sees me free; in vain I sue,
*   Heav'n ne'er relents, and Cloris ne'er relieves."*

Camilla was mightily pleased with the sonnet, but Anselmo transported; he was lavish of his commendation, and added that the lady must be barbarously cruel, that made no return to so much truth, and so violent a passion. "What, must we then believe all that a poet in love tells us for truth?" said Camilla. "Madam," replied Lothario, "though the poet may exceed, yet the lover corrects his fondness for fiction, and makes him speak truth." Anselmo, to advance Lothario's credit with Camilla, confirmed whatever he said; but she, not minding her husband's confirmations, was sufficiently persuaded by her passion for Lothario, to an implicit faith in all he said; and therefore, pleased with this composition, and more satisfied in the knowledge she had that all was addressed to herself as the true Cloris, she desired him to repeat some other verses he had made on that subject, if he could remember any. "I remember some," replied Lothario; "but, madam, in my opinion, they are not so tolerable as the former: but you shall be judge yourself:

A SONNET

I

"I die your victim, cruel fair;
And die without reprieve,
If you can think your slave can bear
Your cruelty and live.

II

Since all my hopes of ease are vain,
To die I now submit;
And that you may not think I feign,
It must be at your feet.

III

Yet when my bleeding heart you view,
Bright nymph, forbear to grieve;
For I had rather die for you,
Than for another live.

IV

In death and dark oblivion's grave,
Oh! let me lie forlorn,
For my poor ghost would pine and rave,
Should you relent and mourn."

Anselmo was not less profuse in his praise of this sonnet than he had been of the other, and so added new fuel to the fire that was to consume his reputation. He contributed to his own abuse, in commending his false friend's attempts on his honor, as the most important service he could do it; and this made him believe, that every step Camilla made down to contempt and disgrace, was a degree she mounted towards that perfection of virtue which he desired she should attain.

Sometime after, Camilla being alone with her maid, "I am ashamed," said she, "my Leonela, that I gave Lothario so easy a conquest over me, and did not know my own worth enough to make him undergo some greater fatigues, before I made him so entire a surrender. I am afraid he will think my hasty consent the effect of the looseness of my temper, and not at all consider that the force and violence he used, deprived me of the power of resisting." "Ah! madam," returned Leonela, "let not that disquiet you; for the speedy bestowing a benefit of an intrinsic value, and which you design to bestow at last, can never lessen the favor; for according to the old proverb, 'He that gives quickly gives twice.'" "To answer your proverb with another," replied Camilla, "'That which cost little is less valued.'" "But this has nothing to do with you," answered Leonela, "since it is said of love that it sometimes goes, sometimes flies; runs with one, walks gravely with another; turns a third into ice, and sets a fourth in a flame; it wounds one, another it kills: like lightning it begins and ends in the same moment: it makes that fort yield at night which it besieged but in the morning; for there is no force able to resist it. Since this is evident, what cause have you to be surprised at your own frailty? And why should you apprehend anything from Lothario, who has felt the same irresistible power, and yielded to it as soon? For love, to gain a conquest, took the short opportunity of my master's absence, which being so short and uncertain, love, that had before determined this should be done, added force and vigor to the lover, not to leave anything to time and chance, which might, by Anselmo's return, cut off all opportunities of accomplishing so agreeable a work. The best and most officious servant of love's retinue, is occasion or opportunity: this it is that love improves in all its progress, but most in the beginning and first rise of an amour. I trust not in what I have said to the uncertainty of report, but to experience, which affords the most certain and most valuable knowledge, as I will inform you, madam, some day or other; for I am like you, made of frail flesh and blood, fired by youth and youthful desires. But, madam, you did not surrender to Lothario till you had sufficient proof of his love, from his eyes, his vows, his promises, and gifts; till you had seen the merit of his person, and the beauty of his mind; all which convinced you how much he deserved to be loved. Then trouble yourself no more, madam, with these fears and jealousies; but thank your stars, that, since you were doomed a victim to love, you fell by the force of such valor and merit that cannot be doubted. You yielded to one who has not only the four S's,[1] which are required in every good lover, but even the whole alphabet; as, for example, he is, in my opinion, agreeable, bountiful, constant, dutiful, easy, faithful, gallant, honorable, ingenious, kind, loyal, mild, noble, officious, prudent, quiet, rich, secret, true, valiant, wise; the X indeed, is too harsh a letter to agree with him, but he is young and zealous for your honor and service." Camilla laughed at her woman's alphabet, and thought her (as indeed she was) more learned in the practical part of love than she had yet confessed. She then informed her mistress of an affair that had been betwixt her and a young man of the town. Camilla was not a little concerned at what she said, being apprehensive that her honor might suffer by her woman's indiscretion; and therefore asked her, if the amour had passed any further than words? Leonela, without any fear or shame, owned her guilty correspondence with all the freedom in the world; for the mistress's guilt

[1] *As if we should say, sightly, sprightly, sincere, and secret.*

gives the servant impudence, and generally they imitate their ladies' frailties, without any fear of the public censure.

Camilla, finding her error past remedy, could only beg Leonela to disclose nothing of her affair to her lover, and manage her amour with secrecy and discretion, for fear Lothario or Anselmo should hear of it. Leonela promised to obey her; but she did it in such a manner, that Camilla was perpetually in fear of the loss of her reputation by her folly; for she grew so confident on her knowledge of her lady's transgression, that she admitted the gallant into the house, not caring if her lady knew it, being certain that she durst not make any discovery to her master; for when once a mistress has suffered her virtue to be vanquished, and admits of any criminal correspondence, it subjects her to her own servants, and makes her subservient to their lewd practices, which she is slavishly bound to conceal. Thus it was with Camilla, who was forced to wink at the visible rendezvous which Leonela had with her lover in a certain chamber of the house, which she thought proper for the occasion; nor was that all, she was constrained to give her the opportunity of hiding him, that he might not be seen by her husband.

But all this caution did not secure him from being seen by Lothario one morning, as he was getting out of the house by break of day. His surprise had made him think it a spirit, had not his haste away, and his muffling himself up as he did, that he might not be known, convinced him of his error, and thrown him into a fit of jealousy that had certainly undone them all, had not Camilla's wit and address prevented it. For Lothario concluded that Camilla, who had made no very obstinate resistance to him, had as easily surrendered to some other; and he fancied that the person he saw come from her house, was the new favored lover, never remembering there was such a person as Leonela in the house, and that he might be a lover of hers. For when once a woman parts with her virtue, she loses the esteem even of the man whose vows

384

and tears won her to abandon it; and he believes she will with as little, if not less difficulty, yield to another; he perverts the least suspicions into reality, and takes the slightest appearance for the most evident matter of fact.

Thus Lothario, distracted by the most violent jealousy in the world, without allowing himself time to consider, gave way to the transports of his rage and desire of revenge on Camilla, who had not injured him; he goes immediately to Anselmo; and having found him a-bed: "I have, my friend," said he to him, "these several days undergone a most severe conflict within my mind, and used all the force and violence I was capable of to conceal an affair from you, which I can no longer forbear discovering, without an apparent wrong to justice and my friendship. Know then that Camilla is now ready to do whatsoever I shall desire of her; and the reason that most prevailed with me to delay this discovery was, that I would be satisfied whether she were in earnest, or only pretended this compliance to try me; but, had she been so virtuous as you and I believed her, she would, by this time, have informed you of that importunity which, by your desire, I used; but finding that she is silent, and takes no notice of that to you, I have reason to believe that she is but too sincere in those guilty promises she has made me, of meeting me to my satisfaction in the wardrobe, the next time your absence from the town should furnish her with an opportunity." (This was true indeed, for that was the place of their common rendezvous.) "Yet I would not have you," continued he, "take a rash and inconsiderate revenge, since it is possible, before the time of assignation, her virtue may rally, and she repent her folly. Therefore, as you have hitherto taken my advice, be ruled by me now, that you may not be imposed on, but have a sufficient conviction before you put your resolves into execution. Pretend two or three days' absence, and then privately convey yourself behind the hangings in the wardrobe, as you easily may, whence you

385

may, without difficulty, be an eye-witness with me of Camilla's conduct; and if it be as criminal as we may justly fear, then you may with secrecy and speed punish her as the injury deserves."

Anselmo was extremely surprised at so unexpected a misfortune, to find himself deceived in those imaginary triumphs he pleased himself with, in Camilla's supposed victory over all Lothario's assaults. A great while he was in a silent suspense, with his eyes dejected, without force, and without spirit; but, turning at last to his friend, "You have done all," said he, "Lothario, that I could expect from so perfect a friendship; I will therefore be entirely guided by your advice; do therefore what you please, but use all the secrecy a thing of this nature requires." Lothario, assuring him of that, left him, but full of repentance for the rashness he had been guilty of, in telling him so much as he had, since he might have taken a sufficient revenge by a less cruel and dishonorable way. He cursed his want of sense, and the weakness of his resolution, but could not find out any way to produce a less fatal event of his treachery, than he could justly expect from the experiment. But at last he concluded to inform Camilla of all he had done; which his freedom of access gave him opportunity to do that very day, when he found her alone; and she began thus to him: "I am so oppressed, my Lothario, with a misfortune which I lie under, that it will certainly for ever destroy my quiet and happiness, if there be not some speedy remedy found for it. Leonela is grown so presumptuous, on her knowledge of my affairs, that she admits her lover all night to her chamber, and so exposes my reputation to the censure of any that shall see him go out at unseasonable hours from my house; and the greatest and most remediless part of my grief is, that I dare not correct or chide her for her imprudence and impudence; for, being conscious of our correspondence, she obliges me to conceal her failings, which I am extremely apprehensive will in the end be very fatal to my happiness." Lothario was at first jealous that Camilla designed cunningly thus to impose her own intimate on him for Leonela's; but being convinced by her tears, and the apparent concern in her face, he began to believe her, and at the same time to be infinitely confounded and grieved for what he had done. Yet he comforted Camilla, assuring her he would take effectual care for the future, that Leonela's impudence should do her no prejudice, and therefore begged her not to torment herself any more about it. Then he told all the unhappy effects of his jealous rage, and that her husband had agreed, behind the arras, to be witness of her weakness. He asked her pardon for the folly, and her counsel how to redress and prevent the ill effect of it, and bring them out of those difficulties into which his madness had plunged them.

Camilla expressed her resentment and her fears; and accused his treachery, baseness, and want of consideration; yet her anger and fears being appeased, and a woman's wit being always more pregnant in difficulties than a man's, she immediately thought of a way to deliver them from dangers that bore so dismal and helpless a face. She therefore bid him engage Anselmo to be there the next day, assuring him she did not question but by that means to get a more frequent and secure opportunity of enjoying one another than they hitherto had had. She would not make him privy to her whole design, but bid him be sure to come after her husband was hid, as soon as Leonela should call him, and that he should answer as directly to whatsoever she should ask him, as if Anselmo were not within hearing. Lothario spared no importunity to get from her her whole design, that he might act his part with the greater assurance, and the better to contribute to the imposing on her husband. "All you have to do," replied Camilla, "is to answer me directly what I shall demand": nor would she discover any more, for fear he should not acquiesce in her opinion (which she was so well satisfied in), but raise difficulties, and by consequence, obstacles, that might hinder her design from having the desired event, or run her upon some less successful project. Lothario complied, and Anselmo in appearance left the town to retire to his friend in the country, but secretly returned to hide himself in the wardrobe, which he did with the greater ease, because Camilla and Leonela willfully gave him opportunity. We may easily imagine the grief with which Anselmo hid himself, since it was to be a spectator of his own dishonor, and the loss of all that happiness he possessed in the embraces of his beautiful and beloved Camilla. On the other hand, she being now certain that Anselmo was hid, entered the wardrobe with Leonela, and fetching a deep and piteous sigh, thus addressed herself to her: "Ah! my Leonela! would it not be much better that thou pierce this infamous bosom with Anselmo's dagger, before I execute what I design, which I have kept from thee that thou mightest not endeavor to disappoint me? Yet not so; for, where is the justice that I should suffer for another's offense? No, I will first know of Lothario what action of mine has given him assurance to make me a discovery of a passion so injurious to his friend and my honor. Go to the window, Leonela, and call the wicked man to me, who doubtless is waiting, in the street, the signal for his admission to accomplish his villainous design; yet, first, my resolution shall be performed, which, though it be cruel, is what my honor strictly demands of me." "Alas! my dear lady," cried the cunning Leonela, "alas! what do you intend to do with that dagger? Is your fatal design against yourself or Lothario? Alas! you can attack neither without the ruin of your fame and reputation. You had better give no opportunity to that bad man, by admitting him, while we are thus alone in the house: consider, madam, we are but two weak and helpless women, he a strong and resolute man, whose force is redoubled by the passion and desire that possess him; so that before you may be able to accomplish what you design, he may commit a crime that will be more injurious to you than the loss of your life. We have reason to curse my master Anselmo, who gives such frequent opportunities to impudence and dishonesty to pollute our house. But, madam, suppose you should kill him, as I believe you design, what shall we do with his dead body?" "What!" said Camilla, "why we would leave him in this place to be buried by Anselmo: for it must be a grateful trouble to him to bury with his own hand his own infamy and dishonor. Call him therefore quickly; for, methinks, every moment my revenge is deferred, I injure that loyalty I owe to my husband."

Anselmo gave great attention to all that was said, and every word of Camilla's made a strange alteration in his sentiments, so that he could scarce forbear coming out to prevent his friend's death, when he heard her desperate resolution against his life; but his desire of seeing the end of so brave a resolve withheld him, till he saw an absolute necessity of discovering himself to hinder the mischief. Now Camilla put on a fear and weakness which resembled a swoon; and, having thrown herself on a bed in the room, Leonela began a most doleful lamentation over her: "Alas!" said she, "how unfortunate should I be, if my lady, so eminent for virtue and chastity as well as beauty, should thus perish in my arms?" This, and much more she uttered with that force of perfect dissimulation, that whoever had seen her would have concluded her one of the most innocent virgins in the world, and her lady a mere persecuted Penelope. Camilla soon came to herself, and cried to Leonela: "Why do not you call the most treacherous and unfaithful of friends? Go, fly, and let not thy delays waste my revenge and anger in mere words and idle threats and curses." "Madam," replied Leonela, "I will go, but you must first give me that dagger, lest you commit some outrage upon yourself in my absence, which may give an eternal cause of sorrow to all your friends who love and value you." "Let not those fears detain you," said Camilla, "but assure yourself I will not do anything till your return; for though I shall not fear

389

to punish myself in the highest degree, yet I shall not, like Lucretia, punish myself without killing him that was the principal cause of my dishonor. If I must die, I shall not refuse it; but I will first satisfy my revenge on him that has tempted me to come to this guilty assignation, to make him lament his crime without being guilty of any myself."

Camilla could scarce prevail with Leonela to leave her alone, but at last she obeyed her, and withdrew, when Camilla entertained herself and her husband with this following soliloquy: "Good Heaven," said she, "had I not better have continued my repulses, than by this seeming consent suffer Lothario to think scandalously of me, till my actions shall convince him of his error? That indeed might have been better in some respects, but then I should have wanted this opportunity of revenge, and the satisfaction of my husband's injured honor, if he were permitted, without any correction, to go off with the insolence of offering such criminal assaults to my virtue. No, no, let the traitor's life atone for the guilt of his false and unfaithful attempts, and his blood quench that lewd fire he was not content should burn in his own breast. Let the world be witness, if it ever comes to know my story, that Camilla thought it not enough to preserve her virtue and loyalty to her husband entire, but also revenged the hateful affront, and the intended destruction of it. But it might be most convenient perhaps to let Anselmo know of this before I put my revenge into execution; yet, on the first attempt, I sent him word of it to the village, and I can attribute his not resenting so notorious an abuse to nothing but his generous temper, and confidence in his friend, incapable of believing so tried a friend could be guilty of so much as a thought against his honor and reputation; nor is this incredulity so strange, since I for so long together could not persuade myself of the truth of what my eyes and ears conveyed to me; and nothing could have convinced me of my generous error, had his insolence kept within any bounds, and not dared to proceed to large gifts, large promises, and a flood of tears, which he shed as the undissembled testimony of his passion. But, to what purpose are these considerations? Or is there indeed any need of considering to persuade me to a brave resolve? Avaunt, false thoughts! Revenge is now my sole task, let the treacherous man approach, let

him come, let him die, let him perish; let him but perish, no matter what is the fatal consequence. My sweet Anselmo received me to his dear bosom spotless and chaste, and so should the grave receive me from his arms. Let the event be as fatal as it will, the worst pollution I can this way suffer is from mingling my own chaste blood with the impure and corrupted blood of the most false and treacherous of friends." Having said this, she traversed the room in so passionate a manner, with the drawn dagger in her hand,

and showed such an agitation of spirits in her looks and motion, that she appeared like one distracted, or more like a murderer than a tender and delicate lady.

Anselmo, not a little to his satisfaction, very plainly saw and heard all this from behind the arras, which with the greatest reason and evidence in the world removed all his past doubts and jealousies, and he, with abundance of concern, wished that Lothario would not come, that he might by that means escape the danger that so apparently threatened him; to prevent which he had discovered himself, had he not seen Leonela at that instant bring Lothario into the room. As soon as Camilla saw him enter, she described a line with the poniard on the ground, and told him the minute he presumed to pass that, she would strike the dagger to his heart: "Hear me," said she, "and observe what I say without interruption; when I have done, you shall have liberty to make what reply you please. Tell me first, Lothario, do you know my husband and do you know me? The question is not so difficult but you may give me immediate answer; there is no need of considering; speak therefore without delay." Lothario was not so dull as not to guess at her design in having her husband hid behind the hangings, and therefore adapted his answers so well to her questions, that the fiction was lost in the appearance of reality. "I did never imagine, fair Camilla," said Lothario, "that you would make this assignation to ask questions so distant from the dear end of coming. If you had a mind still to delay my promised happiness, you should have prepared me for the disappointment; for, the nearer does the hope of possession bring us to the good we desire, the greater is the pain of having those hopes destroyed. But, to answer fairly your demands, I must own, madam, that I do know your husband, and he me; that this knowledge has grown up with us from our childhood; and, that I may be a witness against myself for the injury I am compelled by love to do him, I do also own, divine Camilla, that you but too well know the tenderness of our mutual friendship: yet love is a sufficient excuse for all my errors, if they were much more criminal than they are. And, madam, that I know you is evident, and love you equal to him, for nothing but your sweet charms could have power enough to make me forget what I owe to my own honor, and what to the holy laws of friendship, all which I have been forced to break by the resistless tyranny of love. Ah! had I

392

known you less, I had been more innocent." "If you confess all this," said Camilla, "if you know us both, how dare you violate so sacred a friendship, injure so true a friend, and appear thus confidently before me, whom you know to be esteemed by him the mirror of his love, in which that love so often views itself with pleasure and satisfaction; and in which you ought to have surveyed yourself so far, as to have seen how small the temptation is that has prevailed on you to wrong him. But alas! this points me to the cause of your transgression, some suspicious action of mine when I have been least on my guard, as thinking myself alone; but assure yourself whatever it was, it proceeds not from looseness or levity of principle, but a negligence and liberty which the sex sometimes innocently fall into when they think themselves unobserved. If this were not the cause, say, traitor, when did I listen to your prayers, or in the least regard your tears and vows, so that you might derive from thence the smallest hope of accomplishing your infamous desires? Did I not always with the last aversion and disdain reject your criminal passion? Did I ever betray a belief in your lavish promises, or admit of your prodigal gifts? But, since, without some hope, no love can long subsist, I will lay that hateful guilt on some unhappy inadvertency of mine; and therefore will inflict the same punishment on myself that your crime deserves. And to show you that I cannot but be cruel to you, who will not spare myself, I sent for you to be a witness of that just sacrifice I shall make to my dear husband's injured honor, on which you have fixed the blackest mark of infamy that your malice could suggest, and which I, alas! have sullied too by my thoughtless neglect of depriving you of the occasion, if indeed I gave any, of nourishing your wicked intentions. Once more I tell you, that the bare suspicion that my want of caution, and setting as severe a guard on my actions as I ought, has made you harbor such wild and infamous intentions, is the sharpest of my afflictions, and which with my own

393

hands I resolve to punish with the utmost severity: for, should I leave that punishment to another, it would but increase my guilt. Yes, I will die; but first to satisfy my revenge and impartial justice, I will, unmoved, and unrelenting, destroy the fatal cause that has reduced me to this desperate condition."

At these words she flew with so much violence, and so well-acted a fury on Lothario with her naked dagger, that he could scarce think it feigned, and therefore secured himself from her blow by avoiding it and holding her hand. Thereupon, to give more life to the fiction, as in a rage at her disappointed revenge on Lothario, she cried out, "Since my malicious fortune denies a complete satisfaction to my just desires, at least it shall not be in its power entirely to defeat my resolution." With that, drawing back her dagger-hand from Lothario who held it, she struck it into that part of her body where it might do her the least damage, and then fell down as fainting away with the wound. Lothario and Leonela, surprised at the unexpected event, knew not yet what to think, seeing her still lie all bloody on the ground: Lothario, pale and trembling, ran to her to take out the dagger, but was delivered of his fears when he saw so little blood follow it, and more than ever admired the cunning and wit of the beautiful Camilla. Yet, to play his part as well, and show himself a friend, he lamented over Camilla's body in the most pathetic manner in the world, as if she had been really dead; he cursed himself, and cursed his friend that had put him on that fatal experiment; and, knowing that Anselmo heard him, he said such things that were able to draw a greater pity for him than even for Camilla, though she seemed to have lost her life in the unfortunate adventure. Leonela removed her body to the bed, and begged Lothario to seek some surgeon, that might with all the secrecy in the world cure her lady's wound. She also asked his advice how to excuse it to her master, if he should return before it was perfectly cured. He replied, they might say what they pleased, that he was not in a humor of advising, but bid her endeavor to stanch her mistress's blood, for he would go where they should never hear more of him; and so he left them, with all the appearance of grief and concern that the occasion required. He was no sooner gone, but he had leisure to reflect, with the greatest wonder imaginable, on Camilla's and her woman's conduct in this affair, and on the assurance which this scene had given Anselmo of his wife's virtue; since now he could not but believe he had a second Portia, and he longed to meet him, to rejoice over the best dissembled imposture that ever bore away the opinion of truth. Leonela stanched the blood, which was no more than necessary for covering the cheat, and washing the wound with wine only as she bound it up, her discourse was so moving, and so well acted, that it had been alone sufficient to have convinced Anselmo that he had the most virtuous wife in the world. Camilla was not silent, but added fresh confirmations; in every word she spoke she complained of her cowardice and baseness of spirit, that denied her time and force to dispatch that life which was now so hateful to her. She asked her too, whether she should inform her husband of what had passed, or not? Leonela was for her concealing it, since the discovery must infallibly engage her husband in a revenge on Lothario, which must as certainly expose him too; for those things were never accomplished without the greatest danger; and that a good wife ought, to the best of her power, prevent involving her husband in quarrels. Camilla yielded to her reasons; but added, that they must find out some pretended cause of her wound, which he would certainly see at his return. Leonela replied, that it was a difficult task, since she was incapable even in jest to dissemble the truth. "Am I not," answered Camilla, "under the same difficulty, who cannot save my life by the odious refuge of a falsehood? Had we not better then confess the real truth, than be caught in a lie?" "Well, madam," returned Leonela, "let this give you no further trouble, by tomorrow morning I shall

395

find out some expedient or other; though I hope the place where the wound is, may conceal it enough from his observation to secure us from all apprehension; leave, therefore, the whole event to Heaven, which always favors and assists the innocent."

Anselmo saw and heard this formal tragedy of his ruined honor, with all the attention imaginable, in which all the actors performed their parts so to the life, that they seemed the truth they represented; he wished with the last impatience for the night, that he might convey himself from his hiding-place to his friend's house, and there rejoice for this happy discovery of his wife's experienced virtue. Camilla and her maid took care to furnish him with an opportunity of departing, of which he soon took hold, for fear of losing it. It is impossible to tell you all the embraces he gave Lothario, and the joy and extreme satisfaction he expressed at his good fortune, or the extravagant praises he gave Camilla. Lothario heard all this without taking a friend's share in the pleasure, for he was shocked with the concern he had to see his friend so grossly imposed on, and the guilt of his own treachery in injuring his honor. Though Anselmo easily perceived that Lothario was not touched with any pleasure at his relation, yet he believed Camilla's wound, caused by him, was the true motive of his not sharing his joy; and therefore assured him, he need not too much trouble himself for it, since it could not be dangerous, she and her woman having agreed to conceal it from him. This cause of his fear being removed, he desired him to put on a face of joy, since by his means he should now possess a perfect happiness and content; and therefore he would spend the rest of his life in conveying Camilla's virtue to posterity, by writing her praise in verse. Lothario approved his resolution, and promised to do the same. Thus Anselmo remained the most delightfully deceived of any man alive. He therefore carried Lothario immediately to his house, as the instrument of his glory, though he was indeed the only cause of his infamy and dishonor. Camilla received him with a face that ill-expressed the satisfaction of her mind, being forced to put on frowns in her looks, while her heart prompted nothing but smiles of joy for his presence.

For some months the fraud was concealed; but then fortune, turning her wheel, discovered to the world the wickedness they had so long and artificially disguised; and Anselmo's impertinent curiosity cost him his life.

VIII: THE CONCLUSION OF "THE NOVEL OF THE CURIOUS IMPERTINENT"; WITH THE DREADFUL BATTLE BETWIXT DON QUIXOTE AND CERTAIN WINE-SKINS

The novel was come near a conclusion, when Sancho Panza came running out of Don Quixote's chamber in a terrible fright, crying out "Help! help! good people, help my master, he is just now at it, tooth and nail, with that same giant, the Princess Micomicona's foe: I never saw a more dreadful battle in my born days. He has lent him such a sliver, that whip off went the giant's head as round as a turnip." "You are mad, Sancho," said the curate, interrupted in his reading; "is thy master such a devil of a hero, as to fight a giant at two thousand leagues' distance?" Upon this, they presently heard a noise and bustle in the chamber, and Don Quixote bawling out, "Stay, villain, robber, stay; since I have thee here, thy scimitar shall but little avail thee," and, with this, they heard him strike with his sword, with all his force, against the walls. "Good folks," said Sancho, "my master does not want your hearkening; why do not you run in and help him? Though I believe it is after meat mustard, for sure the giant is by this time gone to pot, and giving an account of his ill life; for I saw his blood run all about the house, and his head sailing in the middle of it. But such a head! It is bigger than any wine-skin [1] in Spain." "Death and hell," cries

[1] *In Spain they keep their wines in the skin of a hog, goat, sheep, or other beast, pitched within and sewed close without.*

the innkeeper, "I will be cut like a cucumber, if this Don Quixote, or Don Devil, has not been hacking my wine-skins that stood filled at his bed's head, and this coxcomb has taken the spilt liquor for blood." Then, running with the whole company into the room, they found the poor Knight in the most comical posture imaginable.

He was standing in his shirt, the fore part of it scarcely reach-

ing to the bottom of his belly, and about a span shorter behind; this added a very peculiar air to his long lean legs, as dirty and hairy as a beast's. To make him all of a piece, he wore on his head a little red, greasy, cast nightcap of the innkeeper's; he had wrapped one of the best blankets about his left arm for a shield, and wielded his drawn sword in the right, laying about him pell-mell; with now and then a start of some military expression, as if he had been really engaged with some giant. But, the best jest of all, he was all this time fast asleep: for the thoughts of the adventure he had undertaken, had so wrought on his imagination, that his depraved fancy had in his sleep represented to him the kingdom of Micomicon, and the giant: and dreaming that he was then fighting him, he assaulted the wine-skins so desperately, that he set the whole chamber a-float with good wine. The innkeeper, enraged to see the havoc, flew at Don Quixote with his fists; and, had not Cardenio and the curate taken him off, he had proved a giant indeed against the Knight. All this could not wake the poor Don, till the barber, throwing a bucket of cold water on him, wakened him from his sleep, though not from his dream.

The shortness of her champion's shirt gave Dorothea a surfeit of the battle. Sancho ran up and down the room searching for the giant's head, till, finding his labor fruitless, "Well, well," said he, "now I see plainly that this house is haunted, for when I was here before, in this very room was I beaten like any stock-fish, but knew no more than the man in the moon who struck me; and now the giant's head, that I saw cut off with these eyes, is vanished; and, I am sure, I saw the body spout blood like a pump." "What a prating and nonsense does this damned son of a whore keep about blood and a pump, and I know not what," said the innkeeper; "I tell you, rascal, it is my wine-skins that are slashed, and my wine that runs about the floor here, and I hope to see the soul of him that spilt it swimming in hell for his pains." "Well, well," said Sancho, "do not trouble me, I only tell you that I cannot find the giant's head, and my earldom is gone after it; and so I am undone, like salt in water." And truly Sancho's waking dream was as pleasant as his master's when asleep. The innkeeper was almost mad to see the foolish squire harp so on the same string with his frantic master, and swore they should not come off now as before; that their chivalry should be no satisfaction for his wine, but that they should pay him sauce for the damage, and for the very leathern patches which the wounded wine-skins would want.

Don Quixote, in the meanwhile, believing he had finished his

399

adventure, and mistaking the curate, that held him by the arms, for the Princess Micomicona, fell on his knees before him, and with a respect due to a royal presence: "Now may your highness," said he, "great and illustrious princess, live secure, free from any further apprehensions from your conquered enemy; and now am I acquitted of my engagement, since, by the assistance of Heaven and the influence of her favor by whom I live and conquer, your adventure is so happily achieved." "Did not I tell you so, gentlefolks?" said Sancho; "who is drunk or mad now? See if my master has not already put the giant in pickle? Here are the bulls,[2] and I am an earl." The whole company (except the innkeeper, who gave himself to the devil) were like to split at the extravagancies of master and man. At last the barber, Cardenio, and the curate, having with much ado, got Don Quixote to bed, he presently fell asleep, being heartily tired; and then they left him, to comfort Sancho Panza for the loss of the giant's head; but it was no easy matter to appease the innkeeper, who was at his wit's end for the unexpected and sudden fate of his wine-skins.

The hostess, in the meantime, ran up and down the house crying and roaring: "In an ill hour," said she, "did this unlucky Knight-errant come into my house; I wish, for my part, I had never seen him, for he has been a dear guest to me. He and his man, his horse and his ass, went away last time without paying me a cross for their supper, their bed, their litter and provender; and all, forsooth, because he was seeking adventures. What, in the devil's name, have I to do with his statutes of chivalry? If they oblige him not to pay, they should oblige him not to eat neither. It was upon this score that the other fellow took away my good tail; it is clear spoiled, the hair is all torn off, and my husband can never use it again. And now to come upon me again, with destroying my wine-skins, and spilling my liquor; may somebody spill his heart's

[2] *In allusion to the joy of the crowds in Spain, when they see the bulls coming.*

blood for it for me: but I will be paid, so I will, to the last maravedis, or I will disown my name, and forswear the mother that bore me." Her honest maid Maritornes seconded her fury; but Mr. Curate stopped their mouths by promising that he would see them satisfied for their wine and their skins, but especially for the tail which they kept such a clutter about. Dorothea comforted Sancho, assuring him, that whenever it appeared that his master had killed the giant, and restored her to her dominions, he should be sure of the best earldom in her disposal. With this he cheered up again, and swore that he himself had seen the giant's head, by the same token that it had a beard that reached down to his middle; and, if it could not be found, it must be hidden by witchcraft; for everything went by enchantment in that house, as he had found to his cost when he was there before. Dorothea answered, that she believed him; and desired him to pluck up his spirits, for all things would be well. All parties being quieted, Cardenio, Dorothea, and the rest, entreated the curate to finish the novel, which was so near a conclusion; and he, in obedience to their commands, took up the book and read on:

Anselmo grew so satisfied in Camilla's virtue, that he lived with all the content and security in the world; to confirm which, Camilla ever in her looks seemed to discover her aversion to Lothario, which made him desire Anselmo to dispense with his coming to his house, since he found how averse his wife was to him, and how great a disgust she had to his company; but Anselmo would not be persuaded to yield to his request; and was so blind, that, seeking his content, he perpetually promoted his dishonor. He was not the only person pleased with the condition he lived in; Leonela was so transported with her amour, that, secured by her lady's connivance, she perfectly abandoned herself to the indiscreet enjoyment of her gallant: so that one night her master heard somebody in her chamber, and coming to the door to discover who it was, he found it held fast against him; but, at last forcing it open, he saw one leap out of the window the instant he entered the room: he would have pursued him, but Leonela, clinging about him, begged him to appease his anger and concern, since the person that made his escape was her husband. Anselmo would not believe her, but, drawing his dagger, threatened to kill her if she did not immediately make full discovery of the matter. Distracted with fear, she begged him to spare her life, and she would discover things that more nearly related to him than he imagined. "Speak quickly then," replied Anselmo, "or you die." "'Tis impossible," returned she, "that in this confusion and fright, I should say anything that can be understood; but give me but till tomorrow morning, and I will lay such things before you, as will surprise and amaze you: but believe me, sir, the person that leaped out of the window is a young man of this city, who is contracted to me." This something appeased Anselmo, and prevailed with him to allow her till the next morning to make her confession: for he was too well assured of Camilla's virtue, by the past trial, to suspect that there could be anything relating to her in what Leonela had to tell him: wherefore, fastening her in her room, and threatening that she should never come out till she had done what she had promised, he returned to his chamber to Camilla, and told her all that had passed, without omitting the promise she had given him to make some strange discovery the next morning. You may easily imagine the concern this gave Camilla; she made no doubt but that the discovery Leonela had promised was of her disloyalty; and, without waiting to know whether it was so or not, that very night, as soon as Anselmo was asleep, taking with her all her jewels, and some money, she got undiscovered out of the house, and went to Lothario, informed him of all that had passed, and desired him either to put her in some place of safety, or to go with her where they might enjoy each other secure from the fears of Anselmo. This surprising relation so confounded Lothario, that for some time he knew not what he did, or what resolution to take;

but at last, with Camilla's consent, he put her into a nunnery, where a sister of his was abbess, and immediately, without acquainting anybody with his departure, left the city.

Anselmo, as soon as it was day, got up, without missing his wife, and hurried away to Leonela's chamber, to hear what she had to say to him; but he found nobody there, only the sheets, tied together and fastened to the window, showed which way she had made her escape; on which he returned very sad to tell Camilla the adventure, but was extremely surprised when he found her not in the whole house, nor could hear any news of her from his servants: but finding in his search her trunks open, and most of her jewels gone, he no longer doubted of his dishonor: so, pensive and half-dressed as he was, he went to Lothario's lodging to tell him his misfortune; but, when his servants informed him that he was gone that very night, with all his money and jewels, his pangs were redoubled, and his grief increased almost to madness. To conclude, he returned home, found his house empty, for fear had driven away all his servants. He knew not what to think, say, or do: he saw himself forsaken by his friend, his wife, and his very servants, with whom he imagined that Heaven itself had abandoned him; but his greatest trouble was to find himself robbed of his honor and reputation; for Camilla's crime was but too evident from all these concurring cir- cumstances. After a thousand distracting thoughts, he resolved to retreat to that village whither he formerly retired to give Lothario an opportunity to ruin him; wherefore, fastening up his doors, he took horse, full of despair and languishing sorrow, the violence of which was so great, that he had scarce ridden half-way, when he was forced to alight, and tying his horse to a tree, he threw himself beneath it; and spent, in that melancholy posture, a thousand racking reflections, most part of the day, till a little before night he discovered a passenger coming the same road, of whom he inquired, "What news of Florence?" The traveler replied, that the most surprising news that had been heard of late, was now all the talk of the city; which was, that Lothario had that very night carried away the wealthy Anselmo's wife, Camilla, which was all confessed by Camilla's woman, who was apprehended that night as she slipped from the window of Anselmo's house by a pair of sheets. "The truth of this story I cannot affirm," continued the traveler, "but everybody is astonished at the accident; for no man could ever suspect such a crime from a person engaged in so strict a friendship with Anselmo, as Lothario was; for they were called the Two Friends." "Is it yet known," replied Anselmo, "which way Lothario and Camilla are gone?" "No, sir," returned the traveler, "though the governor has made as strict a search after them as is possible." Anselmo asked no more questions, but, after they had taken their leaves of each other, the traveler left him and pursued his journey.

This mournful news so affected the unfortunate Anselmo, that he was struck with death almost that very moment; getting therefore on his horse, as well as he could, he arrived at his friend's house. He knew nothing yet of his disgrace; but seeing him so pale and melancholy, concluded that some great misfortune had befallen him. Anselmo desired to be immediately led to his chamber, and furnished with pen, ink, and paper, and to be left alone with his door locked: when, finding that his end approached, he resolved to leave in writing the cause of his sudden and unexpected death. Taking therefore the pen, he began to write; but unable to finish what he designed, he died a martyr to his impertinent curiosity. The gentleman, finding he did not call, and that it grew late, resolved to enter his chamber, and see whether his friend was better or worse; he found him half out of bed, lying on his face, with the pen in his hand, and a paper open before him. Seeing him in this posture he drew near him, called and moved him, but soon found he was dead; which made him call his servants to behold the unhappy event, and then took up the paper, which he saw was written in Anselmo's own hand, and was to this effect:

"A foolish and impertinent desire has robbed me of life. If Camilla hear of my death let her know that I forgive her; for she was not obliged to do miracles, nor was there any reason I should have desired or expected it, and since I contrived my own dishonor, there is no cause——"

Thus far Anselmo wrote, but life would not hold out till he could give the reasons he designed. The next day the gentleman of the house sent word of Anselmo's death to his relations, who already knew his misfortunes, as well as the nunnery whither Camilla was retired. She herself was indeed very near that death which her husband had passed, though not for the loss of him, but Lothario, of which she had lately heard a flying report. But though she was a widow now, she would neither take the veil nor leave the nunnery, till, in a few days the news was confirmed of his being slain in a battle betwixt Monsieur de Lautrec and that great General Gonzalo Fernandez de Cordova, in the kingdom of Naples. This was the end of the offending, and too late penitent, friend; the news of which made Camilla immediately profess herself, and soon after, overwhelmed with grief and melancholy, pay for her transgression with the loss of her life. This was the unhappy end of them all, proceeding from so impertinent a beginning.

"I like this novel well enough," said the curate; "yet, after all, I cannot persuade myself that there is anything of truth in it; and if it be purely invention, the author was in the wrong; for it is not to be imagined there could ever be a husband so foolish, as to venture on so dangerous an experiment. Had he made his husband and wife a gallant and a mistress, the fable had appeared more probable; but, as it is, it is next to impossible. However, I must confess, I have nothing to object against his manner of telling it."

405

At the same time the innkeeper, who stood at the door, seeing company coming, "More guests," cried he, "a brave jolly troop, on my word. If they stop here, we may sing 'O be joyful.'" "What are they?" said Cardenio. "Four men," said the host, "on horseback, *à la Gineta*,[1] with black masks on their faces,[2] and armed with lances and targets; a lady, too, all in white, that rides single and masked; and two running footmen." "Are they near?" said the curate. "Just at the door," replied the innkeeper. Hearing this Dorothea veiled herself, and Cardenio had just time enough to step into the next room, where Don Quixote lay, when the strangers came into the yard. The four horsemen, who made a very genteel appearance, dismounted and went to help down the lady, whom one of them, taking in his arms, carried into the house; where he seated her in a chair by the chamber-door, into which Cardenio had withdrawn. All this was done without discovering their faces, or speaking a word; only the lady, as she sat down in the chair, breathed out a deep sigh, and let her arms sink down in a weak and fainting posture. The curate, marking their odd behavior, which raised in him a curiosity to know who they were, went to their servants in the stable, and asked what their masters were? "Indeed, sir," said one of them, "that is more than we can tell you; they seem of no mean quality, especially that gentleman who carried the lady into the house, for the rest pay him great respect, and his word is a law to them." "Who is the lady?" said the curate. "We know no more of her than the rest," answered the fellow, "for we could never see her face all the time, and it is impossible we should know her or them any otherwise. They picked us up on the road, my comrade

1 *A kind of riding with short stirrups which the Spaniards took from the Arabians.*
2 Antifaz: *a piece of thin black silk, which the Spaniards wear before their faces in traveling to keep off the dust and sun.*

and myself, and prevailed with us to wait on them to Andalusia, promising to pay us well for our trouble; so that, bating the two days traveling in their company, they are utter strangers to us." "Could you not hear them name one another all this time?" asked the curate. "No, truly, sir," answered the footman, "for we heard them not speak a syllable all the way: the poor lady, indeed, used to sigh and grieve so piteously, that we are persuaded she has no stomach to this journey. Whatever may be the cause we know not;

by her garb she seems to be a nun, but, by her grief and melancholy, one might guess they are going to make her one, when perhaps the poor girl has not a bit of nun's flesh about her." "Very likely," said the curate; and with that leaving them, he returned to the place where he left Dorothea, who, hearing the masked lady sigh so frequently, moved by the natural pity of the soft sex, could not forbear inquiring the cause of her sorrow. "Pardon me, madam," said she, "if I beg to know your grief; and assure yourself, that my request does not proceed from mere curiosity, but an earnest inclination to serve and assist you, if your misfortune be any such as our sex is naturally subject to, and in the power of a woman to cure." The melancholy lady made no return to her compliment, and

Dorothea pressed her in vain with new reasons, when the gentleman, whom the foot-boy signified to be the chief of the company, interposed: "Madam," said he, "do not trouble yourself to throw away any generous offer on that ungrateful woman, whose nature cannot return an obligation; neither expect any answer to your demands, for her tongue is a stranger to truth." "Sir," said the disconsolate lady, "my truth and honor have made me thus miserable, and my sufferings are sufficient to prove you the falsest and most base of men." Cardenio, being only parted from the company by Don Quixote's chamber-door, overheard these last words very distinctly; and immediately cried out, "Good Heaven, what do I hear! What voice struck my ear just now?" The lady, startled at his exclamation, sprung from the chair, and would have bolted into the chamber whence the voice came; but the gentleman, perceiving it, laid hold on her, to prevent her, which so disordered the lady that her mask fell off, and discovered an incomparable face, beautiful as an angel's, though very pale and strangely discomposed, her eyes eagerly rolling on every side, which made her appear distracted. Dorothea and the rest, not guessing what her eyes sought by their violent motion, beheld her with grief and wonder. She struggled so hard, and the gentleman was so disordered by beholding her, that his mask dropped off too, and discovered to Dorothea, who was assisting to hold the lady, the face of her husband Don Ferdinand: scarce had she known him, when with a long and dismal "Oh!" she fell in a swoon, and would have reached the floor with all her weight, had not the barber, by good fortune, stood behind and supported her. The curate ran presently to help her, and pulling off her veil to throw water in her face, Don Ferdinand presently knew her, and was struck almost as dead as she at the sight; nevertheless, he did not quit Lucinda, who was the lady that struggled so hard to get out of his hands. Cardenio, hearing Dorothea's exclamation, and imagining it to be Lucinda's voice,

flew into the chamber in great disorder, and the first object he
met was Don Ferdinand holding Lucinda, who presently knew him.
They were all struck dumb with amazement: Dorothea gazed on
Don Ferdinand; Don Ferdinand on Cardenio; and Cardenio and
Lucinda on one another. At last Lucinda broke silence, and, addressing Don Ferdinand, "Let me go," said she; "unloose your
hold, my lord: by the generosity you should have, or by your
inhumanity, since it must be so, I conjure you, leave me, that I may
cling like ivy to my old support; and from whom neither your
threats, nor prayers, nor gifts, nor promises, could ever alienate
my love. Contend not against Heaven, whose power alone could
bring me to my dear husband's sight, by such strange and unexpected means: you have a thousand instances to convince you that
nothing but death can make me ever forget him: let this, at least,
turn your love into rage, which may prompt you to end my miseries
with my life, here before my dear husband, where I shall be proud
to lose it, since my death may convince him of my unshaken love
and honor, till the last minute of my life." Dorothea, by this time,
had recovered, and finding by Lucinda's discourse who she was,
and that Don Ferdinand would not unhand her, she made a virtue
of necessity, and falling at his feet, "My lord," cried she, all bathed
in tears, "if that beauty which you hold in your arms has not altogether dazzled your eyes, you may behold at your feet the once
happy, but now miserable Dorothea. I am the poor and humble
villager, whom your generous bounty, I dare not say your love,
did condescend to raise to the honor of calling you her own: I am
she, who once, confined to peaceful innocence, led a contented life,
till your importunity, your show of honor, and deluding words,
charmed me from my retreat, and made me resign my freedom to
your power. How I am recompensed, may be guessed by my grief,
and my being found here in this strange place, whither I was led
not through any dishonorable ends, but purely by despair and grief

409

to be forsaken of you. It was at your desire I was bound to you by the strictest tie, and whatever you do, you can never cease to be mine. Consider, my dear lord, that my matchless love may balance the beauty and nobility of the person for whom you would forsake me; she cannot share your love, for it is only mine; and Cardenio's interest in her will not admit a partner. It is easier far, my lord, to recall your wandering desires, and fix them upon her that adores you, than to draw her to love who hates you. Remember how you did solicit my humble state, and, conscious of my meanness, you paid a veneration to my innocence, which, joined with the honorable condition of my yielding to your desires, pronounce me free from ill design or dishonor. Consider these undeniable truths: have some regard to your honor! Remember you are a Christian! Why should you then make her life end so miserably, whose beginning your favor made so happy? If I must not expect the usage and respect of a wife, let me but serve you as a slave; so I belong to you, though in the meanest rank, I never shall complain: let me not be exposed to the slandering reflections of the censorious world by so cruel a separation from my lord: afflict not the declining years of my poor parents, whose faithful services to you and yours have merited a more suitable return. If you imagine the current of your noble blood should be defiled by mixing with mine, consider how many noble houses have run in such a channel; besides, the woman's side is not essentially requisite to ennoble descent: but chiefly think on this, that virtue is the truest nobility; which, if you stain by basely wronging me, you bring a greater blot upon your family than marrying me could cause. In fine, my lord, you cannot, must not disown me for your wife: to attest which truth I call your own words, which must be true if you prize yourself for honor, and that nobility whose want you so despise in me; witness your oaths and vows, witness that Heaven which you so often invoked to ratify your promises; and, if all these should fail, I make my last appeal to your own conscience, whose sting will always represent my wrongs fresh to your thoughts, and disturb your joys amidst your greatest pleasures."

These, with many such arguments, did the mournful Dorothea urge, appearing so lovely in her sorrow, that Don Ferdinand's friends, as well as all the rest, sympathized with her, Lucinda particularly, as much admiring her wit and beauty, as moved by the tears, the piercing sighs and moans that followed her entreaties; and she would have gone nearer to have comforted her, had not Ferdinand's arms, that still held her, prevented it. He stood full of confusion, with his eyes fixed attentively on Dorothea a great while; at last, opening his arms, he quitted Lucinda. "Thou hast conquered," cried he, "charming Dorothea, thou hast conquered me; it is impossible to resist so many united truths and charms." Lucinda was still so disordered and weak, that she would have fallen when Ferdinand quitted her, had not Cardenio, without regard to his safety, leaped forward and caught her in his arms, and embracing her with eagerness and joy, "Thanks, gracious Heaven," cried he aloud, "my dear, my faithful wife, thy sorrows now are ended; for where can you rest more safe than in my arms, which now support thee, as once they did when my blessed fortune first made thee mine?" Lucinda, then opening her eyes, and finding herself in the arms of her Cardenio, without regard to ceremony or decency, threw her arms about his neck, and laying her face to his, "Yes," said she, "thou art he, thou art my lord indeed! It is even you yourself, the right owner of this poor harassed captive. Now fortune act thy worst, nor fears nor threats shall ever part me from the sole support and comfort of my life." This sight was very surprising to Don Ferdinand and the other spectators. Dorothea perceiving, by Don Ferdinand's change of countenance and laying his hand to his sword, that he prepared to assault Cardenio, fell suddenly on her knees; and, with an endearing embrace, held Don

411

Ferdinand's legs so fast, that he could not stir. "What means," cried she, all in tears, "the only refuge of my hope? See here thy own and dearest wife at thy feet, and her you would enjoy in her true husband's arms. Think then, my lord, how unjust is your attempt to dissolve that knot which Heaven has tied so fast. Can you ever think or hope success in your design on her, who, contemning all dangers, and confirmed in strictest constancy and honor, before your face lies bathed in tears of joy and passion in her true lover's bosom? For Heaven's sake I entreat you, by your own words I conjure you, to mitigate your anger, and permit that faithful pair to consummate their joys, and spend their remaining days in peace: thus may you make it appear that you are generous and truly noble, giving the world so strong a proof that you have your reason at command, and your passion in subjection." All this while Cardenio, though he still held Lucinda in his arms, had a watchful eye on Don Ferdinand; resolving, if he had made the least offer to his prejudice, to make him repent it, and all his party, if possible, though at the expense of his life. But Don Ferdinand's friends, the curate, the barber, and all the company (not forgetting honest Sancho Panza) got together about Don Ferdinand, and entreated him to pity the beautiful Dorothea's tears; that, considering what she had said, the truth of which was apparent, it would be the highest injustice to frustrate her lawful hopes; that their strange and wonderful meeting could not be attributed to chance, but the peculiar and directing Providence of Heaven; that nothing (as Mr. Curate very well urged) but death could part Cardenio from Lucinda; and that though the edge of his sword might separate them, he would make them happier by death than he could hope to be by surviving; that, in irrecoverable accidents, a submission to fate, and a resignation of our wills, showed not only the greatest prudence, but also the highest courage and generosity; that he should not envy those happy lovers what the bounty of Heaven had

412

conferred on them, but that he should turn his eyes on Dorothea's grief; view her incomparable beauty, which, with her true and unfeigned love, made large amends for the meanness of her parentage; but principally it lay upon him, if he gloried in the titles of Nobility and Christianity, to keep his promise unviolated; that the more reasonable part of mankind could not otherwise be satisfied, or have any esteem for him: also that it was the special prerogative of beauty, if heightened by virtue and adorned with modesty, to lay claim to any dignity, without disparagement or scandal to the person that raises it; and that the strong dictates of delight having been once indulged, we are not to be blamed for following them afterwards, provided they be not unlawful. In short, to these reasons they added so many enforcing arguments, that Don Ferdinand, who was truly a gentleman, could no longer resist reason, but stooped down and, embracing Dorothea, "Rise, madam," said he, "it is not proper that she should lie prostrate at my feet, who triumphs over my soul: if I have not hitherto paid you all the respect I ought, it was perhaps so ordered by Heaven, that having by this a stronger conviction of your constancy and goodness, I may henceforth set the greater value on your merit: let the future respects and services I shall pay you, plead a pardon for my past transgressions; and let the violent passions of my love, that first made me yours, be an excuse for that which caused me to forsake you. View the now happy Lucinda's eyes, and there read a thousand further excuses; but I promise henceforth never to disturb her quiet; and may she live long and contented with her dear Cardenio, as I hope to do with my dearest Dorothea." Thus concluding, he embraced her again so lovingly, that it was with no small difficulty that he kept in his tears, which he endeavored to conceal, being ashamed to discover so effeminate a proof of his remorse.

Cardenio, Lucinda, and the greatest part of the company, could not so well command their passions, but all wept for joy; even

413

Sancho Panza himself shed tears, though, as he afterwards confessed, it was not for downright grief, but because he found not Dorothea to be the queen of Micomicon, as he supposed, and of whom he expected so many favors and preferments. Cardenio and Lucinda fell at Don Ferdinand's feet, giving him thanks, with the strongest expressions which gratitude could suggest: he raised them up, and received their acknowledgments with much modesty; then begged to be informed by Dorothea how she came to that place. She related to him all she had told Cardenio, but with such a grace, that what were misfortunes to her, proved an inexpressible pleasure to those that heard her relation. When she had done, Don Ferdinand told all that had befallen him in the city, after he found the paper in Lucinda's bosom, which declared Cardenio to be her husband; how he would have killed her, had not her parents prevented him; how afterwards, mad with shame and anger, he left the city, to wait a more commodious opportunity of revenge; how in a short time he learned that Lucinda was fled to a nunnery, resolving to end her days there, if she could not spend them with Cardenio; that, having desired those three gentlemen to go with him, they went to the nunnery, and waiting till they found the gate open, he left two of the gentlemen to secure the door, while he with the other entered the house, where they found Lucinda talking with a nun in the cloister; they forcibly brought her thence to a village, where they disguised themselves for their more convenient flight, which they more easily brought about, the nunnery being situate in the fields, distant a good way from any town. He likewise added, how Lucinda, finding herself in his power, fell into a swoon, and that, after she came to herself, she continually wept and sighed, but would not speak a syllable; and that, accompanied with silence only and tears, they had traveled till they came to that inn, which proved to him as his arrival at Heaven, having put a happy conclusion to all his earthly misfortunes.

The joy of the whole company was unspeakable by the happy conclusion of this perplexed business; Dorothea, Cardenio, and Lucinda thought the sudden change of their affairs too surprising to be real; and, through a disuse of good fortune, could hardly be induced to believe their happiness. Don Ferdinand thanked Heaven a thousand times for its propitious conduct, in leading him out of a labyrinth, in which his honor and virtue were like to have been lost. The curate, as he was very instrumental in the general reconciliation, had likewise no small share in the general joy; and that no discontent might sour their universal satisfaction, Cardenio and the curate engaged to see the hostess satisfied for all the damages committed by Don Quixote: only poor Sancho drooped pitifully; he found his lordship and his hopes vanished into smoke, the Princess Micomicona was changed to Dorothea, and the giant to Don Ferdinand; thus, very musty and melancholy, he slipped into his master's chamber, who had slept on, and was just wakened, little thinking of what had happened.

"I hope your early rising will do you no hurt," said he, "Sir Knight of the Woeful Figure; but you may now sleep on till doomsday, if you will; nor need you trouble your head any longer about killing any giant, or restoring the princess, for all that is done to your hand." "That is more than probable," answered the Knight, "for I have had the most extraordinary, the most prodigious and bloody battle with the giant, that I ever had, or shall have during the whole course of my life; yet, with one cross stroke, I laid his head thwack on the ground, whence the great effusion of blood seemed like a violent stream of water." "Of wine, you mean," said Sancho, "for you must know (if you know it not already) that your worship's dead giant is a broached wine-skin, and the blood

415

some thirty gallons of tent, which it held in its belly, and your head so cleverly struck off, is the whore my mother; and so the devil take both giant and head, and altogether, for Sancho." "What sayest thou, madman?" said the Don. "Thou art frantic sure." "Rise, rise, sir," said Sancho, "and see what fine work you have cut out for yourself: here is the devil-and-all to pay for, and your great queen is changed into a private gentlewoman, called Dorothea, with some other such odd matters, that you will wonder with a vengeance." "I can wonder at nothing here," said Don Quixote, "where, you may remember, I told you all things ruled by enchantment." "I believe it," quoth Sancho, "had my tossing in a blanket been of that kind; but sure it was the likest the tossing in a blanket of anything I ever knew in my life. And this same innkeeper, I remember very well, was one of those that tossed me into the air, and as cleverly and heartily he did it as a man could wish, I will say that for him; so that after all I begin to smell a rat, and do perilously suspect, that all our enchantment will end in nothing but bruises and broken bones." "Heaven will retrieve all," said the Knight; "I will therefore dress, and march to the discovery of these wonderful transformations." While Sancho made him ready, the curate gave Don Ferdinand and the rest an account of Don Quixote's madness, and of the device he used to draw him from the Poor Rock, to which the supposed disdain of his mistress had banished him in imagination. Sancho's adventures made also a part in the story, which proved very diverting to the strangers. He added, that since Dorothea's change of fortune had prevented their design that way, some other trick should be found to decoy him home: Cardenio offered his service in the affair, and that Lucinda should personate Dorothea: "No, no," answered Don Ferdinand, "Dorothea shall humor the jest still, if this honest gentleman's habitation be not very far off." "Only two days' journey," said the curate. "I would ride twice as far," said Don Ferdinand, "for the pleasure of so good and charitable an action." By this Don Quixote had sallied out, armed *cap-à-pie*, Mambrino's helmet (with a great hole in it) on his head; his shield on his left arm, and with his right he leaned on his lance. His meager, yellow, weather-beaten face, of half a league in length, the unaccountable medley of his armor, together with his grave and solemn port, struck Don Ferdinand and his companions dumb with admiration, while the champion, casting his eyes on Dorothea with great gravity and solidity, broke silence with these words:

"I am informed by this my squire, beautiful lady, that your greatness is annihilated, and your majesty reduced to nothing, for of a queen and mighty princess, as you used to be, you are become a private damsel. If any express order from the necromantic king your father (doubting the ability and success of my arm in the reinstating you) has occasioned this change, I must tell him that he is no conjuror in these matters, and does not know one half of his trade; nor is he skilled in the revolutions of chivalry; for had he been conversant in the study of knight-errantry, as I have been, he might have found that, in every age, champions of less fame than Don Quixote de la Mancha have finished more desperate adventures; since the killing of a pitiful giant, how arrogant soever he may be, is no such great achievement; for, not many hours past, I encountered one myself: the success I will not mention, lest the incredulity of some people might distrust the reality; but time, the discoverer of all things, will disclose it when least expected." "Hold there," said the host, "it was with two wine-skins, but no giant that you fought." Don Ferdinand silenced the innkeeper, and bid him by no means interrupt Don Quixote, who thus went on: "To conclude, most high and disinherited lady, if your father, for the causes already mentioned, has caused this metamorphosis in your person, believe him not; for there is no peril on earth, through which my sword shall not open a way;

417

and assure yourself, that in a few days, by the overthrow of your enemy's head, it shall fix on yours that crown which is your lawful inheritance." Here Don Quixote stopped, waiting the princess's answer. She, assured of Don Ferdinand's consent to carry on the jest, till Don Quixote was gotten home, and assuming a face of gravity, "Whosoever," answered she, "has informed you, valorous Knight of the Woeful Figure, that I have altered or changed my condition, has imposed upon you; for I am just the same today as yesterday: it is true some unexpected, but fortunate accidents, have varied some circumstances of my fortune, much to my vantage, and far beyond my hopes; but I am neither changed in my person, nor altered in my resolution of employing the force of your redoubtable and invincible arm in my favor. I therefore apply myself to your usual generosity, to have these words spoken to my father's dishonor recalled, and believe these easy and infallible means to redress my wrongs to be the pure effects of his wisdom and policy, since the good fortune I now enjoy has been the consequence of your surprising deeds, as this noble presence can testify. What should hinder us then from setting forward tomorrow morning, depending for a happy and successful conclusion on the will of Heaven, and the power of your unparalleled courage?"

The ingenious Dorothea having concluded, Don Quixote, turning to Sancho with all the signs of fury imaginable: "Now must I tell thee, poor paltry hang-dog," said he, "thou art the veriest rascal in all Spain. Tell me, rogue, scoundrel, did not you just now inform me, that this princess was changed into a little private damsel, called Dorothea, and the head which I lopped from the giant's shoulders, was the whore your mother, with a thousand other absurdities? Now, by all the powers of Heaven," looking up, and grinding his teeth together, "I have a mind so to use thee, as to make thee appear a miserable example to all succeeding

418

squires, that shall dare to tell a knight-errant a lie." "Good your worship," cried Sancho, "have patience, I beseech you: mayhap I am mistaken or so, about my lady princess Micomicona's concern there; but that the giant's head came off the wine-skins' shoulders, and that the blood was as good tent as ever was tipped over tongue, I will take my corporal oath on it. Gadzookers, sir, are not the skins all hacked and slashed within there, at your bed's head, and the wine all in a puddle in your chamber? But you will guess at the meat presently, by the sauce; the proof of the pudding is in the eating, master; and if my landlord here do not let you know it to your cost, he is a very honest and civil fellow, that is all." "Sancho," said the Don, "I pronounce thee *non compos:* I therefore pardon thee and have done." "It is enough," said Don Ferdinand; "we, therefore, in pursuance of the princess's orders, will this night refresh ourselves, and tomorrow we will all of us set out to attend the Lord Don Quixote, in prosecution of this important enterprise he has undertaken, being all impatient to be eye-witnesses of his celebrated and matchless courage." "I shall be proud of the honor of serving and waiting upon you, my good lord," replied Don Quixote, "and reckon myself infinitely obliged by the favor and good opinion of so honorable a company; which I shall endeavor to improve and confirm, though at the expense of the last drop of my blood."

Many other compliments had passed between Don Quixote and Don Ferdinand, when the arrival of a stranger interrupted them. His dress represented him a Christian newly returned from Barbary: he was clad in a short-skirted coat of blue cloth with short sleeves, and no collar, his breeches were of blue linen, with a cap of the same color, a pair of date-colored stockings, and a Turkish scimitar hung by a scarf, in manner of a shoulder-belt. There rode a woman in his company, clad in a Moorish dress; her face was covered with a veil; she had on a little cap of gold tissue, and a Turkish mantle that reached from her shoulders to her feet. The man was well shaped and strong, his age about forty, his face somewhat tanned, his mustachios long, and his beard handsome: in short, his genteel mien and person were too distinguished to let the gentleman be hid by the meanness of his habit. He called presently for a room, and being answered that all were full, seemed a little troubled: however, he went to the woman who came along with him, and took her down from her ass. The ladies, being all surprised at the oddness of the Moorish dress, had the curiosity to flock about the stranger; and Dorothea, very discreetly imagining that both she and her conductor were tired, took it ill that they could not have a chamber. "I hope, madam, you will bear your ill-fortune patiently," said she, "for want of room is an inconvenience incident to all public inns: but if you please, madam, to take up with us," pointing to Lucinda, "you may, perhaps, find that you have met with worse entertainment on the road, than what this place affords." The unknown lady made her no answer, but rising up, laid her hands across her breast, bowed her head, and inclined her body, as a sign that she acknowledged the favor. By her silence they conjectured her to be undoubtedly a Moor, and that she could not speak Spanish. Her companion was now come back from the stable, and told them, "Ladies, I hope you will excuse this gentlewoman from answering any questions, for she is very much a stranger to our language." "We are only, sir," answered Lucinda, "making her an offer which civility obliges us to make all strangers, especially of our own sex, that she would make us happy in her company all night, and fare as we do; we will make very much of her, sir, and she shall want for nothing that the house affords." "I return you humble thanks, dear madam," answered the stranger, "in the lady's behalf and my own; and I infinitely prize the favor, which the present exigency and the worth of the donors make doubly engaging." "Is the lady, pray sir, a Christian or a Moor?" asked Dorothea. "Our charity would make us hope she were the former; but, by her attire and silence, we are afraid she is the latter." "Outwardly, madam," answers he, "she appears and is a Moor, but in her heart a zealous Christian, which her longing desires of being baptized have expressly testified. I have had no opportunity of having her christened since she left Algiers, which was her habitation and native country; nor has any imminent danger of death as yet obliged her to be brought to the font, before she be better instructed in the principles of our religion; but I hope, by Heaven's assistance, to have her shortly baptized with all the decency suiting her quality, which is much above what her equipage or mine seem to promise."

These words raised in them all a curiosity to be further informed who the Moor and her conductor were; but they thought it improper then to put them upon any more particular relation of their fortunes, because they wanted rest and refreshment after their journey. Dorothea, placing the lady by her, begged her to take off her veil. She looked on her companion, as if she required him to let her know what she said; which, when he had let her understand in the Arabian tongue, joining his own request also, she discovered so charming a face, that Dorothea imagined her more beautiful than Lucinda; she, on the other hand, fancied her handsomer than Dorothea; and most of the company believed her more beautiful than both of them. As beauty has always a prerogative, or rather charm, to attract men's inclinations, the whole company dedicated their desires to serve the lovely Moor. Don Ferdinand asked the stranger her name. He answered, "Lela Zoraida." She, hearing him, and guessing what they asked, suddenly replied with great

421

concern, though very gracefully, "No, not Zoraida, Maria, Maria": giving them to understand, that her name was Maria, and not Zoraida. These words, spoken with so much eagerness, raised a concern in everybody, the ladies especially, whose natural tenderness showed itself by their tears; and, Lucinda embracing her very lovingly, "Ay, ay," said she, "Maria, Maria," which words the Moorish lady repeated by way of answer. "Zoraida macange," added she [1]; as much as to say, not Zoraida but Maria, Maria. The night coming on, and the innkeeper, by order of Don Ferdinand's friends, having made haste to provide them the best supper he could, the cloth was laid on a long table, there being neither round or square in the house. Don Quixote, after much ceremony, was prevailed upon to sit at the head; he desired the lady Micomicona to sit next to him; and the rest of the company having placed themselves according to their rank and convenience, they ate their supper very heartily. Don Quixote, to raise the diversion, never minded his meat, but, inspired with the same spirit that moved him to preach so much to the goatherds, he began to hold forth in this manner: "Certainly, gentlemen, if we rightly consider it, those who make knight-errantry their profession, often meet with most surprising and stupendous adventures. For what mortal in the world, at this time entering within this castle, and seeing us sit together as we do, will imagine and believe us to be the same persons which in reality we are? Who is there that can judge that this lady by my side is the great queen we all know her to be, and that I am that Knight of the Woeful Figure, so universally made known by fame? It is then no longer to be doubted, but that this exercise and profession surpasses all others that have been invented by man, and is so much the more honorable, as it is more exposed to dangers. Let none presume to tell me that the pen is preferable to the sword; for be they who they will, I shall tell them they know

[1] Macange *was an Arabic expression signifying the negative.*

422

not what they say; for the reason they give, and on which chiefly they rely, is, that the labor of the mind exceeds that of the body, and that the exercise of arms depends only on the body, as if the use of them were the business of porters, which requires nothing but much strength: or, as if this, which we who profess it call chivalry, did not include the acts of fortitude which depend very much upon the understanding. Or else, as if that warrior, who commands an army or defends a city besieged, did not labor as much with the mind as with the body. If this be not so, let experience teach us whether it be possible by bodily strength to discover or guess the intentions of an enemy. The forming designs, laying of stratagems, overcoming of difficulties, and shunning of dangers, are all works of the understanding, wherein the body has no share. It being therefore evident that the exercise of arms requires the help of the mind as well as learning, let us see, in the next place, whether the scholar or the soldier's mind undergoes the greatest labor. Now this may be the better known by regarding the end and object each of them aims at; for that intention is to be most valued which makes the noblest end its object. The scope and end of learning, I mean human learning (in this place I speak not of Divinity, whose aim is to guide souls to Heaven, for no other can equal a design so infinite as that), is to give a perfection to distributive

justice, bestowing upon everyone his due, and to procure and cause good laws to be observed; an end really generous, great, and worthy of high commendation; but yet not equal to that which knight-errantry tends to, whose object and end is peace, which is the greatest blessing man can wish for in this life. And, therefore, the first good news the world received, was that which the angels brought in the night, which was the beginning of our day, when they sung in the air 'Glory to God on high, peace upon earth, and to men good-will.' And the only manner of salutation taught by the best Master in Heaven, or upon earth, to His friends and favorites, was, that entering any house they should say, 'Peace be to this house.' And at other times He said to them, 'My peace I give to you, My peace I leave to you, peace be among you.' A jewel and legacy worthy of such a Donor, a jewel so precious, that without it there can be no happiness either in earth or Heaven. This peace is the true end of war; for arms and war are one and the same thing. Allowing then this truth, that the end of war is peace, and that in this it excels the end of learning, let us now weigh the bodily labors the scholar undergoes, against those the warrior suffers, and then see which are greatest." The method and language Don Quixote used in delivering himself were such that none of his hearers at that time looked upon him as a madman. But, on the contrary, most of them being gentlemen to whom the use of arms properly appertains, they gave him a willing attention. And he proceeded in this manner: "These, then, I say, are the sufferings and hardships a scholar endures; first, poverty (not that they are all poor, but to urge the worst that may be in this case), and having said he endures poverty, methinks nothing more need be urged to express his misery; for he that is poor enjoys no happiness, but labors under this poverty in all its parts, at one time in hunger, at another in cold, another in nakedness, and sometimes in all of them together, yet his poverty is not so great, but still he eats, though it be later than the usual hour, and of the scraps of the rich, or, which is the greatest of a scholar's misfortunes, what is called among them, 'going a sopping';[2] neither can the scholar miss of somebody's stove or fire-side to sit by, where, though he be not thoroughly heated, yet he may gather warmth, and at least sleep away the night under a roof. I will not touch upon other less material circumstances, as the want of linen, and scarcity of shoes, thinness and bareness of their clothes, and their surfeiting when good fortune throws a feast in their way. This is the difficult and uncouth path they tread, often stumbling and falling, yet rising again and pushing on, till they attain the preferment they aim at; whither being arrived, we have seen many of them, who, having been carried by a fortunate gale through all these quicksands, from a chair govern the world; their hunger being changed into satiety, their cold into comfortable warmth, their nakedness into magnificence of apparel, and the mat they used to lie upon into stately beds of costly silks and softest linen; a reward due to their virtue. But yet their sufferings, being compared to those the soldier endures, appear much inferior, as I shall in the next place make out."

XI: *A CONTINUATION OF DON QUIXOTE'S CURIOUS DISCOURSE UPON ARMS AND LEARNING*

"Since speaking of the scholar, we began with his poverty and its several parts," continued Don Quixote, "let us now observe whether the soldier be anything richer than he; and we shall find that poverty itself is not poorer; for he depends on his miserable pay, which he receives but seldom, or perhaps never; or else on that he

[2] *Referring to the sops in porridge, given at the doors of monasteries.*

makes by marauding, with the hazard of his life, and trouble of his conscience. Such is sometimes his want of apparel, that a slashed buff coat is all his holiday raiment and shirt; and in the depth of winter being in the open field, he has nothing to cherish him against the sharpness of the season, but the breath of his mouth, which, issuing from an empty place, I am persuaded is itself cold, though contrary to the rules of nature. But now see how he expects night to make amends for all these hardships in the bed prepared for him, which, unless it be his own fault, never proves too narrow; for he may freely lay out as much of the ground as he pleases, and tumble to his content, without danger of losing the sheets. But, above all, when the day shall come, wherein he is to put in practice the exercise of his profession, and strive to gain some new degree; when the day of battle shall come, then, as a mark of his honor, shall his head be dignified with a cap made of lint, to stop a hole made by a bullet, or he perhaps be carried off maimed, at the expense of a leg or an arm. And if this do not happen, but that merciful Heaven preserve his life and limbs, it may fall out that he shall remain as poor as before, and must run through many encounters and battles, nay, always come off victorious, to obtain some little preferment; and these miracles too are rare: but, I pray, tell me gentlemen, if ever you made it your observation, how few are those who obtain due rewards in war in comparison of those numbers that perish? Doubtless you will answer, that there is no parity between them; that the dead cannot be reckoned up, whereas, those who live and are rewarded may be numbered with three figures.[1] It is quite otherwise with scholars, not only those who follow the law, but others also, who all either by hook or by crook get a livelihood; so that though the soldier's sufferings be much greater, yet his reward is much less. To this it may be answered, that it is easier to reward two thousand scholars than thirty thousand

[1] i.e., *do not exceed hundreds.*

soldiers, because the former are recompensed at the expense of the public, by giving them employments, which of necessity must be allowed on those of their profession, but the latter cannot be gratified otherwise than at the cost of the master that employs them; yet this very difficulty makes good my argument. But let us lay this matter aside, as a point difficult to be decided, and let us return to the preference due to arms above learning, a subject as yet in debate, each party bringing strong reasons to make out their pretensions. Among others learning urges, that without it warfare itself could not subsist; because war, as other things, has its laws, and is governed by them, and laws are the province of learning and scholars. To this objection the soldiers make answer, that without them the laws cannot be maintained, for it is by arms that commonwealths are defended, kingdoms supported, cities secured, the highway made safe, and the sea delivered from pirates. In short, were it not for them, commonwealths, kingdoms, monarchies, cities, the roads by land and the waters of the sea, would be subject to the ravages and confusion that attends war while it lasts, and is at liberty to make use of its unbounded power and prerogative. Besides, it is past all controversy, that what costs dearest, is, and ought to be, most valued. Now for a man to attain to an eminent degree of learning costs him time, watching, hunger, nakedness, dizziness in the head, weakness in the stomach, and other inconveniences which are the consequences of these, of which I have already in part made mention. But the rising gradually to be a good soldier is purchased at the whole expense of all that is required for learning, and that in so surpassing a degree, that there is no comparison betwixt them; because he is every moment in danger of his life. To what danger or distress can a scholar be reduced equal to that of a soldier, who, being besieged in some strong place, and at his post or upon guard in some ravelin or bastion, perceives the enemy carrying on a mine under him, and

427

yet must upon no account remove from thence, or shun the danger which threatens him so near? All he can do is, to give notice to his commander, that he may countermine, but must himself stand still, fearing and expecting, when on a sudden he shall soar to the clouds without wings, and be again cast down headlong against his will. If this danger seem inconsiderable, let us see whether that be not greater when two galleys shock one another with their prows in the midst of the spacious sea. When they have thus grappled, and are clinging together, the soldier is confined to the narrow beak, being a board not above two feet wide; and yet though he sees before him so many ministers of death threatening, as there are pieces of cannon on the other side pointing against him, and not half a pike's length from his body; and being sensible that the first slip of his feet sends him to the bottom of Neptune's dominions; still, for all this, inspired by honor, with an undaunted heart, he stands a mark to so much fire, and endeavors to make his way, by that narrow passage, into the enemy's vessel. But what is most to be admired is, that no sooner one falls, where he shall never rise till the end of the world, than another steps into the same place; and if he also drops into the sea, which lies in wait for him like an enemy, another, and after him another, still fills up the place, without suffering any interval of time to separate their deaths; a resolution and boldness scarce to be paralleled in any other trials of war. Blessed be those happy ages that were strangers to the deadful fury of these devilish instruments of artillery, whose inventor I am satisfied is now in hell, receiving the reward of his cursed invention, which is the cause that very often a cowardly base hand takes away the life of the bravest gentleman, and that in the midst of that vigor and resolution which animates and inflames the bold, a chance bullet (shot perhaps by one that fled, and was frightened at the very flash the mischievous piece gave when it went off) coming nobody knows how or from whence, in a moment puts

428

a period to the brave designs and the life of one that deserved to have survived many years. This considered, I could almost say, I am sorry at my heart for having taken upon me this profession of a knight-errant, in so detestable an age; for though no danger daunts me, yet it affects me to think, whether powder and lead may not deprive me of the opportunity of becoming famous, and making myself known throughout the world by the strength of my arm, and dint of my sword. But let Heaven order matters as it pleases, for if I compass my designs, I shall be so much the more honored by how much the dangers I have exposed myself to are greater than those the knights-errant of former ages underwent." All this long preamble Don Quixote made whilst the company supped, never minding to eat a mouthful, though Sancho Panza had several times advised him to mind his meat, telling him there would be time enough afterwards to talk as he thought fit. Those who heard him were afresh moved with compassion, to see a man, who seemed in all other respects to have a sound judgment and clear understanding, so absolutely mad and distracted, when any mention was made of his cursed knight-errantry. The curate told him he was much in the right in all he had said for the honor of arms; and that he, though a scholar and a graduate, was of the same opinion. Supper being ended, and the cloth taken away; whilst the innkeeper, his wife, his daughter, and Maritornes fitted up Don Quixote's loft for the ladies, that they might lie by themselves that night, Don Ferdinand entreated the slave to give them an account of his life, conscious the relation could not choose but be very delightful and surprising, as might be guessed by his coming with Zoraida. The slave answered he would most willingly comply with their desires, and that he only feared the relation would not give them all the satisfaction he could wish; but that, however, rather than disobey, he would do it as well as he could. The curate and all the company thanked him, and made fresh instances to the same effect. Seeing himself courted by so many, "There is no need of entreaties," said he, "for what you may command; therefore," continued he, "give me your attention, and you shall hear a true relation, perhaps not to be paralleled by those fabulous stories which are composed with much art and study." This caused all the company to seat themselves, and observe a very strict silence; and then, with an agreeable and sedate voice, he began in this manner:

XII: WHERE THE CAPTIVE RELATES HIS LIFE AND ADVENTURES

"In the mountains of Leon my family had its first origins, and was more kindly dealt withal by nature than by fortune, though my father might pass for rich among the inhabitants of those parts, who are but poorly provided for; to say truth, he had been so, had he had as much industry to preserve, as he had inclination to dissipate, his income; but he had been a soldier, and the years of his youth spent in that employment, had left him in his old age a propensity to spend under the name of Liberality. War is school where the covetous grow free, and the free prodigal: to see a soldier a miser is a kind of prodigy which happens but seldom. My father was far from being one of them; for he passed the bounds of liberality, and came very near the excesses of prodigality; a thing which cannot suit well with a married life, where the children ought to succeed to the estate as well as name of the family. We were three of us, all at man's estate; and my father, finding that the only way, as he said, to curb his squandering inclination, was to dispossess himself of that which maintained it, his estate (without which Alexander himself must have been put to it), he called us one day all three to him in his chamber, and spoke to us in the following manner:

" 'My sons, to per-
suade you that I love
you, I need only tell
you I am your father,
and you my children;
and, on the other side,
you have reason to
think me unkind, con-
sidering how careless
I have been in pre-
serving what should
one day be yours; but
to convince you, how-
ever, that I have the
bowels of a true and
loving parent, I have
taken a firm resolve,
which I have weighed

well and considered for many days. You are all by now of an
age to choose the kind of life each of you incline to; or, at least, to
enter upon some employment that may one day procure you both
honor and profit: therefore I design to divide all I have into four
parts, of which I will give three among you, and retain the fourth
for myself to maintain me in my old age, as long as it shall please
Heaven to continue me in this life. After that each of you shall have
received his part, I could wish you would follow one of the employments I shall mention to you, everyone as he finds himself inclined.
There is a proverb in our tongue which I take to contain a great
deal of truth, as generally those sorts of sayings do, being short sentences framed upon observation and long experience. This proverb
runs thus, "Either the church, the sea, or the court." As if it should
plainly say, that whosoever desires to thrive must follow one of these

431

three, either be a churchman, or a merchant and try his fortune at sea, or enter into the service of his prince in the court: for another proverb says, that "King's chaff is better than other men's corn." I say this, because I would have one of you follow his studies, another I desire should be a merchant, and the third should serve the king in war; because it is a thing of some difficulty to get an entrance at court; and though war does not immediately procure riches, yet it seldom fails of giving honor and reputation. Within eight days' time I will give each of you your portion, and not wrong you of a farthing of it, as you shall see by experience. Now, therefore, tell me if you are resolved to follow my advice about your settling in the world.' And turning to me, as the eldest, he bid me answer first. I told him, that he ought not upon our account to divide or lessen his estate or way of living; that we were young men, and could shift in the world; and at last I concluded, that for my part I would be a soldier, and serve God and the king in that honorable profession. My second brother made the same regardful offer, and chose to go to the Indies, resolving to lay out in goods the share that should be given him here. The youngest, and I believe the wisest of us all, said he would be a churchman; and, in order to do so, go to Salamanca, and there finish his studies. After this, my father embraced us all three, and in a few days performed what he had promised; and, as I remember, it was three thousand ducats a-piece, which he gave us in money; for we had an uncle who bought all the estate, and paid for it in ready money, that it might not go out of the family. A little after we all took leave of my father; and at parting I could not forbear thinking it a kind of inhumanity to leave the old gentleman in so straitened a condition: I prevailed with him, therefore, to accept of two thousand of my three, the remainder being sufficient to make up a soldier's equipage. My example worked upon my other brothers, and they, each of them, presented him with a thousand ducats; so that my father remained with four thousand ducats in ready money, and three thousand more in land, which he chose to keep, and not sell outright. To be short, we took our last leave of my father and the uncle I have mentioned, not without much grief and tears on all sides. They particularly recommending to us to let them know, by all opportunities, our good or ill-fortunes, we promised so to do, and having received the blessing of our old father, one of us went straight to Salamanca, the other to Seville, and I to Alicante, where I was informed of a Genoese ship, which was loading wood for Genoa.

"This year makes two-and-twenty since I first left my father's house, and in all that time, though I have written several letters, I have not had the least news, either of him, or of my brothers. And now I will relate, in a few words, my own adventures in all that course of years. I took shipping at Alicante, arrived safe and with a good passage at Genoa, from thence I went to Milan, where I bought my equipage, resolving to go and enter myself in the army of Piedmont; but being come as far as Alexandria de la Paille, I was informed that the great duke of Alva was passing into Flanders with an army; this made me alter my first resolution. I followed him, and was present at all his engagements, as well as at the deaths of the Counts Egmont and Horne; and at last I had a pair of colors under a famous captain of Guadalajara, whose name was Diego de Urbina. Some time after my arrival in Flanders, there came news of the league concluded by Pope Pius V of happy memory, in conjunction with Spain, against the common enemy the Turk, who at that time had taken the Island of Cyprus from the Venetians; which was an unfortunate and lamentable loss to Christendom. It was also certain that the general of this holy league was the most serene Don Juan of Austria, natural brother to our good king Don Philip. The great fame of the preparations for this war excited in me a vehement desire of being present at the engagement, which was expected to follow these

433

preparations; and although I had certain assurance, and, as it were, an earnest of my being advanced to be a captain upon the first vacancy, yet I resolved to leave all those expectations and return, as I did, to Italy. My good fortune was such that I arrived just about the same time that Don Juan of Austria landed at Genoa, in order to go to Naples and join the Venetian fleet, as he did at Messina. In short, I was at that great action of the battle of Lepanto, being a captain of foot, to which post my good fortune, more than my desert, had now advanced me; and that day, which was so happy to all Christendom (because the world was then disabused of the error they had entertained, that the Turk was invincible at sea), that day I say, in which the pride of the Ottomans was first broke, and which was so happy to all Christians, even to those who died in the fight, who were more so than those who remained alive and conquerors, I alone was the unhappy man; since, instead of a naval crown, which I might have hoped for in the time of the Romans, I found myself that very night a slave, with irons on my feet, and manacles on my hands. The thing happened thus: Vehali, king of Algiers, a brave and bold pirate, having boarded and taken the Capitana galley of Malta, in which only three knights were left alive, and those desperately wounded, the galley of John Andrea Doria bore up to succor them: in this galley I was embarked with my company, and doing my duty on this occasion; I leaped into the enemy's galley, which getting loose from ours that intended to board the Algerine, my soldiers were hindered from following me, and I remained alone among a great number of enemies; whom not being able to resist, I was taken after having received several wounds; and as you have already heard, Vehali having escaped with all his squadron, I found myself his prisoner; and was the only afflicted man among so many joyful ones, and the only captive among so many free; for, on that day above 15,000 Christians, who rowed in the Turkish galleys, obtained their long-

434

wished-for liberty. I was carried to Constantinople, where the Grand Signor Selim made Vehali, my master, general of the sea, he having behaved himself very well in the battle, and brought away with him the great flag of the order of Malta, as a proof of his valor.

"The second year of my captivity, I was a slave in the Capitana galley at Navarino; and I took notice of the Christians' fault, in letting slip the opportunity they had of taking the whole Turkish fleet in that port; and all the Janizaries and Algerine pirates did so expect to be attacked, that they had made all in readiness to escape on shore without fighting, so great was the terror they had of our fleet: but it pleased God to order it otherwise, not by any fault of the Christian general, but for the sins of Christendom, and because it is His will we should always have some enemies to chastise us. Vehali made his way to Modon, which is an island not far from Navarino, and there landing his men, fortified the entrance of the harbor, remaining in safety there till Don Juan was forced to return home with his fleet. In this expedition, the galley called 'La Presa,' of which Barbarossa's own son was captain, was taken by the admiral galley of Naples, called the 'Wolf,' which was commanded by that thunder-bolt of war, that father of the soldiers, that happy and never-conquered captain, Don Alvaro de Baçan, Marquis of Santa Cruz; and I cannot omit the manner of taking this galley. The son of Barbarossa was very cruel, and used his slaves with great inhumanity; they perceiving that the 'Wolf' galley got of them in the chase, all of a sudden laid by their oars, and, seizing on their commander, as he was walking between them on the deck and calling to them to row hard, they passed him on, from hand to hand, to one another, from one end of the galley to the other, and gave him such blows in the handling him, that before he got back to the main-mast, his soul had left his body and

435

was fled to hell. This, as I said, was the effect of his cruelty and their hatred.

"After this we returned to Constantinople; and the next year, which was 1573, news came that Don Juan of Austria had taken Tunis and its kingdom from the Turks, and given the possession of it to Muley Hamid, having thereby defeated all the hopes of reigning of Muley Hamida, one of the cruellest, and withal one of the bravest Moors in the world. The Grand Signor was troubled at this loss, and using his wonted artifices with the Christians, he struck up a peace with the Venetians, who were much more desirous than he of it.

"The year after, which was 1574, he attacked the Goletta, and the fort which Don Juan had begun, but not above half-finished, before Tunis. All this while I was a galley-slave, without any hopes of liberty; at least, I could not promise myself to obtain it by way of ransom; for I was resolved not to write my father the news of my misfortune. La Goletta [1] and the fort were both taken, after some resistance; the Turkish army consisting of 75,000 Turks in pay, and above 400,000 Moors and Arabs, out of all Africa near the sea; with such provisions for war of all kinds, and so many pioneers, that they might have covered the Goletta and the fort with earth by handfuls. The Goletta was first taken, though always before reputed impregnable; and it was not lost by any fault of its defenders, who did all that could be expected from them; but because it was found by experience, that it was practicable to make trenches in that sandy soil, which was thought to have water under it within two feet, but the Turks sunk above two yards and found none; by which means, filling sacks with sand, and laying them one on another, they raised them so high, that they overtopped and commanded the fort, in which none could be safe, nor show

1 *The Goletta was a fortress in the Mediterranean, between that sea and the lake of Tunis. In 1535 Charles V took it by storm.*

436

themselves upon the walls. It has been the opinion of most men, that we did ill to shut ourselves up in the Goletta; and that we ought to have been drawn out to hinder their landing; but they who say so, talk without experience, and at random of such things; for, if in all there were not above 7,000 men in the Goletta and the fort, how could so small a number, though never so brave, take the open field against such forces as those of the enemies? And how is it possible that a place can avoid being taken, which can have no relief, particularly being besieged by such numbers, and those in their own country? But it seemed to many others, and that is also my opinion, that God Almighty favored Spain most particularly, in suffering that sink of iniquity and misery, as well as that spunge and perpetual drain of treasure to be destroyed. For infinite sums of money were spent there to no purpose, without any other design than to preserve the memory of one of the Emperor's (Charles the Fifth's) conquests; as if it had been necessary to support the eternity of his glory (which will be permanent) that those stones should remain in being. The fort was likewise lost, but the Turks got it foot by foot; for the soldiers who defended it sustained two and twenty assaults, and in them killed above 25,000 of those Barbarians; and when it was taken, of 300 which were left alive, there was not one man unwounded; a certain sign of the bravery of the garrison, and of their skill in defending places. There was likewise taken, by composition, a small fort in the midst of a lake, which was under the command of Don John Zanoguerra, a gentleman of Valencia and a soldier of great renown. Don Pedro Puerto Carrero, general of the Goletta, was taken prisoner, and was so afflicted at the loss of the place, that he died of grief by the way before he got to Constantinople, whither they were carrying him. They took also prisoner the commander of the fort, whose name was Gabriel Cerbellon, a Milanese, a great engineer, as well as a valiant soldier. Several persons of quality were killed in those two fortresses, and amongst the rest was Pagan Doria, the brother of the famous John Andrea Doria, a generous and noble-hearted gentleman, as well appeared by his liberality to that brother; and that which made his death more worthy of compassion was, that he received it from some Arabs to whom he had committed his safety after the loss of the fort, they having promised to carry him disguised in a Moor's habit to Tabarca, which is a small fort held on that coast by the Genoese, for the diving for coral; but they cut off his head, and brought it to the Turkish general, who made good to them our Spanish proverb, that the treason pleases, but the traitors are odious; for he ordered them to be hanged up immediately, for not having brought him alive. Amongst the Christians which were taken in the fort, there was one Don Pedro d'Aguilar, of some place in Andalusia, and who was an ensign in the place; a very brave, and a very ingenious man, and one who had a rare talent in poetry. I mention him, because it was his fortune to be a slave in the same galley with me, and chained to the same bench. Before he left the port he made two sonnets, by way of epitaph for the Goletta and the fort, which I must beg leave to repeat here, having learned them by heart, and I believe they will rather divert than tire the company." When the captive named Don Pedro d'Aguilar, Don Ferdinand looked upon his companions, and they all smiled; and when he talked of the sonnets, one of them said, "Before you go on to repeat the sonnets, I desire, sir, you would tell me what became of that Don Pedro d'Aguilar, whom you have mentioned." "All that I know of him," answered the slave, "is, that after having been two years in Constantinople, he made his escape, disguised like an Arnaut,[2] and in company of a Greek spy; but I cannot tell whether he obtained his liberty or no, though I believe he did, because about a year after I saw the same Greek in Constantinople, but had not an opportunity to ask him about the success of his journey." "Then

[2] *A trooper of Epirus, Dalmatia, or some of the adjacent countries.*

438

I can tell you," replied the gentleman, "that the Don Pedro you speak of is my brother, and is at present at home, married, rich, and has three children." "God be thanked," said the slave, "for the favors He has bestowed on him; for in my mind there is no felicity equal to that of recovering one's lost liberty." "And moreover," added the same gentleman, "I can say the sonnets you mentioned, which my brother made." "Pray say them then," replied the slave, "for I question not but you can repeat them better than I." "With all my heart," answered the gentleman. "That upon the Goletta was thus:

XIII: THE STORY OF THE CAPTIVE CONTINUED

A SONNET

"Blest souls, discharg'd of life's oppressive weight
  Whose virtue proved your passport to the skies:
You there procur'd a more propitious fate,
  When for your faith you bravely fell to rise.

"When pious rage diffus'd thro' ev'ry vein,
  On this ungrateful shore inflamed your blood;
Each drop you lost, was bought with crowds of slain,
  Whose vital purple swell'd the neighb'ring flood.

"Tho' crush'd by ruins, and by odds, you claim
That perfect glory, that immortal fame,
  Which, like true heroes, nobly you pursu'd;
On these you seiz'd, even when of life depriv'd,
For still your courage even your lives surviv'd;
  And sure 'tis conquest, thus to be subdu'd."

"I know it is just as you repeat it," said the captive. "Well, then," said the gentleman, "I will give you now that which was made upon the fort, if I can remember it.

439

"Amidst these barren fields, and ruin'd towers,
　　The bed of honor of the falling brave,
Three thousand champions of the Christian pow'rs
　　Found a new life, and triumph in the grave.

"Long did their arms their haughty foes repel,
　　Yet strew'd the fields with slaughter'd heaps in vain;
O'ercome by toils, the pious heroes fell,
　　Or but surviv'd more nobly to be slain.

"This dismal soul, so famed in ills of old,
In ev'ry age was fatal to the bold,
　　The seat of horror, and the warrior's tomb!
Yet hence to Heav'n more worth was ne'er resign'd
Than these display'd; nor has the earth combin'd,
　　Resum'd more noble bodies in her womb."

The sonnets were applauded, and the captive was pleased to
hear such good news of his friend and companion; after that he
pursued his relation in these terms: "The Turks ordered the dis-
mantling of the Goletta, the fort being razed to their hand by the
siege; and yet the mines they made could not blow up the old walls,
which nevertheless were always thought the weakest part of the
place; but the new fortifications made by the engineer Fratin
came easily down. In fine, the Turkish fleet returned in triumph to
Constantinople, where not long after my master Vehali died, whom
the Turks used to call Vehali Fartax, which in Turkish signifies
the scabby renegade, as indeed he was; and the Turks give names
among themselves, either from some virtue or some defect that is
in them; and this happens, because there are but four families
descended from the Ottoman family; all the rest, as I have said,
take their names from some defect of the body, or some good
quality of the mind. This scabby slave was at the oar in one of the

Grand Signor's galleys for fourteen years, till he was four and thirty years old; at which time he turned renegade, to be revenged of a Turk who gave him a box on the ear, as he was chained to the oar, forsaking his religion for his revenge: after which he showed so much valor and conduct, that he came to be king of Algiers, and admiral of the Turkish fleet, which was the third command in the whole empire. He was a Calabrian by birth, and of a mild disposition towards his slaves, as also of good morals to the rest of the world. He had above 3000 slaves of his own, all which after his death were divided, as he had ordered by his will, between the Grand Signor, his sons and his renegades. I fell to the share of a Venetian renegade, who was a cabin-boy in a Venetian ship which was taken by Vehali, who loved him so, that he was one of his favorite boys; and he came at last to prove one of the cruellest renegades that ever was known. His name was Azanaga, and he obtained such riches, as to rise by them to be king of Algiers; and with him I left Constantinople, with some satisfaction to think, at least, that I was in a place so near Spain, not because I could give advice to any friend of my misfortunes, but because I hoped to try whether I should succeed better in Algiers than I had done in Constantinople, where I had tried a thousand ways of running away, but could never execute any of them, which I hoped I should compass better in Algiers; for hopes never forsook me upon all the disappointments I met with in the design of recovering my liberty. By this means I kept myself alive, shut up in a prison or house, which the Turks call a bagnio, where they keep their Christian slaves, as well those of the king as those who belong to private persons, and also those who are called the Almazen, that is, who belong to the public, and are employed by the city in works that belong to it. These latter do very difficultly obtain their liberty; for, having no particular master, but belonging to the public, they can find nobody to treat with about their ransom, though they have money to pay it. The king's slaves, which are ransomable, are not obliged to go out to work as the others do, except their ransom stays too long before it comes; for then, to hasten it, they make them work, and fetch wood with the rest, which is no small labor. I was one of those who were to be ransomed; for when they knew I had been a captain, though I told them the impossibility I was in of being redeemed, because of my poverty, yet they put me among the gentlemen that were to be ransomed, and to that end put on me a slight chain, rather as a mark of distinction, than to restrain me by it; and so I passed my life in that bagnio, with several other gentlemen of quality, who expected their ransom; and though hunger and nakedness might, as it did often, afflict us, yet nothing gave us such affliction, as to hear and see the excessive cruelties with which our master used the other Christian slaves: he one day would hang one, then impale another, cut off the ears of a third; and this upon such slight occasions, that often the Turks would own, that he did it only for the pleasure of doing it, and because he was naturally an enemy to mankind. Only one Spanish soldier knew how to deal with him, his name was Saavedra; who, though he had done many things which will not easily be forgotten by the Turks, yet all to gain his liberty, his master never gave him a blow, nor used him ill, either in word or deed; and yet we were always afraid that the least of his pranks would make him be impaled; nay, he himself sometimes was afraid of it too: and, if it were not for taking up too much of your time, I could tell such passages of him, as would divert the company much better than the relation of my adventures, and cause more wonder in them. But, to go on: I say that the windows of a very rich Moor's house looked upon the court of our prison; which indeed, according to the custom of the country, were rather peeping-holes than windows, and yet they had also lattices or jalousies on the inside. It happened one day, that being upon a kind of terrace of our prison, with only three of my comrades, diverting ourselves as well as we could, by trying who could leap furthest in his chains, all the other Christians having gone out to work, I chanced to look up to those windows, and saw that out of one of them there appeared a long cane, and to it was a bit of linen tied, and the cane was moved up and down, as if it had expected that some of us should lay hold of it. We all took notice of it, and one of us went and stood just under it, to see if they would let it fall; but just as he came to it, the cane was drawn up, and shaken to and fro sideways, as if they had made the same sign as people do with their head when they deny. He retired upon that, and the same motion was made with it as before. Another of my comrades advanced, and had the same success as the former; the third man was used just as the rest; which I seeing, resolved to try my fortune too: and as I came under the cane, it fell at my feet. Immediately I untied the linen, within which was a knot, which being opened, showed us about ten Zianins, which is a sort of gold of base alloy used by the Moors, each of which is worth about two crowns of our money.

"It is not to be much questioned, whether the discovery was not as pleasant as surprising; we were in admiration, and I more particularly, not being able to guess whence this good fortune came to us, especially to me; for it was plain I was more meant than any of my comrades, since the cane was let go to me when it was refused to them. I took my money, broke the cane, and going up the terrace, saw a very white hand that opened and shut the window with haste. By this we imagined that some woman who lived in that house had done us this favor; and to return our thanks, we bowed ourselves after the Moorish fashion, with our arms across our breasts. A little after there appeared out of the same window a little cross made of cane, which immediately was pulled in again. This confirmed us in our opinion, that some Christian woman was a slave in that house, and that it was she that took pity on us; but

443

the whiteness of the hand, and the richness of the bracelets upon the arm, which we had a glimpse of, seemed to destroy that thought again; and then we believed it was some Christian woman turned Mahometan, whom their masters often marry, and think themselves very happy; for our women are more valued by them than the women of their own country. But in all this guessing we were

far enough from finding out the truth of the case: however, we resolved to be very diligent in observing the window, which was our north star. There passed above fifteen days before we saw either the hand or cane, or any other sign whatsoever; though in all that time we endeavored to find out who lived in that house, and if there were in it any Christian woman who was a renegade; yet all we could discover amounted only to this, that the house belonged to one of the chief Moors, a very rich man, called Agimorato, who had been Alcaide of the Pata, which is an office much valued among them. But, when we least expected our golden shower would continue, out of that window we saw on a sudden the cane appear again, with another piece of linen, and a bigger knot; and this was just at a time when the bagnio was without any other of the slaves in it. We all tried our fortunes as the first time, and it succeeded accordingly, for the cane was let go to none but me. I untied the knot, and found in it forty crowns of Spanish gold, with a paper written in Arabic, and at the top of the paper was a great cross. I kissed the cross, took the crowns, and returning to the terrace, we all made our Moorish reverences; the hand appeared again, and I having made signs that I would read the paper, the window was shut. We remained all overjoyed, and astonished at what had happened; and were extremely desirous to know the contents of the paper; but none of us understood Arabic, and it was yet more difficult to find out a proper interpreter. At last I resolved to trust a renegade of Murcia, who had shown me great proofs of his kindness. We gave one another mutual assurances, and on his side he was obliged to keep secret all that I should reveal to him; for the renegades, who have thoughts of returning to their own country, used to get certificates from such persons of quality as are slaves at Barbary, in which they make a sort of affidavit, that such a one, a renegade, is an honest man, and has always been kind to the Christians, and has a mind to make his escape on the first occasion. Some there are who procure these certificates with an honest design, and remain among Christians as long as they live; but others get them on purpose to make use of them when they go a-pirating on the Christian shores; for then if they are shipwrecked or taken, they show these certificates, and say, that thereby may be seen the intention with which they came in the Turks' company; to wit, to get an opportunity of returning to Christendom. By this means they escape the first fury of the Christians, and are seemingly reconciled to the Church without being hurt; afterwards they take their time and return to Barbary to be what they were before.

"One of these renegades was my friend, and he had certificates from us all, by which we gave him much commendation: but if the

Moors had caught him with those papers about him they would have burnt him alive. I knew that not only he understood the Arabic tongue, but also that he could speak and write it currently. But yet before I resolved to trust him entirely, I bid him read me that paper, which I found by chance; he opened it, and was a good while looking upon it, and construing it to himself. I asked him if he understood it? He said, 'Yes, very well'; and that if I would give him pen, ink and paper, he would translate it word for word. We furnished him with what he desired, and he went to work; having finished his translation, he said, 'All that I have here put into Spanish, is word for word what is in the Arabic; only observe, that wherever the paper says Lela Marien, it means our lady the Virgin Mary.' The contents were thus:

" 'When I was a child, my father had a slave, who taught me in my tongue the Christian worship, and told me a great many things of Lela Marien: the Christian slave died, and I am sure she went not into the fire, but is with Alla, for I have seen her twice since; and she bid me go to the land of the Christians to see Lela Marien, who had a great kindness for me. I do not know what is matter; but though I have seen many Christians out of this window, none has appeared to me so much a gentleman as thyself. I am very handsome and young, and can carry with me a great deal of money, and other riches; consider whether thou canst bring it to pass that we may escape together, and then thou shalt be my husband in thy own country, if thou art willing; but if thou art not, it is all one, Lela Marien will provide me a husband. I wrote this myself: have a care to whom thou givest it to read, do not trust any Moor, because they are all treacherous; and in this I am much perplexed, and could wish there were not a necessity of trusting anyone; because if my father should come to know it, he would certainly throw me into a well, and cover me over with stones. I *will tie a thread to a cane, and with that thou mayest fasten thy answer; and if thou canst not find anyone to write in Arabic, make me understand thy meaning by signs, for Lela Marien will help me to guess it. She and Alla keep thee, as well as this cross, which I often kiss, as the Christian slave bid me to do.'*

"You may imagine, gentlemen, that we were in admiration at the contents of this paper, and withal overjoyed at them, which we expressed so openly, that the renegade came to understand that the paper was not found by chance, but that it was really writ by someone among us; and accordingly he told us his suspicion, and desired us to trust him entirely, and that he would venture his life with us to procure us our liberty. Having said this, he pulled a brass crucifix out of his bosom, and with many tears, swore by the God which it represented, and in whom he, though a wicked sinner, did firmly believe, to be true and faithful to us with all secrecy, in what we should impart to him; for he guessed, that by the means of the woman who had wrote that letter, we might all of us recover our lost liberty; and he, in particular, might obtain what he had so long wished for, to be received again into the bosom of his mother the Church, from whom, for his sins, he had been cut off as a rotten member. The renegade pronounced all this with so many tears, and such signs of repentance, that we were all of opinion to trust him, and tell him the whole truth of the business. We showed him the little window out of which the cane used to appear, and he from thence took good notice of the house, in order to inform himself who lived in it. We next agreed, that it would be necessary to answer the Moorish lady's note: so immediately the renegade wrote down what I dictated to him; which was exactly as I shall relate, for I have not forgot the least material circumstance of this adventure, nor can forget them as long as I live. The words then were these:

447

"'The true Alla keep thee, my dear lady, and that blessed Virgin, which is the true mother of God, and has inspired thee with the design of going to the land of the Christians. Do thou pray Her that She would be pleased to make thee understand how thou shalt execute what She has commanded thee; for She is so good that She will do it. On my part, and on that of the Christians who are with me, I offer to do for thee all we are able, even to the hazard of our lives. Fail not to write to me, and give me notice of thy resolution, for I will always answer thee: the great Alla having given us a Christian slave, who can read and write thy language, as thou mayst perceive by this letter; so that thou mayst, without fear, give us notice of all thy intentions. As for what thou sayst, that as soon as thou shalt arrive in the land of the Christians, thou designest to be my wife, I promise thee, on the word of a good Christian, to take thee for my wife, and thou mayst be assured that the Christians perform their promises better than the Moors. Alla, and His mother Mary, be thy guard, my dear lady.'*

"Having wrote and closed this note, I waited two days till the bagnio was empty, and then I went upon the terrace, the ordinary place of our conversation, to see if the cane appeared, and it was not long before it was stirring. As soon as it appeared I showed my note, that the thread might be put to the cane, but I found that was done to my hand; and, the cane being let down, I fastened the note to it. Not long after, the knot was let fall, and I, taking it up, found in it several pieces of gold and silver, above fifty crowns, which gave us infinite content, and fortified our hopes of obtaining at last our liberty. That evening our renegade came to us, and told us he had found out that the master of that house was the same Moor we had been told of, called Agimorato, extremely rich, and who had one only daughter to inherit all his estate; that it was the report of the whole city, that she was the handsomest maid in all Barbary, having been demanded in marriage by several bashaws and viceroys, but that she had always refused to marry; he also told us, that he had learned she had a Christian slave who was dead: all which agreed with the contents of the letter. We immediately held a council with the renegade, about the manner we should use to carry off the Moorish lady, and go all together to Christendom; when at last we agreed to expect the answer of Zoraida, for that is the name of the lady who now desires to be called Maria; as well knowing she could best advise the overcoming all the difficulties that were in our way; and after this resolution, the renegade assured us again, that he would lose his life, or deliver us out of captivity.

"The bagnio was four days together full of people, and all that time the cane was invisible; but as soon as it returned to its solitude, the cane appeared, with a knot much bigger than ordinary; having untied it, I found in it a letter and an hundred crowns in gold. The renegade happened that day to be with us, and we gave him the letter to read; which he said contained these words:

" '*I cannot tell, sir, how to contrive that we may go together for Spain; neither has Lela Marien told it me, though I have earnestly asked it of Her; all I can do is to furnish you out of this window with a great deal of riches: buy your ransom and your friends, with that, and let one of you go to Spain, and buy a bark there, and come and fetch the rest. As for me, you shall find me in my father's garden out of town, by the sea-side not far from Babasso gate; where I am to pass all the summer with my father and my maids, from which you may take me without fear, in the night-time, and carry me to your bark; but remember you are to be my husband: and, if thou failest in that, I will desire Lela Marien to chastise thee. If thou canst not trust one of thy friends to go for the bark, pay thy own ransom, and go thyself; for I trust thou wilt return sooner than another, since thou art a gentle-*

man and a Christian. Find out my father's garden, and I will take care to watch when the bagnio is empty, and let thee have more money. Alla keep my dear lord.'

"These were the contents of the second letter we received. Upon the reading of it, every one of us offered to be the man that should go and buy the bark, promising to return with all punctuality; but the renegade opposed that proposition, and said he would never consent that one should obtain his liberty before the rest, because experience had taught him, that people once free, do not perform what they promise when captives; and that some slaves of quality had often used that remedy, to send one either to Valencia or Majorca, with money to buy a bark, and come back for the rest; but that they never returned: because the joy of having obtained their liberty, and the fear of losing it again, made them forget what they had promised, and canceled the memory of all obligations. To confirm which he related to us a strange story which had happened, as there often does among the slaves. After this, he said, that all that could be done, was for him to buy a bark with the money that should redeem one of us; that he could buy one in Algiers, and pretend to turn merchant, and deal between Algiers and Tetuan; by which means, he being master of the vessel, might easily find out some way of getting us out of the bagnio, and taking us on board; and especially if the Moorish lady did what she promised, and gave us money to pay all our ransoms; for, being free, we might embark even at noon-day: but the greatest difficulty would be, that the Moors do not permit renegades to keep any barks, but large ones fit to cruise upon Christians: for they believe that a renegade, particularly a Spaniard, seldom buys a bark but with a design of returning to his own country. That, however, he knew how to obviate that difficulty, by taking a Tagarin Moor for his partner both in the bark and trade, by which

450

means he should still be master of her, and then all the rest would be easy. We durst not oppose this opinion, though we had more inclination, everyone of us, to go to Spain for a bark, as the lady had advised; but were afraid, that if we contradicted him, as we were at his mercy, he might betray us, and bring our lives into danger; particularly if the business of Zoraida should be discovered, for whose liberty and life we would have given all ours: so we determined to put ourselves under the protection of God and the renegade. At the same time we answered Zoraida, telling her that we would do all she advised, which was very well, and just as if Lela Marien herself had instructed her; and that now it depended on her alone to give us the means to bring this design to pass. I promised her once more to be her husband. After this, in two days that the bagnio happened to be empty, she gave us, by means of the cane, two thousand crowns of gold; and withal a letter, in which she let us know, that the next Juma, which is their Friday, she was to go to her father's garden, and that before she went, she would give us more money; and if we had not enough, she would, upon our letting her know it, give us what we should think sufficient; for her father was so rich, that he would hardly miss it; and so much the less, because he entrusted her with the keys of all her treasure. We presently gave the renegade five hundred crowns to buy the bark, and I paid my own ransom with eight hundred crowns, which I put into the hands of a merchant at Valencia, then in Algiers, who made the bargain with the king, and had me to his house upon parole, to pay the money upon the arrival of the first bark from Valencia; for if he had paid the money immediately, the king might have suspected the money had been ready, and lain some time in Algiers, and that the merchant for his own profit had concealed it; and in short, I durst not trust my master with ready money, knowing his distrustful and malicious nature. The Thursday preceding the Friday that Zoraida was to go to the garden,

451

she let us have a thousand crowns more; desiring me at the same time, that, if I paid my ransom, I would find out her father's garden, and contrive some way of seeing her there. I answered in few words, that I would do as she desired, and she should only take care to recommend us to Lela Marien, by those prayers which the Christian slave had taught her. Having done this, order was taken to have the ransom of my three friends paid also; lest they, seeing me at liberty, and themselves not so, though there was money to set them free, should be troubled in mind, and give way to the temptation of the devil, in doing something that might redound to the prejudice of Zoraida: for though the consideration of their quality ought to have given me security of their honor, yet I did not think it proper to run the least hazard in the matter: so they were redeemed in the same manner, and by the same merchant that I was, who had the money beforehand; but we never discovered to him the remainder of our intrigue, as not being willing to risk the danger there was in so doing.

XIV: THE ADVENTURES OF THE CAPTIVE CONTINUED

"Our renegade had in a fortnight's time bought a very good bark, capable of carrying above thirty people; and, to give no suspicion of any other design, he undertook a voyage to a place upon the coast called Sargel, about thirty leagues to the eastward of Algiers, towards Oran, where there is a great trade for dried figs. He made this voyage two or three times in company with the Tagarin Moor, his partner. Those Moors are called in Barbary Tagarins, who were driven out of Aragon; as they call those of Granada, Mudajares; and the same in the kingdom of Fez are called Elches, and are the best soldiers that prince has.

"Every time he passed with his bark along the coast, he used to cast anchor in a little bay that was not above two bow-shots from the garden where Zoraida expected us; and there used to exercise the Moors that rowed, either in making the salaam, which is a ceremony among them, or in some other employment; by which he practiced in jest what he was resolved to execute in earnest. So sometimes he would go to the garden of Zoraida and beg some fruit, and her father would give him some, though he did not know him. He had a mind to find an occasion to speak to Zoraida, and tell her, as he since owned to me, that he was the man who, by my order, was to carry her to the land of the Christians, and that she might depend upon it; but he could never get an opportunity of doing it, because the Moorish and Turkish women never suffer themselves to be seen by any of their own nation, but by their husband, or by his or their father's command; but as for the Christian slaves, they let them see them, and that more familiarly than perhaps could be wished. I should have been very sorry that the renegade had seen or spoke to Zoraida, for it must needs have troubled her infinitely to see that her business was trusted to a renegade: and God Almighty, Who governed our design, ordered it so, that the renegade was disappointed. He in the meantime seeing how securely, and without suspicion, he went and came along the coast, staying where and when he pleased by the way, and that his partner the Tagarin Moor, was of his mind in all things; that I was at liberty, and there wanted nothing but some Christians to help us to row; bid me consider whom I intended to carry with me besides those who were ransomed, and that I should make sure of them for the first Friday, because he had pitched on that day for our departure. Upon notice of this resolution, I spoke to twelve lusty Spaniards, good rowers, and those who might easily get out of the city: it was a great fortune that we got so many in such a conjuncture, because there were above twenty sail of rovers gone out, who had taken aboard most of the slaves fit for the oar; and

453

we had not got these, but that their master happened to stay at home that summer, to finish a galley he was building to cruise with, and was then upon the stocks. I said no more to them, than only they should steal out of the town in the evening upon the next Friday, and stay for me upon the way that led to Agimorato's garden. I spoke to everyone by himself, and gave each of them order to say no more to any other Christian they should see, than that they stayed for me there. Having done this, I had another thing of the greatest importance to bring to pass, which was to give Zoraida notice of our design, and how far we had carried it, that she might be ready at a short warning, and not to be surprised if we came upon the house on a sudden, and even before she could think that the Christian bark could be come. This made me resolve to go to the garden, to try if it were possible to speak to her: so one day, upon pretense of gathering a few herbs, I entered the garden, and the first person I met was her father, who spoke to me in the language used all over the Turkish dominions, which is a mixture of all the Christian and Moorish languages, by which we understand one another from Constantinople to Algiers, and asked me what I looked for in his garden, and who I belonged to? I told him I was a slave of Arnaute Mami (this man I knew was his intimate friend) and that I wanted a few herbs to make up a salad. He then asked me if I were a man to be redeemed or no, and how much my master asked for me; during these questions, the beautiful Zoraida came out of the garden-house hard by, having descried me a good while before; and as the Moorish women make no difficulty of showing themselves to the Christian slaves, she drew near, without scruple, to the place where her father and I were talking; neither did her father show any dislike of her coming, but called to her to come nearer. It would be hard for me to express here the wonderful surprise and astonishment that the beauty, the rich dress, and the charming air of my beloved Zoraida put me in: she was all bedecked with pearls, which hung thick upon her head and about her neck and arms. Her feet and legs were naked, after the custom of that country, and she had upon her ankles a kind of bracelet of gold, and set with such rich diamonds that her father valued them, as she since told me, at ten thousand pistoles a pair; and those about her wrists were of the same value. The pearls were of the best sort, for the Moorish women delight much in them, and have more pearls of all sorts than any nation. Her father was reputed to have the finest in Algiers, and to be worth besides, above two hundred thousand Spanish crowns; of all which, the lady you here see was then mistress; but now is only so of me. What she yet retains of beauty after all her sufferings, may help you to guess at her wonderful appearance in the midst of her prosperity. The beauty of some ladies has its days and times, and is more or less, according to accidents or passions, which naturally raise or diminish the luster of it, and sometimes quite extinguish it. All I can say is, at that time she appeared to me the best-dressed and most beautiful woman I had ever seen; to which, adding the obligations I had to her, she passed with me for a goddess from Heaven, descended upon earth for my relief and happiness. As she drew near, her father told her, in his country language, that I was a slave of his friend, Arnaute Mami, and came to pick a salad in his garden. She presently took the hint, and asked me in Lingua Franca, whether I was a gentleman, and if I was, why I did not ransom myself? I told her I was already ransomed, and that by the price, she might guess the value my master set upon me, since he had bought me for one thousand five hundred pieces of eight: to which she replied, 'If thou hadst been my father's slave, I would not have let him part with thee for twice as much; for,' said she, 'you Christians never speak truth in anything you say, and make yourselves poor to deceive the Moors.' 'That may be, madam,' said I, 'but in truth I have dealt by my master, and do intend to

455

deal by all those I shall have to deal with, sincerely and honorably.' 'And when dost thou go home?' said she. 'Tomorrow, madam,' said I, 'for here is a French bark that sails tomorrow, and I intend not to lose that opportunity.' 'Is it not better,' replied Zoraida, 'to stay till there comes some Spanish bark, and go with them, and not with the French, who, I am told, are no friends of yours?'

'No,' said I, 'yet if the report of a Spanish bark's coming should prove true, I would perhaps stay for it, though it is more likely I shall take the opportunity of the French, because the desire I have of being at home, and with those persons I love, will hardly let me wait for any other conveniency.' 'Without doubt,' said Zoraida, 'thou art married in Spain and impatient to be with thy wife.' 'I am not,' said I, 'married, but I have given my word to a lady, to be so as soon as I can reach my own country.' 'And is the lady handsome that has your promise?' said Zoraida. 'She is so handsome,' said I, 'that to describe her rightly, and tell truth, I can only say she is like you.' At this her father laughed heartily, and said, 'On my word, Christian, she must be very charming if she be like my daughter, who is the greatest beauty in the kingdom: look upon her well, and thou wilt say I speak truth.' Zoraida's father was our interpreter for the most of what we talked, for though she understood the Lingua Franca, yet she was not used to speak it, and so explained herself more by signs than words. While we were in this conversation, there came a Moor running hastily, and cried aloud that four Turks had leaped over the fence of the garden, and were gathering the fruit, though it was not ripe. The old man started at that, and so did Zoraida, for the Moors do naturally stand in awe of the Turks, particularly of the soldiers, who are so insolent on their side, that they treat the Moors as if they were their slaves. This made the father bid his daughter go in and shut herself up close, 'Whilst,' said he, 'I go and talk with these dogs; and for thee, Christian, gather the herbs thou wantest, and go thy ways in peace, and God conduct thee safe to thy own country.' I bowed to him, and he left me with Zoraida, to go and find out the Turks: she made also as if she were going away, as her father had bid her; but she was no sooner hid from his sight by the trees of the garden, but she turned towards me with her eyes full of tears, and said in her language '*Amexi, Christiano, Amexi,*' which is, 'Thou art going away, Christian, thou art going': to which I answered, 'Yes, madam, I am, but by no means without you; you may expect me next Friday, and be not surprised when you see us, for we will certainly go to the land of the Christians.' I said this so passionately, that she understood me; and throwing one of her arms about my neck, she began to walk softly, and with trembling towards the house. It pleased fortune, that as we were in this posture walking together (which might have proved very unlucky for us), we met Agimorato coming back from the Turks, and we perceived he had seen us as we were; but Zoraida, very readily and discreetly, was so far from taking away her arm from about my neck, that drawing still nearer to me, she leaned her head upon my breast, and letting her knees give way, was in the posture of one that swoons: I, at the same time, made as if I had much ado to bear her up against my will. Her father came hastily to us, and seeing his daughter in this condition, asked her what was the matter. But she not answering readily, he presently said, 'Without a doubt, these Turks have frightened her, and she faints away'; at which he took her in his arms. She, as it were, coming to herself, fetched a deep sigh, and with her eyes not yet dried from tears, she said, '*Amexi, Christiano, Amexi,*' 'Begone, Christian, begone'; to which her father replied, 'It is no matter, child, whether he go or no, he has done thee no hurt, and the Turks at my request are gone.' 'It is they who frightened her,' said I, 'but since she desires I should be gone, I will come another time for my salad, by your leave; for my master says the herbs of your garden are the best of any he can have.' 'Thou mayest have what, and when, thou wilt,' said the father; 'for my daughter does not think the Christians troublesome, she only wished the Turks away, and by mistake bid thee be gone too, or make haste and gather thy herbs.' With this I immediately took leave of them both; and Zoraida, showing great trouble in her looks, went away with her father. I, in the meantime, upon pretense of gathering my herbs here and there, walked all over the garden, observing exactly all the places of coming in and going out, and every corner fit for my purpose, as well as what strength there was in the house, with all other conveniences to facilitate our business. Having done this I went my ways, and gave an exact account of all that had happened, to the renegade and the rest of my friends, longing earnestly for the time in which I might promise myself my dear Zoraida's company, without any fear of disturbance. At last the happy hour came, and we had all the good success we could promise ourselves, of a design so well laid; for the

Friday after my discourse with Zoraida, towards the evening we came to an anchor with our bark, almost over against the place where my lovely mistress lived; the Christians, who were to be employed at the oar, were already at the rendezvous, and hid up and down thereabouts. They were all in expectation of my coming, and very desirous to seize the bark which they saw before their eyes, for they did not know our agreement with the renegade, but thought they were by main force to gain their conveyance and their liberty, by killing the Moors on board. As soon as I and my friends appeared, all the rest came from their hiding-places to us. By this time the city gates were shut, and no soul appeared in all the country near us. When we were all together, it was a question whether we should first fetch Zoraida, or make ourselves master of those few Moors in the bark. As we were in this consultation, the renegade came to us, and asking what we meant to stand idle, told us his Moors were all gone to rest, and most of them asleep. We told him our difficulty, and he immediately said that the most important thing was to secure the bark, which might easily be done, and without danger, and then we might go for Zoraida.

"We were all of his mind, and so, without more ado, he marched at the head of us to the bark, and leaping into it, he first drew a scimitar, and cried aloud in the Moorish language, 'Let not a man of you stir, except he means it should cost him his life;' and while he said this, all the other Christians were gotten on board. The Moors, who are naturally timorous, hearing the master use this language, were frighted, and without any resistance, suffered themselves to be manacled, which was done with great expedition by the Christians, who told them at the same time, that if they made the least noise, they would immediately cut their throats. This being done, and half of our number left to guard them, the remainder, with the renegade, went to Agimorato's garden; and our good fortune was such, that coming to force the gate, we found it open with as much

459

facility as if it had not been shut at all. So we marched on with great silence to the house, without being perceived by anybody. The lovely Zoraida, who was at the window, asked softly, upon hearing us tread, whether we were Nazarani, that is, Christians? I answered 'Yes,' and desired her to come down. As soon as she heard my voice, she stayed not a minute; but, without saying a word, came down and opened the door, appearing to us all like a goddess, her beauty and the richness of her dress not being possible to be described. As soon as I saw her, I took her by the hand, which I kissed, the renegade did the same, and then my friends; the rest of the company followed the same ceremony; so that we all paid her a kind of homage for our liberty. The renegade asked her in Morisco, whether her father was in the garden? She said 'Yes,' and that he was asleep. 'Then,' said he, 'we must awake him, and take him with us, as also all that is valuable in the house.' 'No, no,' said Zoraida, 'my father must not be touched, and in the house there is nothing so rich as what I shall carry with me, which is enough to make you all rich and content.' Having said this she stepped into the house, bid us be quiet, and she would soon return. I asked the renegade what had passed between them, and he told me what he had said: to which I replied, that by no means anything was to be done, otherwise than as Zoraida should please. She was already coming back with a small trunk so full of gold, that she could hardly carry it, when, to our great misfortune, while this was doing, her father awakened, and hearing a noise in the garden, opened a window and looked out: having perceived that there were Christians in it, he began to cry out in Arabic, 'Thieves, thieves, Christians, Christians.' These cries of his put us all into a terrible disorder and fear; but the renegade seeing our danger, and how much it imported us to accomplish our enterprise before we were perceived, he ran up to the place where Agimorato was, and took with him some of our company; for I durst by no means leave

Zoraida, who had swooned away in my arms. Those who went up bestirred themselves so well, that they brought down Agimorato with his hands tied behind him, and his mouth stopped with a handkerchief, which hindered him from so much as speaking a word; and threatening him besides, that if he made the least attempt to speak, it should cost him his life. When his daughter, who had come to herself, saw him, she covered her eyes to avoid the sight, and her father remained the more astonished, for he knew not how willingly she had put herself into our hands. Diligence on our side being the chief thing requisite, we used it so as we came to our bark, when our men began to be in pain for us, as fearing that we had met with some ill accident: we got on board about two hours after it was dark; where the first thing we did was to untie the hands of Zoraida's father, and to unstop his mouth, but still with the same threatenings of the renegade, in case he made any noise. When he saw his daughter there, he began to sigh most passionately, and more when he saw me embrace her with tenderness, and that she, without any resistance or struggling, seemed to endure it; he, for all this, was silent, for fear the threatenings of the renegade should be put in execution. Zoraida seeing us aboard, and that we were ready to handle our oars to be gone, bid the renegade tell me, she desired I would set her father, and the other Moors, our prisoners, on shore; or else she would throw herself into the sea, rather than see a father, who had used her so tenderly, be carried away captive for her sake, before her eyes. The renegade told me what she said, to which I agreed; but the renegade was of another opinion; saying, that if we set them on shore there, they would raise the country, and give the alarm to the city, by which some light frigate might be dispatched in quest of us, and getting between us and the sea, it would be impossible for us to make our escape; and that all that could be done, was to set them at liberty in the first Christian land we could reach. This

461

seemed so reasonable to us all, that Zoraida herself, being informed
of the motives we had not to obey her at present, agreed to it. Immediately, with great silence and content, we began to ply our
oars, recommending ourselves to Providence with all our hearts,
and endeavored to make for Majorca, which is the nearest Christian land; but the north wind rising a little, and the sea with it,
we could not hold that course, but were forced to drive along shore
towards Oran, not without great fear of being discovered from
Sargel, upon the coast, about thirty leagues from Algiers. We
were likewise apprehensive of meeting some of those galliots which
come from Tetuan with merchandise. Though, to say truth, we
did not so much fear these last; for, except it were a cruising
galliot, we all of us wished to meet such a one, which we should
certainly take, and so get a better vessel to transport us in.

"Zoraida all this while hid her face between my hands, that she
might not see her father; and I could hear her call upon Lela
Marien to help us. By the time we had gotten about thirty miles
the day broke, and we found ourselves within a mile of the shore,
which appeared to us a desert solitary place, but yet we rowed
hard to get off to sea, for fear of being discovered by somebody.
When we had gotten about two leagues out to sea, we proposed the
men should row by turns, that some might refresh themselves; but
the men at the oar said it was not time yet to rest, and that they
could eat and row too, if those who did not row would assist them,
and give them meat and drink; this we did, and, a little while after,
the wind blowing fresh, we ceased rowing, and set sail for Oran,
not being able to hold any other course. We made about eight miles
an hour, being in no fear of anything but meeting some cruisers.
We gave victuals to our Moorish prisoners, and the renegade comforted them, and told them they were not slaves, but should be
set at liberty upon the first opportunity. The same was said to
Zoraida's father, who answered, 'I might expect from you any-

thing else perhaps, O Christians; but that you should give me my liberty, I am not simple enough to believe it; for you never would have run the hazard of taking it from me, if you intended to restore it me so easily; especially since you know who I am, and what you may get for my ransom; which if you will but name, I do from this moment offer you all that you can desire for me, and for that unfortunate daughter of mine, or for her alone, since she is the better part of me.' When he had said this, he burst out into tears so violently, that Zoraida could not forbear looking up at him, and indeed he moved compassion in us all, but in her particularly; insomuch, as starting from my arms, she flew to her father's, and putting her head to his, they began again so passionate and tender a scene, that most of us could not forbear accompanying their grief with our tears; but her father, seeing her so richly dressed, and so many jewels about her, said to her, in his language, 'What is the meaning of this, daughter? for last night, before this terrible misfortune befell us, thou wert in thy ordinary dress; and now, without scarce having had time to put on such things, I see thee adorned with all the fineries I could give thee, if we were at liberty and in full prosperity. This gives me more wonder and trouble than even our sad misfortune; therefore answer me.' The renegade interpreted all that the Moor said, and we saw that Zoraida answered not a word; but on a sudden, spying the little casket in which she used to put her jewels, which he thought had been left in Algiers, he remained yet more astonished, and asked her how that trunk could come into our hands, and what was in it? To which the renegade, without expecting Zoraida's answer, replied, 'Do not trouble thyself to ask thy daughter so many questions, for with one word I can satisfy them all. Know then that she is a Christian, and it is she that hath filed off our chains, and given us liberty: she is with us by her own consent, and I hope well pleased, as people should be who come from darkness

463

into light, and from death to life.' 'Is this true, daughter?' said the Moor. 'It is,' replied Zoraida. 'How then,' said the old man, 'art thou really a Christian? and art thou she that has put thy father into the power of his enemies?' To which Zoraida replied, 'I am she that is a Christian, but not she that has brought thee into this condition, for my design never was to injure my father, but only to do myself good.' 'And what good hast thou done thyself?' said the Moor. 'Ask that of Lela Marien,' replied Zoraida, 'for she can tell the best.' The old man had no sooner heard this, but he threw himself with incredible fury into the sea, where without doubt he had been drowned, had not his garments, which were long and wide, kept him some time above water. Zoraida cried out to us to help him, which we all did so readily, that we pulled him out by his vest, but half drowned, and without any sense. This so troubled Zoraida, that she threw herself upon her father, and began to lament and bemoan as if he had been really dead. We turned his head downwards, and by this means having disgorged a great deal of water, he recovered a little in about two hours' time. The wind in the meanwhile was come about, and forced us toward the shore, so that we were obliged to ply our oars, not to be driven upon the land. It was our good fortune to get into a small bay, which is made by a promontory, called the Cape of the Caba Rumia; which, in our tongue, is the cape of the wicked Christian woman; and it is a tradition among the Moors, that Caba, the daughter of Count Julian, who was the cause of the loss of Spain, lies buried there; and they think it ominous to be forced into that bay, for they never go in otherwise than by necessity; but to us it was no unlucky harbor, but a safe retreat, considering how high the sea went by this time. We posted our sentries on the shore, but kept our oars ready to be plied upon occasion, taking in the meantime some refreshment of what the renegade had provided, praying heartily to God and the Virgin Mary, to protect us, and help us to bring our design to a happy conclusion. Here, at the desire of Zoraida, we resolved to set her father on shore, with all the other Moors, whom we kept fast bound; for she had not courage, nor could her tender heart suffer any longer, to see her father and her countrymen ill-used before her face; but we did not think to do it before we were just ready to depart, and then they could not much hurt us, the place being a solitary one, and no habitations near it. Our prayers were not in vain; the wind fell, and the sea became calm, inviting us thereby to pursue our intended voyage: we unbound our prisoners, and set them on shore one by one, which they were mightily astonished at. When we came to put Zoraida's father on shore, who by this time had come to himself, he said, 'Why do you think, Christians, that this wicked woman desires I should be set at liberty? Do you think it is for any pity she takes of me? No certainly, but it is because she is not able to bear my presence, which hinders the prosecution of her ill desires: I would not have you think neither that she has embraced your religion, because she knows the difference between yours and ours, but because she has heard that she can live more loosely in your country than at home.' And then turning himself to Zoraida, while I and another held him fast by the arms, that he might commit no extravagance, he said, 'O infamous and blind young woman, where art thou going in the power of these dogs, our natural enemies? Cursed be the hour in which I begot thee, and the care and affection with which I bred thee!' But I, seeing he was not like to make an end of his exclamations soon, made haste to set him on shore, from whence he continued to give us his curses and imprecations; begging on his knees of Mahomet to beg of God Almighty to confound and destroy us; and when, being under sail, we could no longer hear him, we saw his actions, which were tearing his hair and beard, and rolling himself upon the ground; but he once strained his voice so high, that we heard what

465

he said, which was, 'Come back, my dear daughter, for I forgive thee all; let those men have the treasure which is already in their possession, and do thou return to comfort thy disconsolate father, who must else lose his life in these sandy deserts.' All this Zoraida heard, and shed abundance of tears, but could answer nothing, but beg that Lela Marien, who had made her a Christian, would comfort him. 'God knows,' said she, 'I could not avoid doing what I have done, and that these Christians are not obliged to me, for I could not be at rest till I had done this, which to thee, dear father, seems so ill a thing.' All this she said, when we had gotten so far out of his hearing, that we could scarce so much as see him. So I comforted Zoraida as well as I could, and we all minded our voyage. The wind was now so right for our purpose, that we made no doubt of being the next morning on the Spanish shore; but as it seldom happens that any felicity comes so pure, as not to be tempered and allayed by some mixture of sorrow; either our ill fortune, or the Moor's curses had such an effect (for a father's curses are to be dreaded, let the father be what he will), that about midnight, when we were under full sail, with our oars laid by, we saw by the light of the moon, hard by us, a round-sterned vessel with all her sails out, coming a-head of us, which she did so close to us, that we were forced to strike our sail not to run foul of her; and the vessel likewise seemed to endeavor to let us go by; they had come so near as to ask from whence we came, and whither we were going? But doing it in French, the renegade forbade us to answer, saying, 'Without doubt these are French pirates, to whom everything is a prize.' This made us all be silent; and as we sailed on, they being under the wind, fired two guns at us, both, as it appeared, with chain-shot, for one brought our mast by the board, and the other went through us, without killing anybody; but we, perceiving we were sinking, called to them to come and take us, for we were going to be drowned; they then struck their own sails, and putting out their long boat, there came about a dozen French on board us, all well armed, and with their matches lighted. When they were close to us, seeing we were but few, they took us aboard their boat, saying, that this had happened to us for not answering their questions. The renegade had time to take a little coffer or trunk, full of Zoraida's treasure, and heave it overboard, without being perceived by anybody. When we were on board their vessel, after having learned from us all they could, they began to strip us, as if we had been their mortal enemies: they plundered Zoraida of all the jewels and bracelets she had on her hands and feet; but that did not so much trouble me, as my apprehension for the rich jewel of her chastity, which she valued above all the rest. But that sort of people seldom have any desires beyond the getting of riches, which they saw in abundance before their eyes; and their covetousness was so sharpened by it, that even our slaves' clothes tempted them. They consulted what to do with us; and some were of opinion to throw us overboard, wrapped up in a sail, because they intended to put into some of the Spanish ports, under the notion of being of Brittany; and if they carried us with them, they might be punished, and their roguery come to light: but the captain, who thought himself rich enough with Zoraida's plunder, said he would not touch at any port of Spain, but make his way through the straits by night, and so return to Rochelle, from whence he came. This being resolved, they bethought themselves of giving us their long boat, and what provision we might want for our short passage. As soon as it was day, and that we descried the Spanish shore (at which sight, so desirable a thing is liberty, all our miseries vanished from our thoughts in a moment), they began to prepare things, and about noon they put us on board, giving us two barrels of water, and a small quantity of biscuit; and the captain, touched with some remorse for the lovely Zoraida, gave her, at parting, about forty crowns in gold, and would not suffer his men to take

467

from her those clothes which now she had on. We went aboard, showing ourselves rather thankful than complaining. They got out to sea, making for the straits, and we, having the land before us for our north star, plied our oars, so that about sunset we were near enough to have landed before it was quite dark; but, considering the moon was hidden in clouds, and the heavens were growing dark, and we ignorant of the shore, we did not think it safe to venture on it, though many among us were so desirous of liberty, and to be out of all danger, that they would have landed, though on a desert rock; and by that means, at least, we might avoid all little barks of the pirates of the Barbary coast, such as those of Tetuan, who come from home when it is dark, and by morning are early upon the Spanish coast; where they often make a prize, and go home to bed the same day. But the other opinion prevailed, which was to row gently on, and if the sea and shore gave leave, to land quietly where we could. We did accordingly, and about midnight came under a great hill, which had a sandy shore, convenient enough for our landing. Here we ran our boat in as far as we could, and being got on land, we all kissed it for joy, and thanked God with tears for our deliverance. This done, we took out the little provision we had left, and climbed up the mountain, thinking ourselves more in safety there, for we could hardly persuade ourselves, nor believe, that the land we were upon was the Christian shore. We thought the day long a-coming, and then we got to the top of the hill, to see if we could discover any habitations; but we could nowhere descry either house, or person, or path. We resolved, however, to go further on, imagining we could not miss at last of somebody to inform us where we were: that which troubled me most was, to see my poor Zoraida go on foot among the sharp rocks, and I would sometimes have carried her on my shoulders; but she was as much concerned at the pains I took, as she could be at what she endured; so leaning upon me, she went on with

468

much patience and content. When we were gone about a quarter of a league, we heard the sound of a little pipe, which we took to be a certain sign of some flock near us; and looking well about, we perceived, at last, at the foot of a cork-tree, a young shepherd, who was cutting a stick with his knife, with great attention and seriousness. We called to him, and he having looked up, ran away as hard as he could. It seems, as we afterwards heard, the first he saw were the renegade and Zoraida, who being in the Moorish dress, he thought all the Moors in Barbary were upon him; and, running into the wood, cried all the way as loud as he could, 'Moors, Moors! arm, arm! the Moors are landed!' We, hearing this outcry, did not well know what to do: but, considering that the shepherd's roaring would raise the country, and the horse-guard of the coast would be upon us, we agreed that the renegade should pull off his Turkish habit, and put on a slave's coat, which one of us lent him, though he that lent it him remained in his shirt. Thus recommending ourselves to God, we went on by the same way that the shepherd ran, still wondering when the horse would come upon us; and we were not deceived, for in less than two hours, as we came down the hills into a plain, we discovered fifty horse coming upon a half gallop towards us; when we saw that, we stood still, expecting them. As soon as they came up, and, instead of so many Moors, saw so many poor Christian captives, they were astonished. One of them asked us, if we were the occasion of the alarm that a young shepherd had given the country? 'Yes,' said I, and upon that began to tell him who we were, and whence we came; but one of our company knew the horseman that had asked us the question, and without letting me go on, said, 'God be praised, gentlemen, for bringing us to so good a part of the country; for if I mistake not, we are near Velez Malaga: and, if the many years of my captivity have not taken my memory from me too, I think that you, sir, who ask us such questions, are my uncle Don Pedro Bustamente.'

469

"The Christian slave had hardly said this, but the gentleman, lighting from his horse, came hastily to embrace the young slave, saying, 'Dear nephew, my joy, my life, I know thee, and have often lamented thy loss, and so has thy mother and thy other relations, whom thou wilt yet find alive. God has preserved them, that they may have the pleasure of seeing thee. We had heard that thou wert in Algiers, and by what I see of thy dress, and that of all this company, you must all have had some miraculous deliverance.' 'It is so,' replied the young man, 'and we shall have time enough now to tell all our adventures.' The rest of the horsemen, hearing we were Christians escaped from slavery, lighted likewise from their horses, offering them to us to carry us to the city of Velez Malaga, which was about a league and a half off. Some of them went where we had left our boat, and got it into the port, while others took us up behind them; and Zoraida rode behind the gentleman, uncle to our captive. All the people, who had already heard something of our adventure, came out to meet us; they did not wonder to see captives at liberty, nor Moors prisoners, for in all that coast they are used to it; but they were astonished at the beauty of Zoraida, which at that instant seemed to be in its point of perfection; for, what with the agitation of traveling, and what with the joy of being safe in Christendom, without the terrible thought of being retaken, she had such a beautiful color in her countenance, that were it not for the fear of being too partial, I durst say there was not a more beautiful creature in the world, at least that I had seen. We went straight to church, to thank God for His great mercy to us; and as we came into it, and when Zoraida had looked upon the pictures, she said there were several faces there that were like Lela Marien's; we told her they were her pictures, and the renegade explained to her as well as he could the story of them, that she might adore them, as if in reality each of

470

them had been the true Lela Marien, Who had spoke to her; and she, who has a good and clear understanding, comprehended immediately all that was said about the pictures and images. After this, we were dispersed and lodged in different houses of the town; but the young Christian slave of Velez carried me, Zoraida, and the renegade to his father's house, where we were accommodated pretty well, according to their ability, and used with as much kindness as their own son. After six days' stay at Velez, the renegade having informed himself of what was needful for him to know, went away to Granada, there to be readmitted by the holy inquisition into the bosom of the Church. The other Christians, being at liberty, went each whither he thought fit. Zoraida and I remained without other help than the forty crowns the pirate gave her, with which I bought the ass she rides on, and since we landed, have been to her a father and a friend, but not a husband. We are now going to see whether my father be alive, or if either of my brothers has had better fortune than I; though, since it has pleased Heaven to give me Zoraida, and make me her companion, I reckon no better fortune could befall me. The patience with which she bears the inconvenience of poverty, the desire she shows of being made a Christian, do give me subject of continual admiration, and oblige me to serve and love her all the days of my life. I confess the expectation of being hers is not a little allayed with the uncertainties of knowing whether I shall find in my country anyone to receive us, or a corner to pass my life with her; and perhaps time will have so altered the affairs of our family, that I shall not find anybody that will know me, if my father and brothers are dead.

"This is, gentlemen, the sum of my adventures, which whether or no they are entertaining you are best judges. I wish I had told them more compendiously; and yet, I assure you, the fear of being tedious has made me cut short many circumstances of my story."

471

XV: AN ACCOUNT OF WHAT HAPPENED AFTERWARDS IN THE INN, WITH SEVERAL OTHER OCCURRENCES WORTH NOTICE

Here the stranger ended his story; and Don Ferdinand, by way of compliment in the behalf of the whole company, said, "Truly, captain, the wonderful and surprising turns of your fortune are not only entertaining, but the pleasing and graceful manner of your relation is as extraordinary as the adventures themselves: we are all bound to pay you our acknowledgments; and I believe we could be delighted with a second recital, though it were to last till tomorrow, provided it were made by you." Cardenio and the rest of the company joined with him in offering their utmost service in the re-establishment of his fortune, and that with so much sincerity and earnestness, that the captain had reason to be satisfied of their affection. Don Ferdinand particularly proposed to engage the Marquis his brother to stand godfather to Zoraida, if he would return with him, and further promised to provide him with all things necessary to support his figure and quality in town; but the captain, making them a very handsome compliment for their obliging favors, excused himself from accepting those kind offers at that time. It was now growing towards the dark of the evening, when a coach stopped at the inn, and with it some horsemen, who asked for a lodging. The hostess answered, they were as full as they could pack. "Were you ten times fuller," answered one of the horsemen, "here must be room made for my lord Judge, who is in this coach." The hostess, hearing this, was very much concerned; said she, "The case, sir, is plain, we have not one bed empty in the house; but if his lordship brings a bed with him, as perhaps he may, he shall command my house with all my heart, and I and my husband will quit our own chamber to serve him." "Do so then," said the man. And by this time a gentleman alighted from the coach, easily distinguishable for a man of dignity and office, by his long gown and great sleeves. He led a young lady by the hand, about sixteen years of age, dressed in a riding-suit; her beauty and charming air attracted the eyes of everybody with admiration, and had not the other ladies been present, anyone might have thought it difficult to have matched her outward graces.

Don Quixote, seeing them come near the door, "Sir," said he,

"you may enter undismayed, and refresh yourselves in this castle, which though little and indifferently provided, must nevertheless allow a room, and afford accommodation to arms and learning; and more especially to arms and learning, that, like yours, bring beauty for their guide and conductor. For certainly at the approach of this lovely damsel, not only castles ought to open and expand their gates, but even rocks divide their solid bodies, and mountains bow their ambitious crests, and stoop to entertain her.

473

Come in therefore, sir, enter this paradise, where you shall find a bright constellation worthy to shine in conjunction with that heaven of beauty which you bring: here you shall find arms in their height, and beauty in perfection." Don Quixote's speech, mien, and garb, put the judge to a strange nonplus; and he was not a little surprised on the other hand at the sudden appearance of the three ladies, who being informed of the judge's coming and the young lady's beauty, were come out to see and entertain her. But Don Ferdinand, Cardenio, and the curate addressing him in a style very different from the Knight, soon convinced him that he had to do with gentlemen, and persons of note, though Don Quixote's figure and behavior put him to a stand, not being able to make any reasonable conjecture of his extravagance. After the usual civilities passed on both sides, they found upon examination, that the women must all lie together in Don Quixote's apartment, and the men remain without to guard them. The judge consented that his daughter should go with the ladies, and so, what with his own bed and what with the innkeeper's, he and the gentlemen made a shift to pass the night.

The captain, upon the first sight of the judge, had a strong presumption that he was one of his brothers, and presently asked one of his servants his name and country. The fellow told him, his name was Juan Perez de Viedma, and that, as he was informed, he was born in the highlands of Leon. This, with his own observation, confirmed his opinion, that this was the brother who had made study his choice; whereupon, calling aside Don Ferdinand, Cardenio, and the curate, he told them with great joy what he had learned, with what the servant further told him, that his master being made a judge of the court of Mexico, was then upon his journey to the Indies; that the young lady was his only daughter, whose mother dying in child-birth, settled her dowry upon her daughter for a portion, and that the father had still lived a widower, and was very rich. Upon the whole matter, he asked their advice, whether they thought it proper for him to discover himself presently to his brother, or by some means try how his pulse beat first in relation to his loss, by which he might guess at his reception. "Why should you doubt of a kind one, sir?" said the curate. "Because I am poor, sir," said the captain, "and would therefore by some device fathom his affections; for, should he prove ashamed to own me, I should be more ashamed to discover myself." "Then leave the management to me," said the curate; "the affable and courteous behavior of the judge seems to me so very far from pride, that you need not doubt a welcome reception; but however, because you desire it, I will engage to find a way to sound him." Supper was now upon the table, and all the gentlemen sat down but the captain, who ate with the ladies in the next room. When the company had half-supped, "My Lord Judge," said the curate, "I remember about some years ago, I was happy in the acquaintance and friendship of a gentleman of your name, when I was a prisoner in Constantinople: he was a captain of as much worth and courage as any in the Spanish infantry, but as unfortunate as brave." "What was his name, pray, sir?" said the judge. "Ruy Perez de Viedma," answered the curate, "of a town in the mountains of Leon. I remember he told me a very odd passage between his father, his two brothers, and himself; and truly had it come from any man of less credit and reputation, I should have thought it no more than a story: he said, that his father made an equal dividend of his estate among his three sons, giving them such advice as might have fitted the mouth of Cato; that he made arms his choice, and with such success, that within a few years (by the pure merit of his bravery) he was made captain of a foot company, and had a fair prospect of being advanced to a colonel; but his fortune forsook him, where he had most reason to expect her favor; for, in the memorable battle of Lepanto, where so many Christians recovered their liberty, he unfortunately lost his. I was taken at Goletta, and after different turns of fortune we became companions at Constantinople; thence we were carried to Algiers, where one of the strangest adventures in the world befell this gentleman." The curate then briefly ran through the whole story of the captain and Zoraida (the judge sitting all the time more attentive than he ever did on the bench) to their being taken and stripped by the French; and that he had heard nothing of them after that, nor could ever learn whether they came into Spain, or were carried prisoners into France.

The captain stood listening in a corner and observed the motions of his brother's countenance, while the curate told his story: which, when he had finished, the judge breathing out a deep sigh, and the tears standing in his eyes: "O sir," said he, "if you knew how nearly your relation touches me, you would easily excuse the violent eruption of these tears. The captain you spoke of is my eldest brother, who, being of a stronger constitution of body, and more elevated soul, made the glory and fame of war his choice, which was one of the three proposals made by my father, as your companion told you. I applied myself to study, and my younger brother has purchased a vast estate in Peru, out of which he has transmitted to my father enough to support his liberal disposition; and to me, wherewithal to continue my studies and advance myself to the rank and authority which now I maintain. My father is still alive, but dies daily for grief he can learn nothing of his eldest son, and importunes Heaven incessantly, that he may once more see him before death close his eyes. It is very strange, considering his discretion in other matters, that neither prosperity nor adversity could draw one line from him, to give his father an account of his fortunes. For had he or we had the least hint of his captivity, he needed not have stayed for the miracle of the Moorish lady's cane for his deliverance. Now am I in the greatest uneasiness in the

476

world, lest the French, the better to conceal their robbery, may have killed him; the thoughts of this will damp the pleasure of my voyage, which I thought to prosecute so pleasantly. Could I but guess, dear brother," continued he, "where you might be found, I would hazard life and fortune for your deliverance! Could our aged father once understand you were alive, though hidden in the deepest and darkest dungeon in Barbary, his estate, mine, and my brother's, all should fly for your ransom! And for the fair and liberal Zoraida, what thanks, what recompense could we provide? O might I see the happy day of her spiritual birth and baptism, to see her joined to him in faith and marriage, how should we all rejoice!" These and such-like expressions the judge uttered with so much passion and vehemency, that he raised a concern in everybody.

The curate, forseeing the happy success of his design, resolved to prolong the discovery no further; and, to free the company from suspense, he went to the ladies' room, and leading out Zoraida, followed by the rest, he took the captain by the other hand, and presenting them to the judge: "Suppress your grief, my lord," said he, "and glut your heart with joy; behold what you so passionately desired, your dear brother, and his fair deliverer; this gentleman is Captain Viedma, and this the beautiful Algerine; the French have only reduced them to this low condition, to make room for your generous sentiments and liberality." The captain then approaching to embrace the judge, he held him off with both his hands to view him well; but, once knowing him, he flew into his arms with such affection, and such abundance of tears, that all the spectators sympathized in his passions. The brothers spoke so feelingly, and their mutual affection was so moving, the surprise so wonderful, and their joy so transporting, that it must be left purely to imagination to conceive. Now they tell one another the strange turns and mazes of their fortunes, then renew their caresses to the height of brotherly love and tenderness. Now the judge embraces Zoraida, then makes her an offer of his whole fortune; next makes his daughter embrace her; then the sweet and innocent converse of the beautiful Christian, and the lovely Moor, so touched the whole company, that they all wept for joy. In the meantime Don Quixote was very solidly attentive, and wondering at these strange occurrences, attributed them purely to something answerable to the chimerical notions which are incident to chivalry. The captain and Zoraida, in concert with the whole company, resolved to return with their brother to Seville, and thence to advise their father of his arrival and liberty, that the old gentleman should make the best shift he could to get so far to see the baptism and marriage of Zoraida, while the judge took his voyage to the Indies, being obliged to make no delay, because the Indian fleet was ready at Seville to set sail in a month for New Spain.

Everything being now settled, to the universal satisfaction of the company, and being very late, they all agreed for bed, except Don Quixote, who would needs guard the castle whilst they slept, lest some tyrant or giant, covetous of the great treasure of beauty which it enclosed, should make some dangerous attempt. He had the thanks of the house, and the judge being further informed of his humor, was not a little pleased. Sancho Panza was very uneasy and waspish for want of sleep, though the best provided with a bed, bestowing himself on his pack-saddle; but he paid dearly for it, as we shall hear presently. The ladies being retired to their chamber, and everybody else withdrawn to rest, and Don Quixote planted sentinel at the castle-gate, a voice was heard of a sudden singing so sweetly, that it allured all their attentions, but chiefly Dorothea's, with whom the judge's daughter Donna Clara de Viedma lay. None could imagine who could make such pretty music without an instrument: sometimes it sounded as from the yard, sometimes as from the stable. With this Cardenio knocked softly at their door, "Ladies, ladies!" said he, "are you awake? Can you sleep when so charmingly serenaded: do not you hear how sweetly one of the footmen sings?" "Yes, sir," said Dorothea, "we hear him plainly." Then Dorothea, hearkening as attentively as she could, heard this song:

XVI: THE PLEASANT STORY OF THE YOUNG MULETEER, WITH OTHER STRANGE ADVENTURES THAT HAPPENED IN THE INN

A SONG

I

"Toss'd in doubts and fears I rove
On the stormy seas of love;
Far from comfort, far from port,
Beauty's prize, and fortune's sport:
Yet my heart disclaims despair,
While I trace my leading star.

II

"But reserv'dness, like a cloud,
Does too oft her glories shroud.
Pierce the gloom, reviving sight;
Be auspicious as you're bright.
As you hide or dart your beams,
Your adorer sinks or swims."

Dorothea thought it would not be much amiss to give Donna Clara the opportunity of hearing so excellent a voice; wherefore touching her gently, first on one side and then on the other, and the young lady waking, "I ask your pardon, my dear," cried Dorothea, "for thus interrupting your repose; and I hope you will easily forgive me, since I only awake you that you may have the pleasure of hearing one of the most charming voices, that possibly you ever heard in your life." Donna Clara, who was hardly awake, did not perfectly understand what Dorothea said, and therefore desired her to repeat what she had spoke to her. Dorothea did so; which then obliged Donna Clara also to listen; but scarce had she heard the early musician sing two verses, ere she was taken with a strange trembling, as if she had been seized with a violent fit of a quartan ague, and then closely embracing Dorothea, "Ah! dear madam," cried she, with a deep sigh, "why did you wake me? Alas! the greatest happiness I could now have expected, had been to have stopped my ears: that unhappy musician!" "How is this, my dear," cried Dorothea, "have you not heard, that the young lad who sung now is but a muleteer?" "Oh no, he is no such thing," replied Clara, "but a young lord, heir to a great estate, and has such a full possession of my heart, that if he does not slight it, it must be his forever." Dorothea was strangely surprised at the young lady's passionate expressions, that seemed far to exceed those of persons of her tender years. "You speak so mysteriously, madam," replied she, "that I cannot rightly understand you, unless you will please to let me know more plainly what you would say of hearts and sighs, and this young musician, whose voice has caused so great an alteration in you. However, speak no more of them now; for I am resolved I will not lose the pleasure of hearing him sing. Hold," continued she, "I fancy he is going to entertain us with another song." "With all my heart," returned Clara, and with that she stopped her ears, that she might not hear him; at which again Dorothea could not but choose to admire; but listening to his voice she heard the following song:

HOPE

I

"Unconquer'd hope, thou bane of fear,
And last deserter of the brave;
Thou soothing ease of mortal care,
Thou traveler beyond the grave;

480

Thou soul of patience, airy food,
Bold warrant of a distant good,
Reviving cordial, kind decoy:
  Tho' fortune frowns and friends depart,
Tho' Sylvia flies me, flatt'ring joy,
  Nor thou, nor love, shall leave my doting heart.

II

"The phœnix hope can wing her flight
  Thro' the vast deserts of the skies,
And still defying fortune's spite,
  Revive, and from her ashes rise.
Then soar, and promise, tho' in vain,
What reason's self despairs to gain.
Thou only, O presuming trust,
  Canst feed us still yet never cloy:
And even a virtue when unjust,
  Postpone our pain, and antedate our joy.

III

"No slave to lazy ease resign'd,
  E'er triumph'd over noble foes.
The monarch Fortune most is kind
  To him who bravely dares oppose.
They say Love sets his blessings high;
But who would prize an easy joy!
Then I'll my scornful fair pursue,
  Tho' the coy beauty still denies;
I grovel now on earth, 'tis true,
  But rais'd by her, the humble slave may rise."

Here the voice ended, and Donna Clara's sighs began, which
caused the greatest curiosity imaginable in Dorothea, to know the
occasion of so moving a song, and of so sad a complaint: wherefore she again entreated her to pursue the discourse she had begun
before. Then Clara, fearing Lucinda would overhear her, getting

481

as near Dorothea as was possible, laid her mouth so close to Dorothea's ear, that she was out of danger of being understood by any other; and began in this manner: "He who sung is a gentleman's son of Arragon, his father is a great lord, and dwelt just over against my father's at Madrid; and, though we had always canvas-windows in winter, and lattices in summer,[1] yet I cannot tell by what accident this young gentleman, who then went to school, had a sight of me, and whether it were at church, or at some other place, I cannot justly tell you; but, in short, he fell in love with me, and made me sensible of his passion from his own windows, which were opposite to mine, with so many signs, and such showers of tears, that at once forced me both to believe and to love him, without knowing for what reason I did so. Amongst the usual signs that he made me, one was that of joining his hands together, intimating by that his desire to marry me; which, though I heartily wished it, I could not communicate it to anyone, being motherless, and having none near me whom I might trust with the management of such an affair; and was therefore constrained to bear it in silence, without permitting him any other favor, more than to let him gaze on me, by lifting up the lattice, or oiled cloth a little, when my father and his were abroad. At which he would be so transported with joy, that you would certainly have thought he had been distracted. At last my father's business called him away; yet not so soon, but that the young gentleman had notice of it some time before his departure; whence he had it I know not, for it was impossible for me to acquaint him with it. This so sensibly afflicted him, as far as I understand, that he fell sick; so that I could not get a sight of him all the day of our departure, so much as to look a farewell on him. But after two days' travel, just as we came into an inn, in a village a day's journey hence, I saw him at the inn-

1 *Glass windows are not used in Spain, at least they are not common, and formerly there were none.*

door, dressed so exactly like a muleteer, that it had been utterly impossible for me to have known him, had not his perfect image been stamped on my soul. Yes, yes, dear madam, I knew him, and was amazed and overjoyed at the sight of him; and he saw me unknown to my father, whose sight he carefully avoids, when we cross the ways in our journey, and when we come to any inn: and now, since I know who he is, and what pain and fatigue it must necessarily be to him to travel thus on foot, I am ready to die with the thought of what he suffers on my account; and wherever he sets his feet, there I set my eyes. I cannot imagine what he proposes to himself in this attempt; nor by what means he could thus make his escape from his father, who loves him beyond expression, both because he has no other son and heir, and because the young gentleman's merits oblige him to it; which you must needs confess when you see him: and I dare affirm, besides, that all he has sung was his own immediate composition; for, as I have heard, he is an excellent scholar, and a great poet. And now, whenever I see him, or hear him sing, I start and tremble, as at the sight of a ghost, lest my father should know him, and so be informed of our mutual affection. I never spoke one word to him in my life; yet I love him so dearly, that it is impossible I should live without him. This, dear madam, is all the account I can give you of this musician, with whose voice you have been so well entertained, and which alone might convince you that he is no muleteer, as you were pleased to say, but one who is master of a great estate, and of my poor heart, as I have already told you."

"Enough, dear madam," replied Dorothea, kissing her a thousand times: "it is very well, compose yourself till daylight; and then I trust in Heaven I shall so manage your affairs, that the end of them shall be as fortunate as the beginning was innocent." "Alas! madam," returned Clara, "what end can I propose to myself; since his father is so rich, and of so noble a family, that he will hardly think me worthy to be his son's servant, much less his wife? And then again, I would not marry without my father's consent, for the universe. All I can desire is, that the young gentleman would return home, and leave his pursuit of me: happily, by a long absence, and the great distance of place, the pain, which now so much afflicts me, may be somewhat mitigated; though I fear what I now propose as a remedy would rather increase my distemper: indeed I cannot imagine whence, or by what means this passion for him seized me, since we are both so young, being much about the same age, I believe; and my father says I shall not be sixteen till Michaelmas." Dorothea could not forbear laughing to hear the young lady talk so innocently. "My dear," said Dorothea, "let us repose ourselves the little remaining part of the night, and when day appears, we will put a happy period to your sorrows, or my judgment fails me." Then they addressed themselves again to sleep, and there was a deep silence throughout all the inn; only the innkeeper's daughter and Maritornes were awake, who knowing Don Quixote's blind side very well, and that he sat armed on horseback keeping guard without doors, a fancy took them, and they agreed to have a little pastime with him, and hear some of his fine out-of-the-way speeches.

You must know then, that there was but one window in all the inn that looked out into the field, and that was only a hole out of which they used to throw their straw: to this same hole then came these two demi-ladies, whence they saw Don Quixote mounted, leaning on his lance, and often fetching such mournful and deep sighs, that his very soul seemed to be torn from him at each of them: they observed besides, that he said in a soft amorous tone, "O my divine Dulcinea del Toboso! the heaven of all perfections! the end and quintessence of discretion! the treasury of sweet aspect and behavior! the magazine of virtue! and, in a word, the idea of all that is profitable, modest, or delightful in the universe! What

484

noble thing employs thy Excellency at this present? May I presume to hope that thy soul is entertained with the thoughts of thy captive-knight, who voluntarily exposes himself to so many dangers for thy sake? O thou triformed luminary, give me some account of her! Perhaps thou art now gazing with envy on her, as she is walking either through some stately gallery of her sumptuous palaces, or leaning on her happy window, there meditating how, with safety of her honor and grandeur, she may sweeten and alleviate the torture which my poor afflicted heart suffers for love of her; with what glories she shall crown my pains; what rest she shall give to my cares; what life to my death; and what reward to my services. And thou, more glorious planet, which by this time, I presume, art harnessing thy horses to pay thy earliest visit to my adorable Dulcinea; I entreat thee, as soon as thou dost see her, to salute her with my most profound respects: but take heed, that when thou lookest on her, and addressest thyself to her, that thou do not kiss her face; for if thou dost, I shall grow more jealous of thee, than ever thou wert of the swift ingrate, who made thee run and sweat so over the plains of Thessaly, or the banks of Peneus, I have forgotten through which of them thou rushed, raging with love and jealousy." At these words the innkeeper's daughter began to call to him softly: "Sir Knight," said she, "come a little nearer this way, if you please." At these words Don Quixote turned his head, and the moon shining then very bright, he perceived somebody called him from the hole, which he fancied was a large window full of iron-bars, all richly gilt, suitable to the stately castle, for which he mistook the inn; and all on a sudden, he imagined that the beautiful damsel, daughter to the lady of the castle, overcome by the charms of his person, returned to court him, as she did once before. In this thought, that he might not appear uncivil or ungrateful, he turned Rozinante, and came to the hole; where, seeing the two lasses, "Fair damsels," said he, "I cannot but pity you

485

for your misplaced affection, since it is altogether impossible you should meet with any return from the object of your wishes, proportionable to your great merits and beauty; but yet you ought not, by any means, to condemn an unhappy knight-errant for his coldness, since love has utterly incapacitated him to become a slave to any other but to her, who, at first sight, made herself absolute mistress of his soul. Pardon me, therefore, excellent lady, and retire to your apartment. Let not, I beseech you, any further arguments of love force me to be less grateful or civil than I would: but if, in the passion you have for me, you can bethink yourself of anything else wherein I may do you any service, love alone excepted, command it freely; and I swear to you by my absent, yet most charming enemy, to sacrifice it to you immediately, though it be a lock of Medusa's hair, which are all snakes, or the very sunbeams enclosed in a glass vial."

"My lady needs none of those things, Sir Knight," replied Maritornes. "What then would she command?" asked Don Quixote. "Only the honor of one of your fair hands," returned Maritornes, "to satisfy in some measure, that violent passion which has obliged her to come hither with the great hazard of her honor: for if my lord her father should know it, the cutting off of one of her beautiful ears were the least thing he would do to her." "Oh, that he durst attempt it!" cried Don Quixote; "but I know he dare not, unless he has a mind to die the most unhappy death that ever father suffered, for sacrilegiously depriving his amorous daughter of one of her delicate members." Maritornes made no doubt that he would comply with her desire, and having already laid her design, got in a trice to the stable, and brought Sancho Panza's ass's halter to the hole, just as Don Quixote was got on his feet upon Rozinante's saddle, more easily to reach the barricaded window, where he imagined the enamored lady stayed; and lifting up his hand to her, said, "Here, madam, take the hand, or rather, as

I may say, the executioner of all earthly miscreants; take, I say, that hand, which never woman touched before; no, not even she herself who has entire possession of my whole body; nor do I hold it up to you that you may kiss it, but that you may observe the contexture of the sinews, the ligament of the muscles, and the largeness and dilatation of the veins; whence you may conclude how strong that arm must be, to which such a hand is joined." "We shall see that presently," replied Maritornes, and cast the noose she had made in the halter on his wrist; and then descending from the hole, she tied the other end of the halter very fast to the lock of the door. Don Quixote being sensible that the bracelet she had bestowed on him was very rough, cried, "You seem rather to abuse than compliment my hand; but I beseech you treat it not so unkindly, since that is not the cause why I do not entertain a passion for you; nor is it just or equal you should discharge the whole tempest of your vengeance on so small a part. Consider, those who love truly can never be so cruel in their revenge." But not a soul regarded what he said; for, as soon as Maritornes had fastened him, she and her confederate, almost dead with laughing, ran away, and left him so strongly bound, that it was impossible he should disengage himself.

He stood then, as I said, on Rozinante's saddle, with all his arm drawn into the hole, and the rope fastened to the lock, being under a fearful apprehension, that if Rozinante moved but never so little on any side, he should slip and hang by the arm, and therefore durst not use the least motion in the world, though he might reasonably have expected, from Rozinante's patience and gentle temper, that if he were not urged, he would never have moved for a whole age together of his own accord. In short, the Knight, perceiving himself fast, and that the ladies had forsaken him, immediately concluded that all this was done by way of enchantment, as in the last adventure in the very same castle, when the enchanted

Moor (the carrier) did so damnably maul him. Then he began alone to curse his want of discretion and conduct, since having once made his escape out of that castle in so miserable a condition, he should venture into it a second time: for, by the way, it was an observation among all knights-errant, that if they were once foiled in an adventure, it was a certain sign it was not reserved for them, but for some other to finish; wherefore they would never prove it again. Yet, for all this, he ventured to draw back his arm, to try if he could free himself; but he was so fast bound, that his attempt proved fruitless. It is true, it was with care and deliberation he drew it, for fear Rozinante should stir: and then fain would he have seated himself in the saddle; but he found he must either stand, or leave his arm for a ransom. A hundred times he wished for Amadis's sword, on which no enchantment had power; then he fell a-cursing his stars; then reflected on the great loss the world would sustain all the time he should continue under this enchantment, as he really believed it; then his adorable Dulcinea came a-fresh into his thoughts; many a time did he call to his trusty squire Sancho Panza, who, buried in a profound sleep, lay stretched at length on his ass's pannel, never so much as dreaming of the pangs his mother felt when she bore him; then the aid of the necromancers Lirgandeo and Alquife was invoked by the unhappy Knight. And, in fine, the morning surprised him racked with despair and confusion, bellowing like a bull; for he could not hope from daylight any cure or mitigation of his pain, which he believed would be eternal, being absolutely persuaded he was enchanted, since he perceived that Rozinante moved no more than a mountain; and therefore he was of opinion, that neither he nor his horse should eat, drink, or sleep, but remain in that state till the malignancy of the stars were over-past, or till some more powerful magician should break the charm.

But it was an erroneous opinion; for it was scarce daybreak, when four horsemen, very well accoutered, their firelocks hanging at the pommels of their saddles, came thither, and finding the inn-gate shut, called and knocked very loud and hard; which Don Quixote perceiving from the post where he stood sentinel, cried out with a rough voice and a haughty mien, "Knights or squires, or of whatsoever other degree you are, knock no more at the gates of this castle, since you may assure yourselves, that those who are within, at such an hour as this, are either taking their repose, or not accustomed to open their fortress, till Phœbus has displayed himself upon the globe: retire therefore, and wait till it is clear day, and then we will see whether it is just or no, that they should open their gates to you." "What a devil," cried one of them, "what castle or fortress is this, that we should be obliged to so long a ceremony? Pray thee, friend, if thou art the innkeeper, bid them open the door to us; for we ride post, and can stay no longer than just to bait our horses." "Gentlemen," said Don Quixote, "do I look like an innkeeper, then?" "I cannot tell what thou art like," replied another, "but I am sure thou talkest like a madman, to call this inn a castle." "It is a castle," returned Don Quixote, "ay, and one of the best in the province, and contains one who has held a scepter in her hand, and wore a crown on her head." "It might more properly have been said exactly contrary," replied the traveler, "a scepter in her tail, and a crown in her hand: yet it is not unlikely that there may be a company of strollers within, and those do frequently hold such scepters, and wear such crowns as thou pratest of: for certainly no person worthy to sway a scepter, or wear a crown, would condescend to take up a lodging in such a paltry inn as this, where I hear so little noise." "Thou hast not been much conversant in the world," said Don Quixote, "since thou art so miserably ignorant of accidents so frequently met with in knight-errantry." The companions of him that held this tedious discourse with Don Quixote, were tired with their foolish chatter-

489

ing so long together, and therefore they returned with greater fury to the gate, where they knocked so violently, that they waked both the innkeeper and his guests; and so the host rose to ask who was at the door.

In the meantime Rozinante, pensive and sad, with ears hanging down and motionless, bore up his outstretched lord, when one of the horses these four men rode upon, walked towards Rozinante, to smell him, and he truly being real flesh and blood, though very like a wooden block, could not but be sensible of it, nor forbear turning to smell the other, which so seasonably came to comfort and divert him; but he had hardly stirred an inch from his place, when Don Quixote's feet, that were close together, slipped asunder, and tumbling from the saddle, he had inevitably fallen to the ground, had not his wrist been securely fastened to the rope; which put him to so great a torture, that

he could not imagine, but that his hand was cutting off, or his arm tearing from his body; yet he hung so near the ground, that he could just reach it with the tips of his toes, which added to his torment; for perceiving how little he wanted to the setting his feet wholly on the ground, he strove and tugged as much as he could to effect it; not much unlike those that suffer the strappado, who put themselves to greater pain in striving to stretch their limbs, deluded by the hopes of touching the ground, if they could but inch themselves out a little longer.

XVII: A CONTINUATION OF THE STRANGE AND UNHEARD-OF ADVENTURES IN THE INN

The miserable outcries of Don Quixote presently drew the innkeeper to the door, which he hastily opening, was strangely affrighted to hear such a terrible roaring, and the strangers stood no less surprised. Maritornes, whom the cries had also roused, guessing the cause, ran straight to the loft, and slipping the halter, released the Don, who made her a very prostrate acknowledgment, by an unmerciful fall on the ground. The innkeeper and strangers crowded immediately round him to know the cause of his misfortune. He, without regard to their questions, unmanacled his wrist, bounced from the ground, mounted Rozinante, braced his target, couched his lance, and taking a large circumference in the field, came up with a hand-gallop: "Whoever," said he, "dare affirm, assert, or declare that I have been justly enchanted, in case my lady the Princess Micomicona will but give me leave, I will tell him he lies, and will maintain my assertion by immediate combat." The travelers stood amazed at Don Quixote's words, till the host removed their wonder, by informing them of his usual extravagancies in this kind, and that his behavior was not to be minded.

They then asked the innkeeper if a certain youth, near the age of fifteen, had put up at this house, clad like a muleteer? adding withal some further marks and tokens, denoting Donna Clara's lover. He told them, that among the number of his guests, such a person might pass him undistinguished; but one of them accidentally spying the coach which the judge rode in, called to his companions: "O gentlemen, gentlemen, here stands the coach which we were told my young master followed, and here he must be, that is certain: let us lose no time, one guard the door, the rest enter the house to look for him—hold—stay," continued he, "ride one about to the other side of the house, lest he escape us through the back yard." "Agreed," says another; and they posted themselves accordingly. The innkeeper, though he might guess that they sought the young gentleman whom they had described, was nevertheless puzzled as to the cause of their so diligent search. By this time, the daylight and the outcries of Don Quixote had raised the whole house, particularly the two ladies, Clara and Dorothea, who had slept but little, the one with the thoughts her lover was so near her, and the other through an earnest desire she had to see him. Don Quixote, seeing the travelers neither regard him nor his challenge, was ready to burst with fury and indignation; and, could he have dispensed with the rules of chivalry, which oblige a knight-errant to the finishing one adventure before his embarking in another, he had assaulted them all, and forced them to answer them to their cost; but being unfortunately engaged to reinstate the Princess Micomicona, his hands were tied up, and he was compelled to desist, wondering where the search and diligence of the four travelers would terminate. One of them found the young gentleman fast asleep by a footman, little dreaming of being followed or discovered: the fellow lugging him by the arm, cries out, "Ay, ay, Don Lewis, these are very fine clothes you have got on, and very becoming a gentleman of your quality, indeed; this scurvy

492

bed too is very suitable to the care and tenderness your mother brought you up with." The youth, having rubbed his drowsy eyes, and fixing them steadfastly on the man, knew him presently for one of his father's servants, which struck him speechless with surprise. The fellow went on: "There is but one way, sir, pluck up your spirits, and return with us to your father, who is certainly a dead man unless you be recovered." "How came my father to know," answered Don Lewis, "that I took this way and this disguise?" "One of your fellow-students," replied the servant, "whom you communicated your design to, moved by your father's lamentation of your loss, discovered it; the good old gentleman dispatched away four of his men in search of you; and here we are all at your service, sir, and the joyfullest men alive; for our old master will give us a hearty welcome, having so soon restored him what he loved so much." "That, next to Heaven, is as I please," said Don Lewis. "What would you, or Heaven either, please, sir, but return to your father? Come, come, sir, talk no more of it, home you must go, and home you shall go." The footman that lay with Don Lewis, hearing this dispute, rose, and related the business to Don Ferdinand, Cardenio, and the rest that were now dressed; adding withal, how the man gave him the title of Don, with other circumstances of their conference. They, being already charmed with the sweetness of his voice, were curious to be informed more particularly of his circumstances, and resolving to assist him, in case any violence should be offered him, went presently to the place where he was still contending with his father's servant.

By this Dorothea had left her chamber, and with her Donna Clara in great disorder. Dorothea, beckoning Cardenio aside, gave him a short account of the musician and Donna Clara; and he told her that his father's servants were come for him. Donna Clara overhearing him, was so exceedingly surprised, that had not Dorothea run and supported her, she had sunk to the ground. Cardenio,

493

promising to bring the matter to a fair and successful end, advised Dorothea to retire with the indisposed lady to her chamber. All the four that pursued Don Lewis were now come about him pressing his return without delay, to comfort his poor father; he answered it was impossible, being engaged to put a business in execution first, on which depended no less than his honor, and his present and future happiness. They urged, that since they had found him, there was no returning for them without him, and if he would not go, he should be carried. "Not unless you kill me," answered the young gentleman: upon which all the company were joined in the dispute, Cardenio, Don Ferdinand and his companions, the judge, the curate, the barber, and Don Quixote, who thought it needless now to guard the castle any longer. Cardenio, who knew the young gentleman's story, asked the fellows upon what pretense, or by what authority they could carry the youth away against his will. "Sir," answered one of them, "we have reason good for what we do; no less than his father's life depends upon his return." "Gentlemen," said Don Lewis, "it is not proper perhaps to trouble you with a particular relation of my affairs; only thus much, I am a gentleman, and have no dependence that should force me to anything beside my inclination." "Nay, but, sir," answered the servant, "reason, I hope, will force you; and though it cannot move you, it must govern us, who must execute our orders, and force you back; we only act as we are ordered, sir." "Hold," said the judge, "and let us know the whole state of the case." "O lord, sir," answered one of the servants that knew him, "my lord Judge, does not your worship know your next neighbor's child? See here, sir, he has run away from his father's house, and has put on these dirty, tattered rags, to the scandal of his family, as your worship may see." The judge then viewing him more attentively knew him, and saluting him, "What jest is this, Don Lewis?" cried he. "What mighty intrigue are you carrying on, young sir, to occasion this metamorphosis, so unbecoming your quality?" The young gentleman could not answer a word, and the tears stood in his eyes; the judge, perceiving his disorder, desired the four servants to trouble themselves no further, but leave the youth to his management, engaging his word to act to their satisfaction: and, retiring with Don Lewis, he begged to know the occasion of his flight.

During their conference, they heard a great noise at the inn-door, occasioned by two strangers, who, having lodged there overnight, and seeing the whole family so busied in a curious inquiry into the four horsemen's business, thought to have made off without paying their reckoning; but the innkeeper, who minded no man's business more than his own, stopped them in the nick, and demanding his money, upbraided their ungenteel design very sharply; they returned the compliment with kick and cuff so roundly, that the poor host cried out for help; his wife and daughter saw none so idle as Don Quixote, whom the daughter addressing, "I conjure you, Sir Knight," said she, "by that virtue delivered to you from Heaven, to succor my distressed father, whom two villains are beating to jelly." "Beautiful damsel," answered Don

495

Quixote with a slow tone and profound gravity, "your petition cannot at the present juncture prevail, I being withheld from undertaking any new adventure, by promise first to finish what I am engaged in; and all the service you can expect is only my counsel in this important affair; go with all speed to your father, with advice to continue and maintain the battle with his utmost resolution, till I obtain permission from the Princess Micomicona to reinforce him, which once granted, you need make no doubt of his safety." "Unfortunate wretch that I am," said Maritornes, who overheard him, "before you can have this leave, my master will be sent to the other world." "Then, madam," said he, "procure me the permission I mentioned, and though he were sent into the other world, I will bring him back in spite of hell and the devil, or at least so revenge his fall on his enemies, as shall give ample satisfaction to his surviving friends"; whereupon, breaking off the discourse, he went and threw himself prostrate before Dorothea, imploring her, in romantic style, to grant him a commission to march and sustain the governor of that castle, who was just fainting in a dangerous engagement. The princess dispatched him very willingly; whereupon, presently buckling on his target, and taking up his sword, he ran to the inn-door, where the two guests were still handling their landlord very unmercifully; he there made a sudden stop, though Maritornes and the hostess pressed him twice or thrice to tell the cause of his delay in his promised assistance to his host. "I make a pause," said Don Quixote, "because I am commanded by the law of arms to use my sword against none under the order of knighthood; but let my squire be called, this affair is altogether his province." In the meantime drubs and bruises were incessant at the inn-gate, and the poor host soundly beaten. His wife, daughter, and maid, who stood by, were like to run mad at Don Quixote's hanging back, and the inn-keeper's unequal combat; where we shall leave him, with a design to return to his assistance presently, though his fool-hardiness deserves a sound beating, for attempting a thing he was not likely to go through with. We now return to hear what Don Lewis answered the judge, whom we left retired with him, and asking the reason of his traveling on foot, and in so mean a disguise. The young gentleman, grasping his hands very passionately, made this reply, not without giving a proof of the greatness of his sorrow by his tears:

"Without ceremony or preamble, I must tell you, dear sir, that from the instant that Heaven made us neighbors, and I saw Donna Clara, your daughter and my mistress, I resigned to her the whole command of my affections; and unless you, whom I must truly call my father, prevent it, she shall be my wife this very day; for her sake I abandoned my father's house; for her have I thus disguised my quality; her would I thus have followed through the world: she was the north star to guide my wandering course, and the mark at which my wishes flew. Her ears indeed are utter strangers to my passion; but yet her eyes may guess, by the tears she saw flowing from mine. You know my fortune and my quality: if these can plead, sir, I lay them at her feet; then make me this instant your happy son, and if my father, biased by contrary designs, should not approve my choice, yet time may produce some favorable turn, and alter his mind." The amorous youth having done speaking, the judge was much surprised at the handsome discovery he made of his affections, but was not a little puzzled how to behave himself in so sudden and unexpected a matter: he therefore, without any positive answer, advised him only to compose his thoughts, to divert himself with his servants, and to prevail with them to allow him that day to consider on what was proper to be done. Don Lewis expressed his gratitude by forcibly kissing the judge's hands, and bathing them with his tears, enough to move the heart of a cannibal, much more a judge's, who (being a man of the world) had presently the advantage of the match and preferment of his daughter in the wind; though he much doubted the consent of Don Lewis's father, who he knew designed to match his son into the nobility.

By this time Don Quixote's entreaties more than threats had parted the fray at the inn-door; the strangers paying their reckoning went off, and Don Lewis's servants stood expecting the result of the judge's discourse with their young master; when (as the devil would have it) who should come into the inn but the barber whom Don Quixote had robbed of Mambrino's helmet, and Sancho of the pack-saddle. As he was leading his beast very gravely to the stable, he spies Sancho mending something about the pannel; he knew him presently, and setting upon him very roughly, "Ay, Mr. Thief, Mr. Rogue," said he, "have I caught you at last, and all my ass's furniture in your hands too?" Sancho finding himself so unexpectedly assaulted, and nettled at the dishonorable terms of his language, laying fast hold on the pannel with one hand, gave the barber such a douse on the chops with the other, as set all his teeth a-bleeding; for all this the barber stuck by his hold, and cried out so loud that the whole house was alarmed at the noise and scuffle: "I command you, gentlemen," continued he, "to assist me in the king's name; for this rogue has robbed me on the king's highway, and would now murder me, because I seize upon my goods!" "That is a lie," cried Sancho, "it was no robbery on the king's highway, but lawful plunder, won by my lord Don Quixote fairly in the field." The Don himself was now come up very proud of his squire's behavior on this occasion, accounting him thenceforth a man of spirit, and designing for him the honor of knighthood on the first opportunity, thinking his courage might prove a future ornament to the order. Among other things which the barber urged to prove his claim: "Gentlemen," said he, "this pack-saddle is as certainly my pack-saddle, as I hope to die in my bed; I know it as

498

well as if it had been bred and born with me; nay, my very ass will witness for me; do but try the saddle on him, and if it does not fit him as close as can be, then call me a liar—nay, more than that, gentlemen, that very day when they robbed me of my pack-saddle, they took away a special new basin which was never used, and which cost me a crown." Here Don Quixote could no longer contain himself; but thrusting between them, he parted them; and having caused the pack-saddle to be deposited on the ground to open view, till the method came to a final decision: "That this honorable company may know," cried he, "in what a manifest error this honest squire persists, take notice how he degrades that with the name of basin, which was, is, and shall be the helmet of Mambrino, which I fairly won from him in the field, and lawfully made myself lord of by force of arms. As to the pack-saddle, it is a concern that is beneath my regard; all I have to urge in that affair is, that my squire begged my permission to strip that vanquished coward's horse of his trappings to adorn his own; he had my authority for the deed, and he took them: and now for his converting it from a horse's furniture to a pack-saddle, no other reason can be brought, but that such transformations frequently occur in the affairs of chivalry. For a confirmation of this, dispatch, run, Sancho, and produce the helmet which this squire would maintain to be a basin." "On my faith, sir," said Sancho, "if this be all you can say for yourself, Mambrino's helmet will prove as arrant a basin, as this same man's furniture is a mere pack-saddle." "Obey my orders," said Don Quixote, "I cannot believe that everything in this castle will be guided by enchantment." Sancho brought the basin, which Don Quixote holding up in his hand, "Behold, gentlemen," continued he, "with what force can this impudent squire affirm this to be a basin, and not the helmet I mentioned? Now I swear before you all, by the order of knighthood, which I profess, that that is the same individual helmet which I won from him, without the least addition or diminution." "That I will swear," said Sancho; "for since my lord won ,it, he never fought but once in it, and that was the battle wherein he freed those ungracious galley-slaves, who by the same token would have knocked out his brains with a shower of stones, had not this same honest basin-helmet saved his skull."

XVIII: THE CONTROVERSY ABOUT MAMBRINO'S HELMET AND THE PACK-SADDLE DISPUTED AND DECIDED; WITH OTHER ACCIDENTS, NOT MORE STRANGE THAN TRUE

"Pray, good gentlemen," said the barber, "let us have your opinion in this matter. I suppose you will grant this same helmet to be a basin." "He that dares grant any such thing," said Don Quixote, "must know that he lies plainly, if a knight; but, if a squire, he lies abominably." Our barber (who was privy to the whole matter) to humor the jest and carry the diversion a little higher, took up the other shaver. "Mr. Barber, you must pardon me, sir, if I do not give you your titles; I must let you understand," said he, "that I have served an apprenticeship to your trade, and have been a free-man in the company these thirty years, and therefore am not to learn what belongs to shaving. You must likewise know, that I have been a soldier too in my younger days, and consequently understand the differences between a helmet, a morion, and a close-helmet, with all other accouterments belonging to a man of arms. Yet I say, with submission still to better judgment, that this piece, here in dispute before us, is as far from being a basin, as light is from darkness. Withal I affirm, on the other hand, that although it be a helmet, it is not a complete one." "Right," said the Don, "for the lower part and the beaver are wanting." "A clear case, a clear

500

case," said the curate, Cardenio, Don Ferdinand and his companions; and the judge himself (had not Lewis's concern made him thoughtful) would have humored the matter. "Lord, have mercy upon us all!" said the poor barber, half-distracted, "is it possible that so many fine, honorable gentlemen should know a basin or a helmet no better than this comes to? Gadzookers, I defy the wisest university in all Spain, with their scholarship to show me the like. Well, if it must be a helmet, it must be a helmet, that is all—and by the same rule my pack-saddle must troop too, as this gentleman says." "I must confess," said Don Quixote, "as to outward appearance it is a pack-saddle; but, as I have already said, I will not pretend to determine the dispute as to that point." "Nay," said the curate, "if Don Quixote speak not, the matter will never come to a decision; because in all affairs of chivalry, we must give him the preference." "I swear, worthy gentlemen," said Don Quixote, "that the adventures I have encountered in this castle are so strange and supernatural, that I must infallibly conclude them the effects of pure magic and enchantment. The first time I ever entered its gates I was strangely embarrassed by an enchanted Moor that inhabited it, and Sancho himself had no better entertainment from his attendants; and last night I hung suspended almost two hours by this arm, without the power of helping myself, or of assigning any reasonable cause of my misfortune. So that for me to meddle, or give my opinion in such confused and intricate events, would appear presumption; I have already given my final determination as to the helmet in controversy, but dare pronounce no definitive sentence on the pack-saddle, remitting it to the discerning judgment of the company; perhaps the power of enchantment may not prevail on you that are not dubbed knights, so that your understandings may be free, and your judicial faculties more piercing to enter into the true nature of these events, and not conclude upon

501

them from their appearances." "Undoubtedly," answered Don Ferdinand, "the decision of this process depends upon our sentiments, according to Don Quixote's opinion; that the matter therefore may be fairly discussed, and that we may proceed upon solid and firm grounds, we will put it to the vote. Let everyone give me his suffrage in my ear, and I will oblige myself to report them faithfully to the board."

To these that knew Don Quixote this proved excellent sport; but to others unacquainted with his humor, as Don Lewis and his four servants, it appeared the most ridiculous stuff in nature; three other travelers too that happened to call in by the way, and were found to be officers of the Holy Brotherhood, or pursuivants, thought the people were all bewitched in good earnest. But the barber was quite at his wit's end, to think that his basin, then and there present before his eyes, was become the helmet of Mambrino: and that his pack-saddle was likewise going to be changed into rich horse-furniture. Everybody laughed very heartily to see Don Ferdinand whispering each particular person very gravely to have his vote upon the important contention of the pack-saddle. When he had gone the rounds among his own faction, that were all privy to the jest, "Honest fellow," said he very loudly, "I grow weary of asking so many impertinent questions; every man has his answer at his tongue's end, that it is mere madness to call this a pack-saddle, and that it is positively, *nemine contradicente*, right horse-furniture, and great horse-furniture, too; besides, friend, your allegations and proofs are of no force; therefore, in spite of your ass and you too, we give it for the defendant, that this is, and will continue the furniture of a horse, nay, and of a great horse too." "Now the devil take me," said the barber, "if you be not all damnably deceived; and may I be hanged if my conscience does not plainly tell me, it is a downright pack-saddle: but I have lost it according to law, and so fare it well. But I am neither mad nor drunk sure, for I am fresh and fasting this morning from everything but sin."

The barber's raving was no less diverting than Don Quixote's clamors: "Sentence is passed," cried he; "and let every man take possession of his goods and chattels, and Heaven give him joy." "This is a jest, a mere jest," said one of the four servants; "certainly, gentlemen, you cannot be in earnest, you are too wise to talk at this rate: for my part, I say and will maintain it, for there is no reason the barber should be wronged, that this is a basin, and that the pack-saddle of a he-ass." "May not it be a she-ass's pack-saddle, friend?" said the curate. "That is all one, sir," said the fellow; "the question is not, whether it be a he- or a she-ass's pack-saddle, but whether it be a pack-saddle or not, that is the matter, sir." One of the officers of the Holy Brotherhood, who had heard the whole controversy, very angry to hear such an error maintained: "Gentlemen," said he, "this is no more a horse's saddle than it is my father; and he that says the contrary is drunk or mad." "You lie, like an unmannerly rascal," said the Knight; and at the same time with his lance, which he had always ready for such occasions, he offered such a blow at the officer's head, that had not the fellow leaped aside, it would have laid him flat. The lance flew into pieces, and the rest of the officers seeing their comrade so abused, cried out for help, charging everyone to aid and assist the Holy Brotherhood.[1] The innkeeper being one of the fraternity, ran for his sword and rod, and then joined his fellows. Don Lewis's servants got round their master, to defend him from harm, and secure him, lest he should make his escape in the scuffle. The barber seeing the whole house turned topsy-turvy, laid hold again on his pack-saddle: but Sancho, who watched his motions, was as ready as he, and secured the other end of it.

[1] *All these troops of the Holy Brotherhood carried wands or rods as marks of their office.*

Don Quixote drew, and assaulted the officers pell-mell. Don Lewis called to his servants to join Don Quixote, and the gentlemen that sided with him; for Cardenio, Don Ferdinand and his friends, had engaged on his side. The curate cried out, the landlady shrieked, her daughter wept, Maritornes howled, Dorothea was distracted with fear, Lucinda could not tell what to do, and Donna Clara was strangely frightened; the barber pommeled Sancho, and Sancho belabored the barber. One of Don Lewis's servants went to hold him, but he gave him such a rebuke on his jaws, that his teeth had like to have forsook their station; and then the judge took him into his protection. Don Ferdinand had got one of the officers down, and laid him on back and side. The innkeeper still cried out, "Help the Holy Brotherhood," so that the whole house was a medley of wailings, cries, shrieks, confusions, fears, terrors, disasters, flashes, buffets, blows, kicks, cuffs, battery, and bloodshed.

In the greatest of this hurly-burly, it came into Don Quixote's

head, that he was certainly involved in the disorder and confusion of King Agramant's camp; and calling out with a voice that shook the whole house, "Hold, valorous knights," said he, "all hold your furious hands, sheath all your swords, let none presume to strike on pain of death, but hear me speak." The loud and monstrous voice surprised everybody into obedience, and the Don proceeded: "I told you before, gentlemen, that this castle was enchanted, and that some legions of devils did inhabit it: now let your own eyes confirm my words: do not you behold the strange and horrid confusion of King Agramant's army removed hither, and put in execution among us? See, see how they fight for the sword, and yonder for the horse! Behold how some contend for the helmet, and here others battle it for the standard; and all fight we do not know how, nor can tell why. Let, therefore, my lord Judge, and his reverence Mr. Curate, represent one King Agramant, and the other King Sobrino, and by their wisdom and conduct appease this tumult: for, by the powers Divine, it were a wrong to honor, and a blot on chivalry, to let so many worthies, as are here met, kill one another for such trifles."

Don Quixote's words were Hebrew to the officers, who having been roughly handled by Cardenio, Ferdinand, and his friends, would not give it over so. But the barber was content; for Sancho had demolished his beard and pack-saddle both in the scuffle; the squire dutifully retreated at the first sound of his master's voice; Don Lewis's servants were calm, finding it their best way to be quiet; but the innkeeper was refractory. He swore that madman ought to be punished for his ill-behavior, and that every hour he was making some disturbance or another in his house. But at last, the matter was made up, the pack-saddle was agreed to be horse-furniture, the basin a helmet, and the inn a castle, till the day of judgment, if Don Quixote would have it so. Don Lewis's business

505

came next in play. The judge, in concert with Don Ferdinand, Cardenio, and the curate, resolved that Don Ferdinand should interpose his authority on Don Lewis's behalf, and let his servants know, that he would carry him to Andalusia, where he should be entertained according to his quality by his brother the Marquis; and they should not oppose this design, seeing Don Lewis was positively resolved not to be forced to go back to his father yet. Don Ferdinand's quality, and Don Lewis's resolution prevailed on the fellows to order matters so, that three of them might return to acquaint their old master, and the fourth wait on Don Lewis. Thus this monstrous heap of confusion and disorder was digested into form, by the authority of Agramant, and wisdom of King Sobrino.

But the enemy of peace, finding his project of setting them all by the ears so eluded, resolved once again to have another trial of skill, and play the devil with them all the second bout: for though the officers, understanding the quality of their adversaries, were willing to desist, yet one of them, whom Don Ferdinand had kicked most unmercifully, remembering, that among other warrants, he had one to apprehend Don Quixote for setting free the galley-slaves (which Sancho was sadly afraid would come about), he re-solved to examine if the marks and tokens given of Don Quixote agreed with this person; then drawing out a parchment, and open-ing his warrant, he made a shift to read it, and at every other word looked cunningly in Don Quixote's face; whereupon, folding up the parchment, and taking his warrant in his left hand, he clapped his right hand fast in the Knight's collar, crying, "You are the king's prisoner: gentlemen, I am an officer, here is my warrant. I charge you all to aid and assist the Holy Brotherhood." Don Quixote, finding himself used so rudely, by one whom he took to be a pitiful scoundrel, kindled up into such a rage, that he shook with indignation, and catching the fellow by the neck, with both his hands, squeezed him so violently, that if his companions had not

506

presently freed him, the Knight would certainly have throttled him before he had quitted his hold.

The innkeeper, being obliged to assist his brother officer, presently joined him: the hostess seeing her husband engaging a second time, raised a new outcry; her daughter and Maritornes bore the burden of the song, sometimes praying, sometimes crying, sometimes scolding: Sancho, seeing what passed, "By the lord," said he, "my master is in the right; this place is haunted, that is certain; there is no living quietly an hour together." At last Don Ferdinand parted Don Quixote and the officer, who were both pretty well pleased to quit their bargain. However, the officers still demanded their prisoner, and to have him delivered bound into their hands, commanding all the company a second time to help and assist them to secure that public robber upon the king's high road.

Don Quixote smiled at the supposed simplicity of the fellows; at last, with solemn gravity, "Come hither," said he, "you offspring of filth and extraction of dunghills, dare you call loosing the fettered, freeing the captive, helping the miserable, raising the fallen, and supplying the indigent; dare you, I say, base-spirited rascals, call these actions robbery? Your thoughts, indeed, are too groveling and servile, to understand, or reach the pitch of chivalry, otherwise you had understood, that even the shadow of a knight-errant had claim to your adoration. You a band of officers; you are a pack of rogues indeed, and robbers on the highway by authority. What blockhead of a magistrate durst issue out a warrant to apprehend a knight-errant like me? Could not his ignorance find out that we are exempt from all courts of judicature?—that our valor is the bench, our will the common law, and our sword the executioner of justice? Could not his dullness inform him, that no rank of nobility or peerage enjoys more immunities and privileges? Has he any precedent that a knight-errant ever paid taxes, subsidy, poll-

507

money, or so much as fare or ferry? What tailor ever had money for his clothes? or what constable ever made him a reckoning for lodging in his castle? What kings are not proud of his company? and what damsels of his love? And lastly, did you ever read of any knight-errant that ever was, is, or shall be, that could not, with his single force, cudgel four hundred such rogues as you to pieces, if they have the impudence to oppose him?"

XIX: THE NOTABLE ADVENTURE OF THE OFFICERS OF THE HOLY BROTHERHOOD WITH DON QUIXOTE'S GREAT FEROCITY AND ENCHANTMENT

Whilst Don Quixote talked at this rate, the curate endeavored to persuade the officers that he was distracted, as they might easily gather from his words and actions; and, therefore, though they should carry him before a magistrate, he would be presently acquitted, as being a madman. He that had the warrant made answer, that it was not his business to examine whether he were mad or not, he was an officer in commission, and must obey orders; and accordingly was resolved to deliver him up to the superior power, which once done, they might acquit him five hundred times if they would. But for all that, the curate persisted they should not carry Don Quixote away with them this time; adding, that the Knight himself would by no means be brought to it; and in short, said so much, that they had been greater fools than he, could they not have plainly seen his madness. They, therefore, not only desisted, but offered their service in compounding the difference between Sancho and the barber; their mediation was accepted, they being officers of justice, and succeeded so well, that both parties stood to their arbitration, though not entirely satisfied with their award, which ordered them to change their pannels, but not their halters nor the girths. The curate made up the business of the basin, paying the barber under-hand eight reals for it, and getting a general release under his hand of all claims or actions concerning it, and all things else. These two important differences being so happily decided, the only obstacles to a general peace were Don Lewis's servants and the innkeeper; the first were prevailed upon to accept the proposals offered, which were, that three of them should go home, and the fourth attend Don Lewis where Don Ferdinand should appoint. Thus this difference was made up, to the unspeakable joy of Donna Clara. Zoraida not well understanding anything that passed, was sad and cheerful by turns, as she observed others to be by their countenances, especially her beloved Spaniard, on whom her eyes were more particularly fixed. The innkeeper made a hideous bawling; having discovered that the barber had received money for his basin, he knew no reason, he said, why he should not be paid as well as other folks, and swore that Rozinante and Sancho's ass should pay for their master's extravagance before they should leave his stable; the curate pacified him, and Don Ferdinand paid him his bill. All things thus accommodated, the inn no longer resembled the confusion of Agramant's camp, but rather the universal peace of Augustus's reign: upon which the curate and Don Ferdinand had the thanks of the house, as a just acknowledgment for their so effectual mediation.

Don Quixote being now free from the difficulties and delays that lately embarrassed him, held it high time to prosecute his voyage, and bring to some decision the general enterprise which he had the voice and election for. He therefore fully resolved to press his departure, and fell on his knees before Dorothea, but she would not hear him in that posture, but prevailed upon him to rise: he then addressed her in his usual forms: "Most beautiful lady," said he, "it is a known proverb, that 'Diligence is the mother of success'; and we have found the greatest successes in war still to

509

depend on expedition and dispatch, by preventing the enemy's design, and forcing a victory before an assault is expected. My inference from this, most high and illustrious lady, is, that our residence in this castle appears nothing conducive to our designs, but may prove dangerous; for we may reasonably suppose, that our enemy the giant may learn by spies, or some other secret intelligence, the scheme of our intentions, and consequently fortify himself in some inexpugnable fortress, against the power of our utmost endeavors, and so the strength of my invincible arm may be ineffectual. Let us therefore, dear madam, by our diligence and sudden departure hence, prevent any such his designs, and force our good fortune, by missing no opportunity that we may lay hold of." Here he stopped, waiting the princess's answer. She, with a grave aspect, and style suiting his extravagance, replied, "The great inclination and indefatigable desire you show, worthy knight, in assisting the injured, and restoring the oppressed, lay a fair claim to the praises and universal thanks of mankind; but your singular concern, and industrious application in assisting me, deserve my particular acknowledgments and gratification; and I shall make it my peculiar request to Heaven, that your generous designs, in my favor, may be soon accomplished, that I may be enabled to convince you of the honor and gratitude that may be found in some of our sex. As to our departure, I shall depend upon your pleasure, to whose management I have not only committed the care of my person, but also resigned the whole power of command." "Then by the assistance of the Divine power," answered he, "I will lose no opportunity of reinstating your highness, since you condescend to humble yourself to my orders; let our march be sudden, for the eagerness of my desires, the length of the journey, and the dangers of delay, are great spurs to my dispatch; since therefore Heaven has not created, nor hell seen the man I ever

510

feared, fly, Sancho, saddle Rozinante, harness your ass, and make ready the lady's palfrey; let us take leave of the governor here, and these other lords, and set out from hence immediately."

Poor Sancho hearing all that passed, shook his head, "Lord, lord, master," said he, "there is always more tricks in a town than are talked of (with reverence be it spoken)." "Ho! villain," cried Don Quixote, "what tricks can any town or city show to impair my credit?" "Nay, sir," quoth Sancho, "if you grow angry, I can hold my tongue, if that be all; but there are some things which you ought to hear, and I should tell as becomes a trusty squire, and honest servant." "Say what thou wilt," said the Knight, "so it tend not to cowardice; for if thou art afraid, keep it to thyself, and trouble not me with the mention of fear, which my soul abhors." "Pshaw, hang fear," answered Sancho, "that is not the matter; but I must tell you, sir, that which is as certain and plain as the nose on your face. This same madam here, that calls herself the queen of the great kingdom of Micomicon, is no more a queen than my grandame. For, do but consider, sir, if she were such a fine queen as you believe, can you imagine she would always be sucking of snouts, and kissing and slabbering a certain person, that shall be nameless in this company?" Dorothea blushed at Sancho's words, for Don Ferdinand had indeed, sometimes, and in private, taken the freedom with his lips to reap some part of the reward his affection deserved; which Sancho spying by chance, made some constructions upon, very much to the disadvantage of her royalty; for, in short, he concluded her no better than a woman of pleasure. She would nevertheless take no notice of his aspersion, but let him go on. "I say this, sir," continued he, "because after our trudging through all weathers, fair after foul, day after night, and night after day, this same person in the inn here, is like to divert himself at our expense, and to gather the fruit of our labors. I think therefore, master, there is no reason, do you see, for saddling Rozinante, harnessing my ass, or making ready the lady's palfrey; for we had better stay where we are; and let every whore brew as she bakes, and every man that is hungry go to dinner."

Heavens! into what a fury did these disrespectful words of Sancho put the Knight! His whole body shook, his tongue faltered, his eyes glowed. "Thou villainous, ignorant, rash, unmannerly, blasphemous detractor," said he, "how darest thou entertain such base and dishonorable thoughts, much more utter thy rude and contemptible suspicions before me and this honorable presence? Away from my sight, thou monster of nature, magazine of lies, cupboard of deceits, granary of guile, publisher of follies, foe of all honor! Away, and never let me see thy face again, on pain of my most furious indignation." Then, bending his angry brows, puffing his cheeks, and stamping on the ground, he gave Sancho such a look as almost frightened the poor fellow to annihilation.

In the height of this consternation, all that the poor squire could do, was to turn his back, and sneak out of the room. But Dorothea, knowing the Knight's temper, undertook to mitigate his anger. "Sir Knight of the Woeful Figure," said she, "assuage your wrath, I beseech you; it is below your dignity to be offended at those idle words of your squire; and I dare not affirm but that he has some color of reason for what he said; for it were uncharitable to suspect his sincere understanding, and honest principles, of any false or malicious slander or accusation. We must therefore search deeper into this affair, and believe, that as you have found all transactions in this castle governed by enchantment, so some diabolical illusion has appeared to Sancho, and represented to his enchanted sight what he asserts to my dishonor." "Now by the powers supreme," said the Knight, "your highness has cut the knot. The misdemeanor of that poor fellow must be attributed

512

purely to enchantment, and the power of some malicious apparition; for the good nature and simplicity of the poor wretch could never invent a lie, or be guilty of an aspersion to anyone's disadvantage." "It is evident," said Don Ferdinand; "we therefore all intercede in behalf of honest Sancho, that he may be again restored to your favor, *sicut erat in principio*, before these illusions had imposed upon his sense." Don Quixote complied, and the curate brought in poor Sancho trembling, who on his knees made an humble acknowledgment of his crime, and begged to have his pardon confirmed by a gracious kiss of his master's hand. Don Quixote gave him his hand and his blessing. "Now, Sancho," said he, "will you hereafter believe what I so often have told you, that the power of enchantment overrules everything in this castle?" "I will, and like your worship," quoth Sancho, "all but my tossing in a blanket; for really, sir, that happened according to the ordinary course of things." "Believe it not, Sancho," replied Don Quixote, "for were I not convinced of the contrary, you should have plentiful revenge; but neither then, or now, could I ever find any object to wreak my fury or resentment on." Everyone desired to know what was the business in question; whereupon the innkeeper gave them an account of Sancho's tossing, which set them all a-laughing, and would have made Sancho angry, had not his master afresh assured him that it was only a mere illusion, which though the squire believed not, he held his tongue. The whole company having passed two days in the inn, bethought themselves of departing; and the curate and barber found out a device to carry home Don Quixote, without putting Don Ferdinand and Dorothea to the trouble of humoring his impertinence any longer. They first agreed with a wagoner that went by with his team of oxen, to carry him home: then had a kind of wooden cage made, so large that the Knight might conveniently sit, or lie in it. Presently after, all the company

513

of the inn disguised themselves, some with masks, others by disfiguring their faces, and the rest by change of apparel, so that Don Quixote should not take them to be the same persons. This done, they all silently entered his chamber, where he was sleeping very soundly after his late fatigues: they immediately laid hold on him so forcibly, and held his arms and legs so hard, that he was not able to stir, or do anything but stare on those odd figures which stood round him. This instantly confirmed him in the strange fancy that had so long disturbed his crazy understanding, and made him believe himself undoubtedly enchanted; and those frightful figures to be the spirits and demons of the enchanted castle. So far the curate's invention succeeded to his expectation. Sancho being the only person there in his right shape and senses, beheld all this very patiently; and though he knew them all very well, yet was resolved to see the end of it before he ventured to speak his mind. His master likewise said nothing, patiently expecting his fate, and waiting the event of his misfortune. They had by this lifted him out of bed, and placing him in the cage, they shut him in, and nailed the bars of it so fast, that no small strength could force them open. Then, mounting him on their shoulders, as they conveyed him out of the chamber door, they heard as dreadful a voice as the barber's lungs could bellow, speak these words:

"Be not impatient, O Knight of the Woeful Figure, at your imprisonment, since it is ordained by the fates, for the more speedy accomplishment of that most noble adventure, which your incomparable valor has intended. For accomplished it shall be, when the rampant Manchegan lion [1] and the white Tobosian dove shall be united, by humbling their lofty and erected chests to the soft yoke of wedlock, from whose wonderful coition shall be produced and spring forth brave whelps which shall imitate the rampant paws of their valorous sire. And this shall happen before the bright pursuer of the fugitive nymph shall, by his rapid and natural course, take a double circumference in visitation of the luminous signs. And thou, the most noble and faithful squire that ever had sword on thigh, beard on face, or sense of smell in nose, be not dispirited or discontented at this captivity of the flower of all chivalry; for very speedily, by the eternal will of the world's Creator, thou shalt find thyself ennobled and exalted beyond the knowledge of thy greatness. And I confirm to thee, from the sage Mentironiana,[2] that thou shalt not be defrauded of the promises made by thy noble lord. I therefore conjure thee to follow closely the steps of the courageous and enchanted Knight; for it is necessarily enjoined,

1 *It may be translated the rampant spotted lion as well as the rampant Manchegan lion: for the Spanish word Mancha signifies both a spot, and the country La Mancha. An untranslatable* double entendre.
2 *Mentironiana is a framed word from* mentira, *"a lie," as if we should say* Fibberiana.

515

that you both go where you both shall stay. The fates have commanded me no more, farewell. For I now return, I well know whither."

The barber managed the cadence of his voice so artificially towards the latter end of his prophecy, that even those who were made acquainted with the jest, had almost taken it for supernatural.

Don Quixote was much comforted at the prophecy, apprehending presently the sense of it, and applying it to his marriage with Dulcinea del Toboso, from whose happy womb should issue the cubs, signifying his sons, to the eternal glory of La Mancha; upon the strength of which belief raising his voice, and heaving a profound sigh: "Whatsoever thou art," said he, "whose happy prognostication I own and acknowledge, I desire thee to implore, in my name, the wise magician, whose charge I am, that his power may protect me in this captivity, and not permit me to perish before the fruition of these grateful and incomparable promises made to me; for the confirmation of such hopes, I would think my prison a palace, my fetters freedom, and this hard field-bed on which I lie, more easy than the softest down, or most luxurious lodgings. And as to the consolation offered my squire Sancho Panza, I am so convinced of his honesty, and he has proved his honor in so many adventures, that I mistrust not his deserting me, through any change of fortune. And though his or my harder stars should disable me from bestowing on him the island I have promised, or some equivalent, his wages at least are secured to him by my last will and testament, though what he will receive is more answerable, I confess, to my estate and ability, than to his services and great deserts." Sancho Panza made him three or four very respectful bows, and kissed both his hands (for one alone he could not, being both tied together), and in an instant the demons hoisted up the cage, and yoked it very handsomely to the team of oxen.

Don Quixote was not so much amazed at his enchantment, as at the manner of it. "Among all the volumes of chivalry that I have turned over," said he, "I never read before of knights-errant drawn in carts or tugged along so leisurely, by such slothful animals as oxen. For they used to be hurried along with prodigious speed, enveloped in some dark and dusky cloud; or in some fiery chariot drawn by winged griffins, or some such expeditious creatures; but I must confess, to be drawn thus by a team of oxen, staggers my understanding not a little; though perhaps the enchanters of our times take a different method from those in former ages: or rather the wise magicians have invented some course in their proceedings for me, being the first reviver or restorer of arms, which have so long been lost in oblivion, and rusted through the disuse of chivalry. What is thy opinion, my dear Sancho?" "Why truly, sir," said Sancho, "I cannot tell what to think, being not so well read in these matters as your worship; yet for all that, I am positive and can take my oath on it, that these same phantoms that run up and down here are not orthodox." "Orthodox, my friend," said Don Quixote, "how can they be orthodox, when they are devils, and have only assumed these phantastical bodies to surprise us into this condition? To convince you, endeavor to touch them, and you will find their substances are not material, but only subtile air, and outward appearance." "Gadzookers, sir," said Sancho, "I have touched them, and touched them again, sir; and I find this same busy devil here, that is fiddling about, is as plump and fat as a capon: besides, he has another property very different from a devil; for the devils, they say, smell of brimstone and other filthy things, and this spark has such a fine scent of essence about him, that you

517

may smell him at least half a league." (Meaning Don Ferdinand, who in all probability, like other gentlemen of his quality, had his clothes perfumed.)

"Alas, honest Sancho," answered Don Quixote, "the cunning of these fiends is above the reach of thy simplicity; for you must know, the spirits, as spirits, have no scent at all; and if they should, it must necessarily be some unsavory stench, because they still carry their hell about them, and the least of a perfume or grateful odor were inconsistent with their torments; so that this mistake of yours must be attributed to some farther delusion of your sense." Don Ferdinand and Cardenio, upon these discourses between master and man, were afraid that Sancho would spoil all, and therefore ordered the innkeeper privately to get ready Rozinante and Sancho's ass, while the curate agreed with the officers for so much a day to conduct them home. Cardenio, having hung Don Quixote's target on the pommel of Rozinante's saddle and the basin on the other side, he signified to Sancho by signs, that he should mount his ass, and lead Rozinante by the bridle; and lastly placed two officers with their firelocks on each side of the cart.

Being just ready to march, the hostess, her daughter, and Maritornes, came to the door to take their leave of the Knight, pretending unsupportable grief for his misfortune. "Restrain your tears, most honorable ladies," said Don Quixote, "for these mischances are incident to those of my profession; and from these disasters it is we date the greatness of our glory and renown; they are the effects of envy, which still attends virtuous and great actions, and brought upon us by the indirect means of such princes and knights as are emulous of our dignity and fame: but, spite of all oppression, spite of all the magic that ever its first inventor Zoroastres understood, virtue will come off victorious; and, triumphing over every danger, will at last shine out in its proper luster like the sun to enlighten the world. Pardon me, fair ladies, if through ignorance

518

or omission of the respects due to your qualities, I have not behaved to please you; for, to the best of my knowledge, I never committed a willful wrong. And I crave the assistance of your prayers towards my enlargement from this prison, which some malicious magician has confined me to; and the first business of my freedom shall be a grateful acknowledgment for the many and obliging favors conferred upon me in this your castle." Whilst the ladies were thus entertained by Don Quixote, the curate and barber were busy taking their leaves of their company; and after mutual compliments and embraces, they engaged to acquaint one another with their succeeding fortunes. Don Ferdinand entreated the curate to give him a particular relation of Don Quixote's adventures, assuring him that nothing would be a greater obligation, and at the same time engaged to inform him of his own marriage and Lucinda's return to her parents; with an account of Zoraida's baptism, and Don Lewis's success in his amour.

The curate having given his word and honor to satisfy Don Ferdinand, and the last compliments being paid, was just going, when the innkeeper made him a proffer of a bundle of papers found in the folds of the same cloak-bag, where he got "The Curious Impertinent," telling him that they were all at his service; because, since the owner was not like to come and demand them, and he could not read, they could not better be disposed of. The curate thanked him heartily, and opening the papers, found them entitled, "The Story of Rinconete and Cortadillo." The title showing it to be a novel, and probably written by the author of "The Curious Impertinent," because found in the same wallet, he put it in his pocket, with a resolution to peruse it the very first opportunity: then, mounting with his friend the barber, and both putting on masks, they followed the procession, which marched in this order. The carter led the van, and next his cart flanked on right and left with two officers with their firelocks; then followed Sancho on his ass, leading

519

Rozinante; and lastly the curate and the barber on their mighty mules brought up the rear of the body, all with a grave and solemn air, marching no faster than the heavy oxen allowed. Don Quixote sat leaning against the back of the cage with his hands tied, and his legs at length; but so silent and motionless, that he seemed rather a statue than a man.

They had traveled about two leagues this slow and leisurely pace, when their conductor, stopping in a little valley, proposed it as a fit place to bait in; but he was prevailed upon to defer halting a little longer, being informed by the barber of a certain valley beyond a little hill in their view, better stored with grass, and more convenient for their purpose. They had not traveled much further when the curate spied coming a round pace after them six or seven men very well accoutered. They appeared, by their brisk riding, to be mounted on Churchmen's mules, not carried as the Don was by a team of sluggish oxen. They endeavored before the heat of the day to reach their inn, which was a league further. In short, they soon came up with our slow itinerants; and one of them, that was a canon of Toledo, and master of those that came along with him, marking the formal procession of the cart, guards, Sancho, Rozinante, the curate, and the barber, but chiefly the encaged Don Quixote, could not forbear asking what meant their strange method of securing that man; though he already believed, having observed the guards, that he was some notorious criminal in custody of the Holy Brotherhood. One of the fraternity told him, that he could not tell the cause of that Knight's imprisonment, but that he might answer for himself, because he best could tell.

Don Quixote, overhearing their discourse, "Gentlemen," said he, "if you are conversant and skilled in matters of knight-errantry, I will communicate my misfortunes to you; if you are not, I have no reason to give myself the trouble." "Truly, friend," answered the canon, "I am better acquainted with books of chivalry than with

Villapando's divinity; and if that be all your objection, you may safely impart to me what you please." "With Heaven's permission be it so," said Don Quixote; "you must then understand, Sir Knight, that I am borne away in this cage by the force of enchantments, through the envious spite and malice of some cursed magicians; for virtue is more zealously persecuted by ill men, than it is beloved by the good. I am by profession a knight-errant, and none of those, I assure you, whose deeds never merited a place in the records of fame; but one who in spite of envy's self, in spite of all the magi of Persia, the brahmans of India, or the gymnosophists of Æthiopia, shall secure to his name a place in the temple of immortality, as a pattern and model to following ages, that ensuing knights-errant, following my steps, may be guided to the top and highest pitch of heroic honor." "The noble Don Quixote de la Mancha speaks truth," said the curate, coming up to the company, "he is indeed enchanted in this cart, not through his own demerits or offenses, but the malicious treachery of those whom virtue displeases and valor offends. This is, sir, the Knight of the Woeful Figure, of whom you have undoubtedly heard, whose mighty deeds shall stand engraved in lasting brass and time-surviving marble, till envy grows tired with laboring to deface his fame, and malice to conceal them."

The canon hearing the prisoner and his guard talk thus in the same style, was in a maze, and blessed himself for wonder, as did the rest of the company, till Sancho Panza coming up, to mend the matter, "Look ye, sirs," said he, "I will speak the truth, take it well, or take it ill. My master here is no more enchanted than my mother: he is in his sober senses, he eats and drinks, and does his needs, like other folks, and as he used to do; and yet they will persuade me that a man, who can do all this, is enchanted forsooth; he can speak too; for, if they will let him alone he will prattle you more than thirty attorneys." Then turning towards the curate, "O

Mr. Curate, O Mr. Curate," continued he, "do you think I do not know you, and that I do not guess what all of these new enchantments drive at ! Yes, I do know you well enough, for all you do hide your face; and understand your design, for all your sly tricks, sir. But it is an old saying, there is no striving against the stream: and the weakest still goes to the wall. The devil take the luck on it; had not your reverence spoiled our sport, my master had been married before now to the princess Micomicona, and I had been an earl at least; nay, that I was sure of, had the worst come to the worst; but the old proverb is true again, fortune turns round like a mill-wheel, and he that was yesterday at the top, lies today at the bottom. I wonder, Mr. Curate, you that are a clergyman should not have more conscience: consider, sir, that I have a wife and family who expect all to be great folks, and my master here is to do a world of good deeds: and do not you think, sir, that you will not be made to answer for all this one day?" "Snuff me those candles," said the barber, hearing Sancho talk at this rate: "what, fool, are you brain-sick of your master's disease too? If you be, you are like to bear him company in his cage, I will assure you, friend. What enchanted island is this that floats in your skull? or what succubus has been riding thy fancy, and got it with child of these hopes?" "With child! Sir, what do ye mean, sir?" said Sancho, "I scorn your words, sir; the best lord in the land should not get me with child, no, not the king himself, Heaven bless him. For though I am a poor man, yet I am an honest man, and an old Christian, and do not owe any man a farthing; and though I desire islands, there are other folks not far off that desire worse things. Everyone is the son of his own works; I am a man, and may be Pope of Rome, much more governor of an island; especially considering my master may gain so many as he may want persons to bestow them on. Therefore, pray, Mr. Barber, take heed what you say; for all consists not in shaving of beards; and there is some difference between a hawk and a handsaw. I say so, because we all know one another; and nobody shall put a false card upon me. As to my master's enchantment, let it stand as it is, Heaven knows best: and a stink is still worse for the stirring." The barber thought silence the best way to quiet Sancho's impertinence; and the curate, doubting that he might spoil all, entreated the canon to move a little before, and he would unfold the mystery of the encaged Knight, which perhaps he would find one of the pleasantest stories he had ever heard: the canon rode forward with him, and his men followed, while the curate made them a relation of Don Quixote's life and quality, his madness and adventures, with the original cause of his distraction, and the whole progress of his affairs, till his being shut up in the cage, to get him home in order to have him cured. They all admired at this strange account; and then the canon turning to the curate: "Believe me, Mr. Curate," said he, "I am fully convinced, that those they call books of knight-errantry, are very prejudicial to the public. And though I have been led away with an idle and false pleasure to read the beginnings of almost as many of them as have been printed, I could never yet persuade myself to go through with any one to the end; for to me they all seem to contain one and the same thing; and there is as much in one of them as in all the rest. The whole composition and style resemble that of the Milesian fables, which are a sort of idle stories, designed only for diversion, and not for instruction. It is not so with those fables which are called Apologues, that at once delight and instruct. But though the main design of such books is to please, yet I cannot conceive how it is possible they should perform it, being filled with such a multitude of unaccountable extravagancies. For the pleasure which strikes the soul must be derived from the beauty and congruity it sees or conceives in those things the sight or imagination lay before it; and nothing in itself deformed or incongruous can give us any real satisfaction. Now what beauty can there be, or what proportion of the parts to the whole, or of the whole to the several parts, in a book or fable, where a stripling of sixteen years of age, at one cut of a sword, cleaves a giant as tall as a steeple through the middle, as easily as if he were made of pasteboard? Or when they give us the relation of a battle, having said the enemy's power consisted of a million of combatants, yet, provided the hero of the book be against them, we must of necessity, though never so much against our inclination, conceive that the said knight obtained the victory only by his own valor, and the strength of his powerful arm? And what shall we say of the great ease and facility with which an absolute queen or empress casts herself into the arms of an errant and unknown knight? What mortal, not altogether barbarous and unpolished, can be pleased to read, that a great tower, full of armed

524

knights, cuts through the sea like a ship before the wind, and setting out in the evening from the coast of Italy, lands by break of day in Prester John's country, or in some other never known to Ptolemy, or seen by Marcus Paulus?[1] If it should be answered, that the persons who compose these books, write them as confessed lies, and therefore are not obliged to observe niceties, or to have regard to truth, I shall make this reply, that falsehood is so much the more commendable, by how much it more resembles truth; and is the more pleasing the more it is doubtful and possible. Fabulous tales ought to be suited to the reader's understanding, being so contrived, that all impossibilities ceasing, all great accidents appearing feasible, and the mind wholly hanging in suspense, they may at once surprise, astonish, please, and divert; so that pleasure and admiration may go hand in hand. This cannot be performed by him that flies from probability and imitation, which is the perfection of what is written. I have not seen any book of knight-errantry that composes an entire body of a fable with all its parts, so that the middle is answerable to the beginning, and the end to the beginning and middle; but on the contrary, they form them of so many limbs, that they rather seem a chimera or monster, than a well-proportioned figure. Besides all this, their style is uncouth, their exploits incredible, their love immodest, their civility impertinent, their battles tedious, their language absurd, their voyages preposterous; and in short, they are altogether void of solid ingenuity, and therefore fit to be banished a Christian commonwealth as useless and prejudicial." The curate was very attentive, and believed him a man of sound judgment, and much in the right in all he had urged; and therefore told him, that being of the same opinion, and an enemy to the books of knight-errantry, he had burnt all that belonged to Don Quixote, which were a considerable number. Then he recounted to him the scrutiny he had made among them, what

[1] *Marco Polo.*

he had condemned to the flames, and what spared; at which the canon laughed heartily, and said, that notwithstanding all he had spoken against those books, yet he found one good thing in them, which was the subject they furnished a man of understanding with to exercise his parts, because they allow a large scope for the pen to dilate upon without any check, describing shipwrecks, storms, skirmishes and battles; representing to us a brave commander, with all the qualifications requisite in such a one, showing his prudence in disappointing the designs of the enemy, his eloquence in persuading or dissuading his soldiers, his judgment in council, his celerity in execution, and his valor in assailing or repulsing an assault; laying before us sometimes a dismal and melancholy accident, sometimes a delightful and unexpected adventure; in one place a beautiful, modest, discreet and reserved lady; in another, a Christian-like, brave, and courteous gentleman; here a boisterous, inhuman, boasting ruffian; there an affable, warlike, and wise prince, livelily expressing the fidelity and loyalty of subjects, generosity and bounty of sovereigns. He may no less, at times, make known his skill in astrology, cosmography, music, and policy; and if he pleases, he cannot want an opportunity of appearing knowing, even in necromancy. He may describe the subtlety of Ulysses, the piety of Æneas, the valor of Achilles, the misfortunes of Hector, the treachery of Sinon, the friendship of Euryalus, the liberality of Alexander, the valor of Cæsar, the clemency and sincerity of Trajan, the fidelity of Zopyrus, the prudence of Cato; and in fine, all those actions that may make up a complete hero, sometimes attributing them all to one person, and at other times dividing them among many. "This being so performed in a grateful style, and with ingenious invention, approaching as much as possible to truth, will doubtless compose so beautiful and various a work, that, when finished, its excellency and perfection must attain the best end of writing, which is at once to delight and instruct, as

526

I have said before: for the loose method practised in those books, gives the author liberty to play the epic, the lyric, and the dramatic poet, and to run through all the parts of poetry and rhetoric; for epics may be as well writ in prose as in verse."

XXI: CONTAINING A CONTINUATION OF THE CANON'S DISCOURSE UPON BOOKS OF KNIGHT-ERRANTRY, AND OTHER CURIOUS MATTERS

"You are much in the right, sir," replied the curate; "and therefore those who have hitherto published books of that kind, are the more to be blamed, for having had no regard to good sense, art, or rules, by the observation of which they might have made themselves as famous in prose, as the two princes of Greek and Latin poetry are in verse." "I must confess," said the canon, "I was once tempted to write a book of knight-errantry myself, observing all those rules; and, to speak the truth, I writ above one hundred pages, which, for the better trial whether they answered my expectation, I communicated to some learned and judicious men fond of those subjects, as well as to some of those ignorant persons, who only are delighted with extravagancies; and they all give me a satisfactory approbation. And yet I made no further progress, as well in regard I look upon it to be a thing no way agreeable with my profession, as because I am sensible the illiterate are much more numerous than the learned; and though it were of more weight to be commended by the small number of the wise, than scorned by the ignorant multitude, yet would I not expose myself to the confused judgment of the giddy vulgar, who principally are those who read such books. But the greatest motive I had to lay aside and think no more of finishing it, was the argument I formed to myself, deduced from the plays now usually acted: for, thought I, if plays now in use, as well those which are altogether of the poet's invention as those that are grounded upon history, be all of them, or, however, the greatest part, made up of most absurd extravagancies and incoherencies; things that have neither head nor foot, side nor bottom; and yet the multitude sees them with satisfaction, esteems and approves them, though they are so far from being good; and if the poets who write, and the players who act them, say they must be so contrived and no otherwise, because they please the generality of the audience; and if those which are regular and according to art, serve only to please half a score judicious persons who understand them, whilst the rest of the company cannot reach the contrivance, nor know anything of the matter; and therefore the poets and actors say, they had rather get their bread by the greater number, than the applause of the less: then may I conclude the same will be the success of this book; so that, when I have racked my brains to observe the rules, I shall reap no other advantage than to be laughed at for my pains. I have sometimes endeavored to convince the actors that they are deceived in their opinion, and that they will draw more company, and get more credit by regular plays, than by those preposterous representations now in use; but they are so positive in their humor, that no strength of reason, nor even demonstration, can beat this opinion into their heads. I remember I once was talking to one of those obstinate fellows: 'Do you not remember,' said I, 'that within these few years, three tragedies were acted in Spain, written by a famous poet of ours, which were so excellent, that they surprised, delighted, and raised the admiration of all that saw them, as well the ignorant and ordinary people as the judicious and men of quality; and the actors got more by those three, than by thirty of the best that have been writ since?' 'Doubtless, sir,' said the actor, 'you mean the tragedies of Isabella,

528

Phillis, and Alexandra': 'The very same,' I replied, 'and do you judge whether they observed the rules of the drama; and whether, by doing so, they lost anything of their esteem, or failed of pleasing all sorts of people. So that the fault lies not in the audience's desiring absurdities, but in those who know not how to give them anything else. Nor was there anything preposterous in several other plays: as for example, "Ingratitude Revenged," "Numancia," "The Amorous Merchant," and "The Favorable She-enemy": nor in some others, composed by judicious poets, to their honor and credit, and to the advantage of those that acted them.' Much more I added, which did indeed somewhat confound him, but no way satisfied or convinced him, so as to make him change his erroneous opinion." "You have hit upon a subject, sir," said the curate, "which has stirred up in me an old aversion I have for the plays now in use, which is not inferior to that I bear to books of knight-errantry. For whereas plays, according to the opinion of Cicero, ought to be mirrors of human life, patterns of good manners, and the very representatives of truth; those now acted are mirrors of absurdities, patterns of follies, and images of ribaldry. For instance, what can be more absurd, than for the same person to be brought on the stage a child in swaddling-bands, in the first scene of the first act; and to appear in the second grown a man? What can be more ridiculous than to represent to us a fighting old fellow, a cowardly youth, a rhetorical footman, a politic page, a churlish king, and an unpolished princess? What shall I say of their regard to the time in which those actions they represent, either might or ought to have happened, for I have seen a play, in which the first act began in Europe, the second was in Asia, and the third ended in Africa? Probably, if there had been another act, they would have carried it into America; and thus it would have been acted in the four parts of the world. But if imitation is to be a

529

principal part of the drama, how can any tolerable judgment be pleased, when representing an action that happened in the time of King Pepin or Charlemagne, they shall attribute it to the emperor Heraclius, and bring him in carrying the Cross into Jerusalem, and recovering the holy sepulcher, like Godfrey of Boulogne, there being a vast distance of time betwixt these actions? Thus they will clap together pieces of true history in a play of their own framing, and grounded upon fiction, mixing in it relations of things that have happened to different people, and in several ages. This they do without any contrivance that might make it appear probable, and with such visible mistakes as are altogether inexcusable; but the worst of it is, that there are idiots who look upon this as perfection, and think everything else to be mere pedantry. But if we look into the pious plays, what a multitude of false miracles shall we find in them? How many errors and contradictions? how often the miracles wrought by one saint attributed to another? Nay, even in the profane plays, they presume to work miracles upon the bare imagination and conceit that such a supernatural work, or a machine, as they call it, will be ornamental, and draw the common sort to see the play. These things are a reflection upon truth itself, a lessening and depreciation of history, and a reproach to all Spanish wits; because strangers, who are very exact in observing the rules of drama, look upon us as an ignorant and barbarous people, when they see the absurdities and extravagancies of our plays. Nor would it be any excuse to allege, that the principal design of all good governments, in permitting plays to be publicly acted, is to amuse the commonalty with some lawful recreation, and so to divert those ill humors which idleness is apt to breed: and since this end is attained by any sort of plays, whether good or bad, it is needless to prescribe laws to them, or oblige the poets or actors to compose and represent such as are strictly comformable

530

to the rules. To this I would answer, that this end would be infinitely better attained by good plays than by bad ones. He who sees a play that is regular, and answerable to the rules of poetry, is pleased with the comic part, informed by the serious, surprised at the variety of accidents, improved by the language, warned by the frauds, instructed by examples, incensed against vice, and enamored with virtue; for a good play must cause all these emotions in the soul of him that sees it, though he were never so insensible and unpolished. And it is absolutely impossible, that a play which has these qualifications, should not infinitely divert, satisfy and please beyond another that wants them, as most of them do which are now usually acted. Neither are the poets who wrote them in fault, for some of them are very sensible of their errors, and extremely capable of performing their duty; but plays being now altogether become venal, and a sort of merchandise, they say, and with reason, that the actors would not purchase them, unless they were of that stamp; and therefore the poet endeavors to suit the humor of the actors, who are to pay him for his labor. For proof of this, let any man observe that infinite number of plays, composed by an exuberant Spanish wit,[1] so full of gaiety and humor, in such elegant verse and choice language, so sententious, and to conclude, in such a majestic style, that his fame is spread through the universe: yet, because he suited himself to the fancy of the actors, many of his pieces have fallen short of their due perfection, though some have reached it. Others write plays so inconsiderately, that after they have appeared on the stage, the actors have been forced to fly and abscond, for fear of being punished, as it has often happened, for having affronted kings, and dishonored whole families. These, and many other ill-consequences, which I omit, would cease, by appointing an intelligent and

1 *Lopez de Vega, who wrote an incredible number of Spanish plays.*

judicious person at court to examine all plays before they were acted, that is, not only those which are represented at court, but throughout all Spain; so that, without his license, no magistrate should suffer any play to appear in public. Thus players would be careful to send their plays to court, and might then act them with safety, and those who wrote would be more circumspect, as stand-

ing in awe of an examiner that could judge of their works. By these means we should be furnished with good plays, and the end they are designed for would be attained, the people diverted, the Spanish wits esteemed, the actors safe, and the government spared the trouble of punishing them. And if the same person, or another, were entrusted to examine all the new books of knight-errantry, there is no doubt but some might be published with all that perfection you, sir, have mentioned, to the increase of eloquence in our language, to the utter extirpation of the old books, which would be borne down by the new; and for the innocent pastime, not only of idle persons, but even of those who have most employment; for the bow cannot always stand bent, nor can human frailty subsist without some lawful recreation."

The canon and curate were come to this period, when the barber, overtaking them, told the latter that this was the place he had pitched on for baiting, during the heat of the day. The canon, induced by the pleasantness of the valley, and the satisfaction he found in the curate's conversation, as well as to be further informed of Don Quixote, bore them company, giving order to some of his men to ride to the next inn, and if his sumpter-mule was arrived, to send him down provisions to that valley, where the coolness of the shade, and the beauty of the prospect gave him such a fair invitation to dine; and that they should make much of themselves and their mules with what the inn could afford.

In the meantime Sancho having disengaged himself from the curate and barber, and finding an opportunity to speak to his master alone, he brushed up to the cage where the Knight sat. "That I may clear my conscience, sir," said he, "it is fitting that I tell you the plain truth of your enchantment here. Who, would you think now, are these two fellows that ride with their faces covered? Even the parson of our parish and the barber; none else, I will assure you, sir. And they are in a plot against you, out of mere spite because your deeds will be more famous than theirs. This being supposed, it follows that you are not enchanted, but only cozened and abused; and if you will but answer me one question fairly and squarely, you shall find this out to be a palpable cheat, and that there is no enchantment in the case, but merely your senses turned topsy turvy."

"Ask me what questions you please, dear Sancho," said the Knight, "and I will as willingly resolve them. But, for thy assertion that these who guard us are my old companions the curate and the barber, it is illusion all. The power of magic indeed, as it has an

533

art to clothe anything in any shape, may have dressed these demons in their appearances to infatuate thy sense, and draw thee into such a labyrinth of confusion that even Theseus's clue could not extricate thee out of it; and this with a design, perhaps, to plunge me deeper into doubts, and make me endanger my understanding, in searching into the strange contrivance of my enchantment, which in every circumstance is so different from all I ever read. Therefore rest satisfied that these are no more what thou imaginest, than I am a Turk. But now to thy questions; propose them, and I will endeavor to answer."

"Bless me," said Sancho, "this is madness upon madness; but, since it is so, answer me one question. Tell me, as you hope to be delivered out of this cage here, and as you hope to find yourself in my lady Dulcinea's arms, when you least think on it; as you—" "Conjure me no more," answered Don Quixote, "but ask freely, for I have promised to answer punctually." "That is what I want," said Sancho, "and you must tell me the truth, neither more nor less, upon the honor of your knighthood." "Pray thee, no more of your preliminaries or preambles," cried Don Quixote, "I tell thee I answer to a tittle." "Then," said Sancho, "I ask, with reverence be it spoken, whether your worship, since your being caged up, or enchanted, if you will have it so, has not had a motion, more or less, as a man may say?" "I understand not that phrase," answered the Knight. "Heyday," quoth Sancho, "do not you know what I mean? Why there is never a child in our country, that understands the Christ-cross-row, but can tell you. I mean, have you a mind to do what another cannot do for you?" "O, now I understand thee, Sancho," said the Knight; "and to answer directly to thy question, positively yes, very often; and therefore pray thee help me out of this strait; for, to be free with you, I am not altogether so sweet and clean as I could wish."

"Ah! sir," said Sancho, "have I caught you at last? This is what I wanted to know from my heart and soul. Come, sir, you cannot deny, that when anybody is out of sorts, so as not to eat, or drink, or sleep, or do any natural occasions that you guess, then we say commonly they are bewitched or so: from whence may be gathered, that those who can eat their meat, drink their drink, speak when they are spoken to, and go to the back-side when they have occasion for it, are not bewitched or enchanted." "Your conclusion is good," answered Don Quixote, "as to one sort of enchantment, but as I said to thee, there is variety of enchantments, and the changes in them, through the alterations of times and customs, branch them into so many parts, that there is no arguing from what has been to what may be now. For my part, I am verily persuaded of my enchantment, and this suppresses any uneasiness in my conscience, which might arise on suggestion to the contrary. To see myself thus dishonorably borne about in a cage, and withheld like a coward from the great offices of my function, when at this hour perhaps hundreds of wretches may want my assistance, would be unsupportable, if I were not enchanted." "Yet, for all that, your worship should try to get your heels at liberty," said Sancho. "Come, sir, let me alone, I will set you free, I warrant you; and then get you on trusty Rozinante's back, and a fig for them all. The poor thing here jogs on as drooping and heartless, as if he were enchanted too. Take my advice for once now, and if things do not go as your heart could wish, you have time enough to creep into your cage again, and on the word of a loyal squire I will go in with you, and be content to be enchanted as long as you please."

"I commit the care of my freedom to thy management," said Don Quixote. "Lay hold on the opportunity, friend Sancho, and

thou shalt find me ready to be governed in all particulars; though I am still afraid thou wilt find thy cunning strangely overreached in thy pretended discovery." The Knight and squire had thus laid their plot. When they reached the place that the canon, curate and barber had pitched upon to alight in, the cage was taken down, and the oxen unyoked to graze; when Sancho, addressing the curate, "Pray," said he, "will you do so much, as let my lord and master come out a little to slack a point, or else the prison will not be so clean as the presence of so worthy a Knight as my master requires." The curate understanding him, answered that he would comply, but that he feared Don Quixote, finding himself once at liberty, would give them the slip. "I will be bail for him," said Sancho, "body for body, sir." "And I," said the canon, "upon his bare parole of honor." "That you shall have," said the Knight; "besides, you need no security beyond the power of art, for enchanted bodies have no power to dispose of themselves, nor to move from one place to another without permission of the necromancer in whose charge they are: the magical charms might rivet them for three whole centuries to one place, and fetch them back swift as the wind, should the enchanted have fled to some other region." Lastly, as a most convincing argument for his release, he urged, that unless they would free him, or get further off, he should be necessitated to offend their sense of smelling. They guessed his meaning presently, and set him at large; and the first use he made of it was to stretch his benumbed limbs three or four times; then marching up to Rozinante, slapped him twice or thrice on the buttocks: "I trust in Heaven, thou flower and glory of horse-flesh," said he, "that we shall soon be restored to our former circumstances: I mounted on thy back, and thou between my legs, while I exercise the function for which Heaven has bestowed me on the world." Then walking a little aside with Sancho, he returned, after a convenient stay, much lighter in body and mind, and very full of his squire's project.

The canon gazed on him, admiring his unparalleled sort of madness, the rather because in all his words and answers he displayed an excellent judgment; and, as we have already observed, he only raved when the discourse fell upon knight-errantry: which moving the canon to compassion, when they had all seated themselves on the grass, expecting the coming of his sumpter-mule: "Is it possible, sir," said he, addressing himself to Don Quixote, "that the unhappy reading of books of knight-errantry should have such an influence over you as to destroy your reason, making you believe you are now enchanted, and many other such extravagances, as remote from truth as truth itself is from falsehood? How is it possible that human sense should conceive there ever were in the world such multitudes of famous knights-errant, so many emperors of Trebizond, so many Amadises, Felixmartes of Hyrcania, palfreys, rambling damsels, serpents, monsters, giants, unheard-of adventures, so many sorts of enchantments, so many battles, terrible encounters, pompous habits and tournaments, amorous princesses,

537

earls, squires and jesting dwarfs, so many love-letters and gallantries, so many Amazonian ladies, and, in short, such an incredible number of extravagant passages, as are contained in books of knight-errantry? As for my own particular, I confess, that while I read them, and do not reflect that they are nothing but falsehood and folly, they give me some satisfaction; but I no sooner remember what they are, but I cast the best of them from me, and would deliver them up to the flames if I had a fire near me; as well deserving that fate, because, like impostors, they act contrary to the common course of nature. They are like broachers of new sects, and a new manner of living, that seduce the ignorant vulgar to give credit to all their absurdities: nay, they presume to disturb the brains of ingenious and well-bred gentlemen, as appears by the effect they have wrought on your judgment, having reduced you to such a condition, that it is necessary to shut you up in a cage, and carry you in a cart drawn by oxen, like some lion or tiger that is carried about from town to town to be shown. Have pity on yourself, good Don Quixote, retrieve your lost judgment, and make use of those abilities Heaven has blest you with, applying your excellent talent to some other study, which may be safer for your conscience, and more for your honor: but if, led away by your natural inclination, you will read books of heroism and great exploits, read in the Holy Scripture the Book of Judges, where you will find wonderful truths and glorious actions not to be questioned. Lusitania had a Viratus, Rome a Cæsar, Carthage an Hannibal, Greece an Alexander, Castile a Count Fernando Gonzalez,[1] Valencia a Cid, Andalusia a Gonzalo Fernandez, Estremadura a Diego Garcia de Paredes, Xerez a Graci Perez de Vargas, Toledo a Garcilasso, and Seville a Don Manuel de Leon; the reading of whose brave actions diverts, instructs, and surprises the most judi-

[1] *Fernando Gonzalez, Cid, and the rest here mentioned were Spanish commanders of note, of whom as many fables have been written, as there ever were of knights-errant.*

cious readers. This will be a study worthy your talent, and by which you will become well read in history, in love with virtue, knowing in goodness, improved in manners, brave without rashness, and cautious without cowardice; all of which will redound to the glory of God, your own advancement, and the honor of the province of La Mancha, whence I understand you derive your origins." Don Quixote listened with great attention to the canon's discourse, and perceiving he had done, after he had fixed his eyes on him for a considerable space: "Sir," said he, "all your discourse, I find, tends to signify to me, there never were any knights-errant; that all the books of knight-errantry are false, fabulous, useless, and prejudicial to the public; that I have done ill in reading, erred in believing, and been much to blame in imitating them, by taking upon me the most painful profession of chivalry. And you deny that ever there were any Amadises of Gaul, or Greece, or any of those knights mentioned in those books." "Even as you have said, sir," quoth the canon. "You also were pleased to add," continued Don Quixote, "that those books had been very hurtful to me, having deprived me of my reason, and reduced me to be carried in a cage; that therefore it would be for my advantage, to take up in time, and apply myself to the reading of other books, where I may find more truth, more pleasure, and better instruction." "You are in the right," said the canon. "Then I am satisfied," replied Don Quixote, "you yourself are the man that raves and is enchanted, since you have thus boldly blasphemed against a truth so universally received, that whosoever presumes to contradict it, as you have done, deserves the punishment you would inflict on those books, which in reading offend and tire you. For it were as easy to persuade the world that the sun does not enlighten, the frost cool, and the earth bear us, as that there never was an Amadis, or any of the other adventurous knights, whose actions are the subjects of so many histories. What mortal can persuade another, that there

539

is no truth in what is recorded of the Infanta Floripes, and Guy of Burgundy: as also Fierabras at the bridge of Mantible, in the reign of Charlemagne? which passages, I dare swear, are as true as that now it is day. But, if this be false, you may as well say there was no Hector, nor Achilles; nor a Trojan war, nor Twelve Peers of France, nor a King Arthur of Britain, who is now converted into a crow, and hourly expected in his kingdom. Some also may presume to say, that the history of Guarino Mezquino, and that the attempt of St. Grial are both false; that the amours of Sir Tristram and Queen Iseo are apocryphal, as well as those of Guinever and Sir Lancelot of the Lake; whereas there are people living who can almost remember they have seen the old Lady Quintaniona, who had the best hand at filling a glass of wine of any woman in all Britain. This I am so well assured of, that I can remember my grandmother, by my father's side, whenever she saw an old waiting-woman with her reverend veil, used to say to me, 'Look yonder, grandson, there is a woman like the old Lady Quintaniona'; whence I infer she knew her, or at least had seen her picture. Now, who can deny the veracity of the history of Pierres, and the lovely Magalona, when to this day the pin, with which the brave Pierres turned his wooden horse that carried him through the air, is to be seen in the king's armory? Which pin is somewhat bigger than the pole of a coach, by the same token it stands just by Babieca's saddle. At Roncesvalles they keep Orlando's horn, which is as big as a great beam; whence it follows, that there were Twelve Peers, that there were such men as Pierres, and the famous Cid, besides many other adventurous knights, whose names are in the mouths of all people. You may as well tell me that the brave Portuguese John de Merlo, was no knight-errant; that he did not go into Burgundy, where, in the city of Ras, he fought the famous Moses Pierre, Lord of Charney, and in the city of Basil, Moses Henry de Remestan, coming off in both victorious, and loaded with honor. You may deny the adventures

540

and combats of the heroic Spaniards, Pedro Barba and Gutierrez Quixada (from whose male-line I am lineally descended) who in Burgundy overcame the sons of the Earl of St. Paul. You may tell me that Don Ferdinand de Guevara never went into Germany to seek adventures, where he fought Sir George, a knight of the Duke of Austria's court. You may say the tilting of Suero de Quinones del Paso, and the exploits of Moses Lewis de Falses, against Don Gonzalo de Guzman, Castilian knight, are mere fables; and so of many other brave actions performed by Christian knights, as well Spaniards as foreigners; which are so authentic and true, that I say it over again, he who denies them has neither sense nor reason." The canon was much astonished at the medley Don Quixote made of truths and fables, and no less to see how well read he was in all things relating to the achievements of knights-errant. "And therefore I cannot deny, sir," answered he, "but that there is some truth in what you have said, especially in what relates to the Spanish knights-errant; and I will grant there were Twelve Peers of France, yet I will not believe they performed all those actions Archbishop Turpin ascribes to them: I rather imagine they were brave gentlemen made choice of by the kings of France, and called Peers, as being all equal in valor and quality; or, if they were not, at least they ought to have been so; and these composed a sort of military order; like those of St. Jago, or Calatrava among us, into which all that are admitted are supposed, or ought to be, gentlemen of birth and known valor. And as now we say 'a knight of St. John, or of Alcantara,' so in those times they said, 'a knight, one of the Twelve Peers,' because there were but twelve of this military order. Nor is it to be doubted but there were such men as Bernardo del Carpio [2] and the Cid, yet we have reason to question whether ever they performed those great exploits that are ascribed to them. As to the pin, Count Pierres's pin which you spoke of, and

[2] *It is a question whether there ever was such a man as Bernardo del Carpio.*

which you say stands by Babieca's saddle, I own my ignorance, and confess I was so short-sighted, that though I saw the saddle, yet I did not perceive the pin, which is somewhat strange, if it be so large as you describe it." "It is without doubt," replied Don Quixote, "by the same token they say it is kept in a leathern case to keep it from rusting." "That may very well be," said the canon; "but upon the word of a priest, I do not remember I ever saw it: yet grant it were there, that does not enforce the belief of so many Amadises, nor of such a multitude of knights-errant as the world talks of; nor is there any reason so worthy a person, so judicious, and so well-qualified as you are, should imagine there is any truth in the wild extravagancies contained in all the fabulous nonsensical books of knight-errantry."

XXIII: THE NOTABLE DISPUTE BETWEEN THE CANON AND DON QUIXOTE; WITH OTHER MATTERS

"Very well," cried Don Quixote, "then all those books must be fabulous, though licensed by kings, approved by the examiners, read with general satisfaction, and applauded by the better sort and the meaner, rich and poor, learned and unlearned, gentry and commonalty; and, in short, by all sorts of persons of what state and condition soever; and though they carry such an appearance of truth, setting down the father, mother, country, kindred, age, place and actions to a tittle, and day by day, of the knight and knights of whom they treat? For shame, sir," continued he, "forbear uttering such blasphemies; and, believe me, in this I advise you to behave yourself as becomes a man of sense, or else read them and see what satisfaction you will receive. As for instance, pray tell

542

me, can there be anything more delightful, than to read a lively description, which, as it were, brings before your eyes the following adventure? A vast lake of boiling pitch, in which an infinite number of serpents, snakes, crocodiles, and other sorts of fierce and terrible creatures, are swimming and traversing backwards and forwards, appears to a knight-errant's sight. Then from the midst of the lake a most doleful voice is heard to say these words: 'O knight, whoever thou art, who gazest on this dreadful lake, if thou wilt purchase the bliss concealed under these dismal waters, make known thy valor by casting thyself into the midst of these black burning surges; for unless thou dost so, thou art not worthy to behold the mighty wonders enclosed in the seven castles of the seven fairies, that are seated under those gloomy waves.' And no sooner have the last accents of the voice reached the knight's ear, but he, without making any further reflection, or considering the danger to which he exposes himself, and even without laying aside his ponderous armor, only recommending himself to Heaven and to his lady, plunges headlong into the middle of the burning lake; and when least he imagines it, or can guess where he shall stop, he finds himself on a sudden in the midst of verdant fields, to which the Elysian bear no comparison. There the sky appears to him more transparent, and the sun seems to shine with a redoubled brightness. Next he discovers a most delightful grove made up of beautiful shady trees, whose verdure and variety regale his sight, while his ears are ravished with the wild and yet melodious notes of an infinite number of pretty, painted birds, that hop and bill, and sport themselves on the twining boughs. Here he spies a pleasant rivulet, which, through its flowery banks, glides along over the brightest sand, and remurmurs over the whitest pebbles that bedimple its smooth surface, while that other, through its liquid crystal, feasts the eye with a prospect of gold and orient pearl.

There he perceives an artificial fountain, formed of parti-colored jasper and polished marble; and hard by another, contrived in grotesque, where the small cockle-shells, placed in orderly confusion among the white and yellow shells, and mixed with pieces of bright crystal and counterfeit emeralds, yield a delectable sight; so that art imitating nature, seems here to outdo her. At a distance, on a sudden, he casts his eyes upon a strong castle, or stately palace, whose walls are of massy gold, the battlements of diamonds, and gates of hyacinths; in short, its structure is so wonderful, that though all the materials are no other than diamonds, carbuncles, rubies, pearls, gold and emeralds, yet the workmanship exceed them in value. But having seen all this, can anything be so charming as to behold a numerous train of beautiful damsels come out of the castle in such glorious and costly apparel, as would be endless for me to describe, were I to relate these things as they are to be found in history? Then to see the beauty that seems the chief of all the damsels, take the bold knight, who cast himself into the burning lake, by the hand, and, without speaking one word, lead him into a sumptuous palace, where he is caused to strip naked as he was born, then put into a delicious bath, and perfumed with precious essences and odoriferous oils; after which he puts on a fine shirt, deliciously scented; and this done, another damsel throws over his shoulders a magnificent robe, worth at least a whole city, if not more. What a sight is it, when in the next place they lead him into another room of state, where he finds the tables so orderly covered, that he is surprised and astonished? There they pour over his hands water distilled from amber and odoriferous flowers: he is seated in an ivory chair; and while all the damsels that attend him observe a profound silence, such variety of dainties is served up, and all so incomparably dressed, that his appetite is at a stand, doubting on which to satisfy its desire; at the same time his ears are sweetly

544

entertained with variety of excellent music, none perceiving who makes it, or from whence it comes. But, above all, what shall we say to see, after the dinner is ended and tables taken away, the knight left leaning back in his chair, perhaps picking his teeth, as is usual; and then another damsel, much more beautiful than any of the former, comes unexpectedly into the room, and sitting down by the knight, begins to inform him what castle that is, and how she is enchanted in it; with many other particulars, which surprise the knight, and astonish those that read his history. I will enlarge no more upon this matter, since from what has been said, it may sufficiently be inferred, that the reading of any passage in any history of knight-errantry, must be very delightful and surprising to the reader. And do you, good sir, believe me, and as I said to you before, read those books, which you may find will banish all melancholy, if you are troubled with it, and sweeten your disposition if it be harsh. This I can say for myself, that since my being a knight-errant, I am brave, courteous, bountiful, well-bred, generous, civil, bold, affable, patient, a sufferer of hardships, imprisonment and enchantments: and though I have so lately been shut up in a cage like a madman, I expect through the valor of my arm, Heaven favoring, and fortune not opposing my designs, to be a king of some kingdom in a very few days, that so I may give proofs of my innate gratitude and liberality. For, on my word, sir, a poor man is incapable of exerting his liberality, though he be naturally never so well inclined. Now, that gratitude which only consists in wishes, may be said to be dead, as faith without good works is dead. Therefore it is, I wish fortune would soon offer some opportunity for me to become an emperor, that I might give proofs of my generosity, by advancing my friends, but especially this poor Sancho Panza my squire, who is the most harmless fellow in the world; and I would willingly give him an earldom, which I have long since promised him, but that I fear he has not sense and judgment enough to manage it."

Sancho, hearing his master's last words: "Well, well, sir," said he, "never do you trouble your head about that matter; all you have to do is to get me this same earldom, and let me alone to manage it: I can do as my betters have done before me, I can put in a deputy or a servant, that shall take all trouble off my hands, while I, as a great man should, loll at my ease, receive my rents, mind no business, live merrily, and so let the world rub for Sancho." "As to the management of your revenue," said the canon, "a deputy or steward may do well, friend: but the lord himself is obliged to stir in the administration of justice, to which there is not only an honest sincere intention required, but a judicious head also to distinguish nicely, conclude justly, and choose wisely; for if this be wanting in the principal, all will be wrong in the medium and end." "I do not understand your philosophy," quoth Sancho; "all I said, and I will say it again, is, that I wish I had as good an earldom as I could govern; for I have as great a soul as another man, and as great a body as most men: and the first thing I would do in my government, I would have nobody to control me, I would be absolute: and who but I: now, he that is absolute, can do what he likes; he that can do what he likes, can take his pleasure; he that can take his pleasure, can be content; and he that can be content, has no more to desire; so the matter is over, and come what will come, I am satisfied: if an island, welcome; if no island, fare it well; we shall see ourselves in no worse condition, as one blind man said to another." "This is no ill reasoning of yours, friend," said the canon, "though there is much more to be said on this topic of earldoms, than you imagine." "Undoubtedly," said Don Quixote; "but I suit my actions to the example of Amadis de Gaul, who made his squire Gandalin earl of the Firm Island; which is a fair precedent for preferring Sancho to the same dignity to which his merit also

546

lays an unquestionable claim." The canon stood amazed at Don Quixote's methodical and orderly madness, in describing the adventure of the Knight of the Lake, and the impression made on him by the fabulous conceits of the books he had read; as likewise at Sancho's simplicity in so eagerly contending for his earldom, which made the whole company very good sport.

By this time the canon's servants had brought the provision, and spreading a carpet on the grass, under the shady trees, they sat down to dinner; when presently they heard the tinkling of a little bell among the copse close by them, and immediately afterwards they saw bolt out of the thicket a very pretty she-goat, speckled all over with black, white, and brown spots, and a goatherd running after it; who, in his familiar dialect, called it to stay and return to the fold; but the fugitive ran towards the company frightened and panting, and stopped close by them, as if it had begged their protection. The goatherd overtaking it, caught it by the horns, and,

547

in a chiding way, as if the goat understood his resentments, "You little wanton nanny," said he, "you spotted elf, what has made you trip it so much of late? what wolf has scared you thus, hussy? Tell me, little fool, what is the matter? But the cause is plain; thou art a female, and therefore never canst be quiet: curse on thy freakish humors, and all theirs whom thou so much resembleth; turn back, my love, turn back; and though thou canst not be content with thy fold, yet there thou mayst be safe among the rest of thy fellows; for if thou, that shouldst guide and direct the flock, lovest wandering thus, what must they do? what will become of them?" The goatherd's talk to his goat was entertaining to the company, especially to the canon, who, calling to him, "Pray thee, honest fellow," said he, "have a little patience, and let your goat take its liberty awhile; for since it is a female, as you say, she will follow her natural inclination the more for your striving to confine it; come then, and take a bit and a glass of wine with us, you may be better humored after that." He then reached him the leg of a cold rabbit, and, ordering him a glass of wine, the goatherd drank it off, and returning thanks, was pacified. "Gentlemen," said he, "I would not have you think me a fool, because I talk so seriously to this senseless animal, for my words bear a mysterious meaning: I am indeed, as you see, rustical and unpolished, though not so ignorant, but that I converse with men as well as brutes." "That is no miracle," said the curate; "for I have known the woods breed learned men, and simple sheepcoats contain philosophers." "At least," said the goatherd, "they harbor men that have some knowledge of the world: and to make good this truth, if I thought not the offer impertinent, or my company troublesome, you should hear an accident which but too well confirms what you have said." "For my part," answered Don Quixote, "I will hear you attentively, because, methinks, your coming has something in it that looks like an adventure of knight-errantry; and I dare answer, the whole company will not so much bring their parts in question, as to refuse to hear a story so pleasing, surprising and amusing, as I fancy yours will prove. Then pray thee, friend, begin, for we will all give you our attention." "You must excuse me for one," said Sancho, "I must have a word or two in private with this same pasty at yon little brook; for I design to fill my belly for tomorrow and the next day, having often heard my master Don Quixote say, that whenever a knight-errant's squire finds good belly-timber, he must fall to and feed till his sides are ready to burst, because they may happen to be bewildered in a thick wood for five or six days together; so that, if a man has not his belly full beforehand, or his wallet well provided, he may chance to be crow's meat himself, as many times it falls out." "You are in the right, Sancho," said the Knight; "but I have, for my part, satisfied my bodily appetite, and now want only refreshment for my mind, which I hope this honest fellow's story will afford me." All the company agreed with Don Quixote: the goatherd, then stroking his pretty goat once or twice: "Lie down, thou speckled fool," said he, "lie by me here; for we shall have time enough to return home." The creature seemed to understand him; for, as soon as her master sat down, she stretched herself quietly by his side, and looked up in his face, as if she would let him know that she minded what he said; and then he began thus:

XXIV: THE GOATHERD'S ENTERTAINING TALE

"About three leagues from this valley there is a village, which, though small, yet is one of the richest hereabouts. In it there lived a farmer in very great esteem; and, though it is common for the rich to be respected, yet was this person more considered for his virtue, than for the wealth he possessed. But what he accounted himself happiest in, was a daughter of such extraordinary beauty, prudence, wit, and virtue, that all who knew or beheld her, could not but admire to see how Heaven and nature had done their utmost to embellish her. When she was but little she was handsome, till at the age of sixteen she was most completely beautiful. The fame of her beauty began to extend to the neighboring villages; but why say I neighboring villages? it extended to the remotest cities, and entered the palaces of kings, and the ears of all manner of persons; who from all parts flocked to see her, as something rare, or as a sort of prodigy. Her father was strictly careful of her, nor was she less careful of herself; for there are no guards, bolts or locks, which preserve a young woman like her own care and caution. The father's riches and the daughter's beauty drew a great many, as well strangers as inhabitants of that country, to sue for her in marriage; but such was the vast number of the pretenders, as did but the more confound and divide the old man in his choice, upon whom to bestow so valuable a treasure. Among the crowd of her admirers was I; having good reason to hope for success, from the knowledge her father had of me, being a native of the same place, of a good family, and in the flower of my years, of a considerable estate, and not to be despised for my understanding. With the very same advantages, there was another person of our village who made court to her at the same time. This put the father to a stand, and held him in suspense, till his daughter should declare in favor of one of us: to bring this affair therefore to the speedier issue, he resolved to acquaint Leandra, for so was this fair one called, that since we were equals in all things, he left her entirely free to choose which of us was most agreeable to herself—an example worthy of being imitated by all parents, who have any regard for their children. I do not mean that they should be allowed to choose in things mean or mischievous; but only that proposing to them ever those things which are good, they should be allowed in them to gratify their inclination. I do not know how Leandra approved of this proposal;

550

this I only know, that her father put us both off, with the excuse of his daughter's being too young to be yet disposed of; and that he treated us both in such general terms, as could neither well please nor displease us. My rival's name is Anselmo, mine Eugenio, for it is necessary you should know the names of the persons concerned in this tragedy; the conclusion of which, though depending yet, may easily be perceived likely to be unfortunate. About that time there came to our village one Vincent de la Rosa, the son of a poor laboring man of the neighborhood. This Vincent came out of Italy, having been a soldier there, and in other foreign parts. When he was but twelve years old, a captain that happened to pass by here with his company, took him out of this country, and at the end of another twelve years he returned hither, habited like a soldier, all gay and glorious, in a thousand various colors, bedecked with a thousand toys of crystal, and chains of steel. Today he put on one piece of finery, tomorrow another; but all false, counterfeit, and worthless. The country people, who by nature are malicious, and who, living in idleness are still more inclined to malice, observed this presently, and, counting all his fine things, they found that indeed he had but three suits of clothes, which were of a very different color with the stockings and garters belonging to them; yet did he manage them with so many tricks and inventions, that if one had not counted them, one would have sworn he had above ten suits, and above twenty plumes of feathers. Let it not seem impertinent that I mention this particular of his clothes and trinkets, since so much of the story depends upon it. Seating himself upon a bench, under a large spreading poplar-tree, which grows in our street, he used to entertain us with his exploits, while we stood gaping and listening at the wonders he recounted: there was not that country, as he said, upon the face of the earth, which he had not seen, nor battle which he had not been engaged in; he had killed more Moors, for his own share, than were in Morocco and Tunis together; and had fought more duels than Gante, Luna, Diego Garcia de Paredes,[1] or a thousand others that he named, yet in all of them had the better, and never got a scratch, or lost a drop of blood. Then again he pretended to show us the scars of wounds he had received, which though they were not to be perceived, yet he gave us to understand they were so many musket-shots, which he had got in several skirmishes and encounters. In short, he treated all his equals with unparalleled arrogance; and even to those who knew the meanness of his birth, he did not stick to affirm, that his own arm was his father, his actions were his pedigree, and that except as to his being a soldier, he owed no part of his quality to the king himself, and that in being a soldier, he was as good as the king.

"Besides these assumed accomplishments, he was a piece of a musician, and could thrum a guitar a little, but what his excellency chiefly lay in was poetry; and so fond was he of showing his parts that way, that upon every trifling occasion, he was sure to make a copy of verses a league and a half long. This soldier whom I have described, this Vincent de la Rosa, this hero, this gallant, this musician, this poet, was often seen and viewed by Leandra, from a window of her house which looked into the street; she was struck with the tinsel of his dress; she was charmed with his verses, of which he took care to disperse a great many copies; her ears were pleased with the exploits he related of himself; and, in short, as the devil would have it, she fell in love with him, before ever he had the confidence to make his addresses to her: and, as in all affairs of love, that is the most easily managed, where the lady's affection is pre-engaged, so was it here no hard thing for Leandra and Vincent to have frequent meetings to concert their matters; and before ever any one of her many suitors had the least suspicion of her inclination, she had gratified it; and leaving her father's house (for

1 *Spaniards famous for dueling.*

she had no mother) had run away with this soldier, who came off with greater triumph in this enterprise than in any of the rest he made his boasts of. The whole village was surprised at this accident, as was everyone that heard it. I was amazed, Anselmo distracted, her father in tears, her relations outraged, justice is demanded; a party with officers is sent out, who traverse the roads, search every wood, and, at three days' end, find the poor fond Leandra in a cave of one of the mountains, naked to her shirt, and robbed of a great deal of money and jewels which she took from home. They bring and present her to her father; upon inquiry made into the cause of her misfortune, she confessed ingenuously, that Vincent de la Rosa had deceived her, and upon promise of marriage had prevailed with her to leave her father's house, with the assurance of carrying her to the richest and most delicious city of the world, which was Naples; that she foolishly had given credit to him, and robbing her father, had put herself into his hands the first night she was missed: that he carried her up a steep wild craggy mountain, and put her in that cave where she was found. In fine, she said, that though he had rifled her of all she had, yet he had never attempted her honor; but leaving her in that manner he fled. It was no easy matter to make any of us entertain a good opinion of the soldier's continence; but she affirmed it with so many repeated asseverations, that in some measure it served to comfort her father in his affliction, who valued nothing so much as his daughter's reputation. The very same day that Leandra appeared again, she also disappeared from us, for her father immediately clapped her up in a monastery, in a town not far off, in hopes that time might wear away something of her disgrace. Those who were not interested in Leandra, excused her on account of her youth. But those who were acquainted with her wit and sense, did not attribute her miscarriage to her ignorance, but to the levity and vanity of mind natural to womankind. Since the confinement of

553

Leandra, Anselmo's eyes could never meet with an object which could give him either ease or pleasure: I too could find nothing but what looked sad and gloomy to me in the absence of Leandra. Our melancholy increased, as our patience decreased: we cursed a thousand times the soldier's finery and trinkets, and railed at the father's want of precaution; at last we agreed, Anselmo and I, to leave the village, and retire to this valley, where, he feeding a large flock of sheep, and I as large a herd of goats, all our own, we pass our time under the trees, giving vent to our passions, singing in consort the praises or reproaches of the beauteous Leandra, or else, sighing alone, make our complaints to Heaven on our misfortune. In imitation of us, a great many more of Leandra's lovers have come hither into these steep and craggy mountains, and are alike employed; and so many there are of them, that the place seems to be turned to the old Arcadia we read of. On the top of that hill there is such a number of shepherds and their cottages, that there is no part of it in which is not to be heard the name of Leandra. This man curses and calls her wanton and lascivious, another calls her light and fickle; one acquits and forgives her, another arraigns and condemns her; one celebrates her beauty, another rails at her ill qualities; in short, all blame, but all adore her: nay, so far does this extravagance prevail, that here are those who complain of her disdain who never spoke to her; and others who are jealous of favors which she never granted to any: for, as I intimated before, her inclination was not known before her disgrace. There is not a hollow place of a rock, a bank of a brook, or a shady grove, where there is not some or other of these amorous shepherds telling their doleful stories to the air and winds. Echo has learnt to repeat the name of Leandra, Leandra all the hills resound, the brooks murmur Leandra, and it is Leandra that holds us all enchanted, hoping without hope, and fearing without knowing what we fear. Of all these foolish people, the person who shows the least, and yet has the most sense, is my rival Anselmo; who, forgetting all other causes of complaint, complains only of her absence, and to his lute, which he touches to admiration, he joins his voice in verses of his own composing, which declare the greatness of his genius. For my part, I take another course,—I think a better, I am sure an easier,—which is to say all the ill things I can of women's levity, inconstancy, their broken vows and vain deceitful promises, their fondness of show and disregard of merit. This, gentlemen, was the occasion of those words, which, at my coming hither, I addressed to this goat; for being a she, I hate her, though she is the best of my herd. This is the story which I promised to tell you; if you have thought it too long, I shall endeavor to requite your patience in anything I can serve you. Hard by is my cottage, where I have some good fresh milk and excellent cheese, with several sorts of fruits, which I hope you will find agreeable both to the sight and taste."

XXV: OF THE COMBAT BETWEEN DON QUIXOTE AND THE GOATHERD: WITH THE RARE ADVENTURE OF THE PENITENTS, WHICH THE KNIGHT HAPPILY ACCOMPLISHED WITH THE SWEAT OF HIS BROWS

The goatherd's story was mightily liked by the whole company, especially by the canon, who particularly minded the manner of his relating it, that had more of a scholar and gentleman, than of a rude goatherd; which made him conclude the curate had reason to say, that even the mountains bred scholars and men of sense. They all made large proffers of their friendship and service to Eugenio, but Don Quixote exceeded them all, and addressing himself to him: "Were I," said he, "at this time in a capacity of undertaking any adventure, I would certainly begin from this very moment to serve you. I would soon release Leandra out of the nunnery, where undoubtedly she is detained against her will; and, in spite of all the opposition that could be made by the lady abbess and all her adherents, I would return her to your hands, that you might have the sole disposal of her, so far, I mean, as is consistent with the laws of knighthood, which expressly forbid that any man should offer the least violence to a damsel; yet, I trust in Heaven, that the power of a friendly magician will prevail against the force of a malicious enchanter; and, whenever this shall happen, you may assure yourself of my favor and assistance, to which I am obliged by my profession, that enjoins me to relieve the oppressed."

The goatherd, who till then had not taken the least notice of Don Quixote in particular, now looking earnestly on him, and finding his dismal countenance and wretched habit were no great encouragement for him to expect a performance of such mighty matters, whispered to the barber who sat next him: "Pray, sir," said he, "who is this man that talks so extravagantly? For I protest I never saw so strange a figure in all my life." "Whom can you imagine it should be," replied the barber, "but the famous Don Quixote de la Mancha, the establisher of justice, the avenger of injuries, the protector of damsels, the terror of giants, and the invincible gainer of battles." "The account you give of this person," returned the goatherd, "is much like what we read in romances and books of chivalry of those doughty Dons, who, for their mighty prowess and achievements, were called knights-errant; and therefore I dare say you do but jest, and that this gentleman's brains have deserted their quarters."

"Thou art an impudent, insolent varlet," cried Don Quixote; "it is thy paper skull is full of empty rooms: I have more brains than the prostitute thy mother had about her when she carried thy lump of nonsense in her womb." With that, snatching up a loaf that was near him, he struck the goatherd so furious a blow with it, that he almost leveled his nose with his face. The other, not accustomed to such salutations, no sooner perceived how scurvily he was treated, but without any respect to the tablecloth, napkins, or to those who were eating, he leaped furiously on Don Quixote, and grasping him by the throat with both his hands, had certainly strangled him, had not Sancho Panza come in that very nick of time, and seizing him fast behind, pulled him backwards on the table, bruising dishes, breaking glasses, spilling and overturning all that lay upon it. Don Quixote, seeing himself freed, fell violently again upon the goatherd, who, all besmeared with blood, and trampled to pieces under Sancho's feet, groped here and there for some fork or knife to take a fatal revenge; but the canon and curate took care to prevent his purpose, and, in the meanwhile, by the barber's contrivance, the goatherd got Don Quixote under him, on whom he let fall such a tempest of blows, as caused as great a shower of blood to pour from the poor Knight's face as had streamed from his own. The canon and curate were ready to burst with laughing, the officers danced and jumped at the sport, everyone cried "Hullo!" as men do when two dogs are snarling or fighting; Sancho Panza alone was vexed, fretted himself to death, and raved like a madman because he could not get from one of the canon's serving-men, who kept him from assisting his master. In short, all were exceedingly merry, except the bloody combatants, who were mauling one another most miserably, when on a sudden they heard the sound of a trumpet, so doleful that it made them to turn and listen towards that part from whence it seemed to come: but he who was most troubled at this dismal alarm, was Don Quixote; therefore, though he lay under the goatherd, very much against his will, and was most lamentably bruised and battered, "Friend devil," cried he to him, "for sure nothing less could have so much valor and strength as to subdue my forces, let us have a

557

cessation of arms but for a single hour; for the dolorous sound of that trumpet strikes my soul with more horror than thy hard fists do my ears with pain, and methinks excites me to some new adventure." With that the goatherd, who was as weary of beating, as of being beaten, immediately gave him a truce; and the Knight once more getting on his feet, directed his then not hasty steps to the place whence the mournful sound seemed to come, and presently saw a number of men all in white, like penitents, descending from a rising ground. The real matter was this: the people had wanted rain for a whole year together, wherefore they appointed rogations, processions and disciplines throughout all that country, to implore Heaven to open its treasury, and shower down plenty upon them; and to this end, the inhabitants of a village near that place came in procession to a devote hermitage, built on one of the hills which surrounded that valley.

Don Quixote, taking notice of the strange habit of the penitents, and never reminding himself that he had often seen the like before, fancied it was some new adventure, and he alone was to engage in it, as he was obliged by the laws of knight-errantry; and that which the more increased his frenzy, was his mistaking an image which they carried (all covered with black) for some great lady, whom those miscreant and discourteous knights, he thought, were carrying away against her will. As soon as this whimsy took him in the head, he moved with what expedition he could towards Rozinante, who was feeding up and down upon the plains, and whipping off his bridle from the pommel, and his target, which hung hard by, he bridled him in an instant; then, taking his sword from Sancho, he got in a trice on Rozinante's back; where, bracing his target, and addressing himself aloud to all there present: "O valorous company," cried he, "you shall now perceive of how great importance it is to mankind, that such illustrious persons as those who profess the order of knight-errantry should exist in the world;

now, I say, you shall see by my freeing that noble lady, who is there basely and barbarously carried away captive, that knight-adventurers ought to be held in the highest and greatest estimation." So saying, he punched Rozinante with his heels for want of spurs; and forcing him to a hand gallop (for it was never read in any part of this history that Rozinante did ever run full speed) he posted to encounter the penitents, in spite of all the curate, canon, and barber could do to hinder him; much less could Sancho Panza's outcries detain him. "Master! Sir! Don Quixote!" bawled out the poor squire: "whither are you posting? Are you bewitched? Does the devil drive and set you on, thus to run against the Church? Ah, wretch that I am! See, sir, this is a procession of penitents, and the lady they carry is the image of the immaculate Virgin, our Blessed Lady. Take heed what you do, for at this time it may be certainly said you are out of your wits." But Sancho might as well have kept his breath for another use, for the Knight was urged with so vehement a desire to encounter the white men, and release the mourning lady, that he heard not a syllable that he said, or, if he had, he would not have turned back, even at the king's express command. At last, being come near the procession, and stopping Rozinante, that already had a great desire to rest a little, in a dismal tone, and with a hoarse voice, "Ho!" cried he, "you there, who cover your faces, perhaps, because you are ashamed of yourselves, and of the crime you are now committing, give heed and attention to what I have to say." The first who stopped at this alarm, were those who carried the image; when one of the four priests that sung the litanies, seeing the strange figure Don Quixote made, and the leanness of Rozinante, with other circumstances which he observed in the Knight sufficient to have forced laughter, presently made him this answer: "Good sir, if you have anything to say to us, speak it quickly; for these poor men whom you see are very much tired, therefore we neither can, nor is it reasonable we should, stand thus in pain to hear anything that cannot be delivered in two words." "I will say it in one," replied Don Quixote, "which is: I charge you immediately to release that beautiful lady, whose tears and looks, full of sorrow, evidently show you carry her away by violence, and have done her some unheard-of injury. This do, or I, who was born to punish such outrages, will not suffer you to advance one step with her, till she is entirely possessed of that liberty she so earnestly desires, and so justly deserves." This last speech made them all conclude that the Knight was certainly distracted, and caused a general laughter; but this proved like oil to fire, and so inflamed Don Quixote, that laying his hand on his sword, without more words, he presently assaulted those who carried the image. At the same time, one of them quitting his post, came to encounter our hero with a wooden fork, on which he supported the bier when they made a stand, and warding with it a weighty blow which Don Quixote designed and aimed at him, the fork was cut in two; but the other, who had the remaining piece in his hand, returned the Knight such a whack on his left shoulder, that his target not being able to resist such rustic force, the poor unfortunate Don Quixote was struck to the ground, and miserably bruised.

Sancho Panza, who had followed him as fast as his breath and legs would permit, seeing him fall, cried out to his adversary to forbear striking him, urging, that he was a poor enchanted knight, and one who in his whole life had never done any man harm. But it was not Sancho's arguments that held the country fellow's hands; the only motive was, that he feared he had killed him, since he could not perceive he stirred either hand or foot; wherefore, tucking his coat up to his girdle, with all possible expedition, he scoured over the fields like a grayhound. Meanwhile Don Quixote's companions hastened to the place where he lay, when those of the procession seeing them come running towards them, attended by the officers of the Holy Brotherhood with their crossbows along with them, began to have apprehensions of some disaster from the approaching party, wherefore, drawing up in a body about the image, the disciplinants lifting up their hoods, and grasping fast their whips, as the priests did their tapers, they expected the assault with the greatest bravery, resolving to defend themselves and repel their enemy as long and as much as possible: but Providence had ordered the matter much better than they could hope; for, while Sancho, who had thrown himself on his master's body, was lamenting his loss, and the supposed death of so noble and generous a lord, in the most ridiculous manner that ever was heard, the curate of the Knight's party was come up with the other who came in the procession, and was immediately known by him, so that their acquaintance put an end to the fears which both sides were in of an engagement. Don Quixote's curate in few words acquainted the other with the Knight's circumstances; whereupon he and the whole squadron of penitents went over to see whether the unfortunate Knight were living or dead, and heard Sancho Panza, with tears in his eyes, bewailing over his master: "O flower of knighthood," cried he, "that with one single perilous knock art come to an untimely end! Thou honor of thy family, and glory of all La Mancha! nay, and of the whole world besides; which, now that it has lost thee, will be overrun by miscreants and outlaws, who will no longer be afraid to be mauled for their misdeeds. O bountiful above all the Alexanders in the world! thou who hast rewarded me but for poor eight months' service with the best island that is washed by salt water! Thou who wert humble to the proud, and haughty to the humble! Thou who durst undertake perils, and patiently endure affronts! Thou who wert in love, nobody knows why! True patron of good men, and scourge of the wicked, sworn foe to all reprobates; and, to say all at once that man can say, thou knight-errant!"

The woeful accents of the squire's voice at last recalled Don Quixote to himself; when, after a deep sigh, the first thing he thought of was his absent Dulcinea. "O charming Dulcinea," cried he, "the wretch that lingers, banished from thy sight, endures far greater miseries than this!" And then, looking on his faithful squire, "Good Sancho," said he, "help me once more into the enchanted car: for I am not in a condition to press the back of Rozinante: this shoulder is all broke to pieces." "With all my heart, my good lord," replied Sancho, "and pray let me advise you to go back to our village with these gentlemen, who are your special friends. At home we may think of some other journey that may be more profitable and honorable than this." "With reason hast thou spoken, Sancho," replied Don Quixote: "it will become our wisdom to be inactive, till the malevolent aspects of the planets, which now reign, be over." This grave resolution was highly commended by the canon, curate, and barber, who had been sufficiently diverted by Sancho Panza's ridiculous lamentation. Don Quixote was placed in the wagon as before, the processioners recovered their former order, and passed on about their business. The goatherd took his leave of the whole company. The curate satisfied the officers for their attendance, since they could stir no further. The canon desired the curate to send him an account of Don Quixote's condition from that time forward, having a mind to know whether his frenzy abated or increased; and then took his leave to continue his journey. Thus the curate, the barber, Don Quixote, and Sancho Panza were left together; as also the good Rozinante, that bore all those passages as patiently as his master. The wagoner then yoked his oxen, and having set Don Quixote on a truss of hay, jogged on after his slow accustomed pace the way the curate directed. In six days' time they reached the Knight's village. It was about noon when they entered the town; and as it happened to be on a Sunday, all the people were assembled in the market-place, through the middle of which Don Quixote must of necessity pass. Everybody was curious to know what was in it; and the people were strangely surprised when they saw and knew their townsman. While they were gaping and wondering, a little boy ran to the Knight's house, and gave intelligence to the housekeeper and niece, that

their master and uncle was returned, and very lean, pale, and frightful as a ghost, stretched out at length on a bundle of hay, in a wagon, and drawn along by a team of oxen.

It was a piteous thing to hear the wailings of these two poor creatures; the thumps too which they gave their faces, with the curses and execrations they thundered out against all books of chivalry, were almost as numerous as their sighs and tears: but the height of their lamenting was when Don Quixote entered the door. Upon the noise of his arrival Sancho Panza's wife made haste thither to inquire after her husband, who, she was informed, went a-squiring with the Knight. As soon as ever she set eyes on him, the question she asked him was this: "Is the ass in health, or no?" Sancho answered, he was come back in better health than his master. "Well," said she, "Heaven be praised for the good news. But hark you, my friend," continued she, "what have you got by this new squireship? Have you brought me home ever a gown or petticoat, or shoes for my children?" "In truth, sweet wife," replied Sancho, "I have brought thee none of those things; I am loaded with better things." "Ay," said his wife, "that is well. I pray thee let me see some of them fine things; for I vow I have a hugeous mind to see them; the sight of them will comfort my poor heart, which has been like to burst with sorrow and grief ever since you went away." "I will show them to thee when we come home," returned Sancho: "in the meantime rest satisfied; for if Heaven see good that we should once again go abroad in search of other adventures, within a little time after, at my return, thou shalt find me some earl, or the governor of some island; ay, of one of the best in the world." "I wish with all my heart this may come to pass," replied the good wife; "for, by my troth, husband, we want it sorely. But what do you mean by that same word island? for believe me, I do not understand it." "All in good time, wife," said Sancho; "honey is not made for an ass's mouth: I will tell thee what it is hereafter. Thou wilt be amazed to hear all thy servants and vassals never speak a word to thee without, 'If it please you, madam, if it like your ladyship, and your honor.'" "What dost thou mean, Sancho, by ladyship, islands and vassals?" quoth Joan [1] Panza, for so she was called, though her husband and she were nothing a-kin, only it is a custom in La Mancha, that the wives are there called by their husband's surnames. "Prithee, Joan," said Sancho, "do not trouble thy head to know these matters all at once, and in a heap, as a body may say: it is enough, I tell thee the

1 *This slip in the name of Sancho's wife is Cervantes'.*

truth, therefore hold thy tongue. Yet, by the way, one thing I will assure thee, that nothing in the 'versal world is better for an honest man, than to be squire to a knight-errant while he is hunting of adventures. It is true, most adventures he goes about do not answer a man's expectations so much as he could wish: for of a hundred that are met with, ninety-nine are wont to be crabbed and unlucky ones. This I know to my cost: I myself have got well kicked and tossed in some of them, and soundly drubbed and belabored in others; yet, for all that, it is rare sport to be a-watching for strange chances, to cross forests, to search and beat up and down in woods, to scramble over rocks, to visit castles, and to take up quarters in an inn at pleasure, and all the while the devil a cross to pay."

These were the discourses with which Sancho Panza and his wife Joan entertained one another, while the housekeeper and niece undressed Don Quixote and put him into his bed; where he lay looking asquint on them, but could not imagine where he was. The curate charged the niece to be very careful and tender of her uncle, and to be very watchful lest he should make another sally; telling her the trouble and charge he had been at to get him home. Here the women began their outcries again: here the books of knight-errantry were again execrated, and damned to the bottomless pit. Here they begged those bewitching chimeras and lies might be thrown down into the very center, to the hellish father of them! For, they were still almost distracted with the fear of losing their master and uncle again, so soon as ever he recovered; which indeed fell out according to their fear. But, though the author of this history has been very diligent in his inquiry after Don Quixote's achievements in his third expedition in quest of adventures, yet he could never learn a perfect account of them, at least from any author of credit: fame and tradition alone have preserved some particulars of them in the memoirs and antiquities of La Mancha; as, that after the Knight's third sally, he was present at certain famous tilts and tournaments made in the city of Saragossa, where he met with occasions worthy the exercise of his sense and valor: but how the Knight died, our author neither could or ever should have learned, if by good fortune he had not met with an ancient physician, who had a leaden box in his possession, which, as he averred, was found in the ruins of an old hermitage, as it was rebuilding. In this box were certain scrolls of parchment written in Gothic characters, but containing verses in the Spanish tongue, in which many of his noble acts were sung, Dulcinea del Toboso's beauty celebrated, Rozinante's figure described, and Sancho Panza's fidelity applauded. They likewise gave an account of Don Quixote's sepulcher, with several epitaphs and encomiums on his life and conversation. These that could be thoroughly read and transcribed, are here added by the faithful author of this new and incomparable history; desiring no other recompense or reward of the readers, for all his labor and pains, in searching all the numerous and old records of La Mancha to perfect this matchless piece, but that they will be pleased to give it as much credit as judicious men use to give to books of knight-errantry, which are nowadays so well received. This is the utmost of his ambition, and will be sufficient satisfaction for him, and likewise encourage him to furnish them with other matter of entertainment; which, though possibly not altogether so true as this, yet it may be as well contrived and diverting. The first words in the parchment found in the leaden box are these:

MONICONGO, ACADEMICIAN OF ARGAMASILLA, ON DON QUIXOTE'S MONUMENT

EPITAPH

"Here lies a doughty knight,
Who, bruised, and ill in plight,
Jogg'd over many a track
On Rozinante's back.

Close by him Sancho's laid;
　　Whereat let none admire:
He was a clown, 'tis said,
　　But ne'er the worse a squire."

PANIAGUADO, ACADEMIC OF ARGAMASILLA, ON DULCINEA DEL
TOBOSO'S MONUMENT

EPITAPH

"Here Dulcinea lies,
　　Once brawny, plump, and lusty;
But now to death a prize,
　　And somewhat lean and musty.

For her the country-fry,
　　Like Quixote, long stood steady.
Well might she carry't high;
　　Far less has made a lady."

These were the verses that could be read: as for the rest, the characters being defaced, and almost eaten away, they were delivered to a university student, in order that he might give us his conjectures concerning their meaning. And we are informed, that after many lucubrations and much pains, he has effected the work, and intends to oblige the world with it, giving us at the same time some hopes of Don Quixote's third sally.

Forsi altro cantera
　　con miglior plectro.

This edition of THE LIFE AND ACHIEVEMENTS OF THE RENOWNED DON QUIXOTE DE LA MANCHA *was designed by George Salter. The type used is Linotype Scotch and the illustrations, which are engraved in wood, are by Hans Alexander Mueller. The book was composed, printed and bound by H. Wolff, New York, using paper manufactured by the P. H. Glatfelter Co., and buckram cloth made by the Bancroft Mills.*